CARROT CAKE MURDER

Books by Joanne Fluke

CHOCOLATE CHIP COOKIE MURDER

STRAWBERRY SHORTCAKE MURDER

BLUEBERRY MUFFIN MURDER

LEMON MERINGUE PIE MURDER

FUDGE CUPCAKE MURDER

SUGAR COOKIE MURDER

PEACH COBBLER MURDER

CHERRY CHEESECAKE MURDER

KEY LIME PIE MURDER

CARROT CAKE MURDER

Published by Kensington Publishing Corporation

A HANNAH SWENSEN MYSTERY
WITH RECIPES

CARROT CAKE MURDER

JOANNE FLUKE

KENSINGTON BOOKS
http://www.kensingtonbooks.com

KENSINGTON BOOKS are published by

Kensington Publishing Corp.
850 Third Avenue
New York, NY 10022

All Kensington titles, imprints, and distributed lines are available at special quantity discounts for bulk purchases for sales promotion, premiums, fund-raising, educational, or institutional use.

Special book excerpts or customized printings can also be created to fit specific needs. For details, write or phone the office of the Kensington Special Sales Manager: Attn. Special Sales Department. Kensington Publishing Corp., 850 Third Avenue, New York, NY 10022. Phone: 1-800-221-2647.

Kensington and the K logo Reg. U.S. Pat. & TM Off.

Library of Congress Card Number: 2007942207

ISBN-13: 978-0-7582-1020-3
ISBN-10: 0-7582-1020-5

First hardcover printing: March 2008

10   9   8   7   6   5   4   3   2   1

Printed in the United States of America

This book is dedicated to Dale Constantine.

Acknowledgments:

Thanks to Ruel, my in-house story editor, research team,
and cheerleader.
And to our kids who know that there is no substitute
for butter.
Hugs to the grandkids as they try to convince their moms
that carrot cake is a vegetable.

Thank you to Mary Ann Grossman who gave me the idea
for the victim in this book.

Thank you to our friends and neighbors:
Mel & Kurt, Lyn & Bill, Gina & the kids, Adrienne, Jay,
Bob, Amanda, Dale, John B., Trudi, David, Dr. Bob & Sue,
Laura & Mark, Richard & Krista, and my hometown
friends from Swanville, Minnesota.

Thanks to the Hannah fans at Mysteries To Die For
for taste-testing the Viking Cookies.

Thank you to my Editor-in-Chief, John Scognamiglio.
You're the absolute best.

The same goes for Walter, Steve, Laurie, Doug, David,
Maureen, Magee, Meryl, Colleen, Michaela, Kate, Jessica,
Peter, Robin, Lydia, Lori, Mike, Tami, and Barbara.

Thank you to Hiro Kimura for the incredible carrot cake
on the cover.
And thanks to Lou Malcangi for designing such a delicious
dust jacket.

Thanks also to all the other talented folks at Kensington who keep Hannah sleuthing and baking up a storm.

Thanks to Levy Home Entertainment for inviting me to the 2007 convention in Chicago. Not only did I have a great time, I met some really wonderful people!

Thank you to Dee for Alison Wonderland's stage name. Thanks to John for proofreading and for keeping my computer running. And thank you to Jill Saxton for catching more goofs than anyone else.

Thank you to Dr. Rahhal & Trina for all that you do.

Thanks to Mrs. Line for trying out so many recipes. And hugs to everyone who sent favorite family recipes for Hannah to try.

Massive hugs to Terry Sommers for testing all the recipes and trying them out on her family. Nobody's keeled over yet, right Terry?

Thank you to Jamie Wallace for keeping my Web site, **MurderSheBaked.com** up to date and looking great.

And many, many thanks to everyone who e-mailed or snail-mailed.
Writing is solitary work, but when you invite me into your lives, you make me feel like family.

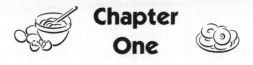

Chapter One

The *Amen* couldn't come fast enough to suit Hannah Swensen. She was sitting in the third pew from the front of Holy Redeemer Lutheran Church in Lake Eden, Minnesota, and her ears were still ringing from the fifth and final chorus of *Jesu Priceless Treasure*. She thought she might have suffered a slight hearing loss from Marge Beeseman's attempt at a high G, but that wasn't her primary concern. Her eyes were trained on Reverend Knudson as he emerged from the small dressing room adjacent to the pulpit. He was wearing an ordinary suit, the type Doug Greerson, president of the Lake Eden First Mercantile Bank, wore every day to work. The minister's vestments had gone the way of his solemn manner, and he was smiling as he walked forward to informally address his flock.

An ecumenical fly droned its way from the open doors at the back of the church, alighting momentarily on Lutherans, Catholics, and Bible Church members alike. The church was packed this last Sunday in August, and much of that was Hannah's mother's doing. Delores Swensen had spent the previous evening on the phone, convincing scores of Lake Eden residents to attend Reverend Knudson's ten o'clock service.

Hannah turned to look at her mother. Delores was watching the reverend with the same intent gaze that Hannah's cat,

Moishe, employed to run surveillance on the chipmunk that frequented the flowerbeds beneath Hannah's living room window. The other occupants of the pew had also drawn a bead on their minister in mufti. Hannah's two younger sisters, Andrea and Michelle, appeared mesmerized by his every move. And their mother's business partner, Carrie Rhodes, was clutching her hymnal so hard Hannah was afraid she'd crack the spine. Even Carrie's son, Norman, looked nervous. This was the showdown, the eleventh hour, the pivotal moment they'd all come to witness.

Reverend Knudson made his way to the head of the center aisle with all eyes upon him. He was still smiling and he didn't look as if he had an important announcement to make, but almost everyone in the congregation, members and visitors alike, knew that he did. The reverend was about to tell them that he planned to marry Claire Rodgers, owner of Beau Monde Fashions, Lake Eden's only designer dress shop.

Startled by a poke in the ribs, Hannah turned to her youngest sister. "What is it, Michelle?" she whispered.

"Two rows back on the other side," Michelle replied, her voice so soft it was almost inaudible. Then she jerked her head in the direction she wanted her oldest sister to look and nudged her again.

Hannah turned around and gave a little gasp as she saw the couple seated two rows behind them on the aisle. It was Mayor Bascomb and his wife, Stephanie. And they were the very couple Hannah had least expected to see at Holy Redeemer Lutheran this morning!

"Mother convinced Mrs. Bascomb to come," Michelle continued, her lips close to Hannah's ear. "She didn't think anyone would have the nerve to object to Reverend Knudson and Claire getting married if they were here for the announcement. I mean . . . what reason could they give in front of the mayor's wife?"

"Diabolical!" Hannah breathed, shooting her mother an admiring look. Rumor had it that Claire had once been

Mayor Bascomb's mistress. No one could prove it, but some members of the congregation tended to look down their noses at Claire. It was the reason Hannah, her family, and the scores of people that Delores had recruited were here to support the reverend's announcement. There was no way Hannah and her extended family were going to let anyone throw a damper on this happy occasion.

"I'm delighted to see so many of you at services this morning," Reverend Knudson said, beaming. And then he proceeded to announce upcoming activities for the week. Hannah learned that Bible study would take place on Monday night, there would be a church rummage sale on Tuesday afternoon, they would hold twilight services on Wednesday at seven with choir practice immediately after the service, and Luther League would meet in the church basement on Thursday night. Friday evening was slotted for Lutherans Without Partners, a new singles club. There would be two weddings on Saturday, and the regular services on Sunday morning.

"And now, if you'll bear with me, I'd like to say something on a personal note. There is someone in this congregation who is near and dear to my heart."

Hannah nudged Michelle. This was it. Reverend Knudson was about to do it!

"That someone is Winifred Henderson, and I'd like to thank her for her years of service in the church nursery. Because of Winnie, many of you mothers have enjoyed worry-free Sunday church services, knowing that your children are well cared for and happy in the nursery. Even though we don't ordinarily applaud in church, I think Winnie deserves a standing ovation."

Hannah stood and applauded along with everyone else, and then she sat back down to wait for the last announcement. Reverend Knudson's eyes met hers for a moment, and then they quickly skittered away.

Uh-oh! Hannah breathed, coming very close to groaning out loud. There was only one reason for Reverend Knudson to avoid her eyes. Claire had gotten cold feet and asked him to delay the announcement again!

The reverend's hand began to rise in a signal for the organist to play the recessional. But Hannah was quicker, and she shot to her feet. "Wait!" she said loudly. "I have an announcement to make."

All eyes swiveled in her direction, and Hannah came close to wishing that the floor would open up and swallow her. But something had to be done right now and she had to do it. Reverend Knudson and Claire were perfect for each other. And Claire was letting her fear of rejection stand in the way of their future happiness.

"I know you're too modest to mention how hard you work to keep all these church activities going," Hannah began, making up a speech as she went. "I didn't realize it before, but you just told us about a meeting, or group, or event every single day of the week. And you go to every one of them. Not only that, you counsel people if they have a problem, you visit the sick at Lake Eden Hospital, and you or Grandma Knudson are always available on the phone if we need you. I know I speak for everyone here when I say that we appreciate all the time and effort you spend looking after us and the church."

"That's right," Marge Beeseman called down from the choir loft. "We think you deserve a standing ovation, too!"

This is nice, Hannah thought as she applauded with everyone else. *They're in the mood to applaud, and they'll go right on applauding when I throw them a curve.*

"Sometimes we take you for granted," Hannah continued. "We forget that you have a personal life in addition to your life as our pastor. And I know that's why you're not mentioning the most wonderful news of all." Hannah looked around at the congregation. She had them on the edges of the pews. Everyone was leaning forward, waiting. "And that wonderful news is that wedding bells are about to ring for you and your bride."

If they lean forward anymore, they'll fall on the floor, Hannah thought fleetingly, noticing that people in the front pew were canting forward at close to a ninety-degree angle. But she went right on despite Reverend Knudson's startled expression. "I'm happy to tell all of you that she's a member of our own congregation. Since the Reverend is too shy to do it, I'm announcing that Reverend Knudson and Claire Rodgers will be getting married at Christmas! And I think our beloved minister and his bride-to-be deserve a standing ovation."

Of course they all applauded. They were programmed for standing ovations. And thanks to Delores and her phone recruiting, more people approved than objected. Now there was only one more thing for Hannah to do and that would be easy.

"I thought we should have a small celebration on this joyous occasion, so I brought several kinds of cookies and Edna Ferguson made coffee. There's juice for the kids, and everything's all set up on tables outside. Please enjoy yourself, and don't forget to tell Reverend Knudson and Claire how much you're looking forward to their marriage."

"Hannah?" Norman came up to her and slipped his arm around her waist. "That was just amazing what you did back there. You could sell kitty litter to nomads."

Hannah laughed. Norman had a way with words. "Thank you . . . I think. Did you happen to notice how fast the Old-Fashioned Sugar Cookies went?"

"They're almost gone. Decorating them with Claire and the reverend's initials was a brilliant touch."

"Thanks," Hannah said, knowing full well that Norman had caught her psychological ploy. Anyone who took a cookie with the two sets of initials encircled by a heart was giving symbolic approval to the marriage. "How about the Viking Cookies?"

"What Viking Cookies? The little sign is still there, but the plate's empty. And I didn't even get to taste them."

"Don't worry. I saved some for you." Hannah was pleased that the Viking Cookies were such a big hit. The recipe was a new one that Lisa had perfected and it was made with her favorite white chocolate.

Marge Beeseman came up to them with a huge smile on her face. "That was an excellent speech, Hannah."

"Thanks. I figured I'd better do something or Reverend Knudson would cop out again. Did Lisa tell you that we saved a few dozen cookies for this afternoon in case some of your relatives come in early for the family reunion?"

"She told me. And that's so sweet of you, Hannah. My sister Patsy and her husband are here already, and so is Lisa's oldest brother, Tim, the one who moved to Chicago."

"How many people do you expect?" Norman asked. Although he wasn't a Lake Eden native, he'd been here for almost three years now and he knew that Lisa's family was huge, and so was the Beeseman family.

"Almost all the out-of-town relatives sent in the card that Lisa and Herb mailed with the invitation. And some locals called instead of filling it out. As it stands right now, I think we'll be over a hundred."

"That's a big party!" Hannah said, wishing she'd saved more cookies. "Did Andrea find enough rentals for you at the lake?"

"I think so. And if we're a little short on room, we'll just double up. The Des Moines Beesemans are bringing their RV and there's room for three more in there, and the Brainerd Hermans are bringing an extra tent in case anyone needs it."

"Are you looking forward to seeing all your relatives again?" Norman asked.

"I'll say! There are some grandnieces and grandnephews I haven't even met yet. It's going to be the most wonderful week! There's only one thing I wish . . ." Marge stopped speaking and looked a bit wistful.

"What's that?" Hannah asked her.

"It's my brother, Gus. I was hoping he'd hear about the family reunion and show up."

"He didn't respond to the invitation?" Hannah was curious.

"He didn't *get* an invitation. I don't have an address for him."

There was a story here, and both Hannah and Norman realized it. Like a good, attentive audience, they remained silent and waited for Marge to explain.

"Gus left Lake Eden over thirty years ago, and no one's heard from him since. I hired a private detective to try to find him when my mother got sick, but he said Gus probably changed his name, and unless he knew what it was, he couldn't get a lead on him."

"Did you try a search on the Internet?" Norman asked.

"Herb did. There are some other August Hermans, but not my brother, Gus."

"He didn't tell anyone where he was going?" Hannah couldn't help but ask.

Marge shook her head. "He just disappeared in the middle of the night. He was staying with my folks at the time. All he took was a change of clothes and some money from the teapot on the kitchen counter." Marge must have seen their puzzled looks, because she went on to explain. "The teapot was a gift from one of my great aunts, the ugliest thing you ever saw! None of us drank tea, so we used it for the family bank when we were all growing up. We knew we could take money out when we needed it, and pay it back later, when we could."

"How much money did your brother take?" Hannah was curious.

"We were never really sure, but my father didn't think it was over a hundred dollars. Nobody ever bothered to count it. They just remembered how much they took so they could put it back."

Hannah did some fast figuring. "Bus tickets weren't that expensive back then," she said. "Your brother could have gone all the way to the west coast. Or to the east coast, for that matter."

"And he would have had seed money when he got there," Marge informed her. "I know my sister Patsy lent him some money about a week before he left town, and he borrowed some from me, too."

"Then his problem wasn't lack of money."

"No. He was living with Mom and Dad, so he didn't have to pay for rent, or food, or anything like that. I was living there, too. I had a job, but I didn't leave home until the next summer, when I got married."

"Was there any indication that he was going to leave?" Norman asked. "I mean, did he act restless or anything like that?"

"Not really. To this day, I don't know why he took off like that. I've been thinking about it ever since Lisa and Herb first mentioned having a family reunion, and I couldn't help hoping that he'd finally come home."

There was a moment of silence. Neither Hannah nor Norman was quite sure what to say. Then there was a honk from the street as a car drove up, a shiny new red car with a classic hood ornament.

"Nice car!" Norman exclaimed, eyeing the new Jaguar with obvious admiration. Then he turned to Marge. "One of your relatives?"

Marge gave a little laugh. "That's unlikely. As far as I know, we don't have any family *that* rich. Can you see who's driving?"

"It's a guy," Hannah told her. "Come on. Let's walk over to see who it is."

By the time they made their way to the street, the Jaguar was surrounded by admirers. They walked around to the street side, and Marge's eyes widened as she saw that her son was sitting in the passenger seat. "Herb?" she gasped. "What are you doing in there?"

"Hi, Mom. I took a quick run by the house to make sure no more relatives came in while we were at church, and look who I found waiting for us!"

Herb leaned back so that Marge could see the driver. "He said you probably won't recognize him, since it's been a really long time."

"Is it . . . ?" Hannah breathed, hardly daring to ask if Marge's wish had come true.

"Yes!" Marge was clearly ecstatic as she ran around the car to hug her brother through the open window. "Oh, Gus! I'm so glad you came home at last!"

VIKING COOKIES

Preheat oven to 350 degrees F., rack
in the middle position.

2 cups butter *(4 sticks—melted)*
2 cups brown sugar
2 cups white sugar
1 teaspoon baking powder
1 teaspoon baking soda
1 teaspoon salt
4 eggs—beaten
2 teaspoons vanilla
½ teaspoon cinnamon
¼ teaspoon cardamom *(nutmeg will also work, but
cardamom is better)*
4 ½ cups flour
3 cups white chocolate chips *(I used
Ghirardelli's)****
3 cups rolled oats *(uncooked oatmeal—I used
Quaker's Quick Oatmeal)*

**** Make sure you use real white chocolate chips, not
vanilla chips. The real ones have cocoa listed in the ingredients. If you can't find them in your market, look for a
block of white chocolate, one pound or a bit over, and cut
it up in small pieces with a knife.*

Melt the butter in a large microwave-safe bowl, or on
the stove in a small saucepan. *(It should melt in about 3
minutes in the microwave on HIGH.)* Set it on the counter
and let it cool to room temperature.

When the butter is cool, mix in the white sugar and the brown sugar.

Add the baking powder, baking soda, salt, eggs, vanilla, and spices. Make sure it's all mixed in thoroughly.

Add the flour in half-cup increments, mixing after each addition. Then add the white chocolate chips *(or pieces of white chocolate if you cut up a block)* and stir thoroughly.

Add the oatmeal and mix. The dough will be quite stiff.

Drop by teaspoons onto a greased *(or sprayed with nonstick cooking spray)* standard-sized cookie sheet, 12 cookies to a sheet.

Flatten the cookies on the sheet with a greased metal spatula *(or with the palm of your impeccably clean hand.)* You don't have to smush them all the way down so they look like pancakes—just one squish will do it.

Bake at 350 degrees F. for 11 to 13 minutes or until they're an attractive golden brown. *(Mine took the full 13 minutes.)*

Cool the cookies for 1 to 2 minutes on the cookie sheets and then remove them to a wire rack to cool completely.

Yield: 10 to 12 dozen delicious cookies, depending on cookie size.

These freeze well if you roll them in foil and put them in a freezer bag.

Hannah's Note: These cookies will go fast, even frozen. If you want to throw the midnight freezer raiders off the track, wrap the cookie rolls in a double thickness of foil and then stick them in a freezer bag. Label the bag with a food your family doesn't like, (something like BEEF TONGUE, or PORK KIDNEYS, or even LUTEFISK—it works every time.)

Chapter Two

Hannah stopped just inside her condo door and stared around her in shock. There had been a blizzard in her living room! Her wall-to-wall carpeting, normally a dark green color that she'd chosen because it reminded her of a lush green lawn, was covered with fluffy white snowflakes. Except it wasn't snow, and it wasn't flakes. And there was the empty couch pillow cover to prove it. Hannah picked up the cover and read the tag listing the contents. What she'd thought was snow was really the "unidentified fibers" Cost-Mart used as stuffing in their decorator sofa pillows.

"Moishe?" she called out, realizing that her orange-and-white feline roommate was nowhere in sight. He hadn't hurtled himself into her arms as he usually did when she came in the door, and that meant he was probably responsible. The pillow was a bit wet on the corner, from kitty saliva no doubt, and at least two paws' worth of claws had shredded the fabric to pull out the faux snow. The male companion who shared her home and her bed knew he'd done wrong and he was hiding somewhere, waiting for her to get over her initial shock and anger before he showed himself.

At least the pillow stuffing was easy to collect. Hannah got a garbage bag from the broom closet and began to fill it with the fluffy white balls. As she bent, retrieved, and stuffed, she thought about the very few times that Moishe had misbehaved.

A month or two after he'd decided to set up residence with her, Hannah had forgotten to empty his litter box when she cleaned the condo. Moishe had given her a one-day grace period, but the following night, when she'd come home from work at her bakery and coffee shop, she discovered that he'd accomplished the task himself and the litter was scattered all over the floor. At that late stage, it had been impossible for Hannah to tell whether her fastidious feline had gotten in to scratch it out, or whether he'd tipped the pan to dump it out and then righted it again. It didn't really matter in the giant scheme of things. She'd never needed another reminder to empty Moishe's litter box.

A more serious infraction had taken place a month or two after the litter box incident. Moishe had taken an immediate dislike to Hannah's mother, and he'd snagged several pairs of her real silk and really expensive pantyhose before Delores had decided that Hannah should visit her, rather than the other way around. Hannah liked to think that her kitty's dislike of Delores came from an effort to protect her from her mother's not-so-gentle reminders that she was over thirty, her biological clock was ticking, and she was still single. Perhaps that was true. Or perhaps Moishe simply didn't like the perfume Delores wore, or the pitch of her voice, or any of a hundred other things.

Hannah glanced at the deflated pillow casing. The litter box message and her mother's shredded stockings had been easy to interpret. This message was not so obvious. Did it mean that Moishe had suddenly developed an aversion to pillows? Although she'd never been to veterinary school, she didn't think it was common for cats to develop pillowphobia. Had Moishe objected to her color scheme for couch accessories and decided to let his preferences be known? The wine-colored pillow was intact, but he'd quite literally beaten the stuffing out of the light green pillow. Perhaps the light green color had reminded him of some traumatic incident in his kittenhood?

"Ridiculous!" she murmured under her breath. If there was a message in Moishe's pillow bashing, it probably had something to do with what was *inside* the pillow. Hannah let her imagination run wild. It was possible that a colony of bugs originating from the country that exported CostMart's unidentified pillow fibers had hatched.

Hannah glanced down at the fibers she'd tossed in the garbage bag. She didn't *see* any bugs. Could they be tiny, almost microscopic insects that would flutter around harmlessly for a day or two and then disappear? Or were they some type of science fiction worm that would invade her body, take over her mind, and . . .

A small pathetic sound brought Hannah out of her late-night horror movie scenario. Moishe was inching across the rug toward her, clearly unsure of her reaction but unable to stay away any longer from the mistress he loved. His expression was wide-eyed innocent, and it seemed to say, *What happened to that pillow? You don't think I did that, do you?* He reminded Hannah of her niece, Tracey, who'd come out of the kitchen at The Cookie Jar with chocolate smears on her face, insisting that she'd given a half dozen chocolate chip cookies to a poor starving man who'd knocked at the back door.

"It's okay," Hannah said, cutting straight to the chase. "I know you shredded that pillow, and I'm not mad at you. I just wish I knew why you did it."

Moishe gave as close to a shrug as a cat could give, hunching his shoulders forward and then back. His tail flicked once and his eyes opened wide. Hannah thought he looked thoroughly bewildered. Perhaps he didn't know why he'd done it either, and she reached down to pick him up.

The moment she lifted him up into her arms, he began to purr. Hannah nuzzled him and gave him a little scratch behind the ears in the spot he loved. He licked her hand to show that he was grateful for her forgiveness. At least she *thought* it was to indicate that he was grateful. It could also have something to do with the fact that she'd packed up the leftover cookies and probably smelled like butter.

"Just let me finish up here," Hannah said, placing him on the back of the couch so that she could pick up the last few clumps of pillow innards. She tied the bag shut, placed it by the door so she'd remember to carry it out to the dumpster when she left for the evening, and beckoned to Moishe, who was watching her intently. "I bet you'd like lunch. I know I would."

After a quick survey of the pantry and cupboards, Hannah turned to her cat again. "How about Salmon Cakes?"

"Yowwww!" Moishe said.

Hannah took that as approval and she selected a small can of red salmon from the pantry. She opened it and dumped it into a strainer, removing the soft backbones and the dark skin for Moishe. Once she'd thoroughly drained the fish and flaked it, she cut the crusts from two slices of sourdough bread and tore it into small pieces. She'd just added the last few ingredients to the bowl when Moishe gave another yowl.

"Can't wait, huh?" Hannah glanced down at her pet. By some miracle, or perhaps it was a deliberate trick, her twenty-three-pound cat managed to look half-starved. If it was a trick, it was a good one. Hannah just wished that she could emulate it when she tried to wriggle into the bronze silk dress she planned to wear to the dance at Lisa and Herb's family reunion tonight.

Moishe gave another yowl, and it sounded so pathetic that Hannah surrendered and dumped the salmon bones and skin in his food bowl. While her cat attacked it with the same ferocity he would have shown to a small, furry rodent, she gave her bowl a final stir. She was just shaping the mixture into cakes about the size of a hamburger patty and preparing to fry them in butter when the phone rang.

Hannah turned to look at her pet. He'd lifted his head from the last of the salmon and was staring at the phone balefully. As it rang again, his ears went back and flattened against his head. The hair on his back began to bristle, and a low growl, more doglike than catlike, rumbled from his throat.

"Mother?" Hannah asked him, already knowing the answer. There was only one person in the universe who got such a negative response from her cat. Surprisingly, mostly because she didn't believe in ESP or any of its cousins, Moishe was right more times than he was wrong. It was probably Delores. Hannah reached for the phone, lifted it out of its cradle, and answered, "Hello, Mother."

"I wish you wouldn't do that, Hannah!" Delores gave her standard reply.

"Do what?" Hannah asked, even though she knew exactly what her mother meant.

"Say *Hello, Mother* before you really know who it is. What if it was someone else?"

"Then I'd be wrong."

"Yes. And you'd feel very foolish, wouldn't you?"

"Not really."

"Well!" There was a long pause while Delores considered it. Finally, she spoke. "You're right. You wouldn't. But I really wish you'd just say hello like a normal person."

"I know you do." Hannah felt a little niggle of guilt for annoying her mother. "It's just that I can't seem to resist."

Delores sighed so heavily, it sounded like a little explosion in Hannah's ear. "You do it because you know it bothers me, don't you?"

"In a way. It's become almost like a game. I say, *Hello, Mother.* You say, *I wish you wouldn't do that.* And I say, *Do what?* And then you give me a reason not to answer the phone that way. It's what we always do before we really start to talk."

"So it's our own private greeting? A mother-daughter ritual?"

"That's exactly right." Hannah nodded even though she knew her mother couldn't see it. There were times when Delores was amazingly perceptive.

"Then we'd better continue to do it, dear. Rituals are important. They're patterns for us to follow to bridge awkward moments."

"That's extremely insightful, Mother."

"Thank you, dear. I've been researching the English Regency period and the number of formal traditions they practiced was truly amazing. Did you know that the dress a debutante wore to be presented at court had to follow strict guidelines? And her curtsy had to be just so?"

"I didn't know."

"And did you know that the number of *removes* at a formal dinner was dictated by the family's social status?"

"No. What are *removes?*"

"They're similar to courses, dear."

Hannah nodded. Unlike some Regency conventions, this one was aptly named. When a meal was served formally, the server *removed* the plates from the previous course before presenting the next. And sometimes the plate or bowl had a cover that was *removed* with a flourish. "Are you doing this research for your Regency Romance Club?"

"Only partially, dear. And that reminds me . . . we're thinking about serving high tea as a fundraiser. Do you think you could help us with the pastries?"

"Sure. Have you set a date?"

"Not yet, but it won't be before Christmas. I'll do more research on exactly what they served and how it was presented. Perhaps, if they had scones in Regency times, Sally could make some of hers."

It was clearly going to be a long conversation. Hannah stretched out the phone cord, put a frying pan with butter on the burner, and turned on the heat. "I didn't know Sally made scones."

"Today was her first batch. She served them to us at brunch, and they were delicious."

"You went out to the Lake Eden Inn for brunch?" Hannah tipped the pan so the butter would melt faster.

"Yes, with all the relatives who arrived early for the reunion. Carrie and I were standing there talking to Marge after you left the church, and Gus practically had to invite us."

"Gus York? Or Marge's brother, Gus?"

"Marge's brother. He asked Marge to recommend a good place for brunch, and then he invited us all."

"That was nice of him."

Delores gave a little snort that Hannah could hear clearly over the receiver. "It was the *least* he could do. He practically broke Marge's heart when he left town in the middle of the night. And Marge's mother and father never stopped hoping that he'd come home. He was the youngest, you know."

"Why did he leave in the first place?" Hannah asked, holding the phone between her neck and her shoulder and cranking her head to the side so it wouldn't fall as she got her plate of uncooked salmon cakes and carried them over to the stovetop. She dropped them into the frying pan and stood back slightly to avoid being splattered by the sizzling butter.

"No one knows why he left, dear." Delores stopped speaking for a moment, and then she asked, "What's that noise?"

"What noise?"

"It's a frying noise. I'm on my cell phone, and it must need recharging. Anyway . . . the real reason I called is to ask you if you have any crackers."

Hannah glanced at the pantry. The door was ajar, and she could see a large package of assorted crackers sitting on the shelf. "I've got some."

"Good. Lisa needs you to bring them. Mike made his Lazy Day Pâté for the potluck tonight, but he doesn't get off work until six and he won't have time to run back into town for crackers."

"Consider it done. Anything else anyone needs?" Hannah flipped a Salmon Cake and it sputtered as it landed on its uncooked side.

"Just your Special Carrot Cake. Lisa and Herb were raving about it at the brunch, and everybody's looking forward to trying it."

"That's good to hear," Hannah said, flipping the other three Salmon Cakes.

"I'll see you there, dear. I've got to go now. That frying noise is getting louder, and I just know we'll get cut off."

Hannah said goodbye and rubbed her sore neck as she walked over to hang up the phone. She supposed she should have admitted that her stove was the source of the frying noise her mother thought was a waning battery, but her lunch was almost ready. Since it was past two in the afternoon and she still had to assemble several veggie and dip platters, there wasn't a lot of time to waste. She had just dished up her first helping and was placing it on the coffee table in the living room when her doorbell rang.

Hannah muttered a few choice words she never would have used around either of her nieces. Whoever it was had lousy timing. Then she picked up her plate (she knew better than to leave one of Moishe's favorite entrees within kitty reach) and carried it to the door. "Who is it?" she asked, rather than squint through the peephole.

"Mike. I need you, Hannah."

Those four little words were definitely the key to Hannah's heart. She couldn't resist a plea for help, even from the ugliest, meanest person in Lake Eden. And Mike Kingston was about as far from that description as you could get. He was ruggedly handsome, a tall Viking-type of a man, and although he was tough and fit and could pulverize an opponent in a fight, she was fairly sure there wasn't a mean bone in his body. "Come in," she invited, unlocking the door and holding it open for him.

"Thanks, Hannah. I had to run out here to talk to your downstairs neighbor, and I thought I'd drop by to pick up those crackers, if you've got them."

"I do. But Sue and Phil aren't in any trouble, are they?"

"Not at all. Phil witnessed an accident on the freeway when he was coming home from his night shaft at DelRay Manufacturing. I just took his statement." Mike glanced down at the plate in her hand and his eyes widened. "That looks good! What is it?"

"Salmon Cakes, hot off the stove . . . or the cell phone, in Mother's case."

"Huh?"

"I was talking to her when I was frying them and she thought . . . never mind. It's not important. Sit down and eat. I've got plenty for two."

There was a yowl from the feline who was watching Mike with half-narrowed eyes, and Hannah turned to reassure him. "That's two and a cat. I have enough for us, and for Moishe."

"You heard her. Relax, Big Guy." Mike gave Moishe a scratch under his chin as he sat down on the couch. Then he cut off a tiny piece of the Salmon Cake and held it out on the palm of his hand. "Here you go. This should tide you over until you get yours."

Hannah watched as Moishe licked it up daintily. She could hear him purring all the way across the room, and she ducked into the kitchen to dish up another plate.

"What's this sauce on top?" Mike asked when she emerged from the kitchen with her own plate. "It's great!"

Hannah didn't want to tell him, but she couldn't lie outright to a man she'd come within a hair's breadth of marrying. "It's one of Edna Ferguson's tricks," she explained, hoping he wouldn't ask for details.

"Tell me. Whenever I visit my sister, she sends me home with fried chicken. It gets kind of dry when I heat it in the microwave, and I bet this sauce would be good on it."

Poor handsome bachelor who had to bring home leftovers from his sister's table! Hannah almost felt sorry for him until she remembered that scores of Lake Eden ladies would jump at the chance to let him taste their home cooking. But he *did* need her, if only for cooking advice, and Hannah couldn't resist telling him the truth. "Okay, I'll let you in on the secret, but you can't tell anyone else."

"If I do, you'll have to kill me?" Mike quipped, flashing the mischievous grin that always made her feel weak in the knees.

"Oh, I wouldn't kill you. I'd lock you up in a closet and . . ."

Hannah clamped her mouth shut. Some things were better left unsaid.

"And what?"

"And leave you there until I decide what to do with you," Hannah finished her sentence with the best ambiguity she could think of on the fly.

"Okay. I promise I won't tell anyone Edna's secret. What is it?"

"Well, I usually make my own dill sauce with fresh baby dill, mayo, and a little cream, but it's better if you make it the night before, and I didn't know I'd be frying Salmon Cakes today."

"Okay. I've had your fresh dill sauce with your Salmon Loaf. It's great, but tell me what this is."

"Campbell's Cream of Celery soup."

"What?"

"It's Campbell's Cream of Celery soup, undiluted. It makes a good sauce in a pinch. Really. All you have to do is heat it in the microwave, and it's even better if you mix in a little dry sherry, but I'm helping Lisa with the potluck buffet tonight, and I thought I'd better not."

"What time are you going out to the lake?"

"Four. I'm stopping by The Cookie Jar first to pick up my cakes, and then I'm heading out. How about you?"

"I should be there by six-thirty as long as I remember to take your crackers with me. Save me a dance tonight, will you?"

"Absolutely," Hannah said, hoping her heart wasn't beating so hard that he could see it through the light sleeveless shell she'd worn to church.

"Tell Andrea, too. And Michelle. I'm crazy about the Swensen sisters."

Hannah smiled, but she would have liked it a lot more if he'd said that he was crazy about just her. Whatever. Mike was Mike, and you had to either take him the way he was or not take him at all.

SALMON CAKES

1 small can salmon***
2 slices bread, crusts removed *(you can use any type of bread)*
1 beaten egg *(just whip it up in a glass with a fork)*
1 teaspoon Worcestershire sauce *(or hot sauce, or lemon juice)*
½ teaspoon dry mustard *(that's the powdered kind)*
¼ teaspoon salt
¼ teaspoon onion powder
2 Tablespoons butter

*** Check the weight on your can of salmon. It should weigh between 7 ounces and 8 ounces—red salmon is best, but pink will do.

Open your can of salmon and drain it in a strainer. Remove any bones or dark skin. Flake it with a fork and put it in a small mixing bowl.

Cut the crusts from two standard-sized slices of bread and tear the middle part into small pieces. Add the pieces to the bowl with the salmon.

Add the egg and mix it all up with a fork.

Mix in the Worcestershire sauce *(or lemon juice, or hot sauce,)* the dry mustard, salt, and onion powder.

Stir it all up until it resembles a thick batter with lumps.

Divide the batter into thirds. *(You don't have to be exact—nobody's going to measure them when you're through. They'll be too busy eating them.)*

Spread a sheet of wax paper on a plate and pick up one of the lumps of batter. Squeeze it together with your hands to form a firm ball. Place it on the wax paper and flatten it like a hamburger patty. The patty should be about a half-inch thick.

Hannah's 1ˢᵗ Note: If you flatten your Salmon Cakes too much and you'd like to make them thicker, just go ahead. All you have to do is gather the batter into a ball again and start over.

Shape the other two lumps of batter into balls and then patties. Let them sit on the wax paper for a minute or two to firm up even more.

Melt the two Tablespoons of butter in a frying pan over medium heat.

Place the Salmon Cakes in the pan and fry them over medium heat until they're golden brown on the bottom. *(That should take approximately 2 minutes.)* Flip the patties over and brown the other side. *(Total frying time will be approximately 4 to 5 minutes.)* Remember that all you're doing is frying the egg. Everything else has already been cooked.

Drain the Salmon Cakes on a paper towel and transfer to a serving platter. Serve with Dill Sauce, or Edna's Easy Celery Sauce. They're also wonderful with creamed peas, or creamed corn.

Hannah's 2nd Note: When I do these for the family, I use my electric griddle and triple the recipe so I have nine Salmon Cakes. If you don't have an electric griddle or you prefer to use a frying pan, you can fry them and then put them in a single layer in a pan in an oven set at the lowest temperature to keep them warm until you've fried them all. Make sure to refrigerate any leftovers. I've put leftover Salmon Cakes in the refrigerator overnight and heated them in the microwave the next day for lunch. They're not quite as good as freshly fried, but they're still very good. (They're also good cold.)

Hannah's 3rd Note: You can also make Tuna Cakes, Shrimp Cakes, Crab Cakes, Chicken Cakes and any other "cake" you can think of. All you need to do is substitute 6 to 8 ounces of the canned, or cooked and chopped main ingredient of your choice for the salmon. (This is why I always keep a can of salad shrimp, a can of tuna, and a can of chopped chicken in my pantry.)

Yield: Serves 3 if you team it up with a nice green salad and a slice of something yummy for dessert. *(If you serve it alone, as a total lunch, it'll work for one person with a big appetite, one person with a little appetite, and a cat.)*

DILL SAUCE

Hannah's Note: This sauce is best if you make it at least 4 hours in advance and refrigerate it in an airtight container. (Overnight is even better.)

> 2 Tablespoons heavy cream
> ½ cup mayonnaise
> 1 teaspoon crushed fresh baby dill (*if you can't find baby dill, you can make it with ½ teaspoon dried dill weed, but it won't be as good*)

Mix the cream with the mayonnaise until it's smooth and then mix in the dill. Put the sauce in a small bowl, cover it with plastic wrap, and refrigerate it for at least 4 hours.

EDNA'S EASY CELERY SAUCE

Hannah's 1st Note: If you make your Salmon Cakes at the drop of a hat, the way I occasionally do, you won't have time to make the Dill Sauce. All Edna's Easy Celery Sauce requires is a can of cream of celery soup and some milk or cream.

Hannah's 2nd Note: The can of cream of celery soup should be in your pantry as a staple, along with a can of

cream of mushroom soup, and a can of tomato soup, and a can of cream of chicken soup. They're a good base for any sauce you want to make on the fly.

One can of cream of celery soup, undiluted *(10 to 11 ounces depending on brand name—used Campbell's).*
Milk or cream to thin

Open the can. Dump it in a small microwave-safe bowl. Heat it in the microwave until it's piping hot. *(Try 30 seconds and see if it's hot enough. If not, heat at 15-second increments until it is. Thin it with the milk or cream to sauce consistency.)*

Drizzle the sauce over the Salmon Cakes, sprinkle on a little parsley or fresh dill if you happen to have it, and serve immediately.

Hannah's 3rd Note: Edna tells me that you can also use undiluted cream of chicken soup (if you're using the chicken variation,) cream of mushroom soup, or cream of garlic soup. She also said something about cream of asparagus soup for Shrimp Cakes, but I haven't tried it.

Chapter Three

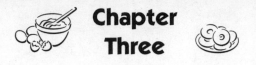

Hannah knew that if she had to hear one more chorus of the *Beer Barrel Polka,* she'd scream. It reminded her of the dance she'd shared with Marvin Dubinski only minutes before, and that wasn't a pleasant memory. Once dinner had been served and the dessert buffet had been set out on the bar, the dancing had begun. Hannah had danced nonstop for at least thirty minutes, going from partner to partner. Her first partner was Mike, and then Norman, followed by Bill, Lonnie, Mayor Bascomb, and Jon Walker. Her last partner, Marvin Dubinski, had finished Hannah off for the night. They'd danced to a polka, and Marvin had stepped on her feet a total of six times. Now she was hiding out in a booth with Marge Beeseman and her family, hoping that Marvin wouldn't spot her and ask her to dance any more polkas.

Mercifully, Frankie and the Frankfurters, the local band Lisa and Herb had hired for the dance, segued into a waltz. At least Hannah *thought* it was a waltz. It had a one-two-three, one-two-three rhythm, but the band played it so rapidly, most of the couples on the floor gave up trying to move to the music and came to a halt. The few that did attempt to dance whirled around as fast as the blades in the window fans, bumping into the stationary couples and making them scramble to get out of the way.

At least Frankie, if that really was his name, realized his

mistake. He led his group into a slower number, one with a cuddle-up-and-barely-move rhythm that restored order to the dance floor. Hannah tuned back into the conversation at hand, just in time to hear Marge Beeseman's question. Since Hannah was sandwiched in the big round booth between Marge and her brother, Gus, she had no choice but to be a party to their conversation.

"Did you find what you wanted to take from your old room?" Marge asked.

"Part of it. I couldn't find my favorite bedspread. I wanted to hang it on the wall in the guest bedroom. That has a western theme."

"Are you talking about the chenille one with Roy Rogers on it?"

"Yeah. The trunks were all labeled, and Lisa showed me the one from my bedroom. I thought it would be there, but it wasn't. I guess I'll have to go to some antique stores to find another one."

"That might be really expensive," Marge cautioned him. "Some of those old memorabilia items go for an arm and a leg."

"Doesn't matter. I don't mind paying for what I want. It's one of the advantages to having money."

Hannah was still watching the dance floor. The havoc was over, and the mirrored ball that hung from the ceiling rotated like the planets in the science project her father had helped her make in ninth grade. As the ball revolved, it sent beams of colored light down to illuminate the dancers who were now moving sedately. Since everything was calm, and there was no bump or tumble imminent, she turned her attention from the dance floor to Marge's brother, Gus. Hannah assumed that he was just trying to impress people, but he certainly mentioned money a lot!

Gus Klein was a handsome, well-dressed man in his fifties. Just an inch or so short of the six-foot mark, he had carefully styled dark blond hair with an elegant streak of silver over his left temple. The silver streak made him look distinguished, and Hannah suspected a beautician had placed it there. She knew she shouldn't make snap judgments, but he seemed to be a man who was all about appearances. Some people believed that if the package was appealing enough, it didn't really matter what was inside. Hannah was not one of them. Naturally, she preferred an attractive package, but it was what was inside that really counted.

What was inside Gus Klein? Hannah hadn't known him long enough to know, but he seemed a bit shallow to her, and she didn't like his continual bragging about his life in Atlantic City. He'd told them all that he had a standing appointment for a manicure at his office, he called in a masseuse when he felt tense, and when he entertained, he ordered food from the most exclusive restaurant in town and had it delivered to his penthouse condo.

She did know that Gus expected everyone else to wait on him. When Marge had asked him to join her at the buffet line, he'd told her he was too busy talking to some Brainerd cousins and practically ordered her to bring him a plate. The same thing had happened with the dessert buffet. It was as if his time was too valuable to stand in line like the rest of the relatives. He'd sent Lisa off to bring a sampler plate of dessert and coffee for the table, and then he'd passed out what he'd said were real Cuban cigars that he'd imported at great expense.

Hannah looked around for Andrea and spotted her on the dance floor with Bill. Andrea was the fashion expert, and Hannah hoped she'd assessed Gus's clothing. While Hannah didn't know a whole lot about men's attire, or women's either for that matter, she knew that the clothes Gus wore weren't mail order. They weren't mall clothing, either.

So what was the bottom line on Gus? Hannah thought about it for a minute. Most would say that he was handsome, charming, and sophisticated. And for those who didn't dig deeper, all of the above would be correct. But Hannah had the feeling that Gus was none of the above. She couldn't help but feel that he was playing a part, trying to appear urbane and elegant when he was really a beer-and-brat guy. Something wasn't quite right about Gus Klein's public persona, but she couldn't put her finger on what it was.

Hannah glanced at Marge. Lisa's mother-in-law was dressed to the nines tonight in an outfit that Hannah termed *aging hippie,* a phrase she'd never utter out loud for fear she'd hurt Marge's feelings. Some ladies liked to look sleek. Delores was a case in point. Her outfits were always tailored to embrace her perfect figure. Other ladies liked flounces, full skirts that swung out like cowgirls at a Saturday night square dance. Marge liked flutter. Butterfly wings and swooping fringes had nothing on her tonight. She was wearing a purple chiffon pantsuit that fluttered around her legs when she walked, and almost cleared off the table when she made a sweeping gesture.

Jack Herman, Lisa's dad, sat next to Marge. He looked handsome in dark slacks and a lavender shirt, but he didn't look happy. His lips were curved in a smile, but his eyes were angry and Hannah could tell that his smiling countenance was nothing but a polite gesture. Several times during the evening, she'd caught him glaring at Gus. Lisa had mentioned that there was bad blood between them, but when Lisa had asked her father what was wrong, he'd refused to discuss it.

Marge's twin, Patsy, looked so much like Marge that Hannah could believe the stories they'd told about how they used to play jokes on their dates by switching places halfway through the evening. There were ways to tell the twins apart, but only if they were standing side by side. Patsy's hair was slightly darker and she was a bit heavier than Marge. Marge's nose was a smidgen longer. Patsy's eyebrows were darker. It wasn't much of a yardstick to tell them apart, and Hannah was glad they didn't dress alike.

Mac, Patsy's husband, sat next to her. He was handsome

and athletic, and Hannah had caught several of the unattached women at the dance eyeing him appreciatively. Patsy had noticed too, but she didn't seem concerned. Either she trusted her husband completely, or she just didn't care. Hannah was betting on the latter since they were sitting right next to each other without touching. If her psychology professor at college was correct when he lectured on body language, the space between them spoke volumes about the health of their marriage.

"I don't think Mother bought your bedspread at a store," Marge said to Gus.

"She didn't," Patsy confirmed it. "I remember we saved box tops for her and she sent away for it."

"That's right! You know the type of thing we're talking about, don't you, Hannah?"

Hannah was jolted out of her musing and back to the scene by Marge's question. It was a good thing she'd been half listening to the conversation. While she'd much rather be ignored and left to her own thoughts, Marge obviously wanted to include her.

"I think I do," Hannah answered. "Andrea and I saved the little proof of purchase circles from something or other so that Michelle could have a fairy princess wand. All we had to pay was the postage and handling."

"Did she like it?" Patsy asked.

"She loved it. Unfortunately, the little bulb burned out the first week, and Dad couldn't find a replacement."

"That's probably what happened to your bedspread," Marge said to Gus.

"It burned out?" Gus gave her a little grin to show he was kidding.

"Close. It must have fallen apart when Mother washed it to store it in the trunk. But you said you found some things you wanted."

"I got some of my baseball stuff."

"The special bat Dad bought you when you made the team at Jordan High?" Patsy asked.

Gus nodded. "It was right on top, my Louisville Slugger, the one I used in high school. I hit my first home run with that bat. I couldn't find my glove, though." Gus gave a little chuckle. "Maybe that fell apart right along with my bedspread."

"You could be right," Patsy told him. "Leather does that if it's not treated."

"And I know Mother didn't treat it," Marge picked up on her sister's comment. "She kept your old room just as it was for a couple of years, and then she packed everything up and put it in the trunk. Dad dragged it up to the attic, and I'm pretty sure they never looked at it again. It was just too painful, you know?"

Gus shifted a bit and Hannah could tell he was uncomfortable. "Well, I'm glad they kept my things for me." He turned to Hannah. "Did you keep anything from your childhood?"

"Let me think about that for a second." Hannah recognized his attempt to steer the conversation in another direction. It was clear he didn't want to answer difficult personal questions. Hannah thought about thwarting his attempt, but Gus was looking at her the way a drowning man might look at a rescue vessel, and she simply had to help him out. "I still have the pink satin toe shoes I bought when I was a kid."

"Ballet?" Marge sounded incredulous. "I didn't know you took ballet lessons."

"That's just the problem. I didn't. When I was about eleven, I got the notion that if only I had the proper shoes, I could dance the lead in *Swan Lake*."

"So you got the shoes and discovered that you couldn't do it?" Marge asked.

"That's right," Hannah replied, dismissing it with a smile and a shrug, not mentioning the disappointment she'd suffered when she couldn't achieve *en pointe* without grasping the back of a sturdy chair and hauling herself up on it. She'd been so sure she was a natural in a field that had no naturals, only dedication, constant practice, and years and years of ballet training. But this wasn't the time or the place to bare her soul. It was best to make light of it "Another childhood dream fractured. You know how it is. But I *did* keep all the Degas prints my mother bought for me."

"So here we all are, reliving old memories," Jack said, staring directly across the table at Gus. "Remember Mary Jo Kuehn?"

The silence that followed Jack's question was so heavy Hannah imagined she could cut with a knife. She wasn't sure what it meant since she'd never heard of Mary Jo Kuehn, but everyone except Jack looked uncomfortable.

"I remember," Gus said, "and I'll never stop missing her. She was such a pretty girl. But I met another pretty girl today, Jack."

"Who was that?" Marge asked, seizing the opportunity to change the subject.

"Jack's oldest daughter, Iris." Gus turned back to Jack. "She doesn't look at all like you, so I guess she must take after her mother. And speaking of Emmy, you're here with Marge. Did you and Emmy get a divorce?"

Jack gave him a look that would freeze lilacs in July. "Emily is dead."

"I'm sorry to hear that." Gus sounded sincere to Hannah's ears. "How about your sister, Heather?"

"She's dead, too," Jack repeated, still glowering.

"Do you remember Mr. Burnside?" Marge trilled, and Hannah's eyebrows shot up. She'd never heard Marge sound so intensely cheerful before.

"Of course." Patsy sounded deliberately cheerful, too. "I thought I was going flunk algebra, but he took pity on me."

"You did all right," Marge reached over to pat her hand. "Did you enjoy the dessert buffet?"

"Oh, my yes! It's absolutely scrumptious. And your carrot cake . . ." Patsy turned to smile at Hannah. "I've always been known for my carrot cake, but yours . . . it's even better than mine. Mac had three pieces!"

"I had four," Gus declared, "and I want more." He turned and winked at Hannah. "I don't suppose you've got another cake stashed anywhere?"

"Actually . . . yes, I do. I was saving it for tomorrow, but I can always put it out if there isn't any left on the platter."

Mac, who was at the edge of the booth, stood up to look. "There's half a platter left."

"Gus just wants you to leave him a private stash so he can eat it later," Marge informed her. "He used to do the same thing with my Cocoa Fudge Cake. I always had to bake two, one for the family and the other one for Gus."

"You're right," Gus admitted. "I'm guilty as charged." He turned to Hannah. "Will you put away a plate of carrot cake for me?"

"Oh. Well . . . sure. How much do you want?"

"At least half a cake," Patsy answered for him. "That's what he used to ask Marge for. And in the morning, it was all gone. Gus was a midnight refrigerator bandit."

"So is Jack," Marge said, in an attempt to bring Jack into the conversation.

Hannah turned to look at Jack. He wasn't having it. He was just staring at Gus and glowering.

"I don't suppose you brought that Cocoa Fudge Cake tonight, did you?" Gus addressed Marge. Hannah was sure he'd noticed that Jack was glowering at him, but he preferred to ignore it.

"Not tonight, but I'm baking it tomorrow. I'll make an extra cake, just for you."

"For me and not for your boyfriend?" Gus glanced across the table at Jack.

"Jack isn't exactly my boyfriend, although I love him a lot. I always have and I always will." Marge shot Gus a level look and took a deep breath. Hannah suspected that she was debating the wisdom of saying more. "And speaking of love," Marge went on, "how could you leave Lake Eden in the middle of the night without saying anything to any of us?"

Gus reared back as if he'd been hit buy a salvo of enemy arrows. "I didn't do it on purpose, Marge. It was just that I had to go then. I don't have to explain myself to you or to anyone else."

"No, you don't," Patsy chimed in. "But you *should* have. It's too late for the people who loved you the most. Our parents are dead now. They deserved an explanation, or at least a good-bye before you left."

"They never stopped believing that you'd come home," Marge added. "And you never even wrote, or called, or anything. We saw their hearts break, and we want to know why."

Hannah's head swiveled to Gus. He looked horribly uncomfortable. For a split second she almost felt sorry for him, but what Marge and Patsy had said was true. Gus hadn't bothered to call, or write, or contact his parents in any way. And now it was too late.

Gus was silent for a moment. And then he leaned forward. "I couldn't," he said. "I had to prove myself first. And that didn't happen until a couple of years ago."

Hannah began to frown. Gus had been bragging about his nightclub business when she'd joined Marge in the booth. "But you said you were successful once your flagship, Mood Indigo, got off the ground. You also said that you paid off the money you borrowed to start it over twenty years ago. You could have come back then. Your parents were still alive."

Gus turned to her, and Hannah fought to the urge to shrink back. He didn't look happy that she'd caught him in an inconsistency.

"What is this? The inquisition?" He gave Hannah a look

intended to warn her off. "I didn't want to put the cart before the horse. There's no way I wanted to contact Mother and say I was a successful businessman and then fail in my plans for expansion."

"Expansion?" Mac leaned closer. "You have more than one nightclub now?"

"You bet. I've got four, and I'm thinking about expanding again. Atlantic City is a great place to own a nightclub, and they're popping up all over."

Mac leaned slightly closer to Gus. "You must be pulling in a good profit to think about opening another one."

"Oh, I am. You don't expand unless you've got the money to do it. That's what I meant about putting the cart before the horse. It always takes a while to get a new club going."

"The construction of the building?" Mac guessed.

"That and the fact you have to get the customers in and then keep them coming back. You definitely have to set aside a big budget for advertising."

"I like the name Mood Indigo," Marge said, and Hannah noticed that she squeezed Jack's hand. "Do all the others have a blue theme?"

Gus looked relieved now that they'd switched to a less personal subject, and he favored his sister with a smile. "It's clever of you to realize that. We play mainly blues in the clubs. And the décor in each club is a different shade of blue. There's Mood Indigo, you already know about that. And then there's the Aqua Room, Sky Blue Heaven, and Midnight Stars. I got that idea from the map of the heavens I used to have on my ceiling. It's one of the reasons I wanted to go through that trunk from my old bedroom. I thought I might come up with another name for a nightclub."

"True Blue," Jack offered. "Except that it wouldn't fit. You've never been true to anyone in your life."

"And you've never minded picking up the leftovers," Gus shot back.

There was a moment of silence when everyone just held

collective breaths. Hannah wondered if they would sit there forever, just wanting for that second shoe to drop. She hated to think of what might happen if it did. Jack was glaring at Gus. And Gus was glaring at Jack. This could be very awkward, especially since she was seated next to Gus.

"Excuse me," Hannah said. And the tension eased as everyone turned to look at her. "I think I'll check my cake platter to see if I need to cut more. Does anyone else want more dessert?"

"I do!" Marge seized the opportunity.

"Me, too," Patsy said, giving Mac a little nudge. "Come on. Slide out and let's get some more of Hannah's Special Carrot Cake."

Marge grabbed Jack's arm and almost pushed him out of booth. "Let's go, Jack. I need some more coffee."

Jack slid out of the booth and held out a hand to Marge. Then he turned to give Gus a final glare. "I'm out of here. And it's not a minute too soon."

And then they were gone, Jack, Marge, Patsy, and Mac. And that left Hannah alone in the booth with Gus.

"You're leaving, too?" Gus asked in a tone she couldn't quite read.

"Well . . . I should probably cut the last cake and refill the platter," Hannah hedged awkwardly. But then she took pity and said, "Why don't you come with me? I'll fix a plate of cake for you and you can stash it somewhere for later."

"Hold on a second. I'll be right with you." Gus popped what looked to Hannah like a pill in his mouth and washed it down with the scotch and soda Marge had gone to fetch for him earlier.

"Should you be drinking and taking meds at the same time?" Hannah couldn't resist asking.

"It's just an over-the-counter antacid. That pâté had too much horseradish for me."

Since they were sitting at the center of the horseshoe-shaped booth, Gus slid out from one direction and Hannah slid out from the other. Gus leaned over to retrieve his glass, and while she was waiting for him, Hannah looked out over the crowd. She was surprised to see Jack standing only a few feet away, holding Marge's arm while she exchanged a few words with another couple in a booth.

Hannah gave a little wave, but all Jack did in return was scowl. He'd obviously heard her talking to Gus, because the look on his face was disapproving. If she had to describe it, Hannah would say that Jack Herman looked as if he'd just overheard her making a pact with the devil!

HANNAH'S SPECIAL CARROT CAKE

Preheat oven to 350 degrees F., rack
in the middle position.

2 cups white *(granulated)* sugar
3 eggs
¾ cup vegetable oil *(not canola, or olive, or
anything but veggie oil)*
1 teaspoon vanilla extract
¾ cup sour cream *(or unflavored yogurt)*
2 teaspoons baking soda
2 teaspoons cinnamon *(or ½ teaspoon cardamom
and the rest cinnamon)*
1 ½ teaspoons salt
1 20-ounce can crushed pineapple, juice and all***
2 cups chopped walnuts *(or pecans)*
2 ½ cups flour *(don't sift—pack it down when you
measure)*
2 cups grated carrots *(also pack them down when
you measure)*

*** *That's about 1 ½ cups of crushed pineapple and a
scant cup juice*

Grease *(or spray with Pam)* a 9-inch by 13-inch cake
pan and set it aside.

**Hannah's 1st Note: This is a lot easier with an electric
mixer, but you can also make it by hand.**

Beat the sugar, eggs, vegetable oil, and vanilla together
in a large bowl. Mix in the sour cream *(or yogurt.)* Add the

baking soda, cinnamon *(and cardamom if you used it)* and salt. Mix them in thoroughly.

Add the can of crushed pineapple *(including the liquid)* and the chopped nuts to your bowl. Mix them in thoroughly.

Add the flour by half-cup increments, mixing after each addition.

Grate the carrots. *(This is very easy with a food processor, but you can also do it with a hand grater.)* Measure out 2 cups of grated carrots. Pack them down in the cup when you measure them.

Mix in the carrots BY HAND. Grated carrots tend to get caught on the beaters of electric mixers.

Spread the batter in your prepared cake pan and bake it at 350 degrees F. for 50 minutes, or until a cake tester *(I use a food pick that's a little longer than a toothpick,)* inserted one inch from the center of the cake comes out clean.

Let the cake cool in the cake pan on a wire rack. When it's completely cool, frost with cream cheese frosting while it's still in the pan.

CREAM CHEESE FROSTING

½ cup softened butter
8-ounce package softened cream cheese
1 teaspoon vanilla extract
4 cups confectioner's *(powdered)* sugar *(no need to
    sift unless it's got big lumps)*

Mix the softened butter with the softened cream cheese
and the vanilla until the mixture is smooth.

**Hannah's 2nd Note: Do this next step at room tempera-
ture. If you heated the cream cheese or the butter to soften
it, make sure it's cooled down before you continue.**

Add the confectioner's sugar in half-cup increments
until the frosting is of proper spreading consistency. *(You'll
use all, or almost all, of the sugar.)*

**Hannah's 3rd Note: If you're good with the pastry bag,
remove ⅓ cup of frosting and save it in a little bowl to pipe
on frosting carrots and stems.**

With a frosting knife *(or rubber spatula if you prefer)*
drop large dollops of frosting over the surface of your
cooled cake. I usually end up with somewhere between 6
and 12 dollops. The dollops are like little stacks of frosting—you'll spread neighboring stacks together, working
your way from one end to the other, until you've frosted
the whole cake. *(This dollop method prevents uneven*

frosting thickness and "tearing" of the surface of your cake as you "pull" frosting from one end to the other.)

If you decided to use the pastry bag to decorate your cake, mix most of the remaining frosting with one drop of yellow food coloring and one drop of red food coloring. Mix it thoroughly to make an orange frosting and pipe little carrots on top to decorate your cake. You can save a bit of uncolored frosting to color green and dab green stems on the large end of the carrots.

Chapter Four

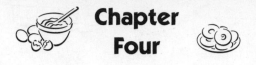

When Hannah's alarm clock went off in her darkened bedroom, she rolled over on her stomach, clamped the pillow over her head, held it in place with her arms, and tried to block out the noise. She wasn't ready to get up yet, certainly not now, and maybe not ever. She'd just closed her eyes, she was very sure of that, and it couldn't possibly be time to get up, get dressed, and drive to work. Perhaps the power had gone off in the middle of the night, causing her alarm clock to malfunction. Or perhaps she'd goofed when she'd set it last night. Whatever the reason, she was absolutely certain it couldn't possibly be four-thirty in the morning.

She really should check on the time, but that meant she'd have to open her eyes. If she kept them closed, she might be able to drift off to sleep again. Quite clearly it wasn't time to get up. She wouldn't be this tired if it were. She assessed her level of exhaustion and decided it had to be two-thirty or three in the morning. If she'd gotten another hour or two of sleep, her eyelids wouldn't feel as if they'd been weighted down with hockey pucks.

Hannah gave a little smile under her protective pillow. How much did hockey pucks weigh, anyway? She seemed to remember that she'd looked it up once, and the regulation weight was between five and a half and six ounces. That was the NHL standard. Then there were the blue four-ounce training puck, and the two-pound steel puck that was used to increase wrist strength. There were also hollow, lightweight, orange fluorescent pucks that were used for road hockey and floor hockey. Roller hockey pucks were made of plastic in light, visible colors. They were available in yellow, orange, pink, and green, but red was the most popular color.

Hannah gave a little groan. Now that she'd recalled almost everything she'd read or heard about hockey pucks, she was wide-awake. And her alarm clock was still ringing. She had to reach out and shut it off. It would wake the neighbors if it continued to ring.

Her eyes popped open, and Hannah sat bolt upright in bed. Her alarm clock couldn't be ringing. It didn't ring. It beeped. Her *phone* was ringing, and that meant something was horribly wrong. Not even her mother called her before six in the morning!

Two-thirty. Hannah glanced at the lighted display on her clock as she reached for the phone by her bed. She snatched it from the cradle, her heart beating hard, hoping against hope that it was a wrong number and nothing awful had happened to her family. "Hello?" she croaked, quickly clearing her throat so that she could talk.

"Hannah?" a young female voice asked.

"Yes. Who's this?"

"It's Sue Plotnik from downstairs. Is everything all right up there?"

Hannah glanced around. Everything looked fine, and she was fine, too, if she didn't count the fact that her pulse was racing. "I'm fine, and everything looks okay. What's the matter?"

"We're not sure. The noise woke us up. Don't you hear it?"

Hannah started to ask what noise Sue was talking about

when she heard it, a low rumbling and thumping like an un-
balanced load of clothing in a washing machine. "I hear it
now. What is it?"

"Phil thought there must be something wrong in your
master bathroom. The thumping is loudest when we stand in
our bathroom and that's right below your bathroom."

"Hold on and I'll go check."

"Wait!" Sue sounded panicked. "Phil says not to go in
there alone. He thinks maybe a burglar tried to get in your
bathroom window and got stuck."

"That couldn't be it. Right after I moved in, Bill put locks
on all my windows. They only open far enough to let the air
in."

"Okay, then. I'll hang on while you go check, and if you're
not back on the line in two minutes, I'll send Phil up with the
extra key."

Hannah's heart was beating hard as she placed the receiver
on the nightstand and headed for her bathroom. The door
was open an inch or two, and the rumbling noise was loud.
She really didn't know how she'd slept through it, but she
supposed that if a person was tired enough, that person
could sleep through anything. After a long night of studying
when she was in college, she'd slept through a tornado siren.
She hadn't learned about the tornado until the next morning,
when she emerged from her apartment to find several large
trees uprooted near the entrance to her building.

Hannah inched the door open and stepped cautiously into
the bathroom. The noise was coming from her tub, and it
sounded like thunder in the space that was enclosed by tile
walls and glass doors that turned the tub into a shower stall.

Something was in there! By the dim nightlight she had
plugged in by the sink, Hannah could see a dark blur racing
around the enclosure. The glass door was open a few inches,
but the dark blur passed by too quickly to identify. It was
short and there was a scrabbling noise as it fought for pur-

chase against the slippery sides of the tub. It had to be some kind of animal, smaller than a dog and about the size of . . .

"Moishe!" Hannah gasped, sliding the glass door open in time to see her feline rounding the back of the tub and heading for the faucets. He skidded to a stop, gave her a *Whatchawant?* look, decided it wasn't something he needed to pursue, and began speeding around the bathtub racetrack again.

There was only one thing to do, and Hannah did it. She stepped into the tub and cornered him as he passed by the faucets again. "That's quite enough, Moishe!" she told him in no uncertain terms.

Moishe studied her expression for a moment or two, and then he jumped out of the tub and ran into the bedroom. Hannah slid the glass door shut and hurried back to the phone. She had some apologizing to do to her downstairs neighbors.

She had been asleep for all of three seconds when it happened again. Hannah got out of bed and dragged her cat out of the bathtub. She remembered sliding the glass door closed, and that meant Moishe had managed to claw it open. Sterner measures had to be taken.

This time Hannah didn't bother to shut the glass door. Moishe would only claw it open again. Instead, she closed the bathroom door and hoped that she wouldn't run into it when she got up out of the sound sleep she was hoping to get before morning. Unfortunately, it *was* morning. One glace at the lighted display of her alarm clock told her that it was ten after three. The term *hellcat* took on new meaning for her as she crawled into bed and attempted to go back to sleep for the hour and minutes that were left before her alarm clock went off.

She was just drifting off when she heard it, a determined scratching at the bathroom door. That conjured up visions of new paint jobs and perhaps even a new bathroom door in

Hannah's mind. Moishe obviously wanted to run more laps in the Bathtub Grand Prix, and he was bound and determined to claw, bite, or tunnel his way in.

Hannah gave a little groan and sat up. She'd been awakened from a sound sleep twice in one night by the ungrateful feline she'd taken in from the cold Minnesota winters, kept healthy with regular vet visits, and fed good nutritious food every day. She'd even bought him his own expensive feather pillow, and she let him snuggle under her comforter. She felt betrayed, and that made her angry, but getting annoyed at Moishe wouldn't solve her problem. She had to calm him down before he found another noisy pastime that would bother her neighbors.

There was only one action to take, one thing that would managed to calm her hyperactive pet so that he wouldn't cause trouble. She flicked on the light, shut off the alarm that would sound in a little over an hour anyway, and headed for the kitchen to put on the coffee. She'd pretend it was morning and feed Moishe. And once he was fed, he'd probably nap on the back of the couch. By then it would be too late for her to try to go back to sleep again, so she'd mix up a batch of Raisin Drops, the new cookie recipe her friend Lois Brown had sent her from Phoenix, and bake them when she got to The Cookie Jar.

RAISIN DROPS

Preheat oven to 350 degrees F., rack
in the middle position.

1 ½ cups raisins *(I've used regular raisins, and also golden raisins—they're both good.)*
1 ½ cups water *(right out of the tap is fine)*

---

3 ½ cups all purpose flour *(don't sift—just scoop it out and level if off with a knife)*
1 teaspoon salt
1 teaspoon baking soda
1 teaspoon baking powder

---

1 cup softened butter *(2 sticks, ½ pound)*
1 ½ cups white *(granulated)* sugar
3 eggs, beaten *(just whip them up in a glass with a fork)*
1 teaspoon vanilla extract

Approximately ½ cup white *(granulated)* sugar for later

Hannah's 1st Note: Hank, the bartender down at the Lake Eden Municipal Liquor Store, suggested that you could soften the raisins in brandy or rum, instead of water. (I used water.)

Put the raisins and the water in an uncovered saucepan. Simmer them on the stove until all the water is absorbed. *(This took me about 20 minutes.)*

Move the saucepan to a cold burner, or on a potholder on your counter, and cool the raisins for 30 minutes. *(If you're in a hurry, you can speed up this cooling process by sticking the pan in the refrigerator until the raisins are approximately room temperature.)*

In a medium-sized mixing bowl, combine the flour, salt, baking soda, and baking powder. *(I stir mine gently with a whisk so that everything's mixed together.)* Set the bowl aside.

Hannah's 2nd Note: I used an electric mixer for this part of the recipe. You can do it by hand, but it takes some muscle.

Cream the softened butter and sugar together until they're light and fluffy.

Add the eggs, one at a time, and beat until the mixture is a uniform color.

Take your bowl out of the mixer and blend in the raisins and the vanilla by hand.

Fold in the flour mixture carefully. The object is to keep the dough fluffy.

Put approximately ½ cup sugar into a small bowl. Drop dough from a teaspoon *(or Tablespoon if you want large cookies)* into the bowl of sugar. Form the drops into balls with your fingers and move them to a lightly greased *(I*

sprayed it with Pam) cookie sheet, 12 to a standard-sized sheet.

Bake the Raisin Drops at 350 degrees F. for 9 to 10 minutes, or until just lightly browned.

Lois Brown's Note: I bake just a few at first to make sure there's the right amount of flour. If they spread out too thin, add another Tablespoon or two of flour. I have been making this recipe for my family for 40 years.

Yield: 5 to 6 dozen deliciously soft raisin cookies.

Chapter Five

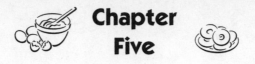

Hannah lowered the driver's window of her cookie truck to enjoy the gentle breeze wafting off the far shore of Eden Lake. Even though the gravel road around the lake was showing wear from the tourists who'd towed heavy boat trailers and campers, she took the ruts at a fast clip to outrun the mosquitoes. She'd been through enough Minnesota summers to know that if she slowed to a crawl, the insects that some people called the Minnesota State Bird would descend on her arm in hungry hordes to gorge on a luncheon of A negative.

It was a perfectly lovely day. The air was scented with a wisp of smoke from a fisherman's shore lunch and a dampness that reminded her of wet swimming suits tossed over a porch rail to dry. The sun was almost straight overhead. When it reached its apex, the shadows of the tall pines that lined the lakeshore would be at their smallest, no larger than a dark circle on the ground around the tree trunks. It was the final Monday in August, and Hannah was playing hooky with her mother's blessing, an occurrence that had never happened during her school days at Jordan High. Delores and Carrie were also playing hooky. They'd closed their antique shop to attend the Beeseman-Herman Family Reunion and sent their assistant, Luanne Hanks, next door to Hannah's cookie and coffee shop. She'd arrived to take charge just as

Hannah was about to turn the CLOSED sign on the front door to OPEN, and now Hannah was free to enjoy this lazy end-of-summer day.

Since she was in no hurry, Hannah took the long way around the lake. Attending Lisa and Herb's family reunion would be fun as long as she didn't get buttonholed by Gus Klein again. She'd spent quite enough time with him at the dance last night.

Hannah let out a groan as she came around a curve and saw that the public parking lot was full. In addition to the relatives who were staying at nearby lake cottages, it appeared that everyone in town had driven out for the day's festivities. It wasn't surprising, considering the size of both families. Lisa was the youngest daughter in the large Herman family. Most of the children had stayed in the area and married into other large families. The same was true for the Beesemans. At last count, over a hundred people had arrived for the reunion.

Since there weren't any vacant parking spots, Hannah created one of her own. That was the beauty of owning a four-wheel-drive cookie truck. When the proper gear was engaged, her Suburban climbed up the three-foot berm of dirt surrounding the parking lot and found a semi-level spot on top.

Hannah took the time to spray on mosquito repellent, a precaution she'd learned early on in life. Then she retrieved the large box of cookies she'd packed to add to the lunch table. Kids loved cookies, and there were plenty of kids at the family reunion. She held the box with both hands, dug in her heels to walk down the berm, and then hurried toward the picnic tables by the shore where a crowd was gathering.

Loud, merry voices floated up to greet her. Hannah spied Lisa standing on top of a picnic table, holding a cheerleading megaphone to her lips. She was wearing a red T-shirt with the legend FAMILY IS EVERYTHING.

"It's time for the family portrait," Lisa called out. "We're going to have the lake in the background, so line up at the edge of the water behind the two chairs for your host and hostess. That's my dad, Jack Herman, and Herb's mom, Marge Beeseman. Norman and Herb will tell you what row you're in if you can't figure it out for yourself. We want the tallest in the back and the shortest in the front."

Hannah set the cookies down on the food table and headed for the shore to watch. She'd heard that Norman had offered to take the group pictures, and perhaps she could help.

"Hannah!"

Hannah knew that voice, and thankfully it wasn't Gus. "Hi, Mother," she said, turning to greet the fashionable, dark-haired woman who would die rather than exceed the petite dress size she'd worn in high school.

"Hello, dear." Delores steadied herself against her eldest daughter's arm and shook the sand from one white high-heeled sandal. "I wish I hadn't worn these today, but I didn't think the beach would be quite this sandy."

Hannah laughed. "It's a beach, Mother. By definition it's sandy."

"You're right, of course. But I didn't think it would be *this* sandy." Delores paused for a moment, and then she gave Hannah a smile. "Did you like the surprise we sent you this morning?"

For a brief moment Hannah was puzzled, but then she got it. "You mean Luanne. That was really thoughtful of you, Mother. I didn't think I'd be able to drive out here until we closed."

"Anything for my dearest daughter."

Uh-oh! Warning bells sounded in Hannah's head. Her mother wanted something . . . but what?

"I hope you can relax and have a good time today. You deserve a little break, Hannah."

The warning bells turned into klaxons, and yellow caution lights began to blink on and off. "Thanks, Mother," Hannah responded. And then, just because she couldn't resist, she asked, "What do you want?"

Her mother reared back in surprise. "*Want?* What makes you think I *want* anything? Just because I called you my dearest daughter and I said I you deserved to relax and have a good time doesn't mean I *want* anything."

"I'm sorry," Hannah said, backpedaling as fast as she could. "I thought there was something you wanted me to do for you."

"Well . . . now that you mention it . . ." Delores gave an elaborate shrug. "You could find Marge's brother Gus for me. No one's seem him since the dance last night. When he didn't show up for the family picture, they sent me to find him. But my shoes . . ." she glanced down at the stylish sandals. "They're just not suitable for trying to locate someone. You know what I mean, don't you, dear?"

Caught like a rat in a trap, like a fly on a sticky spiral of flypaper, like a deer in the headlights, like a moth fluttering helplessly against . . .

"Hannah?"

Delores interrupted her mental chain of similes, and Hannah focused on the here and now. Delores *had* wanted something, and now she knew what it was. "Okay, Mother." she said, bowing to the inevitable. "I'll go find Gus for you."

Nothing was ever easy. Hannah gazed around the small lake cottage. The only living creature inside was a small green frog hopping determinedly from the bedroom closet toward the kitchen alcove. Unless Gus had met a witch who'd turned him into the Frog Prince, he wasn't here. And since his Jaguar was still parked in the driveway, he'd gone somewhere on foot. But where? Eden Lake was far from being the largest body of water in Minnesota, but it would still take several hours to walk around the perimeter searching for him.

The frog gave a croak, and Hannah watched as he hopped up on the counter and into the sink. He landed next to what looked like a green-and-white capsule, and Hannah picked it up just in case it was something that could hurt him. There were markings, probably indicating the manufacturer, but they were so blurred Hannah couldn't read them.

There was no pill bottle on the counter, and the bathroom medicine cabinet had been empty and standing open when she'd checked the bathroom. She didn't know where the pill had come from, so she couldn't put it back. She supposed she could wrap it in plastic and toss it in the open suitcase that Gus had left on the bed, but the green-and-white capsule appeared to be a twin to the over-the-counter antacid she'd seen Gus take at the dance last night, and that meant it was probably expendable.

She glanced down at the capsule again, and her decision was made for her. The powder inside was already starting to leak out of the side. It was dissolving from the slight bit of moisture that had gathered in the bottom of the sink and there was no sense saving a dissolved capsule. She poked it down the drain so the frog couldn't get it, and ran some water to flush it down. That was when she realized that there were no dirty breakfast dishes. It was a cinch that Gus hadn't washed them. The dishtowel hanging on a rack by the side of the sink was bone dry.

"No dishes," Hannah said to the frog, who was looking at her with inscrutable black eyes. The frog didn't comment, not even a croak, as she opened the refrigerator door. A quick peek inside explained the absence of dirty dishes. There was no food. The only contents were a bottle of Jack Daniels and two cans of beer. There was nothing in the freezer compartment, either, except two trays of ice cubes, the old metal kind with the dividers between the cubes that nobody could pry up if they were filled too full. If Gus had wanted something other than a boilermaker for breakfast, he'd probably walked over to the Eden Lake Store to buy supplies.

Hannah ran a little more water in the sink for the frog and then she headed across the road to the store. It had been one of her favorite places as a child. The old-fashioned bell on the door tinkled as she pushed it open and stepped in. Some things never changed, and Hannah found that comforting. The interior of the store still smelled the way it always had, a curious mixture of ring bologna, dill pickles in a large jar on the counter, and elderly bananas that had gotten too ripe for anything except banana bread.

"Hello, Hannah." Ava Schultz came out from the back, pushing aside the curtain that concealed her living quarters from her customers' view. A small woman prone to quick movements and rapid speech, she reminded Hannah of a little brown wren, flitting from one part of the store to another and seldom lighting in one place for long. Ava had fashionably cut, perfectly coiffed, dark brown hair without a touch of gray. Delores and her friends were certain that, she wore a wig, since Bertie Straub, the owner of the Cut 'n Curl, insisted that Ava had never come in, not even once, to have her hair cut, styled, or colored.

"Hi, Ava." Hannah walked over to the main attraction, a shiny metal case filled with every available Popsicle flavor. "Anything new since I grew up?"

Ava gave a little laugh and joined her at the case. "See the three boxes in the middle?" she asked, pointing to them. "Those are Rainbows, Scribblers, and Great Whites."

"Never heard of them."

"Of course not. We didn't have them when you were a kid. All we carried then were the double pops in a variety of flavors."

"Rhubarb," Hannah said with a grin. "That was my favorite."

Ava's mouth dropped open. "They never made rhubarb!" she exclaimed. "You're pulling my leg, Hannah."

"You're right. I should have known I couldn't put one over on Winnetka County's leading Popsicle authority."

"I *do* like to keep up with it," Ava admitted. "The kids enjoy hearing about the new products, and they've got so many nowadays." She pointed to another box. "Look at those Lifesaver Super Pops. From the bottom up, they're pineapple, orange, cherry, and raspberry. And over here are the Incredible Hulks. They're part of the Firecracker Super Heroes series. The Hulk is strawberry-kiwi, grape, and green apple. They've even got Big Foot. It's cherry and cotton candy swirled together and shaped like a foot with a gumball. Get it?"

"Big Foot. Cute. Popsicles have come a long way since nineteen-oh-five when Frank Epperson left his lemonade and stir stick out on the porch and it froze solid overnight."

"You remembered!" Ava gave her the same smile a teacher might bestow on a favorite student.

"Of course I did." Hannah smiled back. Ava had told her the story enough times. But she wasn't here to discuss Popsicle history. She had to find out if Ava had seen Gus. "Did Gus Klein come in this morning?" she asked. "They're lining up for the family reunion picture, and they sent me to find him."

"I haven't seen him since he walked me back here last night after the dance. And before you can ask, it's not what you think. He just wanted me to open the store so he could get some milk to go with that carrot cake you gave him."

"So you opened the store for him?"

"Of course I did. A customer's a customer, even after midnight. He bought his groceries, and then we had a drink together and waited for the cars to clear out of the parking lot. He said he hid your cake behind the bar and he was going back to eat it as soon as no one else was around. I think that was so he wouldn't have to share. We went to school together, you know. Gus never was any good at sharing, not even in kindergarten."

Hannah thought about that for a moment. On the one hand, she was pleased that Gus liked her Special Carrot Cake so much that he hadn't wanted to give any away. On the other hand, she'd given him a half-dozen pieces, and he could have given one to Ava.

"Anyway," Ava went on, "he got the milk and some other groceries."

"Food for breakfast?" Hannah guessed, remembering the empty refrigerator.

"Not what a normal person would eat for breakfast, but that didn't surprise me. Gus was never what you'd call a normal person. From little on, he had his own style, you know?"

"What did he buy?" Hannah was curious.

"Sliced ham, bread, Swiss cheese, a half-dozen little packages of potato chips, and ten Milky Ways, the old-fashioned kind with the milk chocolate, not the dark. The last I saw Gus, he was heading back to the pavilion with his cooler and his sack of groceries."

"Cooler? What cooler?"

"Guess I forgot to mention that he bought one of those disposable coolers. I asked him why he needed a cooler when there was a refrigerator in his cottage, and he said it wasn't working right."

Hannah frowned. When she'd checked the cabin, the refrigerator had been working just fine. The ice cubes in the trays hadn't melted, and cold air had rolled out of the door when she'd opened it. Why would Gus lie to Ava about it?

"He was supposed to come back to pay me for the groceries this morning," Ava went on, "but he never showed."

Ominous music began to play in the recesses of Hannah's mind. It sounded like a cross between Bach's *Toccata and Fugue in D minor,* and the soundtrack of a bad horror movie. But she didn't have time to think about that now. "What time was it when Gus left here last night?"

"A little after one-thirty. I got ready for bed, that takes about ten minutes, and I looked at the clock before I turned off the lights. It was a quarter to two."

Hannah reached reflexively for her steno pad, the kind she

used for murder cases, but she quickly thought better of it. This was nothing more than a missing person, someone who hadn't shown up for the family reunion picture. Gus hadn't left for good, his car was still here, but he could have found a warmer, more hospitable place to sleep than the single bunk in his unheated lake cottage. There had been at least five dozen women at the dance last night. One of them might have thought a good-looking, middle-aged man like Gus was irresistible, especially since he wore expensive designer clothes and sported a Rolex watch and a diamond pinkie ring. Lake Eden women didn't meet many men who drove Jaguars and flashed around money at every opportunity. Gus could have asked one of the women for a late date, and she could have accepted. Then he could have waited with Ava until no one was around, gone back to collect the carrot cake, and walked to the woman's cottage bearing gifts of what appeared to Hannah to be picnic fixings.

The more Hannah thought about it, the more sense it made. Perhaps Gus and his lady friend had decided to skip the group photo this morning, and they were sitting at her kitchen table right now, eating a ham and cheese sandwich, and sharing the carrot cake . . .

". . . or not," Hannah muttered under her breath, and then she turned to Ava. "I'd better get going. They'll be ready to take that photo soon."

"I hope you find Gus. If you do, will you do me a favor?"

"What?" Hannah asked, knowing better than to promise blindly.

"Right after they snap that picture, grab Gus by the ear and march him back here to pay his bill. You can tell him I said that groceries don't grow on trees, not unless they're apples that is."

Chapter Six

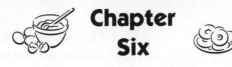

There was only one logical place to look, and Hannah headed straight for it. The Lake Pavilion was clearly deserted. The sandy parking lot was empty of cars and contained only a crumpled cigarette pack, the remnants of what had once been a blue and white bandanna, and a neatly clipped coupon for a two-fer breakfast at Paula's Pancake House.

As she approached the entrance to the white clapboard structure, Hannah felt an odd prickling at the back of her neck. She'd experienced that sensation before, and it had preceded something unpleasant, something bad, something like discovering a body. She told herself that Gus was fine and she'd find nothing but the debris of a party inside, but her feet dragged a bit as she approached the front entrance.

Last night the pavilion had looked majestic, a gleaming white edifice in the moonlight with its open shutters spilling out warm yellow light into the humid blanket of summer darkness. Music had set up joyful vibrations in the walls, the wooden booths, the old chrome-and-black plastic barstools, and the revelers themselves, causing laughter and loud voices to peal out in a cacophony of raucous gaiety. Today it was . . . Hannah paused, in both mind and step, attempting to think of the word. *Sad.* The word was *sad.* The white paint was peeling, the shutters were warped from exposure to the ele-

ments, and there were a half-dozen brown beer bottles leaning up against the front of the building like tipsy sentinels.
The party was over. Everyone had left. All that remained was
the abandoned pavilion with its curling shards of paint.

Hannah tried the front door, but it was locked, just as
she'd thought it would be. She knocked, calling out for Gus,
but there was no answer. Someone else might have gone back
to find Lisa or Herb to get the key, but Hannah had been born
and raised in Lake Eden, and she knew all about the Lake
Pavilion. In a town where Lover's Lane was regularly patrolled,
and the parking lot at the rear of Jordan High was peppered
with arc lights, the Lake Pavilion was the sole haven for
teenage couples seeking privacy.

The shutter was at the back of the pavilion, the third from
the corner. Hannah found the proper one, tugged on the pad-
lock that had been rigged to open, and removed it. Gaining
access to the pavilion was as easy as her high school friends
had told her it was. She lifted the shutter and propped it open
with the stick that was attached to the side of the window
frame. The opening was a bit above waist height, but she
managed to swing one leg up and over the sill. A moment
later, she was sitting on the sill with both legs hanging down
inside the building, preparing to push off with her hands and
jump down.

She landed awkwardly, which wasn't surprising. She'd
never been the athletic type. Since the shutter was at the back
of the pavilion, not visible from the road, she left it open for
illumination.

All was quiet within. The interior had an air of abandon-
ment, and the only sign of life Hannah heard was the buzzing
of several flies that had been trapped inside. As a child she'd
believed that if she recorded the high-pitched buzzing of
house flies and played it back ever so slowly, she'd hear tiny
little voices saying things like, "Dig in. Hannah spilled strawberry jam on the kitchen table," and "Watch out! Her mother's
got a flyswatter!"

A phalanx of giant trash barrels sat against the wall. Several were close to overflowing with plastic plates from the dessert buffet and Styrofoam cups with the remnants of coffee. Another barrel was marked with a familiar symbol, and it contained bottles and cans for recycling.

Hannah wrinkled up her nose. There was an odd combination of scents in the air, a spicy sweetness from the dessert buffet, the acrid scent of coffee that had perked too long in the pot, the lingering fragrance of perfumes and colognes, and the stale odor of spilled beer and liquor. Those smells were ordinary, what you might expect in a place where a large party had been held. But there was another scent under it all, cloying and sharp, and slightly metallic. It reminded Hannah of something unpleasant, something bad, something . . . but she didn't want to think about that now.

She fought the urge to dig in, to start picking up paper napkins, cups, glasses, and bottles, and stuffing them into the appropriate trash barrels. She reminded herself that Lisa and Herb had organized a crew of relatives to clean the pavilion this afternoon, and nobody expected her to do it. Her number one priority was to find Gus so that they could take the family picture.

A light breeze swept across the shaft of sunlight that streamed through the open window, setting dust motes twirling. As Hannah watched, several more flies buzzed by the beam of sunlight on their way to the mahogany bar against the far wall. The top of the bar was empty except for a brown grocery sack and a white, disposable cooler. It was obvious that Gus had been here. Perhaps he'd been so tired, he'd forgotten his groceries and his cooler.

Fat chance! Hannah's rational mind chided her. *He wanted those groceries. He asked Ava to open the store after hours for him. There's no way he would have forgotten them when he left.*

Another group of flies with the same destination in mind

flew in and headed straight for the bar. If this kept up, Lisa and Herb would never get the insects out in time for the slideshow they'd scheduled for tonight. Hannah hurried to the kitchen, soaked a rag with water, and grabbed a bottle of cleanser. They'd set out the dessert buffet on the bar last night, and it was apparent that whoever had wiped it down hadn't done a good job. She'd clean it thoroughly right now so that no more flies would come in.

Hannah had almost reached her goal when she noticed something. She stopped abruptly and peered down at the floor. The flies weren't the only insect group attracted to this particular locale. There was a line of black carpenter ants streaming toward the bar and disappearing behind it. They must be looping around because there was a returning line of ants and they were carrying morsels of something. Carpenter ants seldom foraged for food during the daylight hours, but their scouts must have discovered something tasty enough to call out the troops.

Hannah moved closer and let out a groan when she saw what had attracted the ants. They were retrieving sweet crumbs from a piece of her carrot cake. It had been dropped, frosting-side down, and mashed to a pulp by someone's heel!

For a brief moment, Hannah was livid. Gus had dropped a piece of her Special Carrot Cake and stepped on it. What a waste! But then she spotted something sticking out from behind the bar, something that looked like a shoe, on a foot, attached to a leg that was presumably connected to a person who was on the floor behind the bar. Hannah set the bottle of cleanser on the barstool as the ominous organ music that had been playing in her mind increased in volume, until the crashing chords almost deafened her.

"Oh, murder!" she breathed, hoping that her words weren't prophetic. But she recognized the shoe, the rich buttery leather that shouted designer footwear with an exorbitant price tag. And the trousers. They were part of an expensive suit that had probably cost more than she made all week in The Cookie Jar. She'd seen the outfit last night at the dance, and she knew precisely who had been wearing it.

Hannah took a bracing breath and made her feet move forward. Gus had come back to the pavilion to eat his cake, but he'd only enjoyed a bite or two before disaster had struck. And now, as Hannah stood there staring, he was lying face up on the floor with a bloodstain resembling a peony in full bloom on the front of his shirt.

Stabbed, or shot, Hannah's rational mind told her, but she ignored it. It didn't really matter what the murder weapon was. Gus was dead . . . or at least she thought he was dead.

Hannah tore her eyes away from the sight and focused on the area around Gus Klein's body. Pieces of her carrot cake were scattered on the floor, and the ants didn't seem to mind that there was a dead body in the middle of their picnic. Except for the cake and the ants, the floor was perfectly clear. Whoever had killed Gus had left nothing resembling a clue behind.

She shut her eyes, praying that she'd experienced a slight delusional episode, perhaps from lack of sleep. Then she opened them again to find that nothing had changed. Gus was still on the floor exactly where he'd been before, and there was no doubt in Hannah's mind that he was dead. His chest was perfectly motionless, and any fool could see that he wasn't breathing.

You should check anyway, the rational voice in her mind prodded her. *Think about how guilty you'd feel if he were still alive and you didn't call for help.*

"Right," Hannah said, swallowing hard. The last thing she wanted to do was touch another dead body, but the voice was right, she'd never forgive herself if Gus were still alive and there was something she could do for him.

Hannah glanced around. There was no pay phone in the pavilion. She patted her pocket. No cell phone, either. She'd left it at home again. That meant she *couldn't* call for help, so there was no need to . . .

So you can't call. So what? Ava's got a phone, and your legs aren't broken. If he's still alive, you can hustle yourself right over to the store and call from there.

"Okay, okay," Hannah answered the inner voice that sounded a whole lot like her mother's. "I'll check."

She swallowed again, took a deep breath for courage, and knelt beside Gus. She reached out with one hand to feel the pulse point at the side of his neck.

Nothing. Hannah pressed a bit harder. Still nothing. He was dead, all right, and it wasn't a pretty sight. She wanted to find something to cover him so the flies that were buzzing around couldn't gather. But that would be the wrong thing to do since she wasn't supposed to touch anything. Gus Klein hadn't stabbed himself in the chest so hard that he'd fallen backwards. This was a murder scene, and she had to call . . .

"Hannah?"

The voice startled her, and she shot to her feet. Herb was standing at the open window.

"You can stop looking, Hannah. We took the picture without Uncle Gus. Norman's going to stick around, so if he shows up later, we'll take another one."

"He won't show up." Her voice sounded strained to her own ears, and Hannah cleared her throat.

"What do you mean, *He won't show up?*"

Hannah cleared her throat again. "He's . . . he . . . call Mike and Bill on your cell phone, will you? It's important."

"Okay, but why?"

"They need to come out here. Uncle Gus is . . . gone," she forced out the words, knowing full well that the woman who hated euphemisms had just used one.

"You mean he left the family reunion without even saying goodbye?"

"Not exactly," Hannah said, sighing as she avoided yet another a direct answer. "Just tell them to hurry. And don't let anyone in until they get here."

Chapter Seven

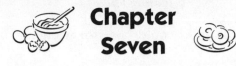

Hannah gazed out across the blue-green expanse of the lake. The sun was shining brightly, the water sparkled as she skimmed it with the tips of her fingers, and a light breeze lifted her hair from the nape of her neck. The warmth of the sun and the serene beauty of the lake was almost enough to erase the memory of Gus . . . almost, but not quite.

Norman rowed smoothly across the water. He'd been waiting for her when she left the pavilion, and he'd led her down to the water and launched the boat.

"Where are we going?" Hannah asked him. They were in the middle of Eden Lake, and she was glad to get away from the continual questions about what had happened, the speculation about who could have done such a terrible thing to Gus, and why.

"We're here." Norman dropped the anchor next to a huge bed of pink and white water lilies.

"Where's here?"

"Eden Lake's water lily garden. Marge told me her father added plants to it every summer."

"It's gorgeous. And all this time, I never knew it was here."

"Are you okay, Hannah?"

"I'm a whole lot better now," she said, admiring the water lilies. "All I need is a white dress and a straw bonnet with a ribbon around it and I could pose for Monet's *The Boat at Giverny.*"

"Or the girl who's not paddling in Renoir's *The Skiff.* But I don't think she has a hat on."

"It's hard to tell with the impressionists. Of course I could always jump in and be a floating face in the middle of any of Monet's water lily paintings. It would be like *Where's Waldo?* and nobody would even spot me."

"Don't do that. Or at least don't do it before you have some lunch." Norman opened the hamper Hannah hadn't noticed before and took out two stemmed glasses. "Let's start with the drinks. Champagne? Or lemonade?"

"I think it'd better be lemonade. Mike hasn't interviewed me yet."

"Smart choice." Norman filled her glass with lemonade from the thermos he'd brought and handed her a sandwich. "Here. You need this."

Hannah accepted the sandwich and bit into it. "Egg salad. My favorite! And this is really good egg salad. Who made it?"

"I did."

Hannah looked at him in surprise. "I thought you didn't cook."

"I don't. But anybody can hard boil an egg, and the rest is just chopping it up, mixing it with other stuff, and spreading it on bread."

"Okay . . ." Hannah stopped and took another bite to be sure. "But this is gourmet egg salad. It even has bits of bacon in it. How did you make it?"

"I'm not sure. I just kept adding things until it tasted right."

"Well, please write it down the next time you make it. I want the recipe."

"Really?" Norman looked surprised.

"Yes, really. Egg salad is one of my favorite comfort foods.

If I eat it, I feel better. It's like macaroni and cheese, or chicken soup. It makes me feel warm and loved."

Norman smiled. "You *are* loved, Hannah."

Hannah wasn't sure what to say. She knew Norman loved her, and she loved him, too. She wanted to tell him she'd marry him and be with him always, but she couldn't. As long as she also had feelings for Mike, it wouldn't be fair to marry Norman.

Norman reached out to put an arm around her. "Sorry. I shouldn't have said that."

"I'm glad you did," Hannah said, reaching out to give him a little hug. And then she changed the subject. "Moishe was really crazy last night. I was so tired, I slept through the noise, but my downstairs neighbor called me at two-thirty in the morning."

"What was Moishe doing?"

"Racing around the tub in my master bathroom. He was making a terrible racket."

Norman began to frown. "Sounds like the Big Guy isn't happy. Is it because you've been gone so much lately?"

"Maybe. He also shredded my couch pillow and left little bits of stuffing all over the floor."

"*Definitely* not happy. I'd invite him out to play with Cuddles, but she's gone on vacation."

Hannah realized she hadn't really talked to Norman for at least a week. They'd both been so busy they hadn't had time to go out to dinner, or just sit over coffee and converse. "What's all this about sending your cat on a vacation?" she asked.

"Oh, I didn't send her. Marguerite dropped by and asked if she could take Cuddles to her friend's house for the week. Since she had Cuddles before I adopted her, I thought it was only fair. Her friend has an older male Persian, and everything's set up for cats. Marguerite thought Cuddles would be in her element."

"But what if she's not?" Hannah was a bit worried. Cats could be finicky about the company they kept.

"She's fine. Marguerite called me this morning to report."

"And if she hadn't been fine, you would have jumped in your car and driven up to get her?"

"Of course. I miss her a lot, but it's good for Marguerite to have this time with her. And after all, I promised we'd have split custody."

Hannah took another bite of her sandwich and gave a little sigh of pleasure. Norman just *had* to write down the ingredients! She'd never tasted an egg salad she liked better. "How about Clara?" she asked, knowing that Marguerite's sister was allergic to cats, dogs, birds, and a whole long list of other things. "Did Doc Knight find a better allergy medicine for her?"

"No, but Clara and Marguerite are taking separate vacations this year. Clara's going to a church retreat, and Marguerite's visiting her friend in Duluth."

"They've never done that before, have they?"

"No. Marguerite says they've always gone everywhere together, but it was Clara's idea to split up this year. Clara's crazy about Cuddles, you know. It's just that she can't be around her without having a reaction. She told Marguerite to bring Cuddles to the condo while she was gone, but Marguerite thought it would be easier to go to her friend's house."

"Kitty dander. It would take a professional cleaning crew to get all the allergens out of the condo for Clara if Marguerite brought Cuddles there."

"Exactly. So tell me more about Moishe. I know you've been gone a lot, but has anything else changed in your routine?"

"Not really, unless you count the cable."

"There's something wrong with your cable?"

"It still works, but our lineup's changed and they haven't sent a new cable guide. We've got over two hundred channels now, and I haven't been able to find Moishe's favorite."

"The Animal Channel?"

"Yes. Do you get it?"

"I get it, but I have a dish. How about Andrea?"

"They've got a dish, too. And Mother never watches it, so she's no help."

"You could always call the cable company and ask." Norman suggested.

"I will, if I ever get a couple of hours to spend on hold. I tried yesterday afternoon, but their business office isn't open on Sunday."

"I think I'm beginning to understand something here," Norman looked thoughtful. "Moishe's lonely because you've been gone so much, and he doesn't have his favorite television channel to watch. Is there anything else he doesn't have?"

"Mice. There's plenty to eat outside right now and the field mice won't come in until the first cold snap. And the maintenance guys replaced the weather stripping on all the doors and windows, so I don't have as many bugs."

"No Animal Channel, no mice, no bugs," Norman reiterated. "Maybe he's bored."

Hannah thought about that for a minute. "You could be right. But what can I do about it? I can't take him to work with me."

"I'll call around. Somebody's bound to know the new cable lineup. I'll get the number of the Animal Channel and tell you."

"That would be great!" Hannah said. Norman was always so good to her. "Maybe I should loosen a little bit of that weather stripping and let some bugs in for him."

"Don't do that. I've got another idea that might work. They're having a sale on Kitty Kondos at the pet store in the mall."

"What are Kitty Kondos?"

"They're three-story activity centers covered with carpeting. The base is the first story. It's a big tub-like thing that supports the rest of the structure."

"*Tub*-like?" Hannah gave a wry smile. "Moishe should like *that!*"

"True, but this tub is carpeted inside and out. He can race around the middle to his heart's content and it won't make any noise."

"That sounds good, especially for Sue and Phil. What's on the next tier?"

"It's the second story of the tub with an opening on both sides. A covered plank juts out and leads to a frame covered in carpet with all sorts of toys on strings. The clerk said she has one at home, and her cats just love to walk the plank and bat at the toys. And on the other side, there's a mesh hammock. She said it's a favorite nap place for older cats because nothing from the floor can bother them."

"And there's another story above that?"

"That's the penthouse, and there's a little outside staircase leading down to the floor. It's a faster exit than ducking down through the tubs."

"So how much does all this grandeur coast?" Hannah asked the important question.

"A dollar."

"*What?!*"

"That's what Moishe's will cost. I'm getting one for Cuddles, and if I buy two, I can get the second one for only a dollar. I was going to do that anyway and give one to Moishe for Christmas. But from what you've told me, I think he needs it right now."

Hannah's eyes narrowed. "Are you *sure* you're buying one for Cuddles and you're not just trying to help me out?"

"I'm positive. I've even got the color picked out. I thought blue would go best in the living room, and that's where I want to put it. She's already got the kitty staircase I built in the den."

The one you built for Moishe, Hannah filled in the unsaid

part of Norman's answer. He'd built the kitty staircase hoping that she'd marry him. And from what he'd said earlier, he still loved her even though she'd turned down his proposal.

"Well . . . if you're sure you're getting one anyway . . ." she said.

"I am. What color would you like?"

"You decide," Hannah told him, because it didn't really matter to her. Coordinating colors in her condo was not a high priority. There was also the fact that almost everything she owned came from the Lake Eden Helping Hands Thrift Store, and if she had a décor at all, it was economical eclectic.

"Okay, where do you want to put it?"

"You can decide that, too."

"How about right next to your desk in the living room? That way Moishe will have something else to do, and he won't bother you when you use your computer."

"Good idea," Hannah said, not willing to admit that the only time she used her computer was when Norman came over to give her a word processing or Internet lesson.

Norman stared at her for a moment, and then he shook his head. "There's something wrong, isn't there," he said, and it was more of a statement than a question.

"What could possibly be wrong? Didn't I just agree with everything you suggested?"

"That's just it. You agreed with everything I suggested. That's not normal for you, Hannah. I think you're still in shock."

"Maybe I am," Hannah said, and only after the words had left her lips did she realize that she was agreeing with him again. "I guess I must be," she concluded.

"Then you need a dose of your own medicine. Hold on a second and I'll get some."

Hannah watched as he reached into the picnic hamper and pulled out a covered cake pan. "Dessert?" she guessed.

"Yes, and you're going to love it. I had a piece while I was waiting for you to come out of the pavilion."

"It's chocolate!" Hannah started to smile as Norman removed the cover and she caught a whiff of the delightful aroma.

"It's Marge's Cocoa Fudge Cake."

"She mentioned it last night. And she said she was going to bake it today."

Norman dished it up on a paper plate and held it out to her. "I forgot forks. You'll have to pick it up with your hands."

"Not a problem." Hannah picked up the cake and bit into it. She gave a little moan of pleasure as she tasted it, and then she took another bite, a bigger one than the first. Once that was gone, she gave Norman a smile that came straight from her heart. "It's incredible!"

"Lisa gave it to me when she saw me packing up the picnic for you. She said you'd need chocolate."

"Oh, I do. I do!"

"She also said to tell you that Marge wrote down the recipe in case you want it."

"*In case I want it?* Of course I want it! Was there ever any doubt?"

"Lisa thought you'd like it. That's why she gave me both cakes. Marge made two so she could give one whole cake to Gus."

"Lisa thought we could eat *two* cakes?"

"No, but she thought seeing them out at the lunch buffet would make Marge sad."

"She's probably right," Hannah said, thinking about what Gus had said at the dance last night and how he was looking forward to a piece of Marge's cake.

Norman glanced at his watch and clamped the lid back on the cake pan. "Time to go, Hannah."

"Go where?"

"To meet Mike and Bill at the yellow cottage. That's where Patsy and Mac are staying. They volunteered to let Mike and

Bill use it as a temporary headquarters to interview the relatives."

"Now I get it." Hannah started to smile. "Lisa probably wants me to dish up that second cake for Mike and his team."

"That's right. She figured the endorphins in the chocolate would put Mike in a good mood and he'll be more likely to answer questions."

"What questions? It's the other way around. Mike's going to interview me. He'll be the one asking the questions."

"Lisa knows that, but she also knows you. She told me she knows that you get all the information you can so that you can investigate. She spent some time with Marge and Patsy this afternoon, and they all want you to help them. They said that the sooner you catch the killer, the faster everyone can get back to normal and enjoy the family reunion again."

"Then they're going on with the reunion?"

"Absolutely. They all got together and took a vote on it. People came hundreds of miles to be here, and it would be heartbreaking if they had to turn right around and go back home again. Granny Truog's here and she's over a hundred. This could be the last chance she has to see some of her relatives."

"Everything you said makes sense. It would be a real pity to call it off."

"So are you going to help Lisa out and take the case?"

"Why not?" Hannah asked, grinning as she threw her hat, the imaginary straw hat with a ribbon around the brim that she'd worn to pose for Monet, into the ring once again.

COCOA FUDGE CAKE

Preheat oven to 350 degrees F., rack
in the middle position.

Hannah's 1st Note: Marge says to tell you that she got this recipe from two girls she met on the bus to Fargo, Sandy and Patricia. They used margarine, but since Marge is from a dairy state and she knows that there's no substitute for butter, she uses regular salted butter in her cake. She says she made a couple of other changes too, but it's been so long she doesn't remember what they are.

Before you start, grease and flour a 9-inch by 13-inch cake pan. *(You can also spray with Pam or another non-stick cooking spray and then dust it lightly with flour.)*

2 cups white *(granulated)* sugar
2 cups flour *(don't sift—just level it off with a knife)*

———————

1 cup butter *(2 sticks, ½ pound)*
1 cup water
3 Tablespoons unsweetened cocoa powder *(I used Hershey's)*

———————

½ cup milk
1 teaspoon vanilla extract
1 teaspoon baking soda
2 eggs, beaten *(just whip them up in a glass with a fork)*

In a large bowl, stir the sugar and the flour together. Set it aside on the counter.

Put the butter, water, and cocoa powder into a saucepan and bring it to a boil over medium heat.

Pour the cocoa mixture over the sugar and flour, and mix it all up together. *(You can do this on medium speed with an electric mixer, if you wish.)*

Hannah's 2nd Note: Marge says you shouldn't be a neatnik and wash your saucepan. If you make the frosting, you'll use it again.

Whisk the milk, vanilla extract, baking soda and eggs together in a small bowl. *(I used a 2-cup Pyrex measuring cup.)*

Add the egg mixture to the large bowl. Stir it until it's thoroughly incorporated.

Pour the batter into a 9-inch by 13-inch greased and floured cake pan.

Bake at 350 degrees F. for 20 to 25 minutes. When the cake begins to shrink away from the sides of the pan, it's done.

Hannah's 3rd Note: This cake is delicious without frosting, or just lightly dusted with powdered sugar. If you want a frosting, try the one below. Start making it 5 minutes before the cake is due to come out of the oven and the frosting and the cake will be ready at the same time.

CHOCOLATE FROSTING

½ cup *(1 stick)* butter
3 Tablespoons unsweetened cocoa powder *(I used Hershey's)*
⅓ cup milk
1 one-pound box of powdered *(confectioner's)* sugar
1 teaspoon vanilla extract

Place the butter, cocoa powder, and milk in a medium-size saucepan *(The one from before that you didn't wash.)* Bring them to a boil, stirring constantly.

Remove the pan from the heat and add the vanilla. Stir in the powdered sugar, a half-cup at a time, until the frosting is thickened, but still "pourable." *(If that's not a word, it should be.)*

Pour the frosting on the hot cake, and spread it out quickly with a spatula.

Hannah's 4th Note: Interruptions happen and it's not always possible to finish the frosting at the same time you take the hot cake from the oven. For that reason I've come up with an alternative fudge frosting, one that can be poured over a piping hot cake, a warm cake, or a stone cold cake. Here it is:

NEVERFAIL FUDGE FROSTING

½ cup *(1 stick, ¼ pound, 4 ounces)* salted butter
1 cup white *(granulated)* sugar
⅓ cup cream
½ cup chocolate chips
1 teaspoon vanilla extract
½ cup chopped pecans *(optional)*

Place the butter, sugar, and cream into a medium-size saucepan *(You can use the one from the cake that you didn't wash.)* Bring the mixture to a boil, stirring constantly. Turn down the heat to medium and cook for two minutes.

Add the half-cup chocolate chips, stir them in, and remove the saucepan from the heat.

Stir in the vanilla and the chopped pecans, if you decided to use them.

Pour the frosting on the cake and spread it out quickly with a spatula. If you're pouring it on a warm cake or a cold cake, just grab the pan and tip it so the frosting covers the whole top.

If you want this frosting to cool in a big hurry so that you can cut the cake, just slip it in the refrigerator, uncovered, for a half-hour or so.

Hannah's 5th Note: Marge says that this cake smells so good, you might have to keep it under lock and key until it's cool enough to cut.

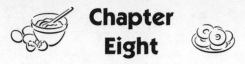

"Thanks, Hannah." Mike snapped his notebook closed to show that their interview was over, but when Hannah made a move to rise to her feet, he reached out to stop her. "Just one more thing."

"What's that?"

"You mentioned that you spent some time with the victim last night at the dance."

Through no choice of mine, Hannah wanted to say, but of course she didn't. "That's true. I told you I was sitting in a booth with Gus and his relatives."

"And they were discussing things they remembered from their childhood?"

"Right." Hannah glanced longingly at the cake that sat on the counter. She'd been closeted with Mike in the kitchen of the lake cottage for over thirty minutes. Normally, being closed up with Mike in an isolated cottage at Eden Lake might have been an opportunity for romance, but not today. Mike was all business. He was the detective, and she was the person who'd found the body. There were guidelines to follow, and Mike was following them.

"Would you like another piece of cake?" Hannah asked, hoping for the diversion of chocolate.

"No thanks. I gained half a pound yesterday and I've got to watch it. But you go ahead if you want to."

Hannah sighed. She could have used another piece of Marge's cake, but she didn't want to admit it in front of the man who curtailed his calories if he gained an ounce. "I'm fine. Did you have anything else you wanted to ask me?"

"Just a couple of things. Let's get back to the conversation you had at the dance last night. From what you told me, it sounds like it was a family discussion that didn't have much to do with you."

"That's exactly what it was, at least most of the time. Marge tried to include me, and so did Gus, but we didn't have a lot in common, especially when they started talking about the people they'd known in school."

"Did they mention anyone in particular?"

Hannah shrugged. "A couple of classmates that Mother probably remembers, and some teachers."

"And you didn't know any of the people they mentioned."

"Only the ones that still live in Lake Eden. And there weren't that many of them."

"So you weren't interested?"

"Not really."

"Then why didn't you make an excuse and leave?"

"I couldn't leave, not without asking them all to slide over and let me out. I was in the middle of a six-person round booth with Gus, Patsy, and Mac on one side, and Marge and Jack on the other."

"How long did you sit there?"

"Through two sets of music. That was probably between twenty and thirty minutes."

"Well, that's long enough."

Mike gave her one of his famous grins, the kind of smile that made her almost believe that she was the only woman in the world who mattered to him.

"Long enough for what?" Hannah gathered herself together enough to ask.

"Long enough to give me your take on the family dynamics."

Yellow caution lights began to blink in Hannah's mind, and warning bells sounded. "What are you asking?"

"I want your personal take on the victim. How did he get along with his long-lost family?"

Hannah hesitated. There was no way she wanted to mention the animosity she'd noticed between Jack and Gus. "I think he got along just fine," she said, "considering that he took money out of the family teapot and skinned out in the middle of the night to disappear for over thirty years. There were bound to be hurt feelings, especially since he didn't contact any family or friends during the time he was gone."

"I heard that the victim and Jack Herman were buddies at Jordan High. Did they appear to be friendly last night?"

Uh-oh! Hannah kept her expression carefully blank. Someone Mike had interviewed must have told him about the animosity between Jack Herman and Gus.

"Hannah?" Mike prompted.

Hannah conducted a lightning-fast inner debate and decided not to mention the fact that there had been some sort of problem between Jack and Gus. "I already told you, there were hurt feelings all around. And hurt feelings lead to resentment. The conversation I heard was polite, if that's what you're asking. But most of the time I wasn't personally involved, so I wasn't paying close attention."

"Do you think you would have noticed if there was any overt hostility?"

"Nobody came out and threatened anybody, if that's what you mean. And there certainly weren't any punches thrown, or anything like that." Hannah told herself she wasn't really being untruthful. After all, Jack hadn't threatened Gus, and they hadn't gotten physical. "When I found Gus, there was blood on his shirt," she said, deliberately steering the conversation away from Jack Herman. "Was he shot?"

"No."

"Then what was the murder weapon?"

"We're not sure yet. Doc Knight said it was something

long, thin, and sharp, like an ice pick or an awl. You didn't touch anything, did you?"

"I know better than that! It was clearly a murder scene. The only thing I did was feel for a pulse on the side of his neck."

"Then you didn't move him?"

"No." Hannah switched gears again. "I did notice one thing I thought might be unusual, especially now that you tell me it was a stabbing."

"What's that?"

"There wasn't very much blood, and I thought stabbing victims bled a lot."

"Not in this case. Doc Knight explained it to me. He said that if there are multiple stab wounds and the first few aren't fatal, the victim bleeds. In this case there was only the one wound, and death was almost instantaneous. Stab wounds don't bleed unless the victim is alive and his heart is still pumping. Gus died so fast, he didn't have very much time to bleed."

Hannah's stomach lurched, but she didn't want to let on that Mike's explanation had made her queasy. "I see. I really hope it wasn't my grandfather's."

"*What* wasn't your grandfather's?"

"The ice pick. If it *was* an ice pick, that is."

Mike looked a bit dazed. "You think the murder weapon belonged to your grandfather, personally?"

"No, not that. He gave them away at his hardware store for Christmas one year."

Mike flipped open his notebook and jotted that down. "Do you know who got them?"

"Almost everyone in town. People still had iceboxes in those days, and they chipped ice off the block for cold drinks."

"But everybody's got refrigerators now. Why would they still have ice picks when they're not needed anymore?"

"Ice picks come in handy for all sorts of things. I've got

one in my kitchen drawer at home, and I just used it to poke another hole in a leather belt."

"Yeah, that would work. I bought a leather punch when I went down a size last year. I didn't want to replace all my belts, so I poked another hole and made them smaller."

Hannah nodded, hoping he wouldn't guess that the hole she'd punched with her grandfather's ice pick was to make her belt larger.

"So what you're telling me is that there are a lot of similar ice picks floating around, and anyone in town could have one."

"Yes, but I don't know how many are left now. That was a long time ago, and they had wooden handles. My grandfather had them painted red and green for Christmas, and the name of his hardware store was stamped on in gold. If the handles broke or splintered, people probably threw them away. But if they were still in good shape, a couple of them could have wound up out at the lake cottages."

"Okay," Mike said, snapping his notebook shut again. "There's not much help there."

"Probably not. Did you find Gus's wallet?"

"Why do you want to know?"

"Because if you didn't, the motive could be robbery. Gus was flashing money around all night."

"Someone else mentioned that," Mike said, not saying where he'd gotten his information. "We recovered the victim's wallet. It was still in his pocket. And it contained a little over two hundred dollars."

"Good!"

"Why do you say that?"

"Because he owed Ava for the groceries he bought last night, and now she'll get her money. It's interesting that robbery wasn't the motive, though."

"We can't rule it out. It's possible that the thief didn't intend to kill him, and fled when he realized what he'd done."

"Or he was after something other than money. Gus was

wearing a Rolex and a diamond pinkie ring last night. When I found him, I didn't notice if he still had them."

"We recovered both of them, and Bill had the guys in robbery take a look. The pinkie ring's a fake. Everybody agrees it's paste. They're still not sure about the watch, so we're having a jeweler take a look at it."

"Why would Gus wear a fake ring?" Hannah asked him.

"Lots of rich people do. They keep the real jewelry locked in a safe and wear paste rings and fake watches."

"Why bother to buy the real stuff when you're never going to wear it?"

"Search me. Some people buy expensive jewelry as an investment. It's probably more interesting than buying a lot of stocks or bonds."

Hannah shrugged. "Maybe. So you think that Gus has a safe at home filled with real jewelry?"

"That's my guess. We'll have someone check it out when we get a minute. In the meantime, we're treating this like a routine homicide."

Was homicide ever *routine?* Hannah doubted it. But she chose not to argue the point with Mike. "Any suspects?" she asked instead.

"Everybody's a suspect until we start weeding them out. It all depends on where they were at two this morning."

"That's the estimated time of death?"

"Doc Knight puts it between one and three. And since Ava says he left her place after one-thirty, and he had time to eat a piece of your carrot cake and drink some milk before he died, we're asking everyone where they were between two and three in the morning."

"I was home at two-thirty," Hannah said, before he could ask, "and I can prove it."

Mike gave a little laugh. "Moishe's testimony doesn't count, Hannah. We don't speak cat down at the sheriff's station."

"Actually . . . it *does* count." Hannah was a bit disappointed that Mike hadn't drawn another conclusion about her middle-of-the-night companion. Or maybe she was pleased that he trusted her. She couldn't quite decide which. "Moishe was chasing around inside my bathtub, and Sue Plotnik called to ask me if everything was all right."

"I guess that clears you. There's no way you could have stabbed the victim, and driven home in time to take the phone call."

"Well *that's* a relief!" Hannah said, but Mike didn't react to her sarcasm. He just stared at her with a frown that knit his reddish-blond eyebrows.

"Why was The Big Guy chasing around inside your bathtub? Do you have mice?"

"No. And that could be part of the problem, right along with the fact that I can't find the Animal Channel on my new cable lineup."

"What do you mean?"

"I've been gone a lot lately, and Norman thinks Moishe's bored. When I came home from church yesterday, he'd ripped open one of my couch pillows and scattered the stuffing all over the rug."

"Maybe he needs a playmate. Why don't you ask Norman to bring Cuddles over to visit?"

"That would probably help, but Cuddles is up in Duluth this week, vacationing with Marguerite and her friend."

"Oh. Well . . . maybe I should drop by for a little cop-to-cat talk. I could tell him about bathtub noise abatement and willful destruction of couch pillows."

"Anytime," Hannah said, smiling at Mike's description.

"Anything else you want to know about the murder?"

Hannah blinked several times. Was she hallucinating, or was Mike actually offering to give her information?

"Hannah?"

"Actually . . . yes. It's been bothering me, and of course I didn't look. What was in that disposable cooler on the bar?"

"A bread wrapper with six ham and cheese sandwiches inside."

Hannah was puzzled. "You mean . . . already made?"

"Right. He must have put them together right there at the bar and stashed them in the cooler. I can't figure out why he'd do that, though."

"He told Ava that the refrigerator in his cabin wasn't working right," Hannah offered. "But I opened it when I went to the cottage to look for him, and it felt cool to me."

"You're sure?"

"Pretty sure. The ice tray was still frozen solid."

"Maybe it was cutting on and off. The old ones do that sometimes. The water in the ice cube tray would freeze right back up again, but he might not have wanted to take the chance with a ham and cheese sandwich, especially with mayo."

"There was mayonnaise?"

"Mayo and mustard."

The light dawned, and Hannah nodded. "I get it," she said, shaking her head.

"Get what?"

"That's one of the reasons he came back here, to use the mayo and mustard in the kitchen refrigerator."

"You know there was some in there?"

"Yes. We ran out of cream for the coffee, and I went to the refrigerator to get another carton."

"And you're sure he didn't buy the mustard and mayo at the store?"

"I'm almost certain. Ava's the type to keep a running tab in her mind, and she named everything he bought last night. She didn't say a word about mayonnaise and mustard."

Mike laughed. "So he took those from the pavilion refrigerator. That's pretty cheap for a man who flashes money around and wears a Rolex and a diamond pinkie ring."

"A Rolex that could be a fake and a diamond made out of paste," Hannah reminded him.

"That's true, but I already explained that. And that suit he was wearing didn't come cheap. Maybe he just forgot the mayo and the mustard. And then, when he started making his sandwiches, he looked around for some."

"Maybe," Hannah said, giving in because fighting about it would be useless. Perhaps that *was* what had happened. She had no reason to think otherwise.

"Okay." Mike gave her a warm smile. "Since you found the body, you don't need copies of the crime scene photos, do you?"

Hannah's mouth dropped open. What was Mike talking about?

"I can call you with the highlights from the autopsy report when it comes in."

"That would be nice," Hannah said carefully, still not sure why Mike was being so cooperative. She had a sneaking suspicion she'd be better off not asking, but she couldn't resist. "Why are you volunteering all this information?"

"Because you're going to get it anyway, one way or the other. There's no sense in trying to keep you from sticking your nose in my case, is there?"

Hannah thought about that for a moment, and then she shook her head. "No. Lisa already asked me to help catch the killer so all the relatives can relax and enjoy the reunion again."

"Okay, then. I've been thinking about it, and I'd rather have you share any information you learn with me. That way we won't be working at cross-purposes. And the only way you'll share with me is if I share with you. Isn't that right?"

"That's right," Hannah said, surprised that she could even find her voice to speak. Mike was actually sanctioning her sleuthing! Or was he? This could be some sort of a trick. She'd have to ask Andrea and Michelle what they thought of his proposal.

"Check it out with your sisters and see what they think,"

Mike continued, practically reading Hannah's mind. "Call me on my cell when you decide."

"Okay," Hannah said, pushing back her chair.

"One more thing . . . I'll give that cake to my team when they report back, but in the meantime, will you cover it for me? It's just too temping. I can smell it all the way over here and it's screaming, *Eat me! Eat me!*"

"I know exactly what you mean." Hannah clamped the cover on the cake pan and gave a little wave as she headed for the door. Was Mike serious about sharing his information? Or would he withhold crucial clues so that he could solve the case first? As she went out the screen door and started down the road to join the women who were counting on her to help them fix dinner for the reunion crowd, she had the uncomfortable feeling that Mike was playing some sort of game with her and he hadn't bothered to tell her the rules.

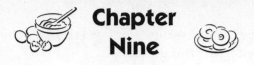

Chapter Nine

They were in the kitchen of Libby Thompson's cottage. Libby was Lisa's great aunt and her cottage was theirs to use for the reunion. It was a huge lime green monstrosity that had grown with the years until it took up three lots to accommodate the Thompsons, their children, the grandkids, and the great grandkids. Because the extended family was so huge and they all lived in the area, the cottage kitchen had been enlarged to hold two sets of double ovens, two stovetops, and two industrial dishwashers. With the exception of Sally's kitchen at the Lake Eden Inn, it was the largest kitchen at the lake and the perfect place for multiple cooks to prepare dishes for the potluck dinner.

"Oh, dear!" Marge said, looking worried.

"What's the matter?" Hannah asked her.

"It's this recipe. I'm just not sure it's appropriate."

Hannah glanced over at the recipe. It appeared to be similar to other hamburger-tomato-macaroni casserole recipes, and Hannah didn't see how it could be unsuitable. "It looks just fine to me. What's inappropriate about it?"

"The name. I mean . . . in light of what happened last night, I thought . . ."

"She's talking about Gus," Patsy spoke up.

Hannah moved over for a second look. She hadn't bothered to read the name before, and it was written in big block letters at the top of the recipe card. FUNERAL HOTDISH, it said.

"It's a really good hotdish," Marge went on. "I got the recipe from Joyce Fuechte. She's on the Funeral Committee at St. Peter's Lutheran in Swanville, and they served it at my cousin Ted's funeral when everybody came back from the cemetery. What do you think, Hannah? Should we use it?"

"I don't see why not. Just don't tell anyone what it's called."

"But what if they ask?" Patsy wanted to know.

"Make up something. I'm sure Joyce and the committee won't mind. You could call it Anniversary Hotdish. They probably serve it for anniversaries, too."

"That's a good idea," Marge complimented her. "An anniversary's a happy occasion."

"Not necessarily."

Marge turned to give her sister a sharp look. "You still haven't worked things out with Mac?"

"The only thing we agree on is not to agree. Would you believe Mac wanted me to ask Gus for the five hundred dollars I lent him right before he left Lake Eden? With thirty years of interest, no less! He even offered to do it for me. Can you believe it?"

"I believe it," Marge said, shaking her head. "Mac's never been shy about money."

"*Tell* me about it! But that's only one of the things we fought about." Patsy glanced over at Hannah. "I don't want to bore Hannah with the details. Hand me the onions and celery, will you, Marge? I'll chop them up and start frying them."

Hannah could see that Patsy was uncomfortable, and Marge didn't look exactly calm and serene, either. Since they were already upset, she figured she might as well introduce another upsetting subject.

"You know that I found Gus, don't you?" When both sisters nodded, Hannah went on. "Are there any questions that you'd like to ask me about how he died?"

Marge and Patsy turned to each other and frowned. "Not really," Marge answered. "The police told us everything we needed to know."

Hannah just stared from one to the other in surprise. Usually the victim's relatives wanted to know everything.

"To tell you the truth, Hannah, none of the relatives really liked him all that well," Patsy confided.

"Why?"

"Well . . ." Marge took over. "He just wasn't like the brother we remember. His personality was completely different."

"In what way?"

"He bragged a lot, and he flashed money around. People from Minnesota don't usually do that," Patsy explained. "And he seemed to think he was a lot better than we were. It was like he was *amused* by us."

"But he came back to see all of you when he saw the notice of the reunion in the paper."

Both Marge and Patsy shook their heads. "No, he didn't," Marge insisted. "Lisa and Herb didn't put any notices in the paper. All they did was mail out invitations to the relatives in our address books."

"So how did Gus find out about it?" Hannah was puzzled.

"We think he must have seen the posters that Lisa and Herb put up on Main Street," Patsy answered.

"You mean, he just stumbled on the reunion when he came back to see his long-lost family?"

"Came back to gloat is more like it," Patsy commented.

"Patsy!" Marge chided her.

"Well, it's true. We both know Gus wasn't like that when he left. He was a little wild, but that was because Mom and Dad spoiled him."

"The high school girls didn't help. The way they fell all

over him made him pretty full of himself." Marge gave a little sigh. "He was never a bad person, though . . . at least not
back then."

For the second time in less than an hour, Hannah kept her
expression perfectly blank. Maybe Gus hadn't been a bad
person when he'd left Lake Eden, but the years that had
passed had turned him into someone she wouldn't describe
as nice. A nice person didn't talk about all he had to the
have-nots in Lake Eden. A nice person didn't try to control
everything, or order other people to wait on him hand and
foot. A nice person would have made allowances for Jack
Herman when he learned that Jack had Alzheimer's. Gus
knew about it. Hannah had heard Marge mention it to her
brother. But Gus had still faced off against Jack the night of
the dance.

"Maybe Gus changed over the years," Hannah offered,
since they seemed to be waiting for her to say something.

Marge exchanged glances with Patsy. "Or maybe there's
another explanation," she said.

"What's that?"

"Neither one of us is sure he really *was* our brother Gus."

"You think he was *pretending* to be your brother Gus?"

"We don't know, for sure." It was Patsy who answered
this time. "We had a family meeting while you were in talking to Mike. Some of the relatives thought he was Gus, but
the others were positive he wasn't."

Hannah felt knocked completely off balance. She hadn't
expected this turn of events! "If he was an imposter, he was a
good one. He seemed to know a lot about your brother's
life."

"Not that much, really." Patsy shook her head. "We compared notes, and all he really knew were the basics. We think
maybe he knew Gus and that's why he was so good at pretending to be him. Marge could pretend to be me around
people who hadn't seen me for over thirty years. Nobody
would know the difference."

"How about his appearance? Did he look like your brother?"

Marge nodded. "We think so, but Mac pointed out that any guy just under six feet tall with dark blond hair who was close to the same age could pass for Gus."

"Did Mac know him well?"

"Oh, yes. They were on several sports teams together at Jordan High."

"Did your brother have any distinguishing features, like moles or birthmarks, or anything like that?" Hannah asked Patsy.

"Nothing."

"How about scars from accidents or operations?"

"He didn't have anything other than the usual scrapes and cuts from playing baseball, and they would have healed a long time ago," Marge answered her. "And he never had surgery that we know about."

"Do you have any idea why someone would try to impersonate your brother?" Hannah asked the critical question.

"No," Patsy answered. "I mean, it's not like there was an inheritance for him to collect or anything like that."

"Marge?" Hannah turned to her.

"I don't know, either. But we all agree on one thing," Marge gave Hannah a long, level look. "We want you to find out for us."

FUNERAL HOTDISH
"Anniversary Hotdish"

Preheat oven to 350 degrees F., rack
in the middle position.
Or
Use an 18-quart electric roaster set
to 350 degrees F.

**Hannah's 1st Note: Joyce says this is easiest with three
people helping: one person to chop and sauté the celery
and onions, one person to brown the hamburger, and one
person to cook the pasta and mix the sauce.**

Start by spraying the inside of your pan, or the electric
roaster with Pam or another nonstick cooking spray. *(I
used a great big disposable turkey roaster sprayed with
Pam.)*

1 bunch of celery *(approximately 10 stalks)*
3 large onions *(We used four because we love onion)*
6 pounds lean hamburger *(We used 8 pounds
    because we like it beefier)*
2 two-pound boxes elbow macaroni *(for a total of
    four pounds—Joyce's Funeral Committee uses
    Creamettes Elbow Macaroni)*
1 large can *(50-ounces)* Campbell's tomato soup,
    undiluted
2 large cans *(46-ounces each)* Campbell's tomato
    juice

1 large bottle *(46-ounces)* catsup *(the Swanville Funeral Committee uses Heinz Ketchup)*
1 Tablespoon brown sugar
1 teaspoon ground black pepper *(freshly ground is
best, of course)*

Clean and chop the celery into bite-size pieces. Put them
in a frying pan with a little butter and start cooking them
over low heat, stirring occasionally.

Peel and chop the onions into bite-sized pieces. Add
them to the frying pan with the celery and continue to
cook them, stirring occasionally, until they're translucent.

Brown the hamburger over medium heat. Be sure to
"chop" it with a spoon or heat-resistant spatula so it
browns in bite-size pieces. *(Joyce and her committee do
this in a pan in the oven.)*

Drain the browned hamburger, and rinse off the fat by
putting the meat in a strainer and spraying it with warm
water. *(We drained the hamburger, but we forgot to rinse
it off with warm water—it was good anyway.)*

Cook the elbow macaroni according to the directions
on the box. DO NOT OVERCOOK. *(Joyce's committee
does not salt the water, but we did.)* Drain it and set it
aside.

Combine the undiluted tomato soup, the tomato juice,
and the catsup. Mix in the brown sugar and the pepper.

(Joyce's committee does this right in the electric roaster and then heats it before they add the other ingredients. We mixed up our sauce in the bottom of the disposable turkey roaster and didn't heat it before we added the other ingredients.)

Add the cooked celery and onions to the sauce and stir them in.

Stir in the hamburger.

Add the cooked, drained macaroni and mix well.

Once everything is thoroughly mixed, cover the disposable roaster with heavy duty foil and put it into a 350-degree F. oven for 2 hours, stirring occasionally so that it heats evenly and doesn't stick to the bottom. *(If you used an electric roaster, put on the lid, turn it up to 350 degrees F., and cook it for 2 hours, stirring occasionally so that it heats evenly and doesn't stick to the bottom of the roaster.)*

Joyce's Note: Joyce says to tell you that cooking the hotdish for 2 hours is mainly to blend the flavors since everything is precooked.

Hannah's 2nd Note: When we made this for the family reunion, we sprinkled shredded Parmesan cheese on the top before we served it. Marge says if she ever makes it at home, she's going to add pitted black olives to the sauce, because Herb and Jack like them so much. She's also going to make garlic bread to go with it.

Yield: The Swanville St. Peter's Lutheran Church Funeral Committee says this recipe will serve 75, but they always serve plenty of other side dishes with it. If you plan to use Funeral Hotdish as your only main course, I wouldn't expect it to serve more than two-dozen people, especially if they're really hungry.

Chapter Ten

"You're going to take the case, aren't you?" Michelle asked, looking young and gorgeous in white shorts to show off her tan and a pink camisole top that played peek-a-boo with her waistband. Her light brown hair was brushed back into a high ponytail held in place with a pink scrunchy, and she looked as if she were still in junior high, except for the fact that her figure was one that most junior high girls would envy.

"I'm taking the case. Lisa already asked me. And Marge and her sister asked for my help, too." Hannah took out another head of cauliflower and plunked it on the cutting board. Edna Ferguson, the head cook at Jordan High, had arrived to join the ladies in the Thompson cottage kitchen, and Hannah had gone to her mother's cottage to make the salad for the buffet table.

"I like Patsy." Andrea adjusted the straps of her gaily flowered, polished cotton sundress. It had an old-fashioned bolero jacket, and it was part of Claire's fifties collection. Hannah had seen it in the window of Beau Monde Fashions.

"We met Pasty when we were walking over here." Michelle explained. "She said she could tell at a glance that we were sisters."

Hannah didn't comment, but she knew it was true. Anyone who saw Andrea and Michelle together was struck by the family resemblance. And if you added Delores to the mix, you could tell they'd inherited their petite figures and lovely features from her.

"What size is that top?" Andrea asked Michelle.

"A five."

"It looks smaller than that. I wear a five and it looks too tight for me."

"It's a little too tight for me, too," Michelle admitted. "I washed it in hot water and it shrunk. I guess it's probably more like a size three now."

Hannah, who'd been listening to their conversation without comment, came very close to groaning. She hadn't worn a size three since preschool. While her sisters had gotten Hannah's share of their mother's petite beauty genes, Hannah had inherited her tall, gangly frame and tendency to be a bit overweight, right along with her frizzy red hair and freckles, directly from their father.

"You look nice today, Hannah," Michelle said, as if she'd suddenly realized that Hannah was feeling left out of the conversation.

Andrea, who was always socially aware, picked up on Michelle's cue. "Yes, you do. I like that shade of green on you."

"Thanks," Hannah said, glancing down at the forest green blouse that she'd paired with tan cotton pants. Forest green was one of her favorite colors. She looked up to see Michelle watching her, and she noticed again how much skin her youngest sister was exposing. "You're wearing sunscreen, aren't you?"

"Yes, and mosquito repellent, too. You don't have to worry about me."

"Right." Hannah exchanged a glance with Andrea. She was willing to bet that they were thinking the same thing. Sunburn and mosquito bites were the least of their worries. While there was nothing indecent about the way Michelle was dressed, her outfit would be certain to produce a loud chorus of wolf whistles if she walked past a construction site.

"Is Lonnie coming to the potluck tonight?" Andrea asked, mentioning the young sheriff's deputy that Michelle had been dating for over a year.

"Yes. And that reminds me . . . I'd better change clothes. Lonnie doesn't like me to wear this top around other men. He says it makes them slobber."

As Michelle headed off to the bedroom to change, Andrea and Hannah exchanged grins. "I think Lonnie's a good influence on her," Andrea commented.

"You could be right," Hannah agreed.

"Do you need some help chopping those vegetables?"

"Not really. This is the only good knife Mother has." Hannah crossed her fingers to negate the lie, a leftover habit from childhood. Their mother had a whole butcher block full of expensive knives on the counter, and every one was perfectly sharpened. But if she let Andrea help her, her younger, less-culinarily talented sister would probably chop off a finger. And Hannah would much rather tell a little white lie than be responsible for that!

"What are you making?" Andrea stepped closer and peered into the bowl. "I see cauliflower and broccoli chopped up into little pieces. It's got to be some kind of salad."

"It is. It's Sally's Sunny Vegetable Salad. I got the recipe from her last year. Lisa's doing a Caesar with black olives, Edna's fixing macaroni salad, and Marge is making coleslaw."

"And I've got my salad," Andrea said proudly. "It's got cottage cheese and grated onions in green Jell-O."

Hannah tried a few comments to that in her mind. *That sounds good,* was an outright lie, and *That's nice,* was too generic. She finally thought of something appropriate to say. "That'll look great with the rest of the salads," she said, just as Michelle emerged from the bedroom wearing white slacks and a lavender top with blousy, chiffon sleeves.

"Nice outfit," Andrea complimented their youngest sibling.

"Thanks. Lonnie loves it when I wear purple and white. I think it's because they're the Jordan High colors." Michelle walked over to stand next to Hannah. "Can I do anything to help?"

Hannah would have loved to ask Michelle to chop up some broccoli, but she'd already told Andrea the fib about the knives. "How about whisking up the dressing?" she suggested. "If Andrea will gather the ingredients, that is. And while you're doing that, I need to ask your opinion about something."

"What's that?" Michelle asked, as Andrea brought over the small cooler that Hannah had brought with her.

"Mike says he doesn't mind if I investigate as long as we exchange information. He sounded sincere, but I'm not sure."

"That's because you can't tell with a cop," Michelle said quickly. "They don't have to be truthful all the time. I think cop school teaches them how to lie to trick suspects."

Both Hannah and Andrea turned to Michelle in surprise. "Do you think Lonnie lies to you?" Hannah asked her.

"Absolutely." Michelle gave a little laugh. "Last night he told me that I was the most beautiful woman in the world."

"That's not a lie," Hannah said.

And at almost the same time Andrea asked, "What's wrong with that? You are."

"Thanks, guys," Michelle smiled at both of them, "but I know that's not true. Lonnie was lying, pure and simple."

"It wasn't a lie, strictly speaking," Hannah informed her. "Lonnie just exaggerated a bit to flatter you."

Andrea agreed. "Men are allowed to say things like that whether they mean them or not."

"But it usually means they want something," Hannah added.

"Oh, he did," Michelle said.

Andrea and Hannah locked eyes. It was clear that both of them were hoping the other one would ask. But the silence lengthened, and finally Hannah broke down.

"Okay, I'll ask," she said. "Are you willing to tell us what Lonnie wanted?"

Michelle laughed. "I was wondering which one of you would cave in and ask me. Sure, I'll tell you what he wanted. Lonnie asked me if he could buy me an engagement ring for Christmas."

"But you've got two years of college to go," Andrea pointed out.

"I know that. I told him it was too soon. And I said that if he still felt the same way next year, he should ask me again."

"Smart sister!" Hannah exclaimed, exchanging a high-five with Andrea.

"But the two years I've got left in school aren't the only reason I didn't want to get engaged now," Michelle went on. "There's someone else I might want to date."

"Someone here in Lake Eden?" Hannah asked, hoping that wasn't the case. Lonnie would be pretty upset if he had a rival he had to face every day in town.

Michelle shook her head. "Someone at school. And he hasn't even asked me out yet. But I think he will, and I want to be free to go if he asks me."

"That's probably smart," Hannah told her.

"I think so. I don't want to commit to anyone until I'm absolutely sure. I'm just like you, Hannah."

Hannah winced inwardly. What Michelle was admiring as a smart choice might actually turn out to be a flaw in Hannah's personality. There were some people who simply couldn't commit to anything. They sat on the fence all their lives, wavering between two choices, and ended up completely alone. Hannah didn't think that was what she was doing, but she wasn't completely sure. In any event, this wasn't the time for deep soul-searching. She needed their opinion of the alliance that Mike had suggested.

"We got off the track here," Hannah said. "We were talking about cops and lying. Do you think Mike was lying to me when he promised to give me access to information he learned if I'd do the same with him?"

Michelle looked thoughtful. "I don't know. Does he have anything to gain by lying to you?"

"Of course he does," Andrea answered the question. "He knows Hannah will play straight with him if she agrees to his deal. But she won't know if he's not playing straight with her."

"I'll know," Hannah said.

Andrea looked surprised. "How?"

"My sister's a member of the sheriff's wife network. Mike has to report everything he does to Bill, doesn't he?"

"Yes, but . . ."

"And it won't be too difficult for you to get a look at those reports, will it?" Hannah interrupted her.

Andrea began to smile. "It won't be hard at all. Tell Mike yes, and I'll check the reports so we can keep him honest."

Michelle manned the whisk while Andrea handed her the ingredients. Hannah chopped the last of the vegetables and as she was chopping, she thought of something she wanted to ask Andrea.

"When Mike interviewed me, he told me that the diamond pinkie ring Gus was wearing was paste, and he thought the Rolex was a fake, too. How about his clothes? Do you think they were fakes?"

"Are you talking about knockoffs?" Andrea asked.

Hannah shrugged, unable to place the word. "I don't know. What are knockoffs?"

"Designer styles that are copied by other manufacturers, mostly in foreign countries. When Bill and I went to Hawaii, we had a four-hour layover in Los Angeles. The taxi driver took us downtown, and I bought a fake Gucci bag for ten dollars. It even had the logo as part of the brass clasp."

"You mean the *G* and the backwards *C?*" Michelle asked her.

"That's exactly right. It was a clutch, really cute, and it smelled like real leather."

"But it wasn't," Hannah guessed.

"Bingo!" Andrea pointed her finger at Hannah. "Of course I knew it had to be hot, or a knockoff. Real Gucci bags sell for anywhere from ten to a hundred times that much. But I liked it, and Bill bought it for me."

"What happened?" Michelle asked.

"Well, the leather smell faded before I even got it home, and the second time I carried it, the clasp fell apart."

"Why didn't you have the clasp fixed?" Michelle asked her.

"Maybe I should have, but I didn't feel like going out of town to have it done."

"You could have taken it to Bud Hauge's welding shop," Hannah told her.

"No, I couldn't have. Bill was a deputy sheriff when we got married, and everybody in town thought he'd bought me a Gucci bag. How would it look for a deputy sheriff's wife to try to pass off an illegal knockoff of a designer bag as the real thing?"

"It would be bad," Michelle said.

"Fodder for the gossip hotline," Hannah added.

"Exactly. And that's why I tossed it in the trash."

"Wise move," Hannah complimented her, and grabbed the bowl with the dressing before Michelle could whisk the daylights out of it.

"Whoa!" Michelle exclaimed, staring at her oldest sister in shock as Hannah added the dressing to the salad. "Why are you doing that now? We're not going to set out the buffet for another two hours!"

"That's okay. There's nothing in this salad to wilt. You can dress it hours ahead of time. It's even a good idea, since it takes that long for the flavors to meld. All you have to do is toss it, cover it with plastic wrap, and stick it in the fridge. Then, when you're ready to serve, you just sprinkle on the bacon pieces and the salted sunflower seeds, and set it out on the buffet table." She stopped, took a deep breath, and got back to the subject at hand. "Now, back to Gus's clothing. Did either of you two fashion experts get a good look at them?"

"I did," Andrea said, which was nothing less than Hannah had expected.

"I didn't," Michelle admitted. "When everybody else was crowding around the car, I was saying goodbye to Lonnie in the church parking lot. He had to work, so I went out to the mall with a couple of my friends, and I wasn't invited to the Inn for the breakfast buffet. Then last night at the dance, Lonnie and I were sitting with Lonnie's parents, and Rick and Jessica. I saw Gus and I thought he looked really good, better dressed than anyone else there, but I didn't really get close enough to catalogue his outfit, if that's what you mean."

"Expensive, expensive, expensive," Andrea categorized, giving a little shrug. "I can't tell you how much exactly, but I'm sure the two ensembles I saw him wearing cost enough for a down payment on a Lake Eden fixer-upper. I'd bet my real estate license on that!"

Hannah just stared at her sister. That was good enough for her. Andrea valued her real estate license only slightly below her husband and her children. "Then the clothes were real even if the jewelry wasn't?"

"That's right."

"That proves that Gus Klein had some money . . . or at least he did until he spent it on master tailors, fine material, and shoes even Mayor Bascomb couldn't afford."

SALLY'S SUNNY VEGETABLE SALAD

5 cups chopped broccoli florets
5 cups chopped cauliflower florets
2 cups shredded cheddar cheese (*the sharper the cheddar the better the salad*)
½ cup golden raisins (*Sally says to tell you she's used sweetened, dried cranberries as a substitute for the raisins*)
⅔ cup minced onion (*Sally uses chopped green onions*)

½ cup white (*granulated*) sugar
1 cup mayonnaise (*Hannah uses Hellmann's—it's called Best Foods west of the Rockies*)
2 Tablespoons red wine vinegar (*I used raspberry vinegar*)

---

6 bacon strips, cooked and crumbled (*or ½ cup bacon bits*)
¼ cup *shelled,* salted, toasted sunflower seeds

Chop the broccoli and cauliflower florets into tiny bite-sized pieces.

Combine the broccoli and cauliflower in a large salad bowl. Add the shredded cheese and mix it up with your fingers.

Mix in the raisins and the minced onion.

In a small bowl, combine the sugar, mayonnaise, and red wine vinegar. Mix it with a rubber spatula, or a whisk until it's smooth.

Pour the dressing you just mixed over the top of the salad. Toss it, or stir it with a spoon or spatula until the vegetables are coated with the dressing.

Sprinkle the bacon bits on top.

Sprinkle the sunflower seeds on top of that.

Hannah's 1st Note: You can make this salad several hours before serving. It's even better that way because the flavors blend. Just toss the vegetables and raisins with the dressing, cover the bowl with plastic wrap, and refrigerate it until your company arrives. Then all you have to do is sprinkle on the bacon bits, and the sunflower seeds, and serve.

Yield: 12 to 16 servings.

Hannah's 2nd Note: I made this for a 6-person dinner party once, and I ended up with about half of the salad left in the bowl. I refrigerated it to see what would happen, and it was every bit as good the next day!

Chapter Eleven

Hannah stifled a yawn as she loaded pots and pans into one of the industrial-sized dishwaters at the Thompson cottage kitchen. She had volunteered for the task to free up the other women who wanted to see the slide show that Lisa, Herb, and Norman had compiled from the old family photos that everyone had brought. Hannah had wanted to see the slide show, too, but she knew she was far too tired to keep her eyes open once she was snuggled down on a blanket on the beach, the alternate venue Lisa and Herb had arranged because the pavilion was still roped off as a crime scene. Norman had rented a giant-screen television, the kind they used for huge outdoor events, from a place in Minneapolis, and the men who'd delivered it had helped to run an extension cord from the nearest cottage. Even though she was across the road and up the equivalent of a city block from the festivities, Hannah could hear applause and laughter from the family members gathered on the beach.

The moths beat themselves silly against the screens as Hannah finished loading one dishwasher and poured in the heavy-duty detergent. Only one more to load and she could go home.

Hannah yawned again as she rinsed out the crock of a slow cooker and found a place for it on the bottom rack of the second dishwasher. She was short on sleep and long on worries. For one thing, she was still having trouble banishing the thought of that ice pick. It didn't make a whole lot of sense, since she'd found victims who'd suffered more violent and much gorier deaths in the past. But there was something about the fact that the killer might have used one of her grandfather's Christmas gifts to his customers as a murder weapon that really disturbed her. Perhaps it was because she had an ice pick just like it at home.

There was another reason Hannah was worried, and it had to do with Moishe. Would she arrive home to find that the cat she'd adopted had shredded every pillow and piece of stuffed furniture in her condo?

"Hannah?" a voice called out, accompanied by a knock on the wooden frame of the screen door. "I need to talk to you, Hannah."

Hannah recognized the voice. It was Ava from the Eden Lake Store. "Come on in, Ava. It's not locked."

"Do you need some help?" Ava walked over to the sink and stared down at a saucepan that was waiting to be scoured.

"Not really. I'm almost done. What's on your mind?"

"There's something I have to tell you. It's about Gus."

Hannah turned to look at her. Ava appeared extremely upset, and Hannah hoped she wasn't about to hear a confession! "What is it?" she asked.

"The Beesemans from Red Wing were in, and she mentioned that they weren't sure the body they found was really Gus."

"That's right. Marge had some doubts, and so did Patsy."

"And this Mrs. Beeseman . . . Betsy, I think her name was . . . said there wasn't any way to tell, since Gus hadn't had any distinguishing marks or scars on him when he left Lake Eden."

"That's right."

"Well . . . he did."

"He did what?"

"He did have a distinguishing mark on him."

"A scar?"

"No, a tattoo. It was two crossed bats and a ball, almost like that major league baseball logo they show on TV before every game."

"Are you sure?"

"I'm sure."

"But why didn't anyone else mention it?"

"I don't think anybody else knew."

"Not Marge? Or Patsy?"

"Neither one of them. It was a tattoo in . . . well . . . a kind of a private place."

Hannah didn't really want to ask, but she knew she should. "What kind of private place are we talking about here?"

"Backside private. On the left."

"You mean . . . ?" Hannah used her own anatomy to pat the area in question.

"That's it. That's exactly where it was."

"And this isn't just hearsay. I mean, you're sure this tattoo was . . . there?"

"It was there. I saw it with my own two eyes way back in high school." Ava stopped and looked highly embarrassed. "But it's not what you're thinking," she added quickly.

"I *wasn't* thinking. I was trying really hard *not* to think."

"Good. It's just that I went over to visit Marge and Patsy one day, and Mrs. Klein told me I could wait up in their room and read some of their movie magazines. So I went up there, and on the way I passed by Gus's bedroom. The door was open, and he was inside getting dressed. And his backside was to me."

"And you saw it?"

"Yes. That was when I saw it. He didn't see me standing there, so I hurried on down the hall as quiet as I could be.

And I went straight into Marge and Patsy's room. I'm absolutely positive he didn't know I was there, and that's all there was to it."

Ava finished her account in a rush, as if she'd rehearsed it several times before delivering it to Hannah. That made Hannah doubt that Ava was being entirely truthful, but she couldn't prove otherwise and it really didn't matter in the long run.

"Thanks for telling me, Ava," Hannah said. "And if Marge and Patsy knew, they'd thank you, too. It's one sure way to tell if the victim really was Gus."

Ava looked worried. "I'm not going to have to testify, or anything like that, am I?"

"I wouldn't think so. It really doesn't have anything to do with the murder. It's just a question of whether he was who he said he was . . . or not."

"Good! I was worried about that, but I thought I should tell you anyway." Ava headed for the door, but she turned back before she got there. "Thanks a lot, Hannah."

"That's okay. I'm really glad you told me."

"So am I, but that's not it."

"Not what?"

"That's not what I'm thanking you for. You see, Bill dropped by and paid Gus's bill out of the money they found in his wallet. So now I've got the money, and I don't have to be worried about that anymore."

"I'm glad," Hannah said, figuring that Bill had pulled some strings to do that. Everyone knew that Ava was on a tight budget and couldn't afford to absorb many losses.

"I'm getting a new Popsicle flavor in next week. Drop in and have one on me."

"Thanks, Ava. I'll do that." Hannah gave her a wave as she went out the door, and then she turned back to her dishwashing chores. At least now she knew how to tell if the body she'd found was really Gus Klein . . . *if* he hadn't had his tattoo removed after he'd left Lake Eden. She'd just finished adding several soup ladles, a bean pot, and two slow cooker crocks to the bottom rack when there was another knock, a very timid knock, on the frame of the screen door.

"Who is it?" Hannah called out.

"Barbara Donnelly. I need to talk to you, Hannah."

"Come in. It's open." Hannah made quick work of stashing a metal spatula on the top rack of the dishwater. She had no idea why Bill's secretary wanted to talk to her, but perhaps she could pump Barbara for information. "I thought you were at the slide show."

"I was, but Norman told me that my pictures of Marge and Patsy at Girl Scout Camp won't come for another half hour. And I wanted to see you, so I came right over." Barbara walked to the sink and picked up a scouring pad. "Do you need some help?"

"Not really, I'm almost through," Hannah said, experiencing a flash of *déjà vu*. "Why did you want to see me, Barbara? You look a little upset."

"It's what Marge said about Gus at the family meeting."

"And that was . . . ?" Hannah asked to encourage her.

"That they didn't have any way of telling whether Gus was really their brother. She said a lot of time had passed and they really couldn't tell by just looking at him. And then she mentioned that Gus didn't have any distinguishing marks."

"Right," Hannah said, that sense of *déjà vu* growing stronger.

"Well, he did except Marge didn't know about it. Patsy didn't either. Nobody did unless they happened to . . ." Barbara stopped and cleared her throat. "Maybe I'd better start again."

Hannah gave her an encouraging nod. "Go ahead."

"It was the summer right before my senior year at Jordan High. A bunch of us went out to the lake to swim, and we needed a place to change into our suits. You've seen the changing rooms, haven't you?"

"Yes." Hannah had used those same changing rooms when

she'd taken swimming lessons as a child. They consisted of a concrete slab enclosed by an eight-foot high block wall on three sides. The fourth wall did not complete the enclosure. Instead it ran parallel to the first wall making a passageway about four feet wide. It also stopped about four feet short of joining the second wall so that a swimmer could walk inside the hallway that was formed, turn the corner into the large part of the enclosure, and have privacy from anyone outside.

"You know how the changing rooms don't have a roof, and they're open on top?"

"I know."

"The Lion's Club had them built that way so they wouldn't get all moldy inside. My dad explained it to me. But the girls' changing room had a low spot on the floor right by the door. If it rained, there was a big puddle full of all sorts of nasty leaves and things and it didn't dry up for a couple of days."

"I understand," Hannah said because Barbara seemed to be waiting for her to say something.

"Well, we didn't want to walk through the leaves and yuck, so we decided we'd use the boys' changing room if nobody was in it. The only problem was that somebody had to check to see. I was the only one that could scale the wall, so I did and I peeked inside. And there was Gus Klein just ready to step into his swim trunks."

Hannah thought she knew what was coming next, but there was only one way to make sure. She clamped her lips shut and waited for Barbara to go on with her story.

"His back was to me, and I saw his tattoo. It was two crossed bats with a baseball in between. And it was on his left side, just about where his back pocket would have come if he'd been wearing pants. I jumped down in a hurry so he wouldn't know I'd seen him. And then we ran back to the car and held up the blanket my dad always kept in the trunk, and took turns changing in the backseat."

"Did you mention what you'd seen to anyone else?"

"Good heavens, no!" Barbara looked shocked. "I didn't want Gus to know I'd seen him and one of the girls would have told. Anyway, that's it, Hannah. I just thought I should tell you right away. I didn't want to mention it to Bill for the obvious reason."

"What obvious reason is that?" Hannah was curious.

"He'd think I was a snoop, or maybe worse. I did date Gus for a while, you know."

"I didn't know, but thanks for telling me." Hannah gave her a warm smile. "And don't worry. I won't mention what you said to anybody."

After Barbara left, Hannah turned back to the work at hand. She scoured two frying pans, a pasta pot, and a scoop encrusted with something that looked like scrambled eggs but probably wasn't. She stashed them in the dishwasher, poured in the heavy-duty detergent, and gave a final look around the kitchen to make sure everything was spotless. Then she turned both dishwashers on, gave a final wipe to the kitchen counters, switched off the lights, and headed for the door. She was just stepping out when she ran smack into Rose McDermott.

"Hi, Rose," Hannah said, wondering if she was going to get the tattoo story for the third time that evening.

"I was looking for you, Hannah. Hal's still at the slide show, and I wanted to talk to you alone."

"Sure, Rose." Hannah sat down in the old porch swing that graced the porch of the Thompson cottage, and pointed to a wicker chair. "Sit down and be comfy."

"Thanks. Your guy is sure doing a great job with that slide show."

Which guy is that? Hannah wanted to ask, but she didn't. She knew perfectly well that Rose was referring to Norman.

"Anyway . . . Marge called a family meeting this afternoon. Hal's her third cousin twice removed, you know, so we went. And she told us she wasn't sure that Gus was really her brother Gus, but since he didn't have any scars, or marks, or anything like that when he left Lake Eden, they had to wait for DNA testing to find out for sure."

"Right."

"Anyway . . . he did."

"Did?" Hannah prompted, even though she was sure she knew what was coming.

"Did have a mark. Gus had a tattoo. He had it when he was a senior in high school."

"And you know this for a fact?"

"I saw it!" Rose said, and Hannah knew she was nodding for emphasis, even though it was dark and all she could see was Rose's slightly darker shape in the chair. "Actually, I saw it twice. But I wouldn't admit it to anybody but you, Hannah. Hal would just die if he ever found out what Gus did."

Uh-oh! Hannah had all she could do not to groan out loud. She really didn't want to know the details of how Rose had seen Gus's tattoo. Twice. Tacked on top of her natural reticence to hearing something embarrassingly personal was the fact that Rose was at least ten years older than Gus, maybe more.

"Just describe the tattoo," she told Rose. "I don't need to know anything else."

"It's okay. I want to tell you. I've kept the secret all these years, and I know you won't say anything to anybody. It was right after Hal and I were married and he was running the café by himself. I was still working as head secretary at the school."

"I didn't know you worked at the school."

"I was there for four years. I started right after I graduated high school, when Mr. Garrison's secretary moved away. He was the principal before Mr. Purvis."

Hannah wasn't sure what being the principal's secretary had to do with Gus and seeing his tattoo, but asking wouldn't do any good. Rose liked to tell things her way.

"Gus was no stranger to the principal's office. He was always getting into trouble. Nothing big, but since the other guys looked up to him so much for being such a fine athlete, he was supposed to set a good example."

"And he didn't?" Hannah guessed.

"Not hardly!" Rose gave a little laugh. "Gus was a hellion, pure and simple. He was always getting into trouble. It was nothing big, just pranks and stuff, but there wasn't a week that didn't go by without Gus being sent to Mr. Garrison's office. And Mr. Garrison was an old Army man. He believed in corporal punishment if the occasion warranted."

"Go on," Hannah said, beginning to get a glimmer of things to come.

"Anyway . . . Gus did something particularly bad the week that school started. I don't remember exactly what it was after all this time, but it had something to do with the drama teacher and three dead frogs."

Hannah's imagination took off like a rocket, and she had all she could do to keep it in check. "And Gus got caught for what he'd done?" she prompted.

"That's right. Anyway . . . I was about to take some reports to the superintendent's office when Gus came in. I knocked on Mr. Garrison's door, showed Gus in, and then I went to deliver those reports. When I got back, Mr. Garrison's door was closed and all I could hear was a loud whacking noise."

"Corporal punishment?" Hannah guessed.

"And how! The first thing I noticed was that the Board of Education was gone. It was a paddle that hung on the wall right outside Mr. Garrison's office. It said *Board of Education* on it, and the *Board* part was in red because it was supposed to be a joke."

"I get it."

"Anyway . . . I knew right away what was happening. Mr. Garrison was spanking Gus with that paddle. And from the sound I was hearing, there was nothing between that paddle and Gus's behind."

"I understand."

"Now normally I wouldn't have done anything at all. I mean, I was only the secretary and Mr. Garrison had a right to punish the students however he wanted. It's different now, of course. But I was a little worried because Gus wasn't making any noise at all. So I went to the door, peeked through the keyhole, and saw the whole thing."

"What whole thing?"

"Mr. Garrison was spanking Gus. His pants were down, he was bent over, and his back was to me. I could see the tattoo as plain as day, Hannah. It was crossed bats with a baseball between them. Of course everything around it was inflamed and I knew Mr. Garrison had been paddling him for quite a while."

"What did you do?" Hannah asked, not able to resist.

"What *could* I do? I was Mr. Garrison's secretary, and I couldn't interrupt him. So I went back to my chair and I waited until he was finished and Gus came out of the office."

"And then you . . . ?"

"Offered Gus some lanolin. I had it in my desk drawer because my hands were chapped. And I figured that if it helped my hands, it might be good for Gus's you-know-what."

"Makes sense," Hannah said. "So you gave Gus some lanolin?"

"That's right. And next time he came in, a week later, he tossed the tube of lanolin on my desk and thanked me."

"That's nice."

"Not really. Because right after he thanked me, he dropped his pants and mooned me to show me that the Board of Education paddle hadn't left any marks."

"Oh." Hannah said, still slightly confused. "But I don't understand why you're so nervous about Hal finding out you gave Gus the lanolin."

"It's not that," Rose said. "It's just that Hal was in the Army with Bill Garrison, and if he ever found out that one of the students Bill disciplined mooned me to show that Bill's paddling had healed, he'd be really angry at me for not telling Bill about it."

"I understand," Hannah said, even though she didn't. It was another case of chalking it up to sensibilities she didn't comprehend. "Well, you don't have to worry. I'm not about to say anything to anybody."

"I know you won't." Rose stood up. "I'd better get back before Hal realizes I didn't just go to the ladies' room. Thanks, Hannah. And I really hope you catch Gus's killer . . . if it really *was* Gus."

Hannah sat there a moment after Rose left, just soaking up the peace of the night. The stars glittered brightly overhead and cast rippling streaks over the water. She could hear the mosquitoes buzzing, but her repellent was still working. It was a perfect summer night except for the puzzle of Gus Klein's murder.

When she felt capable of actually moving, Hannah got up and went down the steps to the path that led to the parking lot. She passed by the picnic area and heard sounds of merriment and clapping as the slide show continued. She walked on for a minute or two and finally arrived at the public parking lot. She was just about to unlock the door to her cookie truck when someone called out to her.

"Hannah! Wait!"

Hannah stopped with the key in her hand and turned to see Delores rushing down the gravel road. Her mother had exchanged the high-heeled sandals she'd been wearing earlier for a pair of ballet-type flats, but she was hobbling a bit, as if they didn't fit her.

"What's the matter with your feet?" Hannah asked, when her mother arrived at the cookie truck.

Delores sighed loudly. "They're Carrie's shoes. She always brings an extra pair. But they're too big and I have to curl my toes to keep them on." Delores stopped and took several short breaths. "I need to talk to you, Hannah. It's important."

"Are you going to give me a lecture about how embarrassing it is for you when I find dead bodies?"

"No."

Hannah reared back slightly in surprise. "You're not?"

"I'm not. I'm responsible for this one, Hannah. I asked you to go look for Gus, but I really didn't think you'd find him dead. It's all my fault!"

Hannah began to frown. In the bluish light cast by the arc lights that ringed the public parking lot, she could see that her mother was agitated. "Are you trying to tell me you had something to do with his death?"

"Of course not. The last time I saw him was when I left the dance with Carrie at midnight."

"But you look upset. What is it?"

"Marge and Patsy told everyone that Gus didn't have any distinguishing marks."

"That's right," Hannah confirmed it, "or at least they didn't *know* about any distinguishing marks," she amended, since she'd found out about one distinguishing mark from three sources so far.

"They wouldn't necessarily know. Marge's mother was death on body adornments. Marge really wanted to get her ears pierced, but her mother wouldn't let her. After Patsy got married, Marge and I went to visit her while Mac was training at Camp Ripley. He was in the National Guard. All three of us went to the doctor and got our ears pierced."

"That's interesting, Mother," Hannah said, even though it wasn't. And then, despite the fact she didn't really want to know, she asked, "But what does that have to do with distinguishing marks on Gus Klein?"

"Gus had a tattoo."

Hannah worked hard to appear unfazed by the question that flashed through her mind. *How did her mother know about Gus's tattoo?*

"This is highly embarrassing, but I feel it's my duty to tell you," Delores went on, "since you've agreed to investigate the murder."

"You don't have to tell me anything," Hannah blurted out.

"Yes, I do. You see, I dated Gus in high school, long before I met your father."

Hannah came close to groaning. The best thing to do would be to cut her mother off at the pass, before she could say anymore. "I don't need to know that, Mother. Was the tattoo two crossed bats with a baseball between them?"

"Yes!"

"And it was on the left of Gus's backside?"

"That's right! But how did you . . . ?"

"Three women already told me about it," Hannah interrupted her mother's question. "And there's probably a couple more waiting to catch me alone."

"And they *all* told you about his tattoo?" Delores looked outraged. "That rat! He told me he *loved* me! Who were they? I have to know."

"No, you don't. They all found out about the tattoo by accident."

"By *accident*? What do you mean?"

"One was visiting Marge and walked by his bedroom door when he was dressing, one peeked over the wall in the boys' changing room at the lake, and the other one . . ." Hannah stopped abruptly. She couldn't mention the principal's office because her mother would be able to identify Rose as the secretary. "He mooned the other one," she settled for saying, only recounting the second part of Rose's experience.

"Likely stories!" Delores gave a little snort. "I guess I shouldn't be surprised. I knew all along that Gus was a *rakehell*."

"Is that the same as a *bounder* and a *scoundrel*?" Hannah asked, exhausting her Regency Romance vocabulary.

"In a way, dear. It's a matter of degree. But it's water over the dam. It happened years ago, and I don't know why I got so upset."

"I do," Hannah said, before she could stop herself.

"You do?"

"Yes. You wonder how you could have been so naïve."

"And gullible. And you wonder how many people know you were that vulnerable back then."

"That, too." Hannah reached out and squeezed her mother's shoulder. Since she'd grown up in a family that seldom showed overt affection, this was tantamount to a hug. "The same thing happened to me when I was in school. But I was older and I really should have known better."

"Really?" Delores gave Hannah's hand a pat, the Swensen family way of returning a hug.

"There was someone in college, an assistant professor. He said he loved me, and I believed him, but I found out that he was engaged to somebody else."

Delores looked shocked. "That's just awful, dear!"

"It was. It took me a long time to get over it. It's one of the reasons I didn't want to go back to college after Dad died."

"Because he was still there?"

"That's right. He probably still is, for all I know."

Delores gave her a shrewd look. "You don't care enough to find out?"

"Not really."

"You're over it, then," Delores pronounced. "The strange thing is, I was sure I was over Gus when I started dating your father."

"But you weren't?"

Delores frowned. "I think I was. And I'm sure it wouldn't have bothered me a bit if your father were still alive. But he isn't. And seeing Gus again brought up old memories."

"I understand," Hannah said. And she did.

"But I almost forgot to tell you something. I talked to Iris Herman Staples this afternoon. She's Lisa's oldest sister, you know."

"I know."

"Well, she remembered some cookies that their mother used to make, and she said they were Jack's favorite cookies. She was just a toddler at the time, but she remembered them. Marge and Patsy did, too. They said their mother used to love those cookies so much, she'd hired Emmy to bake them whenever she had ladies over for meetings."

"What kind of cookies were they?" Hannah asked.

"Patsy said that Emmy called them Red Velvet Cookies. We were eating a piece of Edna's red velvet cake at the time, and they all agreed that the cookies were just like the cake, except that they had more chocolate in the batter and there were chocolate chips inside. They were even frosted with a cream cheese frosting. You've eaten Edna's cake, haven't you, dear?"

"Yes." Hannah thought she knew exactly where her mother's conversation was heading.

"I mentioned the cookies to Lisa, and she looked through her mother's recipe box, but she couldn't find any cookie recipe like that. Jack remembers them, though, and he told Lisa they were the best cookies he'd even eaten."

Hannah couldn't stay silent any longer. "So you want me to try to make a red velvet cookie that tastes like the one Jack remembers?"

"That's right, dear. It won't be too much trouble, will it?"

Hannah felt like laughing, but she didn't. Her mother had no concept of how many batches of trial-and-error cookies she'd have to bake before she found the proper balance of ingredients. And even when she arrived at a cookie recipe that worked, she still had no assurance that it would even remotely resemble the cookie that Jack Herman remembered.

"Dear?"

Hannah gave a tired little sigh and bowed to the inevitable. "I'll do my best, Mother," she promised.

"I asked Edna to write out her recipe for you." Delores

handed her a piece of notebook paper covered with Edna's fine, spidery writing.

"Thanks, Mother. This'll help."

"Then you think you can do it?"

"I'll give it my best shot."

"By tomorrow night? It's Jack's birthday, and I think it would be wonderful to surprise him with a batch of his favorite cookies. Unless, of course, you're too busy to bake them."

"I'll try, Mother," Hannah repeated, realizing that it would be another night with less sleep than she needed.

"Thank you, dear. Just let me know if there's any way I can help you."

Hannah was about to say there was nothing her mother could do, when she thought of something. "There *is* one thing . . ."

"You want me to help you *bake?*" Delores sounded even more panic-stricken than Andrea had when Hannah had once asked her to listen for the timer and take cookies out of the oven at The Cookie Jar.

"No, Mother. I can handle the baking part. It's just that I need to ask you more questions about Gus. Will you drop by the shop around ten for coffee tomorrow morning?"

"Of course I will."

"Good. I'll try to have a test cookie ready for you to taste. And could you ask Marge to let you into the library later tonight or early tomorrow morning to collect any Jordan High yearbooks you can find with pictures of Gus?"

"I'll do it right after the slide show's over. Marge wants to help you any way she can."

"Thanks. I'd better get going, Mother. I want to mix up some cookie dough tonight and bake it first thing tomorrow morning."

Chapter Twelve

Hannah wasn't quite sure what to expect when she opened the door to the condo, but when Moishe wasn't there to leap into her arms, she knew what she'd find wouldn't be good. He was hiding again and that meant trouble.

The living room looked fine at first glance. It even looked fine when she walked through it, eyeing anything that could be destroyed by a determined feline. The one remaining couch pillow was intact, and so were the couch, the crocheted throw from her Grandma Ingrid's farmhouse, and the bouquet of silk flowers Delores had given her for her coffee table. Her desk appeared to be fine, but there was something hanging over it, something new, something . . .

"Good heavens!" she exclaimed, stepping closer. Norman must have had time to deliver the Kitty Kondo because it was standing . . . perhaps *looming* was a better word . . . over her desk.

There was a sound, and Hannah turned to see Moishe sidling into the room. He stepped cautiously closer but stopped short of her, staring at his Kitty Kondo with narrowed eyes. Then he puffed up like a Halloween cat, and the hair on his back stood up. He made a low, growling noise Hannah had only heard him make a few times before, and she knew he was suspicious and fearful of the new piece of furniture that had invaded his living room.

"It's okay. Norman put it there for you," Hannah attempted to explain. "It's a Kitty Kondo, and it's an activity center for cats."

Moishe's ears canted back to flatten against his head, and Hannah knew he wasn't convinced. "Just look at this," she said, stepping up to the carpeted tower and batting at one of the jingling balls hanging from the pole on the second story. "Isn't that fun?"

Moishe's growl was not an assent, and Hannah was wise enough to know it. Some less savvy human roommates might have attempted to pick him up and put him on the activity center, but not Hannah. She valued the skin on her arms too much, and she didn't want to arrive at Jack's birthday party tomorrow night covered in Band-aids. Moishe would have to learn to like his new Kitty Kondo gradually.

"Let's go have some tuna," Hannah said, leading the way to the kitchen without checking the rest of the rooms for damage. Moishe had obviously been traumatized by the forest green Kitty Kondo that had invaded his living room, but a whole can of albacore tuna should take his mind off the carpeted intruder.

Two hours later, Hannah slipped on the oversized T-shirt she wore as a summer nightgown and crawled into bed. Moishe had cut a wide berth around the activity center when they walked through the living room on their way to bed, but he hadn't growled or bristled, and that was a good sign.

She certainly hoped the cookie dough she'd mixed up after two failed attempts would work. She'd read through Edna's red velvet cake recipe, balanced the wet and dry ingredients for drop cookie dough rather than a cake batter, and added more chocolate and some chocolate chips. There was no point in using the vinegar and baking soda, since the cookie dough would sit out on the counter and lose its fizz between batches. She couldn't use buttermilk, either, since she didn't have any in her refrigerator and she certainly didn't want to drive out to the Quick Stop to buy some.

The first batch she'd baked looked fine, but they were too flat and chewy. The second batch solved that problem, but they fell apart when she tried to take them off the cookie sheet. She thought she'd managed to mix up a winner with the third batch, but she was so tired her eyes were beginning to cross. She covered the dough and stashed it in her refrigerator. She'd be risking disaster by baking more cookies tonight. The third batch would have to wait until morning to bake.

" 'Night, Moishe," she whispered, reaching out to give her pet a scratch under the chin. Then she closed her eyes and fell asleep to dream of Red Velvet Cookies dancing around the floor of the Lake Pavilion while Frankie and the Frankfurters played the *Beer Barrel Polka*.

It wasn't morning. It couldn't be morning. But it must be morning, because a rooster was crowing in the living room.

Hannah rolled over and pulled the covers over her head, but that didn't help. The rooster kept right on crowing. Except it wasn't exactly crowing. It was more of a chirping sound, like a cricket on steroids, or a frog croaking in a falsetto, or a mouse being terrorized by a . . .

Hannah's eyes popped open. Her mind was working so hard to identify the origin of the sound she was hearing, it had awakened her. And it was the middle of the night. At least she *thought* it was the middle of the night. It was certainly dark enough to be the middle of the night.

There it was again, a sort of a high-pitched squeak. Perhaps it *was* a mouse being terrorized by a cat! "Moishe?" she called out, flicking on the light.

Moishe was nowhere in sight. He wasn't on the bed, and he wasn't in it, either, because there was no lump under the covers. He wasn't in the bedroom at all. The chirping had stopped, and Hannah knew that meant she had to get up. She gave a tired sigh as she pulled her slippers out from under the bed and put them on. It was a warm summer night, and she didn't need to protect her feet from cold floors. But her slippers were washable, and she did need to protect her feet from any tangible evidence of rodent carnage that might be scattered in her path.

There was nothing in the hallway. Hannah was careful as she walked. And there was nothing in the living room except . . .

Hannah stopped short as she spotted Moishe sitting proudly on the second floor of his Kitty Kondo. He was practically grinning at her, but not so widely that he might drop the prize in his mouth. It was a furry gray mouse with a string attached, and Hannah knew that string had been tied to the pole of kitty toys when they'd gone to bed. Moishe must have gathered his courage and gone up there in the middle of the night to get his prize. And he must be chewing on it right now, even though she couldn't see his jaw working, because it was making a new sound, an electronic beeping sound that seemed to be coming from her bedroom.

Realization dawned and with it, Hannah groaned. The beeping was coming from her alarm clock. It was time to get up and face the morning. She'd had a full four-hours' sleep, and that was all she was going to get.

There was a soft hissing sound from the kitchen, and Hannah sniffed the air. The last of the water had gone into her coffeemaker's basket and it was dripping down through the coffee grounds to join the fresh brew that awaited her in the carafe.

"I should have taught you to shut off the alarm clock," Hannah said, addressing her courageous hunter.

As Hannah turned to go back to the bedroom to shut off her alarm, Moishe made a sound that she took for agreement, but he didn't open his mouth. It was clear he wasn't about to give up his prey for an early-morning conversation.

It didn't take long for Hannah to shower and dress, and

she drained the last of her first mug of coffee as she walked down the hallway to the kitchen again. There she found Moishe still staring at the food in his bowl, the toy mouse held tightly in his mouth. "Can't have your mouse and eat it, too?" she asked, pointing to the food bowl.

Moishe made another pathetic closed-mouth sound, and Hannah took pity on him. "I tell you what . . . why don't I tie the mouse back on the pole, and you can catch him again later? That way you'll have twice the fun." With that said, Hannah reached for the mouse, and surprisingly, Moishe let her have it. As she headed for the living room to tie it back on the pole, she wondered if he'd really understood her and opted for twice the fun, or whether the food in the bowl had simply won out over the nonfood in his mouth.

She had time for one more cup of coffee. Hannah poured her last cup and leaned against the counter to sip it. Once she finished her coffee, all she had to do was retrieve the cookie dough, find her car keys, pick up her purse, and go out the door.

The phone rang, and Hannah mentally corrected herself. All she had to do was answer the phone, pick up the cookie dough, find her keys and her purse, and go.

"Hello," she said, answering normally since Moishe wasn't bristling.

"Hi, Hannah. You were up, weren't you?"

It was Norman, and Hannah laughed. "Of course I was up. I have to be at work in thirty minutes. I'm glad you called, though. I wanted to thank you for putting up Moishe's Kitty Kondo."

"You're welcome. I didn't think you'd mind if Sue from downstairs let me in."

"I don't mind at all!"

"Good. I think it's going to take a while before the Big Guy gets used to it. He made himself scarce while I was installing it, and when I tried to coax him closer, he hid under your bed."

"He's a faster learner than you think. You should have seen him this morning playing with that mouse on the pole. He managed to get it loose, and he looked really proud of himself."

"Great! I'll pick up some replacement toys the next time I'm out at the mall. The girl at the pet store said her cats tear up at least one toy a week."

"Thanks, again," Hannah said. "You're the most thoughtful person I know."

There was a silence, and Hannah knew Norman was a bit embarrassed by her compliment. "Well, you are," she told him.

"Thanks. You threw me off balance there and I almost forgot the reason I called. It's number fifty-seven."

"Number fifty-seven?"

"Five-seven. That's right."

"But *what's* five-seven?"

"The Animal Channel. For Moishe to watch. I asked around after the slide show last night. I thought you might want to turn it on before you left for work."

"Right. Thanks, Norman. I'll do that. And if you can, come in for cookies this morning. I'm trying out something new."

Hannah had no sooner hung up the phone than it rang again. She assumed it was Norman, who'd thought of something he'd forgotten to tell her, so she answered, "Hello again, Norman."

"It's not Norman. It's Mike."

"Oops. Sorry about that. I just finished talking to Norman on the phone, and I thought he was calling back."

"Norman calls you *this* early in the morning?" Mike sounded shocked.

"Sometimes. He knows I get up early."

"How does he know *that?*"

"Because I'm always in the kitchen at The Cookie Jar by six at the latest, and he sees the lights on when he drives by on his way to the dental clinic. Anyway, how did *you* know I'd be up this early?"

There was a pause, and then Mike laughed. "Okay. Let's start over. Morning, Hannah."

"Morning, Mike. What can I do for you at the crack of dawn?"

"I don't think I'd better try to answer that. I just called to say that Ronni says to try seven-five."

Hannah was puzzled. "Try seven-five for what?"

"For the Animal Channel. Ronni turns it on every day for her dog. She's got a Pekingese."

"Ronni who?"

"Ronni Ward. Her engagement didn't work out, and she's back doing fitness training at the station. She just rented the apartment across the hall from me."

"Oh," Hannah said, wondering if she should start worrying about Mike and Ronni. The last time a woman from the sheriff's department had lived in Mike's complex, they'd been involved. And right after that unpleasant thought had crossed her mind, Hannah wondered if Andrea knew that Ronni was back in town. Even though Bill had sworn up and down that he wasn't the least bit interested in the winner of Lake Eden's bikini contest, Andrea had worried that they were more than employer and employee.

"Andrea knows," Mike answered Hannah's unspoken question. "Bill said he told her last night when he got home."

"Oh," Hannah said again, treading on eggshells. She wasn't about to tell Mike any sisterly secrets.

"Bill said Andrea thought they were involved when he went to Florida for that convention."

This time Hannah didn't even open her mouth for fear she'd say the wrong thing. Less was more, or silence was golden, or any one of several phrases that seemed to fit the situation.

"Anyway, I thought I'd tell you. Try seventy-five and see if it works. And if it doesn't work, try fifty-seven. Ronni sometimes transposes numbers."

"Good thing she doesn't do countdowns for NASA."

"Very funny, Hannah. Just try both numbers. It might save you money on couch pillows. And that reminds me . . . are you going to be at the lake this morning?"

"No, I have to work. I'll be at The Cookie Jar."

"Good. I've got a couple of things to do in town, anyway. I'll come in about eleven, and we can compare notes."

"Fine by me," Hannah said. "And thanks for telling me about the Animal Channel. I'm about to leave for work, so I'll try it right now."

Once she'd hung up the phone, Hannah headed for the couch and the remote control that she kept in the drawer of the coffee table. The drawer was fairly cat-safe, but she still pushed it all the way to the back and covered it with an old copy of the TV guide. Moishe had already killed one control, and it had cost her big bucks to replace it.

"Hi, Moishe," she greeted her pet as he jumped up to the seat of the couch and then even higher to perch on the back. "Just for fun, let's see if Ronni Ward got the number for the Animal Channel right."

When channel seventy-five came on the screen, Hannah let out a gasp of pure shock. She didn't know they were allowed to do things like that on television! She resisted the urge to cover her cat's eyes and wasted no time punching in fifty-seven. When a pride of lions replaced the scene that had shocked her on channel seventy-five, she smiled and reached up to give Moishe a scratch. "Okay, this is the Animal Channel. It's number fifty-seven and I'll leave it on for you."

Once she'd stashed the cable control in the drawer and collected her cookie dough, her keys, and her purse, Hannah noticed that one of the lions, probably the adult female, was stalking a zebra. "'Bye, Moishe. Enjoy the show, but don't get any grandiose ideas," she said. And then she headed out into the early morning darkness to drive to The Cookie Jar and bake the day's cookies.

RED VELVET COOKIES

Preheat oven to 375 degrees F., rack
in the middle position.

2 one-ounce squares unsweetened baking chocolate
½ cup *(1 stick, ¼ pound, 4 ounces)* butter at room
temperature
⅔ cup brown sugar, firmly packed
⅓ cup white *(granulated)* sugar
½ teaspoon baking soda
½ teaspoon salt
1 large egg
1 Tablespoon red food coloring
¾ cup sour cream
2 cups flour *(pack it down in the cup when you
measure it)*
1 cup *(a 6-ounce package)* semi-sweet chocolate
chips

Line your cookie sheets with parchment paper. Spray
the parchment paper with Pam or another nonstick cooking spray. *(If you don't have parchment paper, you can use
foil, but leave little "ears" of foil sticking up on the ends,
enough to grab later when you slide the whole thing on a
cooling rack.)*

Unwrap the squares of chocolate and break them apart.
Put them in a small microwave-safe bowl. *(I used an
8-ounce measuring cup.)* Melt them for 90 seconds on
HIGH. Stir them until they're smooth and set them aside
to cool while you mix up your cookie dough.

Hannah's 1st Note: Mixing this dough is easier with an electric mixer. You can do it by hand, but it takes some muscle.

Combine the butter, brown sugar, and white sugar together in the bowl of an electric mixer. Beat them on medium speed until they're smooth. This should take less than a minute.

Add the baking soda and salt, and resume beating on medium again for another minute, or until they're incorporated.

Add the egg and beat on medium until the batter is smooth *(an additional minute should do it.)* Add the red food coloring and mix for about 30 seconds.

Shut off the mixer and scrape down the bowl. Then add the melted chocolate and mix again for another minute on medium speed.

Shut off the mixer and scrape down the bowl again. At low speed, mix in half of the flour. *(That's one cup.)* When the flour is incorporated, mix in the sour cream.

Scrape down the bowl again and add the rest of the flour. *(That's the second cup.)* Beat until the flour is fully incorporated.

Remove the bowl from the mixer and give it a stir with a spoon. Mix in the chocolate chips by hand. *(A firm rubber spatula works nicely.)*

Use a teaspoon to spoon the dough onto the parchment-lined cookie sheets, 12 cookies to a standard-sized sheet. *(If the dough is too sticky for you to work with, chill it for a half-hour or so, and try again.)* Bake the cookies at 375 degrees F., for 9 to 11 minutes, or until they rise and become firm. *(Mine took exactly 9 minutes.)*

Slide the parchment from the cookie sheets and onto a wire rack. Let the cookies cool on the rack while the next sheet of cookies is baking. When the next sheet of cookies is ready, pull the cooled cookies onto the counter or table and slide the parchment paper with the hot cookies onto the rack. Keep alternating until all the dough has been baked.

When all the cookies are cool, peel them off the parchment paper and put them on waxed paper for frosting.

Cream Cheese Frosting

¼ cup softened butter *(½ stick, ⅛ pound)*
4 ounces softened cream cheese *(half of an 8-ounce package)*
½ teaspoon vanilla extract
2 cups confectioner's *(powdered)* sugar *(no need to sift unless it's got big lumps)*

Mix the softened butter with the softened cream cheese and the vanilla until the mixture is smooth.

Hannah's 2nd Note: Do this next step at room temperature. If you heated the cream cheese or the butter to soften it, make sure it's cooled down before you continue.

Add the confectioner's sugar in half-cup increments until the frosting is of proper spreading consistency. *(You'll use all, or almost all, of the sugar.)*

A batch of Red Velvet Cookies yields about 3 dozen, depending on cookie size. They're soft, velvety, and chocolaty, and they'll end up being everyone's favorite.

Hannah's 3rd Note: If you really want to pull out all the stops, brush the tops of your baked cookies with melted raspberry jam, let it dry, and then frost them with Cream Cheese Frosting.

Chapter Thirteen

"We're done!" Hannah said, carrying two mugs of coffee over to the stainless steel workstation in the kitchen of The Cookie Jar.

Lisa glanced up at the clock with a smile. "I know, and it's only seven."

"You got here at six. You really shouldn't have come in, Lisa," Hannah gently chided her partner. "I told you to take the week of the reunion off."

"I took yesterday off. That's enough. From now on I'm coming in at six to help with the baking."

"But that's a lot of work for you, with the reunion and all."

"It's a lot of work for *you*, too! You're baking cookies every morning and then coming out to the lake every afternoon to help with the dinner buffet."

"Okay, you win." Hannah held up her hands in surrender. "I appreciate the help. But don't feel you have to come in if you're too tired, okay?"

"Okay, as long as you don't feel you have to come out to the lake to help with dinner."

Hannah laughed. "Do we have a culinary standoff?"

"I think so." Lisa turned and pointed to the pan of bar cookies she'd baked. "The bars are cool enough to cut. Do you want to taste my new invention?"

"Sure. What do you call them?"

"Rocky Road Bar Cookies, because they remind me of rocky road ice cream." Lisa walked over to cut a piece and brought it back to Hannah.

"I see nuts, and marshmallows, and chocolate, and . . . I don't know what else."

"Go ahead and taste. And give me your honest opinion."

Hannah took a bite and chewed. The bars were delicious. "Yummy!" she pronounced. "On a goodness scale of one to ten, these are a twelve."

"Do they remind you of rocky road ice cream?"

"Yes. And they also remind me of S'mores. We used to make those on Girl Scout campouts."

"What's a S'more?"

"A graham cracker with a square of Hershey's milk chocolate on top. You toast a marshmallow over the campfire, plunk it on top of the chocolate square, and cover it with another graham cracker. Then you eat it when it's hot and everything just melts in your mouth."

"That sounds great! I think I missed a lot by not joining the Girl Scouts."

"Why didn't you?" Hannah asked.

"They met after school on Wednesdays, and I had to get right home. Mom was sick, and Dad worked an extra two hours four days a week so he could take Friday off to do all the stuff that was closed on the weekends."

Hannah kicked herself mentally for not realizing that Lisa would have a selfless reason for not joining the Girl Scouts. "You're talking about things like going to the bank?"

"Yes. And driving her to doctor's appointments and other medical stuff. She went in for dialysis on Fridays."

"That must have been hard on you, Lisa."

"Yes, but worth it. Mom had some good times when she was in remission and all my sisters and brothers would come to visit."

Hannah saw Lisa blink several times and knew she was re-

membering her mother and grieving for her. It was time to introduce a happier subject. "I've got something for you to
taste," she announced.

"What's that?"

"Red Velvet Cookies."

Lisa stared at her in something close to shock. "You mean
you've got Mom's recipe? The one Dad remembers?"

"No, but I put one together that I *hope* is like your mom's.
My mother thought it would be a nice surprise for your dad's
birthday."

"It's great! You're wonderful, Hannah!"

"Don't get too excited. They might not be like your mother's
cookies at all. I understand she stopped baking them years
ago."

"That's what Iris said when she told me about them."

"Do you remember them?" Hannah asked.

"No. I think she'd already stopped baking them. But I get
to taste one anyway, don't I?"

"Of course. I haven't tasted one yet, either."

Mere seconds later, both partners had fresh mugs of coffee
and a cookie on a napkin in front of them to taste. Hannah
tried hers first and pronounced it good, but perhaps not the
exact cookie Emily Herman had baked.

"It's better than good, it's superb," Lisa declared. "The
chocolate melts in your mouth and the cream cheese in the
frosting sends it off the top of that goodness scale you were
talking about earlier."

"Thanks, Lisa. When you get out to the lake will you find
your sister and ask her what she thinks? Have Marge and
Patsy try them, too. If they taste like your mother's, I'll bake
another batch before I come out this afternoon. Maybe
they'll jog your dad's memory and he can tell us more about
the night Gus left town and why there was bad blood between them."

"Do you really think your cookies can cure Dad's
Alzheimer's?"

"No, but the chocolate is bound to be good for him."

"That's true." Lisa gave a little laugh. "And even if your cookies don't give us any answers, they'll be a lovely birthday present for him."

After Lisa left, Hannah got the coffee shop ready for customers. This meant filling the sugar and artificial sweetener containers that sat on each table and setting out dishes with coffee creamer. Once the napkin dispensers were filled and the tables were wiped down a final time, Hannah sat down at her favorite table in the back of the coffee shop and waited for Luanne to arrive.

Nothing was moving on the street except Jon Walker's old Irish setter, who was strolling from the drugstore up the block. Jon was nowhere in sight, so Hannah unlocked the front door of the coffee shop and went out to intercept Skippy. But just as she got there, Jon appeared at the end of the block with a leash in hand. A handsome man of Chippewa ancestry, Jon was the town druggist and the owner of Lake Eden Neighborhood Pharmacy.

"Hi, Jon," Hannah greeted him.

"Morning, Hannah. Skippy started without me this morning. By the time I grabbed the leash, he was halfway up the block and headed for your place."

"He must have smelled the cookies. Want to come in and have one?"

"Sure. Skippy, too? I can take him back to the drugstore if you don't want him inside." Jon bent down and snapped on the leash.

"Skippy, too. The health board's never around this early, and technically I'm still closed so it doesn't matter anyway."

Once Jon was settled in a chair with two of his favorite Molasses Crackles and a mug of coffee, and Skippy was sitting at his feet with one of the dog biscuits Hannah kept for visiting dogs, she asked the question she'd been planning to ask him ever since she'd seen the pill in the cottage Gus Klein had inhabited so briefly at the lake. "I saw someone take a pill the other night and I'm wondering what it was. I found another one the next day, so I got a good look at it."

"Do I want to know who took the pill and where you saw it?"

"Not really."

"Okay. What did it look like?"

"It was a capsule. One end was green and the other end was white."

"A green-and-white capsule," Jon repeated. "Was it a regular size capsule, or a really skinny one?"

Hannah thought about that for a moment. "I think it was a regular size. Mother used to take gelatin capsules to make her nails stronger. It was that size."

"Regular, then. How about markings? Did you see any?"

"There was something there, but it was blurred and I couldn't make it out."

"Do you know the difference between a capsule and a caplet?"

"I think so. Caplets are solid, right?"

"Right. But this capsule you saw was one you could have pulled apart like your Mother's gelatin capsules?"

"That's right. Do you have any idea what it was?"

"I may have, if you described it accurately." Jon leaned a little closer, even though the coffee shop wasn't open yet and there was no one else at the tables. "Does this have anything to do with the murder out at the pavilion?"

"Uh . . ." Hannah dithered for about two seconds and then she decided to play it straight. "It may have. I don't know for sure."

Jon covered his eyes with his hands. "I wish you hadn't said that, Hannah. You could be asking me to give you information that I should be giving to the sheriff's department."

"Have they asked you anything about green-and-white capsules?"

"No."

"I don't think they will, since I'm the only one who saw it and I flushed it down the drain so the frog couldn't get it."

Jon gave a little groan. "I'm not even going to *ask* you about the frog. It's too early in the day. You're going to owe me big time for this, Hannah."

"How about a dozen Molasses Crackles?"

"You got it. But you don't really have to give me cookies. As long as I'm not breaking any laws, I'll be happy to tell you anything I know."

"Great! Tell me, please?"

"It's like I said before . . . if your description is accurate, it sounds like an amphetamine capsule to me."

"Really!" Hannah began to frown. "What, exactly, does an amphetamine do?"

"It increases heart rate, decreases appetite, and makes you feel alert. It used to be prescribed as a diet pill, but it has addictive properties and some nasty side effects, like sleeplessness and occasional hallucinations. It's more tightly regulated now."

"Then the pill I saw couldn't have been an over-the-counter antacid?"

Jon shook his head. "I don't think so, not unless it's something so new I haven't seen it yet. I know I don't have any antacids like that at the store."

"Okay," Hannah said. "Thanks, Jon. You've helped me a lot. Hold on a second and I'll pack up some Molasses Crackles for you."

A few minutes later, Hannah saw Jon and Skippy out the door with a dozen Molasses Crackles, two more dog biscuits, and the steak bone she'd been saving for the Malamute who lived next to Lisa and Herb's neighbors. She still didn't understand what Gus had been doing with an amphetamine and why he'd called it an antacid, but she didn't have time to think about that right now. She had to bake another couple of batches of Red Velvet Cookies before the birthday party tonight, catch Gus Klein's killer without alienating Mike in the process, go out to the lake to make three batches of Wanmansita Casserole to serve at Jack's party, and check on her wayward cat to make sure he was still behaving. She knew she could do it, but it would take all the energy she had to give, and then some!

ROCKY ROAD BAR COOKIES
(S'MORES)

Preheat oven to 350 degrees F., rack
in the middle position.

24 graham crackers *(12 double ones)*
2 cups miniature marshmallows *(white, not colored)*
6-ounce package semi-sweet chocolate chips *(1 cup)*
1 cup salted cashews
½ cup butter *(1 stick, ¼ pound)*
½ cup dark brown sugar, firmly packed
1 teaspoon vanilla extract

Spray a 9-inch by 13-inch cake pan with Pam or other nonstick spray. *(If you like, buy a disposable foil pan in the grocery store, place it on a cookie sheet to support the bottom, and then you won't have to clean up.)*

Line the bottom of the pan with a layer of graham crackers. *(It's okay to overlap a bit.)*

Sprinkle the graham crackers with the marshmallows.

Sprinkle the marshmallows with the chocolate chips.

Sprinkle the chocolate chips with the cashews.

In a small saucepan over low heat, combine the butter and brown sugar. Stir the mixture constantly until the sugar is dissolved.

Turn off the heat, move the saucepan to a cool burner, and stir in the vanilla.

Drizzle the contents of the saucepan evenly over the contents of the cake pan.

Bake at 350 degrees F. for 10 to 12 minutes or until the marshmallows are golden on top. Cool in the pan on a wire rack.

When the Rocky Road Bar Cookies are cool, cut them into brownie-sized bars and serve.

If there are any leftovers *(which there won't be unless you have less than three people)* store them in the refrigerator in a covered container. They can also be wrapped, sealed in a freezer bag, and frozen for up to two months.

Yield: 2 ½ to 3 dozen yummy treats that will please adults and kids alike.

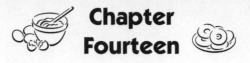

Chapter Fourteen

"This is a wonderful cookie, Hannah!"

"That's what Lisa said. But do you think it's anything like the cookies Iris told you about?"

Delores gave a dainty little shrug. "I'm not sure, dear. It certainly tastes like the cookie she described to me. But there's no way to tell unless she tastes it. Isn't that right?"

"That's right. Lisa took a few out to the reunion. I'm waiting for her to call and tell me what Iris thinks."

Hannah got up to refill her mother's coffee mug. They were sitting in the kitchen at The Cookie Jar, and Delores looked as fresh as the first daffodil of spring in a bright yellow linen suit with a lacy white shell. If Hannah were wearing the same suit, in a larger size of course, she'd look as wilted as an old banana skin.

"What is it, dear? You're staring at me."

"Sorry. You look wonderful this morning, Mother."

"Thank you, Hannah."

"I was just wondering if your suit is real linen."

"Of course it is. You know I don't like to wear synthetics."

"I know that, but . . ." Hannah stopped and sighed.

"But what?"

"I can't figure out how you can wear a linen suit when it's this hot and humid outside and still not get it wrinkled."

"I'm careful, dear. And I take off the jacket and hang it up on the hook in the back of the car when I drive."

"But your skirt isn't wrinkled, either."

"Well, I don't take it off and hang it up in the car, if that's what you're thinking!"

Delores gave a little laugh and Hannah joined in. Her mother was quick-witted this morning. "I'm careful about how I sit," Delores explained. "Your grandmother used to say, *Ladies don't wrinkle unless they assume unladylike positions.*"

Hannah nodded. Her maternal grandmother had been a stickler for proper etiquette, impeccable grammar, and a ladylike demeanor.

"You said you wanted to ask me some questions about Gus," her mother opened the discussion.

"I do. Did you manage to find a picture of him about the time the two of you were dating?"

Delores reached for one of four Jordan High yearbooks she'd stacked on the stainless steel surface of the workstation and flipped it open to a page that was marked with a pink strip of paper. "This is his formal senior picture."

Hannah stared down at the yearbook photo. Gus looked every bit as handsome as Marge and Patsy had claimed he was. She could understand why the high school girls had been wild about him.

"What happened to him after high school? I was going to ask Marge, but I forgot. Did he go on to college?"

Delores shook her head. "Good heavens, no. His grades weren't good enough. He got drafted."

"Into the Army?"

"No, into the minors. Didn't anybody tell you that Gus played baseball?"

"Marge and Patsy mentioned it, but I thought it was just in high school."

"No, Gus was really very good, and he was a first round

draft pick. He still holds the Minnesota state record for the highest batting average."

"Did he ever make it to the majors?" Hannah asked.

"I don't think so. I'm sure Marge would have mentioned it to me." Delores stopped and looked thoughtful. "Or maybe not. I was already engaged to your father by then, and she might have thought it wasn't appropriate to bring it up."

"Was Gus still playing baseball when he came back to Lake Eden to stay with Marge and his parents?"

"No. I know that for a fact. Gus came into the hardware store one day and he told your father he'd quit the farm team."

"Did he give a reason?"

"He said that life on the road with a baseball team just wasn't for him, that he wanted to get a good job and settle down. But I never believed that!"

"Why not?"

"Because it was his chance for a great career if he'd worked at it. I don't think he did. It just wasn't in his nature. For one thing, there were the women. I'm sure he had plenty when he was with the team, and he probably didn't treat them well. He certainly didn't in high school! And then there was the gambling. The Gus I knew when we were in high school made his spending money by cheating at cards and making rigged bets."

"Didn't he ever lose?" Hannah was curious.

"Only when he ran into someone who was a bigger cheater than he was. And when that happened, he just borrowed money from his sisters, or his current girlfriend, and kept right on gambling. He drank a lot, too. It was easy for him to buy liquor, because he looked older than most of the other boys."

"Did you ever lend him money when you were dating him?"

Delores gave a little sigh. "More often than I should have. And he didn't always pay me back. As a matter of fact, I think he still owed me twenty dollars when he left Lake Eden. Gus was a louse, pure and simple."

"Maybe he changed," Hannah suggested, playing devil's advocate.

"A leopard doesn't change its spots." Delores gave a little snort for emphasis. "I'm willing to bet that he was kicked off the team for drinking, or gambling, or romancing the wrong woman, or something like that."

Hannah bit her tongue and didn't say anything about sour grapes or a woman scorned. This was her mother, after all. Instead, she pulled the Jordan High yearbooks closer and smiled at her mother. "Show me the pictures?" she asked.

For long moments, Hannah looked and Delores pointed, giving a brief explanation for each photo she'd marked. The collection of Gus Klein pictures was extensive. There were at least a dozen photos in each book. It appeared that Gus had been awarded almost every high school athletic trophy, although Hannah didn't notice any academic honors.

"That's it, dear," Delores said, closing the last yearbook. "Is there anything else you need to know?"

"Just a few more things. Do you know anything about why Gus Klein left Lake Eden in the middle of the night?"

"I'm not sure why he left. I don't think he told anyone. And I don't know the details, but I heard there was a big fight between Gus and Jack Herman."

"Who told you that?"

"Your father. He was driving home from the store with Uncle Ed, and they stopped to break up the fight."

"What was the fight about?"

"I asked, but your father wouldn't tell me. Uncle Ed wouldn't say, either."

"So nobody knows?"

"Nobody knew except your father and Uncle Ed. And they're both gone now." Delores stopped and blinked hard, several times. "Of course Jack Herman knows, but . . ."

"But he might not be able to remember," Hannah finished her mother's thought.

"That's right. Poor Jack. Your father said he got the worst of it, and they dropped him off at Doc Knight's clinic to get stitched up. That was before the hospital was built. They didn't want to take Jack home that way and scare Emmy half to death. Iris was just a toddler, and Emmy was expecting Tim any day."

Hannah made a mental note to talk to Doc Knight about the night he'd treated Gus. Perhaps Lisa's father had said something about the fight.

"Is there anything else, dear?" Delores asked, glancing at the clock on the wall. "I need to pick up Carrie and go out to the mall. We want to find a little something for Jack's birthday party."

"There's just one more thing. Do you think there's anyone in town who had a grudge against Gus? Maybe somebody who might have wanted to see him dead?"

Delores's eyes widened. If she'd been depicted as a cartoon character, the little balloon over her head would have contained a drawing of a lightbulb. "Yes, I do! I don't know why I didn't think of it right away! Remember when I told you about Mary Sue Erickson?" She waited for Hannah to nod, and then she went on. "Well, that didn't last long. Gus only went out with her twice. But right after that, he dated Bert Kuehn's older sister."

Hannah was puzzled. "I've never heard of Bert Kuehn's older sister. Does she live in town?"

"She doesn't live anywhere, dear. Bert's sister is dead. She died the night of the senior prom in a terrible car accident."

"You told me Gus was a drinker. Was he driving drunk?"

"Not according to the accident report. It said that Bert's sister was at the wheel and her blood alcohol level was normal."

Hannah picked up on her mother's phrasing. "But there was some question about whether Bert's sister was actually driving?"

"Yes, there was. No one could prove otherwise, but the first person on the scene was the Jordan High baseball coach. He pulled both of them from the car before Doc Knight got there. Everyone in town wondered whether Gus had been driving and the coach had covered it up for him."

"Why would he do something like that?"

"To save Gus's career and his reputation as a coach. It was a feather in his cap to have one of his ballplayers drafted. As a matter of fact, he left Jordan High the next year and got a job in college baseball as an assistant coach. I seem to remember it was somewhere in Michigan, but I'm not sure exactly which college."

Hannah flipped open her stenographer's notebook, the one she'd designated as her murder book, to jot down the names. Bert Kuehn certainly had a reason to hate Uncle Gus, and both Bert and Ellie had been at the dance the night Gus was killed. They'd even brought six of their house specials from Bertanelli's Pizza for the potluck dinner. "What was the baseball coach's name, Mother?" she asked.

"Toby Hutchins. But I really don't know where he went when he left Lake Eden. All I can remember is that his new team was the wolves, or something like that."

"Wolverines?"

"That's it, dear. Do they play in Michigan?"

"Ann Arbor. The Wolverines is the team name for the University of Michigan athletic program."

"Really!" Delores looked impressed. "How do you know that?"

"It just stuck in my mind," Hannah said, settling for a half-truth. She wasn't about to tell her mother that she'd worked to memorize the team names from all the big colleges to impress a boy she'd hoped to date in high school.

"I really don't think you could track him down at this late date," Delores told her. "That was years ago, and I doubt he's still coaching baseball."

"If he's still alive, I'll find him," Hannah said, more confidently than she felt. "Is there anyone else who might have wanted Gus dead?"

"I'm not sure. Perhaps one of the girls he stopped dating in high school carried a grudge."

"Who would that be?" Hannah asked, mentally adding her mother's name to the list. Of course the way Delores told it, she'd dumped Gus when she'd caught him kissing another girl. That made her the dumper and Gus the dumpee, not the other way around.

"Oh, dear. I can't really remember all the girls that Gus dated. He was the love-them-and-leave-them type."

"Could you get together with Marge and Patsy when you get out to the reunion, and see if they remember any names?"

"Of course. You know I want to help, dear. I'll just take these yearbooks with me and see if they remember anybody. And I'll see whether I can find any of his old classmates to talk to. Lottie Borge is here. She married a Herman cousin. And she was only a year behind Gus in high school."

Just then Luanne Hanks stuck her head in the door. "Lisa just called and she said to tell you that Iris tasted a cookie. She said she thinks they're perfect."

"Great!" Hannah exchanged a high five with her mother.

"And Mike Kingston's here and he says he wants to talk to you. Should I send him back?"

When Hannah nodded, Delores picked up her stack of yearbooks and headed for the door. "What does *he* want?" she asked as she pulled it open.

"He wants to pick my brain." Hannah gave a little laugh and waved goodbye to her mother. "And since I want to pick his, it amounts to a draw."

"Hi, Mike," Hannah said when he came through the swinging, restaurant-style door that separated the coffee shop from the kitchen. "I'm a little short on time. Do you mind if I mix up a batch of cookies while we talk?"

"I don't mind, especially if you feed me." Mike flashed her his famous grin.

Hannah glanced over at the trays of cookies ready to be packed up and taken out to the birthday party. "I've got Raisin Drops, Molasses Crackles, Red Velvet Cookies, and Party Cookies."

"What are Party Cookies?"

"These." Hannah held up one of the pretty four-color pastel cookies she'd made earlier this morning. "They're for Jack Herman's birthday party tonight, but I've got plenty."

"I'll take one of those and one of the Red Velvet Cookies. I've never had either one of them before."

"You got it!" Hannah said, grabbing the cookies and delivering them, along with a mug of black coffee.

"Thanks, Hannah. I expect you've been asking questions."

"Some."

"Did you find out anything?"

"Not much." Hannah started to melt chocolate for the Red Velvet Cookies to give her a few seconds to think. She didn't want to tell Mike too much, but she had to tell him something. "Marge and Patsy talked to me right before dinner last night," she said.

"And?"

"They had some doubt that the victim, the man who claimed to be Gus Klein, really was their brother."

"Really?

Mike's eyes widened slightly, and Hannah knew she'd handed him a nugget he hadn't panned. "I guess Marge and Patsy didn't tell you that."

"No. But it figures they'd tell *you*."

Hannah stopped in her tracks and turned, six squares of unsweetened chocolate in her hand. "I thought this was supposed to be an exchange of information, not a contest about who's going to get all the clues and catch the killer first."

"It *is* an exchange of information! At least that's what I want it to be." Mike looked very sincere. "Do you think I could be letting my ego get in the way?"

Duh! Hannah thought, but of course she didn't say it. "What makes you say that?" she asked instead, unwrapping the chocolate, which was beginning to melt in her hand, dumping it into a half-pint measuring cup, and popping it into the microwave.

"It's just that I pride myself on my interviewing techniques, and I can't believe I didn't pick up on something like that and pursue it."

Hannah glanced at him as she set the timer on the microwave. "Maybe it's a girl thing," she said.

"And maybe I'm losing my touch and you're just really good at this."

"Fat chance," Hannah told him, melting the chocolate squares and salvaging his ego simultaneously. "I'm just lucky, that's all. And people talk to me because I was raised here. I've got the hometown advantage."

Mike considered it for a moment and then he said, "You're right. That probably counts for a lot. I like these Party Cookies, Hannah. They remind me of something, but I don't know what."

"Old-Fashioned Sugar Cookies."

"That's right!"

"It's close to the same recipe, but with different flavoring and pretty colors."

"Right. So let's get back to the identity of the victim. Why did Mrs. Beeseman and Mrs. Diehl have doubts about it?"

Hannah was stymied for a moment and then she realized that Mike was talking about Marge and Patsy. "It's just that they hadn't seen him for so many years," she tried to explain. "And both of them thought that his personality had changed since he left Lake Eden."

"It probably did. He was pretty young then, wasn't he?"

Hannah did some mental arithmetic and came up with a figure. "He was in his twenties, I think."

"Point taken. You're not the same person you were when you were twenty, are you?"

"I hope not!" Hannah said, without thinking. And then she was a bit embarrassed over the vehemence of her answer. She'd been horribly naïve at twenty, and she preferred to think that she was wiser and more sophisticated now.

"I bet you were cute!"

Hannah felt her heartbeat speed up as Mike flashed his knee-weakening grin. How could one man affect her autonomic nervous system so drastically? Then she remembered that he'd used the past tense. She was about to call him on it, when he spoke again.

"They had enough time to get a good look at him," Mike continued. "Did they think his physical characteristics matched their brother's?"

"Yes, but they pointed out that any guy about the right age and height with blondish hair might have fooled them. Marge told me that Gus didn't have any distinguishing physical characteristics or marks." Hannah stopped speaking, but she quickly convinced herself that telling Mike about the tattoo couldn't hurt. "But he did," she said.

Mike's eyes narrowed. "How do you know?"

"You don't need to know that. Let's just say that four different people told me about one special physical characteristic that Gus had."

"And that characteristic would be . . . ?"

"A tattoo. It was two crossed bats with a ball between them and it was on his left buttock."

"And you know this for a fact?"

"Not me!" Hannah glared at him. "The people who told me about it said that he got it in high school and it was still there unless he had it removed in the intervening years."

"Hold on," Mike said, pulling out his cell phone. "I'll call

Doc Knight and find out. Thanks for telling me, Hannah. This could be important."

While Mike was waiting to be put through to Doc Knight at the hospital, Hannah began to assemble her cookie dough. She mixed the softened butter with the sugars and beat them together until they were light and fluffy. Then she mixed in the baking soda and salt, and added the egg. Once that was incorporated, she mixed the sour cream with the red food coloring and added them to her mixing bowl. As she mixed them in, she half listened to Mike's conversation with Doc Knight while she debated whether or not she should tell him about how Jack Herman and Gus had fought on the night that Gus left Lake Eden.

"Okay, then. Thanks, Doc." Mike clicked off his phone and looked over at Hannah. "The victim has an identical tattoo to the one you described."

"No," Hannah said, nodding her head.

"What does that mean? You said no, but you're nodding yes."

"That means I came to a decision about something else, and I was acknowledging the information you gave me about the tattoo at the same time.

"Then the no you said was for the decision."

"Yes," Hannah said, shaking her head.

"Hold on. This time you said yes, but you shook your head no."

"That's right. Yes, I came to a decision. And no, I won't tell you what it's about."

Mike drained the last of his coffee and stood up. "Thanks for the cookies. And thanks for telling me about the tattoo. I'll let the family know we have positive I.D. I'd better go now. I've got a meeting with my team in twenty minutes."

"Take these with you." Hannah reached for the box of cookies she'd packed up for him to take back to the sheriff's station. "And share them with your team. There's nothing like chocolate to perk you right up."

PARTY COOKIES

DO NOT preheat the oven yet. This
dough must chill before baking.

2 cups melted butter *(4 sticks)*
2 cups powdered sugar *(not sifted)*
1 cup white sugar
2 eggs
2 teaspoons vanilla *(or any other flavoring you
    wish)*
1 teaspoon baking soda
1 teaspoon cream of tartar *(critical!)*
1 teaspoon salt
4 ¼ cups flour *(not sifted)*
Food coloring *(at least 3 different colors)*

¼ cup white sugar *(for later)*

Melt the butter. Add the sugars and mix. Let the mixture cool to room temperature and mix in the eggs, one at
a time. Then add the vanilla, baking soda, cream of tartar
and salt. Mix well. Add the flour in half-cup increments,
mixing after each addition.

Divide the cookie dough into fourths and place each
fourth on a piece of waxed paper. *(You'll work with one
fourth at a time.)* Place one fourth in a bowl and stir in
drops of food coloring until the dough is slightly darker
than the color you want. *(The cookies will be a shade
lighter after they're baked.)* Place the colored dough back
on the waxed paper and color the other three parts. *(You
can leave one part uncolored, if you like.)*

Let the dough firm up for a few moments. Then divide each different COLOR into four parts so you have sixteen lumps of dough in all. Place a sheet of plastic wrap on your counter and roll each lump into a dough rope with your hands *(just as if you were making bread sticks.)* The sixteen dough ropes should each be about 12 inches long.

To assemble, stack the dough ropes, two on the bottom, two on the top, near the edge of the plastic wrap. Squeeze them together a bit and push in the ends so they're even. Flip the edge of the plastic wrap over the top and roll them up together tightly in one multi-colored roll. Twist the ends of the plastic wrap, fold them over on top of the roll, and refrigerate the rolls as you make them. When you're all finished, you'll have four rolls of multi-colored cookie dough chilling in your refrigerator.

Let the dough chill for at least an **hour** *(overnight is fine, too.)* When you're ready to bake, pre-heat the oven to 325 degrees F., rack in the middle position.

Put ¼ cup white sugar *(granulated)* in a small bowl and have it ready next to your greased cookie sheets.

Take out one dough roll, unwrap it, and slice it into ½ inch thick rounds. *(Each dough roll should make about 24 cookies.)* Place each round into the bowl of sugar and flip it over so it coats both sides. Position the sugarcoated rounds on a greased baking sheet, 12 to a standard sheet. Return the unused dough to the refrigerator until you're ready to slice more cookies.

Bake the cookies at 325 degrees F. for 12 to 15 minutes, just until they begin to turn slightly golden around the edges. Cool them on the cookie sheet for a minute or two, and then transfer them to a wire rack to complete cooling.

These cookies freeze very well if you stack them in a roll, wrap them in foil, and place the foil rolls in a freezer bag. You can also freeze the multi-colored unbaked dough rolls by leaving them in the plastic wrap and placing them in a freezer bag.

Yield: Approximately 8 dozen pretty party cookies.

Chapter Fifteen

By the time the hands on the kitchen clock met and pointed straight up at the ceiling, Hannah had finished baking and frosting the Red Velvet Cookies. She was about to call Norman to see if he was free to taste one, when Luanne pushed though the swinging door between the kitchen and the coffee shop.

"Norman just called," she told Hannah. "He's got an emergency patient in the chair, and he can't make it in to taste those cookies you told him about."

"Okay. Thanks for telling me. How are you holding out on cookies?"

"Just fine. It's been only the regulars so far. As far as take-out goes, Mrs. Surma came in for two dozen Orange Snaps for the Brownies, Reverend Knudson picked up some Viking Cookies for his grandmother since she liked them so much after church, and Mr. Purvis came in for five dozen Oatmeal Raisin Crisps for his teachers."

"But school's not in session yet."

"That's what I said, and he told me it's teachers' prep week. They come in a week early to get things done that they don't have time to do when they've got classes to teach."

A mental picture of her second grade teacher flashed through Hannah's mind. Miss Gladke was dressed in a pair of white overalls with a white painter's cap pulled over her curls. And she was up on a ladder with a brush in her hand, painting the walls of her classroom.

Hannah took a step back from the ridiculous image. She knew that painting wasn't the type of work done during teachers' prep week. Miss Gladke would be making up lesson plans, choosing textbooks, and other academic tasks.

"You can leave for the reunion now," Luanne told her. "I can take care of everything here. I'll lock up when it's time and be in tomorrow morning at nine to help you open."

Hannah was grateful for the extra work Luanne was putting in, especially because Delores and Carrie were spending the week at the lake and she was sure Luanne would much rather spend the time with her four-year-old daughter.

"You probably won't have many customers this afternoon. Why don't you call your mother and Nettie, and have them bring Suzie down here for cookies? It's a hot day, and I've got some Pecan Crisps made into ice cream sandwiches in the freezer."

Luanne looked absolutely delighted at the suggestion. "Thanks, Hannah. I'll do that. Suzie just loves to come down here with her grandmas and see all the different kinds of cookies. She says she wants to be a cookie baker when she grows up."

"Great! She can take over for me when I retire . . . unless she changes her mind and decides to be a nuclear physicist or a brain surgeon, of course."

Less than five minutes later, Hannah was zipping down the alley in back of her shop in her cookie truck. She turned west on Third and then made a right onto Main Street. Luck was with her and there was a parking spot directly in front of the Rhodes Dental Clinic. Hannah wasted no time pulling into the spot and shutting off her engine. She grabbed the pink box of cookies she'd packed as a care package for Norman, got out of the truck, and headed straight for the front door that nestled under the green-and-white metal awning that protected dental patients from the sun and rain in the summer and the snow in the winter.

A buzzer sounded somewhere in the interior of the building as Hannah opened the front door and stepped in. The sliding frosted glass windows at the reception desk were closed, but that didn't surprise Hannah. Norman usually hired a student from the Jordan High senior class work-study program to man the desk during the school year, and he took care of things himself during summer vacation.

"Please make yourself comfortable in the waiting room. I'm with a patient, but I'll be with you in just a minute or two."

Hannah smiled as Norman called out to whoever had come in the door. He had no idea who it was, and she decided to surprise him. Since he was expecting a reply, she settled for a one-word response that was unlikely to give away her identity.

"Okay," she replied, keeping her voice deliberately low. Then she walked over to the magazine rack and chose a current issue to read while she was waiting. Norman ordered magazines specifically for his waiting room, and they were delivered directly to the clinic. His patients weren't stuck perusing three-year-old news stories, or movie magazines that featured celebrity weddings that had already ended in divorce.

As Hannah flipped through a gourmet food magazine, she heard voices coming from the examining room just inside the inner door. She didn't consciously intend to eavesdrop, but there were no other patients that she could engage in conversation. That meant the waiting room was perfectly silent, except for the soothing music that was playing at low volume. She could hear every word that was spoken in the examining room.

"I waszh eating an apple and it juszht pulled out."

"That happens sometimes. How old it is?"

"Doc Bennett put it in sheventeen yearszh ago."

"He did a fine job. Most bridges need to be replaced long before that, especially if they're not made of modern amalgams. Just let me clean it up for you and I'll reattach it. It'll only take a couple of minutes."

"Good! I've got shurgery at two, and I need to get back to the hoshpital."

Hannah drew in her breath sharply. She thought she'd recognized that voice! It was Doc Knight, the very man she needed to see!

The sliding glass doors opened and Norman peered out. He seemed surprised but pleased to see her. "Hi, Hannah. I didn't know it was you out here. This isn't a dental emergency, is it?"

"No, it's a cookie deficiency emergency." Hannah carried the pink box over to the window and presented it to Norman. "Is that Doc Knight I heard back there?"

"Iszh me!" Doc Knight answered her. "What kind of cookieszh did zhu bring?"

"Something new I baked today. They're called Red Velvet Cookies. Would you like to try one, Doc?"

"Oh, no you don't!" Norman confiscated the box. "Not until I reattach his bridge."

"Sorry, Doc," Hannah called out.

"Not half aszh shorry aszh I am."

Hannah turned back to Norman. "Is it okay if I go back to keep him company while you're cleaning up that bridge? I've got some questions I need to ask him."

"Not a good idea. Doc's my patient, and I have to protect his right to privacy while he's under my care."

"Okay, but I just wanted to talk to him."

"Sorry, it's not allowed. If I let you back there, I'd be violating our patient-dentist relationship."

"Oh, nonshenszh! She'szh going to catszh me here or at the hoshpital, anyway. Might aszh well get it over wiszh."

Norman shrugged. "You heard him. He's waiving his right to privacy. Hold on a second and I'll let you in."

Hannah smiled as she went through the doorway to the inner sanctum and into the examining room. She liked Doc Knight, and he'd always been good about answering her questions. "Hi, Doc," she said, taking the chair against the wall.

"Hi, Hannah," Doc said, giving her a grin that showed several missing teeth. "Iszh a good thing your name iszhn't Shuszhana or Shally. Sheila would be okay, though."

"Not with me. I like my name," Hannah said with a laugh. "I need to ask you some questions about Gus Klein and Mary Jo Kuehn."

"That'szh easzhy. I don't know anything exszhept that they were girlfriend and boyfriend."

"How about the accident? The night of the senior prom when Mary Jo died?"

"I waszhn't here. I waszh in Boszhton for a two-week medical convenszhon. The county coroner took care of that and he'szh been dead for twenty yearszh."

Hannah came close to groaning. Doc Knight would be no help on that subject. "How about the fight Jack Herman had with Gus Klein? That was the night Gus left town for good, and nobody saw him again until the family reunion."

"I waszh here for that. Fire away, Hannah. I'm your captive audienszh. There'szh no way I'm leaving here until I get my bridge back."

"Mother told me that Dad and Uncle Ed broke up the fight and brought Jack to your office."

"She'szh right. Tha'szh what happened. Jack waszh in pretty bad shape. They didn't want Emmy to szhee him until I got him all cleaned up and looking aszh normal aszh I could. Didn't work, though. She went into labor and delivered that night."

"And the baby was Lisa's brother Tim, right?"

"That'szh right. And Tim waszh just fine. Iszh like I told Jack . . . she waszh ready to deliver, anyway. He didn't do anything wrong. He waszh juszht defending hiszh . . ." Doc

Knight stopped and shook his head. "You didn't hear me szhay that."

"Szhay . . . I mean, *say* what?"

"Szhay anything about defending anybody."

"You just told me that Jack was fighting to defend someone." Hannah peered closely at Doc. "Was it Emmy?"

"You didn't hear me szhay that, either."

Hannah's mind flew, attempting to fit the pieces she'd learned together. There'd been some important verbal salvos at the dance. When Jack had mentioned Mary Jo Kuehn, Gus had retaliated by mentioning Emmy. Then Jack had taken offense at the fact that Gus had used a diminutive name for his wife, and replied with Emily's full name. After that, Gus had mentioned Jack's sister Heather, but Marge had brought up their teacher, Mr. Burnside, and steered the conversation to safer ground.

"Do you know if Gus dated Emmy before she married Jack?" she asked.

"Yeszh."

Hannah gave herself a mental kick for asking an ambiguous question. "Yes, you know? Or yes, he dated her?" she asked, hoping to clear up the confusion.

"Yeszh I know. And that'szh all I'm going to szhay."

There was a knock on the door and Norman came in. "Just let me reattach this, and then you can have one of Hannah's cookies. The only stipulation is that you chew on the other side." He turned to Hannah. "Do you use nuts in your Red Velvet Cookies?"

"No. They have chocolate chips, but they melt when they bake and they're soft. There's nothing at all chewy, if that's what you're asking."

"That's exactly what I'm asking." Norman set the tray he was carrying down on the round shelf that was attached to the dental chair, and turned to Hannah again. "Excuse us for a couple of minutes. This won't take long."

Hannah watched while Norman tilted the chair back, positioned something she assumed was the bridge in Doc Knight's mouth and held it in place. A minute or so later, he removed his gloved fingers and stepped back.

"Okay," he said to his patient. "You're as good as new. I'll go get those cookies and we'll all have one."

The moment Norman left the examining room, Hannah seized her opportunity and moved her chair closer to Doc Knight. "Did the fight have something to do with Emmy dating Gus in the past?" she asked.

"Of course it did."

Now that Norman had reattached his bridge, Doc answered normally. For a brief second or two, Hannah was thrown for a loop. She's gotten used to the lisp. "Was it a love triangle?" she asked him.

"Only in Gus's mind. Emmy loved Jack, and Jack loved her. It was a good marriage, Hannah. Gus was a troublemaker, and he didn't care who he hurt. To tell the truth, I was relieved when he left town. I felt sorry for his parents. It had to be hard not knowing what had happened to their son, especially since he left like a thief in the night, with no explanation and no good-byes. I still don't know which would have been more heartbreaking."

"Which?"

"The way he left and not knowing why. Or the grief he was bound to cause them if he'd stayed."

Hannah took a moment to digest Doc's statement. It was damning, but probably accurate. Doc Knight was a straight shooter, and he didn't equivocate. But there were more questions to ask, and Norman would be back any moment.

"You said Gus didn't care who he hurt. Does that mean there were people who hated him?"

Doc thought that over for a second. "I'm sure there were."

"And some of them were right here in Lake Eden?"

"Oh, yes. I can think of several. You've got to understand that the Gus we knew was concerned only about himself. He used people to get what he wanted. And then, when he didn't need them anymore, he discarded them like old candy wrappers. It was all about Gus, if you know what I mean. He had an ego that wouldn't quit."

"I know the type," Hannah said, remembering the assistant professor she'd dated in college. "Tell me more."

"Gus was a funny bird, at least that's what the psychiatric head at the hospital where I did my internship would have called him. I watched Gus grow up. He was in grade school when I was in high school, and it was all in one building. Gus was a manipulator from early on and everybody, including his family, gave him whatever he wanted."

"Marge and Patsy said he was spoiled."

"That may be too mild a way to describe it. Spoiled kids usually know better. Most of them know right from wrong, and they're aware that other children their age aren't treated the way they are."

"And you don't think Gus was aware of that?"

Doc Knight shook his head. "I'm almost sure he wasn't. Gus grew up with everything he ever wanted. That caused him to be amoral."

"Amoral?" Of course Hannah knew what the word meant, but she'd never actually heard it applied to someone she knew.

"Yes, amoral. I really don't think the question of right or wrong ever occurred to him. If Gus wanted something, he got it. And if something bothered him, he got rid of it. That went for material things, and it also went for people. He lived for the moment, and it was all about Gus. Nothing else mattered. I have no idea how many angry people he left in his wake. And even worse . . . I don't think Gus did, either."

"So you weren't surprised when he turned up dead at the family reunion?"

"Not really." Doc Knight gave a little shrug. "The big surprise is that it took two days for somebody to do it!"

Chapter Sixteen

"**W**hoa!" Hannah held up her hands in surrender as Michelle came barreling through the screen door at their mother's cottage. "Where's the fire?"

"Andrea's talking to Bertie Straub on the road, and I wanted to get here before she did."

"Why?" Hannah picked up the pepper grinder and prepared to grind pepper over the casserole she was preparing.

"Because I've got something I have to tell you. I wanted to talk to you yesterday, but every time I tried, you were with someone. And I don't want anyone else to hear."

"Not even Andrea?"

"*Especially* not Andrea!"

Hannah put down the pepper grinder with a thump. "Why?"

"Because she can be kind of . . . prudish."

"And I'm not?"

"Maybe a little, but nothing like Andrea! I think it's because she's married."

Hannah thought about that for a moment. "You'd think a married woman would be more sophisticated and worldly than a single woman. What you said seems counterintuitive."

"Maybe it seems that way, but it's not. Married women don't date anymore, and that means they don't do any wild and crazy things like single women do."

"I see." Hannah picked up the pepper grinder again and gave it a series of twists. "And since I'm single, you assume that I do wild and crazy things?"

"Well . . . no. Maybe you don't. But you *could,* if you wanted to."

"Hmm." Hannah made the most noncommittal comment of all. "So what did you want to tell me? Or did you change your mind?"

Michelle walked over to the counter where Hannah was working, and pulled up a stool. "It's about Sunday night and the murder. I think I saw the killer."

"Really?!" Hannah was glad she hadn't opened the bottle of cumin. If she'd been in the process of measuring it, the whole thing might have landed in her hotdish.

"Well . . . maybe. It was really quiet and there wasn't anyone else out. It just stands to reason that the person I saw go across the road and around to the front of the pavilion is the murderer."

Hannah drew in her breath sharply. "Did this person see you?"

"No. He didn't even know I was there. Or maybe it was a she, a woman wearing pants and a jacket. I was a long ways away, and I couldn't really tell."

Hannah glanced out the window over the sink. If Michelle had been in the kitchen of the cottage at two in the morning, she would have had a perfect view of the road and the entrance to the pavilion. "You were standing at the sink at two in the morning?"

"Not exactly."

"What does that mean?"

"It means that's not precisely correct."

"I *know* that's what it means!" Hannah gave a little sigh. That made twice today that she'd fallen into a semantic trap. "Why don't you just tell me where you were?" she suggested.

"Down on the dock with Lonnie. We were swimming and we climbed up on the dock to take a rest."

At two in the morning?! Hannah's mind shouted, but she didn't voice the sentiment. And she didn't ask about swimming attire, either, since she was supposed to be the non-prude.

"And you saw this person at two o'clock?" she asked instead of the thousand and one questions she really wanted to ask.

"I think it was about two. I met Lonnie on the dock at one-thirty. Mother and Carrie were asleep by then. And by the time we climbed back up on the dock and got our towels, it was probably close to two."

"But you don't know for sure, because you weren't wearing a watch."

"That's right. I don't have a waterproof watch. As a matter of fact, I wasn't wearing . . ."

"You said you saw this person walk across the road. Did he get out of a car?"

"There was no car. I would have heard it drive up. It was really quiet except for the crickets and the frogs and the mosquitoes. And the lapping of the waves against the dock, and the loons across the lake."

"Describe the person for me," Hannah interrupted her sister before she could hear more than she wanted to hear. "You said you couldn't be sure whether it was a man or a woman?"

"That's right. I just saw him or her through the trees. And this person went inside and didn't come out while we were sitting on the dock."

"And that was how long?"

"I was in bed by two-thirty. I know because I looked at the clock. Do you think I should tell Mike what I saw?"

Hannah shrugged. "You probably don't need to do that. I'm sure Lonnie has already told him."

"No, he hasn't. Lonnie didn't see the person. He was sitting with his back to the road. I was right next to him, facing the other way. I really don't want to tell Mike unless you think I absolutely have to. Mother's bound to hear about it, and I shouldn't have been out that late."

"Let me get this straight," Hannah said, reaching into her purse for her steno notebook and grabbing a pen. She really wanted to cut her baby sister a break, but this was a murder investigation. "Tell me *exactly* what you saw and when you saw it."

"I saw a person walk across the road, go around the side of the pavilion, and enter through the front door."

"You know, for sure, that this person went inside?"

Michelle nodded. "Light spilled out on the concrete when the door opened. A second later, the light disappeared, so the door must have shut again."

"Makes sense. And you were so far away you couldn't tell the identity of this person, or even if that person was a man or a woman?"

"That's right."

"Giving your best estimate, you think it was about two in the morning when the person went inside the pavilion?"

"I think so."

"Would you have seen the person if he or she had come back out while you were still sitting on the dock?"

"Yes. The light would have spilled out again when the door opened, and I would have noticed it."

"So you believe that the person was inside the pavilion for the entire period from two to two-thirty? And two-thirty is the time you left the dock and went back into the cottage?"

"A little before two-thirty. I already told you, I looked at the clock when I climbed in bed, and it was two-thirty. And I know the lights were still on inside the pavilion."

"How do you know that?" Hannah asked, remembering that when she'd checked the next day, the lights had been off.

"Because I saw light leaking out one of the shutters when I passed by the kitchen window on my way to the bedroom."

"Okay," Hannah said, flipping her notebook shut. "I've got it all down."

"So what do you think? Do I have to tell Mike?"

"No. All you saw was a shadowy figure entering the pavilion and not coming out again. That's not going to help in Mike's investigation. He already knows somebody went inside to kill Gus, because Gus didn't stab himself in the chest."

Michelle looked very relieved. "Thanks, Hannah! I'm really glad Mother won't know I was out so late. I'm too old to punish or anything like that, but she gives me that look."

"What look?"

"You know the one. It's her hurt look. And then she says, *Oh, Michelle! I'm so disappointed in you!* And then I know I've let her down, and it just about kills me."

"That's why she does it," Hannah said, remembering the very same phrase with her name in the culprit spot.

The screen door opened, and Andrea hurried in, carrying a Jell-O mold. She headed straight for the refrigerator, opened the door, and found a place for it inside. "I hope my Lemon Fluff Jell-O Mold didn't get hot and melt!"

"What's in it?" Hannah asked her.

"Lemon Jell-O, lemon pie filling, crushed pineapple, and Cool Whip."

"Cool Whip and not real sweetened whipped cream?"

"That's right."

"Then it should be fine. Cool Whip doesn't break down as fast as whipped cream. And even if your mold got a little runny, it'll firm up again before dinner. There's plenty of time."

"Oh, good. And you'll help me unmold it? I'm not very good at that."

"Of course I will," Hannah promised her. "Michelle said you were out on the road talking to Bertie Straub?"

"That's right. I was making an appointment for this weekend. She's going to give me a full weave, and this time it's going to be in four colors. I've never done more than three, but I want a reddish blond in the mix. And I'm having a layer cut to give my hair more body."

"A four-color weave's going to take all morning," Michelle commented.

"You don't know the half of it! I'm also booked for a manicure, a pedicure, and a full makeover. And when I'm all through with that, I'm heading down to Claire's to try on some of her sexy summer sundresses. The next time you see me, I'll be a new me."

"But I like the old you," Michelle said.

"So do I," Hannah added. "I think you look just fine the way you are. I really don't know why you want to be a new you, when . . ." her voice trailed off as the obvious reason occurred to her. Mike had mentioned it on the phone this morning. "Ronni Ward?" she guessed.

"Of course not! I just want to look good, that's all. When you've been married for as long as Bill and I have, you have to work to rekindle the romance every now and then, and . . ." Andrea stopped speaking and gave a little sigh. "You're right. It's Ronni Ward. Bill told me she was back in town when he got home last night. How did *you* find out about it?"

"Mike. He called me this morning to give me the number for the Animal Channel for Moishe, and he mentioned it."

"Did he also mention that Ronni rented the apartment across the hall from him?" Andrea asked.

"He did."

"Are you jealous?" Michelle raised the question.

"Mike and I don't have that kind of commitment. It's true that I date him, but I go out with Norman, too. That means I don't have any *right* to be jealous."

Andrea gave a nod of concurrence. "That's a perfectly reasonable point, but it's not what Michelle asked. Are you jealous?"

"What do *you* think?" Hannah faced them squarely.

"You're jealous." Andrea spoke for both of them. "You just don't know what to do about it, that's all."

LEMON FLUFF JELL-O

3 small *(3-ounces apiece)* packages of Lemon Jell-O
2 cups water
1 large can *(20-ounces)* crushed pineapple
2 cups cold water ***
1 small *(2-cup)* container Cool-Whip *(or any other whipped, non-dairy dessert topping)*
1 can *(enough to make an 8-inch pie)* lemon pie filling****

*** *This is approximate because it all depends on your can of crushed pineapple. You're going to drain the crushed pineapple and save the liquid. Then you'll add the cold water to the juice until it makes a total of 2 cups.*

**** *If you can't find lemon pie filling in a can (Andrea couldn't—Florence didn't have it at the Red Owl) you can use a 3.4 ounce package of lemon pudding and pie filling. Just follow the directions for pie filling and add it to your Jell-O mixture at the proper time.*

Drain the can of crushed pineapple. Save the liquid to use later.

Boil two cups of water in a small saucepan. Take it off the burner.

Empty the three packages of Lemon Jell-O powder into the recently boiled water. Stir until the Jell-O is dissolved. This step should take about 2 minutes. *(There's nothing*

worse than Jell-O powder that doesn't dissolve. It makes a layer of sweet lemon rubber at the bottom of your Jell-O mold and the mixture on top is runny. To tell if Jell-O powder is dissolved, reach in with your impeccably clean fingers and rub a bit of liquid between your thumb and your finger. If it's not gritty, it's dissolved.)

When the Jell-O powder is dissolved, combine the pineapple juice with cold water to make 2 cups of liquid. Add this to your saucepan and stir it in.

Refrigerate your saucepan until the Jell-O is partially set. *(This should take approximately 45 minutes.)*

Put the Jell-O mixture into a bowl and whip it with a whisk or an electric mixer.

Fold in the Cool-Whip.

Fold in the lemon pie filling. *(This is the time to make the instant pudding and pie filling and fold it into your Jell-O if you couldn't find canned pie filling.)*

Fold in the drained, crushed pineapple and blend thoroughly.

Spray a 2-quart Jell-O mold, or a standard-sized Bundt pan with Pam or another nonstick spray. You'll also need a second, much smaller bowl or mold to hold the Jell-O that won't quite fit in the first mold.

Transfer the Jell-O mixture to your molds and chill it in the refrigerator for at least 12 hours before serving.

Chapter Seventeen

The three sisters worked in silence, helping Hannah assemble the casseroles she was making for tonight's dinner. Andrea opened cans, Michelle chopped onions, and Hannah fried hamburger, enough for four batches of Wanmansita Casserole.

"To tell you the truth, Hannah, I really don't know what to do about Ronni Ward, either." Andrea broke the heavy silence that had fallen over them. "It's just that I thought a complete makeover might help. I shouldn't have said that about you being jealous."

"That's true. You were dead wrong, you know. The sinking feeling in my stomach and the overwhelming urge to wrap my hands around Ronni Ward's perfectly shaped throat and squeeze couldn't possibly be caused by jealousy."

Both Andrea and Michelle burst into laughter, and Hannah joined in. It was a good moment sandwiched in between all the bad things that had happened lately, and all three wanted to savor it for as long as they could.

When they'd quieted down again, Andrea turned to Hannah. "How about a makeover for you, too? I can run and find Bertie and make an appointment, my treat."

"No, thanks. I don't think it would help." Hannah carried the first casserole to the preheated oven and slipped it inside.

"Okay then. How about going out to Heavenly Bodies at the mall with me?"

"What's Heavenly Bodies?" Michelle asked.

"It's a new fitness club. Their motto is, *We'll make you look like a star*. That's because of the name. Do you get it?"

Michelle groaned and gave Hannah one of those *I-don't-believe-she-said-that* looks.

"We get it," Hannah answered Andrea. "You know how I feel about fitness clubs. They'd have to open at three A.M. for me to go there before work. And after work, I'm too tired to go anywhere that requires any effort. It would be a waste of money for me to join."

"But this one's different. They give you a key to the outside door and you can come in anytime, day or night, twenty-four seven."

"They have around-the-clock staff?" Michelle looked interested.

"No, but they've got an agreement with the guards at the mall to come in to check every hour."

"That doesn't sound very safe to me," Hannah said. "I wouldn't want to go there by myself at three in the morning, knowing that dozens of other people had keys and any one of them could unlock the door and walk in on me."

"I wouldn't feel safe, either," Michelle added her opinion. "It would be creepy to go to a gym alone at night."

Andrea shrugged. "Go during the day, then. You could always go on your lunch hour. Lisa would be happy to handle the coffee shop by herself for an hour or so, especially if she thought it was helping you."

"That's another point. I don't think it *would* be helping me." Hannah picked up another casserole and slid it into the oven. "I've never been able to stick with an exercise program, and there's no reason to think it would be different this time. I start out just fine, but after a week or so, I start making excuses for not exercising. And then, before I realize what I'm doing, it's been over a month since I've jogged, or used the treadmill, or whatever I planned to do. Besides . . ." Hannah paused to carry the remaining casseroles to the oven, and when she came back, she plunked down on the stool at the counter and sighed. "Look, Andrea . . . it doesn't really matter how cute the club's name is or the promises they make. Let's face reality here. We all know I'm never going to look like a star."

"Well, you *are* a star as far as I'm concerned!" Andrea looked very serious.

"With me, too," Michelle chimed in.

"Thanks," Hannah said. It was nice to get a vote of confidence from her sisters.

"Let's not talk about makeovers, or fitness clubs, or Ronni Ward anymore, then. It's just too depressing." Andrea reached into the briefcase she was carrying and pulled out an envelope. "Let's talk about murder instead."

There was perfect silence for a nanosecond, and then both Hannah and Michelle burst into a volley of laughter. Andrea looked slightly puzzled for a moment, and then she began to smile. "I didn't realize I made a joke," she said, handing the envelope to Hannah. "I brought these for you."

"What are they?"

"Crime scene photos. Bill brought them home with him last night, and I scanned them into the computer after he went to bed. I printed them out this morning as soon as he left for work."

"Thanks, Andrea. These will help me a lot." Hannah didn't mention that Mike had offered to give her a set of the crime scene photos. "Did you look at them?"

"No. You know I don't like gory things. I figured I'd let you look first, and you could show me the ones that aren't too awful."

Michelle began to frown. "Wait a second. How did you scan the photos and print them out without looking at them?"

"It was easy. They go face down on the scanner, so that was no problem. And then, when I brought them up on the screen to print them out this morning, I just peeked through my fingers, clicked on them, and sent them to the printer."

"But they came out face-up, didn't they?" Hannah questioned her. And then, when both of her sisters turned to look at her in surprise, she asked, "Why are you looking at me like that?"

"You've been using your computer!" Andrea exclaimed.

"Of course I've been using my computer. Norman's been giving me lessons. *Mother's* using a computer, for crying out loud! I don't want to be the only holdout in the family."

"It's a matter of pride," Michelle explained to Andrea.

"No, it's actually a matter of necessity," Hannah countered. "I got tired of asking Norman to look up things on the Internet for me."

Andrea gave a smile of approval. "Well, good for you," she said. "And speaking of good, those casseroles you put in the oven are starting to smell great. What are they called again?"

"Wanmansita Casseroles. It's Gary Hayes's recipe. You remember Gary and Sally, don't you? They used to live right across the street from Mother."

"Sally with the apron collection!" Michelle identified her. "You used to take me over there, and she'd let me look at her aprons while you talked about recipes and stuff."

"That's right."

"Wait a second." Andrea began to frown. "That doesn't make sense."

"Sure it does. I used to get home from school early because I had study hall last period. And I'd take Michelle over to Sally's with me."

"Not that. I remember that you went over there. It's just that Sally and Gary lived right here in Lake Eden. And if they lived here, why does Gary call it a casserole?"

For a moment Hannah was confused, but then she realized

what her sister was asking. "You mean, the word *casserole,* instead of the word *hotdish?*"

"Yes. Everybody in Lake Eden says *hotdish.* What's the difference, anyway?"

"I'm not positive, but I don't think there's any difference between a casserole and a hotdish. It's probably another example of regional dialogue," Hannah did her best to explain.

"You mean like *pop* and *soda?*" Michelle asked.

"Exactly right. Sally said it was an old recipe from Gary's family, and I think they came from Oklahoma. They must call a hotdish a casserole there. Or it got passed on to another relative who changed the word *hotdish* to *casserole.*"

Andrea gave a big smile. "That explains the rest of the name, then. There are a lot of American Indians in Oklahoma, and *Wanmansita* is probably an American Indian word. I should ask Jon Walker."

Hannah shook her head. "Jon's Chippewa, and I don't believe they got as far west as Oklahoma."

"Well, what American Indian tribe would it be?"

"It depends on when the recipe was named," Michelle told her. "And there are lots of Indian tribes in Oklahoma. They've got the Delaware, Arapaho, Miami, Iowa, Shawnee, Caw, Creek, Chickasaw, Cheyenne, Cherokee, Witchita, Patawatomi, Peoria, and Osage, plus a couple of others I can't remember."

Andrea looked impressed. "How do you know all that?"

"I took a course in Indian Studies last fall, and it was taught by a visiting professor from O.S.U. The names were so intriguing, I remember them. And besides, there's a mnemonic. It's *Donna Asked Mom In Secret, Can Wally Play Outside?* The first letter of each word stands for the first letter of an Indian tribe."

"But you named more *C*'s than that!"

Michelle laughed. "You're right. You have to remember that there are four *C*'s and two *P*'s. It's not as easy as the word *HOMES* for the Great Lakes."

"Or *Roy G. Biv* for the colors of the spectrum." Hannah added.

"Or *Mother Very Eagerly Made Jelly Sandwiches Under No Protest.*"

"The planets," Michelle said. "I never could remember them without that."

"But now you'll have to, since *Protest* is gone," Hannah reminded her.

"Pluto." Michelle gave a little sigh. "I forgot all about Pluto."

"*What* about Pluto?" Andrea asked.

"It's not a full planet anymore. It's been downgraded to a dwarf."

"Oh, no!" Andrea looked horrified.

"What's the matter?" Hannah asked her. "You look as if you just lost your best friend."

"It's Tracey. I just taught her the planets that way! And now she's going to get them wrong when she goes in to be tested for her Girl Scout badge."

"She's smart enough to remember to leave Pluto out," Hannah comforted her sister. "Just remind her before she goes to the meeting, or wherever they go to be tested."

"It's the school. The scouts are using the auditorium since school hasn't started yet. And Tracey's the youngest one going for a badge, and she really wants to get it right."

"She will," Michelle said with a smile. "But I thought Tracey was a Brownie Scout, not a Girl Scout."

"She is, but Bonnie Surma got a special exception for Tracey to study for her badges early. And it's a really big deal this year because one of the ladies from national is coming to award the badges."

"Tracey will be fine. Don't worry," Hannah reassured her sister again, and then she picked up the envelope and removed a file that was inside. "Let's go over the crime scene photos together."

"Don't look," Andrea instructed Michelle.

"What do you mean, *don't look?* It's not like I'm a child, you know. You don't have to protect me from the ugly side of life."

"You're too young to know anything about the ugly side of life. The ugliest thing you ever saw was the stuffed boar's head that hung over Grandpa and Grandma Swensen's couch!"

"I thought that boar's head was cute! All that bristly hair sticking up. He looked like a character in a cartoon. But getting back to the ugly side, I bet I've seen more ugly things than . . ."

"That's enough, girls!" Hannah interrupted, stepping in with her best big-sister-in-charge voice. "If you don't stop squabbling, I won't let you taste the new cookies I brought."

There was complete silence for a moment, a phenomenon that deeply gratified Hannah. She hadn't lost her big sister touch.

"New cookies?" Michelle was the first to speak.

"Yes. I made them for Jack Herman's birthday party tonight. Lisa's mom used to make a similar cookie years ago."

"Do they have chocolate?" Andrea wanted to know. "I'm going to need chocolate if I'm going to look at anything the least bit gory."

"They've got plenty of chocolate. There's chocolate in the cookie dough and more chocolate chips inside. And there's cream cheese frosting, too."

Michelle gave a little whimper of anticipation. "Cream cheese frosting is my very favorite. Sometimes I make up a batch and spread it on soda crackers."

"Is that *good?*" Andrea asked her.

"Yes, but make sure you buy salted soda crackers. Then you lay them out with the salt side down and frost the other side. You can spread it between two graham crackers, too. Or two chocolate cookie wafers. That tastes almost like Oreos."

With peace restored and cookie hunger kindled, Hannah wasted no time opening her box of Red Velvet Cookies and giving each of her sisters a sample. While they were tasting her newest creation, she paged through the crime scene photos. Since nothing was really gory, she left them all in the pile.

When she was finished censoring the stack of photos, Hannah almost called out, *You can look now,* the phrase her father had used on Christmas morning when they sat by the Christmas tree, eyes tightly shut, until he brought in the presents that had been too large to wrap. But the photos she held in her hand weren't presents. They were grim reminders of what could happen when the sanctity of human life was violated.

"I'm ready with the photos," she said instead.

"These are great cookies, Hannah!" Andrea complimented her, wiping her fingers on a napkin. She picked up the stack of photos, examined the one on top, and then she handed it to Michelle.

"Yuck!" Michelle commented.

"My cookies are *yuck?*" Hannah, who hadn't noticed the photo pass from hand to hand, was clearly astounded by Michelle's remark.

"Not your cookies. They're absolutely fantastic, and they remind me of red velvet cake. I meant this photograph. He was stabbed, right?"

Hannah nodded. "Keep your eye out for something unusual that I might have missed, or anything that doesn't fit with the way you remember the pavilion from the night of the dance."

"But you were right there," Michelle pointed out. "You found him. You saw everything with your own two eyes. How could you have missed something?"

"Hannah was probably in shock," Andrea reminded her. "Finding a dead body isn't fun."

"Okay. You're right," Michelle said, taking the next photo from Andrea and examining it.

Nobody said anything for at least five minutes, an unusual occurrence when the three Swensen sisters got together. But Hannah was busy watching her younger sisters, and Michelle and Andrea were absorbed in examining the photos. Finally the last one was placed facedown on the counter.

Andrea gave a big sigh. "I didn't see anything unusual," she said. "And I'm pretty sure that everything looked just the way it did when I left the dance."

Michelle gave a little nod. "I agree. I'm sorry we didn't learn anything new, Hannah."

"So am I, but I did learn *one* new thing."

"You did?" Andrea looked surprised.

"What is it?" Michelle asked.

"Everything was exactly as I remember it. And that means one of two things. Either being in shock doesn't affect my memory, or I'm getting much too used to finding murder victims!"

Chapter Eighteen

Hannah picked up the photos and returned them to the envelope. There was another file in the envelope that she hadn't noticed before. "What's this?" she asked Andrea. "A duplicate set?"

"No. Those are photos they took of the cottage where Gus was staying right before they searched it. It's standard operating procedure. I heard Bill talk about it once."

"It's a good procedure!" Hannah gave a little grin. "I've seen other places they've searched, and they always looked like the aftermath of a tornado."

"Not this time," Michelle spoke up.

"Why not?"

"Because they confiscated almost everything after they searched, and took it to the sheriff's station. Lonnie said they were going to go through it with a fine-tooth comb to see if there were any clues."

"There wasn't much more than a suitcase full of clothes and some personal items in the bathroom," Hannah said, thinking back in time to early Monday afternoon when she'd walked through the cottage searching for Gus.

"How about the closet? Did you look in there?" Michelle asked.

"The doors were open," Hannah did her best to bring back the mental picture. "I looked at the bed first. The suitcase was on it, and it was open. And then I turned to look at the closet. There was one of those little green frogs. You've both seen the type that lives at the lake. He hopped out of the closet and . . . it was empty inside. I remember now. There were no clothes on the hangers."

"That's because they were all in the suitcase," Michelle said. "Gus probably hadn't gotten around to unpacking yet."

"But why hadn't he? He'd already changed clothes twice." Hannah turned to Andrea. "That's right, isn't it?"

"Twice at the minimum," Andrea said, giving a definitive nod. "I saw him when he drove up at the church. He was wearing an eggshell white linen suit with an Egyptian cotton shirt . . ."

"You could tell his shirt's country of origin by just looking?" Hannah interrupted her sister's recital.

"Not exactly, but Egyptian cotton is distinctive, and it's always been the hot material. It was a wonderful shade of slate blue. You know the color. It's blue, but it's got a lot of gray in it, too. Very subdued, and it looks great with blond or gray hair. The shirt was open at the neck, and he had on a gold neck chain and . . ."

"Then he must have changed clothes, because that's not what he was wearing at the dance," Michelle interrupted her.

"You're right. The suit he wore at the dance was completely different. And he was wearing a different shirt. Not only that, he wasn't wearing a tie when I saw him at the church, and he wore a designer tie at the dance. It's right there in the crime scene photos."

Hannah was grateful that her sisters had noticed what Gus had been wearing when they saw him in the car at the church. She'd only caught a glimpse of him, and she would have been hard-pressed to describe any item of clothing he'd worn.

"There's one thing that really puzzles me." Andrea turned to Hannah. "It's the suit Gus was wearing the first time we saw him."

"What about it?"

"It was linen. I said that before. And linen wrinkles. He wore it to the brunch. I know that, because Mother mentioned it to me. But he had to have taken it off before he showered and changed for the dance. That was an expensive suit. I'd guess it was over five hundred dollars, maybe a lot more. He was staying at a cottage with a nice big closet. Why didn't he hang it up?"

"Are we sure he didn't?" Michelle asked.

"I'm almost positive he didn't." Hannah paged through the photos of the cottage, found the one of the bedroom, and handed it to Michelle. "Here's a picture that shows the closet. Check it out for yourself. It's as bare as Mother Hubbard's cupboard."

"Maybe he spilled something on it at the brunch and it needed to be dry cleaned?" Michelle suggested a possible explanation.

"Maybe, but there aren't any dry cleaners open on Sunday," Andrea pointed out. "And by the time they opened on Monday morning, he was already dead."

"So what would you do with an expensive suit you wanted dry cleaned?" Hannah asked them.

"Toss it on the floor of the closet so your wife will take it to the cleaners," Andrea said. "That's what Bill always does. I try to get him to stuff it in a laundry bag, but he forgets."

"Since there was nothing on the floor of the closet, maybe he just tossed it back in his suitcase," Michelle suggested.

"If he did, it would be right on top." Andrea paged through the photos until she came to the one of the suitcase. "It's not here, so he didn't. And since he was such a nice dresser, he probably wouldn't have thrown it in on top of his clean clothes anyway."

Something niggled at the back of Hannah's mind, and she shut her eyes to concentrate. A second or two later, she had it. "I just remembered something. When I went to the cottage to look for him, his car was parked in the driveway. And I'm almost sure there was a jacket hanging up on the hook in the backseat."

"Was it the jacket to his linen suit?" Andrea asked her.

"I don't know. I really didn't pay much attention. Is the Jaguar still parked in front of the cottage?"

Michelle shook her head. "Mike sealed it up and had it towed to the impound lot. It's going to stay there until they find out if Gus had a will, or any other family members back in Atlantic City."

"I wonder if the jacket's still in it," Hannah said. "I'd like to find out if it's the one to the missing linen suit."

"But why would Gus take it off inside the cottage and then carry it out and hang it in his car?" Andrea asked.

"Maybe he planned to take it to the cleaners, but he was killed first?" Michelle suggested.

Andrea shook her head. "Then he would have just tossed it in the backseat, or the trunk. He wouldn't have bothered to hang it up."

"Wait!" Hannah began to smile. "I know why he hung it in the car!"

"Why?" both sisters asked her, almost in unison.

"Because that's how you keep linen from getting wrinkled. Mother mentioned that this morning. She always hangs up her linen jacket when she drives the car."

"I get it," Michelle said, looking excited. "Gus didn't carry the jacket back out to his car to hang it up. He slipped it off when he left the brunch, and hung it up for the drive back to the lake."

"And forgot to take it with him when he went inside the cottage." Andrea finished the scenario.

"But where are the pants?" Michelle reminded her. "We still haven't found them." Then she turned to Hannah. "Do you think the missing pants are a clue?"

Hannah shrugged. "Search me. But it *is* interesting, and it might mean something. I'm just not sure what."

"Nobody's using the cottage, so you can go back and go

through it again," Andrea told her. "You might find something that the crime team missed."

Hannah gave her a grin. It wasn't the first time she'd found something the crime team hadn't thought was important, but that later turned out to be an important clue. "You say it's vacant?"

"Yes. Lisa thought maybe somebody else would move in, but none of the relatives want to use it."

Hannah was puzzled. "Why not? It's a nice cottage. And it's not a crime scene or anything like that. Why doesn't anybody want to use it?"

"Because Gus stayed there," Andrea explained.

"But he was only there for an hour or so. He didn't even have time to unpack!"

"That's true, but I guess they think it's bad luck." Michelle did her best to explain. "A lot of people are really superstitious."

"Maybe so," Hannah said, turning back to her cooking duties. She was glad that no one else was using the cottage. She intended to go back there at the very first opportunity, but her primary purpose wasn't to search for clues Mike's crime team might have missed. It had more to do with the frog. She hoped he'd hidden out somewhere when the crime team had searched the cottage, or hopped out the door to find a new place to inhabit. Maybe it was silly of her to be concerned, but she'd try to get over there later this evening to check.

WANMANSITA CASSEROLE

Preheat the oven to 325 degrees F.,
rack in the middle position.

2 pounds lean hamburger***
2 medium onions, sliced
1 cup diced celery *(that's about 3 stalks)*
1 green bell pepper, seeded and diced
1 large package of crinkle noodles *(I used egg noodles that were twisted in the middle.)*
2 cans *(14.5 ounces each)* of diced tomatoes with juice
1 can *(5 ounces)* sliced water chestnuts**** *(Sally uses chopped)*
1 can *(4 ounces)* mushroom pieces
2 teaspoons cumin
2 teaspoons chili powder
2 teaspoons salt
1 teaspoon pepper *(freshly ground is best, of course)*
2 cups grated cheddar cheese

*** *If you use regular hamburger instead of lean, you'd better buy 2 ½ or 3 pounds, because there's a lot of fat that'll cook off. If you buy extra lean hamburger it probably won't have enough fat and you'll have to add some.*

**** *Don't worry about the ounces on the water chestnuts—anything from 4 ounces to 8 ounces will do.*

Start by spraying a 9-inch by 13-inch cake pan, or a half-size disposable steam table pan with Pam or another

nonstick cooking spray. If you choose to use a disposable pan, set it on a cookie sheet to support the bottom and make it easier to move it from the counter to the oven, and then out again when it's finished.

Pour 6 quarts of water into a big pot and put it on the stove to boil. You'll use this to cook the noodles. *(If you start heating the water now, it should be boiling by the time you're ready to cook the noodles. If it boils too early and you're not ready, just turn down the heat a little. If it's not ready when you are, crank up the heat and wait for the boil.)*

Crumble the hamburger and brown it over medium heat in a large frying pan, stirring it around with a metal spatula and breaking it up into pieces as it fries. This should take about 15 or 20 minutes.

When the hamburger is nice and brown, put a bowl under a colander so that you can save about ⅓ cup of fat to use with the onions. Dump the hamburger into the colander to drain it.

Put the drained hamburger into the prepared baking pan.

Pour the ⅓ cup of hamburger grease back into the frying pan.

Peel the onions and slice them into ⅛ inch thick slices. *(When you do this they may fall apart in rings and that's perfectly okay.)*

Place the onion slices in the frying pan, but don't turn on the heat quite yet.

Dice the celery. Add it to the onion slices in the frying pan.

Cut open the green bell pepper and take out the seeds, the stem, and the tough white membranes. Chop the remaining pepper into bite-sized pieces. Once that's done, add them to the onions and celery in your frying pan.

Cook the aromatic vegetables *(that's what they call them on the Food Channel)* over medium heat until they're tender when pierced with a fork.

Drain them in the same colander you used for the hamburger, and then mix them up with the hamburger in your baking pan.

Add some salt to your boiling water on the stove. Then dump in the noodles, stir them around, let the water come back to a boil, and then turn down the heat a bit so the pot doesn't boil over. Set your timer for whatever it says on the noodle package directions and cook the noodles, stirring every minute or so to make sure they don't stick together.

Drain the cooked noodles in the same colander you've been using all along, add them to your baking pan, and mix them up with everything else.

Add the diced tomatoes, juice and all, to your baking pan. Wait to stir. You don't want to mush your noodles by stirring too much.

Open and drain the cans of water chestnuts and mushroom pieces in the colander that's still sitting in the sink.

Dump the water chestnuts and mushrooms on top of the tomatoes in your baking pan.

Sprinkle the cumin over the top of your casserole.

Sprinkle the chili powder on top of the cumin. *(Gary says to tell you that if your chili powder has been sitting around for as long as theirs has, it's a good idea to buy fresh.)*

Sprinkle on the salt and grind the pepper on top of that.

Now is the time to mix it all up. This might not be easy if the baking pan's too full to stir with a spoon. If that's happened, just wash your hands thoroughly and dive in with your fingers to mix everything up. When you're through, pat the casserole so it's nice and even on top, and call it a day.

Wash your hands again, and then cover the baking pan with a single thickness of foil.

Bake at 325 degrees F. for 60 minutes, or until you peek under the foil and see that it's hot and bubbling.

Remove the pan from the oven. Remove the foil slowly and carefully to avoid burning yourself with the steam that may roll out. Set the foil on the counter to use again in a few minutes.

Sprinkle the 2 cups of shredded cheddar cheese over the top and return the baking pan to the oven. Bake it, uncovered, for another 10 minutes, or until the cheese melts.

Cover the pan again with that foil you saved, and let your casserole sit on a cold burner or rack to set up for at least 10 minutes, and then serve and enjoy!

Hannah's 1st Note: Sally says to tell you that she made 4 pans of this for a luncheon meeting. There were 25 people and she had one whole pan left over.

Hannah's 2nd Note: Gary says to tell you that they didn't serve seconds, though.

Yield: Judging from the above notes, I'd guess that one pan of Wanmansita Casserole would serve 8 to 10 people, especially if you served fresh buttered rolls and a nice mixed green salad on the side.

Chapter Nineteen

Norman gave a resigned sigh as he perched rather precariously on the top of Hannah's cookie truck. They were parked next to the chain link fence that surrounded Cyril Murphy's impound lot. Any cars that the city of Lake Eden, the Winnetka County Sheriff's Department, or the Minnesota Highway Patrol impounded were stored here. Hannah and Norman had driven here right after she'd unmolded Andrea's Jell-O, put it on a platter, and returned it to the refrigerator. Michelle had promised to remove the Wanmansita Casseroles from the oven when they'd finished baking, and to carry them to the dinner buffet. That meant Hannah was free to pursue the linen jacket lead they'd uncovered, and Norman had agreed to help her.

Hannah glanced at her watch. They had exactly one hour before dinner would be served, and they had to locate Gus Klein's Jaguar, look to see if the jacket was there, and drive back out to the lake in time to join everyone for Jack Herman's birthday party.

"I still think this is breaking and entering," Norman said as he began to climb up the chain-link fence.

"No, it's not. It might be entering, but there's no breaking involved. Go ahead, Norman. You said you could do it."

"I can. I'm just not sure I want to. Do you know for a fact that Cyril doesn't keep guard dogs inside?"

"I do." Hannah shaded her eyes with her hand as she stared up at Norman. He had reached the top of the chain link and was just about to climb over. "Cyril bought two guard dogs when he opened the impound lot, but he ended up taking them both home for pets."

"Okay. What do you want me to do now?"

"Just drop down on the other side and unlock the gate. The sooner we get this done, the sooner we can get back out to the lake."

Norman gave a brief nod and dropped down. Hannah noticed that he landed lightly on the balls of his feet, the exact opposite of what would have happened if she'd jumped from that height. She watched him head for the gate at an easy trot, and she was impressed. Norman had never been in bad physical shape, but he appeared to be more agile and fit than he'd ever been before.

"Got it!" Norman called out, opening the gate for her.

"You picked the lock that fast?"

"Not really. It wasn't locked."

"Sorry about that." Hannah stepped inside and watched as he shut it again. "I should have thought to check it before I asked you to climb over. And speaking of that climb you made, have you been working out?"

"You noticed!" Norman looked pleased. "I've been swimming out at the new fitness club. They've got a lap pool. You should come out with me sometime. Members can bring a guest."

"Are you talking about Heavenly Bodies at the mall?" Hannah guessed. And when Norman nodded, she was almost tempted to give it a try. But then she remembered that her old swimsuit didn't fit her anymore. That meant she'd have to try on suits in a department store fitting room, and that was always depressing.

"Do you want to split up to look for the car, or do it together?"

"Together, but separate," Hannah said, enjoying the apparent contradiction. "Let's do what the police do when they search for something in the woods."

"Walk forward in parallel and meet at a designated point?"

"Exactly. That way you'll hear me if I spot it, and I'll hear you if you do. Let's pick a starting point and walk straight down the rows. Then we'll meet at the fence in back and start up another two rows."

It took three rows out of what must have been at least twenty, but they lucked out. Norman called out from the middle of his row, and Hannah darted between the cars to join him. She found him standing next to Gus Klein's Jaguar with a smile on his face. "This has got to be it. It's probably the only Jaguar in the lot."

"It's the one Gus was driving," Hannah confirmed it, "And there's the jacket I remembered."

"Linen," Norman commented. "I think that's the same one he was wearing when he drove up in front of the church."

"Mother said he wore it to the brunch he hosted at the Lake Eden Inn. He must have hung it up so that it wouldn't wrinkle for the drive to the lake."

Norman stepped up to the window, pressed his nose to the glass, and peered in. When he stopped back, he was shaking his head. "I don't think so," he said.

"Why not?"

"Because his pants and shirt are there, too. They're hanging behind the jacket. And I really don't think he drove out to the lake in his underwear."

Hannah and Norman stood there staring at the expensive linen suit. For long moments, the only sounds were the humming of insects and the far-off drone of cars on the highway.

"This just doesn't make sense," Hannah said at last. "Gus changed clothes at the cottage. His suitcase was open on the bed. And the closet was right there, no more than three or four steps away. I just can't figure out why Gus went outside and hung his suit up in his car."

Hannah smiled across the picnic table at Norman. "It was so nice of you to make Clara and Marguerite's Mexican Hotdish for Jack's birthday party."

"Maybe not. You haven't tasted it yet. I doubled the spice. Marguerite says it's even better that way. She felt so bad about not being able to bake it for Lisa and Herb's family reunion, and I volunteered to do it for her."

"That was really nice of you, Norman."

"It was fun, and really easy. Taste it and tell me what you think."

Hannah took a bite and smiled. "It's excellent, but it's a little spicier than I remember."

"Then Clara must have made it the night you went over there for dinner. She uses only one packet of taco seasoning. When Marguerite makes it, she uses two packets."

"The sour cream on the side is a nice touch."

"That's a little trick I picked up in Puerto Vallarta. We went to a place that was famous for its fish tacos and they were too spicy for Bev. The waitress brought her some sour cream to cut the heat."

"That's nice to know," Hannah said, referring to the sour cream, not to the fact that Norman had taken his ex-fiancée, Beverly Thorndike, to Mexico.

"We should go sometime. You'd love it down there. We could stay at the La Jolla de Mismaloya resort."

"Isn't that the location John Huston used in *The Night of the Iguana?*" she couldn't resist asking.

"That's right. Of course it's all modern and restored now, but they really did a good job of keeping the original ambience."

"Nice," Hannah said, deciding that one-word responses were best. She really didn't care to hear much more about Norman's Mexican vacation with Beverly.

"They run the movie continuously in the bar. The first night Bev and I were there, we sat through it twice."

"Really."

"You'd love the place, Hannah. It's very relaxed, and you can practically live in your swimsuit."

Swimsuits again. It was the second time in less than an hour that she'd been reminded of swimsuits. "Great," she said, not mentioning that if she agreed to go anywhere with Norman, and the way she felt right now the odds of that happening were drastically reduced, it certainly wouldn't be somewhere he'd vacationed with his ex-fiancée.

"I wonder what's wrong with Lisa," Norman said, changing the subject abruptly. "She looks worried."

Hannah turned to look. Her friend and partner was making her way through the crowd toward the picnic table where they were sitting.

"I don't know, but she's definitely upset." Hannah glanced around for Jack Herman and was relieved to see him smiling and laughing with Marge and a full table of relatives. Whatever the problem was, it wasn't with Jack. But there was definitely something wrong.

"Oh, Hannah! I've got to talk to you!" Lisa said, rushing up.

"Of course. What is it?"

"Not here! Mac and Herb are waiting on the dock for us. It's private there. I promised to come and get you right away. You too, Norman."

Hannah and Norman exchanged glances as they got up to follow Lisa. Hannah's glance said, *Uh-oh. This is something big!* And Norman's answering glance said, *You can bet the farm it is!*

The sun had lowered in the sky, changing from a bright yellow ball high in the sky to a huge orange orb at the edge of the horizon. The surface of Eden Lake gleamed with color. Red, yellow, orange, and pink streaks rippled with the waves across its surface, forming a riotous canvas for the darker reflections of the pines that lined the shores. The dock protruded, a dark carpet rolled out to greet the approaching evening. Two motionless figures in silhouette stood at the end of the dock, and as they drew closer, Hannah could see their tense postures and serious demeanors.

"Norman," Herb reached out for his hand. "You've met my Uncle Mac, haven't you?"

"Yes." Norman reached out to shake Mac's hand.

"And thank you for coming, Hannah. You've met my Uncle Mac?"

"Yes, at the dance." Hannah gave him a nod and a brief smile. "Nice to see you again."

For several moments that followed the polite greetings, no one moved or spoke. It was as if they'd been turned into carved pieces on a chessboard, waiting for someone or something to move them.

"So what's wrong?" Hannah asked at last, taking a step closer and breaking the grip of inertia.

"It's Dad," Lisa said, sounding tearful. "We're afraid he killed Uncle Gus!"

CLARA & MARGUERITE HOLLENBECK'S MEXICAN HOTDISH

Preheat oven to 350 degrees F., rack
in the center position.

4-ounce can Ortega diced green chilies (*with the juice*)

2 cups shredded Jack cheese (*approximately 8 ounces*)

2 cans (*14 ounces each*) diced tomatoes (*with the juice*)

1 medium onion, chopped

2-ounce can sliced black olives (*with the juice*)

1 large green bell pepper, seeded and chopped

2 cups UNCOOKED white rice

2 packages (*approximately 1-ounce each*) Taco seasoning (*Clara buys Lawry's*)

3 cups cubed cooked chicken

1 can (*14.5 ounces*) chicken broth

½ cup cold butter (*1 stick, ¼ pound, 4 ounces*)

2 cups Fritos corn chips

2 cups (*approximately 8 ounces*) shredded Mexican cheese *** (*I used the kind with four cheeses mixed together*)

*** *If the cheese selection at your grocery store is limited, just use shredded Monterrey Jack for the first cheese, and shredded sharp cheddar for the second cheese to melt on top of the Fritos. If you can't find Monterrey Jack, use Mozzarella, or Swiss.*

Spray a 6-quart roaster with Pam or other nonstick cooking spray. *(Clara buys disposable half-size steam table pans at CostMart and uses one of those. She says to be careful to set it on a cookie sheet before you fill it, though. The disposable foil could buckle and you could end up with uncooked Mexican Hotdish all over your kitchen floor!)*

Hannah's 1st Note: This hotdish is easy to make because once you've got the cubed chicken, all you have to do is open a bunch of cans. You don't even have to drain them. Just dump them in your baking pan, juice and all!

In the bottom of the pan or roaster, mix together the diced green chilies, the Jack cheese, the two cans of diced tomatoes, the chopped onion, the can of sliced black olives, the chopped bell pepper, and the UNCOOKED white rice. *(Marguerite told Norman that she washes her hands and then just mixes everything up with her fingers, but that's only if no one's around.)*

Sprinkle the Taco seasoning over the top, add the chicken cubes, and mix again.

Add the chicken broth and stir everything up with a wooden spoon. *(You can also get in there with your impeccably clean hands and mix it up that way.)*

Cut the cold stick of butter into 8 pieces and put the pieces on top of the hotdish.

Cover the pan with heavy duty foil *(or a double thickness of regular foil)* and turn down the edges to seal them.

Bake the hotdish for 1½ hours *(90 **minutes**)* at 350 degrees F.

Take the baking pan out of the oven BUT DON'T TURN OFF THE OVEN YET. Remove the foil carefully as steam may escape.

Sprinkle the Fritos on top of the hotdish, spreading them out as evenly as you can.

Sprinkle the cheese on top of the Fritos as evenly as you can.

Don't cover the hotdish. Return it to the oven to cook for another 10 minutes, uncovered, or until the cheese has melted.

Let the baking pan or roaster sit for at least 10 minutes so the hotdish can firm up before you serve it.

Hannah's 2nd Note: When I first had this hotdish at Clara and Marguerite's condo, they served it with white wine margaritas. If you don't want to serve alcohol, it would also be good with ice cold lemonade.

Hannah's 3rd Note: Norman served this with sour cream on the side for those who wanted to put a dollop on top of their serving. (I really liked it that way.) I think it would also be good with guacamole on the side for those who want to add that.

Chapter Twenty

Mac took out a handkerchief and wiped his brow. "It was a little after one-thirty. Patsy was already sleeping, but I was still wound up from the dance and talking to all the people I haven't seen for years. I knew there was no way I was going to be able to sleep, so I got up to get a glass of water and take a couple of those aspirins with the sleep aids."

Hannah knew the type of over-the-counter medication he was talking about. "How did you come to see Jack?"

"I was running water at the sink in the kitchen, and I looked out the window. It faces the pavilion, and I saw Jack walking down the road from his cottage. He cut across to the pavilion and went around to the entrance. I think he went inside, but I don't know that for sure. You can't see the entrance from the window."

Mac stopped speaking and cleared his throat. "I thought about going out to get him and walking him back to his cottage. I was already in my pajamas, but I figured I'd just get dressed again and go out after him. But then I realized that there was somebody inside the pavilion. One of the shutters was still open, and the lights were on. I figured whoever was in there would take care of Jack if he couldn't find his way back, so I took the tablets and went back to bed." Mac stopped speaking again and sighed. "I sure wish I'd gone after him now, but you know what they say about hind-sight."

Hannah glanced at Lisa. Her friend looked as if wanted to break down and sob. Hannah wanted to assure her that her father couldn't have killed Gus, but what Mac had just told them fit perfectly with what Michelle had seen from the dock. Of course Michelle hadn't known that the person she saw was Jack Herman.

"Did you tell this to the police?" Hannah asked, not knowing which answer she'd prefer. If Mac had already told Mike, the matter was out of her hands and she didn't have to worry about when she should tell him, or even *if* she should tell him.

"Of course not!" Mac shook his head. "I haven't told any-body except you four. I didn't even tell Patsy. Since I didn't see Jack go into the pavilion, I don't know for sure if he did, or not. I just saw him walking outside. The awful thing is Jack probably doesn't even remember leaving his cottage."

Lisa bit her lip. "You're probably right, Uncle Mac."

"But don't you get too upset, Lisa. I've known Jack for years. He was almost like a brother to me. He's kind, and loving, and . . . there's no way he'd do anything violent to anybody."

Hannah was silent, but her mind raced. The fight her mother had told her about between Jack and Gus wasn't ex-actly nonviolent. And Doc Knight had backed up that story.

"I knew if I told the cops about Jack, it would just muddy the waters." Mac reached out and took Lisa's hand. "Be-sides," he said, giving her hand a squeeze, "we're family. And family's got to stick together."

"She's a real trooper," Norman said, watching Lisa stick candles on top of the birthday cake she'd made for her father while Herb stood by, ready to light them.

"Yes, she is. And she loves Jack with all her heart." Han-nah thought about how Lisa had given up her college scholarship, two years ago, to stay at home with her father who'd just been diagnosed with Alzheimer's. She'd wanted to become a doctor and Hannah was convinced she would have made a good one. On the other hand, Lisa seemed happy and content with the hand life had dealt her, especially now that she'd married Herb.

"What?" Norman asked, noticing Hannah's determined expression.

"I've got to clear Jack. I just have to do it for Lisa!"

"I know you do, and I'll help any way I can. How about Mike? Will you tell him what Mac told us?"

"I promised him that I'd share information."

"That's not what I asked you," Norman said with a chuckle. "Let me ask again . . . will you tell Mike?"

It was Hannah's turn to smile. "I don't know. I haven't made up my mind yet."

"And you'll put off making that decision to give yourself time to clear Jack?"

"That's probably right. I just hope my conscience doesn't get in the way." Hannah broke into applause as Lisa walked to the table where Jack was sitting, set the cake down in front of him, and led them in singing *Happy Birthday*.

"Make a wish and blow out the candles, Dad," Lisa said, kissing him on the cheek. "It's like you used to tell me when I was a little girl. If you blow out all the candles, your wish will come true."

Jack smiled as he bent over to blow out the candles, and everyone applauded when he extinguished every one. "Marge always tells me I'm full of hot air," he said, and everyone laughed again.

"That was great, Jack," Herb said, patting him on the back. "Now your wish will come true."

"It already did. I wished for enough of Lisa's Chocolate Peanut Butter Cake for everybody. And Marge and her sister are at the back table right now, dishing it up on the plates."

*   *   *

"Why are we here?" Norman asked, following Hannah inside as she opened the door to the cabin Gus Klein had used so briefly.

"I just want to check on the frog."

"What frog?"

"The one I saw yesterday when I came here looking for Gus. I'm just hoping the crime scene people didn't trample him, or anything like that."

"So you're going to check to make sure he's all right?"

"Yes. Don't worry. It'll just take a second and then we'll rush right back for the cake."

Norman chuckled as Hannah turned on the lights and began to look for the frog. "I'm not worried about that. I just thought we were here to check something for your investigation. And now I find out it's for the frog."

"Sorry."

"Don't be. I think it's nice of you to be concerned. Do you want me to check the bedroom?"

Hannah turned to smile at him. "Yes. I'll get the kitchen. That's where he was when I left him."

While Norman looked in the bedroom, Hannah went into the kitchen. She looked in every cupboard and checked the counters and the sink. There was no little green frog hiding anywhere that she could see.

"Hannah?"

Hannah turned to face Norman as he came into the kitchen. He was holding his hands in front of him and they were cupped around something.

"You've got him?" she guessed, hoping that she was right.

"He was under the bed."

"Is he all right?"

"He's fine. Where do you want me to put him?"

"Up here on the counter. I'll run a little water in the sink. I know he can hop down, because he was up here when I saw him the last time."

Norman placed the frog on the counter while Hannah turned the faucet on and off. "Anything else?" he asked her.

"Can you open one of the windows a little in case he wants to hop out?"

"I already did," Norman said with a smile.

"Okay, then. We can go now."

They turned off the lights and started down the road toward the scene of the party. Jack's birthday celebration was still going strong if loud voices and laughter were any indication. Norman held the flashlight in one hand, and he held Hannah's hand with the other. "Have you figured out a time line for Gus?" he asked.

"I think so. Herb took a run to the house after church and found Gus waiting. It's the old family house. Marge and Herb's dad took it over after her parents died. Gus didn't know that she gave it to Lisa and Herb, of course."

"The old family home was the logical place to go."

"That's right. Herb brought Gus to the church, and then he took everyone out to brunch at the Inn. Mother said the brunch ran late and Gus was still there when they left at two. By the time he paid the bill and left, it had to have been at least two-thirty. Then Gus drove back to Lisa and Herb's house and looked through the trunk his parents packed from his old bedroom. It was probably four thirty by the time he left there. It's thirty minutes from Lisa and Herb's house to the lake, so Gus couldn't have gotten to the cottage until almost five. Then he changed clothes and went to the dinner buffet at the pavilion."

"And that started at six. I know. I was there to take pictures. So that means he spent all of an hour at the cottage?"

"That's right, give or take thirty minutes or so." Hannah was almost sorry as they approached the lights and music of the party. She really enjoyed the time she spent alone with Norman. "I'm sorry I didn't explain about the frog, Norman."

"You shouldn't be. I think you've got your priorities straight, Hannah."

"I do?"

"Yes. Maybe a murder investigation is more critical, but the welfare of a frog is important, too."

It was almost nine in the evening by the time the party began to break up. Tomorrow would be what Lisa and Herb were calling, "Games Day." There would be the usual summer picnic games, like kickball, three-legged races, sack races, biking expeditions, tricycle parades, and team softball. There would also be water games, like swimming and diving competitions, water polo, canoe and rowboat races, and even a synchronized swimming demonstration by three junior-high girls who hoped to make their high school team. Anyone who didn't want to or couldn't play in the games was recruited to be a volunteer judge. Others were encouraged to sit in lawn chairs and cheer on the contestants.

Hannah glanced at her watch and turned to Norman. "I'm going to help clean up, and then I'm heading home. I'd invite you over, but I really need to get a good night's sleep. I haven't had my full six hours for at least a week."

"Why didn't you tell me when I called this morning?" Norman sounded surprised.

"Tell you what?"

"That Moishe acted up again. I thought the Kitty Kondo did the trick."

"I think it did do the trick. He certainly enjoyed playing with the mouse this morning. And the fact that I lost sleep last night has nothing to do with Moishe. It's Mother's fault."

"Your mother called you in the middle of the night?"

"No, she gave me a deadline for Jack's Red Velvet Cookies, and I promised to do my best to have them by tonight. When I got home last night, I researched them and mixed up three different test batches. I didn't get to bed until midnight, and Moishe started playing with the squeaky mouse at four in the morning, a minute or two before my alarm went off."

"But he didn't tear up any pillows or race around inside your bathtub?"

"No. I'm beginning to think you were right, Norman, and he was acting up because he was bored."

Once Norman had hugged her and they'd said their good-byes, Hannah started to pick up paper dessert plates and put them in the trash. In the space of fifteen minutes, the picnic tables had been wiped down and the dishes had been scraped and put into the dishwashers. Hannah was more than ready to drive home and go to bed, but there was one more thing she had to do first.

It took a while to find Lisa. Hannah finally spotted her alone at a picnic table under a pine tree. No doubt her partner wanted to be alone to think about what Mac had told them, but thinking alone wouldn't solve the problem.

"Lisa?" she said, sitting down across from her partner.

"What is it?"

Lisa's voice sounded thick, as if she'd been crying, but Hannah didn't mention that. "I need to talk to your dad for a minute," she said. "Do you think you could find us a nice quiet spot?"

"He's in a nice quiet spot right now. Herb took him back to the cottage so they could watch what's left of the ball-game. The Twins had a doubleheader with the Angels today."

"Will he mind if I interrupt him?"

"He won't mind. It's probably over by now, anyway." Lisa got up and led the way. "Are you going to ask him questions about the night of the murder?"

"Yes. I need as much background as I can get. Don't worry, Lisa. I'll do my best not to upset him."

"I don't think you'll upset him. You never have before. And I know that he really likes you."

Lisa opened the screen door and they stepped into the small cottage where Jack and Marge were staying. "Hi, Dad," she greeted her father with a kiss on the cheek, and then moved over to Herb. "How did the ballgame go?"

"Twins won the first, but the Angels won the second," Herb told her.

"Oh, well." Lisa sat down next to her father. "Hannah needs to ask you some questions, Dad. Herb and I are going to leave you with her for a couple of minutes. Hannah's our good friend, and you can tell her anything, okay?"

"Okay." Jack nodded and watched his daughter walk off. "She's a good girl," he said.

"Yes, she is. You're lucky to have her, and she's lucky to have you." Hannah moved a little closer to keep his attention and asked her first question. "Is it possible you went for a walk on Sunday night after the dance?"

"Yes, it's possible. It was the first night in a different bed. I always sleep better at home, you know."

"And you might have gone for a walk if you couldn't sleep?" Hannah asked him.

"I might have . . . Hannah. It's Hannah, isn't it?"

"That's right. You remembered!"

Jack shrugged. "It comes and goes. I just try not to get too . . . what's the word that's the opposite of calm, Harriet?"

Hannah resisted the urge to correct him. "Agitated? Frustrated?"

"Both of those. If I stay quiet, I've got a better shot at remembering. Say, Helen . . . he wasn't shot, was he?"

"No, he was stabbed with an ice pick."

"Too bad. If he'd been shot, I'd be in the clear."

"Really?"

"That's right. Emmy wouldn't let me have a gun in the house. She was always afraid the kids would get hold of it and shoot each other, or some such thing. And now my little girl's a trophy winner in that cowboy game with Herb. Life's iron . . . iron . . . what's the word?"

"Ironic?"

"That's it. Life's ironic, Hazel."

"It's Hannah," Hannah corrected him before she could think better of it.

"I know you're Hannah. I just wanted to see how many times I could call you the wrong name before you corrected me. That must have just about killed you!"

Hannah gave him a startled glance and then she started to laugh. "You're like the guy who got a hearing aid and didn't tell his family he was wearing it."

"And changed his will a dozen times," Jack finished the old joke. "You'd be surprised what I remember and what I don't. There's no rhyme or . . . whatever that other *R* word is . . . to it. Sometimes a smell will spark something I haven't thought of in years. And other times it's something I eat, or a car I see in an old movie, or an antique around the house."

"You told me that once before," Hannah said. "I was hoping those Red Velvet Cookies I made for your birthday would bring back the memory of the fight you had with Gus the night he left Lake Eden for good. I think that's one of the keys to this whole thing, Jack. I wish you could remember what that fight was about."

"So do I. But I've tried and I can't."

"Don't try so hard. Just eat another couple of the cookies tomorrow. You daughter, Iris, said Emmy used to bake them when Iris was really little."

"They *did* taste familiar. It's probably why I thought they were so good. I miss her, you know."

"Your wife?"

"That's the hardest thing about getting old. Everybody you knew when you were young is dead."

"It must be horribly depressing," Hannah commented, feeling horribly depressed just thinking about it.

"It is. But then there's the upside."

"What's that?"

"You get to outlive your enemies. That's the good part . . . unless you're the guy that killed them, of course."

CHOCOLATE PEANUT BUTTER CAKE

Preheat oven to 350 degrees F., rack
in the middle position.

WARNING: THERE ARE PEANUTS IN THIS
RECIPE. MAKE SURE YOU ASK IF ANYONE IS AL-
LERGIC TO PEANUTS BEFORE YOU BAKE AND
SERVE THIS CAKE!!!

Hannah's 1st Note: Lisa says she got the idea for this
cake by watching Marge make her Cocoa Fudge Cake.
Since Herb is crazy about Reese's Peanut Butter Cups,
Lisa's cake combines peanut butter and chocolate.

Butter and flour a 9-inch by 13-inch sheet cake pan.
*(You can also spray it with Pam or another nonstick cook-
ing spray and then just lightly dust it with flour. You can
also do what Lisa did and spray it with a product that
mixes nonstick cooking spray with flour.)*

Hannah's 2nd Note: I was really leery of the nonstick
cooking spray mixed with flour, but Lisa says it works just
fine.

2 cups white *(granulated)* sugar
2 cups flour *(don't sift—just level it off with a knife)*

---

1 cup butter *(2 sticks, ½ pound, 8 ounces)*
1 cup peanut butter *(Lisa used Skippy creamy
    peanut butter)*
1 cup water

½ cup cream *(or evaporated milk, if you're all out of cream)*
1 teaspoon vanilla extract
1 teaspoon baking soda
2 eggs, beaten *(just whip them up in a glass with a fork)*

Hannah's 3ʳᵈ Note: Lisa used the mixer down at The Cookie Jar to make this cake. She says you can also do it by hand if you don't have an electric mixer.

Mix the sugar and the flour together at low speed.

Put the butter, peanut butter, and water into a medium-sized saucepan. Turn the burner on medium heat and bring the mixture ALMOST to a boil. *(When it sends up little whiffs of steam and bubbles start to form around the edges, take it off the heat.)*

Pour the peanut butter mixture over the sugar and flour, and mix it all up together.

Rinse out the saucepan, but don't bother to wash it thoroughly. You'll be making a frosting and you can use it again before you really wash it.

Whisk the cream, vanilla extract, baking soda, and eggs together in a small bowl.

SLOWLY, add this mixture to the large mixer bowl and combine it at medium speed. *(You have to go slowly with*

this step because you have the hot peanut butter mixture in your bowl and you're adding an egg mixture. This cake wouldn't be wonderful if you ended up with peanut butter flavored scrambled eggs!)

Scrape down the mixing bowl with a rubber spatula, remove it from the mixer, and give it a final stir by hand.

Pour the batter into the 9-inch by 13-inch greased and floured cake pan.

Bake at 350 degrees F. for 30 to 35 minutes. When the cake begins to shrink away from the sides of the pan and a long toothpick inserted in the center of the cake comes out clean, it's done.

Hannah's 4th Note: Lisa uses my Neverfail Fudge Frosting on this cake. It's given as an alternative frosting at the end of Marge's Cocoa Fudge Cake recipe, but I'll write it down again here.

NEVERFAIL FUDGE FROSTING

½ cup *(1 stick, ¼ pound, 4 ounces)* salted butter
1 cup white *(granulated)* sugar
⅓ cup cream
½ cup chocolate chips
1 teaspoon vanilla extract
½ cup chopped salted peanuts *(optional)*

Place the butter, sugar, and cream into a medium-size saucepan *(You can use the one from the cake that you didn't wash.)* Bring the mixture to a boil, stirring constantly. Turn down the heat to medium and cook for two minutes.

Add the half-cup chocolate chips, stir them in until they're melted, and remove the saucepan from the heat.

Stir in the vanilla.

Pour the frosting on the cake and spread it out quickly with a spatula. If you're pouring it on a warm cake or a cold cake, just grab the pan and tip it so the frosting covers the whole top.

Sprinkle the chopped salted peanuts *(if you decided to use them)* over the top of the frosting.

If you want this frosting to cool in a big hurry so that you can cut the cake, just slip it in the refrigerator, uncovered, for a half-hour or so.

Hannah's 5th Note: Lisa says to tell you that this cake is absolutely yummy if you serve it slightly warm. It's also wonderful at room temperature. If you keep it in the refrigerator, take it out 45 minutes or so before you plan to serve it.

Chapter
Twenty-One

Hannah had an odd thought as she unlocked her door. If her condo complex had been built next door to the Palace of Westminster, she would be hearing Big Ben strike ten. Of course that didn't account for the time change.

It had been so long, Hannah had almost forgotten to brace herself for the furry orange-and-white cat bombardment. She staggered slightly as he landed in her arms, but she was smiling all the while. "Hi, Moishe!" she said, nuzzling him as she carried him over to his favorite perch on the back of the couch and gave him a pat before she set him down. Things were back to normal. All was right with her world.

But before she could give her pet the scratch behind the ears he'd always expected, Moishe jumped down from the back of the couch and made a beeline for the Kitty Kondo. He whisked inside, and a second later came out on the penthouse floor.

"Oh, that's your favorite perch now?" Hannah asked, walking over to give him the scratch that was part of her coming home ceremony.

She stood there petting him and listening to him purr until the phone rang. Then she hurried to the base station on the end table by the couch to get the receiver. "Hello?" she answered.

"You sound happy. I take it Moishe behaved himself while you were gone?"

It was Norman, and Hannah began to smile. "Thanks to you, he did. All I lost was another squeaky mouse, and I'm sure it's around here somewhere."

"That's the reason I called. The girl from the pet store called me on my cell phone. Their shipment of mice came in, and I stopped out there to pick up some more. If you're not too tired, I'll bring them over. But if you are, it can wait until the next time I see you."

Considerate. Norman was so considerate. And despite the fact that she'd gotten very little sleep this week, Hannah felt energized by the fact that Moishe was back to his old self.

"Come on over," she said. "I just got my second wind, and I'll put on the coffee."

Hannah put on the coffee. And while she was there in the kitchen, she gave Moishe a full bowl of food and fresh water. Then she headed straight to the pantry. She needed to serve something with the coffee when Norman arrived at her condo. It was a Minnesota tradition. The obligation to serve a kind of sweet treat was still in force, even though they'd both eaten generous portions of Jack's birthday cake less than two hours ago. A good Minnesota hostess could not serve coffee all by itself!

It took Hannah all of thirty seconds to evaluate the supplies on her pantry shelves. The *something* would be Scandinavian Almond Cake. It would make her whole place smell wonderful while it was baking, and it was easy to assemble and serve. She even had some sliced almonds to sprinkle on top of the batter. What could be easier?

Ten minutes later, Hannah slipped her loaf pan into the oven and set the timer. She was about to pour herself a cup of the coffee she'd just made when there was a knock at her condo door.

"Already?" Hannah said to Moishe, whose head had emerged from his food bowl when he'd realized that there was someone at the door. She glanced at the clock, calculated the time, and shook her head. "It's not Norman. It couldn't be. Even if he broke the land speed record, there's no way he could make it here this fast!"

Always cautious, especially when she was working on a murder case, Hannah didn't simply open the door. The fish-eye peephole that had been in the door when she'd bought her unit was practically useless. It distorted her visitors' features so much she couldn't even recognize her own mother! From force of habit, Hannah looked through it anyway, and what she saw made her rear back with a start. It *was* her own mother. At least she *thought* it was Delores.

"Uh-oh!" Hannah whispered under her breath. Delores didn't visit her at the condo. She'd stopped when Moishe had shredded her tenth pair of pantyhose. There must be something drastically wrong to have brought her here this late in the evening. But perhaps it wasn't Delores. It could be another woman with dark hair. She wasn't going to open the door until she knew for sure, so she called out, "Who is it?"

"Don't you recognize your own mother?" Delores asked. "We're sweltering out here, not to mention we're getting eaten alive by the mosquitoes. Open the door, Hannah."

Hannah opened the door and saw why her mother had answered in the plural. Delores had Michelle and Andrea in tow.

"I thought you went home after the party," Hannah addressed Andrea.

"I did, but Grandma McCann had everything under control. She said Bill called to say he'd be tied up until late, and then Mother called, and . . . here I am."

"Me, too," Michelle added. "I was getting ready for bed, but Mother decided we needed a family meeting, so she dragged us all over here."

"Well, the family's about to get bigger," Hannah said, ushering them into the living room. "Norman should be here in ten minutes or so."

Delores smiled. "That's just fine. Norman's practically family, anyway. And we don't have any secrets from him . . . do we, dear?"

Hannah was saved from the necessity of a response by an orange-and-white blur that streaked through the living room, tore through the opening in the bottom floor of his new Kitty Kondo, scrambled up two floors, and emerged at the penthouse floor to glare at his archenemy.

"Oh, how cute!" Delores exclaimed, not even noticing that Moishe was puffed up and practically spitting. "You got one of those wonderful Kitty Kondos for my darling grandcat. You must have been saving your pennies, dear."

"I always do. And that's what it cost me. They're having a twofer sale at the pet store in the mall, and Norman bought one for Cuddles. This one cost just a dollar, so he got it for Moishe."

There was total silence for the count of ten, and then Delores cleared her throat. "Who told you that, dear?"

Hannah's eyes narrowed. "Norman did," she responded. "There *isn't* a twofer on the Kitty Kondos at the pet store?"

"Well . . . I haven't checked recently, but . . ."

"Mother!" Hannah interrupted her. "I need to know if there was a twofer on the Kitty Kondos two days ago."

"Well . . . actually . . . I'm not really sure that . . ."

"Give it to me straight, Mother," Hannah demanded. "I can take it."

Delores gave a big sigh and shook her head. "I don't think so, dear. Of course he may have negotiated a special price for some reason or other, but . . ."

"But Norman lied to me about the twofer," Hannah interrupted what was going to be another excuse.

"That would be my guess, dear. But you've got to admit that it was sweet of him to buy it."

"It *was* sweet," Hannah admitted, "but he lied to me."

"You could be right. What are you going to do about it?"

Hannah stared at her mother in shock. "Well . . . I'll just have to pay him back, that's all. I'll find out what it costs, save the money and . . ."

"And make Norman feel really bad that he gave Moishe such a wonderful present," Michelle jumped into the mother-daughter conversation. "Are you really sure you want to do that?"

"Of course I don't want to make Norman feel bad!" Hannah was outraged at the assumption. "But I don't want to accept charity, either. I own a successful business. I can pay."

"But you'd spoil all his fun," Andrea said, frowning at her older sister. "Norman thinks he put one over on you. He's proud of himself, and he's happy he found something to give you. And he's crazy about Moishe, and he wants to give him something, too. And now you want to ruin it all for him?"

"And make him feel bad for even trying to please you?" Michelle added.

"Of course not. But . . ." Hannah stopped and thought about it. Maybe her mother and sisters were right. Maybe she ought to let Norman think he'd put one over on her. And maybe she should be grateful that he cared enough about Moishe and enough about her to try to give them both a present.

"Well?" Delores raised her eyebrows in a question.

"You're right," Hannah said, giving in as gracefully as she could. "I won't say a word about it."

"Good for you!" Michelle said.

"You're doing the right thing," Andrea added.

"It's very smart of you, dear," Delores had the final word on the matter as she took a seat on the couch. "What's that divine scent?"

"Almonds," Hannah told her. "I'm baking Joyce's Scandinavian Almond Cake."

Delores looked pleased. "Is that the recipe Joyce gave me from her friend Nancy?" she asked.

"That's the one. The only difference is that I used clarified butter instead of margarine."

"When will it come out of the oven?" Andrea asked her.

Hannah turned to glance at the clock on her end table. "In about five minutes. And then it has to cool a bit, but I'll serve it warm."

"Marvelous!" Delores gave a nod. "I suppose you're wondering why we're here, dear."

"The thought did cross my mind."

"It's about Gus, of course. Marge and I got together this afternoon and made a list of all the women Gus dumped. And we called every one of them this afternoon. They all have alibis."

"*All* of them?"

"That's right. But I didn't come here just to tell you that. I stopped in at Ava's store when I left Jack's birthday party, and she told me that she talked to the credit card company. It seems the gas card Gus used to fill his tank wasn't valid."

"Uh-oh!" Hannah said, as a couple of the puzzle pieces clicked together. Gus had worn what Mike thought was a fake Rolex on his wrist, and a diamond pinkie ring made of paste. If he had been living a lie and only pretending to be rich, how many other merchants along his route from Atlantic City to Lake Eden, Minnesota, would discover they'd been defrauded?

"When did he gas up his Jaguar?" she asked, recognizing the loose end. She wasn't sure if it was important, but she knew from experience that murder cases were usually solved by asking questions and remembering the answers.

"He filled his tank when he came back from the brunch at the Inn," Delores told her. "And that was a Sunday, so Ava couldn't call in the card. She did it today, and that's when she found out that the gas card he used was no good."

"No good? Does that mean it was stolen?' Hannah asked.

Delores shook her head. "Ava said it was canceled, not stolen. The lady she talked to told her they canceled his account because the bill hadn't been paid."

"That doesn't sound good," Hannah said, taking a moment to digest the information she'd been given. Then she turned to her mother again. "Will you go out to the Inn tomorrow morning and see if Gus's charges for the brunch were accepted on his credit card? Sally must have called them in by now."

"Of course," Delores agreed.

"Great." Hannah turned to Michelle. "Will you ask Lonnie if Gus's Rolex was real? Mike told me he was pretty sure it wasn't, especially when the guys in robbery said the diamond in the pinkie ring he was wearing was paste."

"I'll do it right now," Michelle said, pulling out her cell phone and ducking into the kitchen to place the call.

Andrea began to frown. "What's going on here, Hannah? Do you know yet?"

"Not yet," Hannah told her, wishing her answer could be more definitive. "All I know is that Gus wasn't what he said he was."

"Fake," Michelle said, poking her head through the doorway. "Lonnie got a call from the jeweler today. I'll be with you in a minute, okay?"

"Do you think Gus was deliberately trying to defraud his friends and relatives?" Delores asked Hannah.

"I don't know. I didn't know him when he was growing up, but you did. What do you think?"

Delores thought about that for a long moment and then she sighed. "It's possible," she said. "I don't really want to believe it, but it's definitely possible."

SCANDINAVIAN ALMOND CAKE

Preheat oven to 350 degrees F., rack
in the middle position.

Before you start to mix up this recipe, grease *(or spray with Pam or another nonstick cooking spray)* a 4-inch by 8-inch loaf pan. *(Mine was Pyrex and I measured the bottom.)*

Cut a strip of parchment paper *(or wax paper if you don't have parchment)* 8 inches wide and 16 inches long. Lay it in the pan so that the bottom is covered and the strip sticks out in little "ears" on the long sides of the pan. *(This makes for easy removal after your cake is baked.)* This will leave the two short sides of the pan uncovered, but that's okay. Press the paper down and then spray it again with Pam or another nonstick cooking spray.

1 stick *(½ cup, ¼ pound, 4 ounces)* salted butter
1 ¼ cups white *(granulated)* sugar
1 egg *(I used an extra large egg)*
½ teaspoon baking powder
1 ½ teaspoons almond extract
⅔ cup cream *(you can also use what Grandma Ingrid used to call "top milk" or what we now call Half 'n Half)*
1 ¼ cups flour
¼ cup sliced almonds *(optional—they make your cakes look pretty)*

If you decided to use the sliced almonds, sprinkle a few in the very bottom of your paper-lined loaf pan. *(This cake is like a pineapple upside down cake—the bottom will be the top when you serve it.)*

Hannah's 1st Note: Now don't let this next step scare you. It's extremely easy and it will keep your cakes from turning too brown around the edges.

Place the stick of butter in a one-cup Pyrex measuring cup or in another small microwave-safe bowl. Zap it for 40 seconds on HIGH, or until it's melted. *(You can also do this in a small saucepan on the stove.)* Now pour that melted butter through a fine-mesh strainer, the kind you'd use for tea, *(or a larger mesh strainer lined with a double thickness of cheesecloth.)* After the melted butter has dripped through, dump the milk solids that have gathered in the strainer in the garbage *(or throw away the cheesecloth, if you've used that method.)* What you have left is clarified butter.

Set your clarified butter on the counter to cool while you . . .

Mix the white sugar with the egg in a medium sized bowl, or in the bowl of an electric mixer. Beat them together until they're light and fluffy.

Add the baking powder and the almond extract. Mix well.

Cup your hands around the bowl with the clarified butter. If you can hold it comfortably and it's not so hot that it might cook the egg, add it to your bowl now and mix it in. If it's still too hot, wait until it's cooler and then mix it in.

Hannah's 2nd Note: In the following steps, you're going to add half of the cream, and then half the flour. You don't have to be precise and measure exactly half. Just dump in what you think is approximately half and it'll be just fine.

Add half of the cream and mix it in.

Add half of the flour and mix it in.

Now add the rest of the cream, and mix.

And then add the rest of the flour, and mix thoroughly.

Pour the batter into the loaf pan you've prepared and smooth the top with a spatula.

Bake the cake at 350 degrees F., for 50 to 60 minutes, or until a toothpick inserted in the center comes out clean.

Let the loaf pan sit on a wire rack or a cold burner for 15 minutes. Then loosen the cake from the short sides of the pan *(the non-papered sides)* with a metal spatula or a knife.

Tip the cake out on a pretty platter, and remove the parchment paper. Let it cool and then dust the top with powdered sugar if you wish.

Hannah's 3rd Note: Mother's friends, Joyce and Nancy, have special half-round loaf pans especially for baking Scandinavian Almond Cake. Joyce's cake bakes for the same length of time as mine does. Nancy's pan has a dark nonstick surface. It's heavier than Joyce's pan and the dark surface makes it bake faster. Nancy bakes her cake for 35 to 40 minutes, or until a toothpick inserted in the center comes out clean.

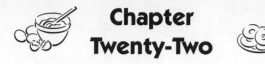

"This is delicious cake, dear," Delores said, sipping the coffee Hannah had brought her and taking a bite of her slice of almond cake. "I think I prefer it warm . . ."

"Thank you, Mother."

"A man would be lucky to have you for a wife. You're such a good cook."

"It's my business, Mother."

"You keep a nice home, too."

"Thank you, Mother," Hannah said again. Then she took a deep breath because she knew that two compliments in a row from her mother were usually followed by a lecture about how she should settle down, get married, and start a family.

"I know you think there's plenty of time for a husband and family, but your . . ."

The start of her mother's biological-clock-is-ticking lecture was interrupted by a knock at the door. Hannah sent up a quick prayer of thanks for Norman's timely arrival and held up her hand.

"Hold that thought, Mother. I've got to get the door."

With that said and her mother momentarily silenced, Hannah hurried over, bypassed the nearly useless peephole, and called out, "Who's there?"

"Mouse delivery for Moishe," Norman announced, and

Hannah opened the door. "I can just drop them off if you're tired."

"Come in and join the party," Hannah said, opening the door all the way so he could see the assembled crew of Swensens.

"Good thing you got your second wind," he said just loudly enough for Hannah to hear him. And then he turned to them. "You came to help Hannah tie squeaky mice to Moishe's Kitty Kondo?"

"Not exactly," Michelle said, laughing. "We were just eating and discussing murder."

"Sounds like a good combination to me. Eating what?"

"Scandinavian Almond Cake," Hannah told him. "Find a seat, and I'll get you a piece with your coffee."

"Moishe's purring, Hannah," Norman remarked, after Delores, Andrea, and Michelle had left. "I can hear him all the way over here."

"That's because Mother's gone. He probably thought I was punishing him when I let her in the door."

"Or he's just glad everything's back to normal and you've forgiven him for past transgressions. You *have* forgiven him, haven't you?"

"Long before you got here. And long before Mother and the girls got here, too. Thanks to you, that's one problem solved. Now all I have to do is figure out who killed Gus."

"If you're not too tired, tell me what you've got so far." Norman took a sip of the coffee Hannah had just refilled.

"I've got lots of motives, but not many suspects. Gus wasn't a very nice person, and there's a long list of people who had a reason to dislike him, even hate him."

"And they are . . ."

Hannah grabbed her shorthand notebook and opened it to the suspect page. "I'll start at the beginning. There are a lot of girls he dated in high school and then dumped for someone else. Mother and Marge made a list. Unfortunately, every single one of them has an alibi."

"Okay. Who else?"

"Bert Kuehn. There's speculation that Gus was driving drunk and he got into the car accident that killed Bert's sister, Mary Jo. The official police report states that Mary Jo was driving, but Gus's high school baseball coach was the first on the scene, and he could have helped Gus put Mary Jo in the driver's seat."

"Did you talk to the coach?"

"No. He left Jordan High and went to coach college baseball at the University of Michigan. I haven't had time to track him down yet."

"I'll help you do that before I leave. Anyone else?"

"There's the possibility of a robbery gone bad. Gus was flashing around money and telling everyone that he was rich."

"But didn't you say that the money in his wallet was still there?"

"Yes. Mike thinks the robber might have panicked when he realized he'd killed Gus, and he fled without anything."

"But you don't agree?"

"Not really. He could have grabbed the Rolex. He wouldn't have had any way of knowing that it was a fake."

"You're sure the Rolex was a fake?"

"Positive. Michelle checked with Lonnie before you got here tonight, and he said he talked to the jeweler. It was definitely a fake, and the ring Gus was wearing was paste. Mike told me that it wasn't unusual for rich people to wear fake watches and jewelry and keep their expensive things in a safe at home. That's what he thinks Gus did."

"But you don't agree?"

"No, but I have more information now. Ava told me that Gus charged gas on a gas card that had been canceled by the company for nonpayment. Mother's going to check with

Sally tomorrow to see if the credit card he used to pay for the brunch went through okay."

"And Mike doesn't know about the canceled gas card yet?"

"No."

"Are you going to tell him?"

"I don't know yet. I'm afraid that if he thinks there aren't any valuables in Gus's apartment in Atlantic City, he might delay sending someone there to check it out. It wasn't high on his list of priorities, anyway. It's really doubtful that someone from New Jersey followed Gus here and killed him."

"That's probably right," Norman said, but he didn't look completely convinced. "But a hired killer could have hidden himself in the crowd of people here for the reunion, bided his time, and killed Gus when nobody else was around."

"Impossible."

"Why? There's got to be at least a hundred and fifty people at the lake."

"And they all get together and talk," Hannah explained. "Somebody who's not a relative would be found out in a hurry. I walked through that crowd enough to know everybody asks everybody else about how they're related, and their background, and the other relatives they know."

Norman thought about that for a moment. "You've got a point. It would be a lot harder than trying to crash a convention or another event like that."

"Back to the suspects," Hannah said, flipping the page. "There's Jack, of course. You already know about that. And then there's the gambling Gus used to do. It could be someone who thought Gus cheated him, someone who carried a grudge all these years. Or it could be someone he borrowed money from and never paid back. Mother told me he was terrible about that. He still owed her twenty dollars from high school when he left Lake Eden for good."

"He sounds like someone I'm glad I met only once," Norman said, shaking his head.

"Well put!" Hannah complimented him. "But that doesn't mean he deserved to die."

"True. Anybody else on your suspect list?"

"Ava."

Norman looked shocked. "Ava Schultz from the store?"

"That's right."

"Because of the canceled gas card?"

"No, Ava didn't know she'd been cheated until today, when she called in the charges. She doesn't have the kind of automatic pumps that accept or reject gas cards. She just writes the number on a form, has the person sign it, and calls them in."

"Okay, but why would Ava want to kill him if she didn't know about the canceled card?"

"Because he didn't stay with her."

"Ava asked him to spend the night?" Norman asked, looking surprised.

"I don't know for sure. What I do know is that she was very quick to tell me that when Gus came back to the store with her after the dance was over, it wasn't what I was thinking. She assured me that the only thing he wanted was to get some groceries."

"Maybe that's all it was."

"Maybe, but I added her to the suspect list anyway. A woman scorned is a prime suspect."

"So Ava's still a suspect?"

"No, I cleared her when Andrea brought me the crime scene photos. Gus is a couple of inches over six feet tall, and Ava's more than a foot shorter. She's also much lighter. I don't think she can weigh more than ninety pounds dripping wet."

"That's about what I'd guess," Norman said.

"So there's no way Ava could stab him in the chest with

enough force to kill him . . . unless she stool on a step stool, of course."

"And there was no step stool?" Norman asked.

"None in the whole pavilion. I know because Patsy was looking for one so she could replace the lightbulb over the back door."

"How about if she knocked him down on his back and then stabbed him?"

"How?" Hannah asked him. "He outweighed her by at least fifty pounds."

"Right. Well . . . you were probably right to take her off the list. She's a pretty unlikely candidate. Anybody else on there?

"Just one. And I'm beginning to think this last one is the one who did it."

"Who's that?"

"The unidentified suspect who killed Gus for some unknown reason. I don't know about you, Norman, but this case has really got me stymied."

"You'll solve it. You always do. Something will happen to put a few of the pieces in place and then the rest will follow."

"Thanks for the vote of confidence."

"You're welcome. Maybe that baseball coach is a piece of the puzzle. Fire up your computer, and let's see if we can find out more about him."

Once the computer was online and Norman was sitting in what Hannah thought of as the driver's seat, he turned to her. "What's the name?"

"Toby Hutchins."

"Is that *Toby* as in *Tobias?*"

"I don't know, and Mother didn't either. I asked. Before I wrote it down."

"Okay, let's go with Toby. I'm going to load the University of Michigan Web site and see what's there."

Hannah watched while the Web site loaded. "There's a place to click for athletics," she said, pointing at the screen.

"Right. We'll try that first." Norman waited, and when the athletics page loaded, he clicked on the link for baseball. Once that page came up, there was another link for history, and then one for coaches.

"We might have something here," Norman said, letting the page for baseball coaches load. But when it came up on the screen, he gave a little groan.

"What is it?" Hannah asked.

"It only gives head coaches and the years they headed up Wolverine Baseball. Didn't you say Toby Hutchins was an assistant coach?"

"That's what Mother said."

"This is a dead end, then." Norman went back to the original screen. "At least we know he lived in Ann Arbor at one time. Maybe there's something about him in the local papers." A few moments later, he asked, "Do you want to try the *Ann Arbor News?* Or the University paper, *Michigan Daily?*"

"Let's try the *Michigan Daily.* Mother was pretty sure he coached there."

Norman pulled up the Web site and did a search for Gus's high school baseball coach. There were several mentions in sports coverage, but then Norman's search took them to another page.

"Uh-oh," Hannah breathed as she saw the heading on the page. Toby Hutchins was dead and had been for three years now. He'd been killed in a boating accident. According to the obituary, there were no survivors and no one to contact. "Another dead end," she sighed. "Literally."

"Let's try the Atlantic City yellow pages," Norman suggested.

"For Toby Hutchins?"

"No, for Gus's nightclub. I want to find out if Mood Indigo actually exists."

It didn't take long to pull up the Yellow Pages and find the address for Mood Indigo. Norman printed it out, along with the phone number, and glanced at his watch. "Too late to call," he said. "They're two hours ahead, and they're probably closed by now."

"What are you doing now?" Hannah asked as Norman typed something in and started loading another Web page.

"Making reservations. Maybe someone at Mood Indigo knows why Gus came back to Lake Eden."

"You're going to fly to Atlantic City?" Hannah was dumbfounded.

"Why not? Doc's filling in for me tomorrow, anyway. I'll drive to the airport, catch the red-eye, sleep on the plane, and get there before noon."

"But don't you have to go back home to pack a suitcase?"

"Not really. I'll pick up what I need at the airport."

"How about clothes?"

"I've got what I'm wearing, and I can pick up another shirt. If Gus's nightclub really is as fancy as he claimed it was, it'll probably have a dress code. I'm just glad I've got my suit hanging in the car, and I can take off for the airport from here."

Hannah just stared at him for a moment as the gears in her brain whirred and then meshed. Pieces of the puzzle clicked into place, and she reached out to hug him. And then, because that wasn't enough, she placed a big kiss on his lips.

"Wow!" Norman said when she released him. "If I'd known that flying to Atlantic City would affect you that way, I would have done it a long time ago!"

"That's not it," Hannah said, still slightly breathless from the way Norman had returned her kiss.

"Then what is it? Not that I'm complaining, of course."

"Remember the suitcase on the bed?" she waited until Norman nodded. "And the empty closet at Gus's cottage?"

"Yes."

"And the linen suit hanging in the Jaguar?"

"Of course I remember. I'm the one who climbed the fence at the impound lot. But what does that have to do with me?"

"Gus didn't unpack and hang up his clothes, because he

knew he wasn't staying. And he hung his linen suit in the car when he changed clothes for the dance because he was planning on leaving later that night."

"How do you know all that?"

"Everything adds up. Ava told me he gassed up his car before he even found out which cabin was his. That tells me he was planning to take off again before Ava opened up in the morning."

"Okay. Anything else?"

"There's the pill I saw him take at the dance. He said it was an antacid, but I described it to Jon Walker and he thought it was a type of amphetamine. Gus wanted to be alert so he could drive back to Atlantic City. That's why he bought all those candy bars and snacks. He told Ava they were for his breakfast, but they weren't. That's why he bought the disposable cooler, too. And made his ham and cheese sandwiches at the bar in the pavilion. He was going to take them with him in the car and drive all night."

Norman thought about it for a moment. "That *does* make sense. But why did he want to leave after only one day? The reunion doesn't end until Saturday night."

"My guess is that he never planned to come to the reunion in the first place. He just saw the posters Lisa and Herb hung on Main Street and thought it was a handy excuse. He came for another reason."

"To see his family?"

Hannah shook her head. "I really doubt that. If he'd wanted to reconnect with his relatives, he would have stayed for the whole reunion. My guess is that Gus came for a purpose. And he must have accomplished it before he hung that linen suit in his car and took that pill to keep him awake."

"Okay," Norman said, standing up and giving Moishe a scratch behind the ears before he headed to the door. "I'll find out why he came here. And I'll check out his apartment to see if he really had a safe with watches and jewelry."

"Be careful," Hannah warned, feeling strangely bereft as he pulled her into his arms for a hug.

"I will be. Where's your cell phone?"

Hannah got her purse and rummaged around until she found her cell phone in the bottom. "Here it is," she announced, handing it to him.

"The battery's low," Norman said, turning it on and pressing some buttons that emitted squeaky sounds.

"Moishe likes those sounds," Hannah said, noticing that her cat had perked up his ears. "It probably sounds like a mouse symphony to him."

Norman laughed as he shut the phone and handed it to her. "Put it on the charger tonight, and don't forget to take it with you tomorrow. I'll call you when I get to Atlantic City, but you have to remember to turn your cell phone on so it'll ring."

"I will. I'll charge it up the second you leave, and I'll take it with me when I go to work tomorrow. And I'll turn it on and leave it on in my purse."

"Good. Don't forget. And be careful, Hannah."

"I will be."

"Do you promise?"

Hannah smiled. Norman really *did* care about her. "I promise," she gave her word.

"If you figure out who killed Gus before I get back, don't take any chances. And whatever you do, don't go after his killer alone. Call Mike and make sure he's got your back."

"Okay."

"Do you promise, Hannah?"

It was a much harder promise, but Hannah could see how much it meant to him. "I promise, Norman," she said.

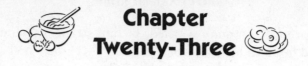

Chapter
Twenty-Three

The coffee was on, Moishe's food and water bowls were filled, and she'd checked to make sure the little locks that Bill had installed on every window were engaged. All she had to do was wash her face, brush her teeth, put on the over-sized T-shirt she used for a nightgown in the summer, and crawl under the covers.

"Come on, Moishe," Hannah said, picking him up from his perch on the penthouse floor of his Kitty Kondo. "It's getting late, and I really need to . . ."

She was interrupted by a knock on the door, three sharp raps that she thought she recognized. A second later, there was a second series of similar raps.

". . . answer the door," Hannah finished her sentence, and put Moishe back on the penthouse floor. "Who's there?" she called out, even though she thought she knew.

"It's Mike. I need to talk to you. You're still up, aren't you?"

No, I'm sound asleep! Hannah felt like saying, but of course she didn't. What she said was, "I'm up. Hold on a second, and I'll get the door."

"Thanks, Hannah." Mike stepped into her living room. "I figured you were still up. I saw Norman driving out."

"Did you talk to him?" Hannah asked, hoping that he'd

say no. Norman was a law-abiding citizen. If Mike had asked him where he was going, Norman would have told him.

"I just waved. I was in a hurry to get over here."

"Is there a break in the case?" Hannah asked, sending up silent thanks to her lucky stars that Mike had been in a hurry.

"Nothing new." Mike did a double take as he saw what was on the wall by her desk. "What's *that?*"

"Moishe's new Kitty Kondo activity center. Norman installed it yesterday." Hannah stopped and thought fast. She didn't want to make Mike feel bad for not thinking of getting one for Moishe. "Thanks to the Animal Channel number you gave me, and his new activity center, Moishe's not destroying things anymore."

"Great! I've got something for him in the cruiser. I'll go down and haul it up here before I leave. I just stopped by to ask you if you learned anything I should know about."

"Actually . . . yes," Hannah said, leading him over to the couch. And then, because she was a good hostess, she asked, "Coffee?"

"Thanks, but I'm all coffeed out. I think it's because I've been drinking the swill at the station. But I wouldn't mind something sweet if you've got it."

"I've got it. I baked almond cake tonight. How about a slice with a glass of milk?"

"Sounds great!"

"Make yourself comfortable and I'll get it." Hannah made a quick trip to the kitchen. When she came back, Mike was sitting on the couch with Moishe in his lap.

"Here you go," she said, setting the cake and the milk on the coffee table. "Try the cake and see how you like it."

Mike took a bite and nodded. "I like it a lot, unless you've been watching *Arsenic And Old Lace.*"

"I haven't seen it for years, and my almonds aren't bitter," Hannah said, referring to the fact that arsenic tasted like bitter almonds. "How did they discover that, anyway?"

"You mean about the bitter almonds?"

"Yes. You can't ask dead people how the poison that killed them tasted."

Mike threw back his head and laughed. "You're right. Somebody must have tasted it without swallowing. Or reported the taste before they died."

"Gruesome. And that reminds me, did Doc Knight run a tox screen on Gus Klein?"

"Yes. It's standard operating procedure."

"Did he happen to find any traces of amphetamine?"

"Why do you want to know *that?*"

Hannah sighed. Mike wasn't being very cooperative. "I saw Gus take a green-and-white capsule at the dance. When I asked him if he should mix alcohol and medicine, he said it was an over-the-counter antacid."

"And you didn't believe him?"

"I believed him at the time. But then I started thinking about it, so I described it to Jon Walker and asked him what it could have been."

"And he told you it could have been an amphetamine?"

"Yes."

"Jon's right. It was an amphetamine. It showed up on the tox screen."

Hannah felt a sinking feeling in her stomach. "When did the tox screen come in?"

"With the autopsy. Doc put a rush on it, and I had it first thing Tuesday morning."

"But I saw you late Tuesday morning at The Cookie Jar! Why didn't you tell me about it?"

"Because it's an official document. It's against regulations for me to share official reports and documents with you."

"So there are things you're not telling me?" Hannah asked him, feeling betrayed.

"A few, yes, but only if they're something confidential that only authorized personnel can know. Besides . . . the amphetamines didn't kill him. He was stabbed with an ice pick or similar object."

The lightbulb of suspicion that had been flickering in Hannah's mind ever since she'd talked to her sisters about sharing information with Mike turned into a steadily glowing globe. She knew the truth now. Mike was holding out on her. Perhaps he didn't mean to. She'd give him the benefit of the doubt. He might truly believe that he was honoring the pact they'd made.

"What about the suitcase on the bed?" she asked. "Were there any more pills in it?"

"Come on, Hannah." Mike gave a weary sigh. "The suitcase is in the evidence room."

"And only authorized personnel can know what's in it?"

"That's right. Some of the contents could be important during the trial."

"*What* trial? You haven't arrested anyone yet."

"No, but we will. And there's no way I want the killer to walk on a technicality because I've been careless with the evidence."

"I understand," Hannah said, and she did. Mike had never said much about it, but Hannah knew that the gang member who'd shot and killed Mike's wife when she was pregnant with their first child had gotten off on a technicality. Bill had told her all about it. It was one of the reasons Mike was so determined to follow police procedure to the letter. No criminal he caught was going to walk free on a technicality if he could help it.

"I'll tell you what I can, Hannah. You know I will."

"I know." Hannah knew that Mike was sharing some information with her. But the information she would get from him wouldn't be critical to the case. He was treating her like an outsider, not a member of his team. And while he might honestly want things to be different, they wouldn't be.

"What's the matter?" Mike asked, frowning slightly.

Nothing that you'd understand, Hannah almost said, but she bit the words back. It was silly of her to be disappointed. She should have known all along that Mike's two-way street was really one-way. He might want to break the rules for her, but he wouldn't.

"Hannah? What's wrong?" Mike asked again.

"I'm just tired," Hannah said, uttering the first thing that popped into her head.

"I'd better go, then. Lock the door behind me, and I'll run down and get that present for Moishe I told you about. I'll knock when I come back up."

Hannah waited, her eye to the peephole. She was expecting to see a distorted image of Mike as he came up the stairs, but instead she saw something huge, bright pink, and fuzzy.

"Okay, Hannah. It's me."

The huge, pink, fuzzy object had Mike's voice, so Hannah opened the door. And then she started to laugh as she saw what he was carrying.

"It's a flamingo," Mike explained unnecessarily. "Didn't you tell me that Moishe liked flamingos?"

"I probably did. He loves to watch them on the Animal Channel. How big is that thing, anyway?"

"It's taller than I am, so it's six and a half feet, at least. And its name is Fred. Where do you want it?"

"Right there," Hannah said, pointing at the corner by the couch. "Will Fred fit there?"

"Sure, if we fold his wing in a little." Mike did just that as Hannah watched. "Too bad Fred doesn't have a tray in its beak, or something. You could use him as a couch table."

Just what I need. A six-and-a-half-foot table shaped like a flamingo, Hannah thought, but of course she didn't say it. Even though Fred wasn't to her taste and he looked dreadful in her living room, she was touched that Mike had thought to get the toy for Moishe.

"Thanks, Mike," she said for lack of anything better to

say. And then, because it sounded so sparse, she added, "Wherever did you find it?"

"Oh. Well . . . actually Fred's recycled. I hope Moishe won't mind."

"I don't think he does," Hannah said, watching her cat approach the big bird and rub up against it. "Is it something the police confiscated?"

"No, it's something I had at my place. Ronni brought Fred back from Florida. She bought him on that trip she took with Bill. And then she moved and she didn't have room, so I kept him at my place. I offered to give him back when she moved in across the hall, but she said she didn't want Fred anymore because he didn't match the colors in her living room."

"I see," Hannah said, wishing she hadn't asked.

"Well, I'd better go. I'm really glad Moishe likes Fred. I got a new 50-inch television and he was in the way."

Hannah walked Mike to the door, thanked him again, kissed him briefly, and sent him on his way. Then she closed and locked the door, and turned to stare at the fuchsia Phoenicopterus.

"I know you like Fred, now," Hannah said, watching her cat rub his head up against the flamingo's legs, "but do you know what he eats?"

Moishe turned to look at her, and Hannah thought he seemed concerned about the diet of Ronni's second-hand shorebird.

"Fred eats shrimp, Moishe, lots and lots of shrimp. Maybe you'd better shred him up now. Then the next time I thaw a bag of shrimp for you, you won't have any competition."

"Rowww!" Moshe responded enigmatically, staring at her with his big yellow eyes.

"You're right." Hannah gave him a smile. "Maybe I'd better take a lesson from you when it comes to Fred's first owner, and shred her, too."

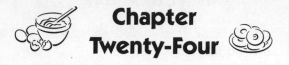

" "Bye, Moishe." Hannah tossed him a few salmon-flavored kitty treats as she headed toward her condo door. "Try to be a good boy again today. I'll be home early this afternoon to feed you."

Her hand had just connected with the doorknob when the telephone rang. Hannah muttered a phrase she wouldn't have used around her nieces in any circumstances and headed back to the kitchen to answer it. The hair on Moishe's back wasn't bristling, so it probably wasn't Delores.

"Hello?" she said, wondering who'd be calling her this early.

"Hi, Hannah."

"Norman!" Hannah began to smile as she recognized his voice. "Where are you?"

"At the airport in Atlantic City. We landed about twenty minutes ago. I'm just waiting to rent a car with GPS, and then I'll be off to find Mood Indigo."

Hannah glanced at the clock. It was five forty-five in the morning. That meant it was seven forty-five in Atlantic City. "It won't be open this early," she reminded him.

"I know. I'll just drive over and take a look at it. Then I'll have some breakfast."

"When are you coming home?" Hannah couldn't help but

ask. It was silly since Norman had been gone for less than a day, but she already missed him.

"If things go the way I hope they will, I should be back early tomorrow morning, maybe sooner if everything works out."

"Well, come by here first thing," Hannah told him. "I don't care how early it is. I want to hear all about it. Or if it's past six in the morning, stop by The Cookie Jar. I should be at work by then."

Hannah had just taken the last two trays of Cherry Winks from the oven and slid them onto the baker's rack when the back door opened and Lisa came into the kitchen.

"Lisa! What are *you* doing here? I thought you were frying pancakes for the big Game Day breakfast this morning."

"That was the plan, but it changed. I got your mother and Carrie to fill in for me."

"Uh-oh!" Hannah winced visibly. "I'm not sure about Carrie, but I know for a fact that Mother's never fried a pancake in her life. Dad always fixed breakfast for all of us."

"Don't worry. Your mother and Carrie are just setting the tables and mixing up the orange juice. That frees up Patsy to help Marge with the pancakes."

Hannah gave a big sigh of relief. "But that still doesn't explain why you're here. I finished the baking, so I really don't need any help."

"Yes, you do. I'm going to help Luanne open so that you can go out to the lake. Dad remembered something this morning, and he won't tell anybody except you."

"Is it about Gus's murder?"

"I don't know. Herb's with him at the cottage, and they're waiting for you to drive out. You don't think Dad might have . . . I mean . . . I just can't believe that . . ."

"Neither can I," Hannah interrupted her, "and I'm positive that he didn't. But maybe he remembered something from the past that'll help catch the killer."

                              *   *   *

Less than twenty minutes later, Hannah was knocking at the door of the cottage. She'd pushed her cookie truck to the limit on the highway and paid no heed to the health of her shocks as she'd flown over the gravel road that ran around the perimeter of Eden Lake.

"Hannah!" Herb greeted her, looking surprised. "How did you get here so fast?"

"Lisa said it was important."

Herb began to frown, and Hannah knew he was mentally calculating the distance and figuring out her average speed. As the only traffic enforcement officer hired by the city of Lake Eden, he'd given out enough speeding tickets to know when someone had broken the law.

"I hope you didn't speed through town," he said.

"I didn't. I did take the gravel road around the lake a little too fast, though."

"How fast?"

"I didn't look at the speedometer, but it was fast enough to bump my head on the top of the truck three times."

"That should teach you to slow down," Herb said, looking very stern. "I really ought to give you a ticket, but it's not my jurisdiction."

"But Lisa *said* it was important," Hannah repeated.

"That's what Jack told us. Come on in, Hannah. Jack's at the kitchen table. He wants to talk to you alone, so after I take you in to him, I'll go down and see if I can help with the breakfast."

Hannah stepped in, and Herb led her to the table where Jack was sitting with a cup of coffee and the box of cookies she'd given him for his birthday. "Here's Hannah to see you, Jack."

"Hi, there," Jack said, smiling at Hannah. And then he turned to Herb. "Thanks for keeping me company, son. Hannah will walk me down to the breakfast when we're through here . . ." he turned to Hannah, ". . . won't you, Hannah?"

"Of course I will."

Jack waited until Herb had left, and then he gestured toward the counter. "Would you like a cup of coffee? Marge made a full pot."

"I'd love a cup, thanks. I'll get it," Hannah filled the clean cup that was sitting by the coffeepot and carried the carafe over to refill Jack's cup. Then she sat down in the chair across from him and waited.

"Your cookies did it, girl!" Jack grinned at her. "I remembered the last time Emmy made them, and that made me remember the reason I got into that fight with Gus. I'll tell you, but you've got to promise me you won't tell anyone else, not even Lisa."

"I promise," Hannah said firmly. What Jack was about to tell her might give her a lead to follow, but it was unlikely that his memories from over thirty years ago would have a direct bearing on the events that had transpired after the dance on Sunday night.

"Gus asked me to lend him some money on the night he left town for good," Jack told her. "We were friends, and I would have given it to him if I'd had any extra, but Emmy and I were barely making it on my salary. Iris was almost two years old, and Emmy was due to have Tim any day. Emmy couldn't work, and it was hard to make both ends meet."

Hannah nodded. She could understand how a young married couple with a toddler and a baby on the way would have trouble paying the bills on only one salary.

"I told Gus I was sorry, but I couldn't help him. And then he said I had to help him because he owed money from a card game, and they'd come after him if he didn't pay it back. I felt awful, but I didn't have anything to give him. All Emmy and I had was the little bit of money we'd put away for Doc Knight to deliver Tim."

"I understand."

"Well, Gus didn't. He wanted me to give him our savings for the new baby. I told him I couldn't. And then I suggested that he ask Patsy. She was working, and she had a pretty good job."

"Did he?" Hannah remembered Patsy saying something about a loan she'd made to Gus that Mac had wanted to collect.

"He said he couldn't, because he hadn't paid Patsy back for the last loan. He owed Marge money, too. And his parents wouldn't help him out again. The last time he borrowed money from them, they'd told him it was time he grew up and accepted responsibility for his own debts."

Hannah was beginning to understand exactly what the fight had been about. "And you got into a fight because Gus wouldn't take no for an answer?"

"In a way, but that's putting it mildly. Now, you need a little background here, or you're not going to understand this next part."

"Okay." Hannah took another sip of her coffee. "Go ahead."

"Well . . ." Jack swallowed hard. "You're sure you won't tell anybody?"

"I swear I won't," Hannah promised.

"Okay, then. I was kind of shy around the girls in high school, but Gus wasn't. We were friends, so I asked his advice about asking Emmy to go out on a date with me. But before I could get up the nerve, Gus asked her out."

"That rat!" Hannah breathed.

"That's right, but it was okay because Emmy only dated him a couple of times and then she said she wouldn't go out with him anymore. When I asked Gus why he'd asked her out in the first place, especially when he knew I wanted to, he told me he was just testing the waters and they were pretty cold."

"That scum!" Hannah stated, a little louder this time.

"Another good word to describe him." Jack gave her a smile. "Of course I didn't believe Gus, but it didn't really matter because the next day Emmy asked me out."

Hannah clapped her hands. "Wonderful! And you fell in love and got married."

"That's right. Not quite that quick, of course, but we got married right after we graduated from high school. Emmy was always a good cook. I think that's where all my girls get it. And her specialty was . . . what did you call these things again?"

"Red Velvet Cookies."

"That's right. Red Velvet Cookies. People used to beg her to make them, and then they started offering her money to bake. Marge's mother hired Emmy to bake for her sewing circle. What do they do at those sewing circles, anyway?"

Hannah blinked. She'd been so wrapped up in Jack's story of the past, his question was a jolt. "I don't know. I've never been to a sewing circle, but maybe it's the same thing they do at the Lake Eden Quilting Club."

"And what's that?"

"They quilt a little, and then they eat cookies and drink coffee. And after that, they gossip about whoever's not there."

Jack threw back his head and laughed. His laughter made Hannah feel good. Except for brief moments with Marge and his children, he'd been solemn and dour for the entire duration of the reunion.

"Go on, Jack," she said, nudging him gently. "Tell me the rest of the story."

"Sure thing. Well . . ." Jack stopped, and all traces of his smile disappeared. "I'm sorry, my dear. I forget."

For a brief moment, the term of endearment puzzled Hannah. Then she remembered that Lisa had taught her father to use *my dear* when he couldn't remember a woman's name.

"That's okay," Hannah said, giving him an encouraging smile. She felt like groaning in disappointment, but of course she didn't. It would have hurt Jack's feelings and served no positive purpose. Instead, she tried to set the scene for him and take him back to the time he'd been describing. "You were just telling me how Emmy used to bake for people," she prompted. "And you said Marge's mother asked Emmy to bake cookies for her sewing circle?"

"That's right! I don't know how I could have forgotten. Anyway, Emmy baked those . . . what are they called again?"

"Red Velvet Cookies."

"Yes. She baked Red Velvet Cookies for the sewing circle. We only had the one car, and she took me to work that morning because she had to deliver them. Her mother was there for a visit, so she was taking care of . . . of . . ."

"Iris?" Hannah prompted.

"Yes, Iris. Our daughter, Iris." There was so much love in Jack's voice that Hannah felt a lump form in her throat. "And when Emmy got to Marge's mother's house to deliver the cookies, she ran into Gus. He wasn't supposed to be there. Everybody thought he'd left the night before. But he missed the bus, and he was waiting around for the next one to take him to camp."

Jack stopped and Hannah could see that he was confused. "What is it?" she asked him.

"That doesn't make any sense. I must be remembering it wrong. Gus was too old for camp. We're the same age, and I was already married to Emmy. Say . . . did I tell you we got married right out of high school?"

"Yes. I think you were talking about baseball camp," Hannah said quickly, before Jack could get off on a tangent. "Wasn't Gus supposed to leave for his Triple A baseball training camp?"

A huge smile spread over Jack's face. "That's it! Gus was supposed to leave the night before, but he missed the bus so he was still home. I bet he was out playing poker and didn't watch the time. He did that a lot. And if you're late for that kind of training, they fine you, and . . ." Jack stopped and looked confused again. "Where was I?"

"You were telling me about the cookies Emmy delivered to Marge's mother. And when she got there, she ran into Gus."

"That's what happened. How did you know that? Say . . . you weren't there, were you?"

"No, but Emmy was. And Gus was. What happened when Emmy saw Gus?"

"She said hello. Emmy was always polite. And then she gave Marge's mother the cookies. Right after that, she went out to the car to come home, but it wouldn't start. And that's when Marge's mother told Gus to take their car and give Emmy a ride home."

This time Hannah had even more trouble stifling a groan. From what she'd learned about Gus and the women he fancied, this couldn't be a good thing.

Jack took a sip of his coffee, and it was clear to Hannah that he didn't want to go on. But she needed to know, and perhaps he needed to tell the story to someone who'd promised never to repeat it. "What happened when Gus took Emmy home?"

"He didn't take her home." Jack's eyebrows met and knit in an angry line.

"Will you tell me? I promise you I won't repeat it. You can trust me, Jack."

"I know. Everybody says that. I didn't know anything, my dear. I was completely in the dark. Emmy didn't tell me about it until I got into that big fight on the night Gus left Lake Eden for good."

"Tell me what Emmy told you." Hannah reached out and took Jack's hand.

"She said Gus got fresh with her and she slapped him and walked over four miles home. Do you know why she didn't tell me about it?"

"She didn't want to worry you?" Hannah guessed.

"No, she didn't want me to kill Gus and go to jail for the rest of my life. She said she needed me and she loved me. And since nothing really happened, she didn't want to tell me about it." Jack stopped talking and blinked back tears. And after a moment, he seemed ready to go on. "Say . . . do you think that's what'll happen? "

"What do you mean?"

"I could have killed him. I was out there walking. Mac saw me from their cottage."

Hannah's eyes widened. "How do *you* know that?"

"Mac told me. He didn't know what to do about it. He said he didn't tell the cops, but he had to tell me."

Hannah was caught off guard. Mac hadn't mentioned anything about telling Jack. She regrouped quickly and asked her own question.

"Do you remember going out for a walk after the dance?"

Jack shook his head. "Marge took her sleeping pill, and we went to bed, the same as we do when we're at home. But I don't sleep very well if it's a different bed. I could have gone out for a walk. That's what I do when I can't sleep."

"You really don't remember walking that night?"

Jack shut his eyes and bowed his head. He kept that position for a long moment and then he raised his head and looked her straight in the eyes. "No, I don't remember," he said. "But there's no reason Mac would say it if I didn't. Will I go to jail if I killed Gus?"

"You didn't kill anybody," Hannah said, purely on instinct. And then, after giving it thoughtful consideration she confirmed it. "I know you didn't."

Jack looked grateful, but dubious. "I hope you're right, my dear. Anyway, I didn't know anything about this Gus getting fresh business until he threatened to tell lies about Emmy."

Hannah felt something niggling in her memory. It was something she heard, and Gus was there. Jack was there, too. It was something from the night of the dance.

"He said if I didn't give him our savings, he'd tell everybody in town that Emmy had . . . Emmy had . . . I can't say it."

"Been unfaithful to you that afternoon?" Hannah guessed, and suddenly she remembered part of the conversation she'd heard in the booth between Jack and Gus.

"Yes! But that wasn't the worst. The worst was . . . was . . . I'm sorry. I forget."

Hannah almost gasped as the section of dialogue between Jack and Gus came back to her in its entirety. Gus had said, *I met another pretty girl today, Jack's oldest daughter, Iris.* And then he'd turned to Jack and said, *She doesn't look at all like you, so I guess she must take after her mother.*

"What is it?" Jack asked, looking confused.

"I just figured it out."

"Figured what out?"

"What your fight with Gus was about. Did Gus claim Iris was his baby?"

Jack's eyes widened, and he clenched his hands into fists. "Yes! That's exactly what he said! I knew he was lying, and I told him so, but he just laughed. And then he said that if I didn't give him our savings, he'd tell everyone in town!"

"So you punched him?"

"You bet I did! Nobody can lie about Emmy like that! Emmy's my wife! I hit him, and I hit him, and I hit him, and the next thing I remember is waking up in the clinic. Doc was stitching up the cut on my face so I wouldn't scare Emmy."

"And Tim was born that night," Hannah said, hoping to bring him back to a more pleasant memory.

"That's right." Jack started to smile. "I was right there. I held her hand until Doc told me to go outside and walk around. And when I came back, there he was! My son, Timmy!"

Hannah knew she should try to bring Jack back to the present. Reliving the memories of his fight with Gus had been painful for him, and it was time to move on. "Timmy's here, you know."

"Timmy's here?" Jack looked disoriented for a moment

and then he smiled. "I know that. He came with his wife and my three granddaughters. They're in that big house thing . . . what's it called?"

"A motor home?"

"That's right. Timmy and his family are in that big motor home parked down by the picnic grounds. He drove it all the way from Chicago for our reunion."

"Actually . . . they're not in the motor home right now. Timmy and his family are at the pancake breakfast with Iris and Marge, and everybody else. Lisa's probably back by now, too. Would you like me to walk you down there?"

"Good idea. I'll join them for breakfast. I hope I didn't eat too many of these cookies and spoil my appetite. What did you call them again?"

"Red Velvet Cookies."

"That's it. Just like the ones Emmy used to bake."

Hannah got up and pushed in her chair. What she'd known all along was confirmed. The only way to clear Jack was to catch the real killer. She motioned for Jack to join her, and when he did, she took his arm.

"Say . . ." Jack said. "Did Emmy give you the recipe?"

Hannah smiled. "Emmy gave me the recipe," she replied. And, in a manner of speaking, she had.

Chapter Twenty-Five

"Good pancakes!" Hannah declared, forking up another bite. "What's the recipe, Patsy?"

"It's just the basic recipe you can find in almost any cookbook. There's nothing special about it."

"But they taste a lot better than that."

"It's because we age the batter," Marge explained. "We mix it up the day before and keep it in a covered bowl in the refrigerator overnight. Then all the flavors blend together, and all you have to do is give it a stir the next morning."

"Look at the one I made, Aunt Hannah," Tracey, Hannah's five-year-old niece, pointed to the pancake sitting on a square of wax paper next to her breakfast plate. "Aunt Patsy helped me make it."

Patsy turned to Andrea. "I told her it was all right to call me Aunt Patsy," she explained. "I hope you don't mind."

"I don't mind at all. Tracey has lots of aunts and uncles that aren't really family members."

"They're pretend aunts and uncles," Tracey told Patsy. "Aunt Hannah is real, because Mom and Aunt Hannah are sisters. And Aunt Michelle's real, too. I don't have any real uncles, but I pretend with Uncle Norman and Uncle Mike and Uncle Herb."

Since Patsy looked thoroughly confused, Hannah stepped

in to change the subject. "That's an interesting pancake, Tracey. Does it taste as good as it looks?"

"I think so. It's from the same bowl as the one I'm eating, so it should be the same."

"And the one you're eating is good?" Andrea prompted her.

"Really, really good. It's the best pancake I ever had. Maybe, if I'm not too full, I'll have one more, but not *this* one." Tracey pointed to the pancake she'd fried.

"You're not going to eat your own pancake?" Michelle asked her.

Tracey shook her head so hard her blond ponytail bounced from side to side. "I have to save it, because it's the first pancake I ever made."

"But food spoils after a while," Hannah reminded her. "You won't be able to keep it forever."

"Yes, I will. Aunt Lisa figured it out for me. She's going to take my pancake home and dry it in her . . ." Tracey stopped and glanced across the table at Lisa. "Would you tell me the name of that machine again, Aunt Lisa?"

"It's a dehydrator. It removes the moisture from fruit and vegetables so that you can store them longer."

"You're going to try to dry Tracey's pancake?" Michelle looked amused.

"Why not?" Lisa gave a little laugh. "And once I dry it, I'm going to shellac it so it won't fall apart."

Herb looked dubious. "But is that going to work?"

"It worked with the cookie ornaments I made for our Christmas tree down at The Cookie Jar. Isn't that right, Hannah?"

"Right. We used those ornaments last year, too, and they held up beautifully." Hannah winked at Lisa. "Of course Norman had to work overtime fixing all the teeth our customers broke trying to get a free cookie from the Christmas tree."

Tracey's eyes widened. "Really?" she asked.

"No, I was just kidding. But it could have happened. Those are real cookies under that shellac."

"And mine's a real pancake," Tracey said, turning to smile at Lisa. "Aunt Lisa's never dried a pancake before. My pancake will be the very first one."

"If anyone can do it, Lisa can," Jack said, leaning over to give Tracey a hug. "What are you going to do with your fine-looking pancake when it's dried?"

"I think I'll hang it on the wall in my room, so I can remember how much fun I had today."

"That's a good idea, but I think you need a fallback position."

"What's a fallback position, Uncle Jack?" Tracey asked him.

"How about calling me *Grandpa Jack?* I'm a little too old to be your uncle."

"Okay," Tracey gave him a smile. "What's a fallback position 'Grandpa Jack'?"

"It's what you do when the first thing you try doesn't work. Do you see that dentist with the camera around here anywhere?"

"He's not here," Hannah spoke up. "Norman had to go out of town, and he won't be back until tomorrow morning."

"Too bad. He could have helped us out. Does anybody else have a camera?"

Lisa gestured toward her husband. "Herb has a digital, Dad. Do you want him to take a picture for you?"

"Not for me, for . . ." Jack reached out and patted Tracey's shoulder. ". . . for my dear, here."

"Tracey," Tracey provided her name before anyone else could do it. "But you can call me *my dear.* I like it, and nobody else calls me that."

"I'm glad you like it, because I'll probably forget your name again." Jack laughed at himself, and everyone else joined in. It was a good moment, and Hannah hoped that he'd forgotten the conversation they'd had and the painful incident he'd remembered.

"So Herb . . ." Jack looked over at him. "Will you take a picture of the . . . the . . ."

Tracey leaned close and whispered something in Jack's ear.

"Right. Will you take a picture of the pancake?" Jack finished his question. "That way Tracey can have the picture framed if the pancake doesn't turn out right."

"I'll do that," Herb promised. "Good idea, Jack."

"Are you through with your breakfast, Grandpa Jack?" Tracey asked him.

"I'm through. How about you?"

"I'm through, too. I wanted another pancake, but I'm too full. Do you want to go to the store for dessert?"

"Did you say *dessert?*" Jack asked, laughing when Tracey nodded. "People don't usually have dessert after breakfast."

"But there's no rule that says you can't," Tracey said, and then she looked a little uncertain. "Is there?"

Jack shook his head. "I don't think so. What did you have in mind?"

"We could get a double Popsicle and ask Mrs. Schultz to split it for us. She's really good at it, and she never breaks them the wrong way."

"Sounds good to me as long as it's not a root beer Popsicle. I don't like root beer Popsicles."

"Me, either. Maybe she'll have lime. That's really good. Or cherry. That's even better." Tracey turned to Andrea. "Is it okay if I go with Grandpa Jack, Mom?"

Andrea smiled. "It's fine with me."

"How about you, Marge?" Jack turned to her. "Is it okay if I go to the store with Tracey?"

Marge laughed. "It's fine with me. I have to start in on the cleanup anyway."

"We'll be right back, so don't worry about us." Tracey stood up and took Jack's hand. And then they walked off together down the road to the store.

"Popsicles for breakfast!" Patsy gave a little laugh as she stood up. "I'd better get started. I have to be down at the lake at eleven to judge the swimming races. I just hope I don't topple off the judge's raft and fall in the lake!"

Andrea laughed. "Falling in the lake with all your clothes on isn't what I'd call fun. That's a nice outfit, and you might ruin it."

"Thanks," Patsy said, glancing down at her light green pantsuit. "It's not just the clothes I'm worried about, though."

"Patsy can't swim," Marge explained.

Hannah was absolutely amazed. The Lake Eden school district had a mandatory water safety program for all of its students. They'd built one of the very first indoor pools, and swimming instruction started in grade school and continued right up until senior lifesaving. "You went to school in Lake Eden and you can't *swim?*"

"That's right, and it's not for lack of trying." Patsy smiled ruefully. "Tell them Marge."

"She can't float," Marge said. "And since she can't float, she can't swim. Patsy can paddle and kick like crazy, but she can't keep her head above water for long."

"They taught me all the strokes and the kicks in the shallow end of the pool. I was really good at those. I know *how* to swim, but I just can't do it. After three or four strokes, I go straight down to the bottom of the pool."

"The swimming teacher came to the house to explain it to our parents," Marge told them. "We were supposed to be playing outside, but we came in and listened. It has something to do with bone density, or specific gravity, or natural buoyancy, or maybe all of those things."

"All I know is, everybody in the whole school tried to teach me to swim, and nothing worked," Patsy said.

"We dressed alike in grade school," Marge went on. "We looked exactly alike, and we had matching pink swimsuits. The swimming teacher couldn't tell us apart."

Patsy gave a little laugh. "Until she told us to get in the pool and float. Marge floated. I sank like a stone. I think that's the reason I don't really want to get out on that raft and judge the swimming races. I get really nervous around deep water. I tried to get Mac to take over for me. He was on the swim team at Jordan High, and he won all sorts of awards. But he's coaching the red softball team, and they've got practice."

"I'll take your place," Michelle offered. "I love to swim, and it won't bother me a bit. You said it starts at eleven?"

"That's right."

"And ends when?"

"It's for all ages, and over a hundred kids are entered. You should be through in two hours."

Michelle gave a little groan. "Uh-oh. I have a conflict. I'm supposed to help with the tricycle parade from noon to two. Unless you want to take my place helping kids decorate their tricycles?"

"I can do that. It's perfect for me. I love kids, and Mac and I never had any of our own. He never really cared one way or the other, but I always wanted to be a mother."

"You would have been a good one," Marge told her. "You sure were good with mine. How about you two?" She smiled at Andrea and Hannah. "What are your plans for the day?"

"We're going out for pizza," Hannah said, motioning to Andrea.

"You're hungry? You can't be hungry! You just had a big pancake breakfast!"

"We're not going for the food," Andrea said, catching on to her sister's agenda. "We're going fishing."

"For information?" Michelle asked.

"Exactly right," Hannah said. "It's about Mary Jo Kuehn and the night she died in that car crash. There are still some people around town who think that it was Gus's fault."

Marge looked sick. "We heard that back then. And he *said* he wasn't driving, but . . ."

"Looking back on it, we think he could have been." Patsy

gave a little sigh. "Do you think that Bert could have killed Gus because he believed that Gus was driving that night?"

"It's a possibility," Andrea said.

"And we won't know until we check out his alibi," Hannah added. "We need to ask Bert where he was between one and three on Monday morning."

"I'll watch Tracey," Michelle promised. "And if you're not back by eleven, I'll take her out to the raft to judge the swimming races with me."

Patsy looked horrified. "Oh, don't do that! What if she falls in the water?"

"It's okay. Tracey can swim," Andrea reassured her. "As a matter of fact, she's entered in the kindergarten races."

"She learned to swim this early?" Marge asked.

"Oh, yes. When Tracey was in preschool, Janice Cox taught the whole class to swim. And this year Tracey's in kindergarten, so she gets to use the school pool."

"I'll make sure I go to the races to cheer her on," Marge promised.

"How long do you think you'll be gone?" Patsy asked, stacking up the plates on the table.

"An hour at the most," Hannah told her.

"You should be fine then," Patsy said with a nod. "I looked at the schedule when I thought I'd have to be a judge, and the kindergarten race is the last one."

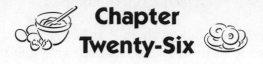# Chapter Twenty-Six

When Hannah and Andrea pulled up in Bertanelli's parking lot, it was far from packed. It was clear that pizza was not the breakfast of choice in Lake Eden. Hannah parked her cookie truck near the door, and they hopped out.

"How are we going to do this?" Andrea asked her.

"We'll just wing it. Do you think you can eat a pizza?"

Andrea thought about it as they went through the door and headed to the main room to find a booth. "I think so," she said. "But only if it's sausage, pepperoni, and extra cheese."

"No anchovies?" Hannah teased her.

"Not before noon. There's something about anchovies in the morning that's just not right, you know?"

Hannah knew. It was a lot like orange juice on corn flakes, a combination she'd once seen a friend attempt to eat when she was out of milk. It wasn't that it was so awful. It was just that it wasn't right.

"Hi, ladies," a waitress came over to greet them a moment after they'd taken a booth near the back of the room. "Can I get you something to drink?"

"Coffee would be good," Hannah told her.

And almost simultaneously, Andrea said, "I'll have coffee, please."

"Two coffees coming right up."

Andrea waited until they were alone again, and then she leaned closer to Hannah. "You mentioned that Norman was out of town. Did he go where I think he went?"

"That depends on where you think he went."

"Atlantic City?"

"That's right."

"To check out Mood Indigo?"

"Right, again. He said he'd call me on my cell phone just as soon as he found out anything at all."

"And you've got your cell phone with you?"

"I do," Hannah said, patting her oversize purse.

"And you remembered to plug it into the charger last night?"

"I did."

"And you've got it turned on?"

"I do."

The waitress came back to their booth with two mugs of coffee. "Here you go," she said, setting a mug in front of each of them.

"Thanks." Hannah decided that there was no time like the present to find out about Bert. "Is Bert in?"

"Not yet."

"How about Ellie?" Andrea asked.

"She's not here yet, either. They're still catching up on sleep from Sunday night."

Hannah and Andrea exchanged glances. "What happened on Sunday night?" Andrea asked.

"The weekly cash register tapes didn't tally with the orders from the kitchen, and we had to find the error."

Hannah picked up on the collective pronoun. "Who's *we?*" she asked.

"Bert, Ellie, and me. I'm the head waitress, so I'm responsible for the others. We went through everything until we found it."

"What was it?" Andrea asked her.

"One of the new waitresses transposed a couple of numbers. It was an honest mistake, but the register was short and we had to account for it."

"So how late were you here?" Hannah asked the critical question.

"Until a quarter to three. We close at midnight on Sundays, so it took us two hours and forty-five minutes to find it."

"I'm glad you found it," Hannah said. And in her mind she added, *in more ways than one.*

"So am I! I'm just glad that nobody had a hand in the till. That happens sometimes in the restaurant business. Would you ladies like a menu? Or do you know what kind of pizza you want?"

"We'd like a medium sausage with pepperoni, and extra cheese." Hannah ordered what Andrea had dictated.

"And mushrooms," Andrea added. "And black olives, too. What other toppings do you have?"

The waitress looked up from her order pad. "How about onions, fresh tomatoes, and anchovies?"

"Yes on the onions and fresh tomatoes," Hannah told her, "but no anchovies." She motioned toward Andrea. "She doesn't like anchovies before noon."

"Can't say I blame her for that!" the waitress said, grinning at Andrea. And then she looked down at her order pad again. "That's a medium sausage pizza with pepperoni, extra cheese, mushrooms, onions, ripe olives, and tomatoes. Is that right?"

"That's right," Hannah said.

"Can I give you ladies a little tip?"

Hannah began to smile. "Absolutely. And if it's a good tip, we'll give you a good tip, too."

"Believe me, it's a good tip!" the waitress said. "You ordered a medium sausage pizza with six extra toppings. Each extra topping is fifty cents and that means you've got an extra three dollars tacked onto your one-topping pizza, okay?"

Both Andrea and Hannah nodded.

"A medium garbage pizza is only a dollar fifty more than a one-topping pizza. And a garbage pizza has all the toppings you just ordered plus anchovies. Do you follow me so far?"

"I think I'm beginning to," Hannah said, starting to smile. "What are you telling us?"

"Why don't you just order a garbage pizza and tell me to hold the anchovies? If you order that way, it'll save you a dollar fifty."

"Good tip!" Hannah said.

"It sure is." Andrea looked delighted. "We'll be sure to double that and add it on to what we would have given you anyway."

"I can't believe we ate the whole thing!" Hannah said, staring down at the empty pizza pan.

"Neither can I. I don't know what got into us."

"That would be pizza," Hannah said, laughing as she glanced around the room. It was filling up for lunch and . . .

"What is it?" Andrea asked, when Hannah's laughter stopped abruptly.

"Déjà vu. Again."

"Very funny," Andrea said, but when she caught sight of Hannah's face she began to frown. "What's wrong, Hannah?"

"Remember the time we came in here for lunch and we spotted Mike with Shawna Lee?"

"I remember. You were really upset."

"That's what I meant about déjà vu."

Andrea looked truly mystified. "What are you talking about, Hannah? Mike *can't* be here with Shawna Lee. She's dead!"

"I know that. It's not Shawna Lee. It's somebody else, but it's like déjà vu because they're sitting in the same booth and she's wearing a tight yellow sweater."

Andrea glanced over at the booth in question. "It's silk,"

she said. "I can tell from here. She's got clothes sense, who-ever she is."

"Do you recognize her?" Hannah asked.

"No. All I can see is the back of her head. Nice hair, but she could be anyone. We'd better look away, Hannah. We're staring too much."

"Why should we look away? They're sitting with their backs to us. They won't know we're staring."

"You don't know that for sure. They might."

"How? Do you think they have eyes in the backs of their heads?"

"Of course not, but maybe one of them is sensitive."

"Sensitive?"

"Like Grandma Elsa," Andrea explained. "I had to sit next to her at church, remember?"

"I remember."

"Well, she used to whisper to me if she thought someone was staring at her, and I'd turn around and look. She was al-ways right. She said she could feel their eyes boring right into the back of her head."

"And you think Mike and that woman, whoever she is, might be able to feel us staring at them?"

Andrea gave a little shrug. "Maybe."

"Okay. We won't stare then. We'll just get up and go over there to see who it is."

"But . . ." Andrea hesitated, and then she shook her head. "I don't think that's a good idea."

"Why? We're all adults here."

"Maybe, but your voice is tight. "

"What does *that* have to do with anything?"

"It means you're all wound up. It's like that windup frog toy Mother bought for Bethany. You wind it and it puffs up. And when you let it go, it spins all over the floor and croaks."

"And you think that if I walk over to find out who that woman is, I'll spin all over the floor and croak?"

Andrea thought it over for a moment, and then she sighed deeply. "Well, maybe not the croaking part."

That did it. Hannah started to laugh. The mental image was just too much to handle.

"Shh!" Andrea warned her. "If you laugh too much, everybody's going to look at us."

Of course that made Hannah laugh harder. And since laughter was contagious, it was too much for Andrea to resist. She began to laugh, too, until both of them were nearly howling with mirth.

"Ronni Ward!" Andrea gasped, clutching Hannah's arm.

"What?" Hannah asked, still in the throes of laughter.

"She's in the booth with Mike. She turned around to look at us, and I saw her face."

If ever there was a sobering thought, a thought that could erase all traces of Hannah's laughter and even her smile, it was the thought of Ronni Ward.

"Are you sure?" she asked, hoping Andrea had laughed herself into a massive hallucination.

"I'm sure. Are you okay, Hannah? You look a little funny."

"That's because I'm turning green. You might have been wrong about the croaking, you know?"

Andrea looked worried. "You mean . . . you're so jealous, you want to die?"

"Not me. I was thinking more of Ronni Ward. And maybe Mike, too."

"Are you serious?" Andrea's worried look grew into something approaching panic.

"Relax. I'm not *that* jealous. I'm just teasing you, that's all."

Andrea let her breath out in a relieved sigh. "For a second there, I thought you were serious. Jealousy can make you . . . who's double-oh-seven?"

"What?"

"Whose ring tone is that?"

"What's a ring tone?"

"I'll explain later. Your cell phone's ringing, and the person who's calling you has the James Bond theme for a ring tone."

"I was wondering where that music was coming from." Hannah reached into her purse, pulled out her cell phone, and answered it. She talked for a moment, and then she turned to Andrea. "It's Norman, calling from Atlantic City."

"Uh-oh!"

"What's an uh-oh?"

"Mike's headed this way. Get up and go to the ladies' room. I'll keep Mike busy, and you can talk to Norman in there."

"It's weird knowing that I'm talking to you in the ladies' room at Bertanelli's," Norman said.

"I know. It feels strange to me, too." Hannah glanced around. The bathroom was neat and clean, but it certainly wasn't a place for lounging or socializing. There was only one place to sit, and Hannah took it. "What time is it there?"

"Almost two in the afternoon."

"Where are you?"

"At Mood Indigo."

Hannah was surprised. "It's open this early?"

"It's open a lot earlier than this. Alison lets them in every day at eleven in the morning. She said they do a lot of business with the lunch crowd."

"Who's Alison?"

"Alison's the . . . uh . . . headliner act at the club."

"Her name is on the marquee?"

"That's right." Norman stopped talking for a moment, and then he came back on the line. "Hold on a second, Hannah. They're about to start the next act, so it's going to get really noisy. I'll try to find a quieter spot."

Norman must not have put her on hold, because Hannah heard a blast of music, followed by raucous shouts from the audience. She couldn't quite make out the words, but it sounded like a boisterous crowd.

"This is fine, thanks," Norman said to someone there.

"Another drink?" a female voice asked.

"No, this orange juice should do it," Norman told her, and then Hannah heard a door shut and the music faded to a dull roar.

"Sorry about that, Hannah," Norman said, picking up where they'd left off. "There's a big lunch crowd today. The construction crew that's been working down the street got paid."

"So they went to a nightclub on their lunch hour?"

"That's right. Except it's not . . ." A blast of music drowned out the rest of Norman's reply, and Hannah began to frown.

"I can't hear you!" she said.

"I know. Hold on again, okay?"

There was a popping sound over the blaring music, and then Hannah heard Norman say, "Thanks, but I didn't order champagne."

A female voice replied, but Hannah couldn't hear her. She did hear Norman's laugh, however, and he sounded fascinated by whatever she'd said.

"It's nice of you to offer, but I'd better pass. I'm talking to my girlfriend."

There was another inaudible utterance by the female, and Norman laughed again. And then the door shut and the music was muted once again.

"What was all *that* about?" Hannah asked.

"You don't want to know. She came in to bring me champagne. It's what Gus told her to do whenever anyone came into his office and shut the door. It was some kind of signal, I guess."

"Do they know he's dead?"

"Not yet. And his name wasn't Gus here at the club."

"Then the detective Marge hired was right, and he *did* change his name."

"That's right. If he hadn't mentioned Mood Indigo, I never would have found a trace of him."

"What was his name there?" Hannah was curious.

"Grant Kennedy. Sounds impressive, huh?"

"Yes, it does. When are you going to tell his employees at the club that he's dead?"

"I'll tell Alison this afternoon when she takes me over to their apartment."

"Alison shared an apartment with Gus?"

"That's right. She says they've been together ever since she came to work here."

"And that was . . . ?"

"Three years ago. She's very good at what she does . . . if you like that sort of thing, of course."

"You don't like blues singers?"

There was silence for a moment and then Norman spoke. "Alison doesn't sing," he said.

"What *does* she do?"

"Uh . . . she dances."

"She dances," Hannah repeated, still having trouble meshing the two mental pictures she had of Mood Indigo, one from Gus and the other from Norman. Gus had described his club as upscale and exclusive, catering to a moneyed clientele. It certainly didn't sound exclusive to Hannah when construction workers came in on their lunch hour!

Since the two mental pictures weren't compatible, Hannah decided to ignore what Gus had told her and concentrate on what Norman had said. Mood Indigo was a place construction workers came on their payday lunch hour to watch the dancers and . . . "Exactly what does it say on that marquee?" she asked Norman.

"Um . . . I told you. It has her name, ALISON WONDER-LAND."

"Oh, boy!" Hannah breathed. She was beginning to understand precisely the type of club Gus had owned. "What else does it say on the marquee?"

There was a long silence and then Norman sighed. "Okay. I was going to tell you anyway, except not on the phone. "It says, FULL FRONTAL NUDITY."

"You're in a *strip* club?"

"Not exactly, if you're thinking of strippers like Gypsy Rose Lee. The talent at Mood Indigo is . . . uh . . . a few notches down on the socially acceptable scale."

Hannah couldn't help it. She started to laugh. She laughed so hard she couldn't talk.

"What's so funny?" Norman asked.

"I was just wondering what your mother would say if she knew you were in a sleazy strip club, drinking champagne."

"I'm not drinking champagne."

Hannah started to laugh again. It reminded her of Andrea's reply to the toy frog comparison, and that made her laugh even harder.

"Do you want me to tell you what would happen if Mother found out about it?" Norman asked, sounding very serious.

Hannah stopped laughing abruptly. Norman sounded grim. "What would happen?" she asked him.

"Even if the people in Lake Eden knew, it probably wouldn't affect my dental business. But Mother would be mortified. She'd be so embarrassed and hurt, she'd want to move away from Lake Eden. And then your mother would lose a partner and a friend. Does any of that sound familiar to you, Hannah?"

"Yes," Hannah said, realizing that Norman had used almost the same words when he'd told her about the Seattle police report and why he didn't want it to be made public.

"You got busted in a strip club when you lived in Seattle?" Hannah could hardly believe she was saying the words.

"That's right. It seems Goldie was running a little side business in the back."

"Goldie?"

"Goldie Lox. She owned the place."

Hannah was beginning to see a pattern here, with names

like Alison Wonderland and Goldie Lox. What was next? Candy Cane? Betty Will? Helen Back? Lotta Moves? And then, because she was getting sidetracked from something much more important, she asked, "What was the side business? Drugs? Prostitution?"

"Numbers. It was just a small operation, mostly sports bets from what I was told. But Goldie got raided, and everyone there was taken into custody."

"But they let you go right away, didn't they?"

"Not until I posted bail for being drunk, disorderly, and resisting arrest."

Hannah was dumbfounded. "You? I've never even seen you take a drink!"

"I did back then. It was my first year at the dental clinic, and we all went out for a drink after work on Fridays. Goldie's place was just down the block, and since she was a client of ours, we used to go there."

"You were Goldie's dentist?"

"It was more than that. She'd bring her girls in to see us whenever they had a dental problem. People might not approve of her line of business, but she was a good boss. I don't think most strip club owners give their dancers free medical and dental care."

It was something that Hannah had never considered before, and it took her a moment to respond. "You're probably right," she said.

"Anyway, that's what happened. They let my partners go because they were smart enough to cooperate with the police. I wasn't, so they kept me overnight."

"Were you convicted?" Hannah asked.

"I pled no contest and paid a fine, but the record stands. And that's why the double scotch I was drinking at Goldie's place was the last drink I ever had."

"Wow!" Hannah said, for lack of something better to say. If someone else had told her that Norman had a drunk, disorderly, and resisting arrest conviction, she would have accused that person of lying. It seemed totally out of character for Norman, and she still had trouble believing it, but she'd heard it straight from the horse's mouth. The Norman he must have been back then was totally different from the Norman he was now.

"So do you understand why I didn't want to tell you about it?" Norman asked.

"I understand. You said you were afraid I'd look at you differently."

"Right."

Hannah heard Norman take a deep breath. "So do you look at me differently?"

"Yes. It makes you seem less perfect and more of a normal person with foibles. And I feel as if I know you better, and I like you even more for telling me about it."

There was dead silence for a moment, except for the muted music in the background. And then Norman chuckled. "Well, that's a relief! I still can't believe you like me better because I've got clay feet."

"Clay is good," Hannah said. "I've got them, too. And so do most of the people I like best."

There was another blast of music, and Hannah knew the door to Gus's office had opened. A second later, it closed again and Norman came back on the line.

"I've got to go, Hannah. That was Alison. She's taking me over to their apartment now."

"And you're going to tell her about Gus?"

"Yes. And I'll ask her if she has any idea why Gus came back to Lake Eden."

"Good. Don't forget to ask her if he had any enemies and if there's anyone from there who might have wanted to kill him."

"Will do. I'll call you right after I leave the apartment. Love you, Hannah."

"Love you too, Norman." The words were out of her mouth before she stopped to think. But she *did* love Norman, so it wasn't a lie. It was possible for a person to love more than one person at once. She was living proof of that!

She punched the button to end the call, and stood up. On her way past the mirror, she fluffed up her hair and pulled her blouse down in back to cover one of her figure faults. Then she hitched up her pants at the waist to hide another figure fault and went out the door to see how Andrea had fared with Mike.

"Hurry, Hannah! Tracey's race is about to start!" Andrea practically streaked across the sand toward the chairs that had been set up on the lakeshore for the audience. Hannah followed, wishing she hadn't eaten that last piece of pizza, and they reached the chairs just in time to hear the whistle blow.

"Which one is she?" Hannah asked, shading her eyes with her hand.

"She's wearing the green bathing cap, the one with the little white flowers on it."

"How far up in the pack is she?"

"She's second." Andrea sounded very proud. And a moment later she let out a little squeal. "She's . . . in the lead! Do you see her? Tracey just passed the boy that was out in front!"

"I see her!" Hannah bounced up and down on the chair. "She's widening the gap, pulling way out in front, and . . . she won, Andrea! Tracey just crossed the finish line!"

"Fantastic! I knew she could do it!"

The two sisters hugged for a moment, and then they sat down again. Both of them were grinning from ear to ear.

"She's just got to join the swim team at Jordan High!" Hannah exclaimed.

Andrea laughed so hard, tears of mirth rolled down her

cheeks. And when she managed to stop laughing, she just stared at Hannah and chuckled.

"What are you laughing about? She'd be great on the swim team. She's fast, and competitive . . ."

"And only six years old," Andrea reminded her. "Tracey's in kindergarten, Hannah. She can't join the Jordan High swim team for at least eight years."

"Right," Hannah said. "Well . . . their loss, kindergarten's gain."

"Did you see me?" Tracey shouted out, racing across the beach to them.

"We saw." Andrea hugged her, wet swimsuit and all.

"You were great, Tracey," Hannah echoed her praise. You outdistanced every one of them."

"Yeah. And Calvin Janowski's pretty fast. I heard his mother say he's got an ear infection and that's why he lost, but I don't believe it. I talked to him before the race, and he was bragging about how he was going to beat me." She stopped and looked up at her mother and her aunt. "Isn't that just like a boy?"

Andrea and Hannah shared a smile, and then Hannah answered. "Pretty much, I guess. But some girls do it, too."

"I know. Karen said that if I got too confident, I was going to come in dead last."

"I think that was just a friendly warning, honey," Andrea said, taking the towel that Tracey was carrying and slipping it around her shoulders.

"Well . . . maybe."

"Karen probably wanted you to be careful not to count your chickens before they were hatched," Hannah added.

"But why not, Aunt Hannah?"

"Why not what?"

"Why not count chickens before they're hatched? You can, you know. Our whole class went out to Egg World on a field trip last year, and the egg lady showed us how to tell a fertilized egg from one that wasn't."

"Really?" Hannah felt dazed. She hadn't known they'd covered all that in kindergarten.

"How did they do that?" Andrea asked, jumping off into deep waters.

"Oh, they put them through the candle machine, and we saw the little baby chicks on the monitor. You could count those, and you'd know exactly how many chicks there would be."

"Well . . ." Hannah was momentarily at loss for words. "I guess you could do that."

"I even asked the egg lady if there was another way to know, because Grandma and Grandpa Todd don't have one of those candle machines."

"What did she say?" Hannah was curious.

"She said that all you had to do was keep the hens away from the roosters, and you wouldn't have any fertilized eggs."

Hannah exchanged glances with Andrea. They were a bit out of their depth, and it was time to change subjects.

"So, honey . . ." Andrea said, doing her best but coming up with nothing.

"Your Mom and I were just wondering what you want to do next?" Hannah bailed her younger sister out.

"I need to change out of my swimsuit and get into my regular clothes. And then I have to find Grandpa Jack, because he said he'd buy me a grape Popsicle and split it with me if I won."

"Do you want to change at Grandma's cottage?" Andrea asked her.

"No, my clothes are in the girls' changing room. If you wait right here for me, I'll just change in there."

Tracey started to scamper off, but she stopped and made her way back. "I almost forgot," she told them. "Mrs. Schultz gave me a message for you, Aunt Hannah. She said that when you got back from your lunch, you should go over and see her."

"I wonder what that's about?" Andrea commented, once Tracey had run off to the changing rooms.

"I don't know, but if she told Tracey it was important, it probably is. I'll head over there now and hook up with you later."

The Eden Lake store was deserted. Everyone was at Games Day. Hannah pushed open the door, and the bell that announced customers tinkled emptily inside. "Ava?" she called out.

Ava emerged from the living quarters in the back, wiping her hands on a dish towel. "Sorry about that. There hasn't been anyone in for an hour, so I washed my lunch dishes."

"Tracey said you wanted to see me?"

"Not really, but I thought I should. It's about the murder, Hannah. It's been eating at me, and I didn't really want to tell you, but then I started thinking about how maybe if I kept quiet some perfectly innocent person would get convicted, and . . ." Ava's voice trailed off, and she gave a little sigh. "He didn't do it, Hannah. He couldn't have. We all went to high school together, and he was the gentlest, the kindest, the nicest . . . I feel like I'm betraying an old friend!"

"Why don't you let me worry about that," Hannah soothed her. "I'm not the police. I don't have to tell them if we decide it's not important."

"You're sure? I don't want to get him in trouble."

"I'm sure. Tell me, Ava."

"It was the night Gus got killed. I did what I told you. Once he left and went back to the pavilion, I got ready for bed. I was about to climb under the covers when the bell rang in front."

"You had a customer?"

"Right. My father installed that bell in case somebody had car trouble or they were running out of gas. Nobody's used it for twenty years, but it worked, and I put on my robe and went to the front door."

"And it was . . . ?"

"Jack. Jack Herman. He was standing there looking confused, so I unlocked the door and let him in. I know about his troubles, and I figured that if he was sleepwalking or something like that, I'd take him back to the cottage and wake Marge."

"So what happened?"

"He wasn't sleepwalking. He was perfectly normal, at least I thought he was. He said he knew it was late, but he saw the light on and he hoped I'd open up and sell him a jar of pickled pig's feet for Marge."

"And you said . . . ?"

"I told him I'd be happy to, but why did he want to buy them now? It wasn't like Marge would want to eat them for breakfast, was it?"

"What was his reaction to that?"

"He laughed and said no, they weren't exactly breakfast food, but they were going to be really busy tomorrow with the family photos and all, and he thought he'd buy them now and have them on hand."

"Did he pay you?"

"Oh, yes. Jack always pays his bills. Even when he and Emmy were poor as church mice, they never charged anything as far as I know."

"Okay. Thanks for telling me, Ava." Hannah fought a feeling of defeat as she turned and headed for the door. She'd hoped that Mac was lying about seeing Jack, but now it seemed that Jack had been out at the time of Gus's murder.

"Hannah!" Patsy looked delighted to see Hannah when she appeared in the kitchen of the Thompson cottage to see if Andrea was there. "I've been looking all over for you."

"Well, you found me." Hannah made herself at home by walking over to the thirty-cup coffee pot the ladies kept going in the kitchen, and pouring herself a cup.

Patsy looked around. The kitchen was crowded with

ladies loading the dishwashers and washing pots and pans in the sink by hand. She motioned to Hannah to follow her into the deserted living room, and they took a seat on the couch.

"Marge just told me what Mac told you last night. You don't think Jack did it, do you?"

Hannah hesitated. What Ava had told her seemed to substantiate Mac's story, but she was on an emotional keel with Ava. There was no way she could believe that Jack had killed Gus. "No. Or at least I'm hoping that Jack didn't do it. I talked to him, and he doesn't remember confronting Gus."

"Would he remember it?" Patsy looked sick as she asked the question.

"I'm not sure, but I'm afraid his memory of that night doesn't count for a whole lot."

"That's what I thought." An angry expression crossed Patsy's face. "I'm so mad at Mac for telling you and Lisa that he ran into Jack on his walk. They were buddies in high school, and I thought they were still good friends. A true friend wouldn't have said anything to anybody."

"Hold on a second," Hannah's mind spun and then screeched to a shocked halt. "You said something about Mac being out on a walk when he ran into Jack?"

"That's right. Mac goes for a walk every night before bed. The doctor told him it was good for his circulation. If he misses his walk, he gets muscle cramps in the middle of the night."

Hannah felt her confusion grow at the two stories she'd heard, one from Mac and one from Patsy, that didn't jibe. "Maybe I'm confused, but this doesn't make sense. Mac told me he saw Jack through the kitchen window at the cottage."

"He did?" Patsy looked shocked. "Where did he say Jack was when he saw him?"

"Coming up the road. And Mac watched him cross over to the pavilion and walk around the side. He said it was the side with the entrance, but he couldn't see whether Jack went inside or not."

"But that can't be right!" Marge looked shocked.

"What do you mean?"

"Mac couldn't have seen Jack walk to the pavilion. There's a big pine tree in the way. We can't see the pavilion at all from the kitchen window. Mac must have run into Jack on his walk. That's the only explanation."

"I don't understand." Hannah was horribly confused. "Why would Mac lie about being out for a walk?"

Patsy just shook her head. "Oh, *that's* easy. Mac hates being in the middle of trouble, and I'm sure he didn't want to answer a bunch of questions from the police. If he admitted he was out for a walk when he ran into Jack, the police might have thought Mac went into the pavilion and killed Gus over the money."

Hannah felt as if her brain was an unfinished sweater that was starting to unravel. Nothing seemed to make any sense. "What money?" she asked.

"I told you before. It's that old loan I made to Gus. Mac wanted to go to Gus and demand that he pay back the money with interest."

"Did he ask Gus to do that?"

"He'd better not have! It was money I earned before we were married, and it was mine to spend as I wanted. I lent it to Gus to keep him from getting into trouble over a big poker game he lost. And I told him he didn't have to pay it back as long as he stopped gambling."

"Did he?"

"For a while, but it was in his blood. Some people are born to take chances, and Gus was one of them. But Mac had no right to try to collect my money. And that's exactly what I said when he told me he was going to do it. It wasn't his business in the first place, and if he'd succeeded, he just would have spent it on the stock market anyway."

"Mac invests in the stock market?"

"He doesn't invest. Investors make money at least part of the time. Mac speculates, and he loses. He's been doing it ever since we were married, and he hasn't made any money yet!"

Hannah decided it was time to get back to the subject. Patsy was getting frustrated, and that wouldn't help. "So Mac didn't want to admit that he was out for a walk, because the police might think he had something to do with Gus's murder?"

"Exactly. And it would be even more suspicious if the police found out about the loan and the fact that Mac had wanted to try to collect it. Mac was afraid they'd take him in for questioning and lock him up. That's why he asked me to lie for him if they came around asking questions. He asked me to say he was home and we were together all night."

"But you weren't."

"No."

"What did you tell him when he asked you to lie for him?"

"I told him I wouldn't, not if they asked me directly. It's just not right to lie. I said I wouldn't volunteer the information, but if someone asked me, I'd have to tell the truth."

Hannah was silent for a moment, adding up the information she'd gotten. "Was Mac angry with you when you told him you wouldn't give him an alibi?"

"He didn't seem to be." Patsy gave a little shrug. "Mac said he could understand how I felt, and he just hoped the police wouldn't nose around."

"He took it *that* well?" Hannah was surprised. "I would think he'd be upset with you for not supporting him."

"I don't think so. Of course with Mac, it's hard to tell. He can smile on the outside and seethe on the inside. We've been married long enough for me to know that."

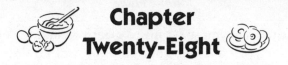

Chapter Twenty-Eight

Hannah was walking down the road from Ava's store to the grassy area that Lisa and Herb had designated for the nonwater games when she heard the James Bond theme again. For a moment she ignored it, assuming that it was someone's radio, but then she realized that it was coming from her purse. Norman was calling her again. She grabbed her cell phone, flipped it open, and answered. "Is it Rhodes, Norman Rhodes?" she asked in her best James Bond voice.

"Hannah! You recognized my ring tone."

"I did. It's the only one that doesn't play the default."

"What's the default?"

"It rings just like a real telephone. Why is yours different?"

"I set it that way before I left for Atlantic City. You can have personal sounds or songs for everyone in your phone book. That way you know who it is before you answer. I'll program it for you when I get back."

"And that'll be tomorrow morning?" Hannah asked, hoping that nothing had delayed him.

"That'll be later tonight. I'm at the airport right now, and I'm catching a flight in twenty-five minutes. It lands at a little after nine. "

"Your time, or my time?" Hannah asked, feeling a bit like a world traveler.

"Your time. Do you want me to meet you at your place?"

"Absolutely! And if I'm not home yet, just go downstairs and get the key from Sue or Phil again," Hannah said. And then she wondered if she'd sounded too eager. "I mean . . . if you want to, that is."

"I want to. Let me tell you what I learned from Alison."

Hannah detoured off the road and into the picnic area. It was deserted since lunch was long over, and she took a seat at a picnic table under a shady tree.

"Okay, shoot," she said.

"Let's start with no safe," Norman said, "and no money, either. The apartment was in an okay area, but it wasn't anything like the penthouse Gus bragged about."

"Then it was all lies?"

"Yes, and that includes the masseuse and manicurist on call, the dinner parties catered by a four-star restaurant, and anything else he mentioned. Everything about Gus was fake. Mood Indigo pulls in enough money to stay in business and pay living expenses, but that's about it."

"How about the Jaguar?"

"Leased. Alison said Gus had one valid credit card when he left, and that was canceled yesterday. She got the notice in the mail. Even worse than that, a month ago he borrowed money from the kind of people who break arms and legs if you're late paying them back, and they charge a lot more than the prime lending rate. Do you get my drift?"

"Oh, yes," Hannah breathed, actually feeling sorry for Gus.

"Alison said they came around looking for Gus at Mood Indigo right before he left. He gave them the money from the till, but they said that if he didn't come up with the rest by the end of this week, they'd have to think of some way to encourage him."

"Uh-oh!"

"Uh-oh is right. Alison said Gus was pretty worried when they closed the club that night, and she tried to distract him with some programs she'd taped. One was an antiques show with appraisers that travel around the country and do appraisals for people."

"I know the one she's talking about. It's one of Mother's favorite shows."

"Well, Alison and Gus were watching it, and all of a sudden Gus got up and started to pack his best clothes. He told Alison that he had to go back to his old home town, because he'd left something there that was worth a whole lot of money."

"What was it?"

"He didn't tell her, but she's almost sure that something he saw appraised on the television show gave him the idea."

"What was on the show that night?" Hannah asked the logical question.

"Alison wasn't sure. She said she was tired and she kept falling asleep. The only things she could remember were a black teddy bear, some kind of famous photograph, and some baseball cards."

Hannah pulled her notebook out of her purse and rummaged in the bottom for a pen. "Okay," she said. "The Antiques Show with a black teddy bear, a famous photograph, and baseball cards. I'll find Mother and Carrie, and ask them if they saw that episode."

"Great. I think we're getting close, Hannah."

"Me, too," Hannah said, although she still didn't have any definitive answers. "You did a great job, Norman."

"Thanks. Just remember what you promised me about calling Mike to watch your back . . . okay?"

"Okay," Hannah said, stacking a second promise on top of her first, and wondering if the penalty was exponential for breaking a double promise.

Hannah spotted her mother on the edge of the crowd, looking like the queen at Ascot. She was sitting up ramrod straight in a green Adirondack lawn chair, and she was dressed in a white chiffon gown that tied at the waist with a wide red sash. As a concession to the bright summer sun, or perhaps as a tribute to outmoded fashion, she wore a wide-brimmed white hat with a red chiffon band around the crown. The band was adorned with red and white flowers, and Hannah began to smile as she approached. No other women in Lake Eden would have the nerve to wear such an outlandish hat, but Delores carried it off with panache.

"Hi, Mother," Hannah took the empty chair next to her mother and turned to Carrie. "Hello, Carrie. I've got a question I need to ask both of you."

"First I've got some information for you," Delores said, leaning closer, even though there was no one close enough to hear. "Carrie and I drove out to the Inn this morning, and we asked Sally about that credit card Gus used for the brunch."

"The charges went through just fine," Carrie picked up the story. "Sally said she always runs it through right away when it's a credit card from someone out of state."

"I'm glad Sally was so prompt," Hannah said. "If she'd waited a few days, she would have been out of luck."

"The credit card's been canceled?" Delores guessed.

"Right. You two watch the Antiques Show on television, don't you?"

Delores nodded. "Every week. Stan says we can deduct it as a legitimate business expense so we watch it live, and then we order the whole season through our Granny's Attic account. Since we own an antique store, it's research for us."

"Makes sense," Hannah said. "Did you watch it last week?"

Carrie laughed. "Of course we did. We haven't missed an episode yet."

"That was the one with the black Steiff bear, wasn't it, Carrie?" Delores asked.

"Yes. And the heart-shaped jewelry box with real diamonds and rubies on the top. There was a signed Ansel Adams, too."

"Maybe I'd better tell why I'm asking," Hannah said. And she proceeded to tell them part of what Norman had uncovered in Atlantic City. Naturally, she didn't mention Mood Indigo's true character. She just said that it wasn't a fancy nightclub the way Gus had described it to them. In her version of events, Mood Indigo was merely a cheap bar, and Alison was Gus's manager.

"So that's why I need to know what was on the show," Hannah wound up her story. "Gus's manager said they watched the show together, and then he told her that he had to go back to Lake Eden because he'd left something there that was worth a whole lot of money."

"And Norman uncovered all that?" Carrie asked, looking very proud of her son.

"Yes, he did," Hannah told her.

"Maybe he should have gone into the detective business. He certainly seems to be good at it."

"Don't even say something like that!" Delores warned her. "Just think of how you'd worry if Norman had to chase around after dangerous criminals."

"You're right," Carrie said, giving a little nod. "I didn't even think of that part of it."

Hannah decided it was time to get off that train of thought before Delores remembered that her own daughter had come into contact with the very same criminals she was warning Carrie against. "Anyway, we're sure that Gus came back here to get something valuable he left behind. I know he went through some of his old things. That night at the dance, he was talking about going through the trunk in Lisa's attic and looking for keepsakes from his childhood. He said he took a teddy bear and the baseball bat he used in high school."

"Maybe the bear was a Steiff," Carrie suggested. "A genuine nineteen-oh-seven black alpaca Steiff was worth a fortune, and it wasn't even in mint condition."

Delores agreed. "There's the bat, too. It could have been signed by a famous baseball player."

"But there weren't any baseball bats on that episode," Carrie reminded her. "There was the young boy with the baseball cards, but no bats."

Hannah realized that they were getting nowhere fast. "Let's go find Marge and Patsy," she said. "You can tell them what items were on the show, and they can tell us if they think Gus might have had something like that in his old room."

They sat around the kitchen table in the cottage where Marge and Jack were staying, sipping fresh coffee that Marge had just made. A plate of the Red Velvet Cookies Hannah had baked for Jack sat in the center of the table, contributed by Jack before Tim had come to take him off to the softball game.

"A Steiff bear?" Marge exchanged glances with Patsy and they both burst out laughing.

"Believe me, it wasn't an antique Steiff!" Patsy said, still chuckling. "The bear Gus took was from Uncle Carl's Five and Dime. Aunt Minnie and Uncle Carl gave every one of us a teddy bear when we were born."

Hannah listened while her mother and Carrie described the items on the show. She was amazed at how much they remembered, but Marge and Patsy kept shaking their heads.

"And then there were the baseball cards the little boy brought in," Delores said.

"They were appraised at eight hundred dollars for insurance purposes, but you wouldn't get more than half of that if you sold them at auction," Carrie said. "That wouldn't be enough to bring Gus back to Lake Eden, would it?"

Marge shook her head. "He spent more than that while he was here. Gus treated over twenty relatives to champagne brunch, and that didn't come cheap."

"Gus did have Grandpa's baseball cards, though," Patsy reminded her. "Dad gave them to him when he made the team at Jordan High."

"He didn't happen to have . . . I mean . . . it's not possible that there was actually a . . . um . . . do you remember if he had . . ."

"Wait!" Hannah interrupted her mother. Delores was so excited she couldn't seem to get the words out. "Take a deep breath, Mother. And then tell us what you're trying to say."

Delores took a deep breath. And then she exhaled with a whoosh. "Honus Wagner," she said.

"You're right!" Carrie's mouth dropped open for a moment, and then she closed it with a snap.

"After the little boy left with his baseball cards, the appraiser mentioned that there was a holy grail of baseball cards. That's what he called it. The last time that card came up for auction, it sold for over two million dollars."

Patsy made a little sound, and they all turned to gaze at her. She looked dazed, almost as if someone had bopped her over the head.

"What is it?" Hannah asked her.

Patsy just sat there motionless, staring at the wall and not blinking. Hannah was wondering if she should call for medical help, but then she seemed to snap out of it.

"Oh, my!" she said. "It's just . . . I think I *remember* that card. Honus Wagner is a really unusual name."

"Do you remember what the card looked like?" Delores asked her.

"I'm . . . I'm not sure. It's been over thirty years, but . . ." Patsy stopped and took a deep breath. "I think it had a picture of short-haired man with a black collar and "PITTS-BURGH" written across his chest in block letters."

"That's it!" Carrie shouted.

And at almost the same time, Delores exclaimed, "Gus actually has a Honus Wagner baseball card?"

"*Had* one," Hannah reminded her mother.

Marge drew in her breath sharply. "Do you think that's the reason Gus was killed? For the baseball card, I mean?"

"It could be," Hannah told her. "If it's worth that much money and the killer knew it, it's certainly a compelling reason."

"Then that means the killer has the Honus Wagner card!" Carrie looked very excited. "If we can find the Honus Wagner card, we'll find the killer!"

Hannah knew she could punch several elephant-sized holes in Carrie's logic, but she chose to refrain. What Carrie had said would work to her advantage.

"The killer doesn't know we found out about the card," Hannah told them. "And that means we can't breathe a word about it."

"Because anybody here could be the killer?" Delores guessed.

"Exactly. And even if you tell someone you *know* couldn't possibly be the killer, news like this is bound to get out. Just one wrong word could do it. Or even a suspicious reaction to something someone says. And if you actually mention it, someone could overhear you, or the person you tell could inadvertently let something slip. We have to keep our guard up and pretend we don't know a thing about it."

"Very true," Delores said with a nod. "Your father used to say that three men can keep a secret, but only if two of them are dead."

That lightened things up a little, but Hannah wasn't through. She had a plan, and she wasn't about to let loose tongues ruin it.

"Just think about how wonderful it'll be if we can recover that baseball card," she said. "I'm sure Mother and Carrie would be happy to help you sell it."

"Of course we would!" Delores said quickly.

"Naturally," Carried echoed. "And since we're friends, our fee would be just a tiny bit of what some antique dealer who didn't know you would charge."

"Of course all that goes up in smoke if the killer gets a whiff of what we know," Hannah reminded them. "It would be a real pity if he tossed a two-million-dollar Honus Wagner card in the lake to keep from being incriminated!"

There were collective sighs around the table. Patsy and Marge exchanged glances, and Hannah knew they'd keep mum. Carrie and Delores would, too, especially since she'd reminded them of the stakes. If the killer thought that they were hot on his trail and ditched the Honus Wagner card, they could be the antique dealers who'd *lost* the sale.

"Let's meet right here after the talent show," Hannah said. "Michelle, Andrea, and I won't be there. We're going to come up with a plan to smoke out the killer, and that's when I'll tell you about it."

Chapter
Twenty-Nine

The mosquito lotion had been slathered on, her coffee cup had been filled, her cell phone was in her hand, and Hannah sat on the end of the dock at their family cottage. To call, or not to call . . . that was the question. She'd made that infernal promise to Norman, not once, but twice. If what they were planning to do was dangerous, she was honor bound to tell Mike. But was it dangerous? Hannah wanted to believe it wasn't, but they were about to search the cottages. The thief who had the two-million-dollar Honus Wagner card had already killed once to get it. There was no reason to doubt that he'd kill again to keep it!

She had to tell Mike. Hannah punched in his number and waited for her call to connect. She half-hoped he wouldn't answer, but of course he did.

"Hi, Hannah," Mike said, before she could even open her mouth.

"How did you know it was me?"

"I could tell by your ring tone."

Prudence warred with curiosity, and curiosity won out. "What's my ring tone?" she asked.

"Oh. Well . . . actually it's . . . an old Beatles song that I like."

Mike sounded embarrassed, and Hannah couldn't resist following up. "What's the name of the old Beatles song?"

" 'Here Comes The Sun.' "

"Why did you choose that one for me?" Hannah asked, although she was secretly relieved that it hadn't been "Eleanor Rigby."

"It's kind of crazy, but whenever I'm around you, I feel like the sun is shining. Whether it is or not, I mean."

Hannah came close to tearing up, it was so sweet. She really didn't know how to respond, but she was saved by an electronic beeping that came over the line.

"Can you hold on a second?" Mike asked. "That's Lonnie, and he's out in the field."

Hannah told him she would, and she sat there contemplating the dusk. The sun had gone down, but the moon appeared brilliant tonight, looming over the opposite shore like a huge silver globe in the sky. It was a full moon, or very close to it, and Hannah thought that if she had a book or a magazine, she could probably read it in this light.

"Sorry about that." Mike came back on the line. "Lonnie's at Bertanelli's Pizza to check on Bert's alibi, but Bert and Ellie took the night off."

"They're out here at the lake for the children's talent show," Hannah told him.

"Thanks. I'll call Lonnie back and send him out."

"Don't bother. Andrea and I checked it out when we were in there for lunch today, and Bert had an ironclad alibi."

"But Bert wasn't there. I asked. That's the only reason I took Ronni out to lunch."

I'll bet! Hannah thought, but of course she didn't say it. She was still too flattered at learning the ring tone Mike had chosen for her.

"How did you substantiate his alibi?" Mike continued, and Hannah knew he'd opened his notebook and was sitting there, pen poised to write down what she said.

"We talked to the head waitress. When they checked the tape from the register after they closed at midnight, it didn't match the total from the order slips. The head waitress, Bert, and Ellie were there until a quarter to three in the morning, looking for the error."

"Bert was there the whole time?"

"Yes. You can cross him off your list." Hannah decided it was time for a gentle nudge. "If you'd mentioned that you suspected him, I would have told you to cross him off right away."

Mike sighed. "My mistake. What else did you find out?"

"Some things you probably know already."

"Like what?"

"Like Gus didn't own any upscale nightclubs. Mood Indigo is a strip joint, and he lives in a little apartment with one of his dancers."

"How did you . . . ?"

"Never mind," Hannah cut off the question. If he didn't ask it, she didn't have to answer it.

"Okay. What else do you know?"

"He changed his name to Grant Kennedy."

"We knew that. It was on his driver's license."

Hannah wanted to ask why he hadn't told her, but she figured she'd just get the runaround again. "Gus borrowed money from some well-connected thugs who have some scary ways of collecting."

"That figures. Go on."

"The night he left Atlantic City, Gus and his girlfriend were watching the Antiques Show, the one where they do the appraisals. She said that before it was over, he got up and started packing a suitcase. And he said that he left something valuable in Lake Eden, something that could get him out of money trouble, and he had to go back and get it."

"Of course!" Mike sounded amazed that he hadn't thought of that himself. "He came back to Lake Eden to get the Honus Wagner trading card. Our appraiser said it was worth over two million."

Hannah gulped audibly. "You *know* about the Honus Wagner baseball card?"

"Sure. We've got it in the evidence room. It was with a bunch of other baseball cards in his suitcase."

"And you didn't *tell* me about it?" Hannah began to do a slow burn.

"It's *evidence,* Hannah. I can't give you a list of the *evidence* unless you're a sworn peace officer."

Hannah counted to three. And then, because she was still seeing red, she counted on to ten. She should have known that Mike wouldn't bend any rules for her. "Do you think Gus was killed for the Honus Wagner card?" she asked.

"I doubt it. If the killer knew about it, he would have searched the cottage, looked in the open suitcase, and grabbed the card. It may be the reason the victim came back to Lake Eden, but it wasn't the reason he was killed."

"Do you have any idea why he was killed then?"

"Not really, now that you cleared Bert Kuehn. But we're working on it. Somebody picked up that ice pick and stabbed him."

"You know for sure it was an ice pick?"

"Not conclusively, no. But Doc Knight found some tiny flecks of red and green paint. That matches what you told me about the ice picks that your grandfather gave for Christmas gifts. I had Rick check with the tool companies, but he couldn't find any that manufactured an awl with red and green paint on the handle, so I figure it's got to be one of your grandfather's ice picks."

"Grandfather wouldn't be happy about that," Hannah said with a sigh. "Did you find the ice pick?"

"Not yet. We got a bad break on that. If the killer was smart, he ditched it in the lake. That's almost impossible to drag."

"Why?"

"Because it's too big, and the murder weapon is too small. It would take months, and if it's under a submerged branch or buried point down in the mud, we'd never find it anyway."

"So where did you look?" Hannah asked him.

"We went through the dumpsters at the pavilion in case the killer dropped it there, but we didn't find it. And then we used a metal detector in the bushes surrounding the building." Mike chuckled slightly. "We found nine beer can openers, too many bottle caps to count, a rusted license plate from nineteen-fifty, and eleven dollars and forty-eight cents in change."

"How about the cottages? Did you search them?"

"Only the one Gus was staying in. I knew getting search warrants would be tricky since we didn't have probable cause, and I decided it would be wasting my team's time to search any of the other cottages. The killer would have to be crazy to hang onto the murder weapon."

"You're probably right," Hannah said, but she wasn't so sure. While it might be true that a cold-blooded killer would get rid of the murder weapon immediately, it might *not* be true for someone who struck out in the heat of the moment and then panicked when he saw what he'd done.

There was another series of electronic beeps, and Mike sighed. "I've got to take that. It's Rick Murphy from the crime lab. He's observing."

Hannah said goodbye and snapped her phone shut to end the call. There was no longer a reason to search for the baseball card, but they could search for the ice pick. Mike wasn't going to do it, and they didn't need search warrants, not if they did it while everyone was at the children's talent show.

The dark shadows from the pines loomed overhead as dusk turned into night. Hannah watched the reflection of the moon on the water and mulled over everything she'd learned until she felt the vibration of footsteps on the dock.

"We're back," Michelle announced, dropping down into a sitting position next to Hannah. "Everyone from the cottages you want us to search is in line to get into the pavilion."

"Let's review to make sure," Hannah said. "Marge and Jack?"

"They're with Herb and Lisa," Andrea reported.

"How about Patsy and Mac?"

Michelle nodded. "They're a little farther back in line, ahead of Edna and her sister."

"Mother and Carrie?"

"They were . . . we're not going to search Mother's cabin, are we?" Michelle sounded thoroughly shocked.

"No. I just wanted to make sure you were paying attention."

In the next minute or two, Hannah cited six more names. When she'd been assured that her sisters had spotted all of them in line at the pavilion, she turned Andrea. "Did you bring the flashlight from your car?"

Andrea patted the Red Owl Grocery bag she'd placed next to her on the dock. "Got it. And we got the two mag lights from your cookie truck. So the search is on, right?"

"It's on, but the objective has changed." Hannah felt a bit like a general, giving instructions to his troops. "We're not going after the Honus Wagner baseball card anymore. I talked to Mike, and he told me it was in Gus's suitcase, and it's locked up in the police evidence room. What we're going for now is an ice pick with a red-and-green painted handle."

"Like the antique ones Grandpa Swensen gave out in his hardware store?" Andrea asked.

"Exactly like that. Doc Knight found flecks of red and green paint and we're pretty sure that one of Grandpa's ice picks is the murder weapon."

"Searching is boring work when you don't find anything," Michelle grumbled as they came out of the pink cottage.

"I know," Hannah said. They'd found two ice picks, but one had a metal handle, and the other one had an orange plastic handle.

"We've searched five places already, and the only even vaguely interesting thing I found is that one of Lisa's brothers and his wife use different brands of toothpaste," Michelle complained.

Andrea shrugged. "It's not that bad. Don't forget that we could be suffering through the children's talent show."

"You've got a point," Hannah said, glancing over at the pavilion, which had been released as a crime scene this morning and reopened for Lisa and Herb to use. "Only two cottages to go."

"Let's get it done," Andrea said, opening the door to the cottage where Patsy and Mac were staying and stepping inside.

Hannah headed straight for the kitchen. "Remember to keep your flashlights pointed down below window level. We don't want anyone to see a light and decide to check it out while we're here."

She didn't turn around to look, but she knew that Michelle was going to the bedroom and bathroom, while Andrea searched the living room. They'd developed a routine, and it was working well for them. Hannah pulled open the drawers, one by one, and examined the contents. Most of the rental cottages had similar items in their kitchens. One drawer held mismatched silverware that had been moved to the summer cottage when the owner had purchased a new set for the house in town. Another drawer contained cooking utensils that had been relegated to the cottage when better ones had replaced them. The pots and pans were from yard sales or closeouts at CostMart.

Hannah moved on to the drawer next to the refrigerator. That was where most summer cottage owners kept the minimal set of tools used to tighten doorknobs, hang pictures, or pry things open. She made her way through a light hammer, two screwdrivers, one of each type, and a pair of pliers. And under those tools was something that made her gasp and step back in surprise.

There it was, one of her grandfather's ice picks. The paint on the red-and-green wooden handle was flaking off, but the point was sharp and wicked looking. Was this the ice pick that had killed Gus Klein? And if it was, what was it doing in the kitchen of the cottage that Mac and Patsy had rented for the reunion?

"Hannah?" Michelle called out. "There's nothing in the bedroom or bathroom."

"Nothing in the living room, either," Andrea added.

"Are you almost done?" Michelle asked.

Hannah was silent. She hadn't heard the question. Her mind was racing, trying to put the pieces together. Was it possible Mac had stabbed Gus when Gus refused to repay the old loan that Marge had told her about? And had he lied about seeing Jack from the kitchen window because he wanted to throw suspicion on someone whose memory was failing, someone who couldn't defend himself?

"Hannah?" Michelle called out again.

"What's wrong?" Andrea asked.

This time their voices broke through the busy workings of her mind, and Hannah whirled to see both of her sisters standing just inside the kitchen door.

"I've found the ice pick," she said. "It's in the tool drawer. And I think I know who killed Gus."

Chapter
Thirty

"Where are you, Hannah?" Mike answered on the first ring.

"Outside the pavilion with Andrea and Michelle. I found the ice pick, Mike."

"Where?"

"In Mac and Patsy's cottage. And I think Mac killed Gus."

There was a moment of silence, and then Mike sighed. "But that doesn't make sense, Hannah. If Mac killed Gus with the ice pick you found, why would he *keep* it?"

"I don't know. Maybe he was afraid that the owner of the cottage would notice it was missing. And since Gus was killed with an ice pick, somebody like you would put two and two together and come up with him as the killer."

"Okay. It's circumstantial, and we don't even know if the ice pick you found was the murder weapon, but I can see why you're suspicious. Do you have anything else to point a finger at Mac?"

"Yes! Mac told me he looked out the kitchen window in the cottage where he's staying with Patsy, and he saw Jack Herman out for a walk right around the time Gus was murdered. And he was lying."

There was a long silence, and Hannah began to frown. "Mike? Did I lose you?"

"You didn't lose me. It's just that Mac told us the same thing. Why do you think he's lying?"

"Patsy told me Mac went out for a walk that night. He goes for one every night, doctor's orders. He couldn't have seen Jack through the cottage window. There's a big pine tree in the way. He saw Jack on the road, all right, but they were *both* out there. And all this time, I've been afraid that Jack killed Gus."

"Me, too," Mike said, "and there's no way I wanted to believe that."

"But you didn't bring him in for questioning," Hannah reminded him.

"No. I probably should have, but . . . why? We all know Jack's memory goes in and out. And . . . well . . . there's no real proof he did it."

"You're a good man, Mike," Hannah said, meaning every word of it.

"Thanks. But maybe I'm not. Maybe I just didn't think I could get anything useful out of questioning somebody with Alzheimer's."

"There's that, too," Hannah said, "but I prefer to think that you cut him some slack because you thought it was the right thing to do."

There was another silence, and then Mike cleared his throat. "You said you found the ice pick. Where was it exactly?"

"It's in the kitchen tool drawer."

"You didn't touch it, did you?"

"Of course not! I left it right where it was."

"Okay. Everything you told me is circumstantial, but it's the best we've got unless we actually find traces of blood on the ice pick. Do you think Patsy will testify that Mac went out for a walk?"

"I'm almost sure she will. She told me that Mac came to her and asked her to lie for him. He wanted her to say he was with her all night, but Patsy refused. She told Mac she wouldn't volunteer the information, but if you asked her directly, she wouldn't lie for him."

"Good for her! I'll be right out to pull Mac in for further questioning. He's definitely a person of interest, if not more. Where is he right now? Do you know?"

"He's watching the children's talent show, and Patsy's with him. Andrea and Michelle saw them in line, waiting to get inside the pavilion."

"Good. Go on in and watch him for him, and don't say anything to anybody. I don't want him to know we're interested in him. I should be there in less than fifteen minutes to take him in for questioning."

"Okay. We'll go inside and watch him. What do you want us to do if he leaves?"

"Don't follow him. If he *is* the killer, it could be dangerous if he thinks anybody's on to him. Just let him go, and we'll find him later."

"Okay. Anything else?"

"Keep an eye on his wife, too. If he thinks she might mention that walk he took, he could try to silence her."

Hannah gulped. "You mean he might . . . kill her?"

"That's *exactly* what I mean." Hannah heard an engine roar into life. "I've got to go, Hannah. I'm on my way, and I need to keep this line open."

Once Hannah hung up, she turned to her sisters and related what Mike had said. "He said he'll be here in fifteen minutes," she concluded.

"Let's go find Mac and Patsy," Andrea led the way to the door of the pavilion. "If we fan out, it'll be easier for us to see them in the audience. Lisa said they were making three aisles. There's one in the middle and one on either side."

"I'll take left," Michelle said.

"And I'll take the middle and look on both sides," Andrea said. "It'll take me a little longer, but that way I can double check for both of you."

"That leaves me with the right," Hannah said. "We'll just walk down the aisles, turn around, and walk back. Then we'll get together right outside the door to see which one of us spotted them."

When they entered the pavilion, the Beeseman sisters were ending their five minutes of song with "Gary, Indiana" from *The Music Man,* a perfect choice since it was their home-town.

The next act started the moment the Beeseman sisters left the stage. It was a group of twelve girls with lighted batons, performing an act to a Sousa march. All eyes were on the stage to see who could twirl her baton the longest without dropping it, and it was the perfect time to canvas the audience without being noticed. Once her sisters had arrived at their starting points, Hannah motioned them forward.

Hannah's eyes scanned the rows as she moved slowly forward, down one row to the end, up to the row in front of it, and then all the way back to the aisle. Like the carriage on an old-fashioned typewriter, she wove her way to the front of the room, and then she started the return trip.

Where only the backs of heads had been visible on her way to the front of the room, Hannah could see actual faces on her return trip. She saw her mother and Carrie, Jon Walker and his wife, Earl Flensburg, and Marge's cousins from Florida, but she didn't spot Patsy or Mac.

Hannah finished first, and she ducked out the door to wait for her sisters. Michelle came out next and she was shaking her head.

"You didn't spot them?" Hannah asked her.

"No, and there were no empty chairs, so they weren't in the bathrooms or anything like that."

"Good for you!" Hannah complimented her foresight. "Let's just hope that Andrea spotted them."

It seemed to take forever, but it probably wasn't more than a minute or two before Andrea came out.

"Anything?" Hannah asked her.

"No. I checked both sides, and they weren't there. I'm sure of it, Hannah."

"What now?" Hannah asked, the sinking feeling in her stomach growing into a full-blown panic. "You saw them in line."

The door opened again, and the three sisters turned to stare as Marge stepped out. "Hi," she said. "I saw you come in, and then I saw you leave. Is something wrong?"

Hannah gave a little sigh. "It could be. We were looking for Mac and Patsy, but we didn't spot them in the audience."

"They decided to skip the talent show," Marge reported, and she looked happy. "They were waiting in line, and Patsy said Mac had a change of heart. He begged her to give their marriage one more chance, and he said he wanted to take her to the water lily garden to propose to her all over again."

"The water lily garden in the middle of the lake?" Hannah asked, feeling her panic grow.

"That's right. It's where he proposed to her the first time. Isn't that just too romantic for words?"

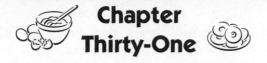

Chapter
Thirty-One

Things happened so fast that Hannah's mind spun, even though she was the one who was making them happen. Hannah and Michelle raced for a canoe, while Marge and Andrea waited on the road for Mike so that they could tell him where they'd gone.

No more than two minutes passed before Michelle and Hannah were paddling out in one of the rental canoes. Lisa and Herb had lined them up on the shore for the relatives to enjoy, and Michelle and Hannah had claimed the one on the end for their own.

"Do you know where the water lily garden is?" Michelle asked her.

"It's just off Sandy Point," Hannah told her. "Norman took me there."

It was a still night, and sounds carried across the water. There was the sound of the waves lapping against the shore, the occasional cry of a night bird, and a splash as some creature of the lake surfaced and then dove back down again.

Hannah held her finger to her lips, and Michelle nodded to show she understood. Their words would carry a great distance if they spoke aloud.

Another minute or two of steady paddling and they could hear voices. At first they were indistinct. Only the intonation was heard. It sounded conversational, rather than confrontational, and Hannah took heart. She couldn't tell how far away they were, but she knew it would take them at least five more minutes of paddling to get to the water lily garden.

Then the tone of the voices changed, and the words became distinct. The woman, Hannah was almost certain it was Patsy, sounded angry.

"I don't understand!" her voice floated over the water. "What difference does it make if the police know you went for a walk? They can't arrest you for murdering Gus if you didn't do it!"

Mac gave a mirthless chuckle. "Oh, but I did," he said.

"You . . . *did?*" Patsy sounded horrified.

"That's right. I told you I wanted to get that money back, and I went over to the pavilion to get it. Gus said *you* gave it to him. And since it was *your* money in the first place, he didn't have to pay *me* back."

"He was right. It wasn't your money."

"Sure it was. You're my wife. I earned it by being married to you all these years."

Patsy didn't say anything. Hannah could imagine how hurt and frightened she was.

"When I told him he had to pay it back, he *laughed* at me. And he wouldn't quit laughing, so I stabbed him to shut him up."

"You . . . killed him," Patsy said, and Hannah could tell she was close to a state of shock.

"That's right, and I'm not sorry I did. The only problem I've got now is you."

"But I won't tell anybody you killed him! I promise, Mac!"

Mac laughed, and it wasn't a pleasant sound. "Oh, sure. You won't tell anyone until I take you back to shore and you can run for help. Don't try to lie to a liar, Patsy. I'm a lot better at it than you are."

"But I love you, Mac!" Hannah could tell by the tone in Patsy's voice that she was desperate.

"Well, that's nice. Too bad I don't love you, huh?"

There was a moment of silence while Hannah and Michelle paddled hard. Mac was going to kill Patsy. Hannah was convinced of it. She just hoped that they could make it to the water lily garden in time!

We're on the way. Just keep him talking until we get there! Hannah urged her silently. And that was when Patsy spoke again.

"I can't testify against you, Mac."

"What do you mean?"

"Even if I wanted to, I couldn't."

"Why not?" Mac sounded suspicious.

"Because a wife can't testify against her husband. And I'm your wife, Mac. Even if I tell somebody what you said, they can't use it against you. That would be hearsay. And hearsay's not admissible in court."

"You're sure about that?" Mac sounded as if he were considering her argument, but Hannah had her doubts. It was more likely he was playing with Patsy like Moishe played with a mouse.

"Of course I'm sure," Patsy said, and to Hannah's ears she sounded desperate again. "I've been a legal secretary for almost thirty years."

"Well that *is* interesting. I've got to admit that. You're positive you're right then?"

Hannah motioned for Michelle to hurry. The water lily garden was just ahead. They'd be on the scene in less than a minute.

"I'd stake my . . ." Patsy stopped suddenly and gave a little sob. "It's all true, Mac. There's no way I can say anything in court to hurt you."

Mac gave a little chuckle and the hair stood up at the back of Hannah's neck. She could tell a crisis was coming with the force of a speeding freight train.

"Patsy, Patsy, Patsy," Mac mock chided her. "You're talking

about a trial here. But there's not going to *be* any trial. There's not even going to be an arrest."

Hannah could hear Patsy crying. They were very close now.

"We're all alone out here, and this canoe is going to flip right over." Mac chuckled again. "And you can't swim, can you, Patsy girl?"

"Stop!" Hannah shouted out, giving a mighty lunge on her paddle to hurtle them forward. "Stop or I'll shoot!"

Michelle gave her a startled glance, but she leaned on her paddle and the canoe leaped forward into the clearing that contained the water lily garden.

Mac didn't wait to see who it was. He just flipped the canoe and Patsy hit the water with a cry. Michelle and Hannah arrived just in time to see her go down into the watery depths.

"I'll get her," Michelle shouted.

"Take her to the point." Hannah gestured toward Sandy Point, which was only a half mile away. "I'll get him."

Hannah watched as Michelle grabbed Patsy and started to swim to shore with her. Patsy didn't panic the way most non swimmers do. Instead she let Michelle support her in the water and kicked with her feet to help them move. Once Hannah was sure they were going to make it, she turned to locate Mac. But before she could do more than glance at the overturned canoe, her own canoe began to tip.

Hannah used an expression she would not have considered around her two nieces, but half of it came out underwater. She was being dragged down to the bottom by Jordan High's champion swimmer.

If you get dumped in the water with all your clothes on, the first thing to do is get rid of your shoes. The words of Hannah's first swimming teacher came back to her in a rush. It was good advice. Hannah hated to lose her favorite sneakers at the bottom of Eden Lake, but it was better than losing her life at the bottom of Eden Lake.

If a drowning person gets you in a stranglehold, don't hold back. Pinch, gouge, bite, do anything you can to get out of it.

The moment that second piece of advice came to mind, Hannah started to fight. She dug her elbow into Mac's ribs, gouged at his eyes, pinched in a place she hoped would do real damage, and bit down on his arm.

The result was explosive. There was a yelp she could hear underwater, and suddenly she was freed. Hannah didn't stick around to see what would happen next. She kicked out with all her might and shot away several feet. After two deep breaths to restore her oxygen, and kicking all the while, she dove underwater, changed directions ninety degrees, and swam as far as she could.

When she came up, she saw she'd been successful. Mac was looking for her about ten feet from where she'd emerged. He hadn't expected her to change directions, but she couldn't play this hide-and-seek game for long. It was like rolling dice and betting on the outcome. She'd keep changing direction, he'd keep guessing where she would surface, and eventually he'd be right. It was the law of averages, and nobody could break that law. And then he'd grab her again and hang on, prepared for her to put up a fight. The element of surprise would be gone, and she'd end up at the murky bottom of Eden Lake with no air in her lungs.

"I see you!" His voice floated across the water to her. "You're a sitting duck, Hannah."

He'd spotted her! Hannah almost groaned. The moon reflecting off the water was just too bright tonight. She waited until he was about six feet away and then she ducked under the water again. She'd run the same pattern she'd run before. He wouldn't expect that . . . she hoped.

Her lungs were burning when she came up for air and discovered that she'd won another round. Mac hadn't expected her to make exactly the same ninety-degree turn underwater. But he would the next time she dove down. And he'd be waiting for her when she surfaced.

"Ah! There you are! Why don't you just give it up, Hannah? You're in lousy shape, and I'm not."

He was trying to distract her. Hannah knew she shouldn't listen. She had to plan out what to do next.

"I can keep this up all night. You know I'll get you eventually. And then I'll get her. And your sister. But you won't be around to see that."

Straight line. Try it, her mind shouted out. *What have you got to lose?*

My life, Hannah answered. But it was a good idea, and she decided to go with it.

A curious thing happened as she dove beneath the surface of the water. She thought she heard something droning in the distance, something like a motor. Was someone coming to help her? Or was she so scared that she was imagining things?

She snagged something with her hand, and for a moment, Hannah thought he'd come under the water to grab her. But it was something slippery like the stem of a plant or . . .

She was on the edge of the water lily garden! Hannah hadn't realized that she was so close. And then she remembered something that she'd said to Norman in what now seemed like eons ago. *I could always be a floating face in the middle of any of Monet's water lily paintings. It would be like* Where's Waldo? *and nobody would even spot me.*

A quick mental picture of the water lily garden the way she'd seen it that afternoon with Norman, and she knew it was about twenty feet across. Could she dive down even further to get under the shallow roots and swim ten feet in to come up in the middle?

What do you have to lose? her mind asked again, and this time she didn't bother to answer. She had something to gain if she made it. And if she didn't, what she'd lose would be lost anyway.

Her lungs felt like they were bursting, but she forced her feet to kick as she propelled herself under the surface, straight for what she hoped was the middle of the water lily garden. She had to surface without a sound. No gasp for breath or splash allowed.

Hannah forced her body on until she knew she couldn't swim another stroke. And then she wound her body through the maze of floating roots, tangled stems, and blossoms. Once she was close to the surface, she willed herself to remain perfectly stationary and silent, and not to gulp at the air her lungs needed so desperately.

She floated and her nose came up. She breathed the beautiful slightly sweet-smelling air. She took two breaths, and then she let her face just break the surface. There were plant stalks around her, taller than her head. That was very good. She straightened her body and let the top part of her head emerge. Carefully, cautiously, she surfaced up to her nose, no further. And nothing, absolutely nothing, happened!

Of course he was looking for her. Hannah expected no less. But he hadn't spotted her here in the middle of the water lily garden. She was part of a Monet exhibit, and he wouldn't think to look for her here.

As she remained there, grabbing roots around her with her legs to keep herself stable, she watched for any sign of him. If he started to swim toward Sandy Point, she'd dive down out of her cover in the water lily garden and grab the nearest canoe. She knew how to right it, and she'd head off after him. A canoe paddle could be a lethal weapon, and she wouldn't hesitate to use it.

But she could see him there, his head bobbing about the surface of the moonlight-clad water, looking for her in all directions. And then she saw something else coming from Sandy Point. It was a speedboat, and the motor was loud across the surface of the lake. There was a searchlight skimming the water, and Hannah knew that help had arrived.

They'd spotted him! Hannah saw someone dive into the water and haul him to the boat. She was safe. And Michelle and Patsy were too, since the speedboat had stopped at

Sandy Point and whoever was on it must know that they were okay.

"Hannah!" an amplified voice called across the surface of the water, and Hannah recognized Mike's voice. "Hannah!"

It was like Marlon Brando yelling "Stella!" in *A Streetcar Named Desire,* and Hannah responded to the anguished cry. "I'm here in the water lily garden."

"Hannah!" Mike yelled again. And this time it was a joyful cry.

Hannah took that as her cue, and she dove down under the garden, deep enough to bypass the roots, stems, and blossoms that had served her so well. This time when she surfaced, there was a smile on her face, and she gave a little wave as she swam out into the bright path of the searchlight that seemed as welcoming as sunlight.

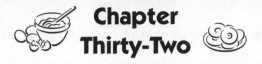

It was Sunday evening, the Beeseman-Herman family reunion was over, and they were gathering in the lobby at the Inn, waiting until they'd all arrived to be seated in the dining room. Andrea, Hannah, and Tracey were sitting on a couch by the mammoth stone fireplace when Michelle walked in.

"Wow!" Michelle said, gazing at Andrea. "You look absolutely fantastic!"

"Thank you," Andrea gave her a smile.

"I love your hair. That four-color weave is amazing. And your outfit's gorgeous, too."

Hannah felt the pangs of guilt begin. Andrea had mentioned she was having a complete makeover this weekend. It was time for a sisterly act of contrition.

"I'm sorry, Andrea," Hannah apologized. "You *do* look wonderful. I just didn't notice."

"Neither did Bill," Andrea said, and she didn't look happy.

"Maybe that's because you always look like you just walked out of a modeling session," Michelle told her, covering the situation smoothly. "I'm sure that's why Bill didn't notice."

"Well . . . maybe." Andrea looked slightly mollified. "You like the dress then?"

"Gorgeous," Hannah said, seizing the opportunity and jumping in quickly.

"Hello, darlings!" Delores breezed in with Carrie and Norman. "Bill and Lonnie just pulled into the parking lot, and Lisa and Herb were right behind them." She turned to smile at all of them and her gaze stopped on Andrea. "You look lovely, dear. Is that a new dress?"

"Yes." Andrea began to smile.

"Well, it's perfect for you. And I like your new hairstyle." Delores turned to Tracey. "Doesn't your mother look wonderful?"

"Mommy's always beautiful," Tracey replied, earning a hug from Andrea.

Once Bill, Lonnie, Lisa, and Herb had joined them, they made their way to the largest table in the dining room of the Lake Eden Inn. As usual, Delores had arranged place cards, and Hannah found hers. She was seated between Mike and Norman again. She gave a little sigh, decided it wasn't worth making a fuss about, and pulled out her chair to sit down. But before she could take her place at the table, Tracey rushed up to her.

"Aunt Hannah?" Tracey looked anxious. "Will you go to the ladies' room with me?"

Hannah nodded and slid her chair in again. There was more to this request than met the ear. Tracey was one of the most independent very-soon-to-be first graders in her class. If she'd needed to visit the ladies' room, she would have told Andrea where she was going, and gone by herself.

Hannah waited until they got out into the carpeted hallway outside the dining room, and then she asked, "Okay, what is it?"

"I want to get three more Girl Scout merit badges before the awards program, and one of them is for cooking. You have to make lunch all by yourself. The only part I can't do is dessert, and I want to have cookies."

Hannah thought she knew what was coming. "And you want me to teach you how to bake cookies?"

"Yes, Aunt Hannah. Will you, please? I can't ask Mom. You know why. I can't ask Grandma Delores, either. I know she doesn't bake. And if I ask Grandma McCann, I might hurt Mom's feelings."

"And you don't think it'll hurt your mom's feelings if I teach you to bake?"

"Why would it?" Tracey shrugged, and it was a miniature duplicate of Andrea's shrug. "You're the professional, Aunt Hannah. Everybody knows that."

Flattery will get you everywhere, Hannah thought, *and that's something you* did *get from your mother!* But of course she didn't say that. She said instead, "I'll be happy to teach you to bake, Tracey. It'll be fun."

"Chocolate Chip Crunch Cookies?" Tracey asked her. "They're Mom's favorites and then I can bake them for her."

"Good idea. Do you want to go on to the ladies' room? Or was that just a ploy to get me alone to ask me?"

"It was just a ploy. Let's go back in, Aunt Hannah. I want to use Mom's cell phone to talk to Bethany. She couldn't come because she's too little for one of Grandma's dinner parties, but I promised I'd call and tell her good night."

It was a lovely meal. Delores had ordered something new on the menu. It was called "A Taste of the Lake Eden Inn," and it was a meal of ten small samples of Sally's best dishes.

"That was great!" Bill said, putting down his fork after eating the last morsel of Sally's Flourless Chocolate Cake. And then he turned to Andrea. "That tasted almost as good as you look tonight. I've got the most beautiful wife in the world."

For one brief second Andrea looked shocked, but then she started to smile. "Thank you, honey," she said.

Thank you, Bill, Hannah thought, but she didn't say it. She was glad Bill had taken her advice when she'd cued him in about Andrea's makeover. "Thank you, Mother," she said instead. "That was a wonderful meal!"

Everyone else jumped on the bandwagon, thanking Delores for inviting them and complimenting her on her menu choice. When the thanks had died down, Delores rose to her feet and gestured toward Carrie. "We have some very good news, but I'll let Carrie tell you. And after she does, I have some personal good news of my own."

Delores sat down, and Carrie stood up. Hannah had a feeling they'd rehearsed this. "I'm not sure you know this, but Marge and Patsy asked us to hold a silent auction for the Honus Wagner baseball card that belonged to their brother, Gus. We sent out notices yesterday morning, and as of two o'clock this afternoon, our Granny's Attic Web site had received five firm offers."

"Tell them about the minimum opening bid," Delores prompted.

"The minimum opening bid for the card was one million, five hundred thousand dollars," Carrie said. "That's the least it could sell for. And the fact that we've received five bids in less than forty-eight hours shows that there are a lot of interested parties out there. I wouldn't be surprised if the winning bid is over two million dollars."

"When does the bidding close?" Andrea asked.

"Next Saturday morning at ten. We gave them a week to discuss it with their clients and enter a bid."

"That's wonderful!" Hannah clapped her hands. And then she asked the question she knew was on everyone's mind. "Who gets the money?"

"It'll be divided evenly between Marge and Patsy," Delores told them. "Gus never married, and he had no children. Marge and Patsy are his only surviving siblings."

Herb gulped so loudly, they all heard it. "You mean Mom and Aunt Patsy could each inherit almost a million dollars?"

"That's right," Carrie told him, "minus our commission, of course. And now Delores has something to tell you."

"It's the real reason we're celebrating tonight," Delores said, smiling at all of them, "but not even Carrie knows why."

Carrie nodded. "It's true. She wouldn't tell me. She said she wanted to tell everyone all together."

All eyes were on Delores, and she clearly reveled in the moment. Hannah decided to ask the critical question. "What are we celebrating, Mother?"

"Remember when we all got together at the Inn the last time?" Delores asked.

"I remember."

"And I said I was working on a secret project, and I'd tell you if it actually happened?"

"I remember," Hannah said.

"Well . . . it happened."

"*What* happened?" at least four of them asked at once, and Delores laughed.

"The secret project was my book. And a big New York publisher bought it."

For a moment they were all shocked speechless, and Hannah was the first to recover. "Congratulations, Mother! Is it a book about antiques?"

"No, it's fiction."

Carrie's mouth dropped open in surprise. "A Regency Romance?" she guessed.

"You're right!" Delores told her, looking very proud of herself. "And I used every one of you for characters. Isn't that marvelous?"

Uh-oh! Hannah said under her breath. "You used all of us?" she asked aloud.

"Of course, dear. One must write from life, you know. My three dear daughters are in it, of course, and I think I did a good job of depicting your true characters." She turned to Carrie. "Naturally you're in it, Carrie. And so is Mike, and Norman, and Lisa, too. You're there, Herb. And Bill. And

Lonnie. I even put some members of my Regency Romance group in it."

"How about me, Grandma Delores?" Tracey asked.

"Of course, darling. I couldn't write a book without putting you in it. You might not be the age you are now, though, so don't look for a six-year-old girl."

"Okay, Grandma. I won't."

"You know what they always say about real people in books, don't you?" Delores asked them, her eyes scanning the crowd.

"No, what do they say?" Hannah finally asked, when no one else spoke up.

"They say that people don't recognize themselves because they don't see themselves the way others do."

Uh-oh! Hannah's mind said again. *This could be very bad.*

"I did my best to be entirely truthful and take off the rose-colored glasses I normally wear to view my friends and loved ones," Delores went on. "I wrote you the way you truly are, the way someone who didn't know and love you like I do, would describe your flaws and your strengths."

"Oh, brother!" Hannah breathed, a little louder than she had intended. She was rewarded by a smile from Norman and a gentle nudge of approval by Mike.

"I didn't quite hear you, Hannah. What was that again?" Delores asked her.

Hannah thought fast. "I said *Oh, Mother* to get your attention. I wanted to ask you when they're going to publish your book."

"Sometime next year."

Perfect, Hannah thought. *That should give me enough time to sell The Cookie Jar and move hundreds of miles away.*

"Will you let me know exactly when?" she asked.

"Of course. Are you going to hold a launch party for me, dear?"

"Oh, definitely!" Hannah said, wondering how much

money it would cost to launch her mother straight to the moon.

As she walked to her cookie truck, still sandwiched between Mike and Norman, Hannah had a sneaking suspicion that the last of the summer evenings had come and gone. There was a crispness to the air that spoke of leaves turning colors, pumpkins ripening on the vine, and chrysanthemums triumphing as the last flower of autumn before winter's icy fingers sprinkled snow on the flowerbeds.

"What time is it anyway?" Hannah asked, since she'd forgotten her watch on her dressing table.

"Almost eight," Norman answered her.

"How about a movie at my place," she suggested, now that she'd finally caught up on her sleep. "I rented two of the newest releases at the video store, and I've got the leftover Black Forest Brownies."

Mike shook his head. "It sounds great, but I've got to pass. I dropped Ronni at the mall on my way here, and I have to meet her and drive her home. Her car's not working right."

A likely story, Hannah thought. As a matter of fact, it was the very same story Shawna Lee had used when she'd lived in Mike's apartment complex. "Ronni's out there shopping?" she asked, just barely managing to keep the pleasant expression on her face.

"No, she's job hunting. She doesn't make that much at the sheriff's station, and she needs to get part time work."

"Well, I hope she finds something. Tell her I wish her luck."

"That's nice of you, Hannah." Mike gave her a warm smile. "I'll tell her."

Hannah was grateful that Mike couldn't read her mind and know that the real reason she hoped Ronni would find work was so that she'd spend less time at the apartment complex with Mike. But some things were better left unsaid, and

Hannah turned to Norman. "How about you? Would you like to watch a movie with me?"

"I'd love to, but I can't. I promised Mother I'd meet them at Granny's Attic and check their Internet connection. Your mother tried to get online this afternoon, and she kept getting error messages. It's probably just a loose connection or a reset problem, but they want to keep up with the bids on the Honus Wagner card."

"You can't blame them for that!" Mike said, grinning at Norman. "It's hard to believe that a little piece of cardboard with a picture on it could go for that much."

They arrived at her cookie truck, and Norman reached out to touch Hannah's shoulder. "See you for coffee tomorrow, Hannah."

"Me, too," Mike said, reaching out to pat her other shoulder. "Bake some more of those Black Forest Brownies, okay? They're the best brownies I ever ate."

And with that the two men in her life walked away toward their respective vehicles. No kisses. No hugs. Nothing but pats on her shoulder.

"Rejected," Hannah said, sighing theatrically as she climbed into her cookie truck. It was an attempt to make light of it, but if she were to be entirely truthful, she did feel a bit abandoned.

She started the engine and gave a little wave as she passed Norman and Mike. Then she drove down the gravel side road that wound through the stand of trees, and turned onto the access road toward the highway.

She zipped along at good speed. There was no traffic to speak of. When she turned on Old Lake Road, it was also deserted, and she was just turning in at her complex when the cell phone in her purse rang. Her first instinct was to ignore it, but it rang again, and then again. Hannah stopped at the gate and pulled out her cell phone. It could be some sort of emergency. Not that many people had her cell phone number.

"Hello," she said, hoping it wasn't a random sales call.

"Hannah. I'm so glad I caught you! I tried your condo, but I got your answer machine."

For a moment that lasted no longer than a heartbeat, Hannah was puzzled by the identity of her caller. Then she recognized his voice, and a smile spread over her face. "Hi, Ross," she said. "Are you in California?"

"No, I'm in Minneapolis."

"That's wonderful! Are you coming to Lake Eden?"

"I'd love to, but I can't. I'm only here for eight and a half hours. I was flying to New York and we had to land here, some kind of mechanical problems. They're transferring us to another flight, but it won't leave here until four-thirty in the morning."

"So you're stuck at the airport until four-thirty?"

"Not the airport. Since the delay is longer than eight hours, they put us up at the Airport Hilton. Do you know where that is?"

"Sure," Hannah said, her smile growing wider.

"How about driving down? I haven't seen you in a long time, Hannah. And I've missed you."

"I've missed you, too," Hannah said.

"So how long do you think it'll take you to get here?"

Hannah did some fast calculations, taking into account the light Sunday night traffic and the fact that she'd just filled her gas tank. "Forty-five minutes," she told him.

"Great! There's an all-night diner across the street at the end of the block. I'll get a table and meet you there. I'm hungry, and all I've had is airplane food."

"I'll be there," she said. " 'Bye, Ross."

She clicked off the phone and tossed it back in her purse. And then she did something she'd never done before. She slid her gate card into the slot, drove in when the wooden arm rose to admit her, did a sharp U-turn over the flowerbed that acted as a center divider, and drove right back out again.

"Not rejected after all," she said, grinning as she stepped on the gas and headed for the highway.

BLACK FOREST BROWNIES

Preheat oven to 350 degrees F., rack
in the middle position.

4 one-ounce squares semi-sweet chocolate *(or the
equivalent—³/₄ cup semi-sweet chocolate chips
will do just fine.)*
³/₄ cup butter *(one and a half sticks)*
1½ cups white *(granulated)* sugar
3 beaten eggs *(just whip them up in a glass with a
fork)*
1 teaspoon vanilla extract *(or cherry extract)*
1 cup flour *(pack it down in the cup when you measure it)*
½ cup pecans
½ cup chopped dried cherries *(or ½ cup well-drained
Maraschino Cherries finely chopped)****
½ cup semi-sweet chocolate chips *(I used
Ghirardelli)*

*** *I used dried Bing cherries in one batch, and
chopped maraschino cherries in a second batch. People
loved both batches, but all agreed that the ones with the
dried cherries were chewier.*

Prepare a 9-inch by 13-inch cake pan by lining it with a
piece of foil large enough to flap over the sides. Spray the
foil-lined pan with Pam or other nonstick cooking spray.

Microwave the chocolate squares and butter in a microwave-safe mixing bowl for one minute. Stir. *(Since choco-*

late frequently maintains its shape even when melted, you have to stir to make sure.) If it's not melted, microwave for an additional 20 seconds and stir again. Repeat if necessary.

Stir the sugar into the chocolate mixture. Feel the bowl. If it's not so hot it'll cook the eggs, add them now, stirring thoroughly. Mix in the flavor extract *(vanilla or cherry.)*

Mix in the flour and stir just until it's moistened.

Put the pecans and dried cherries in the bowl of a food processor and chop them together with the steel blade. If the dried cherries stick to the blades too much, add a Tablespoon of flour to your bowl and try it again. *(If you don't have a food processor, you don't have to buy one for this recipe—just chop everything up as well as you can with a sharp knife.)*

Mix in the chopped nuts and cherries, add the chocolate chips, give a final stir by hand, and spread the batter out in your prepared pan.

Bake at 350 degrees F. for 30 minutes.

Cool the Black Forest Brownies in the pan on a metal rack. When they're thoroughly cool, grasp the edges of the foil and lift the brownies out of the pan. Put them facedown on a cutting board, peel the foil off the back, and cut them into brownie-sized pieces.

Place the squares on a plate and dust lightly with powdered sugar if you wish.

Jo Fluke's Note: The ladies at Delta Kappa Gamma deserve credit for this recipe. After I spoke to them in Camarillo, CA, they gave me a huge box of dried fruit that included the dried Bing cherries that I used in these brownies.

Hannah's Note: If you really want to be decadent, frost these with Neverfail Fudge!

Index of Recipes

Baking Conversion Chart

These conversions are approximate, but they'll work just fine for Hannah Swensen's recipes.

VOLUME:

U.S.	Metric
½ teaspoon	2 milliliters
1 teaspoon	5 milliliters
1 tablespoon	15 milliliters
¼ cup	50 milliliters
⅓ cup	75 milliliters
½ cup	125 milliliters
¾ cup	175 milliliters
1 cup	¼ liter

WEIGHT:

U.S.	Metric
1 ounce	28 grams
1 pound	454 grams

OVEN TEMPERATURE:

Degrees Fahrenheit	Degrees Centigrade	British (Regulo) Gas Mark
325 degrees F.	165 degrees C.	3
350 degrees F.	175 degrees C.	4
375 degrees F.	190 degrees C.	5

Note: Hannah's rectangular sheet cake pan, 9 inches by 13 inches, is approximately 23 centimeters by 32.5 centimeters.

Novels by Andrew M. Greeley

Death in April
The Cardinal Sins

THE PASSOVER TRILOGY
Thy Brother's Wife
Ascent into Hell
Lord of the Dance

TIME BETWEEN THE STARS
Virgin and Martyr
Angels of September
Patience of a Saint
Rite of Spring
Love Song

MYSTERY AND FANTASY
The Magic Cup
The Final Planet
Godgame
Angel Fire
Happy Are the Meek
Happy Are the Clean of Heart
Happy Are Those Who Thirst for Justice

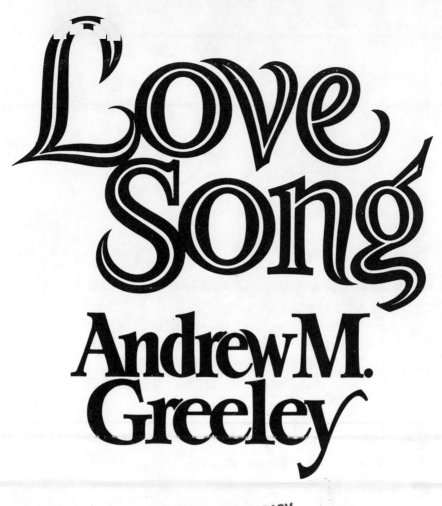

Love Song
Andrew M. Greeley

WARNER BOOKS

A Warner Communications Company

For the Goggin clan
   Gail
   Terry
   Terry
   Bridget
   Sheila
   John
   Colleen

All the events and characters in this story are products of the author's imagination. While the prosecutorial techniques described herein are in use in many jurisdictions, they were not necessarily used in northern Illinois during the time depicted in this story. The Chicago Cubs, however, were REAL!

Warner Books, Inc., 666 Fifth Avenue, New York, NY 10103

W A Warner Communications Company

Printed in the United States of America
First printing: January 1989

10 9 8 7 6 5 4 3 2 1

Book design: H. Roberts

Library of Congress Cataloging-in-Publication Data

Greeley, Andrew M., 1928–
    Love song.

    I. Title.
PS3557.R358L68   1988   813'.54   88-5776
ISBN 0-446-51455-1

Judas, do you betray the Son of Man with a kiss?

—LK 12/47

To be interested in the changing seasons is a happier state of mind than to be hopelessly in love with spring.

—George Santayana

The Egyptian love songs and the Song of Songs are first of all poems about love. The poets reveal their views of love not by speaking about love in the abstract, but by portraying people in love, making lovers words reveal lovers' thoughts, feelings, and deeds. The poets invite us to observe lovers, to smile at them, to empathize with them, to sympathize with them, to recall in their adolescent pains our own, to share their desires, to enjoy in fantasy their pleasures. The poets show us young lovers flush with desire and awash in waves of new and overwhelming emotions. We watch lovers sailing the Nile to a rendezvous, walking hand in hand through gardens, lying together in garden bowers. We come upon them sitting at home aching for the one they love, standing outside the loved one's door and pouting, swimming across rivers, running frantically through the streets at night, kissing, fondling, hugging and snuggling face to face and face to breast, and—no less erotically—telling each other's praises in sensuous similes.

—Michael V. Fox
The Song of Songs and Ancient Egyptian Love Poetry

How is one to understand the Song in terms of human and divine love? It is we moderns who have difficulty with this question. But the Bible suggests that these loves are united and not to be separated. Israel, it is true, understood that Yahweh was beyond sex. He had no consort; and the fertility rites were not the proper mode of worship for him. Yet the union between man and woman became a primary symbol for the expression of the relationship of the Lord to His People. The covenant between God and His People is consistently portrayed as a marriage.

—Roland Murphy O.Carm.

Said Rabbi Akiba: Heaven forbid that any man in Israel ever disputed that the Song of Songs is holy. For the whole world is not worth the day on which the Song of Songs was given to Israel, for all the Writings are holy and the Song of Songs is the Holy of Holies.

—Mishnah Yadaim 3/5

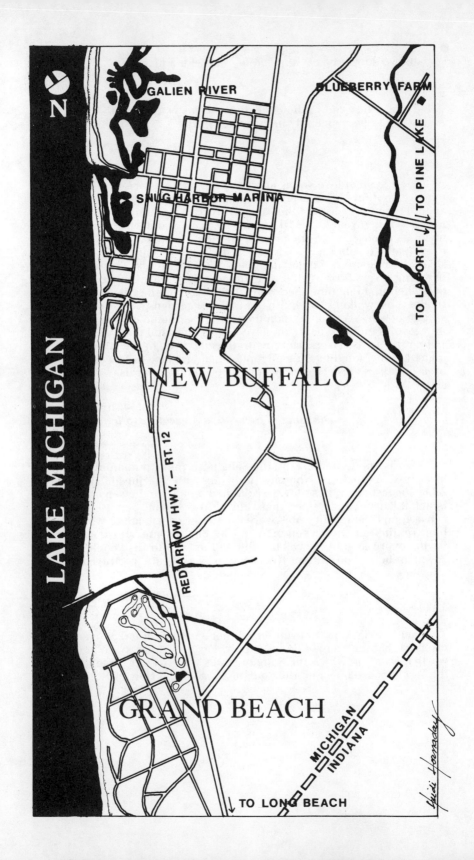

Summer

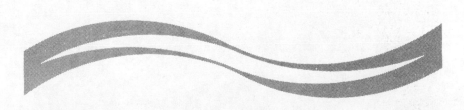

Fifth Song

Lover:

There are many girls, but you're my special one,
Fierce and passionate woman, kindest friend,
Without you my hours never seem to end.
Where have you been, my sun, my moon, my dawn?
There's no escape now, I'm holding you down.
Do not pretend that you want to flee,
Tremble at my touch, you belong to me,
Be still while I slip off your frilly gown!
You were sculpted an elegant work of art,
Dark hair falling on snow white chest,
Honeydews, your high and graceful breasts,
One taste enough to break my heart.
In the curve of your wondrous thighs:
A deep valley flowing with perfumed wine
Around which wheat and blooming lilies twine
Whose sweetness invites my enchanted eyes.
I will seize the fruit, press them to my teeth.
Then, famished, impassioned, and lightly deft,
Swim in the waters of the valley's aromatic cleft
And your delicacy savor, drink, and eat!

Beloved:

I will be dry white wine to slake your thirst
And a tasty morsel to tease your mouth.
A trembling prize from the misty south,
A plundered vessel for your nightly feast,
A submissive trophy you can carry off
To a cool treasure house in your magic lands,
A most willing slave to your artful hands,
A total gift, passionate, loving, soft!

Lover:

She sleeps now, my innocent little child,
Wake her not, good winds, adore her radiant smile!

Love Song, 6:4—8:4

prologue

Diana Lyons felt his eyes undress her. Slowly, carefully, and with lingering movements, his imagination was stripping her and reveling in her nakedness.

On the third hole of Long Beach Country Club.

It was an unexpectedly and powerfully pleasant sensation, a perfumed hot tub of admiration and desire. He was a spoiled, dishonest, overage child. His father had ruined her father's life—poor Daddy, who even at this moment was probably glued to his old radio listening to the White Sox and dreaming of the "old days," of players who were only names: Billy Pierce, Minnie Minoso, and "Little Nellie" Fox.

He belonged in jail. Her office would put him in jail. It was not her case, but still, he was a target of the United States Attorney for the Northern District of Illinois.

His delight in her body was soothing and respectful, hungry and yet somehow not lewd.

"Winner shoots first," she announced, trying to sound calm and self-possessed.

"Don't rub it in." His eyes absorbed her with tender caresses.

The gentleness of his longing was probably part of his act. You had to be pretty skillful at conning women to send out such seductive vibes. He was a phony. Definitely.

Feel vile, Diana; he's exploiting you.

"You blew a three-foot putt," she said, rubbing it in.

He relaxed on the bench, a solid, beautiful man with long blond hair and silver blue eyes, arm and thigh muscles bulging in a Notre Dame T-shirt and cut-off jeans. Cute. No, adorable.

"Mortal sin." He leaned back comfortably. "Sorry about that!"

She sensed that in his fantasy he was caressing her breasts, not harshly or lasciviously but with reverent awe. He wants me. Body and soul. The way a man in a cave wants fresh air. Don't stop.

No, do stop. You have no right to my body. Or my soul.

Damn, I can't tell him to stop without making it worse. I've never enjoyed being a sex object before. Why do I like it when a man I am supposed to hate is objectifying me?

That's not true. He's almost worshiping me, she thought, as she placed her golf bag against a tree, removed her two wood, and walked over to the tee, pretending that she was immune to his intense scrutiny.

I wish he would kiss me.

"Two wood?" He raised an eyebrow.

"Dogleg to the left. I need about two hundred yards."

Her father, incurable sports fan, even now that his health was ruined, had taught her to play golf—at a driving range where a friend let him play for nothing. Now she was betraying him and the skills he had taught her.

"If you need it," he grinned approvingly, "I'm sure you'll get it."

I want to be naked for him, she thought. I want to be spread out on the grass with him on top of me. I want to be covered by his kisses. All of me.

She dismissed the dangerous images that were racing through her mind. She should not be playing golf with a man that her office was investigating for possible indictment. She had been obsessed with him as a possible enemy, wishing that she might be assigned to his case and yet afraid, as a relative newcomer to the office, to seem too ambitious. She could not resist the impulse to spend some time with him. It was not ethically improper, not yet anyway. Know thine enemy, she had told herself.

Now her obsession had been stood on its head. I am infatuated with him. It's not love, nothing even remotely resembling love. She swallowed bravely. Only infatuation. Silly teenage crush.

The eyes of other men had appraised her critically, trying, she supposed, to decide whether someone so tall and strong would be any good in bed. She had been either indifferent or offended. Now a man she ought to despise was evaluating her womanliness, and she was wallowing in his interest.

I am in trouble, she told herself, as she teed up the ball. I must concentrate on my backswing. It's only an afternoon of golf, not a preliminary to a grand jury hearing. Or the beginning of a romance.

"Hit it hard," he urged her with a chuckle.

Straining with all her willpower, she glared fiercely at the golf ball and began her backswing. She sensed his eyes savoring her movement. No, she insisted, I will not think about him.

The ball soared off the tee, straight and true down the fairway. A hundred and ninety yards, not perfect, but adequate.

Thank God. I did not blow my cool.

Maybe he's not evil. Maybe he's just a nice boy with a few problems who needs someone to take care of him, someone to be a lover in bed and a friend out of bed. Someone like me.

Body and soul.

Lover and friend, there had never been a man before who might have been both. Fun and funny, kind and considerate. Masculine yet gentlemanly. Strong and vulnerable. Adorable boy child.

Body and soul.

If only . . . if only his father had not driven Daddy out of his job investigating the commodities racket. If Mama or Daddy knew I was playing golf with him . . .

She did not want to think about that. Mama would blow up like Mount Etna. Daddy would be silent and hurt, musing occasionally that his last child had failed him like all the rest.

"Devastating, Diana!" Conor's rich baritone laughter echoed behind her.

"Is there a comma between the two words?" she asked a fraction of a second before she wished she could bite off her tongue.

I

At the seventh hole, when she missed the three-foot putt, Conor Clarke decided with a shiver that the woman would probably become a hanging judge.

His shiver was inappropriate for a humid day when the temperature was in the high eighties and the smell of gasoline fumes permeated a hazy "inversion" over northern Indiana.

She would be the kind of judge that finally sentenced herself to the noose.

"Judge Lyons, you have been found by a jury of your peers to be guilty as charged. Therefore, I sentence you to be taken to Cook County Jail on the first day of next week and there to be hanged by your neck until you are dead."

"Yes, Your Honor."

"Since I'm your defense counsel as well as judge and jury, we won't have any of this appeal-to-the-Supreme-Court nonsense."

"What was my crime, Your Honor?"

"I forget. But it doesn't matter. You've failed. You're guilty."

"Yes, Your Honor. I deserve to be hanged by my neck until I'm dead."

"Oh yes, now I remember your crime: you missed a three-foot putt at Long Beach Country Club."

A pity to choke the life out of such a lovely neck, Conor thought. It was made for caressing, in the middle of the night preferably—tender, affectionate caressing as a prelude to more love. Not that he had any experience with such assaults on her virtue, since he'd met her for the first time only two hours ago. I need some time to make up my mind whether I am going to fall in love with her.

I think I might appeal for a stay of execution. Amicus curiae. Amator curiae, even. I would plea for a reduction of sentence: life in my bedroom. With her clothes off.

"How much time, Counselor?"

"Could I have the rest of her natural life? And maybe a few years more besides?"

In the real world, which alas interfered too often with his fantasy dialogues, Diana Marie Lyons bent over with a graceful flowing movement that reminded him of an elegant mountain lioness regally picking her way down a desert mountainside, and scooped up her golf ball. "Not too swift," she murmured, more to herself than to him.

I may have seen more lovely rear ends in my thirty years, Conor observed to himself. But never as part of such a comprehensive package.

"One over par," Conor said innocently. He pretended that the sharp stab of desire occasioned by the shifting of her trim breasts under her brown knit tank-top did not belong to him. "With my ten-stroke handicap, I'm still two strokes ahead of you."

"I should have had a bird." She tossed the offending ball into the air and caught it with a quick, angry little jab of her hand.

"Can't make them all." Conor, still entranced by the

lithe and seductive grace of her bending motion, sternly lectured himself that it was chauvinistic to remove a woman's
clothes in your imagination. Especially on a golf course. Actually, I didn't do it all, he insisted piously. Pick up her golf
clubs and carry them off the green for her.

It could be worth his life to offer to carry her clubs to the
next hole. So he picked them up without asking.

It was also, he reflected, not fair that women could do
their evaluations so much more efficiently than men. In one
quick glance she had taken in his long blond hair, blue eyes,
and broad shoulders, filed it all for future reference, and
then treated him as though he were no more important than
the oak and maple trees along the edge of the Long Beach
fairways.

"You should be a better golfer," she sniffed as she firmly
removed her golf bag from his hand. "You have nothing else
to do."

"Except sail."

Actually, he replied to his own prosecuting counsel, it is
a body that is designed to be undressed. God made her
beautiful so that she could attract a man who would love her
and strip her and make love with her and produce children
with her and live together with her to a happy old age.

Is that not so?

It sure is, said counsel for the prosecution, a benign and
understanding fellow. It would be less than human if you did
not find her desirable. Maybe you'd better fall in love with
her.

An excellent idea, Counselor. Why did not I think of
that?

Yes, it would be a very wise strategy for him to fall in
love with Diana Marie Lyons, even if she did scare the hell
out of him. She was the sort of woman about whom poets
wrote. And he was a poet, wasn't he? Of a sort?

Then why haven't you found a metaphor to describe
her? The voice belonged to the young and idealistic assistant State's Attorney who lurked behind his more experi-

enced and tolerant leader. Why don't you stop ogling her and imagine a metaphor?

Ogling, he replied hotly, is a preliminary to a metaphor. You can't just produce them on the spur of the moment. You have to study the subject carefully, sometimes for hours, even days, before the creative powers of the soul erupt and produce, like Venus from the sea, a fully grown, if not a fully clad, metaphor. Right?

You have to concentrate.

"If you sail like you play golf, then your problem is that you don't concentrate," she interrupted his thoughts. "You're a daydreamer. You're not really paying any attention to your game."

"You've already made the argument, and I think I probably need a beer."

Diana had vetoed a golf cart. ("After all, neither of us are elderly invalids. And you look like you need exercise. Dissipation and athletics are incompatible.")

"Your defense for drinking when you sail"—her lips, full and straight, hardened into a severe line—"was that on your boat—"

"Name of *Brigid*."

"—your drink protected you from boredom. Surely an hour of golf is not so boring that you need already to ingest narcotic substances into your bloodstream."

Her lips melted into a faint, very faint, hint of a smile. I amuse her.

"There are chemicals, and then, there are chemicals, fair Diana."

"Come on." The amusement was gone. "Take your expensive golf clubs and their expensive case and let's play golf. We can discuss substance abuse later."

"Yes, Your Honor."

I think she might have actually laughed at me just then. An impatient and not altogether friendly laugh, but we have to begin somewhere.

Chemicals in the blood, is it? Glory be to God, woman, what do you expect?

There had been an instant chemical reaction between the two of them when she had climbed into his Ferrari. Hormones, of course, nothing more, he told himself in the mock Irish brogue he affected when he was feeling shy. As a man whose love life had been marked by sudden and injudicious chemically driven impulses—as often to flee as to pursue—Con distrusted chemical reactions, especially when they were engendered by regal types like Diana Marie Lyons, regal types who could hit a golf ball, bullet straight, for a country mile.

She felt the reaction, too. When she was not bashing the small projectile the said country mile, she was covertly and judiciously considering him. Fascinated, he told himself hopefully, and repelled, he told himself sadly.

She strode ahead of him over the hill toward the next tee. Not a mountain lioness, but a mountain nanny goat, drat her. "You're not very good at sailing either." A judgment which seemed to extend to his general social uselessness. "Are you?"

The poem he was trying to compose in his head would be about double poetry in motion—her golf swing, flawless in its execution and delightful in its womanly grace; arms, back, hips, legs, all swaying in one concerted, controlled, captivating sweep of body and club. Alliteration, too.

Moreover, he could not succumb to the cliché of observing that she was well named—five feet nine inches of shapely, well-muscled nubile elegance: Diana the huntress, Diana the Assistant United States Attorney for the Northern District of Illinois.

Perhaps a symphony in brown—determined eyes with a touch of gold fleck that hinted at laughter (even if she didn't laugh much), long hair, and dark skin suggesting Mediterranean genes mixed with Celtic (armada genes perhaps?). Brown clothes, too—beige slacks, dark brown golf shoes, brown glove, and even a brown strap on her wristwatch. Nothing very expensive, but tastefully chosen and absorbing style from the slender, tough-jawed woman with delicately designed facial bones who wore them.

Not everyone would think her beautiful: too tall; too regal in bearing, too stiff maybe; too dark, perhaps even Arabian; too slender, her curves a trifle understated, or maybe it was only her height (Conor had yet to have an opportunity to evaluate her legs); a face that was perhaps too thin. Moreover, as a matter of principle, Conor tended to prefer his women shorter, fuller, fairer, more bubbly.

Or, alternatively, delicate, doll-like, exquisite.

There was nothing either fair or bubbly or doll-like about Diana Lyons.

To hell with principles.

And what's wrong with having Saudi Arabian genes?

The Saudis produced excellent race horses, didn't they? Or do they buy them from us? I can't quite remember.

He pretended again that the fantasy of slowly removing those clothes was someone else's and certainly not his—after all he had just decided definitely to fall in love with her and—and searched for a metaphor. Regal, imperial, countess, archduchess . . .

"Are you?" she persisted, definitely the United States Attorney, as they pulled up onto the eighth tee.

"Are I what?"

"Your boat was last in class in the Mackinac race this summer, wasn't it?"

"You would mention that." He heaved himself wearily to the bench behind the tee to rest while she drove. The humidity was as thick as heavy drapes; they were playing golf in a steam room. And she didn't even seem to be sweating. Just a bit inhuman. It doesn't matter. My decision to fall in love with her is final and irrevocable. My last and best offer.

Then he had his metaphor. Boats, of course.

"What are you thinking about?" She adjusted the strap

on her glove, tightening it, of course.

You would have loved to lace up your corset in the old days, wouldn't you? Think of the fun I could have unlacing it. "I've been searching for a metaphor."

"You did publish a book of poetry, didn't you?" She inserted her tee into the soft, grass-covered dune—one of the many on top of which Long Beach and its country club had been constructed—with a tough brisk motion that suggested possible dissatisfaction with the glacial eras that had produced such soft turf. "And also a version of the Song of Songs from the Bible. Minor publishing house, was it not?"

"Not too minor. . . ."

"I presume the metaphor is about me?"

"Right." Conor wiped the sweat off his face. "In the sonnet I shall write tonight—a love sonnet of course—I will compare you with Grace O'Malley, the West of Ireland pirate queen of the sixteenth century."

She considered him coolly, repeatedly tossing her golf ball a few inches above her hand: everything she did was cool, even on a day when ordinary mortals like Conor were soaked in sweat. "My grandfather's name was O'Malley and he was from the Cong area in County Mayo." She arched a carefully trimmed eyebrow. "I'd be cautious about publishing such verse; even if the hint that I am piratical was not actionable—and I think most juries would vote that it was—I could still seek redress on the grounds that my privacy was being violated. . . ."

"You never would!" Conor decided that he absolutely adored her. No hurry about getting you in bed, my dearest. I just want to look at you and listen to you.

"Oh, wouldn't I?" she smiled wickedly. "You can't tell about your pirate women, can you?"

For a moment she seemed flattered, flustered, vulnerable. It was the smile, of course. The smile discarded the corset and revealed the real Diana, even more adorable, basking transiently in the warmth of his admiration.

For Conor Clarke that was too much.

"Go ahead, hit your drive, the foursome behind us is already on the green."

"I forgot I was playing with a serious golfer." She actually winked as she turned to address the ball.

She's nothing but a flirt. And if she flirts with me for long, she'll own me body and soul. And the next thing I know we'll be looking at furniture.

So what's wrong with that?

Before she could begin her backswing, Conor slipped deftly off the bench, tilted her chin back, and at the not inconsiderable risk, he thought, of having his head bashed in by her driver, brushed his lips against hers. She was startled, but neither her firm, warm lips nor her relaxed, self-possessed body offered objection or resistance.

"What was the reason for that?" A tiny, wafer-thin tremor in her words. She bent over to tee up the ball, which had fallen to the ground while he kissed her.

"Your smile demands a kiss." The Parousia now begins, Conor announced to himself. Maybe, just maybe, this is the one.

God knows, he warned himself, you're at an age at which anyone who is capable of walking down the aisle of a church and making it on her own power to the bedroom might be the one.

"Really? Excuse me now while I return to golf, which is why I thought my cousin Maryjane arranged this outing."

I bet I disconcerted her. She was pleased and frightened. She'll blow this drive. I'll have won the first round, no matter what her score.

No, it wouldn't be so bad to have to kiss that woman every day for the rest of my life.

Her drive, as always, was arrow straight, cleaving the fairway in two perfectly equal parts. Longer this time—maybe 230 yards. Her lips darted out in the tiny sign of approval that Conor had come to recognize as a stay of execution. Its opposite, an equally quick pursing of the lips, indicated that Diana was not pleased with Diana and would deny all motions for a retrial.

"You should be kissed before every drive," he said cautiously.

She grinned at him—a real live grin. "That's an interesting possibility."

"We'll try on the next hole," he said, lumbering toward the tee.

"We will NOT!" But she didn't sound too convinced.

His drive started out with all the good will in the world—like most of the efforts in Conor Clarke's life. Alas, the streets of hell are paved with well-intentioned golf balls; 150 yards down the fairway it began to wander to the right in a lazy slice that reminded him vaguely and inaccurately of a double by Ryne Sandberg off the left field wall. Into the rough and maybe the next fairway.

"Faded a little." She was smiling at him, not contemptuously, not even disdainfully. Dare he hope it—maternally?

"I amuse you?" He picked up his tee.

"You looked so frightened when I threatened suit," she said, actually smiling again, a big, warm, generous smile from a big, warm, generous woman. Conor noted that the sun, the golf course, and the rest of the cosmos went away in shame when they had to compete with her smile. "I'd be flattered to be in one of your poems."

"With your clothes off?" he blurted.

"That's the kind of poem you write, isn't it?" She pulled out a custom-made two wood—man-size, of course. "I presume you don't write from life very often, but I can't recall any part of the Grace O'Malley legend that would justify such a situation."

Had she really winked at him again? Ah, woman, you're the divil, the very divil!

"You're the divil, woman," he said aloud. "The very divil."

"Come on." She hefted her heavy bag of clubs like it was a quart of milk from the corner delicatessen. "I'll help you find your golf ball."

They found it in the rough bordering the next fairway. "Five iron," she said tersely.

"Just what I thought myself." He put the six iron back in his golf bag, removed the five iron, and with no practice swing and only symbolic aim, he hit it out of the rough and onto the fairway, only fifty yards off the green.

"Seems to help me, too—with a bit of delayed action," he murmured thoughtfully.

"Only in the short run."

She put her second wood shot three feet from the pin and earned her first birdie of the day. His best efforts produced only a double bogie. Well, they weren't really his best efforts. His rough shot had been too hurried, and he had momentarily forgotten that he was trying to lose to her.

She offered more resistance to his kiss on the par-five ninth hole, but the kiss was considerably longer in duration and involved something of an embrace. Her body was both solid and soft, light as air and as substantial as a mountain range. Her heart, he noted, was beating very slowly.

"May I drive now?" she asked coolly.

"Why not? I bet it's perfect."

It was all of that. Another long, high, straight blast that earned a faint smile of approval from the judge.

Her second wood shot was equally effective; again she had come within a few feet of the flag.

"Eagle," she said calmly as she removed the ball from the cup. "You do seem to be a good influence on me, Conor Clement Clarke. "I've managed a par on the first nine."

"Abandon the law," he pleaded, "and join the professional tour. I'll be your caddy. You can also model golf clothes like that woman..."

"Stevens."

"Sure, you're prettier than she is. I'll be your business manager and..."

"Venture capital."

"Right." It was a make-believe scheme, but Conor could get as enthusiastic about jokes as he could about backing new computer chips or sophisticated but really user-friendly accounting programs. "I could learn to do the color on CBS and slip into little advertising hints for the Diana Lyons line of brown knit tank-tops that were not more concealing than they had to be and—"

"Go buy me a Coke, would you please? You can afford it better than I can."

Well, that settled that. I can't tell whether my true love—a lovely Saudi Arabian princess, *"Nigra sum, sed formosa"*—has a sense of humor or not.

"I like kissing you," he observed, as they consumed Diet Cokes under an enormous, gnarled oak tree—a powerful fertility symbol, he hoped—before starting the second nine.

"Do you?" she replied with discouraging indifference. "I hardly imagine I am as satisfying a sex object as your models and cabin attendants and advertising executives."

"Ah, you shouldn't believe everything you read in *INC* and Sneed and Kup's column."

"Shouldn't I?"

"Besides," he continued honestly enough, "most of those gorgeous women are pretty and nothing else. No real passion lurking behind the kiss. Not at all, at all."

"And there is in me?" She arched a skeptical eyebrow over her Coke can.

"A volcano about to erupt. Mount Etna maybe."

"Really? Isn't that a weary metaphor. Surely you can do better even on the spur of the moment."

"Well, let me see. . . . A lake ready to boil into a storm, a landslide about to unleash its first rock— No, no, strike that. An open-hearth furnace . . . what do they do? . . . Uh, lightning about to carve a slice of the night sky. . . . What about a tidal wave?"

"What about a warm fire at Christmastime with 'Greensleeves' playing in the background and marshmallows toasting on the fire and a large jug of cheap red wine and a man and a woman in heavy clothes who have just come in out of bitter cold and twenty feet of snow, wrapped up in a blanket and slowly becoming warm?"

"You're making fun of me!"

"Uh-huh. But I think the best I can do is the Christmas fire."

"You would think of Christmas when it's ninety and the humidity is ninety-nine."

"A red blanket, do you think? And had they been skiing or risking their lives on a snowmobile or trudging in from a car that broke down—a cute little red car maybe—or maybe just walking hand in hand under the naked, you should excuse the expression, trees."

"You're making fun of all my poems!"

"If it were one of your poems, they'd both already be naked in the blanket. As if people in the real world immediately take off their clothes when they come in from the cold."

"Have you ever curled up in front of the fire on a cold night with a man?" he demanded in defense of his muse.

"No. I suppose you and your pretty but sexless sex objects do it all the time. They are the kind of women who romp with you in the subzero snow, aren't they?"

"As a matter of fact, no," he admitted lamely. "They never leave the Lincoln Park bars that time of the year. Maybe you and I can experiment in these dunes come next December."

"And then again, maybe not."

"Besides, you don't expect us poets to be literal all the time do you? Aren't we permitted to use our imaginations?"

"Your imagination seems to have only one track, naked women in various compromising positions." She emptied her Coke can and considered it thoughtfully.

"Another one?"

"No, thank you."

"Sure?"

"All right." She smiled again and once more the cosmos vanished.

"Your morals are falling apart, woman. No self-control at all."

"Maybe I'm just thirsty."

The woman was smart, and clever, too, he thought on his return to the Coke machine. Well, in principle again, Conor liked women who were smart and clever. He would never marry a dummy, he had always insisted. "But, my dear," his friend Naomi Silverman, M.D., had often told him, "when your juices begin to flow, you forget about considering a woman's IQ."

Well, look at me now, Naomi Rachel Stern Silverman, I'm well aware that this woman is as smart as they come. And like I say, I don't object to smart women. So long as they are not too smart.

"Our finest wine, madam."

"Another cliché. But thank you. I'll buy the next two."

"Why are you worried so much about money?" he asked, permitting himself to be just a little bit irritable. "We're talking about sex, not money."

"Are they that much different?"

"Money isn't nearly so enjoyable as a beautiful woman."

"So long as she remains a sex object and does not become a person. Dollars are a lot more submissive."

"In the old days, my lovely 'dark-skinned but shapely'— that's the translation . . ."

She nodded. "I studied Latin in high school, too. And I read your translation of the Song of Solomon."

"*Love Song?* What did you think of it?" He leaned forward eagerly and, honestly, without any conscious thought about it, put his arm around her.

"Less erotic than the original." She eased away from his arm. "And perhaps more lyrical, by our standards anyway. . . . Now what would happen to me in the old days?"

"Well, my Persian princess—"

"Italian. Sicilian, in fact."

"Same difference. In the old days you would have brought a high price in the slave market. A king, at least, or maybe an emperor."

"Disgusting. Besides, they wouldn't have liked a big and sturdy woman."

"Worse luck for them." Conor sighed loudly. Not sure whether he had won or lost that exchange.

Hell, he'd lost it. Going away.

"Why aren't you married?" She did not look at him as she asked the question, but concentrated on freeing a monarch butterfly that was trapped by a discarded paper cup.

"Their arrival"—Conor watched her intently; she would not step on ants, swat flies or even crush mosquitoes, he had noted on the first nine—"marks the beginning of the end of summer. They migrate to a plateau in Mexico."

"Who? Oh, the monarchs." The brown and orange-winged creature soared away. Another possible metaphor for Diana—excessively romantic, but then Conor Clarke was nothing if not an excessively romantic man. "I'd hate to be trapped like that poor thing without anyone to help," she said.

"Have you ever been to Mexico?"

"I was to Detroit once." She actually laughed. "We never had the money to travel and now I don't have the time. You didn't answer my question. You're thirty. If you were married, you wouldn't have to steal kisses from defenseless virgins on the golf course."

I'd love to take you to all the sunny places in the world and swim naked with you in all the warm bodies of water in the world. That's probably too romantic a cliché for my sonnet, but I want to do it just the same.

"There was some abetting of the felony both before and after the fact. My problem is that I don't have an office."

"Pardon?" She laughed again, genuinely amused, it seemed.

Ah, good, I begin to entertain her again, progress of a sort. I should have left out that slave-market cliché. She didn't seem to mind, though. Does she know she's beautiful? What woman does? She probably thinks she's too tall. I'll have to work on that. Reassure her that I've always liked tall women. Even if it isn't true. Not till this morning anyway. At least she resolutely refuses to stoop—a good sign.

"My cultural background is South Side Irish. Beverly Hills. St. Praxides. Right, you know the type?"

She nodded, pursed lips suggesting that she knew them and did not altogether approve, a common enough reaction by those who were not of the tribe. "You might live in Lake Forest now, if you wanted."

"It wouldn't make any difference. It's in my genes."

"Let's stipulate that you're Beverly shanty Irish."

"Thus I must seek a bride from that group. Your Lake Forest or Kenilworth nubiles of the sort I meet at the Junior Orchestra Association threaten me enormously. N'est-ce pas?"

"Not my world."

"You're lucky, believe me. In any event, consider how I appear to young women of a marriageable age and their mothers of the aforementioned Beverly Irish. And I won't accept the word 'shanty' as universally accurate: I am an unemployed lawyer who writes poetry. Would you want your daughter or sister to marry such an unpromising fellow?"

"You're a venture capitalist." Her lovely brow furrowed, doubtless she was trying to figure out whether he was serious or not.

"Indeed." Perhaps she would suspect that, as in most things, he was half fun and full earnest. "Without an office. If I had an office, the title would not be a burden in my unsuccessful pursuit of a bride. But among the South Side Irish, what is a venture capitalist? A gambler, and not a respectable gambler like your cousin or your uncle who speculates on the Board of Trade or the Merc or the CBOE. Does not the very word 'venture' suggest someone a little disreputable, possibly even piratical—which brings me back to my earlier metaphor."

"A pirate who had doubled his inheritance by his twenty-eighth birthday." She frowned, apparently disapproving of this feat.

"Without having an office or seeming to do much work and spending most of his time, as you yourself have hinted, playing golf badly, sailing boats badly, writing poetry badly, and pursuing, with notable failure, fair but passionless women."

"The poems aren't bad." The golden flecks danced in her eyes—amusement, that's indeed what they stand for. "A touch of youthful narcissism and unabashedly romantic, but not bad. Only mildly erotic. Perhaps a bit afraid of the demands of real passion."

Red lights flashed on in Conor Clarke's brain and warning klaxons wailed. "I pay my taxes."

"What . . . oh, you think that the only reason an Assistant United States Attorney would read your poems is that she's checking your tax returns." Diana turned a becoming shade of scarlet. Would she, self-proclaimed virgin (Kiss me, if you want, but no more, fellow), blush like that on their wedding night when he gently removed her elaborate and intricately fastened white finery? "I'm not, really I'm not. Your cousin told me that she had set up this match last night and gave me the book to read. . . . If you weren't afraid of marriage, you'd rent an office, wouldn't you?"

"Ah, not only a pirate and a tax lawyer, but also a woman of wisdom. Can we say, before I tee off for the second and decisive nine in this epic contest, that I'm looking for a woman who would not assign herself the lifelong task of remaking me?"

"An impossible task, I should think." The gold flecked in her eyes. A good sign, she indulges in no self-deception about the corrigibility of Conor Clement Clarke.

Nonetheless, even though she seemed to expect the attempt, he did not kiss her on the tenth tee. As a result, she merely parred the hole. On the next fairway, he opened his counterattack.

"You're not playing against me, are you?"

"Pardon?" This time her brown eyes were startled, not amused.

"I'm not a worthy opponent, but even if I were, it wouldn't matter. You play against yourself. You have a standard of play against which you measure yourself, an impossibly difficult standard if I am to judge by the ratio of these"—he made her disapproving lip movement—"to these"—he mocked her tiny smile of approbation. "It must be hard to live with a hanging judge watching your every move—kind of like what we used to think God did."

Without comment, she turned and put her first fairway shot within ten feet of the pin. Her lips did not move when she walked off the tee. "You live your way, I'll live mine."

"Sorry to pry," he apologized, contrite for the moment, then added with the old verve restored: "I'll leave your psychological clothes on for the rest of the day. Make no promises about the other clothes, though."

"You're impossible." She favored him with her amused mother's smile, waited till he had dubbed his fairway shot, and added: "It's the way I was raised. I guess we couldn't afford to doubt that what we did had to be done well."

"And I on the other hand have come to understand, in the immortal words of G. K. Chesterton, that whatever is worth doing is worth doing badly. Thus we make an exceptionally well-balanced team. However, ought you not by your own terms be a professional golfer? You're playing this tough course even on a week's vacation from the mills of the United States Attorney for the Northern District of Illinois. If you played every day, you'd be one of the top money winners on the tournament, to say nothing of the fortune a figure like yours might earn modeling golf wear."

"A frivolous life," she snapped, distinctly displeased by his compliments. "Play that shot with your nine iron."

To display his independence, he used his eight iron and overshot the green by fifteen yards.

"I won't say I told you so," she said aloofly, then laughed

in embarrassment. "Please don't stare at me that way."

"It's your fault. You made the crack about taking off psychological clothes. It put dirty ideas into my head."

"Nonsense," she snapped. "And it was your phrase, not mine. Moreover, you've been doing that since Maryjane introduced us. Like what you find?"

"Enormously. Do you mind?"

"I should. I'm not an object." She stood on the green, one hand on the red-flagged pin, the other holding her putter, now flustered and vulnerable again. Flattered by his interest, and offended—though not as much as she thought she should be—by his frank inspection.

"I can't quite control what my imagination does, Diana," he tried to speak seriously for a change. "You are a beautiful young woman and I am at a time in life when the genes of our species program a young man to react, ah, vigorously to such as you. But as lovely as you would be standing there on that green with your clothes in a heap next to you, I'd never confuse you with an object."

"Grace O'Malley, pirate queen, becomes golf course exhibitionist. Putt."

He did. Again he forgot to concentrate and putted up to his ability. The ball ran on a straight, unerring line from the edge of the green, up over a slight rise, down into a steep depression, and then, like it had eyes, turned lazily and slid contentedly into the cup, from which Diana at the last minute pulled the pin.

"Wow!" exclaimed Diana Marie Lyons in unfeigned admiration. "Even the hanging judge approves of that one."

"See what my fantasies can accomplish."

"They make you forget that you're deliberately playing beneath your ability." She dropped the pin with sufficient disregard for the green as to give the relevant members of the Long Beach Greens Committee a heart attack.

"Can't make up your mind about me, can you, Diana Marie Lyons?" He essayed his most winsome smile.

"Oh"—she bent over to putt, causing more delightfully

obscene fantasies to race through Conor's brain—"I've made up my mind about you."

"And the verdict?"

"The old Scottish one—guilt not proven." She paused while she tapped her golf ball into the hole. "And tell me about translating poor old Solomon?"

"It's not exactly a translation. More of a paraphrase. I don't know any Greek or Hebrew and only a bit of Latin. I tried to redo the English so it sounds like poetry. I showed it to Father Roland Murphy—you know he comes to Grand Beach every summer—to make sure I hadn't wandered too far from the original."

They trudged on to the next tee.

"And he said?"

"That none of the specialists in the Song needed to worry about their jobs, but I hadn't done too much that was wrong. . . . It's not easy." He leaned his golf bag against the tree and, warming to the subject, began his usual lecture. "Take for example the famous line—that I may have quoted when I kissed a certain woman a half hour ago—in which the Shulamite says, *'Nigra sum, sed formosa.'* Father Roland insisted that I could not render it, 'I'm black and I'm really built.' "

"You're terrible!" She lifted his golf bag and continued the trip to the next tee.

"It is variously translated, 'I'm black and I'm lovely,' or 'The sun has tanned my skin.' "

"And you translate it, 'Dark is my skin and slim my waist.' "

"You really read *Love Song*?" He did not bother to try to hide his pleasure.

"I told you Maryjane had a copy. I compared it with her Bible. Even the original is pretty erotic for the Scriptures. It's all allegorical, isn't it?"

"My priest, Monsignor Ryan, you know . . ."

"Judge Kane's brother."

"Right. He tells me that it's strictly secular love poetry

that was included in the Jewish Scriptures because it was sung at weddings. Maybe written by a woman. . . ."

"I should think so." She dropped his golf bag against the bench and gestured for him to tee up.

"Monsignor says it's not allegorical but sacramental. Human passion, he says, gives us a hint of God's passion for us. We are most like God's love for us when we are aroused in the presence of our beloved. And we best experience a hint of God's love when our beloved pursues us."

"Really?" She searched for a tee in her pocket.

"God is a passionately aroused lover, nice, huh? And kind of scary?"

"Scary?" She considered her golf ball. "I suppose so. Beautiful, too. Now drive, three wood, I think."

Her thoughtful response so influenced Con that he did indeed use his three wood.

He sliced with it, too.

She came in with a par seventy-two. Conor, who settled down to concentrate on his golf on the last seven holes, finished with an eighty-three, giving her a one-stroke victory. If he had not deliberately hit his first putt on the eighteenth green too far, he would have won. Diana seemed about to accuse him again of deliberately losing and then thought better of it.

"Tennis? Squash?" she asked.

"A man as ancient as I am can afford only one loss a day." He carried her clubs into the clubhouse, without protest. "Besides I can hardly wait to see you in a swimsuit."

"The next generation of children"—she sighed wearily and took her golf bag from his hands—"will be raised to understand that it is not proper to consider the body of another human being that way."

"Do you really believe that?"

"Of course."

"How much beauty will God have wasted."

"I read your poems. I know how you react to a woman's body."

"It might not be safe to be in the pool with me."

"I'd be safe enough. But I'd rather not swim." She looked around. "This place is too rich for my blood. All these wealthy idle matrons."

"They're not really wealthy, Diana." He placed his hand gently on her shoulder. "I know some of the truly wealthy ones, too. If you can stay at Maryjane's, you can swim here. Maybe even eat supper with me."

Her lower lip jutted out stubbornly. "Idle rich."

"If you say so."

"The trouble is"—she put the lower lip back in its proper place and laughed at herself—"the trouble is that having swum here everyday with Maryjane, I'm hardly in a position to assert my convictions now, am I? See you at poolside, Conor Clement Clarke."

"A threat?"

"Take it as you want." She sauntered toward the women's locker room.

You could carry it off, woman, he thought, in the most exclusive country club in the world, the kind of place which wouldn't let a Beverly shanty Irishman like me by the guard dogs at the front gate.

A distinctly nasty side of her, Conor considered, as he showered before putting on his swimming trunks. Complex and interesting woman. Potentially dangerous, though I don't quite know why. Worth further exploration. Definitely.

Not that now I have the slightest choice in the matter.

2

Perhaps it is all right to play golf with him, Diana considered as she turned on the shower, but I ought not to have enjoyed his company. His father destroyed my father as casually as a man swats a pesky mosquito. And with so little thought that our family name touches no memories in his son.

But maybe I'm giving in to my Sicilian genes. Why should I have a blood feud with Clem Clarke's son? He's a nice boy.

A playboy, she told herself sternly. A spoiled rich kid. An overgrown Notre Dame sophomore.

As the warm waters of the shower caressed her, Diana thought of the reproaches she would have to write in her diary that night.

Instant obsession, that's the only name for it. They say, Mama had told her often, that the body is a good adviser and a bad ruler.

Diana never knew whether Mama's aphorisms were Sicilian folk wisdom or her own ideas that she had converted into folk wisdom so Diana would listen.

Well, my body gave me treacherous advice about Conor Clarke.

They also say—Diana could almost hear Mama's voice—that only a fool does not listen carefully to the body's advice.

I would like to go to bed with him, she told herself honestly. I would adore spending the rest of my life taking care of him.

Then she thought of the impact of marriage to Con

Clarke on her father and mother and shivered despite the shower's warmth.

She and Mama had been working out at the Nautilus in Mama's shopping mall, an activity about which Daddy was not supposed to know, since he objected to women with "too much muscle." Like a lot of other matters in their family life—including Mama's job as manager of a boutique—Daddy pretended to ignorance.

"Ah, *cara mia*"—Mama wrestled with the back bars, sweat pouring down her face—"the body grows old."

Diana could not describe even to herself her complex relationship with Mama. Usually Mama was a steadfast defender of Daddy's dignity and honor against the assaults of their children and the rest of the hostile world. Diana felt that as the last one in the family, the last hope, so to speak, she was the special target of Mama's ire.

Yet occasionally, and more frequently in the last couple of years, Mama would behave like a co-conspirator, a buddy, a big sister.

"The body does all right," Diana had replied, truthfully enough. In her sweat-drenched exercise suit, Mama might be a mature elder sister.

"Bah! A few more years and I'll be dust."

"Attractive dust!"

They both had laughed. "*Irlandesa*, you inherited your father's tongue."

"He doesn't talk that way much anymore." Diana had leaned against the wall, hoping she'd have as much enthusiasm for working out when she was Mama's age.

"It was all the fault of that Clem Clarke!" Mama went into her Mt. Etna mode, explosive Mediterranean fury. "He ruined your father's life! He took away his job! He stole his career! He ruined his health! He turned him into a hollow man! I hope he rots in hell forever!"

"Shush." Diana had looked around nervously. The others in the workout room were listening.

"I don't care." Mama had lowered her voice. "He was the devil. And his son is as bad. May he die without children and rot in hell, too."

You bet, Diana had thought then, herself a junior-grade Mt. Etna.

Daddy had been closing in on Clem Clarke; he had gathered enough evidence for an indictment. Then Clarke exercised his political clout, quashed the investigation, and arranged for Daddy's transfer to another agency, where he initialed papers all day. The deterioration of his spirit and his body had begun then, never to be stopped.

In the shower at Long Beach, Diana told herself that Con was as bad as his father. He's rich, he's spoiled, he thinks his money permits him to make his own rules. For all practical purposes, he has cheated the poor out of their money and their jobs.

Now that's silly, Diana. You don't believe in family feuds. You're an educated American, not a Sicilian peasant. You know nothing about the case that your colleagues Leo and Donny are trying to build against him. You are not working on the case. For all you know, it's just one more blind alley. Donny rushes down enough of them.

You want to marry him, you silly little bitch. One game of golf and you want to marry him.

Would it be ethical to marry him?

Of course it would, you little dummy. You're not working on his case, are you? All right, now you can't work on it, but so what? They weren't going to ask you to, anyway.

Have you heard ethics mentioned once since you went to work for Donny?

I impulsively asked Maryjane to set up this golf date because I wanted to have a good look at the son of my father's enemy.

Now I'm acting like a silly fourteen-year-old. I hide my reactions better than he does, but I'm not one bit better.

She watched the soap suds slip down her breasts. Conor

had liked them. No, more than that, he wanted them.

Half the time she thought her breasts were too big and the other half of the time she thought they were too small. She knew that she was well coordinated and had been told that she was graceful. Yet she was awkward and uncomfortable with her body.

She rubbed the suds into her belly. Conor Clarke thought it was a splendid body.

I haven't been kissed very often, and never like that. He reached the bedrock of my being. If he'd wanted to kiss me all day long, I would not have been able to fight him off.

She shivered again despite the hot water that was cascading down her body.

His priest says that sexual passion is a hint of how God loves us. . . . Do You desire me the way I desire him?

She pondered that exciting possibility.

Well, maybe You had better help me then, seeing that You know what it's like.

It's all biology, of course. But I thought I was immune to that sort of thing. I didn't need to marry, I told myself up till last night. In a few years I'd adopt a refugee orphan and settle down to be a single parent without having to go through the agony of divorce. That all looks pretty silly right now.

She turned the shower handle firmly to "cold," gritted her teeth, clenched her fists, and waited for the icy water to cure her of her foolish obsession.

It didn't help. Of course, Lake Michigan isn't very cold this time of year.

They say, Mama would have observed, that if you find a man very attractive, no harm is done by getting to know him better.

Could they possibly mean that? Or was Mama imparting sex education through folk wisdom?

Does Mama want to get rid of me?

Probably.

"Men look at you, Diana," she had said recently, "and

they like what they see. Women too." She had eyed her daughter clinically. "Even I sometimes wonder if that beautiful woman is really my daughter."

Men stare at me because they think tall women are freaks. He doesn't seem to think I'm a freak. I think Conor actually enjoys me as a woman.

That's strange. It is also very nice.

And, finally, it's ridiculous. He's a chauvinist like the rest of them. I'd merely be another temporary addition to his harem.

She turned off the shower. It wasn't nearly cold enough.

He is so beautiful. Am I actually thinking that about a man? Be honest with yourself, Diana, like Daddy said you always should be. You're smitten by his physical attractiveness. Curly blond hair, blue eyes, Robert Redford face, strong, strong body in those disgraceful Bermuda shorts he wears. And that sad, hurt-little-boy look of his that makes me want to take him in my arms and mother him, till whatever it is that causes his pain goes away.

Can this be me?

I must be honest. She shivered under a towel and stepped out of the shower room. It is me and I am, as we used to say in college, absolutely whipped.

I should have been offended at that disgusting image of him buying me on the slave block. Instead, I reveled in it. I would be delighted to be naked before him, powerless as he played with me and fondled me, considering whether I was worth his interest or not. Absolutely vile and repulsive. Yet it aroused me even more. Like it is doing now. What is wrong with me?

I shouldn't be playing golf with him, much less permitting myself these dirty feelings about him.

Come on, Diana Marie Lyons, she fought with her emotions and, in control again, walked into the empty locker room. You're human like everyone else. You're not immune to temptations. The nuns warned you about temptation when you were a little girl, before the Catholic church forgot about temptation. Now you're being tempted by a man you hate.

Only I wish the world was different and I didn't have to hate him. Well, as Daddy always says, the world is not the way we want it to be, but the way it is.

Repeating that wisdom over and over, as if to drill it into her brain, she struggled into her swimsuit. Now I'll have to go out there and face him while he devours me with those hurt, hungry, sad eyes of his.

Maybe he won't like me. Maybe there is too much of me. I am terribly big. Too big. Taller even than Daddy. Too many muscles. Ordinarily I'm proud of my tall, strong body and my athletic ability. Today it embarrasses me. I want him to like me. Men don't like tall women. They use them but they are threatened by them. Well, if he doesn't like me, that's too bad. There's nothing I can do to change.

She tossed a dry towel around her shoulders, drew a deep breath like she was about to take the bar exam again, and strode bravely toward the pool.

Just before she opened the door to go outside, she glanced at the woman in the mirror. She stopped in momentary surprise. That is me, isn't it!

Oh, he'll like me all right. No doubt about that.

My obsession will become worse before it becomes better. I'll live to regret this.

Right now, however, I don't care.

3

It does not matter, Conor Clarke told himself sternly, whether she's too thin and has skinny legs. What counts is that she is smart and personable and witty and not unattractive. And passionate, too, virtually by her own admission. Well, she didn't disagree with me when I suggested it. I'm looking for a wife—let's be candid about it at this age—and not a beauty queen.

It did matter, as it turned out. When Diana emerged from the women's locker room, he stopped breathing. Call an ambulance, find me a doctor, I have stopped breathing, perhaps permanently.

By no stretch of the imagination could the young woman be called skinny. And while her legs might have had too many strong muscles for some men, to Conor's dazzled eyes they were more than adequate. I need a metaphor for strength and elegance, solidity and airiness. Quick, someone find me a metaphor.

Her white swimsuit was modest enough, if anything could be modest on such a splendidly sumptuous body, carried with a grace that suggested either modeling school or natural elegance.

"I'm not sure how safe," he said, trying to appear both candid and judicious in his appraisal.

"What do you mean?" she frowned nervously.

"You said you'd be safe with me at poolside. I'm not sure how safe, even with every other man and woman in the vicinity staring in admiration."

She blushed crimson and turned her face away from his gaze. "You're acting like a horny adolescent male," she snapped, sitting on the lounge next to him. "Do you have to be so obvious about your lust? Would you please take me off the slave block in your imagination and treat me like a person instead of an object."

"If there was not a bit of the horny adolescent male in every man"—he picked up his tube of Hawaiian Tropic coconut-smelling suntan cream—"the human race would soon go out of existence. Do I take it that your principles still mean civil action against me if I refer to your, ah, physical charms in the sonnet I will write tomorrow about Grace O'Malley the golfer?"

She lowered her head and bit her lip. "Say whatever you want in your damned sonnet."

"I may require that on the record. . . . Your back need any of this?"

Defiantly she turned away from him and pushed the straps off her shoulder. He anointed her with the respect he would have shown to the back of a mitered abbess, if by some impossibility one such would appear at the side of the swimming pool of the Long Beach Country Club. However, the back of a mitered abbess would hardly stir up in him the same alarmingly delicious fantasies.

Unless, and in the new Church all was possible, said mitered abbess had a body like Diana Lyons.

I want you, my darling. I've never wanted anyone this badly before. I won't hurt you and I won't treat you like an object. But I do want you in my bed, I want your body under mine—or vice versa when it suits your pleasure—on an indefinite, not to say permanent, basis.

He tried to make the touch of his cream-smeared fingers as light and delicate, as reverent and respectful as his pounding heart would permit. Some of the stiffness seemed to ooze out of her.

"I guess," she said softly, "that the human race needs women to act occasionally like horny teenage girls, too. I'm glad you like me. God knows, I think you're extremely attractive."

"Did you really say that?"

"Why not? It's true. If you can say such things, why can't I? Nothing special follows from them. They're simply a declaration of a biological reaction."

A lot of back to cover with cream. And you'd better do it a second time. Despite her dark skin, she could be badly burned by the sun. Couldn't she?

"With no emotional overtones."

"Emotions are biological. How do you separate hormones from affection? Maybe men can. They seem to do a pretty good job of it. Women can't."

He paused, his fingers only a few centimeters from where a full, apparently very firm breast began. "You're a disconcerting young woman, Diana Lyons, an unpredictable mixture of ideology and passion, of affection and anger, of professional competence and breathtaking tenderness."

There were a few seconds of pregnant silence. She swallowed once, nervously. "Let's say I am complex and often inconsistent, but that's the way your golf-course Irish woman pirates are." She readjusted her straps. "Now I'm going to swim a half mile, and when I come back, you're going to tell me about saving the Rust Bowl."

Her progress to poolside was impeded by two girl children of early-grammar-school age, West of Ireland waif children transported across the sea and through several social classes but as appealing as ever.

"Will you tie my straps, Diana?"

"Will you put cream on my back, Diana?"

To the delight of the brats she made a big deal of both projects, kissed them both, patted their little rumps, and then waved at them as she dived—perfectly, of course—into the blue pool.

He joined her later and did notably less than his daily mile for the same reason he had blown the putt on the eighteenth green. He considered a small frolic in which he would dunk her, frolics that teenage girls of every age enjoyed. He decided against it: she would probably not approve and she might well be too strong for him to dunk.

"Ten!" he said as she pulled herself from the pool, engaged in the usual womanly ritual of making sure her straps had not vanished and that her swimsuit had not crept up too high on her quite presentable if not altogether voluptuous, by Conor's normal standards, rear end. She was, he thought (in another hasty and inadequate metaphor), brighter than the sun. Making a disrespectful face that no Arabian slave girl would dare make at an Irish chieftain, she lay on the lounge next to him.

"As in Bo Derek?"

"That too, God knows, but, no, as in performances for an Olympic judge. Ten for golf, kids, dive, and swim."

"You have a certain flair for nastiness, don't you?" Her lips were tight with rage. "Does that come with being a poet?"

He noted that there was a ridge of freckles across her nose and another line just above her breasts. Mick blood in this Arabian. So much the better.

"When some man finally overcomes your prudery and fear and talks you into bed with him"— this was strictly dirty pool, but Conor went ahead with it anyway—"he's likely to enjoy it tremendously until he realizes those invisible judges are there in your brain rating both performances, yours more rigorously than his."

He waited for the explosion as she silently considered the charge before the court.

Oddly enough, her anger vanished as quickly as the sun at the end of a winter day. "You're wrong about the kids, anyway. At least, mostly wrong. That's pure fun. If I wasn't a lawyer, I'd like to be a teacher. It's funny, but since I was in maybe seventh or eighth grade, kids have done that. I must look like a faerie godmother or something."

Only one woman in ten thousand would have let him get away with what he'd said. So he pushed his luck. "You were not so poor growing up that you could permit pure fun a rare place in your life?"

She stiffened, her lips hardened into a bitter line, her face turned white with rage, her eyes turned as hard as the steel of the Daley Civic Center in the loop.

If Grace O'Malley had a sword at hand at this moment, he thought, she'd run me through.

"Am I beautiful when I'm angry?" she asked through tight lips.

Actually she wasn't at the moment. Too much hatred. He lied. "Very, if that matters."

She lay back on her lounge and closed her eyes. "OK, let's stipulate that you have one gotcha. Now tell me about the Rust Bowl."

"Not before I find out more about those kids. They've seen you here before?"

"Once or twice."

"And now they lay in wait?"

"Uh-huh."

"And that happens all the time?"

"Usually."

"And you love it?"

"Obviously. And the next question is why I don't have any children of my own. And the answer to it is that I made a conscious and difficult decision to pursue a career." She spoke, eyes still closed, shapely shoulders sagging just a little. "Maybe the two could mix for others. I don't think I could be a good mother and a good lawyer at the same time. Satisfied?"

"No."

"Why not? Not that it's any of your affair . . . uh, business."

"Because I think you could do anything you wanted to do, Diana Marie Lyons. I sure would hate to have you as an enemy."

"Indeed."

"And I'd love to have you as a . . ."

"Yes?" She opened her eyes and stared at him.

"I was going to say, before I was so rudely interrupted, 'A mother.' "

"Two gotchas!" She threw back her head and laughed. "I'd be very stern with you, little boy. None of this shanty Irish blarney. Now to the Rust Bowl."

Later the mystery would disappear from her response, and Conor Clarke would realize what a fool he'd been not to wonder more about it.

"The point is that the so-called Rust Bowl—the ring of factories in the states around the Great Lakes—is not merely a precious national resource, it is also an incredible economic opportunity." As always when he got into his speech on the subject, Conor abandoned his poet persona and dusted off and donned his politician and pitchman mask. "It doesn't need protection like an endangered species, it doesn't even need a large government subsidy like Lockheed or Chrysler. It only needs investors with imagination and courage."

"And tax breaks," she interrupted.

"We'll take what we get, of course, but I'm in favor of tax reform. If we lose our write-offs, there will be other ways of making money." Absently he touched her hand. "When bright young lawyers like you leave government service and enter the private sector, they figure out the ways for dumb old lawyers like me . . ."

"I'll never do that." She snatched her hand away from him like he had leprosy. He was so preoccupied with his sermon that he hardly noticed.

"Anyway, the Rust Bowl has the buildings, the transportation, the skilled work force, the public transportation, a more mature political and financial structure, and especially water. We Chicagoans don't realize how important water is because we have so much of it down the way in the big melted glacier. Why locate in the Sun Belt when you can

locate in the Rust Bowl and save a lot of money because you
don't have to build new factories or transportation facili-
ties?"

"I don't know, why?"

I have talked for several minutes and not once noticed
her cleavage. I may not be human. I would never hurt her,
never exploit her, never be anything but gentle and kind and
loving with her. I promise.

Mind you, I'm not promising I won't engage in all sorts
of terribly obscene activities. But at her speed.

He trusted that was an adequate if temporary nod of his
head to the Deity.

"Because you think that labor costs are cheaper in the
Sun Belt and because you have never stopped to think that
you can save money on plant construction and because, anyway, your firm is not into rehabilitating old factories."

"So?"

"So I buy the South Works at U.S. Steel for you, buy it
cheap because U.S. Steel thinks it will have to spend money
tearing it down, and I refit it so that you can manufacture
computer assemblies for your robots or assemble Japanese
VCRs or process film or make prefab houses or maybe all of
these things together, along with the software programs to
make them work—and user friendly ones at that. I mean really user-friendly documentation, and I offer to sell it to you
at half the cost of your new plant in Texas and I'm even
ready to take some of my payment in shares of the profits
you make on the products turned out in our rehabilitated
factory. It's an offer you can't refuse."

"In the process, you make a huge profit." She twisted on
her lounge to reach for her sunglasses. Conor did not notice
the allurements involved in her efforts to protect herself
from the rays of the setting sun. Well, he did notice them,
but not forcefully enough to distract him from his argument.

"More than if I put the money in tax-free government
bonds. But the social costs are still less than if the govern-

ment tried to do the same thing. And this administration would rather commit mass suicide than get involved in competition with the Sun Belt."

"How much profit? Twenty-five percent a year?" She reached for the suntan cream. "That used to be considered usury."

"Nothing that easy or certain. Sometimes zero percent and then the next year, if you're really lucky, a hundred percent."

"That's outrageous. Without any risk." She pulled the tube away from his fingers.

"No, that's the point. The risk is high. You read in *Business Week* only about the successes."

"I don't read *Business Week*." She was rubbing the cream furiously into her skin.

"Well, you should. Anyway. You can lose a lot of money on these projects. An ordinary investor should stay out of ventures. There is a saying that lemons turn up quick and pearls take a long time to develop. Federal Express, which is one of the most successful of the ventures—what would we do without it?—required three capitalizations to make it. Even the man who has the resources for ventures had better not expect to win every time. The potential profit is the price paid for taking the risk. If you cut the profits, people won't take the risk. They might as well put the money in municipals or in CDs at the local version of Talman Federal. The possibility of playing the venture game is why we are ahead of the rest of the world in computers."

"Ahead of Japan?" she asked contemptuously.

"In most respects, yes. No one over there"—he felt a faint smile of complacency and self-satisfaction—"has come up with anything like our accounting program yet."

"The one your Notre Dame classmate devised that's made you a hundred percent profit?"

"Five hundred, actually."

"And you don't think that's grounds for arrest?"

"The accountants who use the system," he said, reaching tentatively for her fingers, "think it is grounds for our canonization." She didn't pull them away. A very erratic young woman. Confused probably, poor kid. "Anyway, I plowed most of the money back into other ventures."

"To make more money?" She sounded like she was genuinely curious.

"You promise you won't laugh."

"Of course."

"To make the world a better place. Honest."

Well, she didn't laugh. She merely went on with her cross-examination—without, however, freeing her fingers.

"What about the unions?"

"Some of them—" He took possession very tentatively of her whole hand and then changed the subject: "Have supper with me here at the club?"

She nodded, as if she had expected to be asked and had already made up her mind.

"Great. . . . Where was I? Oh, the unions. Some of them are cooperative, others suspicious. The bright people at United Steel Workers of America know that we can provide jobs for the workers who will never make steel at the South Works again, if our productivity can match the productivity of the nonunion plants in the South. Sometimes we index wages to productivity and profits, sometimes we give workers shares in the company or put union people on the board, sometimes we make products that are less labor intensive."

"So some men and women end up out of work anyway."

"Less than if the factory site is unused. Look, this isn't a perfect world. Some of the people that work in the rehabilitated factory didn't work in the old one. Many of those who worked in the old one, for one reason or another, not the least of which are age and retirement, will not work in the new—or I guess I should say *renewed*—plant. Maybe their children or grandchildren will. But at least there are workers in the community and that means business for the shopkeepers and the tradesmen and the professionals and the clergy and even the undertakers. Maybe things will never be as good in South Chicago as they were when the South Works was operating at full capacity, but they're a lot better than if the buildings are empty or are replaced by high-rise upper-income condominia with marinas attached."

"What about those who say men like you are profiting out of the misery of the unemployed industrial workers?"

"You are a good lawyer." He released her hand, for tactical reasons, not out of boredom, rolled over on his stomach, and jabbed his finger at her. "Marvelous at the adversarial style. The answer is that I make money, when I make it, which isn't all the time despite what you read in *Crain's Chicago Business*, by reducing their misery. I can't do anything about *ressentiment*. That's French, but it doesn't quite mean resentment. It means, well, sort of murderous envy."

"I went to Chicago Circle, not Notre Dame, but I know what *ressentiment* means." She glared at him coldly.

"I didn't learn it at Notre Dame. . . . Anyway, my reward is for putting the package together—political, financial, community support, actual reconstruction of the facility. If I do a good job, I have money to invest in another project. If I don't do a good job often enough, I hang out a law shingle somewhere."

"How much time does all this take?"

"Ordinarily? Three mornings a week. If something big is in a crucial state? A hundred hours a week. That's maybe once a year."

"Nice work if you can get it."

Suddenly he was angry at her snide comments, which he had hardly noticed. He touched her face with his fingers, a firm and even harsh pressure against her cheekbone.

"Look, Diana Marie Lyons," he said grimly, "you're a beautiful and gifted woman. In that swimsuit you're one of the most awesome sights I have ever had the pleasure to observe, so challenging that my poetic imagination is paralyzed in its search for a metaphor. I intend to fall in love with you. I'm halfway there already. However, there are times when you seem to have a ledger book for a soul and a stopwatch for a heart. . . . Is the worth of an activity to be judged by the amount of time spent on it?"

Her eyes flashed dangerously. He prepared for the explosion. Again it didn't come.

"Of course not." She shrugged her wonderful shoulders, notably appeasing his wrath, and made no effort to dismiss his hand, which was, in effect, laying a claim to be exactly where it was. "Like you say, I have a tendency to be adversarial"—she hesitated—"and even judgmental." She grinned and touched his hand, in effect approving its invasion and continued presence. "Your Irish women pirates are that way, you know. You remember what Grace O'Malley did to the Flahertys, don't you?"

He didn't but it didn't much matter.

"It would be a terrible mistake," he continued his summary for the defense, recalling his troops from her cheekbone, "for me to become compulsive about the day-to-day administration of these projects. It's not my talent, I'd goof up, not to use more obscene language, and not devote enough energy to dreaming up new schemes."

"The good Rust Bowl venture capitalist should be a poet?" She rested her head on her hand and smiled at him.

He almost fought back again and then realized that she was serious. "I've never had the nerve to say it."

His face felt very warm. Her smile widened, and his face became even warmer. "Maybe we should dress for supper?"

"Are you really trying to buy the South Works?" She stood up and slipped a John Marshall Law School sweatshirt over her head. Not exactly the quality of his University of Chicago degree. Him and "Fast Eddie" Vrdolyak.

"Not yet. It's too good a site and too much press attention. These things have to be done quietly at the beginning."

"It won't be too expensive?"

"The South Works?"

She blushed. "No, dinner."

He swatted her rear end, playfully, not nearly enough to hurt, but enough to let her know that he'd been there. "Woman, will you stop that?"

"Not if that's your reaction."

"You like having your ass swatted?"

"Occasionally and that way."

"Keep on talking about prices and you might just get even worse."

She considered him with mock seriousness. "An interesting prospect. Do I have a choice, by the way?" She had not resisted his arm around her shoulders as they walked toward the locker rooms.

"In what?"

"In your falling in love? I presume you do it weekly?"

"That's not fair," he said with a chuckle. "You know me too well, too soon. Yes, I do it often. Sometimes, but only sometimes, seriously. And no, you don't have any choice at all."

"That seems rather autocratic," she said lightly.

"Not in the least. It's my falling in love. So I'm the only one who has a choice. You"—they were at the door of the locker rooms—"have the choice of whether to respond. Thus far, the typical reaction, a sad commentary on the taste of female humankind, has been remarkably consistent."

"They decline with thanks?"

"Sometimes." He kissed her longer and more affectionately than before. He thought he detected a faint hint of a response.

"Remarkable." She winked mysteriously. "I at any rate will say thanks for the dinner." She disappeared into the women's locker room, with a last few words thrown over her shoulder: "And the kiss."

Conor Clarke sighed wearily. The woman was presentable enough. She was also exhausting. That was the way of it with Irish women pirates.

What am I to do with her? he asked himself in the shower room.

Now that, Conor Clarke, is a ridiculous question.

Even then, he would remember much later, there was a tiny voice in the back of his head warning him to be careful.

You're the fly and she's the spider, the voice said. You're the one on the block, not she.

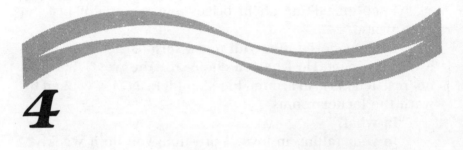

4

She was waiting for him on the terrace overlooking the eighteenth hole, a margarita in hand, appraising him coolly as he walked toward her.

"Jacket and slacks coordinated with your blue eyes? I feel distinctly underdressed."

"You noticed the color of my eyes?"

"I didn't spend all day staring at your chest muscles. . . . What should the score have been down there?" She gestured at the eighteenth green. "I mean if you were playing golf instead of appraising me like a teenage boy?"

It was going to be a long hard evening. Glory be, won't she ever let up?

You'll have to adjust to it, my friend. It's the way she is. You kind of like it, to tell the truth. Fighting with her excites you. It makes you more physically aggressive than you would otherwise be.

"I figure that if both of us are in top form, you're four strokes better than me. But then I'm not good enough to be on the tour and you are."

"So you lied about your handicap?" She shook her head in feigned—at least he thought it was feigned—dismay. "That's fraud, Counselor."

"I underestimated. That's business, Counselor.... Oh well, I shouldn't but I'll have one of what the young woman is having."

She was wearing a light tan, strapless sun dress, one of the new kind that bunched in under the shoulders and flared broadly from there on down, thus enabling a woman to be both formal enough for dinner and comfortably underclad in the summer heat. A touch of makeup, long brown hair at last undone and falling casually on bare shoulders, a simple gold chain around her neck, and, he presumed, panties were all that was required to be acceptable at the country club on a warm night.

"I shouldn't because I feel I've been drinking rich wine all afternoon."

"Blarney, not to use more scatological language. Your health, Counselor. More and bigger ventures!"

Very strong rich wine.

"You came prepared for dinner."

She shrugged. "I hoped that if I was reasonably well behaved, I might be permitted to eat with the beautiful people."

"These aren't the beautiful people," he insisted grimly.

"I know that." She touched his hand again, fingers lingering for what seemed half of eternity while they were there and a millisecond when they were removed. "When I was a little kid and we used to come up to Washington Park in Michigan City for a day, I thought they were the beautiful people."

"They are a lot nicer than the beautiful people." He moved his fingers against hers. Finally she withdrew her hand, but very gently.

"Why did you let me win?" she asked, apparently curious instead of contentious.

"You'll become angry and adversarial again."

"I will not," she snapped stubbornly, blushed, and then added sweetly, "I really won't."

"Well . . ." He decided that it might be a useful tactic to tell the truth, something he rarely risked this early in the game with a woman. And so far in his life, it had been a mistake to risk it at any time in the game.

"Two reasons, I guess. First of all, I wanted to establish early in the game that while I am indeed an insensitive, horny, objectifying, male chauvinist pig, I don't mind contending on the links with a woman who is better at the game than I am. I take it as clearly established that, handicaps aside, you are better at golf than I. Will you stipulate that, Counselor."

"OK." She nodded her head, her curiosity now aroused. "I was to be impressed with your moderate, athletic feminism. I am duly impressed, though skeptical, about your motivation. Secondly?"

There was something special about her nod; it indicated not only intellectual agreement but a sort of personal acceptance and approval.

"Secondly, from the first moment, you fascinated me. I wanted to study you. I kind of felt—hunch more than anything else—that I could learn more about you when you were winning. Angry?"

"I said I wouldn't be. And you learned that I look good when I swing a club, that I'm a hanging judge, and that I have a ledger book for a heart?"

"Among other things."

"Which are?" She traced a pattern on the table with her glass.

"That you are one of the most intriguing, mysterious, and lovely women I have ever known; that, by your leave, I want to know you better; and that from now on, I'll play it straight with you—uh, straighter than you have any reason to expect."

"At least I passed the test well enough to earn my supper."

"With flying colors."

"You found me mysterious?" She raised her quizzical eyebrow again. "No man has ever tried that line on me before."

" 'Tis true just the same. So . . ." Who were the other men? he wondered, instantly and irrationally jealous.

"So . . . what?"

"Do I have your leave to get to know you better?"

"At the present I'll reserve judgment." She continued to work on her designs on the table.

"So what do *you* think?"

"About what?" She sipped her margarita and watched him cautiously over the rim of the glass.

"About Conor Clement Clarke, playboy, patron of the arts and the sciences, entrepreneur, inept, possibly drunken sailor, unsuccessful lover so far but still hopeful, reverse cheater at golf, companion of rich and beautiful women, frequent habitué of Kup's column . . ."

"Oh, *him* . . . Well, I'm a little less persuaded about the hordes of beautiful women than I was this morning."

"I don't know whether to be relieved or insulted." He squirmed uneasily.

"Hold still," she said primly. "Moreover, he is certainly not physically unappealing, he has a kind of hurt, hangdog expression that would appeal to any woman's maternal instinct."

"Hey . . ."

"If you can take off my clothes, I can take off yours." She colored faintly. "Psychologically, I mean. At the moment."

"Of course." Why was his face so hot?

"Well, how much money is it going to take?"

"Huh?"

"Your father was a fabulously successful trader"—she put the margarita glass on the table and began to tick off points on her discreetly lacquered fingernails—"in . . . what was it? . . . pork bellies and soybeans? Made and lost millions on the Board of Trade. What must it feel like in the parlors of the rich and famous, by the way, to say, 'I'm into pork bellies'? Then, at the end of his life in the big run-ups of the early seventies, made more than he'd ever made and lost before put together. The Board was his life. Nothing else mattered, neither the second wife he married late in life nor the one son to whom he paid little attention, especially when it was clear that he was not going to be the only thing the old man wanted, a Notre Dame football star. Your mother and father died within a year of each other, and you inherited an enormous amount of money, millions and millions, because your father, believing in his own immortality, never bothered with a will that would keep it out of your hands. So you set about doubling it in a couple of years and doing it in socially useful ways while you continued to affect the image of playboy and patron of arts and poet. . . ."

"The poet is not an image."

"*D'accord.*" She nodded agreement and continued to tick off the case against him on her fingertips—fingertips that rightly belonged inside his mouth. "As I've said before, you're good at it and probably will become better. But how much more money will it take before you will have proven to yourself and your father's ghost that you can make more money than he did and still be a discount-store renaissance man, a kind of Irish Catholic George Plimpton?"

Well, she'd left him his shorts. Or had she?

"It's not quite doubled." Only much later, after it was too late, did Conor Clarke ask himself why anyone would come to a first date so well briefed, even a lawyer who believed in being prepared.

"Don't turn sullen on me." She picked up her half-empty margarita glass. "You said I had a ledger book for a soul and a stopwatch for a heart. You fantasized my performing in a highly hypothetical bed for the benefit of Olympic judges. What's sauce for the goose . . ."

"Doubling will be enough," he said glumly.

"Then you'll settle down to write poetry?"

"No." Now he was totally in love with her. She was the

best one yet, the best ever, most likely. His cousin Maryjane was a genius for arranging the golf game.

"Why not?" She drained the glass and shook her head when he raised his eyebrow to ask whether she wanted another.

"I like what I'm doing."

"Venture capitalism is fun?"

"Not as much fun as being disrobed by you." He grinned wickedly. That would come, too.

"I'm serious."

"So am I. Well, more or less. It's exciting and useful work. Maybe there's more of the old man's gambling instincts in me than I thought. I don't know."

"You feel you're making a contribution by making money?"

He would not want to be cross-examined by her on the witness stand. No way.

"Something like that."

"Greed doesn't enter in?"

"Maybe it does. I try to keep it out. What more can I say?"

Dusk was rapidly creeping up the golf course, appropriate for his sudden fit of melancholy.

She watched him carefully, folding her hands in front of her like a mother superior. Gradually her facial expression softened and became almost tender. "You can invite me to the dining room to eat some of their poached salmon. You can forgive me for being unbearably rude in my curiosity."

"Let's eat." He grinned and took her arm to guide her into the dining room.

Damn it, in the game of keeping the other off balance that they had played all day, she had won another round. Perhaps by acknowledging her triumph, as every eye in the dining room turned to peer at his striking dinner companion, he could save a little face.

"Diana Marie Lyons," he began, his tongue outracing his common sense, a not infrequent phenomenon when he was in love, "you are a very beautiful and a very smart woman. You use your intelligence, commendably enough, to keep at bay the men who are attracted by your beauty. Small wonder you're still a virgin." I shouldn't have said that. "I want to serve notice on you that, even though I lost today's scrimmage, we discount-store renaissance men are not put off by women who are smarter than we are and more articulate and quicker witted and four-stroke-better golfers."

"Truce!" She held up her hands in mock surrender. "Let's eat our salmon and drink the white wine you're going to buy for me, in peace."

"Truce, indeed," he agreed, wondering if truce would ever be possible with such a one as Diana Marie Lyons, currently his One True Love.

At supper, however, she was charming, playful, eventually slightly tipsy from the margarita and half bottle of wine. Short hitter.

"This is very good wine." She nodded approvingly. He saw a cloud gather in her sparkling brown eyes, a question forming on her lightly defined lips. Then the cloud faded and the question died.

"It is *very* expensive wine," he answered the unasked question.

"I didn't ask." She bowed her head to hide her blush. "I was afraid of your right hand."

"It still hurts from the last time." He examined his hand. "Rock hard muscle."

"Squash does that. We'll have to play that sometime."

He considered a faintly suggestive comment about the attractiveness of her posterior and rejected the notion as premature. Instead, he turned to her work, normally a safe subject.

"So what do you do in the seventy-hour week that Donny Roscoe imposes on you?" he asked when they had returned to the terrace for the final cup of coffee. (Decaf for her. Aha, my love you don't sleep well? In the months ahead perhaps we can find a cure.)

"Government work." She was instantly guarded, defensive.

"I know *that*." He possessed himself firmly of her hand, not intending to let it escape this time. She didn't try to escape. "What kind of government work?"

"Oh, taxes, fraud, that sort of thing." Fireflies were busy punctuating the sticky night air with their bursts of hopefulness. "Well, it's in the papers, so I suppose there's nothing wrong with talking about it in a general sort of way."

"I don't read the local news much." It was a remarkably submissive hand for one which could do such wonderful things with a golf club. Old-fashioned lovers, holding hands on a porch at night—a humid summer night in a resort, at that.

"We're taking a look at your friend Broderick Considine, of the Cook County Board."

"Broddy Considine? That old crook? You have your work cut out for you. My father used to say he was the kinkiest politician in the Cook County Regular Democratic Organization—and that covered a lot of territory."

"He was a good friend of your father's, was he not?"

"They played golf at Olympia, whenever my father got around to golf, which, when I knew him, was a couple of times a summer. He contributed to Broddy's campaigns, of course. Everyone did in those days, I guess. Even today, I suppose I give him a few thousand every four years for old time's sake. He's a fraud and a phony, but like some of the early Chicago architecture, you want to keep him around as a museum piece."

"Isn't he some kind of business associate of yours?"

"Broddy? Hell, no. I have more sense than that, Diana Marie Lyons."

"I can't recall at this hour of night," she replied after a

moment's silence, "with all the alcohol you have forced upon me in your treacherous assault on my virtue"—she giggled and held her hand delicately to her mouth to suppress a hiccup—"but are you not involved with the United Foundry Works?"

"Sure, out in Cokewood Springs at the south end of Cook County. . . . Gosh, you're right, I'd forgotten about it. Broddy does have a piece of that action. It was my idea, too. It's a lot easier to get things done in that end of creation if Broddy is involved. I had my lawyers make sure there was no conflict of interest."

"There's no suggestion of that." Her hand seemed to tighten on his. "It's merely that Mr. Considine's affairs are tangled. It may take years to sort them out."

"Centuries." What a terrible waste of beauty and brains to be sorting out the web of chicanery of an old man who would probably be dead before he ever served a day of his sentence. It was a sin against justice for such a woman to spend her young years laboring to provide a few newspaper headlines for Donny Roscoe, the sleazy character who was currently trying to build a political future in the U.S. Attorney's office, just as Jim Thompson did more than a decade ago. Teflon sleaze. She should be working for Rich Daley and getting some real courtroom experience. Or maybe teaching little kids how to draw, her own especially. Well, we'll see about that.

"It's not one of your big ventures then? Strictly minor league?"

"One of the easiest. As I remember, the company will make machines that test other automatic machines to make sure they work properly. Very skilled engineering and machine-tool stuff, so it will attract a lot of engineers to aging professional suburbs like Homewood and Flossmoor and Olympia Fields that need some new blood."

"Is it one of those five-hundred-percent projects?"

He laughed easily and confidently. "Those come along only once a decade. No, the Cokewood caper is interesting

not so much because of the rehabilitation of the plant—
that's pretty standard stuff—as for the product they'll be
making. If we can get ourselves a head start in automatic
machines to make automatic machines, we'll make south
Cook County the Silicon Valley of the nineteen nineties. So
I'm mainly concerned, both personally and financially, with
the technology, not the reconstruction."

"Have you been to Cokewood Springs?" Her hand
slipped away. Ah well, it was too good to last.

"Once, I think. Perfect plant. The company actually
asked me to find a place for them. The town looked like a
down-at-the-heels Calumet City. Lots of neat little houses
that could stand another coat of paint. Well, if you folks are
poking around, you can look all you want at my tax returns."

"I wouldn't be discussing this matter with you," she said
stiffly, "if we intended to do that."

"I know. Damnit, woman, give me your hand back. I
have no evil designs on your virginal body. Not tonight, anyway."

She complied without comment.

"That's better. I'll make no guarantees for the future."

"As I said, I can take care of myself."

Could she really? he wondered. Tough, strong,
competent—that was the mask. Beneath the mask was a
vulnerable, frightened, and perhaps lonely woman. Both the
mask and the woman were attractive, especially in combination.

"Is that fun?"

"Taking care of myself? It has been so far."

"Hmmn . . . where was I? Oh yes, taxes. The point is—"
how many times had he used that phrase today? Interesting
Freudian implications, Naomi would say. Had indeed said
when he was almost successfully courting her. "—that I
wanted to assure you that I pay my taxes. I've been audited
every year since Dad died. I'm clean as a whistle. If I go to
Lexington or some other federal poky, I'd want it to be for
something that's more fun than cheating the IRS."

"Such as?"

"Taking virgin pirates across state lines for immoral purposes, Indiana-Michigan lines will do for the moment. Though Illinois-Hawaii would be nice, too. It's really not too hot in Hawaii this time of the year."

"Come back in January with your immoral propositions."

She giggled again. The wine, sixty dollars a bottle, was worth a lot more if it made her giggle.

"You enjoy ravishing virgins?" She considered him with the intense seriousness of the slightly inebriated.

"I usually like to put it off to their wedding nights," he replied lightly. "Unless they assault me, which frequently happens, as you can imagine. In fact, I'm actually hiding out from a couple of them over here." He glanced around the room with pretended nervousness. "They might show up at any time."

"I can imagine."

He had told her the truth about his intentions. His poetic sense insisted that a woman who had remained virginal into her twenty-fifth year should be ravished only on her wedding night. However, such a night must not wait till her twenty-sixth year.

Moreover, the woman was exhausting. While he was, he now concluded, hopelessly in love with her, she bore a lot more careful investigation before any premature decisions were made.

She was, he had to admit, a delightful dinner companion once she had forsaken her cross-examination of his lifestyle. Aware that she was being admired, and lightheaded from the Niersteiner, she laughed at his worst jokes, listened appreciatively to his stories about the mores of Silicon Valley, and imitated most of the prominent Illinois politicians. As her boss, Donald Bane Roscoe, she was especially funny.

"This office," she lisped through jutting teeth, "will not tolerate any convictions that will not open the way to the governor's mansion."

"How can you work for the man and make fun of him?" It was his turn to be shocked.

She shrugged her shoulders. "I can make fun of a man who buys me dinner, too." She put on a faintly lunatic face, not unlike one Conor had often seen in the mirror. " 'Once my love and I, on the coldest of winter nights . . .' "

Ignoring anyone in the club who might have been watching, Conor silenced her mocking lips, tasting now of sweet Niersteiner, with a long kiss.

" 'Under the mothering gaze of friendly stars . . .' " she went on, before trailing off in a spasm of tipsy giggles.

A dangerous woman. *Tremendum et fascinans.* I could get in a whole lot of trouble. Tonight.

So it would be a reasonably modest brush of the lips and a quick good-night—though, dear God, that sort of affection can't go on forever in a man's life, can it? Well, it will go on for one more night, anyway.

In companionable silence he drove her back to Maryjane's summer home in Grand Beach.

"Only one light on in the house?" he said as they turned the corner in the Sun Valley Falls subdivision.

"Maryjane and Gerard are coming up together tomorrow morning. He's taking a long weekend. He didn't want her driving back here by herself. The baby, you know."

"In three months?"

"If you ever work up enough courage to marry, you'll be that way when your wife is expecting her first."

He was in no mood for any further sparring with her. "Will you be safe?"

"With Rich Daley's family down the street? I'd be safer only in a cloistered convent."

"They are not so safe these days." He opened the door and bowed her out of the car. She was not consistent enough in her feminism to reject the traditional courtesies. "I'll give you a ring tomorrow."

"I can hardly wait," she said ironically. "No, I won't end contentiously. It has been a very interesting day. Will that do?"

"I've enjoyed every moment of it." He held her arm, guiding her to the door. Most of the effect of the wine had worn off.

"Even the adversarial part of it?"

"I can't think of a more beautiful woman with whom to argue." He leaned over her for a brief and chaste good-night kiss.

"Thank you," she said simply.

Conor's plans for the kiss went awry. Somehow their bodies and their lips locked. Both their hearts pounded. She was soft and warm and appealing—and utterly without defenses. Surrender, he thought dimly as he disengaged himself.

"That was very nice, Diana." He touched her face affectionately. "You kiss even better than you play golf."

"I . . ." She gulped. "Thank you."

"Good night, Diana."

"Good night, Conor."

"I'll see you tomorrow."

Conor realized as he drove back to the Creekwood Inn, in the woods behind I-90, that the woman had been his for the taking. Upright and chaste young women like Diana Lyons don't offer themselves that easily, not unless they are terribly confused, frightened, and lonely.

What if I had taken her up on her offer?

She'd probably hate me forever.

Still, there's something wrong with her. I'd better figure out what it is before I become any more deeply involved.

5

I should go for a long swim in the lake, Diana told herself as she squeezed the yellow number-two pencil she held poised over the blank spiral pages of the latest volume of her diary.

Maybe I should call it a journal, she thought. It sounds more literary.

Mama thought diary keeping was a waste of time. "Who will ever read it?" she asked bluntly. "Don't they say that it is better to write love letters to others than to yourself?"

Sometimes she and Mama were buddies. Sometimes enemies. But they were only enemies when Diana seemed to threaten Daddy's happiness, about which Mama was fiercely protective.

Daddy insisted that it was only proper to keep track of your life. He showed her some of the entries he'd made when he was a young law student, with two children already and another on the way; and later entries when he was chief investigator for the Department of Agriculture, hunting fraud on the Board of Trade, in the years before the Commodity Futures Trading Commission had come into existence.

Diana had been impressed by the fire of his idealism. Even at her most enthusiastic, she never had any illusions about her ability to make the world an appreciably better place. That might be the difference between the eighties and the fifties.

"See, Maria," Daddy had said, "it is worthwhile to have kept this diary if only because my youngest daughter takes inspiration from it."

Mama did not reply. She never did when she disagreed with Daddy.

He did not approve of the imitation-leather diaries high school girls kept intermittently. "No one who is serious spends money on fancy little books. What's wrong with a plain spiral notebook and a number-two pencil? That's what I've always used. What's important about a diary is what goes into it, not what it goes into."

In college, a boy who was sweet on her—and she sweet enough in return to tell him about her journal (as she called it on the rare occasions when she told others about it)—had given her an expensive leather-bound book. She had never used it, but rather put it away in her closet. It was still there along with prom souvenirs and other memories of times in the past before she had decided that she was not the marrying kind.

From her window in the modern summer home with its little porches and vast windows and high beams and eccentric roofs, designed by Catherine Curran, Grand Beach's resident architect, she could see the lake was as calm as a pitcher of ice coffee, black and silent and a bit foreboding under the persistent inversion. Diana had turned off the air conditioning when she came into the house. It was typical of Maryjane's extravagance to have left it on all day even though no one would be inside till midnight and there would be only one person sleeping in the house after midnight.

There might have been two, she thought, and promptly dismissed that terrifying and fascinating possibility from her consciousness.

I shouldn't have wine after two drinks, she told herself firmly.

Furthermore, you didn't need air conditioning on most summer nights. It was a waste of money even to install it when you lived right next to a lake. Maybe if you were a young woman, pregnant for the first time and scared as well as happy, it might help you sleep. But our grandmothers didn't have that sort of luxury.

Anyway, Diana liked hot, sticky summer nights with the thick undefinable acrid smell of August hanging on the air and a layer of heat oozing from her body. It was the kind of night that suggested autumn but promised firm resistance to its coming.

She was sitting up on her narrow bunk—a room no doubt designed for future Delaney children—clad in a thin sleep T-shirt, bent over her spiral notebook, trying to remember the words that had come so easily to her in the shower at the Long Beach Country Club.

All that she could remember was the word "obsession," which had already been scrawled—in large printed letters—on an otherwise virgin page.

Interesting choice of word, young woman. If you're still one tonight, it isn't your fault.

I have never done an imprudent deed all my life. I have always been the cautious, thoughtful, responsible person that my father trained me to be. Today I blew it all right out the window.

"WELL"—Maryjane had poised her ballpoint pen over the list of members of the Long Beach Country Club—"if you don't want to play golf alone today..."

"I don't mind," Diana had replied indifferently, not looking up from *The New York Times*, which, astonishingly, was delivered to homes in Grand Beach. "I merely said that I've practiced enough now, so I think I could hold my own in competition."

"There's no one under *A* or *B* who is acceptable."

"I'm not looking for a husband." She frowned over Anthony Lewis's column. The man was such a bleeding-heart knee-jerk liberal that you could predict the rest of the column after reading the first sentence. That was probably what knee-jerk liberals wanted—a columnist who confirmed their biases without a single challenge to thought. "Only a golf partner. Man or woman or child, it doesn't matter. I can play by myself on the Grand Beach course like I did every other day. Long Beach Country Club is a little too rich for my blood anyway."

A lot too rich. I don't belong there. I barely belong here. If Maryjane and I hadn't been best friends in high school and if she hadn't wanted someone to be with her while Gerry was away, I wouldn't be here. Daddy didn't exactly approve. The Irish over there, he said, put on airs.

Actually, a lot of them don't know how to put on airs.

"Let's see." Maryjane ignored her protest. "Under *C* . . . Cain, no he's a creep. Carmody, no, you'd have to fight him off every inch of the way. Clarke . . . now that's an interesting possibility. Someone says he's over at the Creekwood Inn. How would you like to play golf with our most eligible bachelor"—Maryjane jumped up enthusiastically—"Conor Clement Clarke?"

It would have been so easy to say no and be done with it. Why not meet him face to face, study him up close, do a little bit of intelligence work on him, just in case they ask me to become part of the team investigating him?

It was close to unethical even at the beginning. Not quite, she told herself, after she had asked Maryjane what he was like and was told that he was cute and sweet and that she shouldn't believe what she read about him in the papers and that they'd get along fine together.

Even when Diana listened to her in the next room making the phone call—Maryjane sounding like she was still in high school—she realized that it was stupid to have agreed to a golf date with Conor Clarke. What was wrong with me? she asked herself, actually forcing herself out of the breakfast room chair to march into the living room and protest.

It was too late.

"Well, he DID remember you. Like I say, how could anyone forget you? I go, 'Would you like to play golf today with my friend Diana?' and he goes, 'The wonderful goddess with the brown hair and the brown eyes?' And I go, 'She's a great golfer,' and he goes, 'But she's married, isn't she?' And I go, 'Like, no way,' and he goes, 'How tasteless of male humankind and what's her handicap?' and I go, 'Four,' and he goes like, 'Wow.' And I go, 'What about it?' And he goes, 'Bring on the fair Diana.' And so that's taken care of."

"He's a bit of a playboy, isn't he?" Diana was then nothing more than curious.

"That's newspaper talk. He's really very smart and very sweet and like, well, kinda sad, you know?"

She didn't then, but she did now.

Diana threw her pencil and notebook aside in disgust. Nothing, absolutely nothing. She was hollow, empty, utterly dissociated from herself, like a second-rate private investigator on a dull surveillance assignment, an outside witness listening and watching from a distance, detached, unsympathetic, uninterested. The woman who had played golf with Conor Clarke, bantered with him, argued with him, became tipsy at supper with him, and tried clumsily to seduce him was someone else, a stranger she did not know and did not like.

I couldn't have acted that way. My God, I am a United States Attorney with an oath of office. I despise the man. His father ruined my father's life. If I love Daddy, I wouldn't even think about Con Clarke as a lover. My reactions are base and vile. Obscene, even.

But those words don't help.

Am I that hungry for a man? Why so suddenly? Have I become a repressed spinster so soon?—and that's a male chauvinist category I shouldn't be using.

Restlessly she climbed out of bed and walked out onto the tiny porch with which Cathy Curran had equipped every bedroom in the house. The moist night air against her face was soothing and reassuring.

Like a man's hand, light and tender?

Stop thinking that way, you little fool.

Impulsively, she pulled off her T-shirt and tossed it on the canvas-cushioned chair with which the architect had decorated each porch.

"She goes, 'They have to be exactly those colors, MJ, to

accentuate the brown wood of the house correctly.' And I go, 'Like it's totally your job to design the place, Cathy.' I mean, really! Right?"

Why did I do that? No one can see me out here and it's late at night on a balcony out over the lake, but I'm a prude. I've never stripped to my panties outside before. Do I want a man here with me?

Of course I do. But not him.

The reaction between the two of them had been instantaneous. Their eyes locked the moment he came into the Delaney house. Their hormones screamed across the awkward silence—need, appeal, vulnerability.

"I don't want to play golf with her, MJ." His grin was both attractive and demented. "She'll beat me."

"Are you afraid to lose to a woman?" she snapped nervously. "I'll give you a generous handicap."

"Will you now?" He winked appreciatively and her heart began a drunken waltz. It had staggered for the rest of the day. And quite completely collapsed during dinner, despite the fact that she saw very clearly what he was.

Over dessert he had talked about Silicon Valley, the rise and destruction of Fairchild Camera, Bob Noyce and Intel, integrated circuits and microprocessors, the Atari madness, men who had made thirty million dollars by their thirtieth birthday, industrial espionage, Japanese spies, drugs bought from Hell's Angels, marriages going down the Jacuzzi drain, lawsuits and hints of murder, enough men making the big score so that all could hope for it.

His fair skin glowed as he talked and his eyes danced in merriment. He loved it all, capitalism at its best and its worst. A handsome, immoral pirate. No wonder he thought of her as a pirate queen. Not immoral. Amoral. He loved the game more than the money. Victory was more important than profit. Why win at golf or racing when you had a shot at the Big Score.

And if the laws of God or man got in the way of the Big Score?

Too bad for them.

Yet there was pain in his eyes, too, as well as merriment. His horrible father must have caused him great suffering. That was no excuse. . . .

The arguments for and against him warred in her head till she was too distraught to think about him anymore. Yet he would not leave her imagination. So beautiful. So lonely. So evil.

She stretched her arms heavenward. "Dear God, help me!"

The only response was a slight movement of breeze, a zephyr stirring the hot, moist night air.

Diana slumped into the canvas chair, buried her head in her arms, and sobbed bitterly.

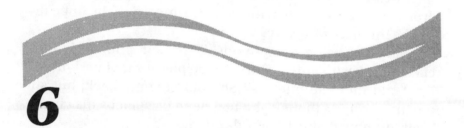

6

Conor did not call Diana the next day as he had promised. The Delaney house, brand new, was not listed in the phone book. In his comfortable room in the Creekwood Inn, secluded in the woods two miles inland from the lake, he thought about consulting directory assistance but concluded that he wanted to consider the whole "affair" seriously and systematically before taking any further steps. His love life consisted of a long series of hasty missteps and wasted opportunities, alternating in a dangerous rhythm of mistakes and blunders and punctuated with the kind of attractive, generally sexless beauties with whom he was pictured in the paper.

None of them, however, not even Naomi, had affected

him like Diana Lyons. Wonderful, delicate, enchanting little Naomi who, on her own skills entirely, God knows, had made successfully the journey from almost lover—dear God, how close—to good friend and confidante.

What would Naomi think of Diana? Naomi and her husband the Rabbi, the scholarly, yarmulke-wearing Cubs fan, who would almost certainly be in Conor's box at Wrigley Field watching Ryne Sandberg et al. this afternoon.

The chain reaction between the two of them had begun the instant he stepped into the Delaneys' wonderful new home. When he reached for her clubs and accidentally touched her hand as she fiercely pulled them away, the hormones broke through the dam that had been holding them back.

"I can carry them myself," she had snapped, her wondrous brown eyes wide with surprise and—dare he hope it—the beginnings of desire.

"I'm not being a chauvinist." He had smiled his most charming Irish smile. "Only a disciple of Stephen Potter."

"And now I'm one up." She didn't smile back, but she did turn away as though she had been dazzled by his charm. Well, he hoped she'd been dazzled.

Already, even then, he was quite explicitly fantasizing about what she would be like in bed.

Dirty old man.

"Really!" exclaimed MJ, shrewd beneath her endless chatter. "Hey, you guys, you have a great time, right? Conor, I'm betting on Diana, like totally!"

Conor didn't like contentious women. He couldn't stand aggressive and ambitious women lawyers. He was not attracted by tall, strong women. Gentleman or not, he preferred blonds.

None of that mattered in the slightest.

However, the disaster of his parents' marriage—always lurking in the back rooms of his memory, as Naomi had graphically put it—forced Conor to caution, just as on other

occasions, including Naomi, it had forced him to reckless-
ness.

Diana Marie Lyons had called his bluff early. Perhaps
unintentionally, and certainly aided by the Niersteiner wine,
she had in effect invited him to put up or shut up.

And wisely or not, he had shut up. For the moment.

Now he had time to think. Unfortunately, before he
could begin his thinking, a call came from San Jose. A new
crisis at Infobase, his program company. The brilliant young
men who had founded it could not believe the handwriting
on the wall: they thought the golden market would never
end. Conor's insistence that they rethink their marketing
priorities did not make it through the software of human
language to the hardware of their brains. Would it be necessary to sell his holdings?

Better that they take his advice and go public with a
stock offering. But the genius behind Infobase wanted to
keep his toy for himself all his life.

Then there were calls from a group of dissidents in a
major hardware company who had a brilliant idea for a
movable fixed disk. Their company would not even think
about putting such boxes into the new series of PCs they
were developing. Conor liked the sound of that, but after the
example of Intel, and then those who broke off later from
Intel to form yet another rebel company, every technician in
Santa Clara county with a new idea thought that venture
capitalists would make him a millionaire overnight.

Finally he listened to a whispered report from one of his
San Jose informants. (Everybody had one, didn't they?) A
group of dissatisfied technicians at National Semiconductor
was about to jump, with a sure-fire voice-to-paper technology. The capital was waiting in line for a piece of the action.

Sure!

The three situations, one a problem, another a possibility, the third an annual madness, kept him on the phone all
day and well into the evening. The Californians seemed to

be incapable of comprehending that five o'clock there—still plenty of time to get in the camper and head for the mountains with your wife or live-in girlfriend—was seven o'clock in Chicago, almost too late to make a supper reservation.

Why wasn't there one time zone for the whole country?

Central time, of course.

Diana as a live-in girlfriend?

Don't be silly. If she is to be tamed at all—and choose whatever nonchauvinistic synonym you want—it would have to be in the marriage bed.

He did call finally, at seven-thirty. He consulted with the bored, superior male voice at directory assistance, and after some difficulty in which he had to explain several times that it was a new number in a new house, he learned the Delaneys' number.

Naturally at that hour on a Friday night in August in the Dunes, there was no one home.

Conor ate supper at a McDonald's outside of Michigan City. "Nothing too expensive tonight, fair Diana." Back in Creekwood he decided on a long walk, despite the continued weather inversion, and enjoyed the solitude of rural northern Indiana, a few miles away from the dunes that ringed the lake, without a single thought of Diana.

She was a passing fancy, nothing else.

The road down which he hiked was asphalt on sand. All this had been lake bed in earlier geological times, long before the last glacier had combined what they now call "Lake Chicago" with a couple of other smaller lakes to form Michigan—an inland sea that ought not to be in the middle of a continent and indeed would not be there unless it had been carved out by repeated glaciers, one of them, it was estimated, two miles high.

Ten thousand feet of ice. And on Labor Day I'm going to race back and forth on it in poor *Brigid.*

I wonder if Diana knows about the glaciers?

Who?

Diana.

Diana who?

That's right, I haven't been thinking about her, have I? Who is she eating supper with? Will she make a pass at him tonight?

If she does, it's her business, not yours.

Right.

Nevertheless, he called the Delaney number when he returned to his room. He remembered it without consulting the paper on which he had jotted it after his go-round with directory assistance.

No one home. Of course. They ought to have a baby-sitter to answer calls. Even if there's no baby just yet. Lovely woman, Maryjane. Daft but very bright. And very loving. She'll make a wonderful mother. Gerry's a lucky man.

And he's two years younger than I am.

Damn. As Naomi says, the longer you wait, the harder it becomes to decide.

Tomorrow. I'll think about it . . . her . . . tomorrow.

Give her a ring then. Maybe.

On Saturday morning the weather inversion had lifted. The day was clear and crisp and there was a brisk northeast wind blowing. Conor drove over to the marina in New Buffalo early in the morning, borrowed a boat that one of his broker friends had offered to lend him for the weekend— poor *Brigid* had been left by herself in Chicago while Conor made his annual ambivalent, bittersweet pilgrimage to the resort of his childhood—and sailed up to Benton Harbor and back.

The challenge of manning a thirty-two-foot sailboat by himself in eighteen-knot winds with four-foot waves did not permit Conor the time to think about his other favorite subject—women. One woman in particular.

But by the time he had tied the borrowed boat to her dock, he found that he had already made his decision.

Diana Marie Lyons was a fascinating woman. Physically attractive, even sexy despite herself, intelligent, witty, challenging—all of these she surely was.

She also was deeply troubled, lonely, haunted by demons the smell of which Conor did not like. She was a hard-nosed crusading ideologue. Conor shivered. Such women scared the hell out of him. Diana should have scared him and probably would have if he hadn't become instantly horny at the sight of her.

Moreover, she had hang-ups about money, curious twisted worries about what things cost that didn't make sense, not in the nineteen eighties. Maybe her crusade was to bring down the wealthy. That meant him.

No, it's not the kind of relationship in which you want to be involved. Naomi would have been horrified if she saw you the night before last. You were lucky your instincts, your better instincts, saved you.

On the other hand . . .

There is no other hand.

Yes, there is. She drank the wine and admitted that she liked it. She turned the cost thing into a joke easily enough. She mellowed easily enough. Your real crusaders can't park their mission at the dining room door like she did.

And she likes you. Face it, she was as dazzled by you as you were by her.

Well, that doesn't show much taste or wisdom on her part, does it? All it means is that she is as horny as you are. So the two of you could have jumped into bed at the Delaney place and had a romp or two—which wouldn't have been much fun.

You're not into one-night stands, remember? You don't want to become a bachelor playboy for real, do you?

Forget her.

Right.

7

"Well." Maryjane could give a pretty good imitation of an outraged Irish mother even though she was still a mother in process. "I thought you'd never answer your phone over at the Creekwood. Have you been like sleeping all day? Anyway, do you want to use our boat over at Pine Lake to water-ski tomorrow? I asked O'Connor the Cat if she would be the third and she goes like, 'Really! I have to be back at eleven o'clock to do my lifeguard thing, but if he's up for an early start, I'd totally like to ski with Mr. Clarke, even if he is an old man. Right?' "

There was silence at the other end of the line, while Conor drank all of that in. "What's an early start?" he finally asked.

"Oh, like eight o'clock or so. Who's the third person? O'Connor the Cat, like you know, the lifeguard. Nancy O'Connor's daughter, the Ryan who writes science fiction. Judge Kane's niece. Oh, the *other* person. Well, Diana, naturally. I mean we can't let the teenagers drive the boat without anyone to supervise, and Gerry's in town. . . . No, Diana is staying one more day. And since Lake Michigan is so cold, I go, 'Like have you water-skied lately?' and she goes, 'Not in five years,' and I go, 'Well, that's excellent then, right?' "

Maryjane hung up and she repeated her judgment of approbation and satisfaction: "Well, that's excellent then, right?"

"I guess," Diana agreed, her disobedient heart racing madly.

"Tomorrow at eight. He'll be here and the kids will meet you in back. It'll be really excellent."

"If you say so." She had been a hollow woman for three days, thinking of nothing else but when would the phone ring. She should have forbade Maryjane's obviously pushy phone call. It simply was not in her power to do so.

Besides she wanted to compete with him on water skis.

"Remember that he is a very dear man, but he had a hard time growing up because his father was such a gelhead. He plays that Irish poet game and it's partly true, but there's a lot of pain there, too. Really!"

"Tell me about it," said Diana wearily.

8

"I MEAN," said O'Connor the Cat—so called not because of physical appearance or personality, but because her name was Catherine or possibly Kathleen, no one was really sure anymore since she had been the Cat from the time of her noisy appearance in the world—"it sure is cute, but the four of us won't fit in it." Hands on pretty hips, snub nose turned up, she regarded the inefficiency of the Ferrari with disdain. "Tell you what, Mr. Clarke, you and Diana go in your little car and John will drive his minivan. Right?"

John was a black-Irish lad, perhaps a year older than the Cat, who was apparently included in the team for purposes of balance. He doubtless had a last name, but Conor never learned it.

"OK, Cat, if you say so."

The legendary Grand Beach lifeguard continued her logistical planning ("a precinct captain's precinct captain," Conor's friend and the Cat's uncle, Monsignor John Blackwood Ryan, had remarked once, rolling his pale blue eyes in a mixture of dismay and pride): "That way, Mr. Clarke, John can bring me back so all the mothers won't panic at the beach, and you can take Diana to Sage's for a chocolate malted milk."

"Sage's?" Only sixteen and already part of the match-making conspiracy. "Is it still open?"

Conor had not missed the fact that from the first moment the kids had made the decision that she was Diana—one of them, more or less—and he was Mr. Clarke—a grown-up, a man of their parents' generation, someone in mortal danger of being described as "real old."

"And their malts are still really excellent. I'm sure Diana wants one, don't you, Diana? Fersure."

"Fersure." Diana had not missed the kid's categories either and was enjoying it enormously. "Mr. Clarke can always have a Diet Coke if he's worried about his figure."

"Really," the two adolescents agreed in unison.

Diana was in great good spirits, a summer resort model in a pink sweatshirt and matching gym pants with GRAND BEACH lettered on them in black and her hair tied with a matching pink ribbon.

His good intentions had faded completely at the first sound of MJ's voice on the phone. One more day won't hurt.

Honest, Naomi, it won't.

He guided the restless Ferrari—a car that always seemed to breathe heavily unless it far exceeded the American speed limits—out of Grand Beach and onto U.S. 12. "It's nice to know," he said, "that I'm dating a teenage girl."

"Really, Mr. Clarke!" She laughed happily.

"You call me that in front of the kids, woman, and that spanking I promised you in jest will become real."

"I can hardly wait." She laughed again. Apparently Diana had reached the same decision he had. Live for the joys of this summer day and forget about autumn and winter.

As they drove through New Buffalo, Conor explained the enormous social problems occurring in the newly named "Harbor Country." The once sleepy, Czech and Lithuanian community was being "gentrified."

"It's Hyde Park and Lincoln Park East," he said, sighing. "Journalists, artists, writers, musicians are buying everything in sight, run-down old homes especially, knocking down the walls and prettying the places up so you'd almost think you were in the Cape or the Vineyard."

"I've never been to either."

"I know, only Detroit once. So what happens? You begin to get notices tacked on trees, and bagel stores, and secondhand-paperback bookstores, and lines of people waiting to buy the Sunday *New York Times*, and folk music groups, and summer workshops in drama. All that kind of stuff."

"Is this bad?" She was still not quite sure whether he was joking.

"Then there's antique stores and writers' colonies and the first thing you know, people will be standing in front of the drugstore on Sunday morning with petitions for you to sign. Your Lakefront Limousine Liberals have to be socially concerned even on vacations, even on Sunday. Then there'll come the protests."

"I agree the process is going on, but so what?"

"Culture, divine Diana with the pretty pink ribbon in your pretty, long brown hair." He stopped at the traffic signal in New Buffalo, signaled a right turn, and said, "I think I'll kiss you now." He leaned across the front seat of the car and kissed her, lightly, playfully. This time there was definitely a movement in response. "I don't think I dare do it when the other teenagers are around."

"You're incorrigible, Conor Clarke" was her only protest. "But do go on about culture in New Buffalo."

"It's not New Buffalo that's the problem. They can have all the culture they want. The problem is what happens when culture sneaks down U.S. 12 and pokes its ugly little head into Grand Beach. If you gentrify Grand Beach, you'll take it away from us Irish. We can't survive the advent of culture. It'll be the death of us all."

"Conor," she placed her hand on his arm, "You are not only incorrigible, you're outrageous."

"I have to do something to impress you, before you rout me completely on the water skis. Anyway, you see my point. When *The New York Times* invades Grand Beach, it will be the beginning of the end. We'll finally have something to talk about at our parties. The world and its problems will have arrived, and that will be the end altogether."

"Maryjane gets the *Times* delivered to her home every day."

"See what I mean?"

"She only reads the food and nutrition section."

"Camel's nose into the tent."

"There's the Ryans. . . ."

He thought about putting his arm around her and decided that he'd better concentrate on the driving, at least on the way over to Pine Lake. Fortified by malted milk at Sage's there was no telling what he might do.

"The Ryans have an exemption. Ever since Ned bought the Old House here when he came home from the war in 1945, everyone has known that the Ryans are crazy. But still, by definition, if a Ryan does it, it's all right, for them anyway. So all their culture is no threat to Grand Beach. It's indigenous culture, if you know what I mean? Can you imagine anyone more thoroughly South Side Irish than the Cat? Yet she wants to get herself a Ph.D. in the classics, can you imagine that? What use is Greek in an age of democracy, I ask you."

"You're absolutely outrageous, Conor Clarke."

"Just showing off for my girl."

"Am I your girl?"

"Would you be, for today anyway? No obligations."

"Fair enough."

"You see that road? The one that turns the corner?"

"Uh-huh."

"That's where I used to have my big beer busts when I was a Notre Dame beer-bust type."

"Oh?"

"My father owned an old house down there, on a blueberry farm, no less. It looks like a Northwest Side nineteen-twenties' two-flat that was wafted away on a magic carpet one night by some comic genie and dropped down in the country for a joke. Legend has it that it was a still during Prohibition and then an Outfit safe house. I don't know how the old man got it, but he turned the farm over to the locals who grow the blueberries—you know, the 'U Pick M' kind of place—and forgot about the house. It was a great place for beer busts. The cops came by once. Most of us were legal, but we still faced a disorderly conduct charge."

"And?" she asked lightly.

He decided it was all right, after all, to rest his right hand on the back of her neck.

"Well, we weren't disturbing anyone. And we weren't all that disorderly. So I used a little clout and took care of things."

"Was that proper?" She sounded more like someone in honest search for truth than a cross-examining attorney.

"Self-defense is a right, delicious Diana, which is prior to all positive law. When the law attacks you unfairly, you still have the right to defend yourself."

"By whatever means?"

"I don't know what that means. Certainly not by immoral means."

"I see."

"Oddly enough," he went on after a moment's silence as they crossed U.S. 20, the old route to Notre Dame before the interstate system was constructed, "I still own the farm. It's all that's left of the Clarke family real-estate empire in this area. Maybe I should have held on to some more of it. With your Lakefront Limousine Liberals from Hyde Park and Lincoln Park moving in on all sides—and displacing the Marquette Park and Jefferson Park peons who know a dumpy old house when they see one—I could have made a nice profit."

"Five hundred percent?"

He squeezed her neck affectionately. "You're right, Diana Marie Lyons. Software is much more profitable than rural real estate."

"Why did you sell it all, Conor? Maryjane showed me the house you owned by the golf course. It's a lovely old place. You enjoy coming back, it would seem, even if you hide—Maryjane's word—over in the woods by I-90."

It was a perfectly reasonable question. A woman has the right to ask about her man's childhood, even if, on the basis of the present agreement, he's only your man for the day. Besides, Maryjane has already told her the rough outline. It was painful, even now. And while he welcomed her already existing tears of sympathy, he was not sure he wanted to run the risk of being drowned in them.

"It's a wonderful place, Diana. It beats the Cape and the Vineyard all hollow, believe me. And I had wonderful times here, too. But with my dad, well, it was all so unpredictable."

"Oh."

He stole a quick glance as they crossed the old Baltimore and Ohio tracks—now, alas, Amtrak—and felt his heart do several somersaults at what it saw. There were tears of compassion in her eyes. For him.

And the day has only begun.

"He was in his middle fifties when I was born. But unlike Red Kane with little Redmond Junior, he didn't want a son and he was already old. I don't know whether Maryjane told you many of the details. He was born at the turn of the century, son of a teamster—chronic alcoholic, of course—and a domestic worker, lied to get in the army in the 1918 war, barely survived the Spanish influenza epidemic, married his first wife when he came out of the army, and was the father of two sons before the stock market crash in 1929."

"I had no idea he was that old." Her soft, gentle voice conveyed reassurance, tenderness. I really am in love with you, woman. No matter how many hang-ups you have.

"He was wiped out like everyone else in the crash. He managed to scrape together a living selling real estate and insurance door-to-door. No brokers in those days, dear heart."

He mustn't sound too serious. It was a serious tale all

right—tragic, even—but not, thank God, totally tragic.

"Anyway, he stayed active in the National Guard. Loved military discipline. When the National Guard was called up after Pearl Harbor, he was over forty, his oldest son had just graduated from Mount Carmel and had received an Annapolis appointment. He could have gotten out of the Thirty-third Division—that was the Illinois National Guard, still is, I guess—God, how many times he told me, drunk and sober, that he could have copped out but didn't. But he fought through the whole war, was wounded twice, and came home a colonel. There wasn't much to come home to, however. His wife and younger son were killed in a train wreck on the IC—the only ones to die—and the Annapolis grad, a company commander in the marines, decorated like his father in the first war, died on Mount Suribachi on Iwo Jima."

"Dear God, the poor man."

"Yeah. He loved his wife passionately and worshiped Matthew, the marine officer. I heard from his old-timer friends that he went through a total character change. Decided that he would devote the rest of his life to money and pleasure. And for the next thirty-three years had plenty of both. . . . I guess he made and lost a couple of fortunes on the Board of Trade before his big clean-up in the early seventies—the hog bellies about which you joked yesterday."

"I'm sorry, Conor."

"Don't be. He had a long string of women, bimbos mostly, not to put too fine an edge on it, up to the bitter end as a matter of fact. My mother was his secretary, a maiden lady, as they would have said then, in her late thirties, who was very skilled at keeping records, good ones and maybe some bad ones, too. I can't imagine how he ever got her pregnant with me. Maybe they were both drunk. Unlike the bimbos, she didn't take precautions. So there he was, stuck with a wife he didn't want and a kid he didn't want, a jab at his memory of Matt that irked him every time he saw the little brat."

They stopped for the signal at I-20. I'd better hurry if I'm going to finish this before we arrive at Pine Lake.

"So to make a long story short—and I figured this all out much later—they didn't cohabit for more than a year after their marriage. He provided well for us; my mother, even when she was on the sauce every day, would not permit a harsh word against him. He would show up intermittently, without warning, sometimes drunk, sometimes sober. It was the unpredictability of it all that got to me. You couldn't tell when he would appear and what mood he'd be in. Was I a wimp who needed to be made into a man or a potential junior partner? I adored him and feared him, loved him and hated him. . . ."

He stopped. The pain was still there.

"Poor little boy."

"He survived, Diana, not too badly, all things considered."

I don't want to see her tears, I really don't.

"I grew up to be a loud-mouthed, smart-assed little punk with a quick tongue and a wild imagination. The teachers and the other kids thought I was great, and in a way I was. Till Dad showed up, usually without warning.

"Matt—how I hated the poor guy—had been a reserve halfback at the academy. And I was a weakling. Matt was a man, and I'd never be anything more than a mama's boy. Well, the genes and the hormones did their work, and I was suddenly big enough and strong enough to play football at Mount Carmel myself. I didn't like it all that much, but I was quick and reckless and durable and thought to be a pretty good college line prospect."

"All-Catholic," she said. "I'd forgotten, but Maryjane reminded me."

"Right, but that wasn't good enough, you see. He came to every game my senior year and picked at my playing. If I wanted to make it at Notre Dame, I'd have to shape up. Well, they scouted me and saw, quite correctly, that I didn't quite have enough of the killer instinct to make it. So Parsegian didn't give me a scholarship. I had rides to other schools. But it was Notre Dame or no school at all. If I concentrated and applied myself, I could make up for my poor performance in high school."

"But you were All-Catholic!"

"Not good enough, I should have been All-State. So I was a walk-on lineman at Notre Dame. You can imagine how much they needed me. There were some mighty unhappy days at Grand Beach—what, ten years ago now—when I was cut. He never spoke to me again."

"Dear God."

They stopped at the intersection of Indiana 39 and Indiana 31, a death corner for the unwary. Across the highway, Pine Lake was dotted with fishing boats, but there were no ski boats yet. And the water was glass smooth.

"The funny thing is, my girl for a day, he was the only one that didn't like me. I got high grades, was always elected a class officer, could hold my liquor better than most. Popular, successful, young, potentially alcoholic Notre Dame yuppie. I won't say he was the only one who counted. He wasn't around enough to count that much, but he counted all right."

"Poor man."

"Right, darling Diana, he was a poor man."

"I agree. I guess I meant you, though. We are all prisoners of the past, Conor, but it doesn't seem fair that yours was so terrible."

"I survived."

With some masculinity and some confidence in dealing with women, he added to himself. Enough? Well, Counselor, as you said yesterday, we're reserving judgment.

He turned off the road into the marina, down a steep slope—another glacial remain—to the side of the lake.

"More than that, I should think."

This time she kissed him, with firmness and determination. Ah, bless the maternal instinct.

"I think we should stop." He backed away, laughing. "Divine Diana. Unless I am mistaken, that Chrysler mini contains the fabled O'Connor the Cat, keeper of the morals of Grand Beach, who even at this moment is raising an eyebrow and announcing with shock, 'Really,' at the sight of an old man like me kissing a teenager like you."

God help me, Diana thought, I'm glad they showed up when they did.

9

"NO WAY am I going into that water first," O'Connor the Cat announced with the full solemnity of a papal bull. "It's FREEZING!"

"Not really." Conor put his hand over the side of the Starcraft 19. "It must be in the middle eighties."

"You don't have any blood if you think that FREEZING water is WARM, Mr. Clarke. No WAY."

"Chicken," sneered John genially. "Girls are afraid. You're a pretty good skier for a girl, Cat, but you're still chicken."

"I'm better than you are, gelhead. No way am I going to be first in that FREEZING lake." She pulled off her green and gold Notre Dame sweatshirt, revealing the most minimal of blue bikini tops.

"We women have to make all the sacrifices, don't we, Cat?" Diana's smile was superior, a fellow member of the conspiracy of womankind.

Diana was as natural with the teenagers as she had been with the little kids at Long Beach the week before. She fit effortlessly into their world and was instantly accepted as one of their own, whereas Conor took the Cat's tirade about the freezing water literally. Only as she put on a ski vest and adjusted the O'Brien slalom ski to her foot size, did he realize her emphatic refusal had been pure ritual. She had already made up her mind that she would be the first skier.

"I'll DIE!" she yelled fervently as she surfaced after a knifelike dive into the water. "Ohmigod, I'll DIE. Mr. Clarke, PLEASE start the boat."

"Girls," John sneered.

Con started the boat, like he was told.

"Do those come off?"

"The jackets?" John asked innocently.

"That's not what I meant."

"If it should ever happen, I'm not saying it does"— John's dialect changed from heavy Russian to light Hispanic— "we are gentlemen and we no look."

"Shut up, you!" Diana ordered. "Conor, the poor girl is *freezing*. Get the boat moving."

So he jammed the throttle forward and both the boat and the Cat leaped out of the water, and with equal grace.

Pine Lake was a three-mile horseshoe of water over seaweed, lined with weeping willow trees, lily pads, and colorfully painted homes—some dating to the Civil War, Con observed, and some to last week. With its sail boards, fishing boats, lazy sailboats, and manic water-ski wakes, it was your typical middle American resort lake, not a huge incomprehensible melted glacier like Lake Michigan.

"She's good," Diana said respectfully.

"For a girl," John agreed.

"For anybody."

Conor stole a hasty glance over his shoulder. The Cat was cutting the water with graceful ease, sending up a wall of spray two stories high. While he watched, she jumped a wake, the way kids used to jump rope.

"I hope I'm that good when I'm as old as she is," he murmured.

"Be quiet and pay attention to the other boats," his woman for the day told him severely.

"I am TOTALLY exhausted," the Cat announced when she finally tossed in her line, sank elegantly into the water, and swam over to the waiting boat. "The water really isn't cold when you get used to it. How'd I do?"

"Not bad," John conceded.

"For a girl." Conor began to remember the way the game was played.

"Gelhead," the Cat replied, admitting him provisionally into the teen culture.

She braced her hands on the side of the boat, drew in her breath, and heaved herself into the craft with a single mighty push.

"You're getting better at climbing in," John admitted. "For a girl."

"What's wrong with the ladder?" Conor threw the Cat a towel that read BUDWEISER for all the world to see.

"Conor!" Diana seemed shocked at the stupidity of the question.

"Only people that are really OLD use the ladder." The Cat huddled under the towel and made sure her swimsuit was properly adjusted.

"Who's next?"

"I am, of course." Diana was wearing the same suit as at the country club, its straps severely and tightly in place, not that it made all that much difference.

"John, you drive, so Mr. Clarke can watch Diana."

"You have a broken hand or something?" John took command of the driver's seat like he was at least a rear admiral. "Oh"—he changed the game—"I forgot. Girls are no good at driving."

"Gelhead!"

Diana dove in with practiced ease, slipped the ski on as if she had done so every day in the summer, and gave John the thumbs-up sign. He pushed the throttle to full speed and Diana surged out of the water.

"Wow!" exclaimed the Cat, scurrying to the back of the boat. "This I gotta see!"

The Cat had charmed Pine Lake with practiced grace.

Diana attacked it with savage power, as elegant as the Cat as she leaned over parallel to the water and twice as strong.

"I mean, she is really a woman of the eighties, isn't she, Mr. Clarke?"

Con agreed without asking what it meant.

"Like, she's really built, but she doesn't look built at all, you know?"

"I agree, though, I think, Cat, we mean different things."

"Keep your eye on that fishing boat, gelhead!" Then with a wicked grin at Con, she added, "That, too, now that you mention it. But, like that's the way we're all going to be in the eighties and the nineties, strong but not gross. No way is that chick gross."

"Tell me about it."

The Cat grinned again.

Woman of the eighties or not, it took Diana two tries to pull herself into the boat. The second time, she contemptuously waved off Conor's proffered hand and hurled herself into the boat, with considerable and delightful bodily movement.

"Moby Dick is landed," Conor announced.

"Monster. Let's see you beat that."

"You're next, gelhead. I'll drive."

Conor reached for the ski as Diana wrapped herself modestly in a vast white towel.

"No, Mr. Clarke"—the Cat laughed—"I meant the other gelhead."

John was a good skier, marginally better perhaps than the Cat, but not as fearsome as Diana. When he was safely landed—over the side of course—Conor announced, "Well, OK, we'll go back to the marina. John, you drive the Cat back to the beach so she can take over as baby-sitter and I'll escort Ms. Lyons to Sage's."

"What?" the three teenagers shouted in unison.

"No way I'm going to compete with you guys. It's a setup."

Diana seemed genuinely displeased with him.

"You gotta ski, Conor," the Cat wailed. "It's not fair to geek out on us."

Diana did a double take; then as she understood she restrained a laugh. Con had been accepted at last into the teenage world and was playing their game, too.

"Boys," she said in protest with a loud sigh.

After considerable argument, protest, threats of dire punishment, recrimination, and excuses, pleas, and complaints, Con was at last persuaded to jump, clumsily, into the water. He struggled awkwardly to put on the ski. In his prime he was surely better at the sport than the others. But he was past his prime, as was evident when he fell on his face in his first try—to the hoots and hollers of his three enemies.

He managed to get out of the water the second time and promptly fell on the opposite end of his anatomy. The hoots and hollers were louder.

Finally the moves came back, he rose, rather shakily from the depths, maintained his balance for the last crucial seconds, and sped across the wake. The hoots and hollers stopped.

He was exhausted but triumphant when he climbed up the ladder into the back of the boat.

"Not bad," the Cat admitted.

"For an old man," Diana agreed, somewhat chastened. "Brute strength, but a lot of it."

"Yeah," the Cat said. "He was probably real good when he was young, twenty years ago or so."

There was no further discussion of his sensational prowess. The conversations turned to the creatures hiding under the waters—muskrats, eels, garfish, and a killer seaweed named Jason (who arguably had a sister named Jessica).

All but the first were patently mythological, but lots of fun.

"Honest, Conor," the Cat insisted, "I SAW it with my own eyes. It looked just like the Loch Ness monster!"

"Really," Conor agreed. "She was here when I was a teenager, twenty years ago."

"I thought it was longer than that."

As she piled into the minivan, the Cat fired her last shot: "You can have two, Diana, but only one for him. He's out of condition. TOTALLY!"

Right! Conor thought. And now comes the hard part.

10

Diana had never been so close to surrender. Watching herself in the boat from a great distance as Conor sliced gracefully through the calm waters of Pine Lake, she had seen a woman entranced by the body of a man, a woman whose flesh was eager to take him inside herself, a woman utterly complacent in her own descent into the bog of erotic need.

Unlike Conor, she was able to hide her desires. He, poor man, was all too obvious in his respectful lust. She hid, as she always had with men, behind her aloof intelligence and quick wit.

Not from the Cat.

"Mr. Clarke really isn't really old, is he, Diana? I mean, like, he couldn't ski that well, could he?"

"Only a couple of years older than I am."

"And that's not totally old at all, right?"

"Right."

"Do you like him, Diana?"

Blunt and to the point is my grandmother, this old woman with the young body.

"I like him, Cat."

"A real lot?"

"A real lot."

Loud adolescent sigh, to be best interpreted as meaning, "Well, that lets me out. Not that I thought I had much of a chance with someone that old."

"He likes you."

"Do you think so?"

"Totally."

Another sigh. This time meaning, "I think you make a beautiful couple. For two people who are not yet totally old."

Her body, Diana knew, was programmed for mating and reproduction. She was not irrevocably determined for such a destiny. She could choose different goals. She might be much happier in such a choice, but her body could accept such a decision only reluctantly.

Until now her body had been cooperative. As soon as Conor Clarke had appeared, however, it rebelled. Give yourself to him, it had insisted, abandon your ideology and your principles and yield yourself. Entrust your life to him. Forget your suspicions. Forget what you know to be true about him. Abandon the walls of the fortress you have built around yourself. Capitulate.

From the great distance in which her mind was watching the rest of herself, she argued that these imperious desires and the resolute preparations her body persisted in making to receive him into herself were absurd. She would not be bowled over by late-summer lust. She would not abandon her career because a man caused a rush of hormones in her blood.

Yet if he tried to make love with her before the day was over, she was not sure that she was capable of resistance. The barriers were down. She was his for the taking.

"Are you, like, going to marry him?" The Cat had per-

sisted in her catechesis as Conor flipped the ski rope and
sank into the water with a graceful bow.

The ham!

"I don't think so, Cat. It's just a summer romance. You
know what they are. As transient as a weekend kiss."

"I dunno." The Cat had sighed again. "Weekend kisses
can be pretty nice. . . . I think you'd be great together."

Conor had tried to climb into the boat, breathing heavily
from his exertions. Cat and Diana had combined forces to
push him back into the water.

The feel of his chest against the palm of her hand had
sent currents of electricity racing through her body.

"Hey, I'm outnumbered!" He had slipped down the side
of the boat to the ladder and tried to vault in again, this time
grabbing Diana in the process. He had crushed her in his
powerful arms and forced her away from the head of the
ladder. The Cat, little traitor, prudently had stayed out of the
battle.

Diana had felt like she was a fiery torch.

"Let me go," she had protested, thinking that if the kids
were not with them she would pull him down on top of herself. "You big ape!"

He had done as he was told, much too promptly, and
reached for his towel. "What were you two biddies talking
about when you should have been watching my sensational
performance?"

"Men," the Cat had sniffed, pulling in the ladder, "and
how dumb they are. Like total gelheads. They forget the
rules."

"Rules?" Conor looked puzzled.

"Skier," Diana recovered herself, "pulls in the ladder."

"Gelheads." The Cat had winked. "Now let's go home."

And I lose my grandmother/chaperone. I'm glad. I want
to be his. Take me, my darling, love me. Please. To hell with
my oath of office.

In the Ferrari she felt her shoulder lean against his. Abjectly, pathetically. She forbade it this indulgence. To hell with you, it replied. You're acting like a total gelhead. If you intend to seduce the man—and you do—get on with the job.

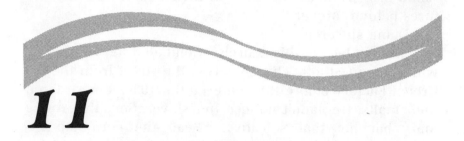

11

"You were wonderful with those kids, Diana." Con glanced at her admiringly as he began to work enthusiastically on his malted milk. "Mmmm . . . as good as they ever were. But like I say, you fit in perfectly with them. I'm sure you're a fine lawyer, but you'd make a great teacher, too."

"It's easy, all you have to do is like them and listen to them and enjoy them." She sipped her own malt. "Hey, this really is the best one I've ever had in all my life. The Cat did not lie."

"The Cat never lies," they repeated in unison and laughed enthusiastically together, discouraging the rather quiet proprietor of the Ice Cream Factory, who probably thought he had adult customers.

The Ice Cream Factory was an old, old place. The glasses and the candy counter and the trays and the soda fountain itself were of a 1920s, 1930s vintage. But the building itself, store in front, living quarters in the rear, was at least a hundred years old. Most of the other houses on the quiet side street in LaPorte, with ancient trees filtering out the sun, were equally old, if not older. Some of them had been thoughtlessly "modernized" thirty or forty years ago—as had been the Ice Cream Factory. Others had been carefully restored more recently so that one could blur one's eyes a bit and imagine that, with younger trees perhaps, one was looking down a street on which young men in blue uniforms were marching off to the Civil War, perhaps singing "John Brown's Body" as they left their homes and their futures behind forever.

Diana shivered.

"Take a look at this church." Con had dragged her to a white stone Catholic church across the street from the Ice Cream Factory before they entered the 1930s and ordered their malts. He hadn't noticed her shiver. Sensitive young man, but not that sensitive. "Read the cornerstone—eighteen fifty-two, a hundred and thirty-two years ago."

"And modernized beyond all recognition fifty years ago. What a pity."

"Can you imagine the funerals in this church—boys killed in the Civil War: Irish immigrant kids or the children of immigrants, most of them no older than our friend John Noname. That'll give you the shivers, too."

So he had noticed.

"I can't remember when I've had so much fun," she said as they consumed their malts. "It's been a marvelous day so far. I hope you can sustain the amusement level."

"I'll try. Drink your malt. Despite the Cat's orders we both can have seconds if you promise not to tell her."

A wonderful day it had certainly been, and it wasn't even half over. Why could not life be like this? No responsibilities, no commitments, no crime to extirpate, no criminals to pursue. Especially beautiful criminals with broad shoulders and blond hair and blue eyes that so quickly changed from happy to sad.

She had resolved to bracket the day, to enjoy it as completely as she could and pretend that what she was doing was not terribly evil. Daddy always said that it is so easy to sin when you make up your mind to have fun and hang the consequences. Now she knew what he meant. Tomorrow would come the reckoning. Today she would have fun. There hadn't been much of that lately.

"You were really very good, Conor." She sipped as slowly as possible, so the good taste would last as long as possible. "When you did your first jump, that little girl's jaw dropped and she whispered, 'Totally awesome,' like an archangel had appeared."

"Give me a chance to excel before two beautiful women"—he made a slurping noise with his drink—"and I'll always be totally awesome."

"She is cute, isn't she? Sometimes I envy girls like that. I mean, not really envy. I don't want to take their figures away from them—I only wish I could wear a bikini once without making a fool out of myself."

Conor drained his malt, his face turned a number of different dark colors. "I will be in trouble, no matter what I say to that."

"No, you won't. I promise."

"I know your kind on this subject, so I don't believe you. Anyway, if there is any problem with your figure in a swimsuit like that, the part of your body where the problem resides . . ."

"Yes? . . ." She lifted her almost empty malt glass as if to throw it at him.

". . . is in your head."

She put the glass back in its place and emptied the remnants from the metal container in which it had been mixed. She felt very warm. "You are a clever one, Conor Clement Clarke."

"If you do try the bikini, I'll come for the show."

"If I lose my taste enough to try it, you'll be the first to be invited."

"Sell tickets— Now don't hit me. I'll tell the Cat."

"Were you like those two when you were that age up here?" She drew in the last of her malt a drop at a time, slurping, but not as loudly as Conor.

"Cat and John? Gosh, no. They're innocents. I mean, they may have a beer occasionally . . ."

"The Cat?"

"Sure, she's almost seventeen . . . And maybe even two on Friday night, but they're not part of the heavy drinking scene. It's impossible to be that athletic when you knock off a six-pack every night."

"You drank that much when you were seventeen?"

"Better say fourteen." He continued to ponder his empty malted-milk tumbler. "I cut back when my mother died. She was drunk every day for maybe the last ten years of her life. I didn't want to go that route."

"You don't drink much now."

"This stuff could be more addictive." He turned over the empty tumbler. "It may not be as good as sex, but almost."

On the ride from Grand Beach to Pine Lake she had been impressed by Conor's candor. He spoke with the calm dispassion of a psychology professor discussing a case with which he had personal experience. He had described his family life with a finely balanced combination of wit and seriousness in his voice, saying in effect that this was pretty bad, but not absolutely destructive. He'd probably gone through some kind of therapy. Momentarily she envied him the money for such treatment. Anyone could talk candidly about himself if he could afford expensive therapy. He was revealing the kind of material about himself that would be very useful background if his case ever came to trial, the kind of background it would have taken months of research to assemble. She felt guilt pangs about what she was doing and quickly reminded herself that this day was to be divorced from the rest of reality.

"I'm afraid I'm a short hitter, as you noticed Thursday night. We never have anything to drink at home, and I rarely drink outside the house."

"But you're Italian! I mean," he quickly amended himself, "your mother is Italian. Don't you drink wine with your meals?"

"My father doesn't approve of drinking. He says that it may be all right in Sicily, but it's wrong among Irish Americans."

"I guess he has a point," Conor agreed dubiously, still

trying to picture an Italian family without wine.

"Anyway, can you tell me more about venture capital?"

"If you'll drink another malted milk with me."

"I was hoping you would ask. . . . Is sex really better? I can't imagine anything that could surpass one of these all that much."

Conor's eyes widened, then he realized she was joking. "I don't know about you, woman. . . ."

The malts were ordered and Conor, lovely blue eyes radiant, returned to his lecture.

"A venture is really nothing more than a good idea looking for money. Three points are important." He began to tick them off on his fingers. "The idea has to be a new one, usually but not always something technical—chips, software, gene splicing. But that's not enough, there also has to be a potential market, even if the market doesn't recognize itself. Five years ago, most writers would not have thought that a PC would be indispensable. Two years ago, accountants were skeptical that they really needed our Infobase. An idea is not much good unless it can create its own market."

"You make people need things they didn't use to need?"

"Not quite." Conor was incapable of being offended, even of sensing criticism when he was wound up. "You help them to recognize needs that they already have but of which they were unaware or to which they paid no attention because they didn't think there was anything they could do about the needs. For instance, writers have always had to revise and they've always wished that they didn't have to type everything all over again. Right?"

"I see, like totally!"

His grin was brief. This subject was too serious for anything more than a very quick joke. "About half the stuff we do is in computers, hardware and software, and other electronics. Medical care is second, hardly a socially irrelevant area. Data communication and consumer products— women's dresses, like the Diana Marie Lyons golf fashion company I'd like to launch—are each about ten percent. Then there's industrial automation, which is my big thing right now, genetic engineering, and energy, each at two percent or so."

"So you're part of the most venturesome."

"Well, kinda ..." It was a compliment, but he had to finish his explanation, didn't he? "Secondly, the idea must need money. Everything needs money, but I mean something special here: money you can't get through ordinary lending channels. Typically in the computer business it is a group of young and ingenious technicians who can't sell their ideas to the established company for which they work—Hewlett Packard, IBM, even Intel, which itself was a venture not so long ago. They don't have the credit lines in an ordinary bank, so they need money from somewhere else."

"No loyalty to the company that gave them their start?"

"Sometimes not much"—he hesitated, with the fingers of his right hand on the third finger of his left—"especially now that the pattern has been established. Every programmer or hardware technician in Santa Clara County thinks he's going to be the head of the new Intel or Lotus. At the beginning of the eighties—and this surge is only three or four years old—they typically did their damnedest to drag the company along and then quit to start their own venture out of desperation."

"And finally the money?"

"Right. Laurance Rockefeller was in many respects the first of the venture capitalists, the modern ones anyway. He was the idealist of the family, philosophy major. He had the idea of putting his money into science-based and/or socially useful ideas. Before the war—Second World War, that is—he salvaged Eastern Airlines. Then after the war he settled down to make the world a better place. Between 1945 and 1961 he spent nine million dollars on such notions, heavily science and aerospace."

"And his profits?"

"They say at least forty million."

Diana thought of what the time after the war meant for her father—hope and then disillusion—and for Con's father.

And a man who already had more money than he could possibly spend made yet more. It didn't seem right.

"That's remarkable."

"It certainly was. And it means scientific progress, jobs for hundreds of thousands of workers, tax for the government, and better technology for all of us."

"Profitable idealism."

"Precisely. A third malted milk?"

"Conor, you'll make me fat. I'm not sure I'll be able to walk out of this place. . . . Well, I'll split one with you. I suppose that there's always money for an idea."

"No way. One of the reasons for the flourishing of ventures during the last couple of years has been favorable changes in the tax laws. Moreover, there are times when you see a wonderful idea and you just don't have the money, so you either take a pass or scrape it together by hook or by crook."

By hook or by crook? Does he worry about morality at all? Or is he so swept away by his enthusiasm that he really doesn't care what he does?

"Then there's China." His wondrous blue eyes seemed far away.

"China?" She poured a little more than half of the final malt into his glass.

"The Middle Kingdom—really the Central Country. The greatest nation in the history of the world. Down and out for the last hundred years or so, one of the periodic dips in their history. Now about ready to return to its rightful place. They—and maybe the Brazilians, but I wouldn't put any money there—are going to be our rivals in the next millennium."

"Help the Chinese be our rivals?"

"If they have a stake in the world, they won't destroy it. . . . Here, you gave me too much. . . . Thank God they've been socialist long enough to give us a head start. Ah, Diana Marie Lyons, forget about Silicon Valley and the Rust Bowl and put your pennies into China. That's where the money is to be made."

Truly a pirate. Or maybe a gentleman adventurer like Sir Walter Raleigh. Came to the same thing.

"Why don't you live in Hong Kong—or Los Altos, if Silicon Valley is all that attractive?"

He seemed surprised. "I'm a Chicago Irish Catholic. How could I live in any of those places?"

All right, an unadventurous adventurer. Odd man.

"Are there times"—she played with her empty glass, avoiding his eyes—"when you need money, Conor?"

"I'm not Laurance Spelman Rockefeller. Come on, woman, finish your malt"—he smiled approvingly at her, his wide, genial, window-shattering Irish smile—"and let's go look at antiques and taste Michigan wine."

The rest of the day was a delightful haze for Diana, a pleasant surrealistic dream, a Disney World of antiques and woods and dry white wine and heart-breaking smiles and paralyzing kisses that made her heart pound and her knees weak and her body ease ever more rapidly downhill toward total gift of itself.

It would, after all, be endlessly pleasant to belong to a man like Conor who would buy you sinfully expensive antiques: "Let's pretend that this little bookcase belonged to one of the boys who came back from the war and read Dickens and Scott, while he courted his sweetheart and fished on Pine Lake." And make you drink wine till you were dizzy: "Try this one, Diana, it's kind of funny. We'll catch up with you Tuscans yet." And spun out poems as they strolled hand in hand through Warren Woods, shoes off: "Do you think there is a Resurrection for wild flowers, Diana? I do. God must be dying of love for them, too." And wouldn't permit you to escape from a state of mild sexual arousal: "It's only a small kiss, Diana, and I've finally persuaded you to kiss back." And never once, not a single time, called you "Di."

When she finally collapsed into her bunk for a late-afternoon nap before supper at The Hunter, begging off from a tennis match that she knew she'd win ("I'm drunk, Conor. And you"—tipsy giggle—"know what happens to me then. . . . All right, maybe that is fine, but not for playing tennis"), she was deliriously happy. Never had there been such a day of excitement and fun and, well, she would say it, love in her life. It could not last, it would not last. It was evil, treacherous, sinful. Tomorrow she would hate herself. Tomorrow and tomorrow and a hundred tomorrows after that.

But in her happy sleep Diana thought that perhaps, just perhaps, tomorrow would never come.

12

"It's not the Indiana Dunes, darling." She had become "darling" so soon. "It's the Vienna Woods, and we're an archduke and an exotic spy on a secret assignation. You are trying to obtain a copy of the secret naval treaty and I'm trying to lure you into my secret harem."

"And the waiter—" She sipped her dry sherry with great caution. No more wine headaches today. I have to work tomorrow morning; he doesn't. "—is Sherlock Holmes with a German accent, in disguise."

The Hunter did not belong in Michiana—the border country of the two states. It was in an old lodge with heavy wood walls, thick drapes, sparkling white tablecloths, antlers, and formally dressed waiters. It could well have been a mountain resort somewhere in Europe. Switzerland, she had thought. But perhaps Con was right. She had never been in either Switzerland or the Vienna Woods. Never east of Detroit.

"So tell me about Diana." He began to dispose of his Wiener schnitzel. "Besides that she is a young woman who has a commendably powerful appetite."

"I'm afraid Lent will have to begin tomorrow." She sighed. "I don't know what there is to tell, Conor. I've had a very placid and ordinary life for my first quarter century."

She hated him for asking. "People are bored when we talk about ourselves," Daddy always said. "And usually embarrassed." She was a dull, respectably lower-middle-class professional for whom the world of venture capital and the Vienna Woods and even of Michiana summer resorts would forever be foreign.

"Maybe we can change the second quarter," he said lightly. He was into summer color coordination tonight, gray shirt, slacks, socks, windbreaker, the kind of gray which set off his haunting blue eyes, into which she ought never to look again. Dear God, I haven't made an entry in my journal since I met him. Four days of silence. How am I going to explain it?

"I'm the youngest of six children, the last one home. My father is a retired government lawyer, a very brilliant man who chose a career of public service instead of a career of profit. My mother is a woman he saved from gang rape when she was ten, in Italy during the war, a very warm and affectionate woman. He went back after the war to marry her when she was old enough. I'm a lawyer, too, like my father I'm proud to say. I want to dedicate my life to the common good just as he did." She felt herself smiling weakly. "I used to be able to beat any smart-mouth teenage punk in the neighborhood on the squash court at the local park on Saturday mornings. I've been so busy lately that I haven't had time for that."

She felt foolish and inadequate, as though she had taken off her clothes awkwardly, clumsily. Conor had shared his life that morning with clarity and self-possession. She was making a mess out of a similar effort.

"Squash is your best sport?" He didn't seem to mind that she had spoken empty pieties.

"That and volleyball. We won State when I was in high school. Of course McAuley always wins State. And I was Junior Women's Squash Champion for a couple of years."

"And you could play golf on the tournament . . . your veal piccata all right?"

"Excellent, and no, I couldn't play on the tournament."

"You mean you don't want to. Which is all right, only it's a little different. Does your mother work?"

"She manages a fashion shop on the mall. I'm sure Maryjane told you that."

He has no right to pry. Why doesn't he leave my family out of it.

"What's she like?"

"She's my mother."

"I know *that*. I mean how does she adjust to life in America?"

Much too pointed a question, Diana thought. I don't want to be on the witness stand, not with those eyes stripping me and reveling in me. "Very well, I think. She's old-fashioned in some ways; quite modern, even chic, in others. She . . ." Diana hesitated, afraid of revealing too much. ". . . had a hard time understanding some of the older kids. Growing up was so different for them from what it was for her. She never was a teenager, never saw the world through the experiences of someone like O'Connor the Cat. But she learned very quickly. She and I are very close."

Sometimes. Other times she doesn't understand me at all and tries to give me advice in the guise of folk sayings— often good advice to which I normally pay no attention. If she knew how strongly I was attracted to you she would observe that they say that "when a woman wants a man, she should stop at nothing to get him. They say," she would continue, "that you do whatever you need to do to get the man you want."

Then if I told her who you were, she'd turn into an angry volcano.

I don't want you. I just feel like I do.

"Your mother has a career then, of a sort?" Conor interrupted her daydreams.

"Mama has a job. It's not easy to send six children to college—even state colleges—on a government lawyer's income. Now, of course, at her age and with the family raised, there's no reason for her not to have a job."

"But career and marriage are incompatible at the beginning?"

Why must he continue to jab at me this way? Why can't he leave me alone?

She put down her fork impatiently. "You will think this very strange coming from a feminist like me, but during the first five years of marriage, a woman's most important responsibility—"

"Is to raise children?" His eyebrows shot up in surprise.

"Let me finish, please. Her principal responsibility is to learn how to make her husband happy and keep him happy. Physically, emotionally, every way. Children, too, of course, but they make the first responsibility more difficult and more important, too."

"Because?" Conor gulped.

She picked up her fork again, a sign that she wished to terminate the conversation. "It should be obvious: the children are influenced more by the quality of the husband-wife relationship than by anything else in their environment."

That sounds like Psychology 101, but I believe it and it's true.

"Lucky husband," Conor said softly.

"I would try to make him feel that, yes. Of course, I would expect the same from him."

"And get it"—Conor winked—"or heaven help him."

"It is unfair," she continued relentlessly, "but it is also true that a man can do that with a career and a woman can't, at least not now and maybe not ever. Intelligent feminism means choice, not trying to do everything. I chose career. There are losses and gains either way."

Damnit, I sound so artificial and phony. I must make it clear to him that we can't have an ongoing relationship. Oh damn, that sounds phony. Our little Disney world must end tonight.

"I suppose"—it was Conor's turn to put down his fork—

"they have Sachertorte here. It's a Viennese chocolate raspberry cake. Better than sex, like malts. . . . I suppose I shouldn't have said that in the context of our present discussion."

"Priests and nuns can choose to be celibate, why can't a lay woman?"

Conor rubbed his chin, a gesture to which she was becoming accustomed and on which she was beginning to dote. "Of course they can. Of course you can. No objections, fair Diana. None at all."

"Except . . ."

"Well, except . . ." He hesitated, groping for the right word.

"Go on."

"Two Sachertortes, please. . . . Except that when you're as old as I am, like TOTALLY old, you realize that the world is not a place which can be divided up into such neat and orderly game plans. A lot of women, and men, too, manage to play different games and play them reasonably well. You seem to foreclose the possibility of doing reasonably well at a number of roles because it would be messy and uncertain and problematic. Couldn't you study your case and study your husband reasonably well, not perfectly, but pretty damn successfully just the same?"

"No," she said flatly. "Do you have decaf? Fine. No, I couldn't. I will not judge others. Only myself and I judge that I couldn't do both the way I want to do them."

"That seems pretty final." He rubbed his chin again. "But it smells a little of perfectionism to me."

"It's easy to say that"—she lost her temper—"when you don't have to work for a living, except to make a phone call or two while your woman for a day takes a nap so she looks fresh and rested as your dinner distraction. Just try to cope with life's complexities when you have to work an eighty-hour week like I do."

"Delightful dinner distraction, delicious Diana. How's that for alliteration?" He leaned across the table and brushed her lips with his and brushed them again on a return trip. "I'll save that for my cycle of sonnets. I think I'll called it 'Doomed Diana, the Delightful, Delicious, Distracting Darling.'"

"Idiot." Why couldn't it be easier to stay angry at him?

"Eat your Sachertorte." He touched her hand. "And enjoy it."

She did. In fact, she ate two of them.

13

As they held hands, watching the full moon, Conor Clarke told himself that one of the woman's many admirable attributes was that she knew when to be quiet.

Instead of reporting in to Maryjane, they had walked down the steps on the side of the dune to the tiny beach that the high waters of Lake Michigan permitted Grand Beach this summer. "Neither beach nor grand," Conor had remarked.

They had watched the moon and listened to the lake and enjoyed each other's hand in compatible and bittersweet silence.

She was magnificent, that was the only word for it. Hang-ups by the bushel basket, but strength enough to fight them off if she had the proper assistance.

Like me. And a good counselor.

I wonder what her mother is really like. Sounds like she's fat and ugly and spiteful, one of those street characters who are shouting all the time in the Fellini movies.

She sure is angry about something. A vocation? Sure.

Why not? But to work for kinky little twerps like Donny Roscoe for all her life? Weird.

Ah, my boy, but the problem is you, not her. OK, you discount the hang-ups. Or should I say hangs-up? You forget about her vocation to be a celibate woman lawyer. Are you strong enough to match yourself against that one on a daily basis for the rest of your life?

You who have been frightened off by less determined women than her?

He glanced at his silent companion. She was wearing the same dress as on Thursday—with apologies: "I wasn't counting on two dates."

"You can wear that anytime you're with me and I won't complain," he had said appreciatively.

"Chauvinist," she had protested with a blushing face and little conviction.

Now, with a shawl over her shoulders, she looked so hapless, vulnerable, so much in need of defense and protection. She thinks she can take care of herself. Actually she's lonely and curious and so hungry for love and affection that she'd be an easy target for anyone with a moderately good line.

He wouldn't have to be nearly as good at blarney as I am. Diana Marie Lyons, you're a sitting duck. If it's not me, it will be someone else. He might be the kind of man who will break that very fragile heart of yours. You can't fool me. You're about as tough as a Sachertorte.

I could break your heart, too, maybe worse than he would. And he might be much better for you than I am.

We will have to think about it. No love tonight, however. Just a gentle good-bye kiss, so we can both withdraw from the field of battle and think about things for a few days. Or weeks.

"Conor . . ."

"You have to get up at five if you are going to drive in with Gerry."

"It would be nice if it could go on forever."

"Yes, but . . ."

"Life is real, life is earnest, life is serious."

"I agree, we should send you up to your bunk bed in the room for a future Delaney."

Still holding hands, they climbed up the steep stairs. The lights of the new house glowed warmly, welcoming them as though they were travelers coming from a great distance. They paused for breath on the platform Cathy Curran had built halfway up the climb, equipped with deck chairs and a lounge: a substitute beach for those times when the Lake, in protest against those who offended its privacy by living too close to its shores, reclaimed all of its beach.

"Conor," she screamed in terror, "the sky is on fire!"

So it was. And with her arms around him seeking protection from the sheets of red and green lights rolling across the sky like giant curtains, so was he on fire.

"It's only the aurora," he said, gently disengaging himself. "You know, the northern lights. Let's go around to the lawn and watch them."

"I'm sorry I panicked." She still clung to his arm. "I've never seen them. We didn't take vacations when I was growing up."

"You can see them in the city, too, though a lot more clearly up here." He freed his arm and extended it around her bare shoulder protectively—he'd pick up the shawl later—as they watched nature's great summer slide show: bursts of white lights and then slow waves of multicolored drapes rising and falling across the clear night sky. It was still hot, in the low eighties even though it was close to midnight. The woman huddling in his arm was hot, too, her arms and shoulders covered with a thin layer of sweat. Conor noted with alarm that she seemed passive, yielding, a captive who was ready to surrender even though he didn't want either a captive or surrender.

"It's so beautiful," she said, sighing. "There is so much beauty and wonder in the world. Why are we too busy with our hatreds to take time to enjoy it and be grateful for it?"

"Now you're the one who sounds like the indolent poet."

Later he was reasonably confident that she made the first move, not that it mattered. At the moment, however, all he experienced was that his protective hug, without any conscious intent on his part, turned into a fiercely passionate embrace, body pushing against body, lips devouring lips, hands desperately exploring.

Then she was beneath him on the damp lounge, her sun dress pulled to her waist, her magnificent breasts, radiantly ivory and gold in the moonlight, at the mercy of his hands, her nipples hard against his lips, her skin eerie in the glow of the aurora. His fingers dug into the firm flesh of her breasts, pushing them gently against her ribs. She moaned and squirmed, resisting, but not really resisting.

Lonely, curious, hungry—quite incapable of defending herself.

Conor Clarke, the real Conor Clarke, not the animal on the sundeck, watched with astonishment and horror. That beast who was pretending to be Conor Clarke was exploiting a lonely and frightened woman. So what if her passivity indicated that she wanted to be exploited? She had too much of the Creature taken. Her virginity should not be ravished at this time and place, no matter how sweet her nipples were against his tongue. You'd better make him stop before it's too late for both of you.

So at the very last second he stopped.

Somehow he made it to the front wall of the Delaney house, where he rested his feverish forehead against a cool window pane.

"It was all my fault." She was standing next to him, miserable and dejected, rearranging her dress. "I'm sorry."

"Sure," he said bitterly, fighting for control of his voice, "teenage boys have no willpower of their own."

"Why did you stop?"

"I don't know. Inhibition, fear, maybe some virtue, a little bit, probably affection and respect." He drew a deep breath and forced a laugh. "Maybe an investment in the future." Then with a mighty effort, he added, "Venture capital."

"Thank you," she said simply. She touched his arm. "I'd better go in the house now."

"I'll give you a ring tomorrow. . . . I guess both of us need someone in our respective beds every night."

"Before tonight I would not have thought so." She turned the key and opened the door to the luxurious new redwood "cottage." "Thank you, Conor Clement Clarke, for a very interesting day."

"From beginning to end?" He kept himself a safe distance from the door and the trap of the empty house.

"Definitely."

"I'll give you a ring."

Autumn

Fourth Song

Beloved:

My lover came to unlock the secret door—
Bathed, fragrant, and unveiled, I waited on my bed—
"Unfold, O Perfect One," he gently said,
Hand in the keyhole, his forever more!
I was powerless, mere putty to shape,
He opened me up, skilled master of the game,
Filled me with his incandescent flame,
And lighted a fire I'll never escape.

Then, my turn to attack, I disrobed my man.
I devoured him, uncovered, full-length,
Explored, then reveled in his youthful strength,
And traced his wonders with my eager hand.
I tickled and tormented my poor darling one,
Embarrassed him, aroused him, drove him quite mad.
"Don't squirm, dearest, you're handsome when you're nude;
I'll stop teasing you only when I'm done.
You are clever, good, and kind, I admit,
And also, belly, arms, and loins, rock hard,
A tree, a mountain, a fiercely loving guard,
In my body and plans I think you might fit.

"Black hair, blue eyes, tawny sunrise skin,
Demanding hands, determined virile legs—
And also an appealing, trustful babe,
Savage chest outside, wounded heart within.
Lie here quietly on my garden couch,
I'll encircle you with affection and love.
My lilies and spices fit you like a glove,
It's fun to torment you with my giddy touch.
On your pleasured smile, I complacently gaze,
Oh! . . . Stay here, my dear, be with me all my days!"

Love Song, 5:2–6:3

14

"We want Conor Clarke." Leo Martin's shrewd little eyes took her in, seeing not a woman but a pawn on his chessboard. "And we want your help in getting him."

The only thing worse than to be evaluated as a woman was to be evaluated by a man who didn't care whether you were a woman or not.

Leo looked out on the plaza with the red Calder mobile. Unlike the young assistants, he had a wooden desk and a plush chair. Like their offices, however, his offered only steel chairs for visitors. Behind his desk was a shelf of pictures of a wife and family, people who were never seen at the office or at parties but who had taken on an elaborate and frequently obscene fantasy existence in the minds of the young people who worked for Leo.

"I see," Diana said cautiously, her stomach knotting.

Leo leaned back in his chair, his thin, almost monastic face content with the power conferred by being First Assistant United States Attorney, the power behind the throne no matter who sat on it. A lean man with high forehead, salt and pepper hair, and quick-witted gray eyes, Leo looked like an Irish Sherlock Holmes. Like her father, he was a career civil servant. United States Attorneys with their driving political ambitions would come and go. Leo would remain to keep the office running and make sure the laws were enforced.

"The IRS people—you know what they're like—will take years. And they may not come up with anything. But Donny wants to put him down and you're going to do it for us."

"I see," Diana said again. The folklore in the office advised that you let Leo tell his story before you interrupted him.

"He's a rat, Diana." Leo folded his hands behind his head. "A mean, rotten little rodent, ripping off the poor in the name of social progress."

Diana waited. Leo considered her, as if expecting an answer.

"He babbles about restoring jobs to the Middle West"—Leo leaned forward on his desk, chin in hand, a Jesuit priest arguing against birth control—"and he takes over these old factories with a flourish and gets rich off them."

"I don't like those kind of men, Leo, but where is the violation?"

"We're convinced that, in addition to his profit, he's robbing the companies."

The words "we're convinced," Diana knew, meant that Leo had a hunch and that Donny, of course, went along with Leo's hunches, especially when a hunch made possible an indictment that could garner lots of TV attention.

"How can I help?"

"Let me emphasize that Donny's need for attention in the press has never been more justified. First of all, we have to control these venture capitalists—most of them are crooks anyway. Secondly, well . . . you read the columns, you know what an arrogant little prick Clarke is. And he's robbing the poor. Sure, he's not a Wall Street prick who makes millions on insider information, but he's worse. He's a hypocrite who takes jobs away from the men who worked in those factories, gives them to yuppies, and then cheats on his own investors while he's doing it. He belongs in Leavenworth, not Lexington where he'll probably end up— and not for long enough if you ask me."

Leo did not like rich people and he did not like anyone who appeared frequently in the columns, except his boss. When he was fired up on the subject of these twin hates, his face glowed with a crusader's zeal.

He also, Diana told herself, is quick at sizing up his new assistants. He knows that this is the kind of appeal that works with someone like me. Too bad he didn't bring this up two weeks ago.

"How do I fit in the picture?"

"Easy." He smiled, a fisherman confident of his catch. "He's involved with your friend Broddy Considine out in Cokewood Springs. Broddy is on the take out there, as always. We're convinced that Clarke is in it with him. You're shaking Broddy. Shake him a little harder and on the subject of Clarke. Have your little Jewish friend help you. When Broddy is shaking real good, you hint that if he sings about Clarke, he won't have to do time."

"I see."

There was always a possibility that the County Commissioner, like other government witnesses, might make something up to keep his interrogators happy. A good United States Attorney did not go to a grand jury without evidence that her witness was telling the truth. Otherwise, as Leo had once said, we look bad in court if they catch us and Donny looks bad on the five-o'clock news.

"Maybe I ought to put myself on the Chinese wall on this one, Leo?"

"In God's name why?" Leo's voice took on the steel edge that was a sure sign of anger, an anger which had meant the end of the career of some of her predecessors.

"I . . . I have a personal relationship with Mr. Clarke."

"You sleep with him?" he barked at her.

"No . . . no, of course not. I played golf with him during my vacation. Had a date or two."

"That's nothing." Leo waved a dismissive hand. "I mean really nothing, Diana."

"I suppose so."

"Are you in love with him?"

"Of course not."

"Donny will be upset if you don't come on board for this one."

When Leo destroyed young United States Attorneys, particularly young *women*, he always attributed the coup de grace to Donny's being upset—as if everyone didn't know that Donny was only upset when Leo told him to be upset.

"I understand."

There was a glint in Leo's eyes, a quick flash of comprehension.

"Look, Diana, you're one of the best new people to wash up on this part of the beach in years. We understand your ethical concerns. If you want to put yourself on the wall, no one will hold it against you."

"Thank you, Leo."

"Frankly, in the world the way it is today, no one would object if you were sleeping with him. We could put a bug on you and call you an agent. In fact, it might help if you sustained the relationship with him. But that's up to you. Follow your own conscience. I must say, though, in all candor, that I don't know of anyone who would accuse you of conflict of interest at this point in time."

"I can see that." She hesitated. "It was only a date or two. Nothing serious."

"Take your time, Diana." Leo was speaking smoothly, reassuringly. "Make sure you are at ease with your conscience. Then let us know."

"Thank you, Leo," she said fervently, well aware that she was being manipulated, but still relieved that she was being let off the hook for a day or two.

"Just one thing, Diana—as a special favor to me?"

"Surely."

"You know where the East Side is? Over behind Lake Calumet, hard against the Indiana line? You can get into it from the rest of the city only on 106th or on Ewing?"

"I've never been there, but I know where it is."

"Yeah, pretty much an out-of-the-way place even for you folks who live in the southern suburbs. Anyway, take a day off tomorrow and ride through it. It's all Republic Steel at 117th and Avenue O. Some of the homes are over a hundred years old. The Church, St. Francis De Sales, is ancient. And there's new bungalows that went up after the war when the steelworkers were doing well. Charming kind of place, real neighborhood, if you know what I mean?"

"Of course. It's the place where the Memorial Day Massacre occurred in the thirties, isn't it?"

"I keep forgetting how smart you are, Diana." He smiled like a cat stalking a canary. "Yeah, in 1937 to be exact. Well, Republic no longer exists. LTV owns the plant. Six hundred workers where there used to be six thousand."

"How terrible!"

"Your friend Con Clarke"—Leo closed for the kill— "according to sources, is planning to buy the plant and turn it into some sort of place for robots to assemble Japanese electronic parts. It will be the end of that community. Friends of Con's will buy out the homes and sell them to yuppies, a few of whom will sit at the computer consoles in the factories. If he isn't a vulture eating corpses, no one is."

Later, much later, Diana wondered if, had her emotions not been so tangled on the subject of Conor Clarke, she might have been inclined to argue with Leo.

In fact, she said bitterly, "He's worse than his father."

Leo did not seem surprised by the reference to Clem Clarke. "I agree. And, Diana, we're the only ones who can stop him."

15

The East Side made Diana cry, not because it was depressing, but because it looked so much like St. Bride's, the neighborhood near the South Works in which she had lived as a little girl.

Superficially there were no signs of deterioration. The stores on 106th Street were all open, girls in parochial school uniforms were loitering in front of St. Frances High School, some of them black. The old homes were still neatly painted, the lawns in front of the new homes were well tended. Women on the streets were dressed neatly if not fashionably. The blight at LTV, at first sight, had not hit the community.

Then you noticed the large number of "for sale" signs; the men walking down 106th Street, heads bowed, shoulders dejected; the old autos; the unhappiness on the faces of the women. The East Side was a community trying to keep a stiff upper lip despite the fact that worry had wrapped its cold fingers around the heart of the neighborhood and the people in it.

When Conor bought the old mill and the yuppies poured into the neighborhood, *Crain's Chicago Business* would doubtless hail the salvation of another Chicago community.

But the people whose lives and heartache and hopes had made the community would be gone.

He was as bad as the blockbusters who turned all-white neighborhoods into all-black neighborhoods for their own profit.

Leo is right. We have to stop him.

Am I in love with him? If I am, even if it's only infatuation, I can't permit myself to become involved in the case.

Mama had exploded, as Diana might have expected, when she tried to share her Conor problem. She changed from confidante to hate-enraged avenger of Daddy, an alto singing a furious aria of vendetta in a Donizetti opera.

"Clement Clarke's son? I spit on you for even speaking to him! Don't you know that your father worked years to assemble the evidence to put Clement Clarke in jail?"

"What does that have to do with his son?" Diana asked timidly, terrified as she always was when Mama did her Mount Etna routine.

Mama did not hear a word. In her operatic temper Mama's beauty was overwhelming. Even Diana, who tried to deny to herself Mama's sex appeal, could not avoid admiring her flushed skin, flashing eyes, heaving shoulders, and full, shapely breasts.

"Years and years he worked, sometimes he slept only two or three hours a night, he took no vacations, he ruined his health, and all because he wanted to put one evil man behind bars. Then when he had all the evidence, Clarke pulled political strings, behind Papa's back. His powerful friends had Papa pulled off the case. He was given an unimportant job—a clerk, a paper shuffler. It broke his heart! Do you understand that, you slut, your boyfriend's father broke your own father's heart! I spit on your grave."

"He's not my boyfriend," Diana had murmured. Yet as it always was, Mama's fury was contagious. She, too, was furious at Clement Clarke, the miserable bastard!

"Then he drove him out of the agency. And he laughed at him in the streets! His son lives off your father's blood! Your duty"—she soared to the high note—"is to seek vengeance! Repay the Clarke family for what they have done to our family! You dishonor all of us!"

"You're right, Mama!" Diana had screamed, joining the orchestra and chorus at the end of Mama's aria. "Send him to jail!"

Mama's Sicilian eruptions were transient. If she met

Conor a half hour after her outburst and he turned on his considerable charm, Mama would forget about her fury. Diana could not forget her only angry response to Mama's virtuoso performance. The taint of a primitive instinct for vendetta had crept into her soul, and infection began to fester.

As Paola had said long ago, Mama forgets about her outbursts. You don't. You have the temper of a Sicilian and the memory of a mick.

She certainly was not seeking vengeance against the Clarke family, was she?

Of course not.

Right?

Even if she was a dangerous mix of two violent and primitive peoples.

Even if the veneer of civilization over her unstable blend of Celtic and Latin genes sometimes seemed pretty thin.

Her angry fingernails had cut deep welts into the palms of her hands.

She did not trust her own emotions. She had to be sure he was out of her system before she went "on board" the team determined to send him to prison.

She was most likely a passing interlude, a woman to paw on hot August nights.

She would wait till next Monday. If she did not hear from him by then, she would assume that she would not ever hear from him. It would be safe to join the team.

Leo wouldn't like the delay but he would grant it.

It's up to him, isn't it? If there's no personal relationship, then there's no conflict of interest.

16

Conor could think of nothing else. The woman haunted his waking and his sleeping—the feel of her flesh, the shape of her body, the sound of her voice, the flash of her smile, the quickness of her wit, the grace of her golf swing, the hot taste of her lips, the softness of her vulnerability.

I want her, more than I have ever wanted anyone.

I can't live without her.

So why don't you call her?

I don't know her number.

You could get it from MJ.

Or look up the United States Attorney's number in the phone book. It's not secret.

In fact, you have looked it up. It's jotted down on that note pad next to your phone. This is Monday morning. She's surely in her office bright and early, as befits a young zealot.

Why don't you call her?

Because you're afraid of her, that's why.

And why are you afraid of her?

Because with this one it could not be a brief and mostly sexless fling.

Why not?

Because she wants you as much as you want her and didn't at the end bother to try to hide it. You're afraid to be the object of a desire as strong as your own.

So what? I'm going to call her.

He picked up the phone, punched in the first six numbers, and then hung up.

17

"Did Clem's boy know what I was doing?" Broderick Considine eased the thick diamond on the ring finger of his left hand, a heavy weight doubtless. "Sure he did. Nothing on paper, if you know what I mean. The boy needed a few extra dollars, not a lot, but a few—some special opportunity, I guess. What do they call it nowadays? A venture?"

"You're quite sure?" Diana tapped her ball-point pen on the thick folder in front of her.

"Didn't he suggest it to me? Would I have run the risk of something like that without his knowing about it?"

In appearance, Broderick Considine reminded Diana of a slender Tip O'Neill, craggy red face, snow white hair, custom-fitted gray suit, expensive rings, equally expensive cologne, a bit too generously applied, a veteran politician's evasive talk, knowing winks, a pretense of explaining, as if to a class of bright but naive undergraduates, how the political system really worked—even though he was talking not about politics but about corruption and fraud. Moreover, he fancied himself as veteran a lady's man as he was a politician. His record, on the desk in front of her, reported a long string of adolescent mistresses, notwithstanding the wife and children and grandchildren, who were proudly displayed each year on his Christmas cards.

It took all the willpower Diana possessed to be patient with him. Yes, he was an old man trying to preserve a few shreds of dignity. But he was not entitled to dignity. He belonged in jail, where all his dignity would be stripped away. He was, however, as Don Weaver put it in a typical cliché, bait for a bigger fish.

"Well," she asked, "was it his idea to misappropriate the funds from the Cokewood Corporation?"

"Didn't I say it was?" He beamed cheerfully and read-justed the diamond stickpin in his tie.

Shelly Gollin came to her rescue. "Please answer the question with a direct statement, sir."

Shelly was a thin, dark little man from New York City, a graduate of Northwestern law school, brilliant and even more ambitious than Don Roscoe, if that were possible. He had been adored by all the women in his life—sisters, mother, grandmothers. He took it for granted when he joined the staff of the U.S. Attorney's office that the young woman from John Marshall, who was hired at the same time, would also worship him. Diana had sliced him up in little pieces on the third day they had worked together. Since then, he had treated her like she was at least an empress. Once he had hinted vaguely at romantic possibilities. Diana was flattered. Shelly was not unattractive, in an intense, Mediterranean way.

"Face it, Shel," she had responded crisply, "our backgrounds don't match. I'm delighted to be under consideration, but it wouldn't work. So let's be friends and cut the romantic stuff now."

He agreed and had become her knight protector, a useful if sometimes embarrassingly protective ally.

"Yes, he did." Considine shook his head, a wise old man, unable to understand the slow perceptions of today's youth. "He told me to talk to Harry McClendon, who is the treasurer, an accountant, like I said, from out there—Clem's boy likes locals in his corporations—and see if he would take a cut, in cash, for fixing the records. Did a good job, too, a hell of an accountant, Harry."

"Why would he bleed his own company through kick-backs?" she asked, to make sure a clear answer was on the record for the grand jury.

"Well now, young lady, like I said the other day, you can never have too much money. I suppose with all his projects, he was strapped for a little cash. He kind of hinted at that, if you take my meaning. Besides, half the money is from the Allen Corporation—you remember, they're the ones taking over the old factory. And he's going to get a lot more back on his investment when he sells the whole plant to Allen. So it's like a little down payment, a kind of advance, if you know what I mean." He made an expansive wave with his hand, gnarled with age, but still capable of a dramatic gesture. "Maybe he even intends to pay it back when he sells some of that computer stock of his that's sitting in a safe deposit box somewhere. Now he needs a little bit of extra cash and no one is hurt much, understand?"

"A million dollars is a little extra cash?"

"Well"—he sounded like he was defending Conor's frugality and integrity—"he only took two hundred thousand of it that day out at Phil Schmid's, you know, the eatery by the Skyway."

"I'm familiar with the South Side of Chicago, Mr. Considine."

Her father had told her that Broderick T. Considine, for thirty years a member of the Cook County Board, had been part of every crooked deal in the south end of Cook County during those years. Her father and Clarke agreed on that, anyway. He was a despicable old man, struggling to salvage a little of his despicable dignity as the stern hand of the law slowly pushed him into the garbage heap where he belonged.

"And the money came back from the overpaid local firms in cash for you and Mr. McClendon. You gave half your money to Mr. Clarke, is that correct?"

"It sure is, honey." He smiled approvingly at her intelligence, a smile that usually turned into a leer as his mean little eyes undressed her again. Shelly, her knight protector, sighed uneasily. "Well, not quite half."

"Wasn't that dangerous?"

"Only if you folks did an intensive audit of the corporation"—he winked knowingly—"and even then you would have had a hard time finding anything wrong. Harry is a damned good accountant."

"I see. So, if it had not been for your willingness to cooperate with us when we began our investigation of your taxes, Mr. Clarke could feel quite safe?"

"Well, when you said you were interested in finding out some dirt on him—"

"That's not what Ms. Lyons said, sir," Shelly intervened. "Strike that from the record, Ms. Jones." The white-haired black stenographer, who knew how the U.S. Attorney's office operated, nodded her head. "Actually, Ms. Lyons asked if you could be of any assistance in our investigation of corrupt practices in the plant rehabilitation industry, is that not correct? And you began to tell us about Mr. Clarke?"

"That's right." He winked. "Mr. Roscoe said that if I cooperated, he might be able to persuade Judge Kane to keep an old man out of jail."

"We made no promises"—she closed her eyes—"and there is no reason to think that Judge Kane will preside over this trial. Obviously we consider a witness's cooperation when we make recommendations to the judge."

"That's what I mean." She could tell without opening her eyes, that he was grinning happily.

A nearly senile fool Broddy Considine might be, but he knew the rhetoric of the game perfectly. If he chose not to use it occasionally, the reason was to maintain his pretense of dignity and to remind the United States Attorneys, both young enough to be his grandchildren, that he had one or two cards left to play.

She opened her eyes. "Did you at any time suggest to Mr. Clarke that a man of his wealth did not need the extra two hundred thousand dollars in cash you gave him last May"—she glanced at her notes—"fourteenth at Phil Schmid's?"

She had bluntly asked Considine if he had any information on Conor Clarke. That was against the rules, but it was a rule that was often bent in government prosecutions.

"Don't worry about the little rules," Leo Martin had told her. "They bend real easy. The bigger ones?" He had raised his thin, nervous hands to heaven. "Well, it takes a little more effort to bend them, but on occasion . . ."

It was a legal philosophy of which her father would not have approved, but Daddy had never worked in a modern U.S. Attorney's office. If he had been trained by a sharp First Assistant like Leo Martin, he might have had more success with Conor Clarke's father.

Her father was still bitter about the restrictions that prevented him from going after crooked traders like Clem Clarke when he worked at DOA. "They were the rules, hon," he had said sadly. "So I had to keep them, but they were rules that were made to help the other side break much bigger rules."

"I repeat, Mr. Considine, did you suggest to Mr. Conor Clarke that he was breaking the law?"

"I sure did, ma'am." He shook his head, sadly disapproving of Clem's boy. "I told him it wasn't worth the risk, any risk, of going to jail. He just laughed and said that it was only a little loan and that he could afford the best lawyers in town and there was nothing to worry about."

It sounded like something Conor Clarke would say. She caught Shelly's eye; he nodded dutifully.

"I think that will be all for today, Mr. Considine. We're grateful for your continued cooperation, particularly this new information about Mr. McClendon. You've been a great help to us."

"Any day I can talk to such a pretty and bright young woman"—she let him take her paw in his slimy hand—"is a happy day for me." He hung onto the hand. "Believe me. . . . You will give Clem's boy a chance to plea-bargain, won't you? He's a little spoiled but not a bad kid."

"That's an improper question, Mr. Considine"—she pulled her hand away—"and you know it."

He also knew that a guilty plea was the way the game was played. A month or two or maybe six and Conor Clarke would be back with his Ferraris and his Peterson Racing Machine boat and his airline cabin attendants. Don Roscoe would have another conviction to build the pavement for his journey to the governor's mansion, the press would have another victim, Conor Clarke would have his freedom, and an expensive, time-consuming trial would be avoided by all. Not much justice, but some.

Three or four months of mild humiliation would take some of the wind out of his sails and some of the glow off his charm.

Leo Martin joined them later in Roscoe's wood-paneled office with its giant American flag.

"What next, Counselor?" he asked Diana with his faintly cynical grin. She felt that he was laughing at her most of the time, affectionately amused at the zealous young woman prosecutor.

"We shake McClendon, real good."

"That would give us two witnesses against Clarke, wouldn't it?" the U.S. Attorney said in the whining tone of a man who wanted to be assured that one and one were two.

Donald Banc Roscoe, the "bane of crooked politicians," as the media called him, was a short baby-faced man with large ears and little hair in his middle thirties. He had brought to a refined art the style of government prosecution developed by James "Big Jim" Thompson, now Illinois' perennial governor: the use of immunized and plea-bargained witnesses to obtain indictments against celebrities, especially political or politically connected; conviction of the "big fish" in the media before indictments were handed down; plea bargaining for guilty pleas and light sentences, judiciously blended with the occasional show trials in which a big fish would be recalcitrant about admitting his guilt and the media coverage would keep the prosecutor's name and face before the public.

"Functional justice," it was called around the U.S. Attorney's office. "A foolish game," in other quarters in town, and "Gestapo tactics," by a few civil libertarians who were consistent enough in their ideologies to believe that even politicians had civil rights. "Di," Shelly Gollin said in awe one day, "we can indict almost anyone we want."

"My name is Diana. I am not an English princess. And that's the whole point. Don't worry about building a road to Springfield for Donny on the bodies of innocent men and women. The public will never vote for a little man that is as ugly as he is. Besides, they're guilty. Otherwise we wouldn't be going after them."

"Suppose, hypothetically, we shake Harry McClendon." Martin rested his chin on pointed fingers. "He's probably filed perfect tax returns."

"Like that bastard Clarke," she cut in furiously. "He defied me to investigate them."

"Let's leave young Conor simmering on the back burner for the moment—" Leo winked at her, causing her face to blaze with heat. They all thought she had gone to bed with Conor. It was taken for granted that most women of her generation in the legal profession would use sex routinely to further their careers. It was an unfair and chauvinistic assumption, but there was no point in challenging it at the present. As for virginity, it was hardly worth mentioning. Even Shelly wouldn't believe her.

"—and worry about Harry McClendon. He's a tricky little bastard. I don't think he'll run the risk of having to testify in a trial unless he thinks that we have enough from Broddy to indict him. Why bother with immunity if you're not under any real threat? And Broddy Considine's word is not enough, in this happy era, to be a threat to McClendon. We'll have to shake all those suppliers that were part of the conspiracy. That makes it public and alerts Clarke and his high-priced lawyers early. It would take years and we might come up with nothing."

"Do you doubt that there is a conspiracy to commit fraud, Leo?" she snapped. "To take money away from the poor people of Cokewood Springs?"

"I don't doubt it, Counselor." He tilted his head whimsically in her direction. "I'm saying that it will be hard to prove without an enormously complex investigation and that we might come up with nothing more than we already have on Broddy. We're a long way from Con Clarke, a long way, and somehow I don't think it's as easy a turnpike as Broddy wants us to believe."

"I'm certain he's involved. You should have heard him talk about Cokewood Springs—a run-down Cal City he called it, and he's only been there once."

"It's not an indictable offense to be a snob and a boor." Leo hesitated. "You'll forgive me for being candid, Diana?"

"Of course." She felt her stomach sink as it always did when someone seemed ready to attack her character, especially someone she liked.

"If we have to face Judge Kane, for example, we might be in serious trouble. She's never forgiven us for the Hurricane Houston case." He made a wry face, recalling deftly that he had been against a trial for the pro basketball player who had been Eileen Kane's client before she was appointed to the federal bench. "Don't let her gentle voice and good looks fool you. She's as tough as they come. If she should find out that we're trying to entrap Con Clarke on the golf course, she'll throw the book at us."

Eileen Kane was Diana's ideal. Someday she wanted to be a distinguished federal judge just like her.

"I didn't sleep with him, Leo," she said mildly, her heart beating rapidly at the memory of what had happened under the northern lights.

"No one is suggesting that you did, uh, Diana." Donny Roscoe waved his hand as if in absolution. "Of course this office would not countenance anything like entrapment. We may take that for granted."

Uncounted press conferences had made Donny sound like a self-righteous hypocrite even when he was telling the full truth—which was less than he was telling right now. If she could find evidence that might convict Conor Clarke by going to bed with him, the United States Attorney for the

Northern District of Illinois would not care in the slightest, so long as she didn't get caught.

"Did you beat him, Counselor?" Leo grinned wickedly.

"Of course," she sniffed, "and giving away ten strokes at that. He's a hollow man."

"Did he make a pass at you?" Shelly's face took on its knight-errant look—part mystic, part angry brother.

She decided to let him down easily. "Certainly he did, Shelly, a rather crude one at that. I can take care of myself."

"It's a delicate matter, I mean, of where the line ought to be drawn." He blushed uneasily.

"I could go on the Chinese wall if you think it proper, sir."

It was an offer she had made before, but never in Donny's presence. Get out of the Clarke case before her maddening obsession with the man deprived her of the last tattered shreds of her sanity.

"That is a possibility we should certainly consider carefully." Roscoe folded his hands like a devout acolyte. "But there is no reason to make a decision on that now, is there, Leo?"

"Not that I can see." Martin frowned uneasily. "We have a long way to go before it would become a pertinent matter. At this point in time, Diana knows the case better than anyone else. It would take weeks to brief someone to replace her. Later on . . . well, it might be a different matter."

"Of course, of course." Donny Roscoe tried to appear judicious, thoughtful. "Then I take it . . ." His voice trailed off, as he waited for someone else to "take it."

"We'll have a few choice words with McClendon"—Leo Martin stood up—"and until then, proceed *very* cautiously."

"Ms., uh, Lyons?" In Donny's office opinions were always asked of women attorneys, just so no one would accuse him of being a chauvinist.

"I concur." She stood up. "For the present we should take one step at a time."

In the corridor, Leo whispered, "Stop by my office for a moment?"

"Sure, Monsignor." She grinned at him. "I'm ready for my weekly sermon."

He waved her to a chair and collapsed like an exhausted man into his own. "You really didn't concur in there, did you?"

"He's a terrible man, Leo. I want to put him in jail. But I'm new here and I know I have to be a team player." She half believed what she was saying. "I can't let my personal crusades blind me to the goals and problems of the whole office."

"I don't especially like Con Clarke, either, from what I read about him in the papers, anyway. He sounds like a spoiled brat." His folded hands, fingers up, found their favorite spot beneath his chin. "Still, you're a very gifted young lawyer with a brilliant career ahead of you, very much like Eileen Kane when she was your age. Con Clarke is beneath your talent and concern. Don't get hung up on him."

"I don't think I'm hung up on him, Leo," she said primly. "And I certainly don't intend to get hung up on him. I disagree, however, that he is beneath my concern. A free society cannot tolerate the kind of privilege that he represents—a young man who has done nothing besides scribble a few chauvinist verses and yet has millions of dollars to play with. It's immoral and demoralizing."

"But not necessarily illegal?" He cocked an inquisitive eye at her.

"Leo, in 1943 when my father was a staff sergeant with a wounded lung in a field hospital at Anzio"—as the words came tumbling out, she knew that she should not have said them—"Clem Clarke was a desk-bound major in Melbourne, bragging about his two wounds, neither one of which was serious and neither one of which resulted from combat. Once, he was so drunk he fell out of a jeep taking his pick of available whores. He came back a decorated hero. Dad came back with a body that's never been well since. That's not fair."

"That was a long time ago, kid," Leo spoke slowly, thoughtfully, not taking advantage of her outburst. "And your father did come home later with a wonderful wife— isn't that more important than fame and medals?"

"I'm sorry, Leo." She sighed wearily. "I didn't mean that quite the way it sounded. There's a statute of limitations on 1943. I know we can't eliminate all inequality from our society. I'm not an ideologue. I was only trying to make the point that a couple of generations of privilege and power produces an attitude, a belief that one is immune to the power of the law and that is pernicious. When some men and women think they are above the law and others feel that they must submit to this immunity, there are grave social results." She sounded like a high school nun lecturing on social justice. "Believe me, Con Clarke thinks he's above the law. Nonetheless, if he does not violate any laws, he is no concern of the U.S. Attorney's office. I accept that."

"Fine," he said, although his tone suggested he was not convinced. "Just remember that you are too important and too valuable to be obsessed with him."

"I will." She stood up to leave, unsure, as always with Leo Martin, where professional respect and concern and man/woman affection parted. What importance could she possibly have for a happily married man with three daughters of his own?

"And, Diana . . ."

"Yes?"

"Sit down for another moment, please."

"Of course." She sat down like a sixth-grade girl summoned to the Rectory.

"Everything I said before was the absolute truth. Don't let him become an obsession. But don't get obsessed with the rules, either."

"I don't understand, Leo."

"Donny about died in there when you offered to put yourself on the wall. Don't you understand the way we play this game yet?"

"Explain it again to me, Leo."

"Look." He sighed patiently. "When Donny stumbles through his little civil liberties talk, he's doing it for the record. In case he has to disown us later on. Actually he's delighted you got your foot into Conor Clarke's door and would be astonished and furious—off the record, of course—if you pulled your foot out now. Understand?"

"But—"

"Later on, we may wire you and call you an agent instead of a prosecutor. Don't worry about it, unless you get caught doing something that would embarrass us."

"Then I'd be disowned?"

"What do you expect?" Leo extended his hands in his what-can-I-tell-you gesture.

"Go to bed with him if I have to, but don't let the media ever find any proof that I did. His word against mine."

"You got it, kid." Leo beamed like a teacher with a bright little student.

"Functional justice?"

He sighed again. "OK, Diana, let me put it this way. Do you want to spend three years up at O'Hare going through the pornography that Customs confiscates?"

"Hardly."

"Then play the game the way it has to be played. Look, I've been here a long time." He laughed at himself—a bit uneasily, she thought. "I've seen hundreds of bright and ambitious young people like you come out of the law schools, not many as bright as you."

"Thank you, Leo," she said impatiently. "Get to the point."

"They divide into two categories: those who bring hangups from the legal ethics class and those who realize that when you're in a hardball world, you play hardball. The former end up with the pornography and crap like that and join some small, dull law firm. The latter become successful trial lawyers and even judges."

"Hardball?"

"Right. If you know someone is guilty, you stop at nothing to get a plea or a conviction. You plant evidence, you bribe witnesses with immunity grants, you persuade FBI or Treasury men to perjure themselves. Sometimes that's easy, sometimes not. You suppress evidence that might help the guy, you use every trick in the game because you know he has the highest-priced defense lawyers in town using every trick in their bag. The only rule is: Don't get caught."

"Was Eileen Kane like that when she was here?"

Leo frowned again. It was the first time in the conversation that his practiced explanation of "hardball" faltered.

"That was a long time ago, kid. The world, the practice of law, has changed in a place like this. You can't turn the clock back."

The office was silent for a moment. "I'm not going up to O'Hare, Leo."

"Good deal. We'd all miss you around here."

They both rose.

"One more thing."

She turned at the door of his office. "Yes?"

"You see the new Bill Murray movie?"

"*Razor's Edge?* Poor man, he's doomed to the Bill Murray persona, no matter how well he can act."

"The title?"

"The line between love and hate . . ." She felt her stomach churn. ". . . as thin as a razor's edge?"

"Do me a favor?" He smiled pleasantly. "Don't let Clarke get to you."

"Screw him if I have to, but don't fall in love with him?"

"Something like that." Leo would not look at her. It was indeed a different world than the one her father knew. The world after Big Jim Thompson.

"I was never about to fall in love with him," she said

primly. "I despise him, but"—with a smile to reward Leo—"I appreciate your concern."

18

"So I go, 'Diana you can't let him cut you off from the human race. I mean, like there are lots of good men in the world.' And my father goes that her father was a good man and pleasant enough but he should have been working on wills and not for the government because, like, he wasn't smart enough to know how it works in law enforcement. So he turned bitter—right?—and then had his heart attack and took it out on the kids and he was always afraid of the Depression again, right?"

Conor wished that he had brought O'Connor the Cat along to translate Maryjane Delaney's running commentary on the problems and perils of Diana Marie Lyons. He was quite sure that Maryjane's father was not present for the discussion with Diana, but it would be a skilled textual critic who could figure that out.

Perhaps the Cat might have a hard time translating. Put up a mountain range between Maryjane's generation and his, plant some Gauls in the mountains to discourage travel, and a new language would emerge as had French from Latin.

"She said you two had a really excellent time on Friday and Monday. Surprised me, really. I mean, I couldn't imagine two people so different would enjoy each other. But she wanted to play with you because she had read so much about you. So I go, 'OK, if you want to be a Conor Clarke groupie, I'll set it up.' "

"Oh."

Outside, Lake Michigan was acting like an ocean. Under swiftly moving clouds, rushing down the lake from the Soo, the lake was sweeping long, gentle breakers against the shore. Give it a few more hours and it would go into one of its dune-destroying snits. The ice age made a mistake in creating a lake right here in the middle of the Middle West. As Alderman Hinky Dink Kenna had once remarked, "Why did they build that terrible lake next to this great city?"

Maryjane continued to babble. "So I go, 'It's your own funeral, Diana.' And she goes, 'I can take care of myself'—which is, like, not what I meant, you know?"

"Oh."

"Really. She's complicated, you know. It's all that father of hers, a total nerd. Like none of the other kids live within a thousand miles of him, and I mean, Diana never wanted to be a lawyer. Like have you seen her with kids? Totally excellent! She wanted to be an artist and an art teacher—for little kids, you know? But no, Daddy is a lawyer and none of the other kids are lawyers, so Diana has to be a lawyer, like because she's the youngest, right? I mean, it's all because he had the heart attack when she was in the room with him after he'd lost some big case at the Board of Trade and was transferred to some other work. And she took care of him and so she's gotta do everything to keep him happy. Isn't that gross?"

"It certainly is. How old was she when he had the attack?"

"Oh, like you know, eight or nine maybe. I mean if she hadn't kept her head and run and got a doctor, like he'd be dead, right? My daddy says that even if he has this gorgeous Sicilian wife he saved from gang rape, he's dull and he has no one but himself to blame that he never made it even as a government lawyer. But she says that it's because of all the crooked politicians and that he's the only honest Irish lawyer in town. Really! I mean they live in this tiny house in Dalton and he has his pension and she works and her mother works and they have to pretend to be poor anyway. It would be totally wonderful if you could get her out of that house."

"She's a hard one to figure out, MJ." Conor tried to cut into the flow of words. "She plays golf and squash and tennis yet claims to be too poor to travel. Those are expensive sports."

"You can play golf at public courses, right? And do squash, you know, and tennis in parks, huh? I mean, she's strictly a park-district athlete. You should see her play basketball, I mean if they were into women's basketball when she was in college, she would have been All-American."

"Just what I need."

"She's really impressive, Con, like totally, you know?"

"But how can someone grow up in an atmosphere like that and be so . . . well, classy? She handles herself over at Long Beach like she belongs."

"WELL"—Maryjane busied herself about refilling their coffee cups—"so what's so classy about Long Beach anyway? You belong, Gerry belongs, I belong, it's just an ordinary country club. Right?"

"Right." Con waved off sugar and cream for the third time.

"And some people are naturally classy anyway. And her mother is a real class act, Sicilian or not. And I guess her father was OK when she was a real little kid. He only turned bitter and sour and cheap later on. And she's so damn smart. Just watch her size up a situation. Like she was a cop or a politician or a priest, you know?"

"Oh."

"And anyway, some people are just classy, regardless."

"If she's so smart, how come she buys all this stuff her father dishes out?"

"I mean"—MJ took a deep breath, winding up for another onslaught of words—"like no way does she really buy.

Deep down she knows better, huh? I go, 'Diana Marie, you know that's a lot of shit, but you're too loyal to your father to admit it. You know what?' I go, 'You really are caught in some sort of split personality. I mean really.' I go, 'One girl is intelligent and sophisticated and can do or be anything she wants and the other still lives under Daddy's thumb.' "

"And she goes?"

"WELL, she goes, 'Maybe you're right MJ, but I'm all he has left of his kids and I have to stand by him. He won't be with us much longer,' and I go to myself, 'He can use that threat to tie you up for twenty more years,' and I go to her, 'WELL, at least you don't have to pretend to yourself that he's right all the time.' And she just sort of laughs sadly, and it would be so cool and neat if you marry her."

"I heard you." He sipped his coffee. MJ made great coffee. Lucky Gerry. Once he learned to speak the language.

"I MEAN, she's a real prize."

"Which woman does the husband get?"

"Huh?"

"Daddy's girl or the naturally classy broad?"

"WELL, that's up to the husband, isn't it? I mean, if you insist on one, that's what you'll get. She's tough, but like, that would make it interesting for you, right?

It was, he decided, time to change the subject and time to leave. The background was emerging. At least there was a corner somewhere in Diana's soul that was still her own. Maybe he could set up camp there for a while and see what the chances were of a permanent occupation.

"It was good of you"—he drained his coffee cup and stood up—"to lend her your book of my poems."

"Oh, I didn't do that. My book is at home. Or maybe at Mom's. Like I don't travel with it, you know what I mean? She had her own copy. So you made some royalties off her!"

"Really?"

"Don't let her get away, Con." With considerable difficulty his pregnant hostess pulled herself out of the chair. "She'd be perfect for you. The two of you would be real cute together. I think I'll ask Gerry if, like, you and Diana could be godparents for the little monster in here." She patted her belly.

"I'll have to give her a ring sometime after Labor Day." Maybe, he added to himself.

19

As she drew a cup of coffee from the machine in the canteen on her floor—no free coffee for government employees—she reflected that Leo did not seem persuaded. Had her emotional mess been that obvious?

In the hundreds of women who had come before her, had there been other pathetically frustrated young creatures who had fallen in love with men against whom they were preparing an indictment?

Given the nature of human nature, it seemed likely as a matter of sheer statistical probabilities. But it's not supposed to happen to paragons of self-control and ethical integrity like Diana Lyons.

And it's just what I am: a pathetic, frustrated, loveless creature, besotted with a charming and plausible man who belongs in jail for the very obvious and simple reason that he enjoys the game too much to keep the law of the land.

Back in her pin-neat, windowless office, a GSA monastic cell, with its beige walls and carpet and government-issued metal furniture, she slumped into her chair, bowed her head, and cupped her hands around the coffee container. *Obsession*—the perfect word. She was obsessed with Conor Clarke.

She opened the file in her briefcase, flipped through the pages, and came to the item from Kup's column she had clipped three days before.

Con Clarke, poet, businessman, and sportsman, promises that his yacht *Brigid* will not be last in its class in the upcoming Labor Day-weekend Tri-State Regatta. Con, pictured here on the *Brigid* with model Lyn Clifford, says that St. Brigid will disown him and demand that he remove her name from the boat.

Lyn Clifford possessed a figure that, to say the least, was well-developed, and a bikini which was not.

She punched the *Sun-Times* number and asked for her contact.

"Hi, Di," he said cheerfully. "Got the info on that picture for you. Promise me first rights on the story when it breaks."

"If it breaks. It's top secret now."

"Gotcha, Di. Anyway, the picture is from last summer. Clarke has a different model each summer."

"Live-in model?" She struggled to keep her voice neutral.

"Opinion is divided. Majority says sure he bangs them. Minority says Con gets his jollies from platonic adoration. Make a difference to your case?"

"When it's a story, if it's a story, it's yours. Thanks, Henry. Bye."

"Bye, Di."

She had neglected to remind him that her name was Diana.

His long disorderly blond hair a banner in the wind, silver blue eyes, fair skin, boyish, innocent face, broad shoulders and chest, solid, well-developed muscles, artist's hands that did such wonderful . . .

The fantasies began again. As always, she told herself she was a mooning teenager, daydreaming over a movie star, and that she should turn off the daydreams at once.

It did no good. They were back on the deck in front of Maryjane's home. Only this time they did not stop. He finished his work of removing her clothes, played wonderful and remarkably detailed games with the sensitive parts of her body, brought her to a pinnacle of need, and then gently opened her up so that, completely powerless to resist, she made herself a willing and total gift to him.

As she slipped into the deep, warm swamp of lustful daydreams, her body began to react as though he were in the room with her.

The phone rang, jolting her out of her fantasy lovemaking. Shelly. Did she want to come with him on the first "informal" visit to McClendon? She struggled for the real world like someone hanging on the edge of a cliff. No, that would make him too defensive this early in the project. You do it.

"Damn," she muttered aloud as she hung up. I hate Conor C. Clarke. Why do I indulge in these stupid daydreams?

"Obsession," she said the word aloud. "Leo is right that I'm obsessed."

She withdrew her journal, which had collapsed into chaotic disarray since her week in Grand Beach. She composed potential entries in her head and then forgot them when she had time to actually write them down with her yellow number-two pencil.

A few seconds ago I had an intelligent entry to make. Now I have the notebook open and already I have forgotten.

She had to talk to someone. Her sisters lived in San Diego. Her mother, thoroughly Americanized in most ways, had ancient Sicilian opinions on men—her husband alone excepted. Her father was upset when one of his daughters dated a boy, only acquiesced to the extent of appearing at Maria's and Paola's wedding Masses when Mom, in a rare display of toughness with him, laid down the law. There was no one else to talk to. A priest?

She did not know any priest very well. She had inherited from her father the Irish respect for the clergy and from her mother the Sicilian suspicion of them.

They say, Mama averred, that priests think God made a

mistake in creating two sexes.

So there was no one to talk to. Back to the journal.

On the top of the page were two words she had scratched on the IC this morning: *Fixated on.*

She crossed them out and substituted *obsessed with.* That phrase seemed to loosen her memory. She wrote rapidly, compulsively.

I am obsessed with Conor Clarke, I, Diana Marie Elizabetha Lyons, who until this summer thought she had so little need of male companionship or physical sex that she would, as a single parent, eventually adopt a little girl, a Cambodian orphan maybe.

I hate him. I detest his arrogant assumption of superiority. I despise the social system of wealth and prestige that he represents. I resent his carefree, playboy life.

She paused and added: with a different buxom wench to bang each summer.

She paused and then scrawled in her carefully preserved margin: *Look at me—I can't stand the man and yet I'm jealous of him. Do I want him to bang me instead of the wench?*

"Well?" she asked herself aloud.

She returned to her text with the question hanging in the Spartan atmosphere of her office unanswered.

I deplore the effect of his celebrity status on public morality. I am determined that he will serve time in a federal prison for his shameless exploitation of unemployed workers in Cokewood Springs. I find his poetry repulsive.

She paused again. There was no point in keeping a diary unless you were as rigidly honest with it as you would be with a therapist—did she need a therapist? Her father would never tolerate it. Besides, they could never afford the cost.

She crossed out *repulsive* and wrote *exploitive in its attitudes toward the bodies of women.*

Was Lyn Clifford in one of those poems? Fat bitch. He compared me with an Irish pirate.... What is his poem about me like? Maybe he hasn't even written it, the pig.

I am currently participating in an investigation of his corruption with the view of obtaining an indictment from a federal grand jury. Yet for all of that I cannot banish the man's physical appeal from my imagination. I started to fall apart—no, I'll use the right term—my demoralization began when he drove up to Maryjane's house in that terrible silver Ferrari of his and I told her that it was a cute little car. I didn't even know what a Ferrari was.

Paragon of virtue that I thought I was, I was bowled over by his physical appeal as soon as I saw him. It's a matter of genes, nerve endings, hormones—an adolescent physical crush, only much worse now because I am not an adolescent anymore.

He didn't even have to try to charm me. I belonged to him—those words are unfortunately the literal truth—by the first tee. I faked it pretty well until the end of the day, when I was perfectly prepared to abandon my virginity, whatever it may be worth on the open market today, which probably isn't much, to a man I abominate at the end of our second date. Under the northern lights, of all things.

Fortunately I came to my senses in time. But, to be candid, there's a strong part of me—or maybe it's a demon woman who has invaded me—that regrets the lost opportunity.

While most of his conversation is puerile gibberish, he did not much miss the mark when he said that both of us may need permanent bed partners.

Perhaps I do need a man in my life besides Daddy. I would have thought until last week that the prospect of regular physical sex with a man was repellent. Maybe I need to reconsider. Certainly I do not need and do not want, as far as my intellect is concerned, an intimate relationship with Conor Clarke.

She considered the final sentence and added: *I do not want to be the Lyn Clifford of the summer of 1984 or 1985.*

It's all biological, she continued to write, *and like all biological obsessions, it will pass with time. Dear God, please let it be over before I have to face him in the grand jury room.*

Again the wave of sweet, enervating daydreams oozed into her brain, again she gave into them, again her body reacted with vigorous enthusiasm.

"It's lust," she told herself as she gathered her papers together for a staff meeting. Not love. Whatever I feel for him has nothing to do with love; it is totally unlike the admiration and affection and respect my mother feels for my father.

She devoured the latest Brother Cadfael mystery by Ellis Peters on the IC riding home that night. Her passion for mystery stories was, she felt, a harmless recreation, but her father, while he would never dream of telling her what to read and what not to read, felt that free time should be spent on professional journals and history and biography instead of fiction. So rather than upset the poor man, she did her novel reading on the train.

Supper was a difficult time, but not because they ever quarreled. When she saw what the battles with the older kids did to her mother, she resolved that she would make the little compromises necessary for family peace, instead of creating anguish and unhappiness by foolish fights, especially since Daddy's string of serious heart attacks.

The problem now was that her father was pathetically interested in her career but did not want to pressure her to violate professional standards by discussing confidential matters with her family. The poor dear, if he only knew how loose the lips were around the office, he would be dismayed.

On several occasions, while adhering to the strictest rules that anyone she knew obeyed, she had started to mention a case or an investigation, but he had put up his hand like a traffic cop and said, "I didn't hear that, Diana, and I don't want to hear any more."

So they were reduced to discussing points of law or matters that were on the public record—and even that was difficult because he was so bitterly opposed to court decisions of the last twenty years, rulings that her professors and her colleagues took for granted.

One night, unwittingly, she mentioned with approval a new, tighter interpretation of the Miranda decision that gave police somewhat more discretion.

"So you're defending Miranda?" His thin sad face, under a vast bald head, drooped in discouragement, his warm brown eyes became dull with disappointment. "Every criminal in the country is grateful for it. I wonder if you know how many small shopkeepers have been robbed and murdered, how many women have been raped by criminals who walk the streets because of that doctrine?"

"I'm not defending the decision, Daddy," she had said, one lawyer talking to another, "but since it is the law of the land and we have to work within it, I am saying that this interpretation, which is on its way up to the Supreme Court, does restore power to the police that some courts have denied."

"Maybe you do know more law than I do," he said with a sigh. "Young people always think they know better. I guess we are getting old, Maria. My daughter thinks she knows more about the law than I do."

"Then she is a fool," Mama had hissed, not angry particularly at Diana, but at anyone who caused her adored husband pain. "Eat your rice pilaf, both of you, and stop fighting at the supper table. I do not know"—her eyes flickered in wild humor—"why you Irlandesi must argue all the time, especially when you should be enjoying my Sicilian cooking."

"Always when I am trouble, I am Irlandesa." Diana went along with the joke to cheer her father up.

"When you're Sicilian, you don't do anything wrong. Eat, girl, you are too thin."

"I weigh the same as you do." Diana welcomed the change of subject. "And I'm exactly your height."

"And I'm an old woman." Which she certainly was not.

That night in her small bedroom, in the bed she had slept in since she was a little girl, Diana tried to come to terms with the fact that she was indeed a better and a smarter lawyer than her father. "Never dodge the facts, hon," he had often said, "even when they're unpleasant and about people you love."

It had been Paola he was talking about then, and a marriage he had bitterly opposed.

But the same dictum had to be applied to him, too, no matter how painful it was.

Poor man, he had never been bright enough or flexible enough to understand about functional justice. He thought that if you kept the rules, that was enough for justice to triumph. It wasn't. Daddy had never played hardball.

She cried herself to sleep. The next morning she refused to discuss with herself the obvious question of why it had taken her so long to realize what was obvious.

When the IC bumped into Chicago Heights the night she had offered to put herself on the Chinese wall, an offer of which her father would have strongly approved if it were ever possible for him to hear and understand the circumstances, she tucked her book—about Shropshire at the time when King Stephen and the Empress Maud were struggling for power—into her bulging briefcase. She stepped off the train, from the humidity of ineffective commuter air-conditioning into the worse humidity of a late August Chicago evening. As she sliced her way through the uncomfortable curtain of wet air toward her dad in his waiting VW bug, she yearned for the deck in front of the Delaneys' at Grand Beach and a cool margarita. Her parents would be shocked to know that she drank, with considerable relish, if the truth be told, an occasional margarita.

"My little girl rarely gets off the train laughing," Dad said as she kissed him. "Interesting traveling companion these days?"

"No, just a little joke I remembered. I read all the way home. A lot of work." She patted the bulging briefcase.

She was shocked, as she was each night now, by how old her father was. He had visibly aged since his heart attack and retirement, forced out of his job, as he claimed, by "affirmative action." He was theoretically at least ten years older than Mom, though the children guessed the truth was closer to fifteen or sixteen years older. He had been so handsome as a younger man, even when Diana was in her early teens, that the age difference had hardly seemed to exist. Now Mama, Anna Maria in her shop ("because they say it has more class"), looked twenty years younger.

Mama's life was interesting and lively, even if she rarely heard from her other children and saw her grandchildren hardly at all. She was a competent and successful manager of a clothing shop in the Flossmoor Mall and enjoyed her work thoroughly. Diana often wondered how she had persuaded her father to let her get the job. The store was never mentioned in the house.

"Anything interesting today?" she asked him as the car picked its way down the suburban side streets.

"Someone called about a real estate closing over the weekend. Needed a good lawyer cheap, I guess. And I finished rearranging my notes about Anzio. I think I can get at the book finally after Labor Day."

An occasional real estate closing, clippings and scrapbooks from the war, military history, law journals, notes for a book he would never write—no wonder Dad was aging rapidly. She softly cursed to herself—a good old-fashioned Sicilian curse—at the bureaucrats who had forced him out of the job that had been so much a part of his life.

She had begged him to undergo the open-heart surgery, pleading with him that it would prolong his life.

"There's no evidence of that, hon," he said with a sad smile, "I read an article about it just the other day."

"No evidence because there hasn't been time enough since the procedures began to be used routinely, but there is every reason to think there will be such evidence soon. Most of the people who have the surgery are still alive and walking the streets."

"So now, Maria, our daughter is a physician as well as an attorney. Aren't we lucky?"

That was always the end of the argument. She was sure Mama pleaded with him, too, but with no more effect. Was he afraid or did he want to die?

He would not live much longer. She did not want to admit that the thin, haggard man next to her in the VW did not want to live much longer. If only she could win a major case before he died, he would know that his life had not been pointless during all the years since he had fought at Anzio and later, in the last days of the American military in Sicily when he'd killed the bandits who were tormenting a skinny little Sicilian girl.

"I think I'll have a big one for you soon, Daddy," she said as they turned down the street of tiny homes on which they lived.

"I hope I live to see the day," he said, sighing. "You're the only one in the family, besides your mother, of course, who cares about my values."

"You'll live to see the day," she said with confidence she did not feel. When Mama was trying to mediate, in her own hot-tempered fashion, between the other kids and Daddy, she sometimes said that the war had taken a terrible toll on him. Diana had read some of the history books and found that they agreed with her father that the Anzio landing had been a terrible mistake caused by rivalry among ambitious generals. Her father had every reason to be angry.

"I hope I see it," he said. "I'm still paying the price for that piece of shrapnel at Anzio. Still, I intend to hang on."

She normally repressed the thought of her father's death and the terror that accompanied the thought. Now it was impossible to do so. He would not last long, she told herself, her stomach churning. What will Mama do? Her culture condoned the role of the permanent widow. Yet the other day she had heard Mama say on the phone to a woman she worked with that a widow was a fool not to remarry if she could.

Who was Mama? she wondered. All her life Mama had been the protector and reflection of Daddy. The children had rarely asked themselves what she thought or what she wanted. Yet at her shop she was a smart, strong-willed woman, a self-consciously sexy woman.

Was she, Diana wondered with horror at her own blasphemy, waiting patiently till the debt she had acquired in Sicily forty years before was finally paid?

If Daddy died and Mama remarried, what would happen to her? She would be completely alone in the world. She quivered involuntarily and told herself as she climbed the steps to her bedroom that it was a foolish and childish reaction. The Clarke case was getting to her.

At supper Daddy tapped his fork lightly on the shining white tablecloth—a clean one every night—and cleared his throat with a raspy little cough. Diana winced. It was the certain sign that she had done something to upset him.

"Have I ever tried to tell my children what they should or should not read, Maria? Have I ever interfered in their intellectual development?"

"Only when Huberto hid *Playboy* under his bed." Mama's eyes flashed at Diana with dangerous anger. "What foolish thing have you done now to upset your father?"

"I don't know," Diana replied, feeling shamed and guilty even before the charge.

"If Diana wants to read erotic trash, if she has the time to do that and still live up to her career responsibilities—after all, she is an adult, a grown woman of twenty-five—do we have any right to criticize her?"

"She is a little fool," Mama snapped. "She lives in our house; she obeys our rules. Yes?"

"Ah, that is the point, isn't it, Maria. We may not criticize what she reads outside of this house." He folded his hands reverently on the tablecloth. "Yet we are surely within our rights, perhaps our obligations, to insist that under no circumstances she bring pornographic trash into this house—not as long as she proposes to enjoy the convenience of living with us. If she wants to leave books of obscene verse lying around where anyone may read them, she ought to perhaps rent her own apartment, should she not?"

"We certainly don't need her paycheck." Mama began to clear away the plates. Automatically Diana, face burning with humiliation, began to help her.

Unlike her older brothers and sisters, Diana understood that Mama's rebukes were only for the record. She supported Daddy because she felt that was her obligation. She did not necessarily agree and rarely felt any real anger toward Diana, even if there was little for them to talk about to each other.

"I did not leave the book lying around the house," she barked back at them. "It was on my dresser, under a pile of papers."

"Ah, see how it is, Maria? After a certain age, they think they have the right to hide things from their parents, even to deny the parent a right to inspect his own home."

Poor Daddy, nothing to do all day but to roam the house, remembering the old angers against the generals whose stupidity sent everyone else in his platoon to death. She should not have left Con Clarke's poems where he might find them.

"Tell your father you're sorry," Mama demanded, eager as always to have peace restored.

"Clement Clarke's son is a vile, immoral man." His voice turned into the shrill whine it always became when he was angry. "He thinks he is above the law because he has inherited so much money. His life-style is a public immorality. His poems should make a respectable young woman blush, especially one who claims to be a feminist."

"I know, Daddy," she said humbly.

"I would not even look at your mother the way he looks at his casual friends. Why are you reading such vile trash, Diana, answer me?"

"I can't talk about it, Daddy," she said miserably.

"Of course you can talk about it if your father wants you to talk about it." Mama began to pour the coffee; long practice enabled her to go on with the usual dinner table activities while her husband battled, in his usual quiet, hurt fashion, with their children. "Answer his question like a good daughter."

"If I answer him, he will say that he doesn't want to hear any more." She sat down at her place, remembering all the pain of countless other sessions like this one, pain that would end only when she pleaded for forgiveness.

"I fail to understand, Maria, what she means by that remark."

"I mean"—suddenly Diana was furious—"that it is a government matter about which I cannot talk. Is that not enough? Did you talk at the family dinner table about confidential matters in your office? Come on, Daddy, give me a break."

"You have no respect," Mama insisted, though her heart did not seem to be in it. "Perhaps you should move out of the house. Tonight."

"Now, Maria, let's not be hasty." He beamed happily. "I think I understand what the child is saying. I don't want to hear anything more about Conor Clarke or his dirty poems."

The crisis was over, but only because she had told her father that she was investigating Con Clarke.

"Of all the men that grew rich and powerful when Dick Daley was mayor"—her father turned to his favorite subject—"Clement Clarke was the most repulsive. He contributed to Daley's campaign even when he ran for sheriff in 1946. When Daley was elected mayor nine years later, Clarke enjoyed a license to steal, not only from the poor farmers on the Board of Trade, but from the poor people of Chicago in his real estate speculations. That young man was conceived in sin. His mother was only one of Clement

Clarke's mistresses and not the last of them, either. She was three months pregnant when he was forced to marry her to avoid a paternity suit. That was in the spring of 1955, right after Daley was elected. You'd think that such a disgrace—there were many rumors that Clement Clarke was not his father—would have caused a so-called family man like Richard Daley to disown him."

"Terrible," Mama commented routinely, refilling the coffee cups.

"The Daley years will be regarded by history as a replay of the decline and fall of the Roman Empire."

Neither she nor Mama said a word. Daddy, in this case agreeing with the Hyde Park liberals whom he ordinarily despised, was wrong about Mayor Daley. Perhaps even Mama thought so, because she never agreed with him in his attacks on the mayor and his family. From Mama, no agreement meant silent disagreement.

Yet Daddy was entitled to a few eccentric opinions. He was nothing more than an old-fashioned moral man. His standards of morality might be out of date, but it didn't mean they were wrong. If all your life you stood by principles that others pretended to believe but did not honor, it was understandable that you might seem to have a few strange ideas when you grew old.

"I'm sure justice will finally be done," he concluded as the three of them stood up from the table, she and Mama to finish in the kitchen, Daddy to return to his study and his clippings about the Anzio beachhead.

Daddy's principles were right even if sometimes his applications of them were wrong.

She remembered him the way he was when she was a little girl—handsome, lively, proud of his six kids, confident of his career. All that had changed because he would not sacrifice his principles when he was working for the Department of Agriculture in the days before the CFTC had been established, and was fighting the high rollers at the Board of Trade—most notably, Clement Clarke, the president of the

Board of Trade at the time Daddy was transferred to HUD.

Despite her anger at the Clarke family, she reread Con's *Love Song* before she fell asleep, like a novice doing her spiritual reading in the convent dormitory.

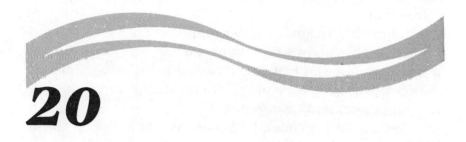

20

This is a pretty creepy trick, Con Clarke rebuked himself as he climbed out of his Ferrari in the huge parking lot of the Flossmoor Shopping Mall. I ought to be ashamed of myself. Still, I'm going to do it and that's that.

He had done well, or well enough, in his efforts to extirpate Diana Marie Lyons from his imagination until the Tri-State race. Then, in the excitement of the fleet boiling past Grand Beach, colored spinnakers ballooning the fresh northeast wind, he lost control of the helm of *Brigid* at a particularly important tack. His crew shouted frantically. At the last minute he regained control and narrowly avoided a collision.

"What the hell happened out there?" the captain of the other boat and an old racing friend demanded that night in the bar of the Michigan City Yacht Club. "I've never seen you do something that dumb before."

"I've never done anything that dumb before. Momentary distraction at the wrong time. Sorry."

"A woman?" the man asked skeptically.

"'Course not. Something much more serious. A business deal."

They both laughed.

Yeah, big joke.

He could still feel her firm, sweaty flesh against his fingers, still taste her nipples on his lips. Some of the time, he kicked himself for wasting such a spectacular opportunity. The rest of the time he congratulated himself on his heroic restraint and his utterly admirable respect for a vulnerable virgin.

Vulnerable virgin . . . alliteration. I am a poet.

He worked hard at avoiding the central issue, which was not whether he had been wise or foolish that night on the deck half up the side of the dune with the aurora flaring all around, but what came next.

Life would be violently passionate with Diana Marie Lyons more or less routinely in bed next to you. She was a violent and passionate woman, despite her pretense at cool, rational self-control. Remember the way she attacked Pine Lake? If she were angry at you, she'd attack you the same way.

And if she loved you, she'd love you the same way.

Not only is she violent and passionate—and breathtakingly beautiful in the light of the moon and the aurora—she is also thoroughly confused. That's the problem. It's obvious that she has a big father fixation, loves him and hates him. Suppose that gets transferred to me? What do I do with it?

As Naomi says, a little bit of psychiatric knowledge and a little more psychiatric jargon is an obstacle to a happy life. A few years ago I would have run after her barefoot, like Zola Budd racing the five thousand meters. Now I slink away and wonder. Damn.

He had not mentioned her to his two trusted confidants—Naomi and Monsignor Ryan. On the one hand, he was afraid that they would both say, Conor, no way. You don't need that kind of wench in your life.

And on the other, he feared perhaps even more that they would say, Conor, this is the one. Go for her.

What if they split?

That was unlikely. The two of them always agreed, even when he was hoping for a split ballot.

So, mostly but not completely sober, he devised a new scheme in his bunk on *Brigid* that Sunday night of Labor Day weekend in the harbor of Michigan City, inspired by the lead he had built up in the first two legs of the Tri-State and feeling like a strategist of greater skills than Nathan Bedford Forrest and Stonewall Jackson combined.

It called for more research. There was lots of time, no rush at all. Learn more about the girl, right?

What if someone else, someone less heroically generous than you are, gets to her first?

Well, that's too bad. Besides, maybe she's learned to be cautious.

He pondered The Fashion Shop in Flossmoor mall. From the outside it looked especially chic and elegant. Only top-of-the-line stuff, he wagered.

He paused to savor the feel and the smell and the taste of the day, brisk, nostalgic early autumn, though technically still summer. Conor liked all the seasons, even winter. Whatever season it happened to be, that was his favorite. Today it was autumn.

So I'm checking up on the girl's mother. So what's wrong with that? If she works in a shop like this, can she be one of Fellini's shrill street women? What's wrong with being curious?

He mentally reviewed his story. He did not want to become tongue-tied. It was the Delaney baby for whom he wanted to buy something. He had checked by phone earlier in the day and had been informed that, of course, they had a small and select line of gifts for infants.

Small and select, that was the theme.

In point of fact, the Delaney baby was not due for two and a half more months. Well, the gift could keep. But she already existed in a story and had a name, Geraldine Diana. He would not reveal to Mama the child's second name. As for his claim to be her godfather, it was probably a specious anticipation, but it was not an absolute impossibility.

He considered the window display of The Fashion Shop. Autumnal night wear. The kind of wine or purple or maroon gown that you could wear at most one night before you would have to launder it most carefully by hand. Not Frederick's of Hollywood, but tasteful and discreet, a good buy if you had a husband whose passions were likely to be stirred up to the point of madness by sheer lace in copious amounts. A hundred years ago a whore wouldn't have dared dress that way. Today your ordinary suburban matron would argue that if it cost that much, it must be conservative.

Conor did some mental calculations. Papa's pension, Diana's salary, Mama's income from managing this place: it would come to not much less than six figures, maybe a little more. Why, then, the need to pretend to be poor? Why didn't she own a car?

Something badly wrong in that family.

He took a deep breath and manfully strode into The Fashion Shop. Inside it was quiet, discreet, respectful. It could have been the entrance to a very high-class and elegant Continental house of assignation, except that Con Clarke had no idea what one of those would be like. Still, a man walking into the place would feel very much that its soft colors and softer lights and tastefully arranged displays said to him, "This is strictly a woman's world, buster, but because it's you and because you're well-heeled, we'll let you come in and share a few of the secrets."

Well, they wouldn't say "buster" or "well-heeled." They'd only think those words.

His eyes squinting as he adjusted to the dim light after the autumn sunshine in the parking lot, Conor peered around the shop. Two of them, neither one Mama. I blew it. Came at the wrong time.

"Can I be of assistance, sir?"

"Uh, well, I want to buy a dress for a very special young woman, a very young, very special young woman. You see,

she's only a week old and I find that I'm her godfather"—he
smiled his blarney smile—"and I think the assumption of
spiritual responsibilities should be marked by the gift of an
appropriate dress. Don't you?"

"Ah." The woman smiled warmly, a hint of flirtation,
mind you, the barest of hints. "The responsibility of a
padrino is very serious. Would you come this way, please?"

Padrino! Ohmygod! It is Mama! How could I have
missed? She's a dead ringer for Diana!

And, he thought, not at all unlike Claudia Cardinale, not
at all. She doesn't remind me of the Cardinale of *8½* but of
the wondrous mature woman in *Fitzcarraldo* or *The Gift*.
What am I getting into with the Lyons family?

He covered his confusion with a rush into smooth, facile
Italian—with horrendous grammar and a terrible accent.
Perhaps the *signora* would suggest a baptismal robe. Nothing but the best for his first goddaughter. Only the birth of
his own daughter would be more important. No, he was not
married, but he hoped to be soon. A very beautiful woman?
Oh, yes, indeed. You have bambini, *signora*? Six of them?
And ten grandchildren, six of them girls? But that is impossible, you cannot be a grandmother. I will not believe it.

Mama finally put her hands up to her face to hide, ineffectually, her laughter. "Oh, sir, you make a wonderful Italian. Most Americans would hesitate or be embarrassed by
grammar and vocabulary and pronunciation. You understand that it is truly Italian to rush ahead, no matter what the
mistakes."

"Do I now?"

"I do not offend you?" A sudden burst of compunction.

"*Signora*, you charm me, but your accent is Roman, is it
not?"

God forgive you, Con Clarke, for that bit of blarney.

Maybe Mama was a year or two or three older than fifty.
Instead of trying to look younger, which she could easily
have done, she had chosen to look mysterious—touches of
silver and gray left in her hair, some facial lines not ob-

scured, luscious figure deftly understated. You had to discover the long, trim legs, the disciplined hips, the smooth stomach, the deep, sumptuous breasts.

Nothing blatant about Mama. She had designed herself for delayed impact. You noticed her figure not at rest but in motion. She knew what she was doing.

A sophisticated woman of the world? That was the illusion, the mask, the image. In fact, she was a peasant girl turned suburban matron.

And a good actress. Who probably devoured the fashion magazines.

Conor's imagination began to do what a young man's imagination automatically does to a beautiful woman. He instructed it to stop immediately. She was old enough to be his mother-in-law.

What difference does that make, his imagination replied? Do we discriminate against mothers-in-law?

Not if they look like that, Conor replied.

Mama could certainly wear Diana's clothes and vice versa. Moreover, Diana would not be any more attractive than Mama in the white sleeveless dress she was wearing. Surely her makeup was done with great care. Surely her hair had been touched up with equally great care. But Mama was, nonetheless, a stunning woman, tall and slender like her daughter, though perhaps without so many solid muscles, but with a whimsical, mobile face that was, if anything, prettier than her daughter's.

What Mama lacked in youth she made up for in the hint of vast experience and wisdom.

Like wow! as Maryjane or the Cat would have said.

"You flatter me, sir," she replied with a dazzling smile. "It is merely dressed-up Sicilian. I think that maybe you studied in Florence but not—"

"Not too hard. Spent my time on Chianti and Florentine women who are not nearly as lovely as Sicilians."

"You must be Irish! It is called blarney, is it not? Come let us look at a dress for the *bambina!*"

"Where in Sicily?" he persisted as he examined delicate baby dresses and lamented that the imaginary Geraldine was not his own daughter.

"A little village down the coast from Agrigento. Other Italians say it is almost Saudi Arabia. I tell my Irlandesi friends that I have Moorish blood. Is that not true, Elaine?" she called to the other woman. "Am I not part Moorish?"

"If you say so, Anna Maria." The other woman laughed tolerantly.

Not one but two Arabian princesses. Schcherazade and daughter. What must it be like to bring your boyfriends around home with a mother like that. Would teenage boys appreciate the fine points of Mama's appeal?

Don't be silly. Look at that figure, those legs, even a fourteen-year-old ape would notice her.

Conor Clement Clarke, he warned himself, stop imagining her with her clothes off. You're a fourteen-year-old, too.

What will a woman be like in twenty years? Take a look at her mother, he had been once advised.

All right, that's what I'm doing.

As MJ would say, like totally awesome.

Does she dress like that around the house? Conservatively she's wearing five hundred dollars' worth of clothes and jewels and perfume. Discount prices, but still . . .

The baptismal dress was duly purchased. Two hundred dollars' worth of handmade Irish lace and linen. Doubtless worth every penny. What if the *bambina* was a *bambino*? Well, there would be others.

He exchanged final flirtatious blarney with Mama and beat what he hoped was a not-too-ignominious retreat. The woman was a shrewd salesman—oops, salesperson. Charming and helpful, but out to make a buck, too. What was this poverty bit?

Back in the Ferrari, cooling himself in the light autumnal breeze, Conor Clarke exhaled slowly. So you wanted to know what herself would be like twenty-five, thirty years from now, so you found out. Does that help you any?

She'll be gorgeous, with any breaks. And maybe as mellow and cheerful as Mama. So now what are you going to do?

You're going to try to figure out how this fits with the picture you were given of Mama and family life at Grand Beach. There's a piece of the puzzle missing.

Conor had noted that the store closed at six that evening. He drove over to Cokewood Springs and had a few beers with the construction crews. The project seemed to be on schedule, a little ahead. Telephones and bars, that's where venture capitalists learn the truth.

At quarter to six he parked the Ferrari in front of The Fashion Shop, put on sunglasses and a cap, slouched down, and waited. The other woman left the store a few minutes before six. Five minutes after closing time, the door opened and Mama appeared, completely transformed.

Had it not been for the slim waist and the long legs, he would have thought it was someone else, maybe a worker coming home from a factory. She wore thick glasses, jeans, low-heeled shoes, a T-shirt, and a man's dress shirt hanging out over her jeans. Her expensively groomed hair was covered by a scarf and she carried not one, but two paper shopping bags.

Conor wasn't close enough to get a good look at her face, but he was sure that the makeup had been scrubbed off.

She didn't look at the Ferrari as she walked by it, so his disguise was unnecessary. He followed her down Halsted and into the side streets of Dolton. She turned into a driveway. He stopped four or five houses behind her. The woman who got out of the Datsun was not even the same one who had climbed into it. She was transformed as if she were a special effect in a film—Mr. Hyde becomes Dr. Jekyll, Anna Maria becomes Mama.

The erect, self-confident grand duchess who had sold

him Geraldine's baptismal dress, had been replaced by a weary, discouraged Sicilian housewife.

With an effort that hinted at exhaustion from a lifetime in a sweatshop, she dragged the shopping bags out of the back seat of an old, two-door Datsun.

What the hell!

It's one way to keep your sanity in that little madhouse, Conor reflected. What does it do to your youngest daughter, however? Does she grow up to be someone like you or someone like her father?

Or with a personality tugged in both directions, in danger of being ripped apart?

Conor waited a long time before he started his car and began the long ride up the Dan Ryan toward his Lincoln Park apartment.

Daddy, he thought, must be a real winner.

Indian Summer

First Song

Beloved:

A captive enslaved by your amorous lips,
A prisoner of your sweet embrace,
Drawn after you in passionate chase,
Helplessly bound by your searing kiss,
Dark is my skin, I know, and slim my waist,
My breasts, dear brothers tell me, inferior.
Yet I undress swiftly when you draw near,
Of my prudish modesty you see no trace.
I am yours, my love, for what I am worth,
Play with me, I beg, however you will,
Fondle me, use me till your pleasure is filled.
I live only for your delight and mirth.

Lover:

But I am the one enraptured as slave,
Captured completely by your form and face.
Chained forever to your numinous grace,
O mistress of love whose favor I crave.
Firm and full your bosom, an exquisite gift,
Your slender legs lead to a perfumed cave.
I am, that I might draw near that sacred nave,
A meek servant to your slightest wish.

Duet:

Lay your head against my breast,
Sooth me with your azure eyes,
Heal me with your gracious thighs,
In my arms forever nest.
You are as soft as raisin cake,
You're as warm, dear, as new-baked bread,
You are a blossoming apple grove,
And a sandalwood treasure trove.
Drink me like expensive wine!
Consume me, I am only thine!
Beneath this star-dense sky,
Lay quiet now on my chest.

Then again, after a little rest,
Drown me in your happy sighs.
My wondrous love, softly sleep.
Your gift tonight I'll always keep.

Love Song, 1:1–2:7

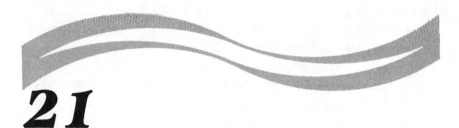

21

Brigid was first in class and fourth in fleet in the Tri-State Regatta (yachting news was relegated to the bottom of the last page of the *Tribune* sports section because of Cub mania). Con Clarke told the poor reporter who was deputed to write the story that almost no one would read that he had been granted a temporary reprieve by St. Brigid, but only temporary. "If I do as bad next summer as I did my first summer with her boat, she'll make me change the name for sure. She's a terrible woman once she gets angry. You know what your Irish women are like."

Diana sniffed impatiently, but nonetheless she clipped the photo of Con, with the usual scantily dressed woman in tow (not as attractive, she thought disdainfully, as Lyn Clifford), and slipped it into the growing file of photos she was collecting. Evidence, she told herself piously, knowing that it was not so.

Then she thought about it for a moment and opened the file again.

A new boat. When did he buy it? The lunch at Phil Schmid's restaurant near the soap works in Hammond had been in early April.

She phoned a yacht equipment store and they gave her the number of the company which made the Peterson 41 Racing Machine. Fitted with a full complement of sails and equipped with radar and computerized navigational devices, the *Brigid* would have cost approximately the amount of money Broddy Considine claimed to have given Con Clarke at lunch.

Diana leaned back in her chair and smiled happily. Somehow this confirmed that, obsession or not, her instincts about Con Clarke were correct. A jury—grand or trial—would love it: a playboy stealing money that was supposed to help the unemployed and using it to buy a big yacht which he dared to name after a Catholic saint.

The next week he phoned her at the office.

"Diana Marie Lyons, what have I done to you?" he demanded cheerfully.

My God, does he know about the investigation?

"I'm afraid I don't understand," she stammered.

"You said you would phone me and give me a chance to regain my honor on the golf course. And here it is, Labor Day come and gone, autumn for all practical purposes, and never a word from you."

"I was afraid that if I beat you again, St. Brigid might really disown you."

"Ah, no. She's the patroness of poetry and spring and new life and Irish television, but she has no venue when it comes to golf."

The phone was wet in her hand, she was on the verge of hyperventilation. "My vacation is over, I'm afraid I don't have any time for golf. Some of us have to work for a living."

"And that's unjust. In the old days, the affluent of both sexes did not have to work. Then in the Dark Ages, the nineteenth century I mean, men began to work to show that they could be socially useful even if they didn't have to. Now women work, too—it's hard on the arts."

"I'm afraid my family was never part of that social class."

"Mine neither, which means we're entitled, doesn't it? Anyway, it wasn't the golf I had in mind, but the symphony. My good friend Sir Georg is doing Handel's *Messiah*, the whole thing, on Thursday night next, not because it's Christmas, which you may have noticed, but in honor of the three hundredth anniversary of the composer's birth. Come wish happy birthday to George Frederick Handel with me. I have two tickets in the boxes."

"At Wrigley Field?"

"No, you idjit, at Orchestra Hall. Dinner at the Cliff Dwellers at six before—that's on the eighth floor of Orchestra Hall, as I'm sure you know."

She didn't and didn't care to.

"No nubile Junior Association women from Lake Forest available?"

"They're always available. I haven't asked any of them." Did he sound a little hurt or was this just part of his tiresome act? "I'll see you at six?"

"You will not." It was surprisingly easy to say. End, she thought with relief, of her obsession. "I have to work on a case."

"Nothing I can do to change your mind?"

"Nothing," she said flatly.

"Maybe when they come home from their European triumph in January?"

"You're not going with them?" she asked sarcastically.

"I'd thought of it. I'll do it if you'll come along."

It was a joke, but the prospect made her heart do a number of awkward flip-flops. Dear God, what is the matter with me?

"No, thank you."

"It would have been fun. Oh well, some other year maybe. But when they come home?"

"I have a very busy case load just now."

"I see." Did he sound relieved? "Well, no harm in trying. I won't promise not to try again. If you have a change of heart, cruel maiden, my number is 642-2222—that's so my not-too-intelligent friends can remember it easily. Or if you are old-fashioned in these matters, as I am, it's Michigan 2-2222. That's five twos in a row. Got it?"

"How much does it cost to obtain a personalized number like that?"

"Doesn't cost a thing if you have some clout. Maybe an occasional seat in my box at Wrigley Field. I do have one there, too. But you have the number?"

"I'm sure I won't need it. Now, if you don't mind, I have to return to my work."

"Sorry to have kept you," he murmured, like a disappointed little boy.

A spoiled little boy. He had yet to learn that there were some things in life that he could not have. And I'm one of them.

Well, she thought, aware that she was exhausted, that wasn't so bad after all.

Of course, I could have found out when he purchased his boat. I can get that anytime I want from the state registration people. I've never been to Orchestra Hall, never to a live symphony concert.

She knew that she was flirting with deadly temptation. This was the turning point: if she stuck to her guns now, there would be no more trouble. If she yielded to temptation, she was running terrible risks with her family, her career, maybe her life.

"Nothing, nothing good could come from such a date," she said aloud and picked up an IRS analysis of his income tax returns and estimated net worth. The conclusion— unusual for the IRS—he seemed to be paying more taxes than their net-worth estimate.

"I won't do it," she insisted.

But the telephone seemed to leap into her hand and her fingers punched 642 almost of their own volition.

She hung up virtuously. Then, knowing that what she was doing was stupid and immoral and dangerous, she deliberately lifted the phone and punched his number.

"Con Clarke." Brisk, businesslike, efficient.

"I presume I'm interrupting a poem?"

"Only a fantasy that might lead to one."

"What fantasy?"

"I won't tell you."

"You did say six?"

"I did."

"I'll see you then."

Having plunged into sin and knowing the dangers of the sin, she did not even feel guilty. Indeed, so quickly did Diana Marie Lyons become acclimated to a life of sin that she left her office during the lunch hour, behavior which was unofficially frowned upon unless the lunch was business related, to buy a late-summer cotton-knit pastel dress with a wide white belt to emphasize her twenty-three-inch waist.

In Marshall Field's basement of course.

And while she was at it, she checked the late-September bargains in swimsuits and made a purchase that was so daring that her hands began to sweat again.

Who was it that said if you are going to sin, sin bravely?

"A very famous Catholic priest said it," Con observed cheerfully as he walked with her, over her protests, to the IC station at Randolph Street. Michigan Avenue seemed warm and soft on this end-of-summer night. "Father Martin Luther. And you were not planning for this to be a night of brave sinning, were you? I thought we'd put that off till next weekend on the *Brigid*."

"I don't think I agreed to go sailing with you next weekend," she said.

He squeezed her hand, of which he had not relinquished control since the beginning of the second half of the *Messiah* after the intermission.

"You should never have had that second glass of wine. You are strictly a short hitter, by your own admission. Certainly you agreed. Call me at the number, remember it's . . ."

"Michigan plus five twos. . . . How long have you had *Brigid*?"

Her Judas question slipped out without thought or plan. She was doing penance, she supposed, for a sinfully enjoyable evening. Con had been charming but restrained, the tone set by his conservative three-piece gray suit— "Pretending I'm a hardworking young lawyer on a date with one of my hardworking, if sensationally lovely, young colleagues," he said after kissing her very modestly on the cheek.

The Cliff Dwellers, scarcely an exclusive and elite club, seemed a magical place to Diana, gentle, a little run-down, civilized, and charming. Orchestra Hall was not run-down; its mixture of red and ivory colors suggested Hapsburg elegance (as she imagined Hapsburg elegance, since the closest she'd been to Vienna was Detroit). Moreover, Sir Georg Solti with his precision direction and his courtly bows also seemed to hint at the Austro-Hungarian Empire.

Diana had the good sense not to admit that she had never been to Orchestra Hall before and to restrain any remark about how much tickets for a box cost.

She did think to herself that his box, empty save for the two them, would feed a family in Cokewood Springs for a month.

Then the wonders of the *Messiah* as no record could ever capture it.

"Probably poor old George Frederick never heard it played so well," Con had whispered, as Sir Georg sat briefly for the second intermission so that those who couldn't stay the whole route—to 10:50—could catch their trains to Lake Forest. "Even the first time when it was played in Dublin, no less."

"I'm an incurable romantic," she said, tears running down her face at the end of Handel's birthday party.

"Welcome to the club." He looked like he was preparing to kiss her, but he did not. She would not have minded. If the real world would have vanished permanently at that moment and left only the two of them and Handel's doxology, she would have been perfectly content.

"Your favorite?"

"Next to Mozart."

"We'll have to see the film version of *Amadeus* when it appears. Did you see the play?"

"No," she said, not willing to add that she'd never seen a real play. High school and parish productions didn't count.

"It's very powerful, about Antonio Salieri, who was a contemporary and rival of Mozart. The author argues, not so much as a historical fact but as a premise for the story, that Salieri killed Mozart because of envy."

"How ugly! I wouldn't want to see it!"

"That was a quick reaction. Don't you like to think about envy?"

"Nor to talk about it," she insisted.

Con, who was in a laid-back mood, did not insist.

He did insist after the final ecstatic curtain calls that he would drive her home in his "cute red car."

"Maryjane and her big mouth," she said, feeling like an untutored little fool.

"It's my one concession to an affluent life-style," he chuckled.

"The *Brigid* isn't a rich man's boat?"

He considered carefully. "No, the *Brigid* is an obligation, not an indulgence."

"Anyway, I'll ride the IC home. My dad will meet me at the train."

"Ride the IC at this time of night?" he exclaimed. "That's dangerous."

"Some of us don't have Ferraris and have to ride public transportation." They were standing in front of Orchestra Hall as the crowds flowed out—one river toward the parking garages under Grant Park, another toward the waiting taxis and the ride to the late, late commuter train for Lake Forest.

"You could certainly afford a car. . . ." He held his car keys in his hand, confused by her refusal to accept a ride home.

"I give my paycheck to my parents and they give me an allowance. When they think we can afford another car, they'll buy me one."

She expected him to be dismayed that someone still lived in such a patriarchal world, as her friends usually were when she told them of her financial arrangements.

"I'll walk you to the train," he said mildly, "if you're absolutely certain you won't let me drive you home. It'll only take twenty minutes or so. Hester is pretty fast."

"Hester?"

"My Ferrari."

"You seem to enjoy riding women," she said, realizing too late the obscene implications of what she had said.

He hardly seemed to notice. "Hester is definitely womanly in temperament. She was preceded by a Porsche named Otto."

"You think it strange that I live at home and give my paycheck to my father?"

"I didn't say that, did I?" He had become distant, withdrawn.

"You think I'm some kind of freak?"

He squeezed her hand. "We're both romantics, Diana, my darling. Handel makes both of us want to cry."

Then he announced that she was sailing with him the next weekend and seemed to recapture his good spirits.

And she asked her Judas question.

"*Brigid?* Oh, I bought her late. End of April, beginning of May. Had a little trouble arranging the financing."

"You had trouble with money?"

"Doesn't everyone? Most of it's tied up in projects, and April is income-tax month. I finally managed to scrape a few dollars together."

In a lunch at Phil Schmid's, she thought with a heart that unaccountably wanted to sink. It had been too easy.

He kissed her cautiously as she was boarding the silver IC car, much like the first kiss on the golf course. "No northern lights to drive us mad tonight, worse luck for me."

"Good night, Conor," she said softly, "I had a wonderful time."

"Yeah." He was back in his withdrawn mood. "I bet."

He is a strange man, she prepared her diary entry mentally, as the train pulled out of the station and began its desultory trek to the south end of Cook County. *His charm is practiced and clever. I suppose that comes with wealth. If you have money to fall back upon, you do not have to push or hurry, you can afford to pretend to be laid back and thoughtful, even adopt the occasional attitude of silent vulnerability. He is very good at it; even though I, of all people, ought to know better, I am practically defenseless when he uses his ingenious techniques on me. I suppose that demonstrates how inexperienced I am with men, particularly with men who think that they can have whatever and whomever they want as a matter of right.*

I have to say that I enjoyed the evening. It was in the most adolescent sense of the term a "good date," so good that it was very easy for me to forget who I am and who he is—even to wish that it could be different between us. I have to admit grudgingly that when I am with him, it is hard not to like him, even though I am fully conscious that he is shallow, superficial, and spoiled. I am traveling on very thin ice. I should not have gone to the concert with him. My obsession is worse tonight than it was this morning. I learned enough perhaps to justify the evening in terms of my investigation: he bought his boat shortly after the lunch at Phil Schmid's with money he had scraped together despite a temporary cash shortage. There can't be much doubt that it was the money from the kickbacks. I could have learned from the state about when he bought the boat, though not about his cash shortage. It is useful to have such information, but I could hardly use it in court. Learning what I did was not worth the danger I incurred. I am certainly not so stupid as to sail with him next Saturday. This was the first date and the last one.

It was not altogether true that the IC was safe at that hour on a Thursday night. Three teenagers hassled her enough that she thought perhaps it would have been better to run the risk of driving up to the family bungalow in Con's Ferrari. She flashed her government card at them and they backed off as though she was a witch who had muttered a terrible curse. The line between civilization and barbarism was porous.

"Dangerous time to be riding the IC," her Dad grumbled at the station. "Wouldn't it have been better to listen to your expensive tapes and records at home with a good book—a safer and more productive use of time?"

"I suppose so," she agreed, relieved to have escaped from the whole evening relatively uninjured.

In her nightmares, Con was dressed formally in a white tie like Sir Georg Solti and chased her with a baton that changed into a switchblade.

When she finished brushing her teeth the next morning, she interpreted her dream for her diary.

I think Conor Clarke represents death for me. Daddy said his father actually had men killed who broke their word to him. Would Con do the same thing? There is a part of him, hidden most of the time, that is violent and dangerous. It was that part of him that almost raped me the night we were watching the aurora. I am afraid of him. Might he really want to murder me someday? Perhaps someday soon?

22

"How much does that one cost?" Con pointed at what he suspected was the most expensive ring in the store—a very exclusive Michigan Avenue jeweler, in the Art Deco shadow of the gleaming-white dowager building that shared its name with a gum business and a ball park.

"The one with the rubies?" the handsome blond woman asked, smiling gently. "Let me see."

"That is thirty thousand dollars, sir," her equally handsome and equally blond male partner intervened. "And a real bargain at that. We maintain such items in our inventory only as a courtesy to a rare customer. There is, as you imagine, little demand for such an item."

"I suppose"—Con sighed heavily—"it depends on the woman."

"Of course," they replied in mystified unison.

"Well, I'm not sure the woman is worth that much," he grumbled "Maybe a little less; let me see some of the others."

The fair Diana was worth much more, but Con, however much in love he felt himself to be on that cold, rainy, foggy autumn morning, was not about to be had in a bargaining session. He had bought diamonds before, three by actual count, and eventually returned them all. Such experience had prepared him for the protocol of the purchase of engagement rings.

"Here is a very nice item." The woman held up a glowing sapphire.

"That's only ten thousand dollars," the man said with a display of studied indifference.

"Really." Con made a face at the ring, indicating that it would scarcely be worth his notice.

"What sort of ring did you have in mind, sir?" the woman asked, trying to be conciliatory.

"Well, I was out walking and saw your window display and realized it was about time to look into a ring and thought that maybe it was a good reason to come in out of the rain."

"You would, of course, make a down payment?" the man murmured suavely.

"I don't think so." Con sighed again. "I mean, if I find the right ring, I might just purchase it outright. You do take credit cards?"

"Of course, sir," the woman whispered, as though they did not really like to admit that their clients used such things.

"It would depend on the price of the item." The man rubbed his hands together easily.

"Of course."

Con let the silence hang in the expensive air. Come on, guys. Time is money. Make me a deal.

"There would be a discount if this were a cash purchase." The woman smiled sweetly.

"Yeah?" Con contrived to look surprised. "How much on that one?" He pointed to the enormous ruby.

"Well, I think . . ." the woman began.

"We might be able to bring it down to, oh, twenty-five. Of course, management would require a certified check."

"Twenty-two fifty in currency." Conor reached for his wallet. "Wrap it up."

"Certainly, sir," they agreed enthusiastically.

Conor counted out twenty-three $1000 bills while the jewelers tried not to stare at either him or his money, and to conceal their suspicion that both he and his money might be counterfeit. Making sure that they would see it, he put the two remaining $1000 bills back in his wallet.

They had to break one of them to pay for the sales tax.

The point is, he told himself as he put the box into the

pocket of his windbreaker, that I'm different from both my mother and my father. She would have given them the asking price on the spot. He would have hassled them down to twenty.

And I don't love the game as much as he did.

Not that I dislike it, either.

Only when he had left the store did he realize that his unreliable imagination had been indulging in some rather interesting fantasies about the handsome blond woman. Not harsh or exploitive fantasies, he told himself, merely appreciative ones. If God didn't want us to admire older women and to imagine the fun of undressing them, he wouldn't have made them so attractive, would he?

That one would almost certainly have been wonderful in bed. I bet she's propositioned often. . . .

Love one woman and you find yourself loving them all. Will it be this way for the rest of my life?

I kinda hope so.

He hadn't been fibbing when he said he'd been out for a walk and stopped in their store on impulse. On the other hand, it was certainly true that he'd cashed a check at the First Chicago yesterday afternoon because he knew it was time to do some ring shopping.

I mean if the girl says yes, you have to be ready to wrap up the deal, don't you?

If I'd had a ring ready for Naomi . . .

We might be married and we'd certainly be unhappy.

Later in the day, when he put the box—still wrapped in the silver-foil paper that screamed "expensive!"—in the locked drawer of the antique secretary in his study, Con considered his two worries. First of all, when would he try to give her the ring? And second, would she wear a jewel so flamboyantly and deliberately expensive?

As to the second, he was not certain. As to the first, even though his heart was singing spring melodies and his poetic imagination was spitting out reams of unconnected lyric verses, he was not yet certain he would ever make the offer.

Better, however, to be safe than sorry, he told himself.

23

I reread what I wrote the other morning and I feel like a little fool. Conor is not a threat to my life. To my sanity, maybe, but that's my fault more than his.

From his viewpoint he's a suitor. He likes what he sees in me and wants it. I'm flattered and, I'll admit it, puzzled.

It's the pursuit game that goes on at our age. His intentions are not evil, no more than those of any man are evil. Which is to say that they are not exactly honorable either.

The point is, as he would say, that I don't want to marry him or anybody else. Moreover, even if I were in the marriage market, Conor Clement Clark would be a bad risk. His mother was an alcoholic, his father a lecher and a brute and a thief—all of which he is perfectly prepared to admit. So he's been through some sort of expensive therapy and can talk casually about his background; that doesn't solve the problem.

I must tell myself over and over again that this is the son of the man who ruined Daddy's career because Daddy had caught him in a violation of the law. Yet it's hard to hate Con for what his father did to Daddy. After all, his father persecuted Con even more than he persecuted Daddy.

Yet, like father, like son, as Daddy always says.

And there is that strange, silent, brooding part of him. I didn't notice it at Grand Beach, but it was obvious at the concert the other night. What is in that silence?

My subconscious said "murder," and that's why I had those terrible dreams. But it's not me that he would like to murder. It's his father and perhaps his mother, too. Rage like that against such terrible parents is understandable. But it maims the personality. I am not its target, not yet; but I could become the target if I permitted myself any kind of intimate relationship with him.

The most obvious target is himself. Maybe that's why he takes big chances in his business and why he runs the risk of a prison term for a sum of money that must be trivial by his standards. Like the Kennedy family, he is gambling with death.

Poor man.

But he's not my problem.

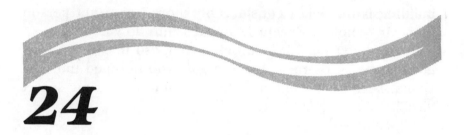

24

Diana was thinking of Conor when she bumped into Mick Whelan, literally.

She charged off a Dirksen Federal Building elevator with a load of law books in her arms and crashed into Whelan. The books flew out of her arms as Diana bounced off the tall senior partner of Whelan, Bishop, and James.

"I'm sorry," she mumbled scrambling for her books, her face flaming. "I'm terribly clumsy."

To add to her humiliation, Whelan had been talking to Judge Eileen Kane, Diana's role model and heroine.

Larry Whelan was a tall basketball-player type with curly brown hair and the twinkling eyes and quick smile of a ward committeeman. In fact, he was not a politician but one of the best trial lawyers in town. While his integrity was as unquestioned as his courtroom skills, Diana was as suspicious of him as she was of an Irish politician. The smile was too charming, and Diana was too likely to be charmed by it.

"Ms. Lyons, isn't it?" He helped her up off the floor and arranged her stack of books. "Diana, right? You know Judge Kane, don't you?"

"Oh, yes." Diana wished that the floor of the Everett McKinley Dirksen Federal Building would open up and consume her.

"Good morning, Ms. Lyons." The judge's expression was neutral but not unfriendly. Her cool green eyes seemed to be appraising Diana thoughtfully. "If it's any consolation to you, when I was your age and working for the United States Attorney, I charged into the Senator after whom this building is named, a considerably more important person than Mr. Whelan. Except I knocked him down."

"He didn't jog," Whelan chuckled, "so he wasn't in as good shape as I am. . . . But I'm glad you bumped into me, Diana, because I wanted to talk to you about your secret vice."

"My what?"

Her face flamed again. She felt off balance, embarrassed, awkward. She wanted to turn and run away. But you simply don't flee from a past president of the Chicago Bar Association.

"I hear on very good authority, Your Honor"—he bowed to Judge Kane—"that young Ms. Lyons here"—he flashed his damn Irish smile—"is a superb golfer, three handicap."

"Four," Diana said automatically, and instantly wished that she could cut off her tongue.

"A lot better than mine." The judge actually smiled at Diana.

"I thought you were six at Long Beach Country Club." Diana's tongue was now out of control.

"It's nice to see that government prosecutors are still observant; but my dear, that was before my younger son was born. I'm afraid little Redmond has ruined my game."

The judge smiled contentedly, more pleased with her two-year-old than with almost anything else in the world.

"Only temporarily," Larry Whelan said smoothly. "But

I've been thinking, Your Honor, that it's time to provide equal opportunity on the bar association's annual golf tournament. If a woman lawyer would be the chairman next year, particularly a woman who might just win the tournament, a lot of other women would come and it might notably improve the, uh, ambience. Wouldn't you agree?"

"What he means, dear"—the judge actually winked—"is that a woman chairman would force the men to clean up their language and cut down on their drinking."

"I couldn't. . . ." Diana stammered.

What would Daddy say if he knew that I even thought of going to a golf tournament?

"You'd probably have to play with himself here"—Judge Kane nodded in Whelan's direction—"and the State's Attorney. It would be good for their souls to lose to a woman."

"If everywhere else, why not on the course? Could we tempt you, Diana?"

God damn Conor Clarke's big mouth!

"I'm too young. . . ."

"Men your age have been chairman."

"Mr. Roscoe . . ."

For one terrifying moment Diana was afraid that she would say yes. He was smoother even than Conor. And someday, she had hoped, maybe she could join Whelan, Bishop, and James.

"I'm terribly busy." She grasped for an excuse, anything to escape. "Maybe next year."

"I'll hold you to it, young woman." He shook hands firmly with her. "Next year."

Judge Kane seemed to be on the verge of saying something, but then, noting Diana's acute embarrassment, changed her mind.

That's not my world, she told herself as she fled to an elevator that would take her back to her office where she could reorganize herself. I don't want to be part of it. I would be as out of place as I was trying to talk to the two of them.

It's Conor's fault. He knows how I feel. Why did he get

me into such a mess? It's his idea of a practical joke. He knows that I would have to refuse. It's not funny.

God damn you, Conor Clarke.

She dialed his number.

"God damn you, Conor Clarke!"

"Who, me?" He sounded frightened. "What have I done now?"

"You violated my privacy, you bastard!"

She was dangerously close to tears.

"You don't know anything about my lascivious dreams." He tried to laugh.

"This is not funny. The whole Chicago Bar has no right to know about my golf game."

"Oh." His voice was very small. "I didn't tell the whole bar—"

"You told Larry Whelan when he said he wanted a woman to be chairperson next summer. I suppose you think that's funny!"

"I think it would be delightful."

"You know I couldn't do that, even if I wanted to associate myself with one of those drunken male chauvinist brawls. You told him just so I would be embarrassed! That's not funny. It's . . . cruel!"

"There is nothing to be embarrassed about. Larry himself said you would be the perfect choice—"

"Then you're more stupid than I had thought you were. Mr. Whelan didn't even know who I was until you told him."

"Dauntless Diana, every male lawyer in Chicago who has ever seen you in court knows who you are."

The compliment, which she later told herself was sexist, was too much. She burst into tears and slammed down the phone.

She was furious at him for the rest of the day. One part of her, which was like Mama, told her that she was being foolish. Conor should have kept his big dumb Irish mouth shut. But he had meant no harm.

Nonetheless, she silenced the Mama within and nurtured carefully her sense of outrage. If she could stay angry at him, she would not be so infatuated with him. She stored up the hurt, sensing that in the days and weeks to come, she would need one more excuse to hate Conor Clarke.

But before she fell asleep that night an unruly imp inside her whispered that she would have no trouble beating Larry Whelan and Rich Daley on the golf course, even giving away strokes.

25

During the following week, she and Shelly Gollin met several times with the two Internal Revenue agents who had been assigned to review the tax returns of Clarke, Considine, McClendon, and the contractors most likely to be involved in the kickback scheme.

The agents were tough, uncommunicative men, like her father utterly dedicated to their work, but they had an agenda and a time frame of their own, which often meant three years of careful preparation for a single case, a span of time as long as the average term of a United States Attorney. Moreover, while they were politely formal with young U.S. Attorneys and never hinted that they thought they were hardly dry behind the ears, they confided only as much as they had to and not always that.

This was the final session with the IRS before Diana and Shelly reported on the case, first to Martin and then to Roscoe. Shelly was improving rapidly, no longer the flashy boy wonder from New York City, but now—for public consumption—a humble young man, eager to learn. "As I understand you, Mr. Leahy, Mr. McClendon's returns seem unassailable, short of a long and very careful investigation."

"That is correct, Mr. Gollin." Leahy was the less dour of the two, a hint of Irish wit lurking behind his elaborate courtesy. "If there are tracks to be covered, he has covered them very well. Moreover, if he is taking money out of the cash economy, there is little hint of it in his personal life-style."

"He was very cautious in his interview with me," Shelly said, rubbing his nose (perhaps reconstructed, Diana thought irrelevantly and uncharitably). "He gave the impression that he was not terribly concerned about Mr. Considine's charges."

"That was to be expected, wasn't it?" Diana shifted her file of papers. "I gather you were more successful with Mr., ah, Corso, the electrical contractor?"

"His returns do leave something to be desired," Krause, the other agent, short, stout, and grim, admitted slowly. "In fact, they give the impression of a man facing serious financial problems. That could not be said of the other three men—Kline, Rodriguez, and Crawford. Of course, our investigation of them will continue as long as Mr. Roscoe requires it."

"I assume"—she tapped her pen on the top of her stack of files—"that you're reasonably close to being able to seek an indictment against Mr. Corso?"

That was a question the elite IRS types never liked. Given their preferences, they would continue to work on a case till even the Archangel Michael could not argue an effective defense.

"If Mr. Roscoe so decides." Kraus studied his stubby fingers.

"Of course," she agreed crisply. "As for Mr. Clarke. . . ."

The agents looked at each other hesitantly. Con Clarke was what the meeting was all about. Corso and Crawford would have been left to routine, computer-indicated audits, had they not been associates of his.

The exchange of glances apparently elected Leahy to give the reply. "It's a textbook return, Ms. Lyons. He has obviously instructed his accountant and lawyers to lean over backward to keep the law. Given the amount of publicity he receives, that is probably a good policy. We could subpoena his records, but I doubt that we will find anything that is different. If Mr. Clarke is cheating the government of the United States out of its proper share of his income, his evasion is buried very deeply indeed. We could work on him for years and find nothing. Candidly, I don't think there's anything to find."

"Cash economy?"

Leahy shrugged. "You'd have to come after that through another agency. As far as we can tell, the man pays his taxes."

"I see. Does it strike you as strange that his returns are so cautious."

Leahy scratched his head. "Yeah, it does, kind of. I mean, you read about him in the papers, and you think this is a young dingbat, a punk with more money than is good for him. Then you look at his returns and say he's smart enough to think there are IRS agents who read the papers and might think just that."

"I see. Tell me, Mr. Leahy, have you looked at the purchase of this much publicized yacht of his last spring. It is my information that he purchased the craft at a time when he was experiencing something of a cash-flow problem."

Leahy's eyes flickered momentarily with something like respect. This was not just another ambitious, ball-breaking, hot-shot woman lawyer. This one was shrewd. "Yeah." He made a note. "That might not be a bad idea."

"You impressed those ghouls," Shelly said when the IRS men had left. "That was a good shot about the boat. What made you think of it?"

"Talent, Shelly."

"Despite that"—he grinned—"and God knows, Diana, I wouldn't question your talent, I think this is a blind alley."

"Oh?" Part of her wanted it to be a blind alley. The weak, feminine part of her, she supposed.

"Look." Shelly adopted what he called his peddler's mode. "All right, so Broddy and McClendon have got something going with the major contractors out in Cokewood. Nothing big, nothing sensational, just a little baksheesh under the table."

"A half-million dollars?" she said.

"All right, I share your sense of outrage. Still, it's a minor part, maybe a wing brace, for a jet fighter. Construction people like my uncle say you have to do that once in a while to stay in business in that business. Right? Are we going to put every construction contractor in the country in jail?"

"If necessary."

"Come off it, Diana. You know better than that."

"I'll do whatever is necessary to get a conviction or a guilty plea, and to tell you the truth, I'd prefer a trial and a conviction against that man."

"You'd do anything?" Shelly's bright brown eyes opened in dismay.

"Absolutely anything. We're playing hardball in this office. With white collar criminals like these, we can't afford to observe all the niceties of the rules."

"Leo's functional justice?"

"Why not? Do you want to spend a couple of years reading pornography at O'Hare?"

Shelly stood up and began to pace back and forth nervously. "I had this uncle back in Brooklyn, Uncle Lad, short for Ladislas, you know?"

He had an apparently limitless supply of uncles, all with stories to back up his arguments.

"So what did Uncle Lad say?"

"So Uncle Lad was an assistant D.A. in New York right out of NYU law school, right? Worked at it for five or six years, big success, lots of convictions, even a profile in the *Times*. Then he quit one day without warning and went into tax work, where he made a lot of money and had a quiet life."

"So?"

"So when he hears what I'm doing, he calls me up and he says, 'Sheldon boy—'"

"What can I tell you?"

"How did you know?" Shelly's grin was broad and infectious, a little like Con's, as a matter of fact. "You been listening into my stories? Anyway, he says, 'Sheldon, it's all right to be good at what you do, it's all right to fight like hell to put the goddamn crooks behind bars. But, Sheldon, I was your age once, I know what ambitious young lawyers are like. You wanna know what they're like? Sheldon boy, I'll tell you what they're like—they got no goddamn experience staying awake all night wondering whether just once or maybe a couple of times they sent an innocent man or woman to jail because they fudged a little evidence. Yeah, sure they say the slob is a crook, what does it matter if we violate his rights a little bit? 'Course they never been inside a place like Attica. Then they visit a jail or they talk to someone that's been there, and in the back of their heads they wonder whether maybe they made a mistake. Then they get a little older, like maybe thirty, real old, you know, and they know enough about life to worry a lot about their mistakes, which might have put innocent people in jail. Sheldon boy, you're going to be goddamn thirty someday, too."

"The point, I suppose, is that I'm going to be thirty in a little less than five years?"

"Yeah. Kinda."

"I'll never lose a night's sleep worrying over Conor Clarke."

Which was not the truth at all.

"What can I tell you? It's hardball."

"And we're, I believe the expression is, taking off the gloves."

"OK, we've got Broddy anyway. Did you see this DEA report?" He held up a thick sheaf of papers. "Broddy is laundering drug money for the Outfit, the Hispanic Outfit at that, which will not please our friends out on the West Side, as you Chicagoans call them. A man in his position at his age!

Talk about natural criminal types. So we maybe can get Corso on his taxes anyway. We won't crack Harold McClendon, I can guarantee you that. He's a shrewd little bugger who will just sit tight and wait us and the Big Bane out. So we have nothing on Con Clarke at all, other than the bastard made a pass at you. . . ."

"Shelly, I'm not your sister or your daughter. . . ."

"For sure." He laughed. "Anyway, it's inherently unlikely that a guy with his money and his caution would take such a crazy chance. Even to buy a Peterson 41 Racing Boat—"

"Racing Machine."

"—Well, whatever they call it. You watch, there'll be an unassailable answer to your question about his goddamn boat."

"I'm sure he's a criminal, a rich one—which means he has to be dragged down and destroyed."

Shelly stopped in midflight, shocked and astonished. "I'm sure you didn't mean that, Diana. So I'm going to forget you ever said it. But what jury is going to believe that a man with his kind of money—who gives so much of it away and uses a lot of the rest of it for socially desirable projects and keeps such excellent records and pays so much income tax—will jump into bed with a couple of small time sleazebags?"

"You don't understand about people who have a lot of money," she pleaded helplessly, thinking of how happy her father would be if Con Clarke had to serve even a few months in jail. "They want more money not because they need it but because they have to have it."

"Maybe. I don't know." Shelly stood up and made an unsuccessful effort to rearrange his tie. "But maybe I know a little bit about juries. At first they might not like Clarke because he's a rich playboy. First thing you know, a good lawyer will persuade them that the government is picking on him because he's young and handsome and generous. That's going to make the great Bane look very bad. When he looks very bad, he becomes very unhappy. He has been known to offer up his young colleagues—that's us—on altars of sacrifice. Have you been on any altars of sacrifice lately, Diana?"

"It would never go to trial. The Bane and his lawyers would do a plea bargain."

"Yeah? Have you taken a close look at that guy? He's a clown some of the time, but he's a competitor some of the time, too."

"Not with me on the golf course."

"Diana, my dear"—he smiled broadly and took her arm as they walked into the corridor—"if I ever persuaded you to come to a good Jewish country club and play golf with me— and I'm not bad, you'd only have to give me a few strokes—I'd shoot a hundred and twenty-five. Maybe on the first nine yet. So he messed up the Mackinac—he came back to win in his class in the Tri-State. We try to shake him and the first thing you know he's likely to think it's the Tri-State and fight us every inch of the way."

"Then he'd go to jail even longer."

"Only if we have the evidence to convince a jury of his peers, which, fair lady, I'm trying to tell you, we don't have."

"You're going to recommend we drop the investigation then?"

"For the time being anyway. If something turns up later, it's a different ball game. No hard feelings?"

"Of course not," she said briskly. "I'm a professional." Then a broad smile for Shelly. "At least I try to be some of the time."

Leo Martin concurred with Shelly. Later in the day the three of them reported to Donny Roscoe in his office. The Big Bane strode back and forth in front of his enormous oak desk while they sat quietly in their chairs, the only truly comfortable ones in the whole Everett McKinley Dirksen Federal Building.

Diana could not quite get over her embarrassment at Roscoe's naked ambition and shameless posturing, no matter how often she had witnessed them. He was acting out the usual scenario of response to a recommendation from his staff: a response pattern as certain as the rising of the sun in the morning.

"This office," he thundered (or tried to in his high fal-setto voice), "will not countenance criminal behavior by a rich and famous man, no matter how rich and famous he is."

The Bane always argued against a staff recommendation so that when he was finally persuaded to accept the recommendation—as he always did—the blame, if it turned out to be bad advice, would be theirs, not his.

Diana thought uncomfortably about being bound on a sacrificial altar.

"Yes sir," Shelly murmured, properly rebuked and not yet understanding the scenario.

"I quite agree, Donny," Leo Martin nodded sagely, "though I think we learned in the Hurricane Houston case that leaning too far in the other direction can cause trouble, too."

Hurricane Houston was a black basketball star whom Donny had indicted on the charge of falsifying a loan application. It had been a mass media trial with Donny leading the prosecution, against Leo's better judgment. Donny had told the TV camera every night that he intended to make an example of the defendant to prove to young Americans that athletic superstars were not above the law. Donny had looked pretty silly when the jury brought in a "not guilty" verdict.

Leo must be in a hurry to get home or he wouldn't play such hardball.

"That bitch," Roscoe exploded, meaning Eileen Kane, who had been the black basketball player's lawyer before ascending to the federal bench. "Pardon me, Ms., ah, Lyon."

"Lyons," she said maliciously.

"Of course."

"Well, if the wheel should put her on the bench in this one—and with our luck lately that could happen—we'd have to be extra careful. It just won't fly, Donny. Not now. As Mr. Gollin properly pointed out, Con Clarke might be quite capable of fighting back, in the media as well as the courtroom. It could be counterproductive to seek an indictment at this point in time."

Leo was an expert at manipulating the boss. First you mention adverse media reaction to scare him and then use the words "this point in time" to give him an out. Suspend the investigation for "the present." Soothe everyone's conscience.

"What about you, Ms. Lyon?" He contemplated the American flag behind his desk. "As I remember, you have been instrumental in developing the case against Conor Clarke. Do you concur in the recommendation?"

"Yes sir. Reluctantly."

What else could she have said and remained honest?

"Reluctantly?" He spun around again, surprised and a little displeased that she had disrupted his scenario.

"Yes sir."

"Why, may I ask?"

"Nothing better than a gut instinct, sir, that he's a criminal. I admit that, instinct or no, I have not been able to sufficiently develop the case against him to move ahead toward a grand jury presentation."

"Hmm. . . ." The Big Bane seemed satisfied. Then he broke out of the scenario, an exceedingly rare event. "Can you think of any compromise approach?"

She moved in quickly to the opening he had given her, conscious that he did not really want her to do so and that her two colleagues would be upset. "The IRS will surely continue its investigation of John Corso. Perhaps we could ask them to give it top priority. If they make any discoveries that are pertinent to Conor Clarke, then we will reconsider today's decision."

"Excellent, Ms. Line. Brilliant." He rubbed his hands together briskly. "I will so instruct them and request that they keep you informed. You may report to me directly should it eventuate that there are reasons to reverse this afternoon's decision. Are we agreed?"

Of course they were.

"Congratulations, Diana, you won," Leo said wryly in the corridor. "Clarke is not a free man yet."

"I don't see it that way, Leo," she pleaded. "The Boss asked me for a suggestion. I gave it to him. The investigation is technically concluded unless we find more evidence, which would have been true anyway. How does that mean I won?"

"By the pricking of my thumbs, something wrong this way comes. I'm sorry, kid. I don't like this one. I admire your energy and dedication, but *my* gut instinct tells me that we should leave Con Clarke alone. If he really is a crook, he'll overreach eventually and we or our successors will nail him."

"Gut instinct against gut instinct? Well, yours is more experienced than mine, God knows. What exactly does it say?"

"It says exactly that we are all going to rue this afternoon, you more than any of the rest of us."

"That sounds like a kind of frightening prophecy, Leo." Shelly sounded spooked.

"Celtic foreboding," Leo said grimly. "From this day on, Diana, it's your case. If nothing comes of it, Donny will forget about it. If you come up with something, you'll be a heroine around here. If it explodes on us, you'll end up with your ass in a sling."

"Oh?" Well, he hadn't used John Mitchell's threat of tits in a wringer.

"You'd be the kind of sacrificial victim the media would love to hang on a cross. Remember that, kid. They're looking right now for professional women they can portray as castrating whores. Remember what they did to that Cunningham woman at Bendex. Do you want to be the next one?"

Diana shivered. Someone had perhaps walked on her grave. "I guess I'll have to take my chances, won't I?"

26

Her next chance was the Saturday cruise on *Brigid*. She explained to her parents that she had to work all day and much of the evening, changed in her office from dress to swimsuit (the one purchased at a sale price in Marshal Field's basement store, where not so long ago she had worked part-time) sneakers, jeans, and a McAuley sweatshirt, and rode in a taxi to the Chicago Yacht Club. It was the first time in her life that she'd ever been in a yacht club. She was crossing the fateful boundaries that separated her world from the world of the rich.

Dear God, she prayed, help me not to gawk like a complete little fool and protect me from other harm, too.

She was afraid to specify what the other harm might be.

Nevertheless, she did gawk inside the club. Not because it seemed so expensive but because it was so lovely—a Hollywood set for a yacht club: glass walls looking out on the lake and the boats already under sail, crisp white tablecloths, a colorful and attractively arranged Saturday brunch on a buffet, ship pictures and banners hanging on the walls, expensively dressed and well-maintained men and women, an atmosphere of casual and informal but skilled and enthusiastic competency.

When she worked in Field's basement during her law-school days, she would often eat her lunch in Grant Park and watch the boats, like graceful birds, soar out to the breakwater beyond and into the open and deep blue lake. She supposed it was envy, but she resented that some people could do that and she could not. On the other hand she was glad that she was not one of the idle rich. They were not happy, she told herself.

Now she wasn't so sure. They certainly seemed happy.

"Light winds, ten to twelve knots, one-foot waves, perfect day for a landlubber." Con also in grubby jeans and sweatshirt appeared next to her. "Nice place, huh? Don't worry about them. Someone as beautiful as you, they are convinced, has to belong to a member. Let's have a cup of coffee and a roll before we see whether *Brigid*—the boat not the saint, that is—will tolerate us for a few hours."

His idea of coffee and a roll was bacon, eggs, coffee cake, fruit juice, English muffins (two), a whole grapefruit, and a large pot of English breakfast tea.

"Don't you eat breakfast in your apartment?" she asked as she nursed her own cup of decaffeinated coffee.

"Nope, no wife to make it for me. So I catch up here. What's the matter? Why aren't you eating? One of the many things I liked about you down in the dunes was your appetite—for food, that is."

"I guess I'm nervous."

"About me?" He arrested the progress of a sweet roll from plate to mouth. "Hey, don't be nervous about me, Diana. There's nothing to be afraid of. I'll never hurt you."

She nodded, struggled against foolish tears, and changed the subject. "It looks like a lot of the boats aren't being used. Is it that way all the time?"

"On the best days of the summer"—he was wolfing down an English muffin—"at least a third of them are covered up. Monsignor Ryan, the Rector of the Cathedral—you know, Judge Kane's brother—says that it is not a sin exactly to own a boat, only to own one and not use it. So I'm just avoiding the occasion of sin. Isn't that expressway ugly?"

"Straightening out the Lake Shore Drive S curve," she said, following the direction of his hand out the window. "Spoils the rich people's view of the city. Terrible."

"Right. The construction people are making a lot of money. I suppose they are entitled to earn a living, but like Lord Keynes suggested, maybe they ought to be building pyramids instead of messing up the lakefront."

"I assume there's a lot of corruption in such a project?"

"Hell, I don't know." He filled his tea cup again. "You're the stern-eyed federal prosecutor. I have the impression, though, that the big frauds are too risky these days. Too much press, too many stern-eyed young lawyers. Small kickbacks here and there, well, they're pretty hard to stop. The real corruption, however, is to build this vast kinetic wall of rushing cars to cut off the people from their lake."

She was not especially interested in his aesthetic ideals. "You think a few hundred thousand dollars of bribery is a minor affair?"

"Don't look at me like the stern-eyed prosecutor on this lovely September morning." He was smearing raspberry jam on yet another English muffin. "No, I didn't say that at all. It's immoral and illegal, too, and probably unstoppable on big projects without the kind of regulation that would make big projects impossible."

"Hard to catch?"

"Unless someone on the inside snitches. I think you folks did a wonderful job eliminating the worst of it. Sanitary district trustees, some of whom are so dumb that even the other trustees noticed it, don't die multimillionaires anymore. My point is that you've probably got it down to the irreducible minimum now."

"You oppose government regulation?"

"On Saturday morning she wants to discuss government regulation. OK, let me finish the subject for the day, all right?"

Conor managed to sound like a very patient kindergarten teacher.

"All right."

"For the last couple of decades there has been a battle between investors and speculators on the one hand and the feds on the other. The former want to make money, the latter, when push comes to shove, want to keep them from making money. Take the commodity markets. The investors made a lot of money in that game ten, twelve years ago.

Then the CFTC moved in and pretty much closed down the action. OK, I know as well as anyone that a few of the traders were crooks. But any mature capitalist economy needs something like a commodity market. If all the feds do is go after the big crooks, I'm a hundred percent behind them, but if they want to take away the financial action, I'm agin' 'em, woman, because you need action in a capitalist economy. And so far no alternative seems to be better than capitalism. Ask Mr. Deng about that."

"So the smart money moved away from commodities into ventures?"

"Some of it." He grabbed a cup of hot chocolate from a passing waiter. "The exchanges, to be fair, have a lot of problems of their own which the feds, you feds, if you don't mind, didn't create. The venture people don't cheat much because they figure with a good idea you don't have to. Still, the feds are closing in with threats to take away most of the profits with high taxes. If that happens, it's bye-bye American ventures."

"You think government regulation ought to be minimal?"

"I think"—he stood up—"that if you have a social consensus in favor of capitalism, you don't violate the consensus by trying to prevent people from making money. If that means you have to risk a little crookedness, then that's too bad. . . . Come on, woman, let's go sailing. You have a swimsuit?"

"New one." She rose with him, wondering why she'd said that. "Underneath my sweatshirt and jeans."

"I can hardly wait."

"I hope you like it. I think you will."

Conor rolled his eyes appreciatively. "How could I not like it?"

"Do you tolerate such small corruption on your projects?"

"I see the tender is waiting for us, the pilot is doubtless impressed by my lovely companion. Huh? You still talking shop? No, I don't tolerate it. I do everything I can to mini-mize it. If I find out it's going on, I get rid of the people in-volved. But I don't kid myself that in this imperfect world you can eliminate it completely without turning the country into a police state. Take my project out in your neighbor-hood. There's a contractor out there who I find out is into the books."

"Books?"

"Bookies. Horse racing, basketball games, almost any-thing you can gamble on. Outfit books. And pretty deep. I kind of wonder if he's trying to get out of trouble with my money. So I have a hard-eyed local accountant named Harold E. McClendon keeping a close eye on him. I even tell him to tell Johnny—the contractor, that is—that I'll give him a long-term low-interest loan if he needs it to bail himself out. McClendon says it's all clean. Here, give me your hand. I don't want you falling into the water here on the dock. Em-barrass me terribly."

"Do you believe this er, Mc . . . ?"

"McClendon. Absolutely last serious conversational ex-change. This is a day off work for you. Understand? If the corruption is small enough as a percentage of the gross, whatever the gross is, you can't stop it. A lumber yard worker takes a few boards. A bank teller removes ten or fifteen dollars a week. How's anyone going to catch it? And is it worthwhile trying? How much time and money you go-ing to spend searching each teller every night?"

"That's condoning immorality."

"Tolerating it as the lesser evil. There she is, woman, *Brigid*. Isn't she lovely now?"

"That cute little blue boat with the white trim?"

"You're putting me on." He swatted her rump playfully, the first minor erotic contact since the night under the au-rora. Head already whirling from the conversation in the yacht club, Diana was even more disconcerted. "Ouch."

"Didn't hurt you. I'll climb on. Mr. Tanner will hold the boats together and I'll pull you up. I've lost a few women this way, but only the kind that beat me on the golf course. Here we go."

Flustered, scared, and eager, Diana struggled on to the gently swaying *Brigid*.

Maybe the way to defeat an obsession, she told herself with a mixture of terror and delight, is to succumb to it a few times.

On board *Brigid* Con became a patient teacher who explained clearly the names of the various ropes and sails and masts and booms and told her exactly what she must do in her role as "novice." "Not to worry about it." He laughed. "It's for fun, no grades or homework. This time."

She remembered the agony of learning to drive a car with Dad as her teacher and then berated herself for her disloyalty.

"*Brigid* is made for a day like this," he said, as he guided the boat, under motor power, through the harbor and toward the breakwater mouth. "Anyone can make speed on a windy day. It was the days with light breezes on which the Aussies took the America's Cup away from us. Like their boat, though at considerably less cost, *Brigid* here is at her best on a day like this. That's why we won the Tri-State."

"Are you going to try to bring the Cup to Monroe Street?" she asked innocently.

"Now that, Diana Marie Lyons, would be a waste of money as a venture. Fun? Maybe, especially if you'd come with me to Fremantle in Australia. . . . Watch it, I'm going to come about, uh, turn. I don't want any blood on that pretty head and long brown hair."

With the wind filling up her mainsail, *Brigid* bounded forward briskly. Con cut the auxiliary motor. The surge of boat against the water and the tension of the wind against the sails made Diana want to sing.

"It's hot and going to be hotter." Holding the tiller with one hand, Con shed his Chicago Yacht Club sweatshirt. "Do I get a chance to see that new swimsuit?"

"If you want." She shrugged indifferently. "I don't suppose you'll find it very interesting."

Trying her best to be graceful and nonchalant and feeling like she imagined a neophyte stripper might, she pulled off her plain gray sweatshirt and stepped out of her jeans.

"Glory be to God," he said, his fake Irish brogue thickening. "What do you call that?"

"I think," she said, her face burning, "you call it a tab-tie bikini. Kind of a descendent of the three-ring, but it suffices with two tabs. Do you like it?"

"I certainly do," he said softly, almost reverently.

She felt her self-possession return and began to bask complacently in his admiration. "I bought this in Marshall Field's basement day before yesterday."

"On sale, I bet."

She giggled. Oh dear God, Diana, when you sin, you really do sin bravely. "What else at this time of year? How do I compare with Lyn Clifford?" She pretended to be concerned with the jib sheet—yes, that was the proper word. Why was a rope a sheet? The old nuns in school would not have approved of a man and a woman, not yet married, anywhere near a sheet. Sometimes, however, a rope was a line. Ought not a sail be a sheet? Oh well, no homework this time.

"So that's the way the land lies, is it? A reader of my friend Kup? Well, let's see." He adjusted the tiller with one hand and rubbed his handsome jaw with the other. "Lyn is a very pretty girl. With some luck, lots of exercise, careful dieting, and a man who loves her, she'll be a very attractive woman twenty years from now. Even thirty. Those categories don't even apply to you. You're a classic, lovely Diana"—he looked sad for a fleeting moment—"unbearably beautiful, like your mythological namesake, at the risk of a cliché a modern poet should avoid."

"And what will I be like thirty years from now?"

"Ah." He thought about it, teasing her with his hesitation. "Well, that's mostly up to you, of course. But you could grow up to be a truly sensational woman, especially if you smile more, maybe even as attractive as Mama."

"Whose mama?" she demanded, suddenly furious at him.

"Your mama, Anna Maria, who else? She's a real knock-out. Wow!"

"My mother is not a sex object!" she screamed.

"Now, that's where you're wrong." He was enjoying himself immensely. "She is certainly many other things, but she is also one spectacular sex object."

"Where did you meet her!" She had knotted her fists angrily and was standing over him, a Fate demanding vengeance.

"Would you mind standing a little bit to one side? You beat both the lake and the Chicago skyline as scenery, but you're much too solid for a navigator to see through. That's right. Oh, I went to her shop looking for some clothes for Maryjane's daughter. I admit that the child won't appear formally for another six weeks, but I was out looking at Cokewood Heights—you disturbed my conscience a little on that—and I thought I'd do my baptism shopping early. So I checked out Mama. We had a nice little talk in Italian. She made fun of my Florentine accent. So I did my Sicilian dialect bit. She thought it was hilarious."

"You had no right to pry into my family." She shook her fist at him. He knows I have good reason to be angry. He's just having his sick little joke.

"I wasn't prying into your family. I was just checking out Mama. . . . Hey, cut it out, you're hurting me! How can I steer the boat and fight off an almost naked Irish woman pirate?"

"Sicilian pirate, you miserable bastard!" She continued to pound him, not completely without effect.

"Saudi Arabian." Then his powerful right arm swung around her and drew her close in a hug that combined restraint with affection. Her fury vanished.

He slipped a line over the tiller—at least she thought it was a line—and held her very close, an embrace of protection more than sexual suggestion. She accepted his protection completely. He looked down at her with silver blue eyes, not hard with lust the way other men had occasionally looked at her, but soft with another emotion to which she did not want to give a name.

"Mama won't talk Italian." She sniffed. "She says she's an American."

"She talked to me in Italian. Maybe she finds my silver blue eyes more irresistible than her daughter does."

"There's nothing wrong with your eyes," she said, astonished at herself. She tried to pull away from his embrace. He would not release her. *Please, someone make him stop looking at me that way.*

"So," he said, nudging her jaw around so that he could stare more deeply through her own eyes into all the secrets of her soul. "First you are jealous of Lyn and now you're jealous of Mama!"

"I am not!" she screamed, furious again, especially since he had read her mind perfectly. *Am I that transparent?*

"Cool it, witch." He drew her even closer and held her even more protectively. "I won't let them hurt you."

Meaningless words. No one was trying to hurt her. Yet oddly reassuring. His gentleness paralyzed her, reduced her to the condition of a contented domestic pet. She was willing to huddle within the warmth of his big, strong, smooth body for the rest of her life. The real world, back there on the receding skyline, no longer existed. She felt no need to talk, to respond, to protest. It was enough merely to be passive in his protecting arms.

His fingers relinquished her jaw, slipped down her throat and chest, and came to rest between her breasts. With awkward delicacy, he slipped out the tab tie of her bikini top, gently pulled it away, and tossed it to the floor of the cockpit.

She was startled, shamed, exhilarated. She felt at one with the wind and waves and the movement of the boat, the rhythms and needs of her body and her life melting into the rhythms and energies of the universe.

"Don't pretend I wasn't supposed to do that." Still no

hard light of lust in his eyes, only soft silver kindness. "Anything that detaches that easily was meant to be detached."

"I'm not fighting you, am I?" she said hoarsely.

He moved her away from him, holding both her upper arms, as if to have a better perspective from which to inspect her. His fingers tightened possessively, digging into her flesh. Embarrassed now, she averted her head from his consuming gaze.

"Damnit, woman, look at me when I'm admiring you."

"Obviously I want you to admire me, Conor," she spoke through gritted teeth. "Or I wouldn't have dressed this way. It's a new experience for me. I feel strange."

"Look at me," he insisted again.

Obediently she turned her head and felt tears form in her eyes because of the pathos on his face.

What a strange man he is, she managed to think, half wise old sage, half silly sad little boy.

Then, his voice deadly serious, like a judge pronouncing sentence, he uttered his second strange sentence: "Don't expect that I will ever let you get away, Diana Marie Lyons: no matter what happens, I'll always be there pursuing you, like a bloodhound."

"Hound of heaven?"

"Something like that."

"I am warned."

"I read an article," he said, hugging her again, "in *Esquire* I think it was, about the etiquette of topless beaches. You are absolutely not to stare. No matter what a woman isn't wearing or how spectacular the display, you are not supposed to look below her chin."

"Really." She was among the damned now and didn't care. "I suppose you've had a lot of experience with such beaches. I've never been to one."

"They don't have them in Detroit."

"Not that I know of, but what I was about to say is that I don't mind if you stare. That's what it's supposed to be about, isn't it? I mean, it embarrasses me, but I love it."

"No trouble with your candor, Diana Marie Lyons."

"Sometimes." Wantonly she snuggled closer to his comforting bulk.

"The article also said that the most erotic of all the women—and the writer didn't think the scene was all that erotic—were the young mothers with their children."

"Youth, experience, and fruitfulness."

He kissed her forehead. "You ought to be the poet."

Brigid heaved in one direction and then tilted abruptly back. Con released Diana and grabbed for the tiller. "Damn jealous woman." He laughed boisterously. "She will do anything to get my attention back. Here." he tossed her a tube of suntan cream—"I'd love to do the honors, but not quite yet. Better use it liberally. We don't want Anna Maria asking any pointed questions."

"Mama doesn't inspect my boobs every Saturday night," she fired back at him, turning away to smear herself with the coconut-smelling Hawaiian Tropical.

He seemed to think that was a very funny crack. The poor man is besotted, she told herself.

"Would you ever go into the cabin and bring my notebook and pen?" He was tightening the winch on the jib line, no sheet.

"I would."

She carefully edged her way forward, fearful that jealous *Brigid* might toss her over the side. Inside the cabin, she glanced out the window and decided that it would be very easy to be seasick. She found his notebook—an ordinary red covered spiral affair, much like her own journal—and quickly stumbled back to the cockpit. His blond hair was flying in the breeze and he looked breathtakingly beautiful. I am going to be seduced, she thought. I want to be seduced. I want to be finished with being a virgin.

"Would you take the tiller please, ma'am." He bowed ceremoniously and removed the pen and notebook from her hand.

She was feeling quite natural now in her advanced condition of undress, as she mentally called it. It was appropriate, was it not, for women to so appear in certain times and

places at a certain age in their lives? Ought not she be admired? And was not this a time and a place where it would
be wrong not to permit admiration?

"What are you doing?" she asked, as he bent over his
notebook. *Brigid*, now docile as a lamb, responded quickly
and gently to her slightest touch on the tiller. Aha, we're allies, are we, my girl?

"Writing poetry. What else?"

"Why?"

"Keep my hands occupied and out of trouble." He
looked up from the notebook and grinned wickedly. "You
seem to like being ninety percent naked."

"Ninety-five, I should think. . . . What are you writing
about?"

"Come on, now you're fishing for compliments."

"Still doing your Grace sonnet?"

"Cycle."

"Cycle?"

"Whole series of sonnets."

"Let me see." She leaned forward.

"Only when I'm finished." He put his fingertips on her
belly and pushed her back. "*Brigid* gets restless when
there's no firm hand on the tiller."

"You have her bewitched, too."

"Too?" He cocked an interested blue eye in her direction.

"Yes," she said passively, "too."

He scribbled a few lines, crossed them out, and began
again. Then he looked up at her, dreamy eyed and blissful.
Shame jabbed at her and she turned away.

"Damnit, woman, don't look away when I'm adoring
you."

She forced her gaze back to face his adoration, shaming,
flattering, frightening.

"I'm new at this bare-breast business, give me a
chance."

"You'd stop traffic even at St. Tropez."

"Where you've been to ogle all the tits."

"An exercise that has its own amusements. Not worth going back now, though." He closed his notebook. "You do realize, don't you, that you are a fantastically beautiful woman?"

"Not really."

"Come on."

"It doesn't seem fair that some women are more beautiful than others."

His fingers touched her thigh, of which, tall girl that she was, there was a lot. "God passes his blessings around his way, not ours. Some have one kind, others have other kinds."

"Some women resent me." She was alternating between waves of exhilaration and shame, as *Brigid* glided peacefully away from the Chicago shoreline. Exhilaration was winning. "In school, a lot of them hated me because I was a class leader as well as—OK, I'll use your words—slightly attractive, if you happen to like tall women."

"As I do. Now, anyway." His fingers were not progressing anywhere. "So you don't think it's right that you should be both bright and gorgeous."

"Not fair to others." Please kiss me now, she thought.

"But those other young women don't have to rate themselves at everything they do, like a hanging judge, do they?"

"What do you mean?" Anger exorcised both shame and exhilaration.

"You stand off at a distance, legal-size notepad in hand"—he was frowning now, clearly upset with her—"evaluating everything you do: What score for my behavior at the Cliff Dwellers? What rating for my first approach to Orchestra Hall? How did I do when I walked into the Chicago Yacht Club? How many points for my novice try as a sailor? Even, what kind of score for my first experience with naked tits and a man staring at me like he was demented?"

"Bastard." Now thoroughly ashamed, she covered herself with her arms.

"The point is," he plunged ahead grimly, "that you don't have to do any of that. You are pure grace, whatever you do.

I'm sorry if I angered you. But the point is—my favorite phrase, you've doubtless noticed—that beautiful and bright, you still have your share of pain."

"I want to go back to shore." She reached for the top of her bikini.

Brigid took a hand in the matter, heaving to one side, tossing her away from the tiller and into Con's arms, and knocking away his notebook. The boom began to swing dangerously. He pushed her aside and grabbed for the tiller.

Brigid settled down, somewhat huffily.

"Come here, woman," he ordered. "Sit next to me."

She hesitated, then dropped the yellow fabric and obediently sat next to him.

"What score do you give yourself on the performing-with-naked-breasts scale?" He put his arm around her.

"I don't think of it in numbers. My ratings are either good or bad." She hesitated. "But if I try to translate my self-evaluation on the subject, not much more than three." She found herself giggling uncontrollably. "What do you give me?"

"Not even that high!"

"Son of a bitch!" she shouted and began to pound his marvelous chest.

He fended her off with one arm and kept *Brigid* in line with the other. They engaged in a brief but delicious wrestling match. She decided that if it came to it, she could probably take him in wrestling, too.

"I surrender, pirate woman," he finally shouted. "I lied. Truth is, at least eight."

"Really?" She stopped struggling with him. "You're not making it up?"

"Really," he said with conviction.

"Is *Brigid* a company boat," she asked, not really intending to say something provocative, "or do you own it . . . her . . . personally."

"Goddamnit, woman." He jumped away from her, suddenly and violently angry. "Will you please leave me alone!"

"I'm sorry—" She tried to appease him.

"Sorry nothing. Take my love or reject it, whatever you want. But stop this everlasting judge-looking-down-her-aristocratic-nose act. I'm fed up with feeling that you're an auditor from the IRS looking for an indictable offense. I'll spend my money the way I think best and you spend or don't spend yours the way you think best—but for the love of God, leave me alone."

He had pulled her out of the cockpit bench, dug his fingers into her bare arms, and was shaking her like a cat would shake a captive bird.

"Conor," she cried, frightened now of his rage, "you're hurting me!"

His face stricken with grief, he lowered her gently back to the bench. "I'm sorry, Diana, forgive me. I don't want to hurt you. Ever."

"You really didn't hurt me." She rubbed her arms. "More scared me."

"I don't lose my temper often. I don't want to scare you, either. I really am sorry."

The sincerity of his contrition dissolved her anger and fears. "It was a damn-fool question, Conor. And none of my business."

"Perfectly harmless question." He adjusted the main sheet (got it right that time, she thought) and sat contritely next to her, shoulders slumped. "My temper kind of builds up and then explodes. I should let it out gradually, but that's hard. Anyway, I own her personally, bought her with cold hard cash."

"Really!"

"The sale is registered, don't worry." He patted her jaw. "You are wondrously beautiful, fair Diana. My emotions are volatile today because I'm so much in love."

It was the third time he had offered his love to her. She wanted desperately to accept it and give her own in return. But the words would not come.

She found herself wrapped in his arms again, protected

and treasured, cherished and respected, rather than assaulted.

Now he will seduce me, she thought with relief. Any moment the second tie tab will go, too. How will I react?

I'll always remember that I lost my virginity, she thought complacently of her journal entry that night, in a cute little boat named *Brigid* on a glorious golden autumn day in the middle of Lake Michigan. That's a better memory than most women have.

But there was to be no seduction that day. The precarious tie tab remained untouched. He might swat her rear end, jab a tickling finger into her belly, absorb her with his hungry eyes, kiss her lips and her eyes and her chin and her throat and her shoulders, but strange, mysterious, wonderful man, he would do no more. She might be a powerless captive, powerless and more than willing. Still she would be treated like a treasure, a work of art to be cherished and protected, a sacred vessel to be reverenced and worshiped.

For Diana, whose experience with men was minimal, this sacred status was beyond comprehension. As the day wore on, she perceived dimly that, somehow, it was more important to her, too, that she be reverenced today instead of seduced. Next time perhaps. Only, dear God, I cannot permit there to be a next time. So she accepted his adoration with grace and gratitude, mixed with laughter.

And joined happily the celebration of her youth and beauty and presumed fertility.

Finally the wind died and *Brigid* sighed her way to a contented stop. They lowered the sails—she found that, half-naked or not, she could skip over the deck and pull on the lines and the sheets with considerable grace—started the motor, and glided back toward the city.

"We'll anchor off Navy Pier and swim. Incidentally"—some embarrassment—"maybe you'd better put this back on." He handed her the top of her swimsuit.

"Oh." Her face burned again, one of the many times during the day. "I almost forgot."

"You know"—he fastened the tab for her, fingers still uneasy, poor man—"I think you did."

Daddy—she had not thought of him all day—would be terribly angry. Mama? Mama was becoming more mysterious. Had she flirted with Con? He seemed to have the ability to bring out the mildly flirtatious in every woman he smiled at.

Would Mama have bared her breasts on a sailboat when she was twenty-five? Would she do it now if given a chance? She could certainly get away with it. Would she rate an eight for her self-possession, half-naked—or even, Diana thought resentfully and jealously, a nine?

Those were absurd speculations. She was ungrateful and disrespectful for even thinking them.

They swam in the warm waters of the lake off Navy Pier, tied *Brigid* to her float, rode the tender into the yacht club, showered, and ate supper. In the shower she admitted to herself she was even more happy today than on the day they had water-skied at Grand Beach. And less intoxicated. With liquor anyway.

"I'm going to drive you home," he announced after supper.

"No!" she begged.

"I'll drop you at the station in Harvey, you can ride on to Chicago Heights and your father can meet you there."

"No, I'll ride the train," she insisted, frightened that he had so easily learned about the need to deceive her father. "That's final."

He considered her with a critical eye. "You are, Diana Marie Lyons, a well-built young woman in a number of different ways, all of them pleasurable. But if it comes to a straight-out physical brawl—for which, if you want, I will find a barroom—I can take you, despite what you thought out there on the boat when I wasn't fighting back seriously. I will do so, if necessary, rather than permit you to ride home late Saturday night on public transportation. Is that clear?"

"I'll have to change into my work clothes," she said obediently enough.

"Then it's settled." He filled her wineglass again with
the best red wine she'd ever tasted. "Eat your steak."

How did he know about Daddy and the train? Had he
made an investigation of her? Was he using her the way she
thought she was using him?

She had not thought about the investigation since they
boarded "cute little *Brigid*."

"You really do think that we have to tolerate corruption
to make society work?"

Would he shake her again, violently and, to be honest,
deliciously?

"Hmm? Oh, we're back to that again. There's a difference between morality and law, you know—and this is my
last lecture on the subject. You can't legislate detailed
morality"—he toasted her with his glittering wineglass—
"and if you try, you may end up making illegal some things
that are not immoral. Take Geraldine Ferraro's poor husband. The man is probably one of the most upright real-
estate operators in Queens. But we have so hemmed in that
business with needless regulations that no one can make it
work and keep all the laws. Too much law is as bad as too
little law. Now don't ask me the obvious question about
swinging pendula—note the Latin plural, by the way." He
sipped the wine and smiled, whether at the wine or her she
was not sure. "My point is merely that in some sectors of
society we have overlegislated in an attempt, usually
unsuccessful, to stamp out every trace of corruption."

"You'd take bribes, then, or give them to achieve your
goals?"

He seemed genuinely surprised at her question.

" 'Course not. Whatever made you think I'd do that?" He
put down the wineglass and touched her chin again. "Diana
Marie Lyons, I'll never end up in a federal court fighting for
my freedom. Despite the public image, I'm a straight arrow.
Almost as straight as you are."

She was supposed to believe him and almost did. But not quite. In the corner of her head—way far back—a voice warned her that he was tricking her, that the whole day was part of an elaborate trick. She resolved that she would enjoy the rest of the day and worry about the tricks tomorrow.

They were both quiet for a time in the Ferrari, as it tooled its way along the Dan Ryan Expressway. I didn't really do that out there, did I? I must have lost my mind. If Daddy should find out. . . . And poor Mama, she'd be horrified. Or would she? Suddenly, after all these years, Mama seemed to be a stranger. Conor would not make up the story—but Mama flirt, mildly enough, with a perfect stranger? Diana had never seen it, but it was not impossible.

"I agree it's an interesting question. I think she would, in the proper circumstances, of course."

"What?" She was startled at his intrusion into her thoughts.

"I think you could persuade Mama to strip to the waist on a sailboat. I bet she'd love it. Heaven knows she'd be well worth the gasoline for *Brigid*'s auxiliary motor. Anna Maria is in the Antonelli/Loren class."

"She is not!" Diana shouted at him through furiously clenched teeth.

"Then you haven't looked at her very closely for the last twenty-five years. My point is that if you get rid of that Lotus One Two Three that's tabulating your mistakes in the back of your head, you will be too at her age."

"I don't need your advice on how to age."

"It's free." He patted her arm tentatively.

"I will not have you making obscene remarks about my mother." She shoved his hand aside.

"Hey, don't hit me while I'm driving. . . . Hester is even more nervous than *Brigid*. Not obscene thoughts. Just teenage-boy thoughts. Wondering whether Mama has as much of the teenage girl left in her as her daughter has. Maybe being a hundred percent non-Irish, a little more. That's all."

"Teenage girls are exhibitionists?"

"Aren't they? By the way, does she turn over her paycheck to Daddy, too?"

"No. I don't know. I don't think so. And it's none of your goddamn business, either." He knew everything. Certainly he knew about the investigation.

"I know it isn't. Just curious."

"I suppose you think we're weird?" She was about to shed foolish, humiliating tears. Damn him.

He placed his hand on the back of her neck and squeezed it very gently. "Ease up, kid. Some day, when I know you a lot better, I'll tell you more of the gory details about my family life. What you got in New Buffalo was carefully expurgated. I win first prize in the weird sweepstakes. I admit I wanted to have a look at your mother. Maryjane said she was gorgeous. I was—well, OK, I'll admit it—I was interested in what you might look like in thirty, forty years."

"And?" she said stiffly, but not pulling away from his caress.

"I told you. So I am fascinated by Anna Maria. She seems to be an amazing woman. Sorry for prying."

Persuasive like all his words. But not convincing. "She's nothing more than a suburban wife and mother who has had a hard life."

"I don't think even you believe that, but it has been too fine a day to ruin with an argument."

They were ten minutes early for the IC train in Harvey and it was ten minutes late. They put the twenty minutes to use in carefully restrained affection, nothing like the manic embraces under the northern lights, but enough to leave Diana starry eyed and devastated.

They say—she imagined Mama's words—that a good woman should be a whore in the bedroom or with a man she wants.

How horrid, she would reply.

Not if the woman learns to enjoy it.

So, I'm learning to enjoy it. . . .

The restraint was his, not hers. He could do anything he wanted to her and they both knew it. But having somehow calculated both their limits, he chose to stay well within them.

Finally she asked him bluntly, "Why do you treat me so reverently?"

He kissed her and sighed. "I've made a lot of mistakes with women, but in the process I've learned that you can never be too gentle, even with the occasional one who seems to hint that you don't have to be gentle."

"Meaning me?" She dodged a repeat kiss.

"Certainly not." He seemed shocked that she would suggest it.

"And you're also a little afraid of me?"

"Ah, getting your own back now, are you?"

"That's not an answer."

"No man in his right mind would not be a little afraid of you, Diana Marie Lyons. Now be quiet and let me kiss you a little more before the train arrives."

Am I that tough? she wondered as she complied with his request. Or is this part of his game, too?

"Good night, Diana," he whispered as the train pulled into the station. "It's been a magic day. I'll never forget it."

"I enjoyed it, too." She sighed, her emotions too shattered to risk anything stronger.

"We'll see you at Wrigley Field next Saturday. The Cubs may win it that day."

"What?" She struggled to climb out of the car. It would be a disaster to miss the train.

"I don't know what happens to your memory when you drink wine. You've already forgotten that we're meeting in my box at Wrigley next Saturday with my friends the rabbi and the psychiatrist. See you then. Don't miss the train. Your father will worry. Give my love to Mama."

"I certainly will not," she shouted in the teeth of his laughter as she raced for the train.

Her father was sullen and uncommunicative in the car.

For once she did not care. Despite the fears and uncertainties, she had been deliriously happy for most of the day. The troubles could wait for tomorrow. Before she fell into bed and the deepest sleep of many years, she scrawled in her diary: *He makes me happy, happier than I've ever been. Can this possibly be wrong?*

27

Her happiness lasted until after the eleven-o'clock Mass. Then, like an avalanche snuffing out a ski resort, remorse hit her. He had used, exploited, rejected her. He was an evil man, and she, naive little goof that she was, had fallen for it completely. Oh, dear God, I'm so ashamed of what I did. I let myself be a sex object for his perverted lusts for at least four hours.

He had violated her privacy, fondled her, molested her. And she had let him get away with it.

After their routine Sunday brunch at Napoli's, she borrowed her mother's Datsun and drove over to the United Foundry in Cokewood Springs. The infectious touch of unemployment and poverty had long ago aged the small bleak industrial community with its streets of tidy little wooden homes, trying their best to look neat and well maintained, even on unemployment-compensation checks. An early autumn rain, the first nasty hint of a mean winter, made the houses and the stores and the somber people coming home from church look even more drab and depressing.

The foundry was a mess, an untidy and hollow old shell surrounded by construction equipment and materials and several dilapidated trailers. Would it ever really turn out smart machines to make even smarter machines? And if it did, what difference would that make to the people she had seen dodging the rain as they emerged from the small and run-down ethnic churches?

Con Clarke might be wonderfully attractive and very clever with women. Nonetheless, he was profiting from the misery of these poor people and robbing them and his own company, too.

He belonged in jail.

She wrote in the diary when she returned home in the now driving rain.

I'll never forgive him for what he did to me yesterday. He used me. I am no more important to him than one of his cheap little whores or those poor dear people in that awful town. Now I have more reason than ever to want to see him rotting in jail.

From this moment on, there will be no more hesitation about Conor C. Clarke. I will stop at nothing to put him in jail.

28

Conor considered the view from the big bay window in the front of the Astor Street house. In a pinch it would do. Down the street there was the green of Lincoln Park, beginning to robe itself in its autumn vestments of red and gold. The complacent, quiet lake was around the corner, even if you could not see it. Every house on the street in either direction was an architectural gem. The most beautiful street in Chicago, it was often said.

And the most expensive.

Hang the expense, man, you're sounding like herself. If you have an empress to house, you should provide her with a palace.

Besides, it's a bargain. You could sell it next year and make a couple of hundred thousand on it.

"Now, Mr. Clarke"—the lovely real estate person (but not as lovely as Mama by a long shot) indicated the direction with a gracious wave of her hand—"if you wish to see the swimming pool."

"Why not?"

He told himself that his image of Mama and Diana both on *Brigid* was obscene, perverse, disgusting, and exploitive. That did not make it any less insidiously appealing. He calculated his chances of witnessing such a marvel and concluded that while they were not very good, they were not zero, either. Not a venture in which he would normally invest, but still . . .

Horny bastard.

"It's not a large pool," she said, turning on the lights in the basement, "but it is well lighted and the photo murals on the wall give an illusion of the outdoors that is very warm and sunny."

"Very nice indeed. The other staircase leads to the coach house?"

"But it can be locked of course, so that one could be perfectly alone when one so wishes."

"Of course." He tried to keep his tones casual as though he and his wife—to whom the salesperson constantly referred—would ever wish to be apart from each other.

"And you can see that the exercise gym equipment is all new and in excellent condition."

"It certainly is."

"Is your wife devoted to physical fitness, Mr. Clarke?"

"Very much so. To say the least."

So eventually we put Mama in the coach house.

"As you know, Mr. Clarke, the heirs are offering the house completely furnished just as is. Your wife will be able to confirm for you that the antique furniture is worth a fortune." She guided him back up the stairs.

"I'm sure she will."

I'm the expert on antiques, not my un-wife who thinks they cost too much, but we'll let it go.

"It is perhaps a little odd to use the term of a house like this, but I think you'll agree that it's a real bargain."

Education would not be a problem. Sacred Heart and Hardy were just a bit up Sheridan Road. And there was always good old St. Ignatius, of whom we usually made a meal in my days at Carmel.

Education of the kids I don't have yet, to be born of a wife to whom I haven't proposed yet.

"The floors are all parquet."

"Naturally. Seven bedrooms?"

"Plus the two in the coach house. And the two dressing rooms. And ten baths."

"That should be enough."

Con did not live extravagantly. *Brigid* was his only big expense. *Brigid* and maybe the Ferrari. But he'd bought them both at bargain prices, the former because he was willing to pay cash—and that had been hard to dig up on the spur of the moment. But beyond those two items of conspicuous consumption, he spent little on himself. His apartment overlooking Lincoln Park was small and simply furnished, only a few antiques to offend the woman if I ever manage to persuade her to come into it. He did not, in fact, have any clear ideas of how the money he made might be spent on himself. So he gave it away or plowed it back into other ventures.

Just now, unlike last April, he had a good-sized cash surplus. So why spend it on Diana, not perhaps the real Diana, but on the empress who was living in his imagination?

Partly because he was a romantic, partly because Diana deserved the best even if she didn't want it, and partly because there was a demon inside of him forcing him to spend money on a young woman whom—even money—he might never marry. Or even propose to.

A laughing demon that chortled, "Wait till she sees this!"

And partly because a house like this on Astor Street was a hell of a good investment.

"And the rugs, needless to say, are all authentic Persians."

"Clearly. What did the heirs say they were asking?"

"Two-one."

"Two million, one hundred thousand?" He wanted to kick himself for such a stupid reply. What other kind of two-one was there on Astor Street?

"But to let you in on a little secret, I think they would be willing to consider very seriously an offer of one-eight, one-nine. As you know, the market is a little soft right now and they are eager to settle the estate."

I bet they are. "I could see myself offering one-three, one-four without much difficulty. And a reasonably good-size down payment."

You won't reach in your wallet for that, buster, but there are always ways of finding some extra money when you need it.

"Oh, I'm afraid that will be out of the question." She sounded as shocked as if he had told her an obscene story. "Naturally, I will pass that offer on to them, if you intend it to be formal."

"Well, let's call it an informal communication for the present."

The actual value of the house, Con felt certain, was somewhere been one-five and one-seven. If he held out long enough he could probably get it for the low number. That's what his father would have done.

I'll offer him one-six with half of it down. He gulped. Even for me that's a lot of money. Of course, I can afford it over the long haul without having to cut back on too many ventures. And I can always scrape together the down payment somehow.

"We will certainly stay in touch with you." The woman smiled pleasantly.

"By all means do."

Fog was rolling down Astor Street from the park when Conor started his walk back to his apartment. Lonely apartment, he admitted.

What kind of a nut is it, he wondered, that is prepared to buy a palace for a grand duchess who would be horrified by it, who will probably not marry you anyway, and to whom you are afraid to propose?

A happy nut.

29

The confusion in this journal reflects my confusion about Conor Clarke all too vividly. Only the other day, I was firmly asserting that he belonged in jail and I would put him there. Now I know, clearly and without any doubt, that I should withdraw from the case. It is absurd to think that someone as conflicted as I am can possibly be objective on the subject of Conor Clarke. I am persuaded by the evidence that he has committed crimes, probably many more than we can prove by the testimony of that disgusting fraud Broddy Considine. Yet I am equally persuaded that I would not be an asset to the prosecution team in an indictment and trial. I would overreact, against Clarke mostly, but at the last moment perhaps in his favor.

Leo Martin was right: even in a crusade for justice, one must keep a certain dispassionate distance. Shelly, poor darling Shelly, was right, too: I don't want to be so driven by my *own confusions to embrace legal tactics of which I will be ashamed later in life.*

Finally, I am convinced that much of my obsession with Clarke is the result of the curious ambivalence in which I find myself. If I withdraw from the case, it is very likely that much of the obsession will vanish and I'll be able to deal with this problem rationally.

As I am doing, at long last, in this journal entry.

I will talk to Leo soon about going on the wall. He will not like it and neither will Donny. But I'm sure they will accept my decision.

As for Conor . . . foolishly, I am very angry that he has not called me in the last several days.

30

In his whimsical moments Conor Clarke used to assert that he had more lovers than friends, and more friends than confidants. The statement was true enough so long as lover was defined in a very loose sense. There were only two confidants, Naomi Stern Silverman and Monsignor John Blackwood Ryan, S.T.L., Ph.D. The former was a gorgeous young psychiatrist, who for a few seconds had almost been a lover, the latter the Rector of Holy Name Cathedral. He even managed once to have them at the same dinner table. Father Blackie, as almost everyone in the parish called him, charmed "Dr. Silverman" as he seemed to charm all women, but spent most of the evening in conversation with her husband, a youthful academic rabbi, about the Hassidic genius Baal Shem Tov—Ezekiel Silverman's specialty, concerning whom the Monsignor seemed inordinately well informed.

Naomi was a delicate little woman just his own age, with enormous green eyes, who looked like she should be a model for a line drawing in a book by Shalem Aleichem and sounded like a native of Brooklyn who had studied at Oxford (which she had). She was part innocent waif and partly wise old grandmother, a delectable combination for Con even after they had transformed a near love affair into a trusting friendship.

His relationship with Naomi had almost ended disastrously. Despite her apparent total self-confidence, the gorgeous little psychiatric resident's head had been completely turned by his Irish charm, more turned than he realized. The little scene in her room had not been a preview of the drama with Diana on the Grand Beach deck under the northern lights. It had been less spontaneous and explosive, more deliberate and more intense.

He could have made love with Diana because her emotions were temporarily as out of control as his were. Willing consent was not an issue on either side in those turbulent moments.

Naomi wanted to stop, to salvage her virginity, too (Con had a genius, he guessed, for stumbling on the few virgins that were left in Chicago), but felt that she had led Con on and must submit. They had not thrown themselves into an embrace of the Grand Beach variety but were about to begin when, his fingers reveling in her dainty little breasts, some deep, sensitive instinct in the dark attic rooms of Conor Clarke's personality whispered, "She doesn't want to do it."

(It was an instinct which, it seemed, continued to haunt him. He had argued philosophically that it was a useful instinct in dealing with the other half of the race and it could probably be relied on to send the opposite message, too, when that was appropriate. He had no evidence to sustain the second and more hopeful component of his reasoning. There were no messages at all about Diana on *Brigid* the other day. He had simply elected to play it cool or had lost his nerve.)

So that night in Naomi's room—little more than an ascetic monastic cell—he had wrapped a blanket around her tiny, pathetic shoulders and held her in his arms while she wept bitterly. They both mourned a little the lost opportunity—"My dear, the issue is not whether you would be a sumptuous lover. I'm sure you would"—but they emerged from the long night of talk with a permanent fondness for each other that nothing would ever destroy.

It was Naomi who, several weeks later, kicked his ass (his description) into the therapy that gave him a little more understanding of the complexities of his personality and character.

He would never forget the image of the frail, frightened little girl in white lace whose body he had covered with the blanket that night. In their subsequent friendship, she adopted the role of the maternal adviser and confidante, which was perfectly appropriate. But they both knew that there were much stronger ties than that holding them together, passions held in strong restraint now, but perhaps deeper than they had been four years before, a poignant, nostalgic, bittersweet network of interacting emotions that were never quite tamed and which added vitality and excitement and richness to both their lives.

"We must never think we are safe, my dear. That is not to be. But we must neither let fear stifle our memories or the affection which comes from the memories."

Religion was the problem. Con's casual Irish Catholicism was as evident as his blond hair and blue eyes. Naomi's devout, nearly Orthodox Jewish piety was much less obvious, indeed practically invisible till that night.

"I have tried to hide it, even from myself, Conor," she had sobbed in his arms, "but it is who I am. I cannot escape it. Freud was wrong—religion is not an illusion. I no longer want to escape it."

So chastity was important and marriage to a gentile

practically unthinkable. "Not that our personalities or backgrounds would ever blend well in any event, my dear," she had said much later with a smile.

Con wasn't so sure about that, though her wisdom seemed more plausible now than it did then. But the point was—he was using that phrase even four years ago—that was the way this lovely little woman wanted it.

He was genuinely fond of her husband the rabbi and had no doubt, even from the beginning of their quaintly formal and old-fashioned courtship, that they were happily matched. Still, when he returned to his apartment, almost always to be described as his lonely apartment, after their wedding, at which he wore the prescribed yarmulke—done in Kelly green—he felt intensely jealous.

"I would have been disappointed if you did not, my dear. When you are married, I shall surely love the fortunate woman. That will not prevent me from occasional bouts of furious jealousy. How could it be otherwise?"

The pose of his Jewish mother, not to say grandmother, was a useful fiction to channel the intense emotions they both felt. And God knows he needed a Jewish mother, not to say grandmother. Everybody should have one, he told her once.

Yet there were times after their highly stylized exchanges that he went back to his lonely apartment and a day on the telephone, dreaming of delicate little limbs in delicate little lace, and cursing his propensity to be a gentleman.

Not, he told himself grimly, that he would behave differently if he were given another chance. The Grand Beach fiasco seemed to confirm that. His real problem might be just the opposite, might it not? Maybe he didn't quite have the masculinity to find himself a woman. Maybe he was doomed to a life of restless and erratic Irish bachelorhood.

Naomi dismissed this fear as ridiculous, but she had a vested interest in such a response.

So he was very cautious when, at their regular Monday morning breakfast at L'Escargot in the Allerton Hotel he told Naomi about his new love. She listened with quiet attention and then excused herself and rushed out of the dining room.

Is she brokenhearted because I have found another woman? he asked himself dubiously, then thought of a more reasonable and happy interpretation as she returned, pale but smiling.

"So the rabbi is going to be a father?" He kissed her gently. "Congratulations to all."

"We are both so happy. It has been a long time and we feared there might not be any . . . The sickness is not too terrible, my dear. I don't really mind."

"So you're blossoming as well as blooming this autumn. Marvelous."

"Not too much blossom yet, I fear. That will come in due course."

It's time that I become a father, too.

"And this will not prevent the rabbi from being in my box at the Cub games for the rest of the season?"

"With these added responsibilities"—she smiled lovingly—"does not the hardworking scholar need his recreation even more?"

Even that morning, with memories of the glorious Diana branded into his memory and with his joy over Naomi's approaching motherhood, he was not in the least immune to her diminutive appeal in her crisp light-blue jacket and skirt.

"In love again, Con, oh my." She looked at him disapprovingly over her orange juice. "And with a big woman, you who always like them tiny and demure."

"Witch." He leaned forward enthusiastically. "I didn't say she was fat, just tall. From close personal observation I would say her waist was not more that twenty-two and a half or twenty-three inches."

"How close?" She smiled archly, searching for the ground rules of this love affair.

"Not close enough, worse luck for me."

"You become more the reluctant suitor with each passing year."

"Tell me about it. I'm six months away from being a chronic Irish bachelor."

"I think, my dear"—she smiled, though she was seriously concerned about him—"that you may have a few more years before you cross that line."

"Your fault," he said, jabbing his finger at her. "Anyway, I want you and Zeke to meet Diana. Wrigley next Saturday."

"To approve?" She raised her eyebrows. "Has it gone that far already?"

"Maybe. She's sensational, Nai, everything I've always dreamed about. . . ."

"I have heard that from you about others, including, I fear, myself."

"She's a lot like you, Naomi." Do I sound that enthusiastic? he wondered. "Not physically, but . . ."

"So what, then, my dear, is the problem?"

"Weird family. Her father is a retired, small-time government lawyer. Rigid, punitive, resentful. Even collects her paycheck and gives her an allowance. Wonderfully beautiful mother, Sicilian war bride. Father apparently saved her from gang rape and has been collecting tribute ever since. The other children—Diana is the youngest—have put as much distance between themselves and the family as they can."

"The youngest is Daddy's little girl?" Her brows knitted in serious concern.

"I'm afraid so. With my background I don't need a wife who has been messed up by her father."

"Incest involved?" She coolly refilled his teacup.

"Dear God, I never thought of that. . . . No, I doubt it, not in the ordinary sense of the word, anyway. She's a good deal more explicit about virginity than some other people I might mention. It's more like emotional domination, which might not be much better."

"Arguably worse, darling. You must excuse my candor,

but it does not sound very promising."

"I know. Still, candor is what I want."

"So you expect me to make a psychiatric evaluation during the baseball game while you and my husband, who is a scholar and ought to know better, make fools of yourselves cheering for this goyische baseball team? You want me to tell you it is all right for you to chase your little—no, wrong word—your well-developed goddess of the chase despite her anal-retentive father? Surely, my dear, you must realize that this is an impossible request?"

"I just want to know whether you like her," he said defensively, though not so defensively that he didn't gobble down several dollar-size pancakes.

"So, if I like her, what does that mean?"

"It means that I'm not completely out in left field."

"Are you going to marry her, my dear?" she asked bluntly.

"Probably."

"Then, what can I tell you, my dear? Naturally, Ezekiel and I want to meet her, even at that horrid old baseball park. I will tell you whether I like her, though candidly, my dear, if you are so enamored of her, I don't see how it will be possible not to like her. You will make your own decision, no matter what I say."

"Of course," he agreed, with a wave of his pancake fork. "I'm mature enough to know that no one else can make my decisions for me."

"Just barely and then only sometimes." She smiled sweetly.

On the whole, Con Clarke was not dissatisfied with the conversation. Naomi had paid due reverence to maturity and to the distinction between therapist and friend. Nonetheless she would turn her keen and critical eye on Diana Marie Lyons and render a blunt opinion. The sort that said, in effect, "Hey, it's your decision and you must make it, but this is what I think, and if you don't follow the advice implicit in what I think, God have mercy on your soul."

After Diana was vetted by Naomi and before his fears about marrying the wrong woman would be completely silenced, there would come final approval from Monsignor John B. Ryan. That would be an interesting meeting indeed.

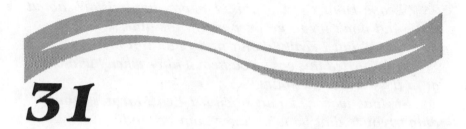

31

Diana spent what seemed like hours staring at the blank page of her journal before she began to write. *I'm numb. Like I was frozen in a glacier for a hundred years. I told Leo today I wanted out of the Clarke case. He gave me a choice: resign from government service or continue on the case. Pornography at O'Hare is no longer an option.*

I sat in the chair in his office stunned. I couldn't believe my ears.

"You made your bed, Diana," he said tersely. "In more ways than one. Now you're stuck with it."

"But conflict of interest—"

"That's not likely to arise. If it does, heaven help you. It's your problem. We'll wire you if you want, turn you into an agent. Do you want to carry a mini mike around in your bra?"

"Of course not."

"Well, that's one possibility. You could cover your ass that way. Otherwise, you'll just have to take your chances."

"But it would ruin the case for everyone if his lawyers ..."

"First of all, should we ever get a case against him, which I doubt, his lawyers will scurry to plea bargain. We might have to settle for that." He rested his chin on his fingers

as he always does, but somehow it didn't seem a cute and charming pose anymore. "Which would be our fault. And even if they don't, I don't think they'll want to bring you up. It will make their client look pretty bad, too."

"Does Donny agree?"

"Leave Donny out of this. I make the decisions about staff. And don't try to go over my head, either."

"I see." But I really didn't understand at all.

"You started this case. You kept it alive when I wanted to drop it. Now it's all yours."

So that was it. I had offended Leo Martin's vanity. I didn't realize that he was either vain or vindictive.

"You can let it slide if you want. No one is peeking over your shoulder."

"I won't do that, Leo. I have an oath of office."

"Still the Girl Scout. Well, then your possibilities are two: you stay on the case or you leave this office. And without a recommendation from us. If you want to cover your ass a little more, then we'll wire you and make you an agent."

"It's not my ass I'm worried about, Leo. I don't want to hurt the case."

"Sure." He sneered. "I'll assume you're staying on the case unless I have a written resignation on my desk by this time next week."

Shelly warned me about Leo at the beginning of the summer. "He likes to play the uncle game, kindly old veteran that keeps the office going, giving tips and advice to the young lawyers. That's fine, so long as you don't trust him too much. People tell me that he has pets and goats. You do exactly what he says and you stay a pet. You deviate one bit and you become a goat. Kindly old Leo turns into an ogre, especially if you're a woman."

"That's just malicious gossip, Shel."

"Sometimes you become a goat even without doing anything wrong. He just decides he doesn't like you anymore. Then you're really dead. It's a kinky way to get your kicks, but there has to be something that keeps a guy around this

place for all those years. Power over young people, that's his thing. Particularly over young women."

I remember sniffing and saying that professional dedication was also a possible motivation. Shel told me a story about his Uncle Zak that I can't remember.

I won't be wearing a mike. That is something I would regret the rest of my life. I won't let the case slide. Conor Clarke is a legitimate target for a federal grand jury. I can't back off now because I'm afraid. That leaves resignation or staying on the case.

I think I'd like to resign. Some of the law firms that tried to recruit me last year might still be interested. But how could I explain that to Daddy? And he's had pains in his chest again. Mama thinks he might have had another heart attack. He won't see a doctor; he still blames the doctors in the field hospital at Anzio for ruining his health.

I can't walk out on him, not now. I guess I'll have to stick with the case.

I'm numb and I feel like I'm trapped in ice.

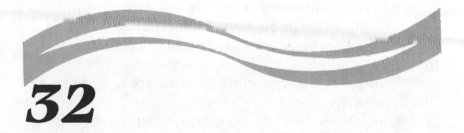

32

Diana was superb at the Cubs game. As at Long Beach and the yacht club, her first moves were quiet and cautious, the natural Irish politician sizing up a situation, studying the people, planning a course of action, before committing to anything. Although it was still blisteringly hot, she wore a light gray shirt-dress with a matching belt, pushing up to the limit of what would be out of place at the ball park, without quite crossing the limit. The woman had excellent taste in clothes. Even if she had little respect for her figure, she certainly knew now to display it subtly and elegantly. Sexy, sure, but tasteful, dignified, classic. Naomi rolled her eyes in appreciation of her good looks and refined taste when Diana turned to shake hands with Zeke.

"My dear," he could imagine her saying, "she really is quite aristocratic."

Which isn't in doubt and isn't the issue.

"I'm delighted to meet you, Rabbi," she said formally. "I've never been to a baseball game with a rabbi before"— and then with just a hint of reckless wit—"but then I've never been to a baseball game before, either."

"Do not call him 'rabbi,' my dear. He will think you are angry at him. That is the only time I use the word."

"In Jewish culture," Zeke, a short, darkly handsome man who looked like a diminutive Omar Sharif with a neatly trimmed beard, explained in his most rabbinic voice, "the *rebbetzin* always treats her husband with enormous respect. But, my child, the very serious question that we must face with due inter-religious respect for the opinions of those from different cultures than our own, is whether you think Rick Sutcliffe will win his fourteenth game in a row?"

He heard Naomi ask her whether she was not interested in sports.

"I don't watch games much because we don't have TV. But I play a lot."

"Which ones?" Naomi asked respectfully.

"Volleyball, squash, some golf and tennis. A little basketball."

"And you are very skillful, no doubt?"

Instead of listing her trophies, Diana nodded in Con's direction, saying, "So far I can beat himself at golf. I can hardly wait to entice him on to the squash court."

Neat answer. And she knows it, too.

So it began. Diana listened with due respect to Con's explanation of the stakes in the game, as ready to learn about baseball as about sailing. Doubtless Daddy didn't approve of baseball, and certainly he didn't watch the games on TV because no TV was tolerated in the Lyons home. Cultural deprivation. A real winner. How could anyone with two such beautiful women in the same house be such a wet blanket?

The Cubs magic number was three. The Phillies were a safe distance behind, but the Cubs, nervous with their prize so close, were losing with alarming consistency—and to bottom-of-the-league teams like the Expos, whom they were playing today. Con was not one of those fainthearted September fans who thought they would collapse as previous Cub contenders had. They would win the division and then, bright, able young men, would have to face the Padres and Steve Garvey in the playoffs. Garvey was the problem, with all his playoff experience, not the Expos. Except they had to beat the Expos first.

Diana handled the scene brilliantly. She cheered for the Cubs at the right time, devoured hot dogs and beer, did not fuss about the mustard on her dress, and still managed to maintain a serious conversation with Naomi. Poor kid, she doesn't know that those sharp little green eyes are dissecting her every emotion.

Or does she? Does she realize that she's being vetted by a shrink who has always half loved me? More than half for an hour or so.

There were layer upon layer of mysteries in Diana Marie Lyons, most of them attractive, some of them ... well, *dangerous* was the word that kept coming into his head.

The Cubs were still slumping. Sutcliffe was as sensational as ever, but he wasn't getting the hitting he needed. In the last of the eighth, they were down two to nothing. The fans were caught in nervous despair. Even Ezekiel, a man of great faith, was muttering about another "September slump."

Then Keith Moreland singled and stole second. Ryne Sandberg doubled, scoring Moreland. The fans went mad. Another wild Cub ending. Alas for their enthusiasm, Sandberg died on second.

The heat, rather than the Expos, got to Sutcliffe in the top of the ninth. He struck out the first batter but then walked the second. Jim Frey ambled to the mound. Sutcliffe nodded reluctantly and trudged off to the showers.

Lee Smith, the colorful relief pitcher who kept the hearts of a nation in their mouth, strode bravely to the mound and, after his warm-up, walked a second man on five pitches. Two on, one out, and the Cubs down by one.

"Con, they simply CAN'T lose," Diana shouted above the pandemonium.

"That's my girl." He hugged her, a behavior to which he was becoming addicted.

She squealed cheerfully and Con Clarke realized that there were realities in life more important than the Cubs. Marginally more important.

Lee Smith struck out the next batter with three straight pitches. The Wrigley Field crowd was delirious.

Then the Expo catcher hit the first pitch, a sharp bouncing ground ball toward left field.

Two runs, Con thought with a sinking heart, promptly forgetting the delightful rear end of his beloved.

He had forgotten about Ron Cey, who picked up the grounder on the first hop and with leisurely step beat the runner to third base.

Last of the ninth, Cubs down one.

"If they don't score, they lose?" Diana whispered in his ear.

"Right, and if they get two runs, the game is over."

"Suppose they get one run?"

"Then the game goes into extra innings."

"How many?"

"Until one team scores. But if the Expos score first, the Cubs get another chance in their half of the inning. That's because they're the home team."

"That seems fair. . . . I hate to admit it, Con, but I think I love this game."

He patted her this time, and she merely smiled affectionately at him in return. You're in love as much as I am, Diana Marie Lyons.

Leon Durham looped a Texas Leaguer over the short-stop and made it to first base, though just barely ahead of the throw from the left fielder.

"Tying run on base!" Con exulted.

"Winning run at bat!" Zeke shouted with the religious professional's special commitment to hope.

Jody Davis took two mighty swings and suffered two mighty misses. He waited out the next pitch, which the ump, with apparent hesitation, called a ball.

The Expo pitcher and catcher and manager shouted loud protests. The Cub fans booed noisily. Diana, sensing if not understanding the drama, clutched at Con's hand.

Then Jody put the next pitch out into Waveland Avenue.

Con and Diana did a little dance of victory in the box. So too did Zeke and Naomi, the latter more of a fan, it would seem, than she was willing to admit.

Well—he thought, after he had deposited his true love, suitably hugged and kissed and embraced, in the train station in Harvey later that night—they saw you at your best.

The next stop was to receive the doctor's report.

33

I hated it. Every moment. And I hate them. Well, the little Rabbi was kind of cute. But that sniveling, prying little green-eyed bitch! How dare she patronize me! What sports do you play, my dear? You must be good at them? You find your work fulfilling? I do hope we see you soon again, Diana! And a phony little kiss.

How dare Conor Clarke bring in one of his former mistresses to examine my mental health. He's the one who has to see a therapist, not me. I should have a doctor's certificate from him before I ever talk to him again.

I don't break the laws. He thinks the laws shouldn't apply to rich people like they do to poor people, and I'm the one who needs psychiatric evaluation at a baseball game!

The jerk. No, that word is out of fashion. He's a total gelhead, that's what he is.

And I was taken in. I actually enjoyed the game. And thought I liked his two friends. Only on the train coming home did I realize what he'd done to me. I'll give him a good piece of my mind the next time he dares to phone me. He did me a favor anyway. Whatever ambivalences I might have about the case are gone. I'll stay on it till hell freezes over.

I'm worried about Daddy. He looked terrible when he picked me up. I had a hard time explaining why I had the afternoon off to go to a baseball game. He never took a dubious half day off in all his years of government service.

Not that it won him any rewards from those bastards.

Well, it was mostly true what I told him. It was a morale day. It certainly helped my morale.

Right now I could kill Conor Clement Clarke. Easily.

Later: The woman who wrote the above paragraphs is a jealous little bitch and is thoroughly ashamed of herself. What right do I have to be jealous?

I am a terrible mess.

Will it ever be over?

34

"My dear, you did not exaggerate." Naomi delicately chewed a small bite of unbuttered toast. "She is indeed spectacularly beautiful."

"And?" Con felt like he was facing a surgeon who would have to render a verdict about major surgery.

"And obviously very gifted and charming. Your grand duchess metaphor is not overdone. Neither, I suspect, is your Irish woman pirate, an image that I find even more fascinating. Moreover, there is a kind of—well, naive innocence about her, unspoiled sincerity, if you will, for which I can find no other word but sweetness, as much as that poor word is so frequently misused. I like her. I like her very much indeed. And now you will excuse me, darling, while I run discreetly to the women's room?"

Conor waited impatiently for her return.

"The doctor says it will not last much longer."

"I know: we men don't know how much you women suffer."

"Nor do you know the rewards, about which we don't talk lest you become truly envious. As I was saying, she is a sweet and appealing young woman."

"But?"

She broke off another piece of toast. "Moreover, she obviously has quite strong libidinal energies. Barely repressed at the moment. My dear, if you truly have not bedded her, that is not her doing." She considered him quizzically.

"She might hurt easily."

"You are an old-fashioned romantic." Naomi smiled in approbation. "Like my Ezekiel. Yes, I dare say she is quite vulnerable. Still, you treat her as though she were a sacred vessel."

"That's wrong?"

"Don't be defensive, my dear. I approve of old-fashioned romantics."

"I'm so old-fashioned that I worry about what some other man might do to her."

"Not without reason. Her greatest vulnerability is curiosity. Mind you, my dear"—she grinned impishly over her teacup—"I speak as one who has had some experience with that weakness."

"Tell me about it."

"The young woman has had, I would surmise, even less experience of men than I did before I began to date you. For her contemporaries in school, she would have been too smart, too successful in sports, too large. She is not the kind of woman about whom an adolescent boy fantasizes. From older men, she has come to expect the crude proposition. So she withdraws from the field and remains very vulnerable to her first love affair, which, my dear, is certainly with you."

"But . . ." He gave up all pretense of being able to eat. "You haven't come to the 'but' yet, Naomi."

She put down the toast. "But, my dear, her father must be one of the most anal-retentive men who has ever lived."

"I hate the bastard."

"Not as much as she hates him, but naturally she cannot acknowledge her hatred. The youngest and presumably the most gifted and attractive child. A mother whose background leaves her ill equipped to mediate between such a father and American children. Endless conflict. The little girl becomes Daddy's special favorite. Her whole life is dedicated to keeping Daddy happy. She is completely co-opted. Daddy's rigid, punitive, angry, resentful world view is absorbed. Ugh." She wrinkled her face in distaste. "It is very ugly. Such beauty and talent slowly crushed by an iron corset of resentment and envy."

"I was afraid you'd think that."

"I must caution you," she went on, putting down her cup carefully, as she did all things, "that these are the impressions of an analyst in training based on a few hours of observation at a baseball game—observation which curiously seems to have flattered her, though doubtless she was angry after and then guilty about her anger. I offer them, Conor, with caution and only because you insist. I might be wrong."

"About the details."

Naomi smiled sadly. "Precisely."

"She wouldn't see *Amadeus* when I told her it was about envy."

"Naturally, she wouldn't see it. There is something . . . how shall I call it"—Naomi touched his fingers sympathetically—"less than fully honest in her relationship to you. No one can be better than Daddy. But you seem to be better than Daddy. Therefore, it is necessary to make you into someone you are not, so she can hate you and not have to choose between you and Daddy. If she persists in this, I must warn you, my dear, she might become dangerous to you. It is very sad and, as you can see from the ease with which I describe it, very common."

Con felt like he'd just come out of a wake. There was no room for disagreement. Naomi had put her finger on just what he feared: the constant testing suspicion, as if she was trying to find blemishes in his character on which to bring in a guilty verdict.

"What's the prognosis?" he asked grimly.

"What is the prognosis for any of us? Not very bright. She might grow out of it, you know. Some humans become mature adults despite all the efforts of us psychiatrists to prevent it. She might one day see Daddy for what he is. There may come a man who can—you will perhaps enjoy the metaphor—unlace the corset. She is not a moral cripple nor a psychological infant. There is always hope."

"How much?"

"If I were forced to guess, I would say that the odds are that she will wither. I can hardly be critical, given my biography, of a twenty-five-year-old virgin. I think, nonetheless, that she has become quite practiced at fending off men. Her future looks like a lonely, crabbed replay of her father's life. Frustration, bitterness, resentment."

"Grim."

"There is, my dear, still hope."

"But hardly with a man who has the kind of father background I have?"

Naomi's green eyes widened. "I didn't say that. I believe your father is not an issue. Surely his excesses were in the opposite direction, were they not? And you are not insensitive to your own emotional dynamics. Quite the contrary, perhaps at the present state of your life, despite your carefree playboy image, you are too much aware of the twists in your own psychological energies. Oh, no, I hesitate to say this because I know how your romanticism will react, but her best chance is someone like you."

"But she is not my best chance?"

Naomi returned to her unbuttered toast. "That's why we're here this morning, isn't it? What can I tell you, darling?"

"What you think."

"In my ethnic group that is a rhetorical question."

"You're not sure, are you, Naomi?" He began to relax. "If you were certain that I should dump *la belle Diane*, you'd tell me bluntly. But you're not."

"I will not take you off the hook on which you have chosen to suspend yourself, my dear."

"Ah?"

"In point of fact, rescuing *la belle Diane* may be just the sort of challenge your romantic heart desires. Good hunting, you should excuse the expression."

35

Conor picked up the phone. "Oh yes indeed. I'm very interested in their counteroffer. One-six with a quarter in down
payment? That seems reasonable."

My father would jigger them down to one-five or one
four and a half. But I'm not my father, thank God.

"No, I won't need time to think about it. I'll have my attorney give you a ring. . . . Fine, I'm delighted, too. Oh yes,
I'm sure my wife will love the house."

I won't even have to do much scraping to raise the cash.

As to my wife, I haven't talked to her since the Cubs
game. I'd better give her a ring. I can't tell her about the
house yet. But soon. Soon. First I must check it all out with
Father Blackie.

He punched in the number on his portable phone and
walked into the parlor of his apartment to marvel at the autumn finery in Lincoln Park.

"Hi, Diana, it's Conor. . . . What's wrong? . . . What verdict? What doctor? . . . Naomi? She liked you a lot, said you
were charming and intelligent and sweet. . . . No, I wasn't
putting you through a test. . . . Psychiatric clearance? Diana,
you're out of your mind. . . . No, that's not what Naomi said,
that's what I'm saying now. They're my friends. I wanted
them to meet you. There was no 'trial' or 'exam.' . . . Well, if
that's the way you feel, I don't want to talk about it."

He slammed down the phone, as angry as she was.

The stupid bitch. How dare she accuse me of such a
crude trick. She needs a good kick in the teeth.

He stormed back into his study and turned on his
Deskpro4 computer.

The nerve of her.

She was absolutely right, you idjit. She saw through the
_whole thing. You're angry because she caught you at it. Now
how are you going to get out of that?

Apologize.

All right, no problem with that. But I still have to explain. Think of a good explanation.

There aren't any. Wait a minute. . . .

He punched the number again.

"Can a guy apologize for losing his temper? And for not
explaining? Look, the phone is no place to do it, but— No, I
never went to bed with her. Almost did once but . . . that's
not the point. The problem isn't you, it's me. I mean you
know enough about my family background to know that I'm
a bad risk in marriage. . . . Well, I don't think *that* bad. Anyway, my only problem was whether— No, I realize that
we're not engaged, not thinking about it. . . . No, not even
talking about it"—he was sinking deeper into the swamp—
"but at our age, well, my age anyway, I mean I wanted to
know whether . . . God, Diana, haven't you ever made a mistake? I could lie to you. I'm trying to tell the truth."

Well, a lot of the truth, more of the truth than you have
any right to expect. Not the whole truth.

"They really did like you. If you want to call it a test, you
passed with flying colors. Or if it's a jury verdict"—he had a
brilliant insight—"it was . . . magnificent as charged. . . .
Yeah, sure, I know you have work to do. Yeah, I'll talk to you
later."

All was not completely lost. She had not been exactly
warm or receptive, but she had simmered down. You just
learned an important lesson about your true love, my friend,
never underestimate how smart she is.

So I have a house, but not yet a bride. And right now
she's more than a little annoyed with me. I'll be able to talk
her out of it, but it will be tough. She's a handful, that one.

And I still must run her by Father Blackie.

36

"May I have a word in private with my client?" Tad Canfield, Harold McClendon's lawyer, simpered politely.

"Certainly." Diana nodded gravely in the direction of the corridor, already savoring triumph.

Canfield and McClendon were like two peas in a pod, short, lean bald men, with hard little eyes, beak noses, and the look of busy squirrels hoarding food for a rapidly approaching winter.

Johnny Corso had been sweated and came running to seek immunity. So had Miguel Rodriguez, the plumbing contractor, on whom they had nothing but who panicked because of his own guilty conscience. Rodriguez had run faster, so Corso had not been given immunity. "Let him do time," Donny Roscoe said, dismissing Corso's two-hour tardiness. "If he wants to bargain, OK, but no immunity."

Because he was two hours late in accepting her offer of immunity if he testified against Con Clarke, Johnny Corso, the father of seven and sometime President of the Parish Council of Infant of Prague Church in Flossmoor, would do time in the federal correctional facility in Lexington. Too bad. He should have thought of that before he went along with Con Clarke's scheme of kickbacks—not knowing his trouble with the books would be passed on to a United States Attorney by Con Clarke in an unguarded moment.

That had been the turning point: Corso had fallen apart when confronted with his indebtedness to Syndicate bookies. Now, surrounded by an immunized Rodriguez, a plea-bargained Corso, and a probably immunized Broddy Considine, McClendon was preparing to come into camp.

Shelly sat next to her, impassive and expectant. Her colleagues had enthusiastically applauded her triumph. On the day at the end of October during which Corso and Rodriguez had made their slapstick race for immunity, even Leo Martin had handsomely complimented her. "You were right, Diana, there's a conspiracy out there."

"Clarke is in it?" she demanded, requiring a complete victory and not giving the slightest hint she remembered his earlier cruelty. I'll fight you, Leo Martin, I'll beat you, too, if I have to.

"He's got to be."

So he dares to bring out his pet psychiatrist to evaluate me at a baseball game, does he? she had scrawled triumphantly in her diary that night.

"We don't have all day, Mr. Canfield," she snapped impatiently. "Does your client or does he not know of Mr. Conor Clarke's involvement in a conspiracy to defraud the Cokewood Springs Company?"

"My client"—Canfield cleared his throat with a dry little rasp—"is in the awkward position of wanting to testify, but realizing that he has certain constitutional guarantees that protect him against self-incrimination."

So would begin the tiresome playacting in which lawyers would save face and clients would save freedom.

"At the present time," she replied briskly, "this office has no desire to force Mr. McClendon to incriminate himself."

"We appreciate the sincerity of that position. Nonetheless, my client realizes that the personnel of your office are subject to change and would appreciate some, ah, more formal reassurance."

Well aware of the defection of Corso and Rodriguez, they had come to the interview to test the waters and discover whether the government wanted more witnesses against Conor Clarke. They had read the signs correctly.

"We could ascertain whether the United States Attorney would be willing to apply for a grant of immunity for Mr. McClendon." Shelly was reciting his lines on cue. "Such grants are by no means automatic, but I think I can say, can I not, Ms. Lyons, that we are prepared to argue strongly for immunity if there is some indication that your client will cooperate fully."

"Oh, I think I can guarantee that, Counselor." When he smiled, Canfield looked like a fourth-string Mephistopheles. "My client will be satisfactorily forthcoming."

She hated these vile little men. It would be better to send them all to jail. However, as Leo Martin had said, if you want the big fish, you have to throw the pip-squeak fish back in.

The rope was tightening around Conor Clarke. If he knew what was happening, he certainly did not seem disturbed. "Some of your colleagues are poking around in the 'Save the Rust Bowl' arena," he'd said last week while they sat in his apartment, sipped wine, held hands, and mourned the instant destruction of Walter Mondale and Geraldine Ferraro on election-night TV.

"Oh," she murmured, still unsure whether he was using her or she was using him.

"They've subpoenaed records of a couple of my companies. Other companies, too. If there's anything wrong going on, I hope they root it out. That's one of the things government is for. If we have a government after another Republican administration."

"Are you concerned personally?" she asked tentatively.

"Me, hell no. I told you I was a straight arrow. If anyone is cheating me, I hope they catch him."

"It's probably only a routine inquiry," she said. Just then, Dan Rather awarded seven more states to Ronald Reagan.

She persuaded herself that Conor was a devious man, pumping her for information. Still, she did not remove her hand from his. It seemed to belong there these days.

Why else continue his relationship with her unless it was to spy on the U.S. Attorney's office? He surely had no plans to lure her into his bed. She was certain that if such an attempt was ever to happen, it would have occurred when she was invited to his apartment to watch the Cubs hemorrhage away their two-game playoff lead.

Yet he drove her to the Harvey IC station and the continued charade with Daddy—who hardly spoke to her now, so certain was he that she was lying to him—with her unwanted virginity still intact. Con Clarke knew not just how far the affection could go before it became uncontrollable. He stopped safely short of the limits. He was left eager for more, indeed, but she felt physically and emotionally content, soothed, reassured, protected.

Maybe she was the kind of woman who appeared in Ann Landers' survey that fall who claimed she would rather cuddle than screw. Heaven knows she liked to cuddle. Making up for the past, she supposed.

So they went to the concert and the opera, watched the Cubs and the Bears in his box or on TV, sailed one final time on *Brigid* (too cold this time to remove even a heavy jacket), and ate a pleasant dinner with the Silvermans.

Naomi was a green-eyed bitch, but a nice green-eyed bitch.

The day that Harry McClendon broke, she reread what she thought was a crucial entry in her journal.

I am two different women. When I am not with him, I am Diana I, a tough-minded, resourceful prosecutor who is determined to pull down a rich criminal and put him in jail if only for a few months. When I am with him, I become Diana II, little better than a whore. I forget my professional standards and code and want only to be in his arms, reveling in that strange but overpowering protection he offers me. I would go to bed with him in a moment if he asked me and stay in bed with him for the rest of my life if he wanted that—no matter what the price. Is this love? I don't know anymore. What is love anyway? I can't return his verbal gift of love to me, but that's about all I wouldn't or couldn't do to keep his protection.

I don't know what is the evil from which I think he is protecting me, but the protection itself at the moment is so wonderful that I don't need to ask.

In the transition between these two women, I justify myself by arguing that I am gathering clues for an indictment or that he is exploiting me to spy on our office. If his lawyers find out about this relationship, it could cost us the whole case. I don't know whether to trust Leo's assurances or not. I can't think clearly on that subject anymore. I simply plow ahead.

I'm obsessed as I ever was. I hate him. I despise him. Yet I like him enormously when I am with him. Do I love him? What more could love add?

The next day she went over to Judge Kane's court to obtain an immunity grant for Harold McClendon. The Chief Judge was away at a professional meeting, and it was Judge Kane's turn on the wheel to consider such routinely granted applications.

The judge's bright green eyes, much greener than Naomi Silverman's, seemed to regard her as though she were a particularly loathsome form of insect life. Her hostility towards the United States Attorney's office filled the courtroom like a powerful scent. Eileen Ryan Kane was far too skilled a lawyer, however, to give any hints that would provide Donny Roscoe with grounds for complaint.

"I will be unavailable, Ms. Lyons," she said in a tone she might have used to ask that an offending spot be removed from the floor, "for any of these rubber stamps next week. Like the Chief Judge, I'll be away at a meeting."

"Yes ma'am."

"I will be attending a convention of women judges."

"Women judges, Your Honor?" Some day, please God, Diana would attend the same convention, perhaps with Judge Kane.

"Indeed. Male judges can and do belong to the association. Does that shock your principles, Ms. Lyons?"

"No ma'am."

"There are a good many women judges now; I suppose that it is a sign of progress that some of them are no better than men judges." She looked at her bailiff, dismissing Diana without even a nod. "Next matter?"

Diana fled from the courtroom close to tears. She adored Judge Kane and hoped that when she sat on the federal bench, she would be as beautiful, as womanly, as competent, and as honest.

Why does she hate me so?

That night in her journal she found an answer, after she had noted that Daddy's chest pains were worse and that Mama was frantic.

She hates me because I am despicable. Con quoted T. S. Eliot the other night at supper, before we heard Pavarotti sing Aida: *"When good does evil to fight its enemy, it becomes indistinguishable from its enemy." I am not worth much to begin with. I am betraying my principles by a love affair with a man I should despise. I am spying on him while pretending to respond to his affection. I am working for another man whose legal style I find disgusting. I am as worthless and corrupt as that which I am opposing. Yet I know as I write these words that I will not change. It is too late to change. I will never be a judge. I locked myself out of that the first day at Grand Beach. I hate myself. I guess maybe I always have. When this case is over I always will.*

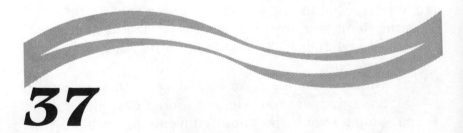

37

Monsignor John Blackwood Ryan, the Rector of Holy Name Cathedral, had worn an aged Quigley Seminary jacket over his clerical shirt in back of church after Sunday Mass since he had been appointed rector of the Cathedral by Cardinal Cronin. Shortly after the Cubs lost to the Padres, he emerged on a Sunday morning after Mass, wearing a brand-new, red, white, and blue Chicago Cubs jacket.

"Loyalty," he murmured by way of explanation.

"Father Blackie," as everyone in the parish called him ("They only call me 'Monsignor' when they are mad at me or want to make fun of me"), was a funny little man with thick rimless glasses, a bland round face, and a manner that was equal parts bemusement and amusement. Con had heard it said that his nieces and nephews accused him of deliberately cultivating the image of G. K. Chesterton's Father Brown and that one of his sisters, who was a psychiatrist, had responded that the truth was that he had been born with the persona and developed the personality to fit it.

Cardinal Cronin, who served on a couple of charitable boards with Con, observed, "Take Blackwood seriously, Conor. He's almost always right."

"I have something to show you, Father Blackie," Con said to him on a blustery mid-November Sunday morning.

"A design for a craft that will bring America's Cup to Chicago?"

"No."

"A check for our school deficit."

"No."

"Hmm . . . A new book of harmlessly erotic poetry."

"No."

"Then it must be an engagement ring." His nearsighted eyes rolled in mock dismay. "A substantial proportion of the female half of the race will surely go into mourning. As G. K. Chesterton—or was it Cardinal Sylvio Oddi—put it, *'C'est la guerre!'* "

"You knew all along!" Conor, somewhat disappointed that his secret was so easily perceived, popped open the tiny box with its precious red stone.

"To quote my beloved niece, O'Connor the Cat, 'Like wow! I mean totally.' " His watery blue eyes blinked rapidly. "You are not displaying it in front of this church"—the priest looked around with feigned nervousness—"without having properly insured it?"

"I know about the legends of crime in front of the Cathedral. Do you like it?"

"It is indeed remarkable, thought I dare say not as remarkable as the woman who will wear it."

"Do you know her, too?"

"Her name? Oh no. Her heroic sanctity is patent, however, from her choice of husband. Am I to meet her?"

"Sure, as soon as I work up enough nerve to bring her around."

"She does not know that she is your intended yet?"

"Well, not exactly. She knows I love her."

"Indeed."

"You might know her actually. She's a friend of my cousin Maryjane Delaney—the one who just had the baby girl. They want me to be little Geraldine's godfather, can you imagine. Anyway, the young woman's name is Diana Lyons, Diana Marie Lyons."

"Tall brown person with a golf club, quite striking. Rather, what should I say, vigorous." Father Blackie nodded his head in approbation. "Gives the impression she can take care of herself."

"Gorgeous."

"Indeed. What other good things have you purchased for her? A house?"

"You've been following me."

"In the parish, I trust."

"Astor Street. Pool in the basement."

"Naturally." Blackie Ryan smiled like a benign leprechaun. "What else? But tell me, when does the good Diana acquire this precious stone?" He peered at the still-open box as though he were assaying its worth, and touched it with his finger as if he wanted to be sure that a marriage symbol for Con Clarke was not an illusion. "And learn about the house?"

"Midnight Mass here. Marriage at Easter, if she'll agree. Do you think it is too expensive?"

Blackie's pale eyes opened in genuine surprise. "Is this the Con Clarke we all know and love? The owner of the most expensive craft ever named after the patroness of poetry?"

"I don't know." He slipped the box back into his Harris tweed jacket. "I'm afraid Diana might think so."

"Indeed." Blackie frowned thoughtfully, apparently troubled. "Tell me, have the two of you seen *Amadeus*?"

"What does that have to do with it?" Conor was miffed. This wasn't the kind of response he expected from his pastor and confidant.

"A woman who would worry about the cost of an engagement ring—or rather that it might have cost too much—hints at the vice of Antonio Salieri."

"Envy?" Con was suddenly scared. "Actually, she doesn't want to see the film, but—"

"Insist." The pastor turned to greet some elderly women who were waiting patiently to fuss over him. "I do not joke, Conor Clement Clarke, not this time. Insist."

Con walked back to his apartment on Lincoln Park, feeling like he had just walked through a haunted house.

Or a graveyard at midnight.

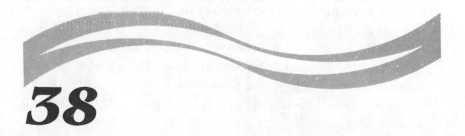

38

"Donny, I don't think we can do it." Leo Martin untangled his long legs, pushed himself to his feet, like an aging but still graceful spider, and strolled over to the window of the United States Attorney's corner office to peer out at the red Calder flamingo in the plaza beneath. "It's too risky."

"Yes, Leo?" Donny knew his limitations well enough not

to attempt an argument with his resident keeper.

"I'm sorry, Diana. I know how hard you worked on this and you've convinced me that that little pimp is a thief besides all the other things he is. But we can drown ourselves in the big muddy on this one."

"I respect your judgment, Leo," she began, "but—"

"But nothing, honey," he turned—spun, viciously, she thought—from the window and began to tick off his argument on slender fingers. "We've got to assume that Con Clarke will have the best defense team in town. We've got to assume that Eileen Kane is waiting to shoot us down. We've got to assume that Clarke is just tough enough a competitor to fight, especially if his lawyers tell him he's got a good chance of winning. We've got to assume that juries are less impressed by immunized or plea-bargained witnesses than they used to be. We've got to assume that while envy will turn them against Clarke initially, his lawyers will be able to win sympathy for a nice, generous young man who is being hounded by an evil government. We've got to assume that jurors, especially women jurors, will be offended by a woman as pretty as you being a mean prosecutor. I'm sorry, Diana, but this is the real world and we have to expect that. Furthermore, we have to assume that the whole crowd of witnesses we have will look sleazy to a jury. A corrupt politician like Broddy? A tight-assed little sociopath like McClendon? Against a clean-cut young man? I tell you, Donny"—he nodded at the boss—"Diana"—he barely glanced at her—"envy is a powerful emotion, maybe even more powerful than sex, but I don't think it's strong enough to carry this case."

"We're not building a case on envy," she protested hotly.

"Aren't we?" Leo was more worked up than she had ever seen him. "Then what the hell is it built on? We wouldn't even be talking about this case if our target wasn't a rich celebrity that jurors are likely to resent and the media likely to eat alive. Come on, Di, you're not that naive."

"I don't envy him," she replied, now fighting mad.

"If you think that, you don't understand human emotions very well, your own or prospective jurors. I want to do the rich bastard in, too. But, Donny, without a smoking gun, we could kill ourselves in a great big media spectacular. Right now, it's not worth the risk. No way."

"I cannot permit this office"—every decision of the Big Bane had to rise to the level of solemn, high, press-conference cliché—"to expend taxpayers' money on bootless prosecutions."

"We have to figure that he'll fight it all the way, don't we, Diana?" Shelly did not look at her as he asked the question. Did he know about her relationship with Con Clarke?

"I agree that we have to assume that," she hesitated. "Yet I am not convinced that we lack a case that we could win."

"Look at it this way, Diana." Leo collapsed back into his chair at the side of Roscoe's desk. "Suppose you're a juror. You resent Clarke's good looks, you envy him his money, you feel that he's a smart-assed spoiled punk; at first you think he belongs in jail; a sentence would reestablish proper balance in the world. You're ready to convict him of the crime of being rich and handsome and famous; then, influenced by skillful lawyers, you begin to wonder whether you really want to put him away for ten or fifteen years because of the testimony of a crooked, self-serving politician like Broddy Considine. You take a good hard look at the government's case, you listen to ironic instructions from Judge Kane—I know we might not get her, but with our luck lately it could happen—which raise even more questions about the credibility of the government's witnesses. You've got a reasonable doubt. You vote 'not guilty.' And Donny here is holding a great big empty bag."

"At least we've made his carefree life a little miserable."

"The difference between the two of us," Martin fired back, "is I'm willing to admit that I envy him."

"Envy is not the point," Roscoe pounded on his desk.

"Expediency is the point. Is it expedient to go ahead with grand jury testimony at this time? I can't justify such an expenditure."

"What do we need, Leo?" She pushed her fingers against throbbing temples.

"The proverbial smoking gun."

"Such as?"

"The money itself, the two hundred big ones that he is supposed to have picked up at the second lunch at Phil Schmid's. Find that or some record of it and, Diana, you have yourself a case."

"I'll find it," she promised bitterly. "No matter what it takes."

Later, in her office, she buried her head in her arms, worn out from exhaustion and multiple frustrations. The phone rang.

"Diana Lyons."

"I wasn't expecting her royal highness the Princess of Wales."

"I'm in a bad mood today, Conor," she warned him.

The sound of his voice on the phone sends electric shocks through my nervous system.

"That's why I called. You're tired, you're not eating, you're losing weight, you're working too hard, you're probably not sleeping much—"

"All right," she snapped irritably, "I fell asleep last night during *Eugene Onegin*. Creepy Russian music anyway."

And she had been barely awake after the concert when Maestro Bartoletti bowed over her hand and kissed it with Florentine elegance—commenting on her beauty to Con in lyrical Italian.

Oh, please, my darling, take me into your arms and protect me from all of them.

"You're not getting enough exercise or else you're pining from separation from me. I propose to deal with both causes by giving you a lesson in squash at the East Bank Club tomorrow at noon."

Until she had run afoul of Con Clarke, she had played squash almost every week in the local park's fieldhouse, routing tough teenage boys who thought they were hot stuff. "I'd beat you easily, but I can't go to the East Bank Club."

"We'll keep it a secret. A quarter to twelve in the lobby. Bye."

She sat at her desk, head in her hands, her body still aching for him. She should think about her interview with Broddy Considine in the afternoon. Yet the memory of the warmth in Con's voice, the solid feel of protection in his arms, the promise of complete abandon with him soon, crowded out all other thoughts and feelings.

Slowly she forced her way out of the daydream and reached for her ever faithful journal.

I will not play squash with him tomorrow, she wrote. *I will not see him ever again. I promise that. The investigation is concluded. There is no reason to see him anymore.*

She paused and then decided that there was one more entry that she had to make:

Even he would not be such a romantic fool.

39

Purgatory, Diana was convinced, would be an endless interview with Broderick Considine, his English Leather scent, his elaborately convoluted sentences, and his locker-room bonhomie tormenting you until the day before eternity began.

"You have to understand, Miss Lyons"—he waved a freshly manicured hand—"that there are certain prerequisites and expectations that attract a man to political endeavor. These emoluments"—his watery blue eyes glowed—"were taken for granted at an earlier time and place. My position has always been that the county was much better governed in those times and places. The costs were a minor price to be paid for effective government. Now what do you have? You have reform, that's what you have." He adjusted one of his diamond rings, something no reformer would wear. "Good government, but not effective government. I have always contended that you can have one or the other but not both. You pays your money and you takes your choice, I always say."

The nausea that was tormenting her stomach, the headache that was pounding against her brain, the tension that was twisting at her arms and legs made it impossible to employ the indirect circumlocution that was imperative when interrogating such a devious character as Broddy Considine.

"What did Conor Clarke do with the money, Mr. Considine?"

"Do with it, Miss Lyons?" His eyes opened in dismay at such blunt questioning. "Why, he counted it and put it in his briefcase. What else would he do with it?"

"I will be completely candid with you, Mr. Considine. Our case against Clarke is on the verge of collapse. That means your cooperation against him will be irrelevant in your own case. I don't want that to happen. But I have to find the money or at least find out what he did with it. Am I being clear enough?"

The man's fingers were trembling as he lit a cigarillo, very much against her explicit rules. "Very clear, Miss Lyons, very clear indeed. Let me think." He leaned back and exhaled vile smoke. The English Leather was better.

"Well, as I remember, he counted the money—we were in one of the private rooms at Phil Schmid's—and locked it in his briefcase. Then he said . . . let me see if I can get his exact words . . . he said, 'I'm going to stash this stuff'—'stash this stuff' were his exact words—'I'm going to stash this in one of my old childhood hideouts.' That's what he said, Miss Lyons. So help me God, that's all I know."

"It might help," she mused. "It might just help."

"I had the impression it was not all that far away. Maybe over by the Dunes someplace."

"Thank you, Mr. Considine. You've been a great help."

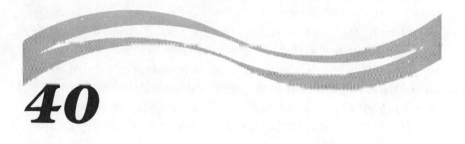

40

Conor was waiting for her inside the squash court he had reserved. "Is it true what they say about the women's locker room at the East Bank Club?"

"What do they say?" She accepted his kiss on her cheek. It would make life much easier if his physical beauty didn't take her breath away. In athletic shorts and T-shirt he was a dazzling male warrior.

"That a lot of women prance around in there without any clothes on at all, at all."

"Enough bare boobs"—she swung her racket at him, delighted to be with him despite what she intended to do—"to provide a feast for your teenage male imagination."

It was always that way: guilty in the transition from Diana I to Diana II and then suddenly a relaxed, reckless hedonist.

"Didn't trouble your Irish Catholic modesty?" He fended her off with his own racket.

"Italian Catholic. After my recent past, I'm not sure I can claim much modesty, but yes, a little. Now, if you've satisfied your fantasies, can we play squash?"

"My fantasy"—he patted her rump with his racket—"is

right here on the squash court with me. With her shirt off already. And a waist," he touched her belly, "that's down to twenty-two at the most."

Her exercise bra was fancied up in blue and white so that it was perfectly presentable as a halter—especially presentable if you wanted to distract a male opponent.

"Play," she ordered, swinging her racket against his rear.

"Ouch, the pirate queen is in a feisty mood today."

"Spoiling for a fight," she agreed.

Squash is more a game of speed and grace than of brute strength. Coordination and quick reactions are more important than physical prowess. But Con, playing today to win, was in better condition than she was and won the first game twenty-one to sixteen.

"Had enough?"

"My serve," she replied grimly. Damnit, I was champ once.

They played in silence now, fiercely, violently, colliding with one another, pushing each other out of the way, ducking each other's furious swings.

Diana won twenty-one to nineteen.

Panting for breath, Con leaned against the wall of the court. "I suppose you've had enough and will settle for a tie?"

Her chest hurt as if a huge iron strap was being tightened against it. "You should be so lucky. Serve!"

The game turned wild, then dangerous, as they battled for every point. She pushed him furiously and knocked him down. "You tried to block my volley, you bastard!"

"Serve," he said grimly.

Then he knocked her down.

"That was deliberate," she wailed.

He grinned crookedly. "That's an Irish woman's reaction, not Italian. Everything you do is innocent."

"Serve," she ordered.

The ball took a fierce pounding and gradually Diana

pulled ahead, this time on her own merits. She was better than he at squash. If she stayed in condition, she always would be better.

Always—what an absurd word for their future.

She won twenty-one to fifteen.

Con banged his racket against the wall in ill-concealed humiliation. Then he turned on her furiously. "Damnit, you did knock me down deliberately!"

"I did not," she crowed. "You lost to a woman."

"A woman who wants to win so badly she'll stop at nothing." His face contorted, his skin purple with fury, he began to advance toward her, the racket becoming suddenly a club.

She stood her ground. "You knocked me down, too. You're acting like a spoiled little boy."

She thought he was about to hit her. His blue eyes were as hard and steamy as dry ice. Rage, she thought as she raised her racket to fight back, murderous rage.

Instead, he threw his racket against the wall and burst out laughing. "Con Clarke, the final, ultimate, and definitively last playboy of the Western world is a bum loser! You're right, demonic Diana, I am a spoiled brat."

Instead of hitting her, he swept her up into his big, strong arms, kissed her savagely. She responded in kind. The heat leaping back and forth between their two squirming bodies made the embrace under the northern lights seem chaste.

She freed her lips momentarily for breath.

"Are you planning to rape me right here in the squash court?"

"Wonderful idea." He forced her back into a sustained kiss. Then his lips sought out her breasts, pushing away the fabric of her bra.

I don't care whether anyone sees us, she thought recklessly.

Finally, when she thought they could never turn back, they released each other.

"So that's how you reassert your masculinity when a woman wins a game from you," she gasped, desperate for breath.

Con picked up both their rackets. "Same thing would have happened if I'd won. You awe me, woman. I'm overwhelmed."

"Take a cold shower," she advised, tying a sweat shirt around her shoulders. "I think you need one."

"You don't?"

"By now you know how much the teenage girl is still in me."

"Long may she live." He saluted her with his racket.

The benign effect of her own cold shower did not survive the soothing warmth of the whirlpool. She permitted herself to lean against his bare chest in the surging waters and to accept once again his protection from the nameless furies against which he always protected her.

"Let's stay here forever," he suggested. "And cuddle."

"Like the women in Ann Landers' poll?"

"Not quite." He laughed.

"For a moment out there, Conor, I thought you wanted to kill me."

"I certainly did." He drew her closer. "You beat me, you humiliated me, you knocked me down, then you lectured me. Aren't those sufficient grounds, Counselor?"

"I mean, you really frightened me. There's a lot of rage inside of you."

"I'm sorry I frightened you. I'd never hit you, Diana. You can count on that."

"But the anger . . . could you . . . could you kill someone?"

"Well, I haven't. Could I? Defending my life or my family if I ever have one? I suppose. But, hey, woman, I told you that I had a temper. Rage, murderous rage against my parents. Mother more than father, Naomi says. But I've pretty well forgiven them. I work on it, anyway. I don't know. Maybe I'm a bad bet for intimacy. In my defense, I have to say my tantrums are pretty short. That was a long one out there. They usually end the same way—I laugh at myself."

"I see." She cuddled closer.

"Do you think I'm a bad bet for intimacy?"

"Who is a good bet, Conor? You kiss passionately. God help me, I guess I do, too. But you've always been gentle with me."

"A marvelously evasive response. Reminds me of our mutual friend Broddy Considine, but thanks anyway."

At lunch in the salad bar, she asked her final Judas question, betraying the lover she had so recently kissed.

"Did you hide things when you were a kid, Conor? From your parents, I mean?"

"Another trick we have in common, huh? Like Daddy and the train?" He squeezed her shoulders to guard her from all snooping parents. "All kinds of hiding places—in Beverly, where we had our main house, over in Long Beach, even in the place in Naples, Florida. You have to understand that my father was a real weirdo. He'd take things from me capriciously, making up, I guess, for the discipline he thought I wasn't getting from Mom. Jackets, gym shoes, transistor radios, books, records, even prizes I won in school—yeah, I did win prizes in school. I was smart in those days."

"How terrible."

He hardly seemed to hear her. Dear God, I am shamelessly exploiting him. "So I found secret places—an old trunk in the attic in Beverly, a corner behind the dryer in the laundry in Long Beach—where I would hide my treasures when I knew he was coming. That way, he could only take away things which were of less importance."

"Did this continue into adolescence?"

"Right up to the time the old bastard died, when I was a sophomore at ND. Remember that house on the blueberry farm outside of New Buffalo?"

"I didn't see it. We drove by the road." That's it. The smoking gun. God forgive me.

"That's right. Creepy place. It was all boarded up, let me see, eleven years ago now, but I found a key and hid my drums—yeah, I played the drums—and my rock records and my beer over there. We even used the place for some all-night bashes when I was a freshman at the Golden Dome, only got in trouble with the state police once. But I guess I told you that. Funny, it would never have occurred to the old man that I was devious enough to think of a trick like that. In his view I was a worthless naif."

Diana heard their damnation, both Con's and hers, in those words.

"Well, it's all over now and I'm still alive and reasonably whole and"—he kissed her, quickly and chastely this time—"I have you."

She told herself then and on the way back to the Dirksen Federal Building that she would not use the information. The investigation was over. Leave well enough alone.

41

Geraldine Diana Delaney was an outstandingly ugly baby. Bald, fat, red-faced, she made nasty faces at the world whenever she deigned to consider its existence—a rare event because she spent most of her time in contented sleep. There was no reason, apparently, in her placid view of reality, to wake up for her baptism.

"She's a darling," her maternal grandmother enthused. "She looks just like Maryjane at the same age."

"Maryjane was placid like her, too," the maternal grandfather agreed. "Quietest baby in the world."

"She's made up for it, hasn't she, Gerry?" Conor asked the proud father.

"Conor, you're like totally worthless. I think we should find a different godfather for poor Geraldine."

"Then give me back that dress!"

It was a happy, unsolemn baptism.

"We celebrate today," the young priest began his homily, "the persistence of life. This quiet little Delaney represents the first fruit of the married love between her father and mother and God's ingenious designs to continue that love on and on till the end of time. We wash her with the waters of baptism because water is the source of all life. It is in the world of nature what human love is in the world of spirit—the guarantee that nothing can finally interfere with God's love for us."

The little girl punk was born fortunate, Conor thought to himself. Her mother and father loved one another. She was an American. Her family was unlikely ever to know serious want.

And her godmother, in a white knit two-piece dress, was one of the most beautiful women in all creation. In that godmother's eyes, as she looked down adoringly at the minor miracle in her arms, there was an obvious yearning for one of those live dolls that would be her own.

I'll have to see if I can take steps toward fulfilling that wish, Conor told himself. Around Easter would be a good time to begin the project, wouldn't it?

42

Geraldine Diana Delaney woke for a few seconds when the priest poured the water on her head. The little kids who were gathered round the baptistry jumped enthusiastically. As they had all predicted, the baby was going to protest with tears her initiation into the Church.

Diana cooed soothingly. Geraldine, reassured that she was still in good hands and receiving her proper attention, shut her eyes and went back to sleep.

I wish Conor would stop looking at me like I'm a madonna, she told herself.

On the other hand, I must admit that I dressed in my best clothes today to impress him more than anyone else. Including you, my sleepy little girl imp of a godchild.

I want him. I want him soon.

And then I want someone like you, little sweetheart. One of my very own.

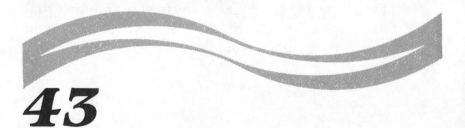

43

At lunch in the Ciel Bleu on top of the Mayfair Regent, Diana realized that she had been imprisoned by her love for Conor Clarke, surrounded by a delightful, sweet-smelling rain forest from which there would be no escape even if she wanted to escape. Too much chastity for too long. Now her body was insisting that her obsession be brought to its proper conclusion.

Consummation.

In such an environment of need, her oath of office, her duty, her character, her father's principles counted for nothing at all.

"See that condo building over there, let me see, the fourth one down from Division. Would you want to guess what's behind it?"

She forced herself out of her reveries to attempt an answer. "State Parkway, Ritchie Court, Astor Street."

Across the deserted beach beneath them, Chicago lay like a corpse, bare trees, brown lawns, laid out against a somber gray sky. A few snow flurries danced against the window above East Lake Shore Drive, laying claim to the rest of the year.

"Eat your fruit salad," Conor insisted. "What's the matter, don't you like your fruit salad?"

"It's fine. I guess I'm a little preoccupied."

It was fine. Everything at the Ciel Bleu was fine. Conor had wonderful taste in food, music, art, sailboats. What would he be like as a lover?

Tasteful, delicate, refined. And passionate. And finally turning a woman on so that she became decadent, wanton, abandoned.

Oh, how much I want to be abandoned. What is it like? Would I even know how to begin?

Curiosity. Dear God, I am so curious. What will— No, I won't even think that. . . . What would it be like?

"Well," Conor raved on, "you haven't guessed what's on Astor Street."

No, and I don't want to guess. "I suppose you finally moved out of that horrible little apartment . . . and bought yourself a townhouse or something."

"Or something."

"Well, maybe a mansion. Rich men are entitled to a

mansion, aren't they? I mean doesn't Hugh Hefner have a Playboy Club."

"I'm not a playboy, Diana." The poor dear man sounded hurt. "You should know that by now."

"I do." She touched his hand and felt shock waves of affection race through her nervous system. "In fact, you are astonishingly abstemious, considering *a)* your money and *b)* your reputation. A strange kind of hypocrite," she added, warming to her subject, "a far better man than he pretends to be."

"Wow!" He squeezed her fingers and then slipped away from them. "The next thing, they'll be putting me up for canonization."

"I don't think that's an immediate prospect."

"Would you like to see my new house?"

"And the electric train, too?"

He thought that was wonderfully funny. Poor man, does he want me as much as I want him? There have been other women. So he's not as curious as I am. Or maybe he is. Maybe each time you're curious.

"I'm not exactly moved in yet. The apartment is my headquarters still, but I've just about got the house shaped up. It's a great investment, too. A real bargain. I can resell it in a year or two with a quarter-million-dollar markup, if I'm willing to wait. With a house like that you have to be willing and able to wait."

She eased her salad plate to one side. "So you bought it as an exercise in venture capitalism and not as a place to live."

"Are you"—he cocked an eyebrow—"making fun of my Calvinism, woman?"

"I am."

"Just so long as I know. . . . Would you like to see it? I mean the first of many grand tours?"

"Today?"

"Well, if you're free this afternoon . . ."

Say yes, yes, yes, her body screamed.

I am not, after all, Molly Bloom.

"I have a lot of work to catch up on," she temporized. "We've just abandoned a case that looked promising."

Yes, the case of the United States of America versus Conor Clement Clarke is closed before it was opened. Unless I ask for a court order to search your blueberry farm.

"After all the wine you've drunk with that fruit salad, you will have a hard time staying awake this afternoon anyway. The walk over to Astor Street will do you good."

"I doubt it."

That's the problem. Too much wine.

"The wine is called sauterne. It's particularly good with fruit. Why don't you call the office and tell them you've encountered a nefarious suspect who has made immoral advances to you and—"

"Conor!"

"Well, you can pretend they're immoral and not just showing off my new house."

"I would like to see it. I'll call Shelly and see if there's anything urgent."

There was nothing urgent. And Shelly was perfectly happy to cover for her while she tended to a "personal matter."

For many of her colleagues of either sex, that would mean an afternoon romp. So assured and unquestioned was her virtue that no one would even think it would be true of her.

As she tried, lightheaded from the sauterne, to walk a straight line back to Con's table, she was not altogether sure that she was flattered any longer by that reputation.

44

Does she expect me to make love? Conor wondered, as with arms linked and heads bent against the nasty November wind, they walked down Division toward Astor.

She is nestling closer to me than would be strictly required by the exigencies of the weather conditions.

I am of many minds about that possibility, Con told himself. First mind: Great! Second mind: It would be a great symbol for taking possession of our house. Third mind: I'm scared.

Con was not nearly the experienced lover that his carefully cultivated reputation and his erotic verse might have led the world to believe. And he had no experience at all with a woman like Diana, who was likely, after her initiation, to be as demanding in bed as she was satisfying.

I mean, I'll have to eventually, but now?

"Am I boring you?"

"Huh? No, I was thinking. I do that occasionally, you know."

"With a woman on your arm."

"Best time for thinking."

"Better thoughts with a dull woman?"

"Best with a gorgeous one." He squeezed her arm.

"Sure." She sniffed skeptically.

"Well, there it is." He pointed at the rambling, turn-of-the-century house, which in the half light of a November afternoon looked like it might be on lease from the Addams Family cartoon book.

"Does it come with its own ghost?"

"They're extra and they don't add to the resale value, though you'd think they would, wouldn't you? There are secret rooms and hidden staircases. Wanna go in?"

"Is the tour free?"

"More or less. No cost to get in. Maybe a minor charge to get out."

He opened the gate, which squeaked appropriately, guided her arm up the steep steps, and unlocked and shoved open the big oaken door. It squeaked, too.

"The squeaks are for atmosphere." He bowed her into the foyer. "They come extra, but I thought they would add to the resale value."

"Conor!" she exclaimed after she had stepped into the foyer and with a quick glance took in the crystal chandeliers, the paneled walls, the antique furniture, and the Persian rugs on parquet floors. "It's magnificent."

"You're not offended?" he asked uneasily.

"Why would I be? ... Oh"—she laughed—"because of the cost? Well, I'm sure you can make a case for the resale value of every item in the house. It's not conspicuous consumption. It's venture capitalism."

"Let me take your coat and I'll conduct the tour."

He helped her take off her faded cloth coat. She was wearing a dark brown shirtwaist dress with bronze buttons and a matching leather belt, a garment that left no doubt about her flowing classical lines but still suggested busy, competent professional woman.

"You don't live here yet?"

"I still make the apartment my headquarters." He hung up their coats carefully in the closet off the foyer. "And come down here to hassle the workmen—no one today—and swim in the pool."

"Pool?" she exclaimed.

"Well," he said sheepishly, "it's only a small one. Down in the basement. But it will serve if you want to swim in the middle of November."

"How delightfully decadent!" She looked around. "Where do you keep the orchestra? And why isn't it playing in my honor?"

"A minute, Your Highness." He ducked into the alcove behind the foyer, turned on the high-fidelity system, and flipped the switch that piped music to every room in the house.

"That's better." She had crept up behind him. "Mozart, nice."

"We haven't seen *Amadeus* yet."

"And we won't. Where next in the tour?"

"The woman's favorite place. The kitchen. I think you'll find it—" He ducked a playful blow from her strong right hand.

He almost grabbed the hand as a preliminary to dragging her into his arms. But thoroughly dismayed by her refusal to be offended, Con resisted physical contact.

No telling what that might lead to.

The real trial would come in the bedroom.

45

Diana drifted through Con's castle—a woman in a wonderful fairy-tale dream, in love with him, in love with the house, in love with the pervasive smell of furniture polish, and in love with love.

She ought to be offended by the expense. She ought to resent his wealth. She ought to be thinking about how ridiculous and impossible love between them was. She ought to tell him that it was unthinkable that she could ever be the lady of this castle, which was obviously what he had in mind.

But she was powerless to reason with herself or to argue with him—as when she was a teenager, a freshmen with her first crush on a senior boy to whom she had never spoken.

I will go mad, she thought, if we do not make love this afternoon. Grand Beach, on *Brigid*, the squash court—each time he could have had me and he decided against it. Now I want him to make love more than I have ever wanted anything. Does he know that? He's keeping his distance from me. Should I try to seduce him? How would I do that?

Even the agony of these questions was a joy as she followed him about his castle, touching the furniture, admiring the wall hangings and art, bantering with his wit, admitting grudgingly that he displayed the beginnings of good taste.

She was sure that he would disrobe her and have his way with her in the master bedroom. She tried to prepare herself as they walked down the corridor. I must not permit myself to act like a frightened prude. "If you are going to give yourself to someone," Mama told me, "do it generously."

I'm sure as hell going to try.

"The master bedroom," he announced. "Two dressing rooms and two bathrooms for those who want privacy. Warm, cozy, convenient."

"For a basketball game. In fact, you could get a whole basketball team in that bed."

"Plenty of room."

"A wife could easily escape in a bed that size."

"Or a husband."

"That stained-glass window reminds me of church."

"Bed your mate in church. Both decadent and perverse." He turned off the light and led the way back into the corridor. "Speaking of decadence, would you like to see the pool?"

"Certainly," she said. I hope I don't sound disappointed. I never thought I would leave that room still a virgin.

They rode in an elevator down to the pool.

"Admittedly, this is unnecessary." Con pushed a button,

opening the door. "But it came with the house and it would have cost a fair amount to pull it out."

"And detracted from the resale value." She stepped into the pool area. "Oh my, it *is* decadent! And the Mozart comes down here, too."

The pool was more than the oversize bathtub she had expected. It was perhaps forty feet long and fifteen feet wide. An array of exercise torture machines were lined up against one wall. On the opposite side were yellow patio chairs and lounges and several thick plastic rubber floats. The walls were lined with backlit pictures which suggested, if it wasn't for the faint chlorine smell, that you were on North Avenue Beach facing the lake in the middle of a hot summer day.

"No excuse for being out of condition in this house."

"Except the best excuse of all, laziness." She knelt on one knee and touched the water with her fingertips. "Inexcusably warm, Conor."

"Only eight-five. If you're going to be decadent, you may as well go whole hog."

"With emphasis on the hog. Still, the water looks inviting."

"I should have suggested you bring a swimsuit."

It is now or never she told herself.

Well, it won't be now. I am not that shameless.

"Who needs a swimsuit down here?" She unbuttoned the top of her dress. "Except a prude. And we know"—she giggled—"that I am not a prude, don't we?"

"We do." Conor's eyes popped as she reached the third button.

Serves you right, she thought as she tried to unfasten the belt. Her fingers seemed to lose all sense of touch, to have "fallen asleep" on her as if circulation had been cut off.

What do I do now? I can't turn back.

"Clever old seductress has lost her nerve, Conor," she pleaded. "Please help me."

"Gladly." He undid the belt and the rest of the buttons

and helped her out of the dress just as he had helped her out of her coat upstairs.

Only then did he take her in his arms and kiss her with savage delicacy.

Her heart was thumping, her throat was dry, her head pounding. She was quaking with fear and shame and anticipation. Don't let me panic now. I must be generous. Keep saying over and over, "Be generous."

"Don't be afraid, Diana," he whispered softly. "I won't hurt you."

"I know you won't," she murmured back to him. "I trust you, Conor. Completely. Do whatever you want."

As they moved into the ritual, old as humankind and yet always new, she realized that Conor was not as experienced a lover as his public image portrayed him. His fingers trembled and fumbled as he unhooked the front of her bra. And he had a difficult time with the complexities of slip, panty hose, and panties. But that did not matter. He was a sensitive and gentle lover. His every touch and movement gauged to her sighs of response.

First lesson, Diana Lyons. Love and gentleness are more important than experience.

Naked at last, she suppressed an instinct to cover herself with her hands. How ungraceful can you get? Instead she stood erect and, she hoped, proud, hands at her side. A generous gift, his for the taking.

"I hope you're not disappointed." She tried to sound casual, as though she stood naked before a man every day, if not several times a day.

"You'll do, woman." Con grinned at her, not a lewd grin though he was entitled to that, too, but a grin of approbation and appreciation. "Till we get Venus de Milo here, anyway. And you're a little better because you have arms."

"Thank you." She gulped. Don't lose your nerve now, Diana. Actually you like this. You enjoy slipping deeper into a sensual rain forest.

"We have some matters to attend to before we swim,

don't we?" Conor seemed to be asking her permission. The dear sweet man. I am out of my mind with love for him. What do I do now?

"We need a naked man first." She loosened his belt and pulled his turtleneck shirt over his head. Why should the woman always be the passive one? Mama had argued. Well, I agree, Mama. Let's see how it works. "You seem to be the only one available."

"You're a provoking woman," he said as she dragged the shirt off him.

"Be quiet till I'm finished," she insisted. "Well, if I am Venus, you look rather like a somewhat older David, though perhaps with other things on your mind than he had on his."

Am I the one saying these bawdy things? No, it can't be me.

Then she lost her nerve completely. What happens now?

I tell him.

"I'm losing my nerve, Conor. Help me. Please."

He folded her into his arms and began to help her. His hands roamed her body, breasts, belly, thighs, loins—touching, caressing, challenging, demanding. He knew her every fantasy, her every whim, her every need. As his lips followed his fingers, it was no longer necessary for Diana to will generosity. She became generosity, conveying to him her innocence and her passion with all the love and all the unrestrained sensuality she could find.

Then he lowered her to one of the rubber floats and continued his assault on her intimate self with even more fervor and skill.

I have no secrets left, she thought as she protested her love for him between deep hungry sighs.

Then finally, after an eternity of agonizingly sweet preparation, he entered her, smoothly and easily, and they struggled up the final mountain of love together. The spasm of joy and the shout of triumph that escaped from lips at the same moment was less an explosive paroxysm of pleasure than a sound of complacent satisfaction. We did it!

It will always be this way, Diana thought, as everything in her universe merged into a caldron of love. There is nothing more to worry about ever again.

46

Balancing a bottle of champagne and an ice bucket and at the same time holding the towel he had tied insecurely around his waist was a bit too much for Conor Clarke, at least in the advanced state of euphoria and exhaustion in which he found himself as the elevator bumped from the kitchen to the swimming pool. In his anxiety to salvage some tatters of modesty, he spilled several ice cubes.

Absurd behavior, he told himself. Recapturing control of the ice bucket, he stumbled out of the elevator and onto the pool patio.

Diana, sprawled quite naked on the rubber float that had been their mating bed and looking simultaneously lascivious and innocent, was still sound asleep, her rib cage moving evenly up and down. The sight of her so captivated Con that he almost dropped the champagne bottle. Solid, well-orchestrated womanly curves; a big strong, shapely woman, yet fragile and vulnerable and needing protection.

How much I love her, more than I would have thought possible to love anyone.

He was quite pleased with himself. It was no great accomplishment, he assumed, to initiate a virgin, but to do it skillfully, so that the experience was memorable for her, required more self-control and sensitivity than he would have either imagined or thought he had. Yet he had carried off the whole process with éclat, the happy smile on her face assured him on that point.

But if points were to be awarded for performance—and since he was opening the champagne bottle, he was in a mood to award points—she would have easily been the winner. Indeed, his accomplishment in producing the peaceful smile and the contented glow that suffused her body would have been impossible if she had not given herself to him without restraint or restriction: I am yours, I trust you, do with me anything you want, absolutely anything.

From any woman such a total gift was unlikely; from the strict and rigid Diana, it was utterly unexpected. She had reason to be pleased with herself.

Mama's influence I bet. And that's reason enough for hope for both of us in the years ahead.

The pop of the champagne cork caused her to move her head slightly, but she did not awaken.

Well, we can't spend all the afternoon in our new house sleeping.

He touched her hair, then her face, lightly with his fingertips. She opened her eyes and smiled at him.

"I love you, Conor," she murmured happily. "Thank you for loving me."

"I'll drink a toast to that." He handed her a bubbling goblet. "Why don't you drink to it, too?"

"You want to get me drunk." She reached for the glass, every sensuous movement of her body pure delight for Conor. "So you can seduce me again."

"That's not a bad idea." He raised his glass. "To our future."

"Well, to more of the same."

She struggled into a sitting position, quite unembarrassed by her nakedness. Con felt that the towel around his loins made him look ridiculous. On the other hand to make a big deal of casting it off would make him look even more ridiculous.

"Today is our unofficial wedding day," he told her, touching her breast, "we'll have an official one soon."

His hand remained at her breast, warm, firm, reassuring.

"I hope I didn't disappoint you."

"You know better than that."

"I guess I do. It's hard to understand. You are trying to seduce me again, aren't you?"

"Surely you don't mind?" He felt her nipple rise to his fingers.

"After we've finished our champagne and used that pool for what it's intended to be used for." She quaffed a large gulp of champagne. "O, Conor. . . ."

His lips descended to the aroused nipple and his other hand, having carefully set aside the goblet, entered the forest lands at her loins.

"I think we should swim first." She did not pull away from him. "Drink your champagne. I'll keep and it won't."

"All right." He picked up the goblet but continued with his other hand the captivity of her breast.

"Finally got what you wanted on the golf course"—she grinned at him over the top of her glass—"my clothes off and me under you."

"That isn't the only position I remember, and I think you got what you wanted, too." She wants to be playful and I want to be solemn. Guess who's going to win.

"I don't deny it"—she held out the goblet for more sparkling wine—"but I do object to this towel." She pulled it away from him. "No prudery in this swimming-pool love‑nest."

"I've never seen you so happy." Con began to play with her still imprisoned breast, moving it slowly from side to side and relishing its solid fullness and smooth exterior.

"I've never been so happy, idiot." She took the goblet from his hand. "Now let's frolic."

Con found himself thrust, quite without ceremony or respect for a highly accomplished ravisher of virgins, into his own swimming pool. He bobbed to the surface in time to see a large, naked woman execute a perfect shallow dive into the pool, split the water next to him, and plunge for his ankles.

Before he could evade her, she had upended him and sent him tumbling head over heels back under the water. That's the way they show gratitude for your servicing their passions.

Diana the beloved wanted to play and frolic, so they played and frolicked like two children celebrating the freedom-granting wonders of their youth. She was a tough, strong women, not the kind you would choose to wrestle with if you could avoid it. On the other hand, she seemed to want him to fight back. So Conor did what was expected of him.

The name of the game was capture the girl. It was not an easy game to win because the girl, eminently worth capturing, was big, strong, slippery, and determined. She was also quite capable of treating her lord and master, her recent conqueror, with monumental disrespect. In fact, the game was designed and played in such a way that he could only win it—and then do whatever might appropriately be done to the captured girl—when she wearied of the game and permitted herself to be captured and put to such uses as he might have on his mind.

Diana Marie Lyons, for all her newfound capacity to make herself a splendid gift, did not weary easily, as Con discovered to his dismay if not exactly to his surprise.

"Is this any way to treat your devoted and skillful lover?" he demanded between embarrassing gasps for breath when he temporarily cornered her at the deep end of the pool.

"Yes," she replied promptly, before feinting to the right and then diving by him on the left and pushing his head underwater as she passed him.

Con finally captured her, if the term could be used of what was clearly her decision to change the rules of the game, by pinning her against the wall of the gym on one of her periodic explosions out of the pool.

She slumped into his arms. "I guess you win, Tarzan."

Her mood changed from violent playfulness to abject fragility, a transformation that, perhaps by design, was enough to break poor Conor's pounding heart. He absorbed her in his arms, listening happily to the rhythm of her own throbbing heart.

"I'm not sure that I'll ever be the winner is this conflict, Diana, but I don't mind. I love you."

"I love you, too." Her wet flesh pressed against his flesh, capitulation and invitation. "Oh, Conor, my darling, I never thought it would be like this. . . . Is it what you expected?"

"A thousand times better," he said honestly enough, his hands beginning their seditious explorations. "I never imagined a woman could be as generous with herself as you are."

She intercepted a hand creeping down her belly. "Really!" she shouted happily. "Was I really generous? I wanted to be, but I wasn't sure I knew how."

"You certainly did know how. I've never been so effectively seduced."

"Seduced." She pretended to shove him away. "Well, I like that. My will is weakened with liquor, I am dragged over to this house, bemused by its luxury, tricked into coming down to this sybaritic pool of yours, stripped, and forced to submit to your obscene designs, and then— Hey, speaking of liquor"—she shoved him away for real this time—"we can't waste the rest of your Dom Perignon. Waste not, want not, I always say."

She scampered to the ice bucket, pulled out the bottle, filled both their goblets, and gave him his.

"Ten thousand years, Diana Maria Lyons."

"At least that, Conor Clement Clarke," she returned his toast. "And I did seduce you, didn't I, my poor darling?" She drew close to him and reinstated his hand on her belly. "I'm sorry."

"I'm certainly not."

"Surprised, though?"

"Astonished."

"Me, too." She nodded thoughtfully. "I guess I didn't understand my emotions very well. . . . Oh, that's so nice. Are you going to make love to me again?"

"Do you think I was chasing you just to burn up calories? Might we not go upstairs to our marriage bed?"

"Sure, if you think you can find me in it."

"I can manage."

She swept up her clothes and wrapped a towel, sarong style, under her arms. "In case we walk by any windows."

"We don't." Inside the elevator he rearranged the towel at the same height his had been located earlier in the afternoon.

"So you can stare at my oversize boobs on the ride up?"

"I'll not accept that false adjective. They are the proper size for you. Anything smaller would be too small. And in addition to staring at them, I intend, with all proper respect, to play with them."

"Be my guest." She sighed with pleasure. "There's enough of them to play with, heaven knows."

"And every centimeter an added joy."

"Poor line for a poet. But go ahead and amuse yourself. I suppose I have to pay for the high-class champagne."

"I also propose," he continued, "to receive full value for my expensive champagne, to kiss them, hold them firmly against your ribs, tickle them, nibble on them, bite them, and perform a number of other amusements for my conquering male fantasies."

"Bite?" she exclaimed.

"Like that." He held her against the elevator wall, ignored the opening door, and demonstrated, touching his teeth lightly against her skin and applying gentle pressure.

"Oh, Conor!" she leaned helplessly against the wall as the door closed and the elevator returned to the basement. "How I wish I had mother's milk, so I could nurse you."

An image that almost destroyed the remnants of Conor's sanity.

Well, that's an amusement that has useful results. I must not forget it.

"On the happy day when I'm able to claim that nourishment, I'll take you up on your promise. Until then, there are a number of other— We seem to have returned to the pool. You distract me, woman." He pressed the up button. "As I was saying there are a number of other delightful obscenities in which I propose to engage. It will do you no good to resist."

"I'm all yours, Conor. Do whatever you want. I'm sure I'll love it. But I don't think I have the strength to walk to the bedroom."

"Then I'll carry you."

Fortunately he did not have to live up to that foolish promise.

This time he locked the door open and turned to his woman, who was still sloped against the side of the elevator, her protecting towel on the floor in front of her, tears pouring down her face.

"Is there something wrong, Diana?" He held her upper arms protectively. "Did I hurt you?"

"Oh, no, darling, I'm sorry." More tears. "I'm crying because I'm so happy and because you keep doing such perfect things."

"Now you're making me cry, too." He crushed her into his arms and decided that heaven must be rather like this moment.

So after the second ride up the elevator and in what he considered their marriage bed, Conor amused himself with various dimensions of his woman's anatomy with considerable imagination and for what he thought was an inordinate amount of time, while she purred and cooed and sighed and praised him as the greatest lover that had ever lived.

An exaggeration, he thought as, sweating from his exertions and almost out of his mind with need, he entered her waiting and willing body. But maybe not that much of an exaggeration.

47

It is much better this time, Diana thought as Conor slipped into her wet and waiting body. How much better can it become? A man can't know this joy. He doesn't feel my body swelling inside of his. Maybe it is the opposite for him. I have so much to learn.

I knew I would do it this afternoon. I kidded myself that it wouldn't happen, but I knew it would. I was ready to seduce him if necessary. It was necessary and I did.

Proudly and shamelessly.

A little slower, Conor. Yes, that's nice.

I can be as good at this game as I am at golf. That's what it is: a wonderful game.

And I can play it without shame or guilt and with reckless immodesty. Who would have thought it? First time out I shot par! I certainly wouldn't have thought it. Neither did he. He almost died on the spot when I unbuttoned my dress. Oh, darling Conor, I have you and I'll never let you go.

Problems? They'll work out. Nothing can be strong enough to blot out this joy.

I'll lose my mind if this doesn't stop soon. I'll tear myself apart. Hurry, Conor, hurry. Don't slow down. You're tormenting me. Don't, please don't. It's so wonderful.

I'm a playboy fantasy. I never thought I could be that. And like all fantasies, I scare the hell out of him when I come alive.

Not that he isn't doing very well with me just at the moment.

She cried out a plea for Conor to have pity on her and finish the game. He only laughed triumphantly.

Make it last forever, she begged.

It could not last forever, but there was hint of eternity in the next few seconds. Her final pleasure started, not in her loins, but deep within the base of her brain, spread like a high-voltage current through her body, and raced back and forth through every nerve cell back to her brain; it rushed out again with even higher voltage and coursed back. She would die the next time the energy burned through her. She heard herself screaming from a great distance, then the electricity between brain and loins enveloped her whole body in a paroxysm of pleasure; she was swept away into eternity and, utterly drained and ecstatically happy, knew nothing at all as she plunged through the starlight years of forever.

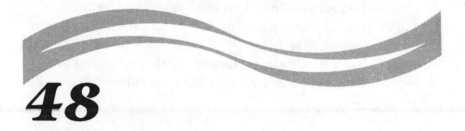

48

Well, one of the great lovers of the Western world met his match this afternoon.

Sure, the woman did in the last playboy of the Western world.

And then some, me boy.

You have had it.

And you don't even mind.

Con stretched, thoroughly satisfied, on his badly rumpled marriage bed. He had dressed to take Diane down to get a cab to the IC station and had helped her to dress, a task about which she seemed quite indifferent in her after-love lassitude.

"Do I have to wear clothes?" she had murmured. "I've decided I like being naked."

He was afraid she meant it.

"I'll ride with you," he argued, buckling the belt on her dress. "You're in no condition to be permitted out on the streets by yourself."

She had insisted that, since her father made one of his rare trips to the Loop today, he should not come to the station with her.

"Don't worry, I'll take care of Daddy," she said, kissing him as she climbed into the cab, "but not today."

He was fully prepared to believe that she could take care of any male.

He had staggered back to his room, thrown off his clothes, and fell back into bed for the sleep of the just. And the worn-out.

When he had awakened an hour later, he continued the pleasant task of remembering the pleasant activities in which he had engaged.

Your shy Catholic virgin, Conor Clarke, turns out to be a lioness in disguise. She's like to become more fierce with more practice.

Are you sure that's what you want?

You bet.

But who would have thought that Diana would be so delightful in bed. The first time.

She is a strong-willed witch. She makes up her mind to something and it happens. So today she made up her mind that she would be . . . *generous* is the only word I can think of . . . and damnit, generous was what she was. Despite fear and shame and embarrassment and inexperience.

I think you call that noble.

Noble Diana. Imperial Diana. Not like Father Blackie's alliterative adjectives.

Alliteration . . . Hey, you're a poet and you've just had the sexual experience of your life and you haven't even thought about hunting for a mctaphor.

Just now, who needs a metaphor?

And face it, last playboy of the Western world, you were

seduced. Deliberately, consciously, willfully, that woman made up her mind at lunch that you were going to screw her this afternoon and you did just that. And when she lost her nerve for a few moments, she made you help her.

Some dame.

Dame Diana.

Well, you always said you'd never marry a weak, clinging woman.

She was terrified. She didn't care, she jumped in anyway. It's not that she isn't vulnerable. She jumps in anyway.

Fragile and determined. Dear God, what a woman.

And, by the by, thank you for her. A very nice pre-Thanksgiving present.

I wonder if I'm overinterpreting. It was just a roll in the hay. She was fed up with a life without sex and decided that it was time she got some. I happened to be around.

I think it's more than that.

But I'm not sure.

He dragged himself out of bed and lurched toward the shower.

I had better check this out with Father Blackie.

Now how the hell am I going to explain this to him?

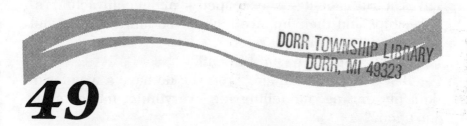

49

"Our child seems entirely too happy," Daddy said at the supper table that night, "for someone who has spent a day of hard work at her office desk. But then, young people don't work like they used to, do they, Maria, my dear?"

Mama studied her carefully. Too carefully, Diana thought.

"She doesn't look any different to me." Mama removed the vegetable dish. "A little prettier, maybe, but that's because of the dress I gave her."

Mama is lying to protect me. She knows or at least suspects. Well, she's almost as much responsible for what happened as I am.

"It's an exciting case," she said calmly as she removed the potato plate. Daddy is so gray these days. How can I ever stand to lose him?

"Exciting enough to make you radiant?"

"Come on, Daddy." She touched his hand. "You're the one who is always saying there is nothing more satisfying than discovering a critical legal point by yourself."

Behind Daddy's back, where she was making the decaf cappuccino, Mama looked like she was about to laugh. Please don't. I'll laugh too, and we'll all be sorry.

"All right"—he glared at her through narrow, hurt eyes—"tell me what your great legal breakthrough was."

"I can't discuss the specifics, you know that, Daddy." She searched desperately for a general statement but found it hard to remember even what law was about. "Let's say it was a very old truth that most of us have to discover for ourselves, a truth about"—she stopped—"about contractual relationships and their implications for certain common but not unimportant procedures."

Whew, not bad for off the cuff.

"I see." Daddy beamed. "And you do have a wonderful skill, my darling, for telling me everything and nothing, don't you?"

"That's what you would expect from an ethical lawyer, isn't it?"

Mama's head was turned so that Diana could not see her face, but she was certain that Mama was laughing. What had happened to Mama lately? Did she know it was Con? Would it have made any difference?

Diana fled to her room immediately after the supper cleanup, pleading brief preparation. She read through Con's book of poems and fantasized about the poems he would write to describe their afternoon of love.

I've probably given him enough material, she giggled to herself, to last for ten years of verse scribbling.

She took off her dress, threw it on the floor negligently, as she had done by Con's pool, and then, ashamed of herself, retrieved it and hung it up.

I'm not THAT decadent.

Then she lay back on her bed to revel in her own complacency and delight in the continued afterglow.

Carefully and methodically, she went through the remembered images, cataloging them for future study. You improve at this game, she told herself piously, like you improve at all games, by practice and concentration.

She shivered blissfully.

But I was very good as a beginner, wasn't I?

And how lucky to have a man like Conor. I would not have trusted anyone else enough to take the risks I did. Such a dear, sweet, wonderful man.

And mine. She shivered again. All mine.

I am still a novice, she admitted, considering her performance that afternoon judiciously. I did creditably on the giving side and encouraged him to take all kinds of risks the poor dear would never have taken with another woman.

And he definitely has more of a modesty problem than I do. Remember when I had to pull that towel away from him?

But I'm not much of a sexual aggressor yet. I want to be. I am a very aggressive woman.

Am I really? Well, let's say I have some strong aggressive strains in my personality. So I should be aggressive some of the time in bed.

Will that threaten him? Probably. But he'll also love it.

So I'll have to learn more about that part of it. There's no rush. I'll have a lifetime to experiment.

I wonder how many women approach marriage with

that thought—a lifetime to experiment with an available man whom you can set on fire anytime you want?

Wow.

Probably not many.

Ten hours ago I wouldn't have thought that way, either.

I certainly was Mama's daughter this afternoon. I'll have to tell her someday when I straighten out all the problems.

Such wonderfully pleasant thoughts.

I've never in all my life been this happy.

Or, damnit, this satisfied with myself.

They had lied to her about the first time. The folk wisdom said it was terrible or at best dull. Maryjane had hinted that it was not necessarily true. It must be that the women whose first experience was memorable were afraid to talk about it for fear that they would be ridiculed. Well, there's no need to talk about it. I can treasure all the sweetness in my head until I instruct my own daughters.

Mama said it all: "If you give yourself, do it generously."

And was I spectacularly generous!

She felt her face become warm at the memory. I don't believe it was me.

What if I'm pregnant? Not likely, but not impossible.

Well, if I am, so what? He wants to marry me. He was the one who had to sanctify what we did by talking about marriage. Dear God, he is sweet.

Dear God, thank You for Conor. I hope You're not mad at me. If You are, I promise I'll be a good wife and make up for anything I've done wrong in winning him.

And don't blame him. I didn't give him a chance.

She giggled again, sure that God was enjoying her joke.

You made us to love. You said that You love like we do, only more so. I think with Conor this afternoon I began to realize for the first time what You're like.

I love him and I love You, too.

He wants to marry me. He can't find a woman like me among the models and cabin attendants. He'd better tie me down before I find someone I like more.

She laughed loudly at that and grabbed a pillow to hold in her arms, imagining for a moment that it was Conor.

And I'll marry him. Soon.

Daddy . . .

Dear God, what am I to do about Daddy?

She tossed the pillow aside and sat up on the edge of her bed. I knew I'd have to ask that question. I was afraid of it, but I have to ask it. Tonight, while all the memories are strong in my brain.

It will kill him. He doesn't want me to marry anyone. Clement Clarke's son? He won't come to the wedding. He probably won't live to come to the wedding.

I wish I could talk to Conor. He doesn't dare call here, I pleaded with him not to. And I don't dare go down to the phone to call him.

She buried her face in her hands, still too happy to cry, but feeling that the happiness was slipping away like a sand pile slipping through her fingers.

I have to choose. There's no way around that. I can't keep them both. Conor wouldn't object to Daddy at all. He doesn't even remember the case in which his father destroyed Daddy's life. But Daddy . . . he's the one forcing me to make the choice.

It would ruin his life; he would think that he had failed at everything. I can't do that to him, poor man.

Still.

Still, what?

Still, I can't betray Conor's love. Not now.

Maybe there's a way out. We could disappear. Run away to Paris. That sounds delicious. Talk about decadence!

But, whatever, if I have to choose, I'll have to choose Conor.

Later, when her dream of love was transformed into a nightmare of hatred, Diana would cite that resolution as the only evidence in her favor.

Much good it would do. Even when the jury was her own conscience.

50

"If it was sinful, Father Blackie, I can't tell you how sorry I am. I wouldn't use her for anything."

In his huge easy chair, feet extended on a tattered ottoman, which he claimed was really Ottoman because it had been purchased in Turkey, and clad in his turn-of-the-century smoking jacket, the little priest looked like a minor Middle Eastern vizier in the dim light of his study, so dark that one could barely see the saucy medieval Madonna who presided authoritatively over the pastor's suite.

"You seem contrite about what you clearly consider a remote possibility and not very sorry about the actual event." The priest sighed noisily. "Indeed, unless I misread the evidence, which we both know is unthinkable, you are quite pleased with yourself and merely want me to reassure you that such pleasure is legitimate. You must know you've come to the wrong priest for that, Conor Clement Clarke. No certain answers offered on this segment of the beach."

"I'm guilty because I don't feel guilty," Conor admitted sheepishly. "I don't think she feels any guilt, either."

"I'm sure not. Lovers rarely do until—you must pardon my expression—chickens come home to roost."

"You mean she might be pregnant?" Conor had not thought of that possibility. "My God!"

"Not so soon if I understand the process. By tomorrow at this time, who could say?"

"I feel rotten already."

"On the other hand," Blackie went on inexorably, drumming his fingers on the book that was open, facedown, on his stomach, "given the fact that both your bloodstreams were drenched with reproductive hormones, I would not think that either of you enjoyed sufficient freedom to be capable of serious sin." He sighed again, somewhat less noisily. "Serious sin is rather hard to commit."

"I love her, Father Blackie, and she loves me."

"Doubtless. Need I add that such is the argument of everyone?"

"That's what they all say? I guess." Conor squirmed uncomfortably.

"I don't approve of premarital sex, Conor C. Clarke, even if it is statistically probable. Too many people are hurt, which is the reason behind the prohibition. On the other hand, it is not the worst offense in which we humans frequently indulge. I might, if pushed, even go so far as to suggest that your faintheartedness in presenting the dazzling Diana with the well-merited engagement ring is more likely to be displeasing to the Lord God than an unplanned and casual afternoon romp."

"I'm going to marry her, really!" Conor clenched his fists. "I'll give her the ring."

"Because of what happened this afternoon?" Blackie glared at him over the top of his rimless glasses. "A single incident, however lamentable, ought not to constrain a life decision."

"Because I love her, damnit!"

"Ah." Blackie beamed.

"And because I can't live without her."

"It would appear not."

"And she can't live without me."

"Patently."

"All right, Father Blackie"—it was Conor's turn to sigh—"I'm ready to take the big risk. I guess I have no choice."

"None whatever." Blackie struggled to his feet, dumping the book, *Letters of William James*, on the floor, and stumbled over to the Madonna. "Consider this young woman, so passionately and defiantly holding her boy child." He lifted the statue off its pedestal and waved it like a giant sword. "Presumably the real-life model died seven centuries ago and her child only a few years after that. Yet her defiant and tender embrace suggests to us, quite pointedly, that Madonna love animates the universe. If such be the case, both the French mother and her child are now in the tender hands of an even more defiant passion. Under those circumstances, if indeed we are all caught up in Madonna love, then your fears and your guilts and that of the defiant Diana are hardly all that much to the point, are they?"

"A sermon I needed to hear," Con admitted.

"You hear it in some form"—Blackie returned the saucy Madonna to her place, with a careful precision that was lacking in most of his disorganized movements—"every Sunday, but never mind. The issue now is to cement the union you began at Long Beach this summer and, ah, furthered this afternoon, as quickly as possible, if indeed you truly intend to do it."

"Why is time so important?" Conor wondered. "I want her in our castle soon, but you seem to think it even more urgent than I do. I won't make love with her until—"

Blackie waved a pudgy paw impatiently. "The two of you live on an edge created by your families' histories. Your love is precarious until you jointly climb off those edges."

Conor did not understand. He did not in fact take seriously the priest's warning. Not, he would tell himself ruefully in a few weeks, until it was too late.

"I don't want to be indelicate and shock you," he began, approaching the principle item on his agenda.

"I have been shocked only once since I was eleven." Blackie eased himself contentedly back into his dark brown chair. "And that was by the lamentable, indeed intolerable, failure of the Cubs to win the fifth game of the playoffs."

"Well." Con felt his face flame. "I suppose the only way to put it is that Diana surprised me."

"Indeed?" Blackie's interest seem to be reawakened.

"She gives the impression of being, ah, well, kind of uptight. Influenced by her father, you know?"

"So I've been led to believe. Delightful but inhibited."

"It turns out that the latter adjective is not justified."

"So." Blackie's face was an unreadable mask.

"The only adjective I can find is *generous*. I trust I don't go beyond the bounds of delicacy, Father."

"Her mother"—the priest ignored the question—"must be a remarkable woman. So much the better for all concerned."

"She is," Con said enthusiastically. "My point is—"

"That this datum challenges previous tentative conclusions. And may offer us grounds for a much happier prognosis."

"Something like that. What I want to know, Father Blackie, is whether you agree that—"

The little priest pointed his finger at Con, a somber challenge from the man Cardinal Cronin once called Merlin on Lake Michigan. "God help you, Conor Clement Clarke, if you let this one get away!"

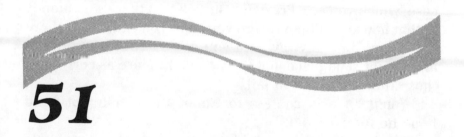

51

The next day, as the IC train chugged through a dark November morning toward the Loop, conscience caught up with Diana. About sin she did not worry. As Mama once told her, "If you really want a man, do everything you need to do to get him. Don't listen to the priests. They are good but they don't understand how it is with a woman and a man at that time."

She would fight Daddy if need be. That would hurt her terribly, but if it would be necessary, it would be Daddy's fault, not hers.

Her oath of office would not yield so quickly. She had evidence that Conor Clarke had stolen money from the poor. She could not believe it to be true of the wonderfully kind and patient lover who had introduced her to the joys of sexual passion the day before. It was unthinkable.

But the unresolved possibility would haunt the marriage that Conor seemed to want and which she now seemed to want, too. The allegations of Broddy Considine had to be checked out and disproved.

That would be the end of it. The case against Con was closed. She could in conscience leave it closed, once she found out about the blueberry farm outside of New Buffalo.

But if she didn't settle it now, the doubt would fester all her life, eating away at her love for Con.

You can forget it in bed with him for a while, because the pleasure is so great. But it would blight even lovemaking. You know that Diana, you really do.

You can fend off Conor for a week or two. Tell him you love him, which you do, and that you are on an important case, which you are. Prove to yourself that there's no money in that house and then resign your job. You can't work there and marry him, anyway. And you don't want to work there any longer. The place and the people in it are as corrupt as those they try to put in jail.

You'll have to confess to Conor the whole story and hope he forgives you.

Maybe you should call him now and explain the whole thing to him. You owe the poor man an explanation. Tell him about Broddy's allegations.

You can't do that, either.

As she walked across the Loop into the teeth of the bone-chilling November wind sweeping in from the prairies, she considered again the position she had taken before lunch the day before: Leave well enough alone. Conor was a good man. She loved him. It was impossible for him to be guilty of such a crime.

Forget it, Diana. You've proved you're not a prude, now prove that you're not a scrup.

Spit that bone out of your mouth.

Yet she realized as she rode up the elevator that it was beyond her power to suppress what she knew. She did not want to request a search warrant for the house on the blueberry farm just across the state line in Michigan on Highway 39. But it no longer mattered what she wanted to do. She would do what she was driven to do—even if it meant sure destruction for both of them.

It's my oath of office, which compels me to see that the law is enforced, she told her diary, before she collected Leo and Shelly to seek an audience with Donny Roscoe.

"I learned of the blueberry house from a confidential informant," she said later in response to Donny's question. "I can't guarantee that the money is there, Mr. Roscoe. If you are reluctant to seek a search order in another jurisdiction, perhaps we should forget about it."

"I've got to hand it to you, Diana." Leo smiled approvingly again, though she was not sure she would ever trust him. "You're a damn good cop as well as a damn good lawyer. Donny, we gotta do it. The people over in Western Michigan owe us a few favors."

52

So on a cold Saturday morning after Thanksgiving, after pleading with Con for just a couple of days more to finish her important case, Diana and three glum FBI agents drove to the New Buffalo exit on I-90, turned left, and then right just short of the railroad tracks. The fields were brown and barren, the trees stripped of their foliage, the air cruel with the threat of a snow-belt winter.

The decrepit old two-flat, as out of place as a strip joint on Mt. Athos, was where it should be, deserted and forlorn. There was no blueberry farmer or anyone else in sight. The door yielded to pressure from two of the agents and sprang open.

They searched the house from top to bottom for several hours and found nothing. Finally, chilled to the bone and sullen, the special agents suggested it was time to leave.

This will be the end, she thought. Nothing more. It will be all over and I can forget the nightmare forever.

What will happen next? If he is really innocent, what would be wrong with marrying him? I am not cut out to be a perpetual celibate. I have to marry someone.

Then she thought of Daddy.

But Daddy won't live forever.

She recoiled in horror from her obscene treason. It's caught up with me finally. I need a long vacation.

"Let me look in the basement once more," she said apologetically. I must satisfy my conscience that I've done my best.

The basement somehow seemed too small for the rest of the dirty, creaking house. There ought to be more room behind the old and long-unused coal furnace. Squeezing behind, with little concern for the layers of dirt being absorbed by her slacks and sweatshirt, she found a door, elaborately wood-paneled, leading to a room that had been added to the basement before the furnace had been installed. A perfect hideout for an Outfit soldier on the run.

Some of the dust had been wiped off the door. It had been used recently. Sick with horror, she called the special agents.

Five minutes later, the four of them stared in astonishment at the open briefcase with its neatly wrapped stacks of tens and twenties.

"Congratulations, Miss Lyons," said the awed senior agent. "Do you want us to count it and record the serial numbers now?"

"Every last one of them," she said dully. "And get the cameras, too. Inside and outside pictures. The grand jury should enjoy the show."

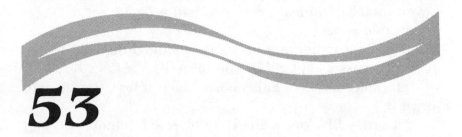

53

Blackie Ryan, wearing a Bears jacket now in honor of the re-surgent Monsters of the Midway, prowled around the car like an Irish countryman critically examining a heifer whose purchase he was contemplating. He rubbed the finish, wet with snow flurries, kicked the tires, opened and closed the door.

"Three-eighty SL, red convertible. Very dear. For the dynamic Diana, I gather."

"Who else? And I got a deal on it."

"That I take as a given." He lifted the hood, peered in and frowned. "Crowded."

"It didn't cost as much as your father's reconditioned gull-wing. Besides, next year its resale value will be at least five thousand dollars more than I paid for it."

"With the long leather raincoats thrown in. But then few creatures are as costly as the old fella's toys."

"You like it?"

"She does not know of its purchase yet." Blackie opened the trunk and nodded.

"Not exactly, no."

"Nor have we been properly introduced."

"Next Sunday, I promise."

"She has been given her seal of approval by the reb?"

"Naomi? Definitely. Naomi's pregnant, you know?"

"So I understand."

"You do?"

"I do."

The priest stood back from the car and squinted. "Only seven thousand miles. Truly you had a deal."

"I told you."

"Tell me something else." He jammed his cold hands into his Bears jacket. "Will she drive it?"

"I think so. With a guilty conscience at first, but she will drive it."

"Then"—Blackie sighed with relief—"there is still much reason to hope."

54

Two weeks later, on a cold Wednesday night in early December, she sat at an isolated table in Ricardo's—the plastic chic restaurant where all the "in" journalists in Chicago did their eating and drinking and back stabbing—with her contact at one of the Chicago papers. "I promised you the story," she had told him on the phone. "Now I'm ready to give it to you."

She felt like a permanent zombie, Diana III, drained of emotion, empty, psychologically and spiritually dead. After the first few hours of triumphant acceptance of congratulations from her colleagues—and an awkward and distasteful kiss from Don Roscoe—she felt only despair. What would happen now, would happen. It was in the hands of the Fates. Her father would be proud of her. She had dragged down one of the rich and famous. He deserved to be dragged down, he was a criminal. Crime does not pay, right? Not even if you're wealthy and sexually attractive and own a cute little blue boat named *Brigid*.

"I suppose Donny doesn't know you're here," the reporter said over their first martini.

"Of course not."

"He would be horrified, however, if he thought you were not spreading the story before it gets to the grand jury. Diligent Assistant United States Attorneys are expected these days to leak the news of indictments to the press."

"That's your inference."

"Well," he said, with twist of distaste to his lips like that of Judge Kane, "it's one way to do it: try a person in the court of public opinion before a grand jury indictment. Saves time and money that way. Who's the victim this time?"

"Con Clarke, haven't you guessed that?"

"I guessed it, but I couldn't believe it. You'd better have good stuff. He has a lot of friends."

"It's good all right, but he has a lot of enemies, too. If you're rich and famous, you're a fair target for destruction. Pull down the rich and famous and you win the cheers of the masses."

"That's pretty cynical."

"Come on, Henry." She drained her martini and signaled for another one, thinking that she might well be the Leo Martin of her generation. "We're both in the business of pandering to the masses. We go after the politicians, the gangsters, the celebrities, the influential—though not the too influential, no newspaper editors. Now we're going after the rich. People like us"—she was echoing Leo Martin in her faintly drunken condition—"survive on envy, feed off it, drink it like it was a Lake Michigan of dry martinis."

"You're right." Henry was watching her curiously, as if she was a visitor perhaps from another planet. "Most government lawyers aren't that candid."

"I'm in a mood for candor tonight. Now do you or don't you want the dirt on Con Clarke?"

"I want it. To use your terms, there couldn't be a better person just now to drag down into the mud. The public is tired of political scandals. So let's drink to one-to-five years at hard labor for Conor Clement Clarke."

She responded to his toast and downed half of her new martini.

"So what do you have on 'Playboy Con Clarke,' as our headline is sure to call him?"

"Would robbing the poor do?"

"Oh boy, would it!" He pulled a notebook out of the pocket of his Harris tweed jacket. "How is the playboy robbing the poor?"

"Would you believe stealing from his own company, which is supposed to be fighting unemployment?"

She told him the whole story, leaving out only the money found in the "secret hideaway," a "Mafia safe house." That would wait for more headlines. She described the case against Clarke, objectively and dispassionately, like a robot devoid of emotion.

"Wow!" Henry considered his notes. "Why the hell would a guy with all his money get involved with scumbags like Broddy Considine and Harry McClendon and small-timers like Johnny Corso and Mike Rodriguez? It doesn't make sense."

"Envy isn't the only cardinal sin."

"Pride, covetousness," Henry began to count them.

"Stop right there."

"Covetousness . . . avarice. In more simple language, greed. Our editorial writers will have a field day. Who will hear the case?"

"We don't know yet. Cases are assigned only after indictments are handed down. Off the record, Leo Martin has Donny lighting vigil lights that it is not Eileen Kane."

"The Big Bane will love that. I hear he shit in his pants the day she was appointed."

"Judge Kane is a distinguished jurist. We have nothing to fear from her."

"Yeah, sure. But if you draw her in the lottery and don't have a good case, she'll cut off Donny's balls. . . . You're not telling me everything, are you?" His shrewd little eyes—too close together around his big nose so that he looked like a bird, a crow perhaps—gleamed. "You wouldn't be going up against Eileen Kane and Con Clarke's fancy lawyers just with immunized and plea-bargained witnesses."

She was in no mood—and now, with her third martini glass almost empty, in no condition—to play games with him. "I'll give you the rest of the story the day the indictment is handed down."

"When will that be?"

"Just before Christmas, I think."

"Merry Christmas, Playboy Con Clarke, from the United States of America and Donald Bane Roscoe."

"And," she added, "from Diana Marie Lyons."

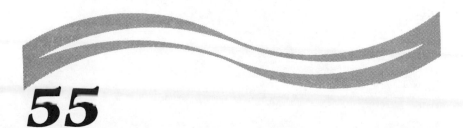

55

Two days later, Con Clarke emerged from the office of his travel agent on Oak Street, pockets stuffed with brochures about cruises to the Greek islands after Easter, warm honeymoon vacations. He would pile them up in the new house, into which he'd move after Christmas, next to the deed to the Mercedes and the insurance policy on his engagement ring.

Midnight Mass. It has to be, no matter how scared I am. Which am I more scared of, a "yes" or a "no?"

He considered. I want her to say "yes." That's official.

The early edition of the Chicago papers was already in

the boxes. Con leaned over, put a quarter in the slot, and saw his name on the front page.

PLAYBOY CLARKE TO BE INDICTED, the headline screamed.

CHARGED WITH THEFT FROM THE POOR, the trailer added helpfully.

Winter

Third Song

Beloved:

On my bed in the dark of night
I took off my gown for the one I love.
I prayed to God and the saints above
But he did not come, my life, my light.
So I sought him everywhere in town,
In alleys, streets, and decrepit bars.
Recklessly I begged the unfeeling guards,
"Tell me, my love where is he to be found?"
I lost all I had, freedom, hope, and fame,
Those who were my friends cruelly pulled me down.
I still wait for him, cold and harshly bound,
Stripped, humiliated, and ashamed.
I dream of him.

Lover:

In the silent, windless heat of day,
Wine sparkling in our goblets, you and me,
Two alone under the eucalyptus tree,
Still your lips, listen to what I must say.
While we recline in our aromatic bath,
And my teeth your taut nipples gently bite,
Let me sing, dearest, of your blazing light,
As my fingers roam your fertile garden paths:
Your lips are chocolate, dark for a feast,
Your mouth is as sweet as honey and milk,
Your unblemished skin the finest silk,
Your love-filled eyes sunrise shining in the east.
Your hair is as smooth as imported lace,
Your complexion like the rising moon,
Irish linen your flesh, and roses in bloom.
An artist's miracle your lovely face.
Your ivory throat, strong, supple, clean,
Your determined shoulders shapely and bare,
Invite me to a bed warmed by loving care,
A house of grace where I'll be free to dream.
And your flowing breasts, one prize in each hand,
Generous and rich, thick cream in my mouth—
I suckle and drain them, thirsty after drought.
Your hips sweet flowing hills round for my hand,

Your belly a peach sugared to my tongue.
Your flanks burnt cinnamon tart to my teeth,
Then a mountain forest, fragrant and neat,
Whose depths I'll explore before I'm done.

Beloved:

I am deprived of my sense, dear poet mine,
Swept away by the winds, the song in your voice.
Here are my poor favors, what is your choice?
I am your harvest, darling . . . reap me and dine!

Love Song, 3:6—5:1

56

I seem to have no feelings about the Clarke indictment, almost as thought it were not my case. I must prepare for the grand jury, but I seem to lack the energy. It will be a routine. I'm surprised that Clarke's lawyers are letting him appear. Apparently he is insisting. A lawyer who acts in his own case has a fool for a client. Unless they want to find out what we have on him before it explodes in the media. Do they think we won't leak it fifteen minutes after the grand jury goes home that night?

Daddy is beside himself with joy. He has shed fifteen years and says he has no more chest pains. He knows I can't discuss the case until the indictment is handed down. But that doesn't matter. He says that no matter what happens to him now, his life will continue in me. Mama is more restrained. She watches me curiously, like I am a customer she's evaluating. Does she recognize Con from the pictures in the paper?

It was only one purchase on an afternoon several months ago, but he does make an impression.

Daddy told her it was all right to buy a TV—so long as it was black-and-white—to watch the news about the case.

"It will be months, maybe longer, before it comes to trial, Daddy."

"Don't worry, Hon. I intend to hang on that long."

I wonder how long I will hang on. I am so cold. They say on the radio it may be the coldest December in history. I feel that way inside. I've won my first legal victory, made my reputation, I suppose. Or begun to make it anyway. I've brought back happiness to poor Daddy's life. I'm convinced that I'm right. I have no regrets.

Yet I am so cold.

In a few days I'll get over it, I suppose. When the indictment is handed down and I settle down and begin sleeping again at night.

No regrets at all.

57

"What did you do with the money, Con?" The seedy, bearded TV journalist, his breath smelling strongly of midday martini, shoved a microphone in front of his face. "Spend it on women? Which ones?"

"No comment." Con tried to keep his face an expressionless mask.

"Did you think you wouldn't get caught?" A young woman, hardly out of college, blocked his way into the building. "Did you think you were above the law?"

Con sidestepped her. "No comment."

"Are you ready to admit your guilt?" A young man with a faint Hispanic lilt to his voice.

Con pushed his way into the lobby. They flocked after him like a starving pack of wolves pursuing a faltering elk.

"Are you prepared to admit your guilt and go to prison?" The man with the gin smell shoved the mike over Con's shoulder.

Con turned and faced the cameras, paused to make sure they had him in the lenses, and said with his top Irish grin, "I am innocent and intend to prove it. Moreover, when I am finished with this case, Donald Bane Roscoe will be sorry he ever heard of me."

He smiled again and ducked into the elevator.

Con pretended to the world that he was detached, objective, in control, quiet but charming as ever. Inwardly he was seething, determined to fight back, to get even, to destroy his enemies. It was as if his father was alive and he was planning revenge against him. All the old rage had surged back from the dungeons of his personality where he had imprisoned it. Now it was a disciplined, harnessed rage—no longer master of the self, but it's servant.

Lee West, his lawyer, or rather the chief of a team of lawyers from Minor, Grey that would defend him, was considering the newspaper clippings. "Thought you were innocent until proven guilty, didn't you?" West, a Gregory Peck–handsome WASP lawyer from Boston, Choate, and Harvard law school, was reputed to be one of the five best, non-Outfit, criminal defense lawyers in Chicago. In the background, attempting to appear almost invisible—without much success—was the associate working with Lee on the case, a freckle-faced, red-haired firebrand named Patricia Anne Slattery. Oh boy, Con thought, when he saw the fires raging in her exuberant blue eyes, this is one of your bomb-throwing Irish revolutionaries. I'll have to get to know her better. I wonder if she'd drive a Mercedes 380 SL convertible?

"I feel like an inkblot. Look at this 'man on the street' poll in the *Trib*. How can these women be so sure that I'm a spoiled brat that ought to be spanked? Or that I've stolen a lot more money in my life and wasted it all on women?" He tossed the clippings on the other side of the Chippendale table that served West as a desk. "And the *Sun-Times* editorial talks about exploiting government tax breaks for personal gain like my guilt has already been proven. And the woman commentator on Channel 7 wonders whether the government would let me bring my harem of models to jail with me. Is any of this libel?"

"All fair comment." West shook his head gracefully—everything he did was graceful. "At least Walter Jacobson had the sense to wonder whether any jury of Cook County citizens in their right mind would believe Broddy Considine on a mountain of Bibles."

"The man is a pig." Naomi had been sitting silently on the couch, legs curled under her, like a hovering protective angel in a black pantsuit. "He should not be permitted to testify."

His two friends had insisted on being present for the first meeting with the lawyers.

"The whole intent, Dr. Silverman"—Lee bowed his head, courtier to a queen—"of this media offensive, is to preclude the need for anyone to testify. Conor has been pursued by reporters and TV crews for the last forty-eight hours. His friends have been harassed by phone calls, every Chicago columnist except Kup has taken a cheap shot at him. His name has been dragged through the mud as was the name of every woman who has ever associated with him, yourself included."

"I am honored," she spat back.

"In your case"—another courtly bow—"Con showed exceptional taste. But to continue . . ." Lee paused, his head thrown back for dramatic effect. For him, as for every good trial lawyer, all the world was a courtroom and all the people in it jurors. "Con has been tried, convicted, and sentenced without even an indictment being handed down. The purpose of this is, as I have indicated, to eliminate the necessity of a trial. The government of the United States has served notice that it is prepared to make his life miserable for the next two years and to cost him an enormous amount of money in fees for high-priced lawyers like myself. It will then ask, in due course, whether it would not be better to enter a guilty plea—"

"I'm not guilty," Con said coldly as he watched the snow pile up below on Jackson Boulevard, in front of the Board of Trade. Baghdad on Lasalle Street.

"I take that as given," Lee agreed, "because you have told me so, but that issue is almost moot. The United States Attorney for the Northern District of Illinois will at first propose to you a guilty plea on one of the lesser counts, perhaps no more than an admission that you should have kept a closer eye on Harry McClendon and Broderick Considine. In return for such a plea you would spend a few months in a federal country club with tennis courts."

"No way."

"I should hope not. Mr. Roscoe and his associates"—he glanced at his list—"Mr. Martin, Mr. Gollin, and Ms. Lyons . . ."

Con shook his head slightly at Naomi, whose face twisted in fury.

". . . will hope to bluff you into accepting this proposal—after the indictment and before arraignment. Failing that, and I take it that we agree that they will fail, they will try to make a quick deal on probation in the courtroom the morning of arraignment."

"Why will they do that?" Naomi wrinkled her pretty nose in distaste.

"Basically to avoid the cost, the work, and the dubious outcome of a long trial. They have a crew of immunized and plea-bargained witnesses, possibly a hostile judge, especially if my former partner Eileen Kane is assigned the case, and if I may say so, opposition attorneys with far more competence than they possess. If you can win with a deal, why risk a loss in a courtroom?"

"So," Ezekiel Silverman murmured. "Nazis."

"I'll fight them every inch of the way. And beat them."

Con stared grimly at the snowflakes. "And destroy them in the process. All of them."

Lee West rubbed his tongue quickly along his lip. "I must say, Conor, on the basis of the short time I've been involved in this sorry matter, you hardly fit the image of a playboy. More likely a gallowglass warrior."

"Playboy of the Western world." Con's grin was mirthless. "Let them think that. Roscoe will never be elected to public office if it takes every penny I have."

"Splendid sentiments. May I recommend, however, that you don't repeat them in public or in the presence of any but the most friendly witnesses for the present."

Con turned away from the window. The snow was so thick now that the gray building next door had disappeared. "Do you think they have any more evidence, Lee, anything we don't know about?"

"The office of the United States Attorney for the Northern District of Illinois leaks like a deliberately perforated sieve. They are claiming that they have some kind of smoking gun."

"More fraud."

"Probably. The point is that I can't imagine evidence of the sort that would lead to a conviction, especially not in a courtroom run with scrupulous respect for the legal processes. No promises, Conor, but if you persist in fighting this charge, I imagine you will win in the long run. A very long and expensive run, I might add."

"I have nothing else to do." Conor shrugged indifferently. "It might even be kind of fun."

"We will, of course, decline to appear before the grand jury," Pat Slattery said, speaking for the first time.

"No, we won't, Pretty Patricia." Con favored her with his best Irish smile. "We'll sail in with colors flying and guns blazing."

"You're a lawyer," she snapped. "You should know better than that."

Ah, why do I always draw the feisty ones?

"But as your colleague Mr. West said, this is a media battle more than a legal battle. If I refuse to confront the grand jury, the people of Chicago will promptly be told that I have something to hide. Won't they, Lee?"

"Of course, but you won't receive any points for testifying. I think Ms. Slattery is right."

"I'm sure she is. Still, I want to give the other side a hint of what they're up against."

West and Slattery nodded dubiously, not altogether sure that they knew what they were up against.

Ah, well, they'll learn in time. I shouldn't be enjoying this so much.

With infinite slowness, they returned in a taxi to the tiny Silverman apartment in Rogers Park where Naomi made him quiche for lunch, poured him some white wine, and chatted happily about her pregnancy.

"It is like your mother and father all over again, is it not, my dear?" she said finally.

"The so-and-so's died before I could tell them what I thought of the way they fucked up—'scuse me, Naomi—messed up my life. Now they're back again. And I'm going to get them."

"Mr. Roscoe and, uh, *la belle Diane?*"

"You got it."

"I understand, my dear." She helped him on with his overcoat. "Yet neither history nor biography repeat themselves exactly. Do not invest too much of yourself in revenge."

"Revenge?" He kissed her lightly. "Who me? Good old laid-back, happy-go-lucky playboy? Don't be silly, Nai. I just want to see them all rotting in hell!"

58

Con was a good witness, cool, self-possessed, crisp and calm in his answers. His hair had been cut short and he was wearing a conservative dark-blue suit. His idea or the lawyers'? He did not look like a playboy, but rather like a careful and responsible—and very successful—businessman. That would be the public image until the trial was over. Very clever. We are not facing a pack of fools on the other side.

Only his dull, hard eyes hinted at rage, a rage that scared Diana. Yet the exchange between them was terse, civil, restrained.

"Now, Mr. Clarke, your occupation as a, uh, venture capitalist does not require much work, does it? Is it not true that you only work three hours a day?"

"Office hours, that is correct."

"What sort of other hours are there?"

"Telephone hours. In the venture business, especially with computer hardware and software, that's often nine or ten hours a day—hunting for facts and information mostly."

"Leaving you hardly enough time to visit such minor projects as the Cokewood Foundry?"

"I did visit the foundry."

"How often?"

"Once or twice."

"Not very often, but then it wasn't a very large project in your portfolio—if that is the right term—of ventures. Do you consider one or two visits responsible behavior?"

"I visited Cokewood Springs many more times. Nine or ten, anyway. I didn't go into the foundry, however."

"And what did you do?"

"Talked with the workers—in bars mostly. That's the way you find out how the job is going. Even if they know you're the president of the company, they'll talk to you in bars."

"That's very interesting, but it is hardly an effective way of maintaining financial supervision, is it?"

"On the contrary, Counselor. If the job is on schedule, you can be pretty sure that there isn't much waste."

"I had forgotten, a mere million dollars in kickbacks isn't much waste in your scale of values, is it? Now, tell me, Mr. Clarke, you admit that you had lunch with Broderick Considine at Phil Schmid's on April 24, 1984?"

"I had lunch with him that day, yes."

"So you admit that you had lunch with Broderick Considine at Phil Schmid's on April 24, 1984?"

Diana felt that she had not projected a "ball-breaker" image to the grand jury, despite her headache and the pain in her stomach that twisted her body. The grand jury would surely indict him—that was the reason for its existence. So the four-hour-long interrogation was mostly ritual. It was also, however, a dress rehearsal for a trial that she devoutly hoped would never come.

"I don't think 'admit' is the proper word, Counselor." He smiled faintly, just enough to win sympathy with some of the women on the grand jury. "As far as I know, having lunch with a family friend at Phil Schmid's is not something to admit."

"You deny, however, that you received any money from him at that time?" She had made only a few mistakes. "Admit" was the wrong word. Still, he was winning. Oh, they'd indict him all right, but he had brilliantly dispelled the playboy image that the jurors had held in their imaginations only a few hours before. A practice round, but it was his.

"Yes, I do."

"You own a blueberry farm in southern Michigan, do you not, Mr. Clarke?"

His eyes flickered momentarily, surprised. Then they

widened. He had guessed what was coming. "Yes, I do."

"And is there an old house on the property that was once used by organized crime as a hideaway?"

"There's an old house, Counselor. I have no certain knowledge of its use prior to my ownership."

"Is this a picture of the house, Mr. Clarke?"

She flipped back the cover on the show-and-tell stand that stood at one end of the windowless room. The ventilation fans hummed as Con considered the picture.

"Yes, I believe it is."

"When was the last time you were in the house, Mr. Clarke?"

"I was a junior at Notre Dame, I think."

"For what purpose?"

"A beer party, but we were all of drinking age, Ms. Lyons."

Titter from the grand jury. Bastard.

"Not since then?"

He thought briefly. "Not that I can recall."

"Not shortly after your lunch with Mr. Considine?"

"No."

"Not the day of that lunch?"

"No."

"Mr. Clarke, do you recognize this briefcase?"

"I do not."

"Are you sure?"

He would not be tricked into losing his temper, but his hard eyes and his tight lips said he was furious. Too bad for him, he had it coming.

"Yes, I'm sure."

"Would it surprise you to learn that this briefcase was found in your house in southern Michigan by special agents of the Federal Bureau of Investigation?"

"I have no knowledge about that, Ms. Lyons."

She flipped the cover open with a dramatic gesture, showing it simultaneously to the grand jurors and to Conor.

The grand jury gasped. Con's face twitched briefly.

Gotcha, bastard. "Can you identify the contents, Mr. Clarke?"

"Rather easily," he said lightly, his cool restored. "They are legal tender of the United States of America."

"Two hundred thousand dollars, Mr. Clarke."

"You must have counted it."

The jury tittered again.

Damn him. Smooth Irish bastard. "Do you have any idea how this sum of money found its way into your house?"

"None."

"You didn't put it there, Mr. Clarke?"

"Certainly not."

"You are aware that it is exactly the sum of money that Mr. Considine alleges he gave you in Phil Schmid's?"

"Really? No, I was not aware of it. How could I be?"

Another point for him. He's cool and I'm flustered. We've changed roles.

"You deny that you hid this money in your house on the fringes of New Buffalo, Michigan?"

"I certainly do."

"How did it come to be there, Mr. Clarke?"

The jurors leaned forward expectantly. Con hesitated, choosing his words carefully. "I don't know, Ms. Lyons. It's a deserted house in the country. Almost anyone could have put it there."

"Mr. Clarke, is it not true that two days after your lunch with Mr. Considine at Phil Schmid's restaurant, you purchased a new yacht named"—she pretended to consult her notes—*The Brigid?*"

"Brigid," he said, "no article. She's blue with white trim."

"I stand corrected. How much did that yacht cost, Mr. Clarke?"

"Fully equipped? I suppose a little over two hundred thousand dollars. I couldn't have used that money in the briefcase to buy it, could I? Not if it had been in the briefcase since last April."

"Thank you, Mr. Clarke, that will be all."

He remained an extra moment or two in the witness chair. She would not get away with that ending in a courtroom. The defense would take up the point immediately on cross-examination. But this wasn't a trial, not yet.

"You're welcome, Ms. Lyons."

He turned his head so the jurors could not see him. He glared at her with an expression of absolute hatred. Diana, for the first time in the investigation, began to fear for herself. Who would have expected exuberant Con Clarke to be such a vehement hater?

That night, in a headline locked into type before the grand jury testimony, the *Tribune* announced PLAYBOY CLARKE'S MONEY HORDE FOUND BY FBI.

That should be that.

Merry Christmas, Con Clarke, from Donald Bane Roscoe.

And Diana Marie Lyons. And her father.

The next day the indictment was handed down. At the press conference, Donny Roscoe delivered a stirring oration. "This office will not tolerate corruption of any sort, especially when that corruption feeds on the misery of the unemployed. No one, no matter how wealthy, will be permitted to exploit the need of these hard-pressed people."

You could almost hear the applause of the political meeting Donny imagined himself addressing.

There was a one-sentence expression of gratitude for the work that Diana and Leo and Shelly had done. You would have thought that Donny was in the grand jury room every second.

The headlines said PLAYBOY CLARKE FINALLY INDICTED. A gentle stab at Donny Roscoe, she thought.

His hogging of the limelight made no difference to her. Nor did the congratulations of her colleagues, nor the ecstatic happiness of her father.

"This is the most joyous day of my life, since I married your mother. I am genuinely proud, finally, of one of my children!"

Mama's praise was perfunctory. Diana thought that she would be happy because Daddy was happy. Instead, she seemed to be regarding her daughter as if she was a not particularly appealing stranger.

Diana ate little supper, her appetite had failed her completely.

"You'll get it back," her father boomed, "now that the strain of this investigation is over."

"There's still the trial."

"He'll plea-bargain, won't he? I know the type—afraid to face a jury of his peers."

"I wonder," Diana said dully. "I wonder."

Having thoroughly drugged her emotions by something that she thought might be despair, Diana slept deeply that night. No dreams. Or nightmares.

None that she could remember.

59

"How did she find out about the house?" Lee West demanded.

Already Pat Slattery had a crush on him, a fierce, protective, maternal crush. Con warned himself that he wanted no part, just then, of attractive young women lawyers.

"Oh, I know that," he replied to Lee's question. "I told her."

"You what?" Lee exclaimed. "When? Where?"

"In November. I can find the exact date if it matters. As to the place . . . well, would you believe in the whirlpool in the East Bank Club?" He reflected briefly, then added, "She beat me at squash just before."

"You were . . . associating with her socially?" Lee looked incredulous.

"You might say that. At the risk of sounding adolescent, we were dating."

"How long?" Pat Slattery exploded with ancient anger of outraged Irish womankind, bad enough when they were angry at their men, but far worse when they were angry at those who were persecuting their men.

"Since August."

"Were you, ah, well . . ." Lee West had lost his way on the desert between propriety and curiosity.

"No, I was not spending my nights with her. Tell you the truth, I think I could have on any number of occasions."

"Why didn't you tell me?" It was worth it to see Lee West lose his patrician cool. "Does Roscoe know?"

"As to the first"—I should be enjoying this scene, but I'm not—"I figured it would come out anyway. As to the second, I assume so."

"He can't," Pat Slattery shouted. De Paul law school. Not a Blue Demon but a red one. So much the better. "He'd kill her."

"What my, mmm, passionate young colleague is suggesting"—Lee was struggling to regain his cool—"is that Donny would be humiliated out of public life if it developed that one of his assistants was using sex to entrap a suspect. Judge Kane, who, thank God, has been assigned the case, would dismiss the charges and probably cite both of them to the bar association."

"We didn't sleep in my apartment. I thought I made that clear."

Lee ran his hand through his perfectly cut hair. "Since it's you, my dear Con, I believe it. But virtually no one else will. Can you prove it?" He actually blushed. "I mean can you prove that you were dating?"

"There are certainly people who saw us together."

"We will get affidavits from them, go to Roscoe with the affidavits, and that will be the last you ever hear of the indictment. It will be dropped for lack of evidence."

"That's not exoneration."

"It's better than a two-year struggle."

"Maybe."

"Why would she do it?" pretty Patricia, the pure-hearted purple demon, demanded.

"Maybe they wired her and intend to claim that she was an agent. Don't overlook that possibility, Lee." Con winked, enjoying himself again. "And even if they didn't, they can always claim that. Right?"

Lee jammed his hands in his pocket and paced back and forth rapidly, not the cool WASP insider anymore. "Donny and that grinning psychopath Leo Martin might do anything, no matter how kinky. They overreach, Conor. They overreach. This time they've gone too far."

"Precisely. If this comes out, they wouldn't look good in the media, but alas, neither would I."

"Ambitious, inexperienced kid fresh out of law school," said Pat—not so long ago, Con was sure, Patty Anne—who was also an ambitious, inexperienced kid fresh out of law school. "Figures she would fuck her way to the top. Probably she thought we'd plea-bargain, but what a terrible chance to take."

"As it turned out, she found some interesting evidence." Lee West took control of the conversation away from his youthful colleagues. "However, the question for you, Conor my friend, is whether we choose to fight this issue. We don't have to decide now and we don't have to fight it now, but I assure you it is the ace up our sleeve of which the other side must be terrified."

"Do you want to spend fifteen years in jail because you're a gentleman?" Pat thundered.

Ah, the Irish genes run true, don't they?

"If it comes to that, Patty Anne, no, though I might change my mind if you promised to visit me every month. But will it come to that?"

Lee threw up his hands. "I don't know. Trials are unpredictable. I doubt it, to be candid. Anyone, as you so ably suggested to the grand jury, could have planted that money, including the rather vicious Ms. Lyons."

"So we use it if we have to?"

"She's not worth protecting," Pat protested hotly.

"Probably not, Patty Anne. I propose to deal with her myself in my own way." He permitted himself a faint grin. "Maybe I don't want to admit that I was so completely taken in. Anyway"—he realized that his voice had become ominous—"I can think of a lot of ways to win this case. Fire against fire, if need be."

There was dead silence in the office. Maybe I've overdone it, Con thought. They're not altogether sure about me. First I insist on confronting a grand jury, then I protect a scheming bitch. Then I make threats. They suspect I may be a handful. Well, finally, for the first time in my life, I am.

"Let me propose a compromise for the present," Lee said cautiously. "Let us collect, through private investigators, the affidavits we will need—while it is easy to do so. We can hold them in reserve."

"Fine." Then he repeated his threat. "There are lots of ways of winning and doing them in, too, without revealing my, uh, romance with Diana Marie Lyons."

The two lawyers stared at him strangely, frightened by the plans lurking in his head.

In fact, he didn't have the faintest idea of what he might do. Not yet. But we would get them all, by hook or by crook.

60

That night, in his apartment, a fire blazing cheerfully in the fireplace, Anton Bruckner agonizing on the compact-disc player, and a bottle of Bailey's Irish Cream open next to him, Con Clarke finally worked up enough nerve to pull himself up from the depths of his easy chair and walk uneasily to the Early American secretary where he stored a few memories from a past that didn't have many memories worth treasuring. He removed a key from one tiny drawer and opened an even tinier locked drawer on the other side, one that was designed to hold envelopes so small that they were not made anymore. Envelopes for love letters probably. He removed the little square blue box that had the drawer all to itself and flipped it open.

A now useless diamond-encircled ruby. He tossed it into a waste basket in disgust. Twenty-five thousand dollars wasted, not twenty-two thousand five hundred. What difference did money make? His legal fees would be many times that before this mess was cleared away. Sell the Mercedes and the Astor Street house with the pool in the basement.

He returned to his poem, poured himself another Bailey's and pondered.

Then he rose from the chair again, fished through the waste basket, removed the ring box and returned it to its hiding place.

Never can tell when you'll need an engagement ring.

61

"You understand, gentlemen," Donny was using his press conference voice again, "that this meeting is not occurring at my instigation and that my office is not committed to any solutions that may be discussed at this meeting. Is that understood?"

"I think it is, Donny." Leo Martin did not treat his boss with any more respect in the presence of adversaries than at staff conferences.

"Quite," said Lee West smoothly.

It might be understood, but it wasn't true, thought Diana, sick now with a lingering cold. This "informal and unofficial" conversation was the first scene in a scenario that was supposed to lead to a plea bargain. In fact, Donny wanted the conference. He would be angry if his staff failed to arrange it. Yet he had to pretend for his own self-image that a worried defendant had begged for it.

"We have a very strong case against your client, Mr. West," he continued. "This sort of crime is particularly offensive to me personally. I believe that such violations should be punished to the fullest extent of the law."

Lee West had not been eager for the conversation. Leo had to almost beg him to come. Con and his attorneys, including that cute little red-haired bitch with the blazing eyes, were hanging very tough.

And Con himself, clearly under stern wraps from his counsel, looked as menacing as a silent Viking pirate, ready at a moment's hint to pull out his sword and run them all through. Or to produce a battle axe and bash in all their heads. Diana thought he was terrifying. Even Leo was uneasy in the face of that deadly blond presence.

Yet Diana knew him well enough to know that he was enjoying the fight. A Viking warrior with powerful battle lust who delighted in the sound and smoke, the blood and violence of battle. Who would have expected that?

"This is a case in which a sentence of fifteen years to life would not be inappropriate. There are, after all, nineteen counts of fraud and conspiracy to commit fraud in the document the grand jury handed down."

"That means at least ten years in prison, probably maximum security, hard labor most of the time," poor Shelly chimed in on cue.

Con turned to at look at Shelly as though he had noticed him for the first time. "I did pass the bar exam, Mr. Gollin," he said, his voice as icy as his eyes. "The first time."

A dig at Shelly, whose great dirty secret was that, boy genius or not, he'd had to take it twice.

Donny went on with his oration. "However, if there were some sign of, ah, early rehabilitation and genuine, ah, compunction and regret, we might be able to agree on something much less stringent, providing Judge Kane would accept such an arrangement, something we cannot guarantee."

"I can imagine Judge Kane imposing a harsher sentence," the red-haired bitch cut in derisively, "than one you recommend."

She was right, but it broke Donny's rules to say it. West smiled faintly. Embarrassed a little by his resident alley fighter, but probably glad she had said it.

Donny went on with his script as though he had not heard her, and he probably hadn't. "I must insist that some time be served in prison. That is essential, if only so that the young people of this district will be taught that even the wealthy must go to prison if they break the law. But the term need not be long, if everything else is proper—oh, say, no more than two years, including time off for good behavior."

There was a long pause. Then Con spoke. "Geez, Lee,

I've never been known for my good behavior."

"It's your decision, Conor." Lee smiled faintly, a man who had heard a joke at a wake.

Conor rose and bowed to the staff of the United States Attorney. His words were pleasant, his manner polite, his tone respectful, only the hardness of his eyes, whose cold color reminded Diana of pictures of Glacier Bay she'd seen in National Geographic, hinted at his fury and contempt and delight. "You good people have a lot of work to do, protecting the United States of America from malefactors of one kind and another." Diana quickly glanced around the room. Donny, Leo, and Shelly looked as if they felt as threatened as she felt by his arctic calm. "Mr. West, Ms. Slattery, and I will not detain you any longer from your responsibilities. We appreciate the time you've given us. I sincerely hope you all have a very happy Christmas."

West and Slattery rose obediently to their feet.

"Our proposal?" Donny sputtered from behind his massive desk.

Con opened the door and bowed his lawyers out. Then he turned to Donny and spoke so softly that he could barely be heard.

"I'm afraid you have a fight on your hands, Mr. Roscoe, to the bitter end. And a happy new year, too."

"Same guy you played golf with, Diana?" Leo asked ironically.

"Not at all. I was not afraid of him. This man terrifies me."

"We have a tiger by the tail, Donny." Leo sighed. "He'll fight us every inch of the way."

"Class act," Shelly breathed softly. "A real class act."

"I don't understand." A violation of one of his scenarios always disturbed Donny. "What does he have to gain?"

"Our scalps," Shelly said grimly, "for starters."

62

"You will spend Christmas day at a Hassidic Yule dinner?" Monsignor Ryan poured out a healthy shot of Jameson's Twelve-Year Special Reserve ("twenty years old now and very dear"), considered the level in his Waterford tumbler, and then added a tad more. It was after the Cathedral's midnight Mass, which the choir and Cardinal Cronin had celebrated with polyphonic exuberance. Con had encountered Blackie Ryan in back of the Cathedral, shaking hands and wishing "Merry Christmas" to his parishioners, as if he wasn't really sure that it was Christmas or this was his parish.

"Cheery midwinter festival, Conor"—he shook hands warmly—"or to a poet of the erotic, should I say, 'fertile saturnalia'? Come back to my room for a touch of Christmas cheer, lest the cold overcome you."

Now, wearing bedroom slippers and his Chicago Bears jacket, the priest in characteristically convoluted fashion was preparing to tell Con that he was concerned about him.

Monsignor Ryan's room had an air of cultivated eccentricity—rolltop desks, decrepit book cases, piles of magazines, newspapers, and books, a certain refined mustiness that suggested, deliberately, a character from Charles Dickens. On one wall were three vast posters—"the three Johns of my adolescence." When he was first led into the inner sanctum, Con observed that he knew John Unitas from the old films but who were the other two guys?

Blackie grinned like a hurt little leprechaun. "For many years I have been hoping someone would say that. Most of your generation know the President and the Pope, but would not appreciate that Unitas was the best two-minute-warning quarterback ever to cheat our hapless Bears out of certain victory." He sighed for the lack of respect of the younger generation. Next to the famed Baltimore Colt was the late-medieval Madonna. Con considered it carefully. Probably original and of extraordinary warmth and beauty, a very saucy Madonna with an even more saucy babe.

"Herself"—Father Blackie nodded at the sculpture—"was a gift of my father, Ned Ryan, when I was ordained. He thought she looked like my late mother."

Con wondered what Christmas would be like with the Ryan clan. "Zeke says that Baal Shem Tov believed in all celebrations."

"Doubtless. Well, in the words of Hilaire Belloc"—he handed Con the tumbler, picked up his own, and raised it in a toast—'Noel, noel . . .' "

" 'May all my enemies be damned to hell . . .' " Con continued the Carol from *Cautionary Verses.*

" 'Noel, noel,' " Blackie finished the chorus with his noisy West of Ireland sigh which had been described as sounding like the advent of a serious asthma attack. "It is surely generous of them to celebrate the winter solstice—however the various religions of Adonai Yahweh may name it. Light does come back. Eventually."

"They are good friends."

"Indeed. You plan to venture to San Francisco to see our stalwarts battle the vile 'Niners in search of a chance to play Miami at Leland Stanford Junior Memorial University for the Super Prize?"

"They don't have a prayer without Jim McMahon. I had planned to fly out there for the game, but I'm being arraigned the day before. Wouldn't look right, I suppose."

"Not guilty?"

"You'd better believe it. There will be guilty people in that courtroom, but I'm going to beat them eventually and then they'll have to face a judge."

"So, you are confident of victory in the struggle with the United States Attorney, the worthy, not to say inestimable, Donald Bane Roscoe."

"We'll cream them, Father Blackie, and then I'm going to destroy the whole lot of them."

"The whole Everett McKinley Dirksen Federal Building?" He rolled his nearsighted eyes. "A mighty task. Doubtless it would save our financially strapped republic considerable sums of money."

"No, just the team that framed me, Roscoe and Lyons in particular. When I'm finished with them, they'll never practice law again. Roscoe will not dare run for public office and Lyons won't even be able to hold a job in this city."

The priest considered him through the rainbow reflections of his crystal tumbler. "Ah. I believe you fully intend to do just that. Perhaps you haven't quite figured out how yet."

"I'll stop at nothing."

The little priest pondered silently. "I have no doubt—and enjoy the process, at that."

"I'll clear my reputation first."

"Then you do the learned Donny and the fair Diana in, more or less permanently."

"Got it."

"It is most considerate of you. God will surely be pleased."

"Huh?"

"Well, you will spare Him the need to exact His own repayment. She is very busy these days, what with the administrations in Washington and Rome, and will doubtless be happy that you have done some of Her work for Her."

"Revenge is mine, I will repay?"

"I think that's the way it is written."

"Someone has to strike a death blow to this whole immunity/plea-bargain strategy."

"Indeed. You assume that the fair Diana is the one who planted the money?"

"Who else? . . . I was going to give her the ring tonight, Father."

"Treason, bred in envy, a most unattractive response to love."

"I don't know. . . ." He didn't want to talk about Diana. "There are two ways we could end it next week. . . . Maybe I should forget about it all, let someone else take on Roscoe."

"Ah?"

"I could do a plea bargain, which would mean no jail and the case could drop out of the papers."

"Or?"

"I could release the story about Diana spying on me."

"And that would clear your name better than a plea bargain?"

"Maybe. You can't tell how it would play. Make me look like an idiot with women." He felt himself grin; he didn't do that much anymore. "Not that it's any great secret. It would not be a satisfying way to win."

"In addition, it would humiliate, quite possibly destroy Diana?"

"That wouldn't bother me. No, it would. I want to destroy her myself."

"And not be smeared in the process?"

"You got it, Father Blackie." He felt himself grinning happily. "I want to win and win big and win with class."

"Like the inestimable Bill Walsh and Joe Montana?"

"Why not?

"Why not, indeed, but are you, nonetheless, strongly considering the two options you have mentioned?"

"Sometimes. There's a lot of strategies available, none of which would absolutely guarantee that I won't have to go to jail for a crime I didn't commit."

"Enough to make a man insecure in the face of all the paranoids who roam the world. And worse luck for you, you are not completely cured of your infatuation for the fair Diana. Or should I call her the dark Diana?"

"I hate her guts."

"Doubtless, but it does not follow—"

"OK. There are times when, yes, I still love her. It's absurd, but I guess love is absurd."

"Indeed yes." He had sipped halfway through his Jameson's and was considering the tumbler carefully, as though he suspected that somehow the consumed liquid had been stolen away by magic. "It is most intelligent of you to recognize that, and the new model Conor Clement Clarke—a 560 SL, if you permit me the analogy—is intelligent as well as self-possessed and determined. Love is not a pretty dynamism, despite the St. Valentine's Day lace. It is rather a messy, violent, implacable, not infrequently destructive impulse toward union. We would not have dared, if we had not been so instructed, to predicate it of God."

"It was infatuation, nothing more. I'll get over it in time."

"More likely obsession." The priest replenished Con's glass. "If one is to judge by the haunted young woman one sees on the TV screen, she is the kind that attracts obsession. And I'm not so sure you'll get over her."

"Depend on it, Father Blackie, I'm going to do her in."

"Which, you may depend on it, Conor Clement Clarke, will solve nothing. You have not moved into the new house?"

"No, I'll probably put it back on the market."

"Ah, but surely you have resold—I take it for granted, at a profit—the red Mercedes?"

"No, not yet."

"I will not even ask about the ring, which doubtless will pass this Christmas in the jeweler's safe."

"I still have it."

Blackie leaned back in his enormous easy chair and sighed.

"You must think I'm a terrible fool, Father Blackie."

"Perhaps." The little priest raised his Waterford tumbler in salute. "It would be an arguable position. Though others might submit that, as a shrewd investor, speculator, and now venturer, you are not the kind of man to sell short on a promising future commodity."

63

Christmas Day.

We have never made too much of Christmas. Daddy thinks the commercialization is disgusting. Why give gifts when we are already gifts to one another? And he loathes midnight Mass—pagan festival, he calls it, religion and drunkenness combined.

I think this bothers Mama a lot. The Italians, especially the Sicilians, she told me once, love Christmas.

This year she broke the rules and gave me a present, a lovely green knit suit that fits perfectly and makes me look festive even if I don't feel it.

Daddy was upset with the present. "Much too expensive display for simple people like us."

Mama laughed. "It cost practically nothing. I bought it with a big discount."

"It nonetheless looks expensive. Well, I suppose with her big victory our daughter is entitled to a new dress."

I was astonished at the gift. Mama has hardly said a word to me since the first news story. She just stares at me kind of strangely. I wonder what she is thinking. I wonder if there is a special message in the bright green color of the dress.

I usually go over to Maryjane's on Christmas afternoon. This year I was disinvited rather dramatically. "And I go to the detective, 'You bet your life I will testify that they were dating each other. They were even godparents for little Geraldine, poor child.' And he goes, 'That will be very useful information, Mrs. Delaney.' You're like a total geek, Diana. I never want to see you again."

She was sobbing when she hung up. There's nothing wrong with the child, other than that her godmother is a geek. A corrupt geek at that.

So Conor has the detectives out collecting evidence against me. I am truly afraid of him.

Otherwise, at this Christmastime, I feel vile and corrupt. The indictment is proper. He is a cheap little criminal who belongs in jail. But my hardball, functional justice is equally cheap. He may be a vile man. I am a vile woman. I seem to be buried in my own filth, out of which I can never climb.

It all happened so quickly. If only I had not permitted Maryjane to set up that golf match. That's when my character began to disintegrate.

I was so proud of my character. I might not have much fun or many suitors. But at least I had character.

Or so I thought.

And all the time it was held together with paper clips, bent, used paper clips like those in Daddy's study.

64

"I certainly appreciate the Jewish Christmas party." Con looked from one to the other of his friends. "It's warmed both the body and the heart."

The Silvermans' tiny dining room, dark with old family furniture and the thick drapes that helped to drown out the roar of the el train by the kitchen window, was illumined in a misty glow of a single large red candle.

"So why is it strange? Do we not celebrate today the birthday of someone who, whatever else he may be, was one of my most distinguished rabbinic colleagues?"

"I guess. Sometimes, Zeke, I suspect that you think it's the same religion."

"Shush." He looked around in mock caution, like an Interpol agent with a trusted source. "Never quote me on the matter, Conor, but it is—temporarily and unfortunately separated into two branches that, please God, will sometime unite."

"Then you might be the Rector of the Cathedral?"

"And Father Blackie the chief rabbi."

"And we could then join all the country clubs!" Naomi laughed brightly, her eyes glowing with happiness and port.

"As the blessed and holy rabbi, Nahum of Detroit, has said so well"—Zeke Silverman raised his glass in a salute not unlike Father Blackie's earlier in the day—'Adversity does some people a world of good.' "

"Nahum of Detroit!" Hand on the appealing little bulge in her stomach, Naomi filled their port glasses again. Not Mogen-David either. "Ezekiel, you've associated with this goy too long."

"But does our friend not look better than ever despite the unjust persecution?"

"What can I tell you?" She returned very carefully, as though protecting the child's sleep, to her couch. "Our friend has found at last a cause into which he can direct his rage. A most useful and functional adjustment, in the short run."

"Short run, Doctor?" Con tilted his head to one side as though dialoguing with a bright junior colleague.

"Surely. You are now very mature and disciplined, my dear. And hence very appealing and attractive. And also just a bit frightening." She shivered ever so slightly. "You will win, I think, but I do not know whether this present adjustment will be functional over the long run, and the trial, should it occur, will be in the long run."

"I'll run out of steam?" He finished his port and resolved that he would not attempt another.

"Oh, surely that. And find that revenge is only transiently sweet. And worse still, I fear that in your present Irish ... what is the word from your heritage? Wild Geese ... *configuration*, you may do something reckless, dangerous, and possibly self-destructive."

"I'll stop at nothing"—Con's fingers tightened around the Waterford cordial glass, his holiday present to the Silvermans—"to reclaim my reputation and defeat those people."

"And then when the old Conor returns, more chastened doubtless and more adult, what compunction might you feel? You should ask yourself, my dear, before you rush into anything foolish, whether you will be able to live with that twenty-five years from now."

"I'll remember that advice, Naomi," he promised. "But it would prevent me from doing what has to be done."

"Ought not our friend be angry at that poor woman?" Zeke whispered.

"Our friend should be very angry at her. She betrayed him unspeakably. But what comes after anger?"

"She hasn't yet thrown the thirty pieces of silver on the floor of the temple treasury." Con stood up to leave, every muscle in his body tight with disciplined anger. Fight her, don't waste energy in hating her.

"The poor woman"—Naomi sighed almost as loud as Father Blackie—"didn't even get thirty pieces of silver."

65

"Very well, Mr. Roscoe." Judge Kane sighed audibly. "I will grant you time for a private consultation, but in the court-room, not in my chambers."

Her facial expression indicated that she did not want to have to fumigate her chambers.

Diana watched the proceedings in Judge Kane's court as though she were a detached spectator, one of the report-ers who had jammed into it for the formal charges against Playboy Con Clarke.

Johnny Corso and Pete Kline had pleaded guilty to one count of conspiracy to commit fraud. Broddy Considine would be arraigned at another time, once they decided which of the scores of charges against him would look least incompatible with probation. Judge Kane had regarded the whole proceeding with a dyspeptic visage which could have meant, under other circumstances, that she was pregnant again and suffering from morning sickness.

Donny Roscoe had asked for a few moments' delay be-fore the arraignment of Conor Clarke and then scurried across the courtroom with Leo Martin to huddle in final con-versation with Con and his lawyers.

"The Bane can't believe that they won't accept proba-tion and end all the nonsense," Shelly, next to Diana, behind the government prosecutor's table, whispered.

She nodded. "We underestimated him."

"Face it, Diana, the man has class. You watch: six, nine months from now, you or I will be back in this courtroom with a quiet motion to dismiss charges. No way those two guys will risk a trial against him."

"He won't let us out of it quietly, Shel."

The stern-faced, unnaturally calm defendant, wearing a conservative dark brown suit, his hair cut even shorter, was not the same boisterous, charming young man with whom she'd played golf at Long Beach Country Club four months ago.

He has matured while I have deteriorated, she had written in her diary the night before. *I'll always love him.*

Her father continued to be almost intolerably happy, so pleased with her that he had raised no objection when she bought a small color television so that she could watch the media commentary on the case.

"The color is important, Daddy, to assess the psychological environment of what is happening."

"It seems like an unnecessary expense, but I suppose the bright young lawyer knows best, eh, Maria?"

Why is she Maria at home and Anna Maria at work? More chic, I suppose, Diana mused as she smuggled the small black-and-white set into her mother's tiny "sewing room," once Paola and Eugenia's bedroom. Her mother acknowledged the present with a tiny smile and a nod of her head, but she was still silent and withdrawn. *The woman is a stranger to me. Why have I never looked at her before as anything but Mama? Who is she?*

How precarious Dad's happiness was. If Con refused to accept Donny's last plea-bargain offer, her secret would almost certainly be revealed.

Maryjane Delaney had phoned her last night to excoriate her once more for betraying Con.

"I go to the detective that it's a gross-out. It was your idea not mine to set up the golf game," she had shouted. "They ought to put you in jail, not Con."

So, she had thought, as a matter of abstract and theoretical interest, *he is not such a romantic as to go to jail to protect my honor.*

Why did I do it? she had asked herself often in the last two weeks. *Why did I take such chances to convict him that* the conviction now becomes impossible?

Somehow it seemed that after that fateful golf game she had no choices, that she'd been locked into a grim fate that had predetermined this courtroom scene and everything else that would come after. She hated Con Clarke more than ever; he was a rich man's son who had exploited the poor. He belonged in jail. Moreover, he had destroyed her life. She was one more of his victims, though God knows a willing victim.

I would still like to go to bed with him. Will I ever escape from this obsession? she had asked her diary. *Or will I be that man's prisoner the rest of my life?*

Roscoe seemed to be doing all the talking. Lee West nodded occasionally. The Slattery bitch seemed barely able to control her rage. Is he sleeping with her already?

Con did not appear to be paying any attention. The press was buzzing expectantly. There was a deal in the works. They would pretend to be outraged and give Donny a hard time at the press conference. He would mouth his usual line that his office was interested in punishing and preventing crime and not providing public entertainment.

God, she hated Donny Roscoe. Almost as much as she hated Con Clarke. And, truth to tell, herself.

"Are you ready for the charge, Mr. United States Attorney?" Judge Kane's green eyes flashed dangerously. "The gentlepersons of the press have deadlines to meet."

Donny flushed. Even he was not insensitive to Judge Kane's contempt, and he had already felt the hot fire of her wit several times, a hint of what a trial might bring. "One more moment, Your Honor."

She glanced at her watch. "Very well. Just one."

The lawyers all turned to Con Clarke, expecting an answer. He looked bemused, as though he was not altogether sure of the question. West whispered in his ear.

Con raised his right hand and, so all the reporters could see, turned his thumb dramatically down. A wave of laughter swept the courtroom. Even Judge Kane smiled. Roscoe

strode back to his side of the court, his face purple with humiliation and anger. "We will not give him another chance,
Leo," he said to Leo Martin, as though the final discussion
had been Leo's idea instead of his own. "We'll go for the
maximum sentence. Understand, Miss Lion? Mr. Golden?"

"Yes sir," they responded dutifully.

The charge was read, a ridiculous nineteen counts of
fraud and conspiracy to commit fraud that she herself had
written.

"How do you plead, Mr. Clarke?"

Con turned on all of his charm in a warm smile for
Judge Kane. "Not guilty to all of them, Your Honor."

So it was done. There were preliminary motions, legal
scrimmaging in which the lawyers from Minor, Grey demonstrated that they could maneuver rings around even Leo
Martin. Next came a press conference during which Donny
blustered that there had never been a suggestion of plea
bargaining and that the conversation before arraignment
had been at the request of Mr. Clarke's attorneys. The reporters didn't believe him.

Con had an expressionless "No comment" for the reporters and the cameras as he left the courtroom. The stern
face was replaced at the very last second, so the cameras
would have to catch it, with a wide grin—not a playboy's
grin of pleasure, but a happy warrior's grin of victory.

Later Diana boarded an elevator by herself to ride to the
lobby for a whiff of fresh air. The only other person on the
elevator was Con Clarke. For a few seconds she thought that
she had begun to hallucinate. What was he doing in the
Dirksen Building so long after he had left the courtroom?

Then, with a shrug of her shoulders, she walked in and
let the door close behind her. She had as much right to be on
an elevator in the federal building as he did.

He gave no sign that he recognized her, or that he was
aware that anyone else was in the elevator with him. She ignored him in return for a few moments of eternity as the car
plummeted to the lobby.

"No witnesses now, eh, Counselor? Just the two of us before God's great judgment seat?"

"Trust you to quote a cliché from Kipling," she said briskly.

"As good with the riposte as ever, huh, Diana Marie Lyons? Well, let's see you respond to this. I'm going to destroy you."

Terrified, she involuntarily cowered against the wall.

"Destroy?" she stammered.

"When I'm finished with you, you'll never practice law again or work at any job in this city. I will drive you out of Chicago forever. I promise you that, if it takes every penny I have and every day for the rest of my life. When I'm finished with you, you'll regret that you were ever born. The door is open, Counselor. After you."

He strode through the high, glass and steel lobby of the Dirksen Building, oblivious of the people who, recognizing him from TV, turned to watch him—a grim-faced avenger who had given fair warning.

We could have just as easily fallen into each other's arms.

66

The small-time mobster had whispered in Con's ear while he was standing on Monroe Street admiring the Christmas lights around the Chagall mosaic in the First National Plaza.

"It's going to be all right, Mr. Clarke," he rasped. "Everything's been taken care of. No problem."

Con and Patty Anne Slattery had eaten supper at the Italian Village on Monroe Street. It was not exactly a date and not exactly business, either. He had met her coming out

of the Minor, Grey offices and rode down on the elevator
with her. She had shyly accepted his shy proposal of a "good
Italian meal with no strings attached."

"There's always strings attached," she murmured as
they walked out into the bitter cold, "when there is a man
and a woman."

"Not in weather like this." He linked his arm with hers.
"No way."

Patty was a delightful dinner companion, more than capable of carrying a light conversation entirely by herself. In
fact, it would have been hard for Conor to get a word into the
monologue about her adventures in the legal profession.

"You should write your memoirs, Patty Anne," he interrupted once. "They'd destroy most of Chicago's law firms."

"Only after I'm a partner.... Now, did I ever tell you
about the time when this drunken judge—'course I never
told you—came into the women's room at the federal court-
house and ..."

What went on under the roaring red hair? What did
pretty Patty want out of life? Besides being a partner?

It was not the night to ask. He contented himself with
some mild fantasies about what Patty Anne might be like under her thick Aran Isle sweater. His daydreams lacked persistence and erotic fascination. In principle, a naked Patty
Anne would be an interesting matter. In practice, however,
Conor's sexual energies were spent, his hormone system in-
active.

Ah, sure, they've killed the last playboy of the Western
world.

"Look at that," she said when, filled with pasta and
wine, they emerged from the Village. "Isn't that a picture of
something you'd only expect to see in heaven?"

"What? ... Oh, the Chagall ... yes, it is lovely ... colors
and lights and snow, like a delicate sixteenth century miniature."

"The most beautiful scene in Chicago at Christmas."

"Do you expect to get to heaven, Patty Anne?"

"What?"

Before the discussion could turn serious, the little man in a shabby overcoat and a fur hat sidled up to him and spoke to him in a grating stage whisper.

"Oh?" Conor knew from past experience that when you deal with such people, you let them speak in their own language and respond in like fashion.

"Right," the punk continued. "In a couple of days, everything will be copacetic. OK?"

"If you say so."

"I won't never forget what you did for my family when I was in Joliet, Mr. Clarke, never."

The little man faded away into the cold night air.

"What was that all about?" Patty Anne sounded frightened and suspicious.

"Damned if I know."

"Who is he?"

Conor took her arm and walked briskly away from the Chagall plaza.

"A small-time punk who use to hang around my father. Harmless old man. Always down on his luck."

"Outfit?"

"Extreme fringes. Like I say, harmless. Probably making stuff up so he can feel important."

But any magic that there might have been that night between himself and Patty Anne had been destroyed. She did not, he was convinced, altogether trust him.

Wise woman.

67

Blackie Ryan sat up with a start. Aha! So that was the way it was supposed to go down.

Stupid of him not to have thought of it.

Thought of what? he inquired of the medieval Madonna.

He had been engaged in the devout clerical piety of reading the ancient fathers of the Church.

An exercise that, to the rest of the world, would have looked like sleeping in his chair.

He was entitled to that, he had argued with the Madonna. Had he not spent much of the night working to make sure that the Cathedral's ancient heating system would function well enough so that the grammar school and the high school might open on Monday morning?

Had not such activity on Super Sunday, which was also the coldest day in Chicago's history—coldest recorded day he always added to the Cathedral associates—earned him the right to a few minutes' rest for his eyes?

Admittedly his associates had complained that he knew nothing about boilers and was only in their way. Admittedly, the Cardinal, a veteran of frozen boilers from his days as a curate in an inner-city parish, finally got the system working again. Admittedly, the Rector would never hear the end of this latest cardinalatial achievement.

What was I thinking just before I woke up? he asked the Madonna. It was the Clarke matter, and I was saying to myself that if one looked at it from this alternative perspective, it became clear. . . .

Certainly. But then why did he awaken with a sense of urgency. What might happen?

Then he saw what would happen.

No, that must not be permitted.

He hunted up his Chicago phone directory, thumbed several times in the blue pages that listed government offices, and finally found the number he was looking for.

He dialed 353-5300.

"U.S. Attorney's office."

"Ms. Diana Marie Lyons."

Ms. Lyons, it developed after several transferrals of the call, was in conference.

"Would you request that she call Monsignor Ryan at the Cathedral—787-8040. It is urgent. Yes, Ryan, R-Y-A-N, 787-8040. Extremely urgent. Thank you."

How else was it spelled?

He drummed his fingers uneasily on the arm of his chair.

Please do call back, Diana Lyons. The furies could be unleashed anytime.

68

Diana picked up the message late in the day. Call Monsignor Rhind. Urgent. Who was Monsignor Rhind? And why would he urgently want her?

Rhind?

She dialed the number anyway.

"Holy Name Cathedral."

Ryan!

Diana hung up. She did not want to talk to Conor's priest. It was unethical for him to attempt to intervene anyway.

He was Judge Kane's brother, wasn't he?

That made it more unethical.

She crumpled the note up and threw it away. She did not want to be late for her parents' anniversary dinner. Perhaps she would reconsider tomorrow.

Cold December had turned into colder January. The cold inside Diana did not change. She struggled with her conscience, poured out reams of journal notes, and understood nothing. She should not have agreed to the golf match, but could so much filthy corruption come from one hasty and imprudent decision?

Was my character always so weak that it required merely a slight push to come tumbling down? she wrote. *The answer must be yes. I am a terrible human being. I wish I could afford therapy. It probably wouldn't do any good. I'm beyond help.*

She watched the New Year's Day games on TV, not altogether understanding football, but fascinated by its gracefully choreographed violence. She thought she saw Con in the crowd at the Notre Dame/Southern Methodist fiasco. Perhaps he wasn't there— she thought she saw him in every crowd.

Her new assignment was a cocaine case, a pathetic businessman with five kids who turned to selling cocaine to pay off his golf-course gambling debts. He would have to do time, a few months, regardless of what this meant to his vague, hassled wife and children. The Con Clarke case languished in legal bickering. It would not come to trial for at least another nine months. Shelly continued to predict confidently that Leo and Donny would get rid of it as a millstone around their necks despite the airtight case she had put together for them.

"Case or no case, those two are not so dumb that they don't know when they're in a losing situation. It would be a long, hard-fought trial with mountains of media coverage. Donny doesn't like to do those unless he's sure he's going to win. If he loses this one, the papers will start to wonder out loud whether Donald Bane Roscoe might be losing his magic touch. And he can't drop the load on us and blame us for the loss because the first thing Walter Jacobson would ask on Channel 2 is why he didn't try it himself."

"I don't know what to think, Shelly. They certainly aren't interested in discussing it anymore, are they?"

"Well, they won't dare ship you up to the pornography shop at O'Hare like Leo threatens all the new lawyers here. You're a celebrity too now, Diana."

"I certainly am not."

She had turned down several invitations, demands really, that she grant interviews for feature stories. "You're hot copy now, Diana," Henry had told her. "It's a chance of a lifetime."

"What can I tell you, Diana?" Shelly raved on. "It's all that guy. He's scared the shit out of them. He'll say you planted the stuff to get him. People hate the government so much these days that they might just believe it."

"I didn't plant it. It's his cache."

"You know that and I know that, but Donny doesn't and Leo's not sure. You gotta admit it, Diana, that guy Conor Clarke has class."

"You're already on record with that opinion, Counselor."

She did not tell Shelly, much less Martin or Roscoe, that private investigators in Con's pay were swarming all over, trying to unearth evidence that the government had suborned perjury and had planted the money at the blueberry farm. Probably Leo knew anyway; he didn't miss much. They were also, according to Shelly, probing into every corner of Broderick Considine's life. "They'll try to tear him apart if they ever get at him on the stand, Diana," Shelly said uneasily. "Even now he's running scared."

"Tell him he'll run even more scared"—she dismissed Shelly's fears with a wave of her hand—"if he tries to back out of our deal."

There was no hint of any attack on her ethics, save for Maryjane's phone calls. Why not? she wondered. In her mood of frigid fatalism, she didn't much care why not. The game would be played out.

The 'Forty-niners wiped out the Miami Dolphins at Leland Stanford Junior Memorial University on the coldest day in the history of Chicago—twenty-eight degrees below zero. The cold suited her mood perfectly. She had not felt warm since the night at Riccardo's with Henry.

That day, the Monday after Super Bowl XIX, it was still bitter cold, but it was also her mother and father's wedding anniversary—the precise number not quite clear because it was never said exactly when they were formally married. Had Mama lived in sin with him? Did she seduce him?

Mama, Diana was beginning to believe, was capable of anything.

Mama and Daddy making love, even producing a child or two before their union was blessed—it hardly seemed possible. Yet Mama might have been willing to make any sacrifice to escape the poverty of her life in Sicily.

The family custom, for as long as she could remember, was a dinner on the anniversary day at Napoli's, whose Sicilian cooking Mama pronounced at least tolerable. Often, when the other children were still living at home, the dinner was an occasion for bitter quarrels. Now, however, Daddy was in an expansive mood, still proud of his daughter's great prosecutorial success.

"I hope I live to see the day when the jury brings in a guilty verdict against that man," he crowed, tapping in the general area of his fragile heart.

"Certainly you will live to see it," Mama said impatiently. "It will be in the autumn, will it not?"

Daddy had been talking about his death on the anniversary day for as long as she could remember. Mama's quick dismissal of the prospect seemed less confident now than in years gone by. Does she still love him at all? Diana found herself treasonably worrying.

And then, with a clinical clarity that shocked her, she wondered whether, with Daddy's bad health, they ever made love anymore. Is Mama as much a celibate now as I am?

Before she could chastise herself for thinking about such subjects, her heart sank. Broddy Considine, face strawberry colored from the January cold, entered the restaurant with a couple of cronies. He looked fit and well groomed as always, and chatted cheerfully with the owner and the hatcheck person and the waiters as he shed his fur coat and cashmere scarf. Diana tried to shrink from his view, but in vain. He saw her and promptly strode across the room, hand outstretched, as though it were the day before the election and she would cast the deciding vote. "Miss Lyons, what is a lovely young woman like you doing out on a cold night like this? I know, you're brightening up this wonderful Italian restaurant." He apparently fought off the cold with an even stronger dose of his cologne. "I haven't had a chance to congratulate you"—he played with his diamond stickpin—"on your brilliant discovery of the money that Clem Clarke's boy stole. Poor kid. I hope he learns his lesson. It's hard to grow up rich, if you know what I mean. Well, you'll go far in your career as a prosecutor, believe you me. Your parents? Mr. and Mrs. Lyons, congratulations on your wonderful daughter. Believe you me, you have every reason to be proud of her."

Mama was polite. Daddy was barely civil.

"I wish you would not associate with men like that," he said uneasily. "He is disgusting."

"He's my case, Daddy. I don't like him much, either, though I think he's pathetic more than anything else. If we're going to convict Con Clarke, we need him."

"I suppose so, still we don't want to have to talk to him on my wedding anniversary, do we, Maria my love?"

"Is he not the one who gave the money to that poor boy?"

"Yes. He's not a poor boy, Mama. He's a very rich boy."

"There is fear in that man's eyes." Mama paid no attention to her. "Is it always there?"

"I didn't notice, Mama. I'm so used to the shiftiness, I didn't look for anything else."

"He was Dick Daley's ally on the County Board." Daddy was not listening to either one of them. "That's the kind of man Daley brought into public life. We resent having to talk to him on my wedding anniversary, don't we, Maria?"

"He is a pig."

Daley's allies on the County Board had been Dan Ryan, then John Duffy, and finally George Dunne. None of them, Daley included, would touch Broddy Considine with a ten-foot pole. But Diana had given up on the Daley subject long ago and was in any case too busy watching Considine and his cronies to pay much attention to her father.

Mama's right, she thought, he is more scared than usual. He's drinking too much.

She lost interest, however, as she concentrated on forcing the tortellini into her stomach, washing it down with inexpensive Chianti—the only wine her father ever bought. She would probably vomit it up when she returned home, as she usually did with her suppers these days, but Mama and Daddy were entitled to a bit of festivity on their anniversary.

What happened next was like something occurring in a film—it could have been out of *Cotton Club*, which she had seen the other night in a desperate attempt to take her mind off herself. Out of the corner of her eye, Diana watched the door of Napoli's swing open and three men in dark overcoats, hats pulled down over their faces, enter. She would hardly have noticed them, except that Mr. Napoli, who had stepped forward to greet them as he did all guests, fell back in terror, pressing himself against the wall like he wanted to disappear.

After that it all happened like a videotape replay in slow motion. Waiters, waitresses, and guests scurried out of the line of march of the three men, as children caught in vandalism would run from the police. Unhurried but implacable, the men walked across the room toward Broddy Considine's table. Broddy's two cronies dived desperately away from him. Broddy himself rose to meet the men as though they were guests, even perhaps voters. Only at the last fraction of a second did terrible fear contort his face.

Three silver toys appeared in their hands. Sounds popped through the room like a string of firecrackers on the Fourth of July. Broddy's face turned into a mass of blood. Women screamed. Men vomited. Blood spurted out of Broddy's chest in little fountains. He hesitated, as though he were not sure, and collapsed rather than fell to the floor.

The three men turned and, as deliberately and implacably as they had come, departed from Napoli's. Diana remembered the line from Elmore Leonard's *Glitz* that she'd read in a review: "You'd think they'd stay away from spaghetti joints."

"That's the city Dick Daley created." Daddy's words were choked and far away.

Diana rushed across the room and knelt next to the bleeding, bullet-ridden corpse that only a few minutes before had been Broderick Considine of the Cook County Board. Heedless of the blood staining her navy blue skirt, she said the act of contrition for him and for all the troubled, haunted men and women in the world.

"O my God, I am heartily sorry for having offended You. I detest all my sins because I dread the loss of Heaven and the pains of Hell, but most of all because I offended You my God, Who art most good and deserving of all my love."

As she prayed, she watched her case against Con Clarke bleed its last on the floor of Napoli's.

69

"This office," Donny Roscoe was fuming like a coach who had just lost a bowl game on a bad call by the head linesman, "will not stand idly by while professional criminals and their allies in high places obstruct the course of justice and threaten the lives of government witnesses. We will push our investigation of this crime and all related crimes to the fullest extent of the law, and we will expect the full cooperation of all local law enforcement agencies."

That's right, hint broadly that Rich Daley and the State's Attorney's office are somehow to blame. Never assume responsibility. That's not the way to be elected governor.

"Mr Roscoe," a woman reporter asked, "do you have reason to believe that this was a mob-style, gangland execution?"

"That is a determination which will have to be made by the local agencies. I suggest you address it to the State's Attorney."

Yep. What goes right is your doing. What goes wrong—as you would say Donny, "irregardless"—is his fault.

"Donny, why wasn't there police protection for Broddy Considine?"

"This office is fully determined to offer full protection to all key government witnesses."

"Yeah, but isn't that a case of locking the barn door after this witness is dead?"

Forced at last to answer a straight question, Donald Bane Roscoe admitted the truth, sort of. "We were not informed by local agencies that the witness's life might be in danger."

"What does this do to your case against Con Clarke?"

"We intend to proceed with the full resources of this office against Conor Clarke. We are fully determined that no one will profit from murder in this jurisdiction."

"Are you suggesting that Mr. Clarke may have been involved in the murder of Broddy Considine?"

"No one will be permitted to benefit from the shedding of innocent blood as long as I am United States Attorney."

Cut to a pale Diana Lyons, her navy blue suit stained with blood.

"I was celebrating my parents' wedding anniversary at Napoli's. I saw Mr. Considine shot. I felt that someone should pray during his last minutes."

"Did you admire him, Diana?" A black woman reporter.

"Broderick Considine," she said carefully, seeming in full control of herself, "was a man who, like all of us, had his faults. But they were not such as to justify the taking of his life. He was entitled to that life—it was the only one he had—until God was ready to call him home. The one responsible for his death should be made to pay for this terrible crime."

"Do you mean Con Clarke, Diana?"

"Who else would benefit from his death?" She seemed surprised that there would be any doubt.

"You're saying that Conor Clement Clarke put out a contract on Broddy Considine?"

"I'm saying that no one, no matter how rich or how influential or how famous or how attractive, should be permitted to get away with murder."

The tape stopped. Silently Pat Slattery flipped the rewind switch. The murder of Broddy Considine had taken the wind out of her flaming spinnaker.

"Was I accused of murder? Con asked lightly.

"Reckless disregard of the truth," Pat said listlessly.

"She slandered you, all right." Lee West nodded mildly. "A jury might feel that a man having just bled to death in her arms, she wasn't fully responsible."

They were in West's office at Minor, Grey the day after

the murder of Broderick Considine. The headlines pro-
claimed SUSPECT CLARKE INVOLVEMENT IN CONSIDINE MUR-
DER and DALEY TO QUESTION CLARKE IN KILLING.

"Prepare a complaint just the same. We may want to use
it." There is more to be done, he thought, before this is
finished.

"I've talked to the State's Attorney's office. As you can
imagine, they're furious at Roscoe. He's put the blame on
them for his bungling. Someone from over there will want to
talk to you, but they have no reason to link the crime to you.
It was what the papers call a gangland execution. Which
means that it will never be solved. As my friend over there
put it, there are hundreds of people in Cook County who
would have wanted to put down Broddy."

"Noise for a few days and then put it in the files?" Pat
asked, her pretty face twisted cynically.

"What else can they do? I must say, incidentally, Conor,
that our friend Ms. Lyons acted with grace and courage."

"Her faults don't lie in that direction. . . . Can Roscoe go
ahead with the charges against me?"

"Absolutely not. Harry McClendon will turn cute and
the rest of it will collapse. Whoever put down Broddy did you
a weird kind of favor."

Lee watched Con intently. He and Patty think I'm responsible.

"Tell me about it. Instead of being suspected of theft for
the rest of my life, I am now suspected of murder."

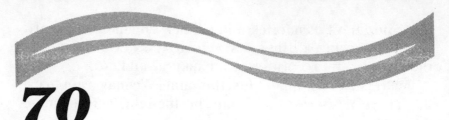

70

She was scribbling furiously in her diary when the phone rang with a hint of coming doom. No one called her this late.

You can get away with murder, she had written, *if you're rich enough and powerful enough and immoral enough. I guess I knew that all along. The men out on the West Side do it all the time. Why not white-collar criminals, too? His father is reputed to have done the same thing to men who refused to pay their debts to him. Self-defense, Conor told me the day we had our fight at the East Bank. He meant it.*

We underestimated him badly. Thank heaven Shelly isn't telling me about Conor's "class" anymore.

The case is finished. I hadn't thought about that. I believed Donny on TV when he said we would continue the prosecution with all our resources. Leo was blunt enough about it this morning. "Diana, don't even mention it in his presence if you want to have a job at the end of the week. He feels it's already a black mark on his record and he blames you. I had a hard time selling him on not firing you outright."

"That wouldn't look good, Leo, would it?" I said bitterly.

"Watch yourself, kid." He looked at me sternly. "Or you'll be in even more trouble. We don't like the way you stole the limelight the other night."

"I shouldn't have been at Napoli's? I shouldn't have prayed over that dying man?"

"You shouldn't have been on television accusing Con Clarke of murder."

"Do you doubt that he put out the contract?"

"Not for a moment, but it was our job to say that, not yours. You were not hired, young lady, to upstage the United States Attorney."

Then the phone interrupted her work on the diary. Diana rushed down the stairs and answered it. One of the other kids had read about it in the papers and was phoning? At last.

"Di? Henry. Be sure you catch Skippie on the ten-o'clock. You've had it, kid. You're so far up shit creek that you're under the waterfall."

Her parents had appropriated the television for the living room. She watched the beginning of the ten-o'clock news with them, her heart thumping, her stomach twisting and churning. Con, she assumed, had released the information his private detectives had gathered about her. She felt calm, fatalistic. It was bound to happen. Her remark about the death of Broddy Considine, as Leo Martin had added, was also a "bit of an embarrassment. A little too blunt. Donny doesn't want anything to be too blunt." Now there would be more embarrassment.

"We have an astonishing story tonight." Walter Jacobson had on his funeral director's mask. "A voice from the grave to denounce both organized crime and organized anticrime prosecution. Channel 2 received a stack of home video tapes in the mail today. They appear to have been made by Broderick Considine, longtime member of the Cook County Board, who was gunned down in a gangland-style execution slaying last week."

Cut to Broddy Considine, wearing the same light-gray suit in which he was killed.

"Well, if you are watching these tapes, it means that Tony 'the Tipster' Corrielli didn't believe me. Know what I mean? I told the Tipster that if he put out a contract on me, these tapes plus all the evidence sent with them would be turned over to the media." He smiled genially. "The Tipster acted like he believed me. He even said that he'd give time to repay him the money. That's another story. So probably no one will ever see these tapes. Still, you can never tell with a man like him, know what I mean? First of all, I thought I'd tell you about how his cocaine distribution system works. He was afraid I was going to tell the feds about it. I kept telling him the feds were more interested in Con Clarke than in him because they could convict a millionaire but they couldn't convict an Outfit heavy. If you're watching this tape, the Tipster didn't believe me. I suppose that 'Little Julie' DeSteffano will be the one to put me down. He's the Tipster's favorite contract man."

Back to Jacobson.

"Broderick Considine has given richly detailed descriptions, complete with names and places, of the south Cook County narcotics racket. Channel 2 will play this segment of his tapes tomorrow night at ten-thirty on an hour-long special, after making them available to federal and local law-enforcement agencies. The most sensational segments of Considine's last will and testament deal with the federal government's case against poet and playboy Con Clarke."

Back to Broddy, smiling like he'd just made a daily double at Washington Park.

"One thing I have to clear up if I'm really dead by now"—big politician's laugh—"is poor Clem Clarke's son. Clem and I were friends, man and boy, for forty years. A great man, Clem. Well, when the feds began to poke around in my business enterprises, they found that I was on the board of one of the Clarke kid's projects out in my end of the county, one of those things to try to put people back to work. I always say that there's nothing more important to a man than having a job of his own. A woman, too, for that matter. Give 'em work, not welfare, I always say.

"Anyway this young woman prosecutor, Diana Lyons, tells me that if I can give them anything on the Clarke boy, they might go easy on me when it comes to a jail sentence. A man my age is too old to go to jail, especially for doing a few minor things that didn't use to be against the rules. Heh-heh! Well, it so happens"—a wink of the eye from a man who imagines himself a great raconteur—"that a few of us have a little thing going on the side out in Cokewood Springs. Nothing big mind you, just a way of recovering some of the expenses of our work. 'Course, Clem's kid doesn't know anything about it. He's as straight as they come, unlike his old man, who never turned down a chance to make a buck. We hide things pretty well, so he's not likely to find out unless he turns an army of accountants loose on us and that's going to cost him more than the money he's losing.

"Well, this young woman really wants to get Con Clarke. I don't know why but that's her business I guess." Another wink. "Anyway, I kind of hint that he's on the take and eventually persuade the others that we should let young Con take the fall for us. We figure that it's going to be one of those things in which he'll get off with a slap on the wrist and nobody gets really hurt, know what I mean?

"Well, it works out that they need more evidence. This young woman fed wants to know where Clem's kid might've put the money. I remember that when he was a kid, he used to hide things from his father over in an old farmhouse outside of New Buffalo, Michigan. I got him out of a little trouble with the Michigan state police when he and some of his Notre Dame buddies had a little beer party there, know what I mean?" Another wink. "So I turn around and tell her that he said he's going to hide the money in one of his favorite hiding places, and I find some spare cash, which the Tipster would have liked to get his hands on—but that's another story, heh-heh—and I plant it over in that house. I hear this Lyons woman is hanging around Clem's kid, kind of spying on him and probably willing to sleep with him if it'll help the feds' case against him, know what I mean? I tell you, these young government attorneys have no morals whatsoever.

"If she's as smart as she thinks she is, she'll find out some night when she's in bed with him where he used to hide stuff from his old man and she'll have her evidence. If she doesn't find out, I'll turn around and see that she gets some anonymous tips, know what I mean?

"Hey, don't get me wrong. I was not about to let the poor

kid go down on this one. Maybe take a little heat, sure, but that'll be good for his character. Help him grow up a little, know what I mean? But no one is going to do time on this one. Clem's boy's got good lawyers, and anyone could have planted that money."

A huge laugh at a great joke shared with his audience. "Anyone did, know what I mean?"

Jacobson again. "So a voice from beyond the grave comes back apparently to clear Conor Clarke and to raise serious questions about the propriety of United States Attorney Donald Bane Roscoe's investigation of the Cokewood Springs corruption charges. Even a hint of sexual involvement between Clarke and a member of Roscoe's staff. We'll hear a lot more"—Walter nodded his head significantly—"about this case."

"I had better report down at the office," Diana said mechanically.

Her father had slumped down in his favorite easy chair, face buried in his hands. "Maria, take her to the train. Tell her not to bother reporting back here. I never want to see her again. She's betrayed us all, Maria. There's nothing to live for anymore. My last hope has been snatched out of my life. She is a worse disgrace than any of the other children."

"I'm sorry, Daddy," she said, a last desperate plea in her voice. "I really am."

"A daughter of mine, Maria"—hand clutching at his chest—"not only a crooked lawyer, but nothing more than a common whore."

"Pack some things, Diana." Mama rose from her chair. "You'll have to stay at a hotel in the Loop tonight, anyway. I'll drive you downtown."

"You don't have to drive me. I'll take the train."

"I want to drive you."

The two women rode in silence down the nearly empty Dan Ryan.

As they turned off at Washington, Mama asked, "You'll stay at the Midland like you usually do?"

"I guess so."

"I'll wait till you check in and then drive you over to your office."

"That won't be necessary."

"I said I'd wait."

In front of the hotel, Mama stopped the car and, before Diana could get out, muttered, "It is my fault, Diana. You must forgive me if you can."

"How is it your fault?"

"I should have protected you from him. With the others, I did not understand what was happening. I tried to keep peace. With you I understood. I saw it. I was afraid to stop him."

Diana hugged her mother. "It's not your fault, Mama, none of it's your fault. I will always love you."

"You will need this money." Mama gave her a thick envelope.

"No, I won't."

"Take it, child. Your hell is only beginning."

Diana accepted the envelope, checked into the faded Midland, threw her bag into her room, returned to her mother's car, and rode over to the Everett McKinley Dirksen Federal Building to end her career as a government prosecutor and probably her career as any kind of lawyer.

I should not have gone to Grand Beach last summer. I did not belong in a place like that.

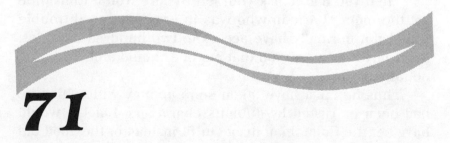

71

"I tried," Blackie Ryan protested to the Madonna, who looked very unhappy with him. "I tried. She did not return the call, poor unhappy young woman. How was I to know that it would go down that night?"

The excuse did not satisfy the French girl. Excuses never did.

Now the Furies were loose and God alone knew how long it would take to put them back in the box. The victimizer had found herself the victim, not that at some level of her personality she hadn't been searching for that all along.

He sighed, reached for the phone, and then thought better of it.

At some point I may of use. But not now. Not for a long time.

If one assumed, *causa argumenti*, that both star-crossed lovers were in error, then new perspectives opened up. Con took it as a given that Diana had set him up. She, for her part, supposed that he had hidden the money in the old safe house.

But what if they were both wrong? What if someone else had done so?

Who would that someone be?

He had been unconscionably slow to understand that Broddy Considine, God be good to him, was the obvious suspect. Con had spoken of getting out of trouble when there had been a bust at the house during a beer party in his Notre Dame days. Someone with clout had taken care of it. Who would have clout in Northern Indiana besides a County Commissioner from the south end of Cook County?

Then you had to ask yourself, Where would Considine get the money? A man who was in grave financial trouble would not normally have access to two hundred big ones. And there was no reason that anyone should lend it to him, not anymore.

Thus he must have taken some money with which he had been entrusted by dubious characters. Blackie would have bet the Colombian drug Outfit instead of the good old Chicago Prohibition Outfit. Perhaps they owed him enough favors to tolerate such behavior. Perhaps not.

So Blackie had called Diana to warn her that her witness was in grave jeopardy.

And she did not call back.

So his thesis had been proven. Not that it will help Conor Clarke much, he thought when he heard the morning news about "another gangland-style killing." They won't be able to try him and he won't be able to exonerate himself.

Now it appeared that Considine had fooled them all.

What would God think about that?

It's Your problem, not mine. I did what I could.

Not enough, he imagined the Madonna observing.

Now what was there to do?

As his father, Edward "Ned" Ryan, sometime Rear Admiral in the United States Navy and longtime Chicago political lawyer, put it several times a week: "When all you can do is wait, then you wait."

Poor Broddy Considine. Poor Conor Clarke. Poor Diana Lyons.

Poor everyone.

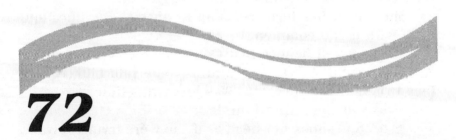

72

"We will not tolerate this sort of abuse in this office." Some of the wind had been taken out of Donny Roscoe's self-righteous sails. He was stumbling over words and repeating words at a much higher than normal rate. "I promise a full investigation of every aspect of the Cokewood Springs investigation. We will leave no stone unturned till we have answered all the unanswered questions."

"Will charges be dropped against Con Clarke, Donny?"

"That question is premature at this time."

"Will Diana Lyons be fired?"

"I have asked for her resignation from government service. However, I will not accept that resignation until I have completed my personal investigation of the entire matter. I fully expect the full cooperation of all state and local agencies in that investigation."

Then a clip of Diana, worn and tired, emerging from her office, and fighting her way through a viper's tangle of reporters.

I know what it's like, bitch, Conor said under his breath, and now you do, too.

"My behavior was injudicious," she said dully. "I deeply regret the embarrassment I have caused Mr. Roscoe and the rest of my colleagues. My enthusiasm for the investigation seems to have deprived me of good judgment."

"Is Con Clarke innocent?"

"Of this charge, it would seem so." She tried to push by the cameramen.

"Did you sleep with Con Clarke, Diana?"

She shook her head refusing to answer the question, even with a "no comment."

"Do you still believe that Con Clarke is a criminal?"

She hesitated. "Of course he is," she said bitterly, her face twisting with fury. "He was lucky this time."

"Did you sleep with him?"

"No." She shook her head as if she were trying to wake up from a nightmare. "I did not."

"Did he try to sleep with you?"

"No comment."

Con turned off his TV. He should feel triumphant, but oddly he did not. Yeah, I was real lucky. Somehow it was incomplete. They'd taken his fight away from him.

"Well"—Naomi Silverman's sigh certainly was not all that different from Blackie Ryan's—"you appear to have triumphed completely, my dear. Does victory taste sweet?"

"Reasonably sweet, there are still a few cards to be played before it is over."

"They have taken your game away from you, have they not?"

"I guess so. You *do* read minds don't you?"

"It was only a game, my dear. A dangerous and fascinating game. It is not real life, which is much less exhilarating and much more serious. It is well that you can return to real life."

"Give me a few more days to wind it up and then a few weeks to get over the letdown—then, I promise, back to the monotony of real life."

"The poor woman," her husband said gently, "never did get her thirty pieces of silver. . . . She will not hang herself, will she, Conor, to make the analogy complete?"

"And be buried in a potter's field? I don't think so."

"She looked like she wished she were dead."

"Diana has many faults, Zeke, but she's not the kind who will destroy herself."

"Not all at once," Naomi agreed. "She will spend the rest of her life working at it."

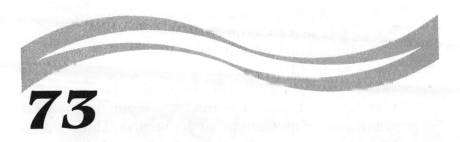

73

Only Patty Slattery, a bailiff, and a court reporter were with Diana in Judge Kane's courtroom. Patty acted as if Diana had the Black Death.

"Where is the United States Attorney, Ms. Lyons?" Judge Kane demanded, her eyes as cold as the walls of the 333 Wacker Building.

"He was unable to come this morning, Your Honor." She could not lift her eyes off the floor. Would anything but death end her humiliation?

"Indeed. I note that the press is, ah, underrepresented."

"Yes, Your Honor."

"You are not accompanied even by Mr. Gollin or Mr. Martin. Do they not want to be seen with you, Ms. Lyons?"

"I don't know, Your Honor."

"Solemn high arraignment, secret dropping of charges. Typical, I fear. . . . Ms. Slattery, I take it you have no objection to the motion to dismiss charges against your client?"

"None, Your Honor. However, we feel that he's entitled to a full exoneration, morally if not legally."

"I quite agree. Ms. Lyons, I think I ought to inform you that I intend to cite you and Mr. Roscoe to the bar association. Apparently there is no limit to his abuse of the power of a government prosecutor."

"I am the one to blame, Your Honor. I take full responsibility."

The judge considered her reply. "That admission may be the only thing you've done in this case which does you credit. Nonetheless, your conduct has been most injudicious, not to say improper."

"I am leaving government service, Your Honor."

"You should leave the practice of law, too, Ms. Lyons. You have done a grave disservice to all lawyers, and especially to all women lawyers."

"I know, Your Honor. I will not practice law again."

Judge Kane considered Diana for a moment, her face expressionless, her quick mind undoubtedly making a precise and detailed assessment for her citation to the bar association.

"Next matter," she said, her eyes still probing Diana.

"Patty," Diana called hesitantly to the other counsel as they left the courtroom. They had studied for the bar in the same crash course.

The lovely redhead turned around sharply. "I don't want to talk to you, Diana. You're a fat disgusting bitch."

74

I am not fat. I weigh less now than I have since I was fourteen. But I am both disgusting and a bitch. I don't blame Patty for her contempt. I feel even worse about myself. If only I could straighten it all out in my own mind, get a handle on it, figure out what I did wrong, besides playing golf with Conor that humid day last August. Can I make up for the disgrace? Probably not. But at least maybe I can pull my life back together and not make the same kind of mistakes again.

I'd like to see a therapist. But I wouldn't know where to start. I could call Dr. Silverman, I suppose, but she would hang up on me. And anyway, I can't afford therapy. I'm not even sure if I can pay the rent next week.

Diana was living in a one-room apartment across the street from a lovely old Polish church and a block away from the Kennedy Expressway and the el train to the Loop. She had applied for her former job in Marshall Field's budget store and had been promised it tentatively.

The buyer was candid. "If you can keep your name out of the papers for another week or two, you can have it."

She was not sure whether she could. It was beyond her control. They were meeting tomorrow with Conor and his lawyers. It would not be a pleasant session. Donny wanted to forget the case; he refused at first even to attend the meeting until Leo insisted: "They've got us by the balls, Donny. If you're not there, they'll turn around and walk out."

"I will not issue a formal statement of exoneration. There is no question of that. The Cokewood matter must remain open."

"Donny, why don't you listen to me just once. This time

you won't get away with merely throwing Diana to the mob. You're going to have to do something yourself. Eat a little bit of humble pie before they make you eat a lot."

"No exoneration and that is final." Donny pounded the desk.

"You'd better hope that's all they want."

Diana to the lions, she wrote with a sick little chuckle. *I deserve to be punished. But how do I begin again? Can I begin again?*

75

"I won't pull any punches." Con's anger had not abated, and now he was enjoying it more than ever, a bitter, much older, and much more self-confident version of the boy with whom she'd played golf centuries before. "I don't have to listen to Lee's cautions anymore. So I can make threats. Either you call one of your famous press conferences and exonerate me of all charges, or I'll put you and Martin and Golden here out of the law business for the rest of your lives."

"Gollin," Diana said softly.

"If your boss can get away with using the wrong name, so can I."

Shelly actually seemed to snigger. Class, huh, Sheldon? Diana thought.

"This office does not issue exonerations," Don Roscoe was sputtering. "We are continuing our Cokewood Springs investigations. We reserve the right to reinstitute charges at any time."

"You're not talking to reporters now, Donny. Let me list what I propose to do—civil suits for libel and for malicious prosecution, complaints to the Illinois Supreme Court's ethical practices board, citations to the bar association.... Have I left out anything, Lee, Patty Anne?"

"The criminal complaint"—Pat looked up from her notebook—"to the State's Attorney, we have an excellent case for that."

"Moreover, I guarantee you that if you ever are so foolish as to try to seek public office, I'll run against you and see that you are beaten."

"He means every word of it, Donny." Lee West smiled gently. "I'd advise you to bend your principles a bit and have that press conference as soon as possible while my client is still in a mood to, ah, grant amnesty."

"We're dismissing Miss Lyon." Donald Roscoe was confused. Was not one sacrificial victim enough? Why would you want your name cleared, too?

"The name is Lyons, Donny, I don't think you'll ever forget it. The amnesty doesn't apply to her. She's going to do time, just like she intended me to do time. If you don't call that press conference, you may just do time, too. Is that right, Leo?"

"You'd better do it, Donny," Leo agreed, almost as though he were enjoying the whole performance.

Con *was* magnificent. Future U.S. Attorneys would be much more careful with immunized and plea-bargained witnesses.

"All right," he muttered grudgingly.

"Tomorrow!"

"Very well."

"OK, gang, let's sell this cheap hotel. See you in court, Diana Marie Lyons."

For one terrifying, chaotic moment she almost ran after him to tell him that she was sorry and beg his forgiveness and spill out her love in his big, strong arms.

Both forgiveness and love would be granted immediately. She saw it in his eyes. He didn't enjoy hating or punishing her.

They would be back where they were at Long Beach

Country Club. Of that she was certain. Four words—"I'm sorry! Forgive me!"—were all that would be necessary. The final three—"I love you!"—could come later.

It would be much easier to kill herself.

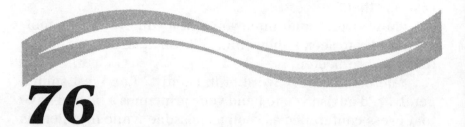

76

The confrontation with Maryjane in the perfume section of Marshall Field's shook Diana to the center of her being. Not because Maryjane was wrong, but because she was probably right.

Even two weeks later, sick with a cold that she was resigned to as a permanent illness and shivering with a chill that was real and not imagined, Diana, pencil poised over her journal, could not exorcise her former friend's terrible words. In one way they absolved her from guilt, but in another and more important way, they made her corruption far worse.

She had bought a bottle of cheap scotch to mix with hot lemonade and aspirin, telling herself that it couldn't make her cold any worse and might, as her solicitous Polish landlady insisted, help a little. Until then she had avoided liquor, fearful that she might drink herself into a permanent alcoholic stupor.

Not much chance of that. I hate the taste of the stuff.

She lived in one room with a tiny kitchenette. It was warm at least, and she welcomed the church across the street, though no one there seemed ready to listen to her prayers yet.

She had dutifully phoned Minor, Grey and given Pat

Slattery her phone number and address so that they could serve the papers on her for whatever actions were being contemplated. Pat had seemed to want to say something, but at the last second cut herself off. "Good-bye, Diana."

Nothing had happened yet, and it was already early March. Had Conor decided to forget about his threats and let her off the hook? Or was he enjoying her torment as she continued to dangle? Somehow the latter tactic didn't seem much like Conor, but she understood the new Conor even less than she did the old Conor.

The first hint of publicity in the paper would mean the end of her job. It was made very clear almost every week that she had better keep her name out of the papers—as though that were a matter still under her control. Maybe life would be easier in jail.

Have you ever been to a jail? Shelly's Uncle Lad. She shuddered. Maybe, she laughed bitterly, I could plea-bargain.

She and Maryjane literally bumped into each other in the perfume department on the first floor. For a second or two, her friend's face shone in delight. Then Maryjane remembered.

At first Diana listened to the recrimination patiently and humbly, thinking of how well Maryjane had recovered her figure after her first pregnancy.

Then Maryjane said the wrong words: "And it's all because of your father. He drove you to do it. Face it, Diana, your relationship with him was totally unhealthy. I mean REALLY gross!"

It was Diana's turn to blow up. "None of this would have happened if you hadn't made me play golf with him."

"That's like totally sick, I really mean it, Diana. You're in trouble because you let yourself be taken in by a wicked old man. What does that have to do with a golf game or a couple of dates with Conor? He's too good for you, anyway."

And further deponent sayeth not. In fact she stormed away, doubtless to her beloved Gerald to report to him what a total gelhead poor little Geraldine's godmother was.

Diana looked over her notes. There was truth there if only she could focus on it. It was not written in stone that I had to push poor Broddy Considine to plant evidence. Why did I do that? Nor was there any necessity that I ask Con about hiding things when we played squash. In fact, even if I was so besotted with him that I had to keep dating him, why did I have to use the relationship to spy on him?

Those were the bad decisions, not the harmless choice of a day of golf on the shores of Lake Michigan.

Why did I make those decisions? Why did my character collapse in the face of those challenges?

For an instant she thought she saw the answer. Then she turned away from it in horror and lost it as the phone rang.

"Cara mia." Mama in tears. Dear God, NO! "Come quickly. Something terrible has happened to Papa. I think he is dying."

77

Conor Clarke was in the Airport Hilton at SFO, not as elegant as the Stanford Court, but much more convenient if he wanted to catch an early-morning flight the day after tomorrow. He would have liked to depart tomorrow afternoon, when his crucial conversations in San Jose were completed. But at that hour in the afternoon, you could not fly from San Francisco to Chicago. He did not feel like celebrating, either—even if, as seemed likely, the decision to go public with Infobase made him vast sums of money.

He never felt at ease in this strange part of the word. Los Gatos, Freemont Avenue, Park Mill, the Bayshore, Stanford Industrial Park, all-night bashes with cocaine and booze and women "sales consultants" at poolside in the hills—the "laid-back" weekends out here made him long for the winds off Lake Michigan's dunes.

Diana once asked why he didn't live here. Had she understood him so poorly? Didn't she know that unlike the rootless folk here he wanted roots that he never had growing up? Wasn't that obvious to everyone?

Joe Murphy, his shrink, had figured it out in thirty seconds.

He had barely finished unpacking his briefcase when the phone rang. "A long-distance call from Chicago, Mr. Clarke."

He glanced at his watch. Midnight already in Chicago. It can't be good news.

"This is Father Ryan."

"Conor Clarke here, Father Blackie."

"Hmmn, oh yes, I called you, didn't I?"

"I think so." He smiled, never quite sure whether the shrewd little priest was as confused as he sometimes appeared. "More so, I think," Joe Murphy, Blackie's brother-in-law as well as Con's therapist, had once said. "Only it doesn't make any difference."

"Indeed . . ."

"What is it, Father? Bad news? Someone die?"

Dear God, not Diana!

"Mr. Frank Lyons."

"Diana's father?"

"Indeed . . . I am not altogether sure why I feel constrained to report this to you, but I do. Massive stroke, he lingered for several days but did not regain consciousness."

"Oh. Does she blame herself?"

"I have no information on that matter. I presume she does. Would that not be the typical response?"

"I suppose so. What can I do?"

"I suggest no particular action. I merely felt that you ought to be informed."

"How did you find out, Father?" Had Diana phoned him, seeking help perhaps?

"The usual sources."

"What usual sources? Sorry if I shouted."

"What my late mother, God be good to her and She'd better be or She'll hear about it, was pleased to call the Irish comics."

"Huh?"

"The death notices. The funeral is the day after tomorrow."

Oh.

"I'm glad you called, Father. I'll pray for him. I'll get over to see you when I come home. I promise."

"Indeed."

His hand rested on the phone. Call her. Where? And for what purpose? Go home for the funeral? But would his presence not make her grief all the worse? And he had important meetings. . . .

He took his hand off the phone.

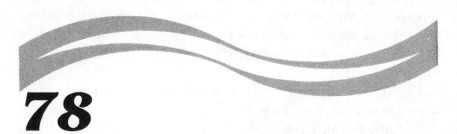

78

The cloudless blue sky, Diana thought, was heartlessly cruel, suggesting warmth but in fact presiding over ten-below-zero cold—with a wind-chill index of thirty-five below. Dear God, please let it end soon. The tears are freezing on my cheeks.

Her cold lingered; she had a slight fever still, and sniffled constantly. I'll be very sick tonight, but I must be at work tomorrow if I don't want to lose my job. The kindly old priest droned on with his prayers. She could not understand a word of what he was saying, just as she did not understand his sermon. He was an elderly, retired pastor, helping out at their parish. He was so kind and sympathetic that it didn't matter that he was incoherent and probably a little senile.

Next to her, Mama was shaking with sobs, accepting Diana's protective arm, but not welcoming it. She blames me too. Why shouldn't she?

Daddy had died slowly, a little bit more of life slipping out of his haggard, hollow body every hour for four long days and nights. She and Mama kept vigil and prayed, rarely talking to each another. What, after all, was there to say?

Then without any warning, his labored breathing stopped. Mama became hysterical and shouted terrible oaths in Italian at Diana, heaping blame on her for not loving her father enough. "You killed him, you killed him. . . . It's all your fault."

It was indeed. Fortunately most of Mama's curses were in a Sicilian dialect that Diana—who knew only a little bit of Italian, which she had studied in college without telling her father—could not understand. At the end of her husband's life, Maria had become once more the fiery little Sicilian he had saved thirty-eight years ago.

Larry Whelan and his attractive wife came to the wake, the only legal couple in the handful of mourners.

"His whole life was integrity, Diana," Larry shook her hand warmly.

How would he know? Clever Irishman probably made some phone calls.

"Thank you, Mr. Whelan."

"If you're looking for a job," he spread his hands as if to indicate that there was no big deal involved, "We're searching for associates at our firm."

"Thank you, Mr. Whelan, I'll never practice law again."

"Never say never, Diana," he winked at her. "It's a hell of a long time."

"That is a nice man," Mama said as the Whelans left.

"Smooth-talking Irishman." Diana told herself that she would never be able to face colleagues in a law office. Even if never were a hell of a long time.

Of the other children, only Paola, who had fought the most with him, returned for the funeral—a matured, gracious Paola who was charming to both Mama and Diana. She left for the airport right after the Mass to return to her husband and family in San Diego. Neither of the boys even returned Mama's call.

So at the graveside there were only the two of them, the poor doddering priest, a neighbor couple, a man who had worked with Daddy at DOA twenty years before, and one or two others whom Diana did not recognize.

Sixty-five years of life and this was all that remained. Dear God, why? Why didn't anyone else love him the way I did?

Then, finally, the prayers came to an end. The priest stumbled over, shook their hands, tried to remember their names, and then followed the undertaker away to the waiting hearse. Poor dear man.

She hugged Mama as hard as she could. "I'm sorry, Mama. I'm sorry."

How many times had she said that in the last week?

"He was a good man!" Mama insisted vehemently. "He was a good man!"

"I know he was, Mama. I know he was."

She helped Mama to the limo, eased her into the car, and closed the door to keep her warm. There were a few questions she must ask the undertaker.

"Diana . . ." An attractive woman she didn't recognize, in a very expensive fur coat. "I am so sorry for you and your mother."

"Judge Kane . . ."

Instantly she was sobbing in the judge's arms. Why had she come? The Ryans had a reputation for taking people under their wings . . . but not worthless people like me.

"Thank you so much for coming. I don't know . . ."

The judge's luminous green eyes were glistening with tears.

"Diana, life is too short to waste opportunities."

What did she mean by that? Diana wondered later, as, sick and cold, she rode the el back to her one-room apartment.

79

Pat Slattery was the first one to put it in words. "Conor Clarke, you're still in love with the fat bitch?"

"She may be a bitch, Patty Anne"—he tried to laugh it off—"but she's not fat. Lovely breasts, actually. Not too large at all for someone as tall as she is."

"Really! I know THAT. She's gorgeous. I'm envious. But how can you still love her?"

Conor had come to Minor, Grey's offices to see his tax lawyers about a new regulation that meant he would have to sign papers for much of the morning. Patty met him, perhaps accidentally, perhaps not, in the corridor.

"Does that seem crazy, Patty?"

"Totally crazy, but not necessarily wrong." The young woman considered the subject thoughtfully. "Not after all that has happened. I mean you must REALLY love her!"

"I'm not sure, Patty."

"WELL, you certainly look like your heart is breaking."

"Then I guess I'll have to get over it, won't I? It will be all right in a little while."

"Don't count on it."

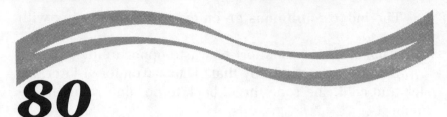

80

It's St. Patrick's Day. My cold is no better. And my spirits were not improved by the green glad good cheer in Marshall Field's basement today.

However, I came home and had three quick drinks in honor of the Irish side of my family. Then I called Mama, who seems to be rebounding better than I am. She wants me to come home, live with her, and work with her in her store at the Flossmoor Mall.

"I will pay you better than they are, and we get to know each other, yes?"

But I can't go home yet. There are too many memories, too much guilt. And how could Mama and I ever work together? She knows I killed him, and I know, from what Conor said, that she flirts. That would tear my heart out. Poor Daddy.

I remember when I was a junior in high school and I had a date for the Shamrock Festival at St. Titus. At the last minute Daddy wouldn't let me go. The Irish drank too much on St. Patrick's Day, he said. And the St. Titus party was notorious among all the Irish lawyer drunks on the South Side.

Later, the girls that went to the party told me it was a real drunken bash. Daddy was right: I shouldn't have gone.

Yet now, somehow, I feel glad that Daddy can no longer say "no" to me anymore. Even relieved that he's gone. It's hard for me to admit that. If I didn't have three drinks in me, I wouldn't dare write it. I guess such feelings show what an evil and worthless person I am.

I've stayed home today, afraid to appear on the streets of Chicago for fear I'll encounter Conor. I often fantasize about such a meeting. Sometimes I picture myself ripping him to pieces with a denunciation that will silence him forever. Then I think I'll turn on my heel coldly and walk away from him without a word. Or would I throw myself into his arms—or on my knees—and beg his forgiveness?

It would be all over then. I know I'd never do it, but I have images of warmth and peace afterward. The strongest memories are not of the two times we made love, but of the day on his boat when he held me in his arms and protected me. From what, I still don't know, but I felt protected, God knows. I don't know why, but I want protection now.

I'm an adult woman. I can take care of myself. I don't need him to take care of me.

I would indeed turn on my heel and walk away in cold, aloof silence.

And, to be honest, as I must in this journal, my heart would be stuffed with raw pain. Just as it is now.

That I could write such a sentence with my poor father's body hardly in the ground shows how worthless I am.

81

"So, my dear, you are completely triumphant? But it does not make you happy."

The Silvermans were celebrating St. Patrick's Day with him in Les Nomades, next to the picture of the Paris railroad station. The terrible weight of cold had lifted temporarily from the city. The day had actually been warm and pleasant instead of the routine annual blizzard that wiped out the wearing of the green in mid March, not that too many of the

Chicago Irish noticed the weather as the day wore on. Con had been urging on his friends the virtues of Les Nomades' monkfish—"wonderful health food for pregnant Jewish psychiatrists."

"Yeah," he said in response to Naomi, "I'm victorious because of a Mafia hit man and a kinky old pol with a weird code of ethics. No great triumph."

"You'll be in your box in Wrigley Field this summer"—Zeke grinned happily—"instead of in the courtroom."

"You won't be there, Rabbi. You'll be home taking care of the baby."

"And, my dear, what are you doing with your time now that you have humiliated Mr. Roscoe, who, if I may remark on it, seems to have a kinkier code of ethics than the late Mr. Considine?"

"Trying to put the pieces back together out in Cokewood"—he shrugged indifferently—"making a lot of money on Infobase. Have some more wine, Zeke, it's from California, but it's still good or it wouldn't be served here. Scratching out a few poems. Thinking about investments in China. Nothing much else."

"There is no cure for a broken heart in that activity, is there, my dear? Would it not have been better to leave Chicago for a time and search for another love?"

"I'm not sure I want another love just now," he said with some asperity, "and I don't have a broken heart."

"Nonsense, my dear, you do too. A sensitive young man, hiding behind a humorous mask, which is not altogether fallacious, falls deeply in love for the first time in his life and then is cruelly betrayed by that love—what else is a broken heart?"

"Modern Americans"—Ezekiel raised his head from the careful attention he had been paying to the rice-cream-with-raspberry-sauce dessert and knotted his thick black eyebrows—"think it is a sign of maturity not to complain about their woes. I will tell you that it is much wiser to follow the example of Jeremiah in the scriptures and bellyache loudly so the whole world hears."

"I don't know whether I was in love." He pushed aside his own white chocolate mousse, feeling like it was improper to enjoy dessert with this conversation. "I certainly made a fool out of myself."

"And you still want her, don't you?"

I still want you, too, Con thought, remembering with pleasure and frustration the night he had this delicate little doll mostly unclothed and almost into bed. Not the same way, though, and that's the point, isn't it? "If it's a broken heart, it will cure itself in time."

"Would you find yourself able to forgive her?" Naomi asked bluntly.

"How can I forgive her for what she did?"

"Have you not dropped all the charges and complaints against her?"

"I don't see any point in it anymore. I guess I made up my mind after Roscoe's press conference that I wouldn't press any of those charges. I've hung on to them, cruelly maybe, because I didn't want to let go of my anger. She's been thrown out by her family, lost her father, lost her job, is living in a near poverty apartment, and is back working as a salesperson in Field's basement. Isn't that enough revenge? Besides, the sweet taste of revenge turns sour all too quickly—as you well know, damnit. Why couldn't it have lasted a little longer?"

"You still want her, don't you?" Naomi insisted. "You have not given up that dream."

"That's not true, Naomi." Con slammed a spoon down on the table. "She betrayed me, I hate her, can't you leave it at that? My broken heart, if that's what it is, will heal in a few weeks or a couple of months at the most."

"It will not, my dear," she shot back at him just as hotly, "not unless you behave rationally."

"Let not the sun go down on your anger," Ezekiel observed mildly. "A certain well-known rabbinic colleague. In *your* scriptures not mine. What can I tell you?"

"All right, what is rational?" he demanded, signaling the waitress for his check.

"Rational is making a clear decision. Either you take the sensible choice and determine that she is a traitor and you wish never to see her again and forget about her, or you do the crazy thing, realize that forgiveness hardly matters when you love, and pursue her with implacable reckless- ness."

"Pursue her?" He glanced at the bill and reached for his checkbook. "There's every sign that she doesn't want to be pursued. Why should she? She thinks I'm a rich, spoiled crook who has destroyed her career. She hates my guts. Why pursue?"

"Only one reason, my dear, and I'm not suggesting that you do it. As I said, I think it would be a mad choice. But her present attitude should have no impact on such a choice. You are, after all, not without some skills as a pursuer."

"What's that reason?" He was so angry that he wrote the wrong sum on his check and had to tear it up and write a new one.

"That you cannot live without her. If that be the case, forgiveness is hardly important, is it?"

"I agree that it would be a mad choice." This time he did the check right.

"God is usually mad in his pursuit of us. Take Hosea, for example," Ezekiel observed with rabbinic patience. And added again, "What can I tell you?"

"I will not pursue her. I won't hold any grudges against her, but I'll be damned if I'll chase her. I can live without her, Naomi, just wait and see."

"I will wait and see, my dear, but I am not convinced. You give no signs of being able to live without her."

"She isn't worth it."

He stood up, so did Naomi and Zeke. She was now mar- velously pregnant. Lucky Zeke, he thought again.

"That may be true, Con, and then again it may not be true. But I am not persuaded that you believe it to be true."

"I do," he insisted. "My love for her is as dead as last summer's golf."

"If St. Patrick's Day come"—the rabbi folded his long, slender hands as if in prayer—"can spring be far behind?"

"In Chicago," Conor shot back, "it can be a hell of a long way behind."

Spring

Second Song

Beloved:

On my garden path a hint of eager feet,
At the window ardent eyes strive to see,
Then my lover's arms reach out strong for me,
My sick and defeated heart begins to beat!

Lover:

Rise up, dear one, the snow is gone,
We are drenched in lemon-scented dew,
The lake again is melted blue,
See, flowers bloom and green the lawn.
Time, I insist, to play and sing and dance.
Let me see once more your laughing face
As together we run our ardent race
And, with darkness gone, we renew romance.

Beloved:

My lover left, quiet with the morning breeze,
Back to the city's busy squares and streets.
On my bed I shivered in icy air,
Unclothed, frightened, alone—what if I freeze?
All day, I pined, I missed him so,
At dusk wanton and wild, I ran to the gate,
"Welcome, my darling, I could hardly wait,
I've caught you now, I'll never let you go!"

Lover:

Enough of your running, my darling, my dove,
Ah, off with your dress, and lie at my side,
My woman now I claim you, and my bride,
In triumph I possess you and seal our love!

Love Song, 2:8—3:5

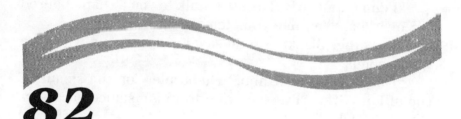

82

"Don't be afraid of me, Naomi." Diana tried to smile. "I don't assault pregnant women."

"I am more worried about what I should say"—the tiny psychiatrist glanced up ruefully as she returned her tea bag to the teapot—"than that you will do harm to me."

They had encountered each other on Wabash Avenue. Dr. Silverman had been walking north, presumably toward her office. Diana on a late lunch break from her job at Marshall Field's was walking south. Recognition came with a shock to each of them at the moment they passed each other. Diana had looked back to make sure it was Naomi and discovered that the other woman had done the same.

"May I talk to you, Naomi?" she had blurted without thinking.

The psychiatrist had hesitated and then, her professional reactions taking over, murmured, "A cup of tea, at the coffee shop here in the Palmer House?"

The Palmer House was not the superior Chicago hotel that it used to be. The elite trade had moved up Michigan Avenue to the Water Tower, leaving the convention trade to Chicago's most famous hotel name. But its coffee shop—beige walls, black countertops, photographs of old Chicago scenes—was more like a lunchroom in an elegant art museum than a greasy-spoon hole in the Wabash Avenue wall. It was an appropriate place to sit in a booth, with a clean table, across from a woman who had been a Rhodes scholar.

"I don't know why I asked to talk to you." Diana poured her own tea. "You like your tea strong?"

"As Father Blackie would say, it is too strong when the spoon bends."

"I have never met him." Diana blew on the steaming cup of Earl Grey. "I've seen him from a distance occasionally at the lake."

"A remarkable man. He and the rabbi have raised to a refined art the practice of ecumenical leg pulling."

There was an awkward silence, like the moment a priest opened the door on your side of the confessional.

"I don't know what to say." Diana wanted to run back on Wabash Avenue.

"Perhaps ..." Naomi finally poured her tea. "... whatever was on your mind when you spoke to me out there."

"I wanted to ... to explain, to apologize ... I don't know."

"I see."

"I was two different people, one loving him, one hating him."

"Is it not that way in all human intimacies?" She sipped her tea, Lapsang Souchong, and nodded approvingly.

"What do you people call it ... dissociation ... becoming completely distinct from one part of yourself?"

"We all do that, Diana. It comes with being human."

"Not to that extent."

"No, that is true."

"He loved me, Naomi." She felt the sting of tears and willed them to disappear. "He wanted to marry me. He bought that huge house to be my castle."

"I believe that to be true." Naomi was studying her jet black tea.

"I hope he will sell the house."

"Father Blackie advises him to retain it for a year so that he will make a nice profit and assuage his Calvinist conscience."

They both laughed weakly.

"He wanted to marry me despite your advice?"

Naomi arched her carefully trimmed eyebrows. "You misunderstand, my dear, both my role and my attitude. I don't give advice even to my clients, much less my friends and—let us be candid about it—almost-but-not-quite lovers." She smiled lightly. "His sensitivity, not my virtue."

"But . . ."

"The most I offer"—she smiled again—"is a series of impressions, which someone may want to call advice but which I can always disown."

"But—"

"Let me finish, my dear."

"I'm sorry." The woman might be fragile, but she possessed enormous moral force. We ought to have been friends.

"My impressions of you after that baseball game, the purpose of which you perceived and tolerated with considerable grace, were rather in the opposite direction than the one you seem to think."

"Oh." Diana felt her throat turn dry and her heart pound. "Now you know that they were wrong."

"I do not know that at all," the other woman said promptly. "I know only that terrible things have happened."

"Too terrible ever to be erased." Diana tasted her tea again.

"Perhaps." Naomi shrugged enigmatically.

"I don't understand what happened . . . how the two me's came apart."

Naomi nodded. "That would seem to be your first challenge, wouldn't it?"

"Is what I have"—Diana leaned forward eagerly—"curable? Can I get over it?"

With small economical motions, Naomi filled her tea cup again. "Curable is a term that we don't like to use in my profession. The most we hope for is that our clients are able to live with their problems, understand them, control them to an extent, and have happy and productive lives." She shrugged again, a pure Brooklyn gesture, Diana supposed, though she had never been to Brooklyn. "Sometimes that can be accomplished at least provisionally."

"But hardly by someone who is as messed up as I seem to be?"

The other woman spoke very slowly, considering every word carefully. "I am in no position, Diana, to offer any prognosis for you." She considered Diana meditatively. "No, I will not evade the responsibility of this conversation with that professional caveat. I will be blunt. While I don't understand, naturally, the origin of your ambiguities—psychological, moral, human, I think that you are the sort of person of whom it might be said that . . ." She smiled again, as if she were bargaining in a marketplace. ". . . with the right sort of help and hard work the prognosis would be quite hopeful."

"Oh."

"What you hoped to hear and yet what you hoped not to hear?"

"Do you read minds?"

"Only faces. Especially lovely and transparent faces."

Diana felt her face flame. "I guess that's what I wanted to talk about. I have to run back to work." She grabbed the check. "My treat."

"This time." It was an offer of help, of friendship, of a way out of the cave.

"This time." Diana agreed, not wanting the offer, but not wanting to refuse it, either. She turned to dash to the cashier's desk.

"Diana . . ."

She turned to face the psychiatrist, whose face seemed to be shining with a magical radiance.

"Yes?"

"It would be utterly improper and unwise for me ever to act as your therapist . . . yet . . . in a transitional situation and for a short time, I would be willing"—she was becoming confused, but the radiance was not fading—"to do whatever I can."

The woman actually loves me. She wants to help. Diana was embarrassed, frightened, and somehow exultant.

"I'll"—she gulped—"I'll keep that in mind, Naomi. Thank you." She gestured in the general direction of the psychiatrist's belly. "Good luck with the kid."

Then she hurried from the coffee shop so that she could weep in the private anonymity of the Wabash Avenue crowds.

Back behind her counter in Marshall Field's basement, she told herself bitterly that she had made a fool of herself with a women she despised, whose help she did not want and would never accept.

83

"It is a great blessing"—Blackie Ryan raised his Waterford tumbler, normally reserved for use only with the Cardinal, to his learned guest—"not to be a Methodist."

"I agree completely." Zeke Silverman toasted in return. "Mind you there is much to be learned from the disciples of John Wesley. Excellent hymns."

"Intense spirituality."

"Dedicated sense of vocation."

"In any restructured Christianity or, if you will pardon my term, Yahwehism, they have an important contribution to make."

"Precisely."

The pieties having been observed, they sipped their "little jars," as Blackie might have called them. John Kennedy, John XXIII, and John Unitas looked down in silent approval.

"Unfortunately, they do not appreciate the full sacramentality of all God's creatures."

"We would use the term sacramental in a perhaps less expansive meaning and then only applied to wine, but as I believe you might say, Monsignor, I take your meaning."

"It must be admitted, Rabbi," Blackie continued piously, "that excessive use of this particular sacramental creature is dangerously inappropriate. It must further be conceded that in the land of my forebears certain of the clergy were indistinguishable from the Methodists in their opposition to such harmless pastimes as dancing. Yet if all that was prone to abuse was to be forbidden . . ."

"Life itself would go under—your term again—interdict."

"We don't have them anymore, God She be praised. Excuse me, Rabbi. For the sake of interreligious harmony, I should say in your presence, Lady Wisdom be praised."

"God's attractive self-revelation in the order and charm of creation."

"Indeed . . . Where was I? . . . Oh yes . . . finally, any tradition that rejects in principle the appropriate use of John Jameson's Twelve-Year Special Reserve cannot be fully acceptable."

"Precisely."

There was a pause while they both considered with satisfaction their skill at dialogue.

"Our young friends," the Monsignor began, "have made a mess out of their lives. Frankly, if Conor were not such a hesitant lover I think this matter might have satisfactorily arranged itself some months ago."

"No one listens to their clergy anymore, Monsignor."

They sighed in unison.

"Did they ever?"

"On the other hand," the rabbi continued, waving his hands in a gesture that equivalated the sigh, "did not Diana encounter my wife on Wabash Avenue two days ago and discuss the problem with her?"

"Really?" Blackie's myopic but appealing blue eyes flickered with interest. "And what is that excellent mother-to-be's evaluation of the situation?"

"She feared greatly for Diana's health, mental and physical. She is clearly under enormous strain."

"Indeed." The little priest sipped his tumbler reflectively. "But then, that is to be expected."

"My good wife also thinks that there are powerful self-destructive dynamics at work. She sees them as long-term energies, the mutilation of her life instead of its termination. She does not rule out, however, the latter horrendous possibility."

"Not likely." Blackie balanced his glass as if balancing the possibilities. "Women in our heritage much prefer prolonged to abrupt self-destruction."

"What, then, is to be done?" The rabbi spoke as a man finally arriving at the point of the discussion.

"Those who will not be helped cannot be helped."

"A harsh prognosis."

"Albeit a temporary one. The two-minute warning has yet to be sounded."

He rose from his chair, reclaimed the Jameson's bottle, and filled both their tumblers.

"James Joyce's favorite, too. Poor man. Have you ever, Rabbi, in the course of such harmless enjoying as this, had the distinct sensation that an imp spirit, of the sort in which your tradition in its folk forms abounds, has slyly slipped into the room and consumed at least half your glass?"

"I take it"—the rabbi nodded—"as proved that such events occur with depressing regularity."

"The issue," Blackie returned to his subject, "is Con."

"I believe he has forgiven her, Monsignor."

"That, Rabbi—you should excuse the expression—together with a dollar bill, will get you a ride—no transfer—on the subway that at this very moment rumbles beneath my church."

"It must be expressed to her in the most—you too should excuse the expression, Monsignor—passionate possible terms."

"Indeed."

"Salvation for the fair Diana will be achieved only through him."

"And then perhaps not."

"Precisely."

They remained silent, perhaps in prayer. They would have assured anyone coming by the Rector's study that they were praying. Should it have been Cardinal Sean Cronin, he would have said "scheming."

"What chances are there, do you think, Monsignor, of that happening?"

"You mean, Rabbi, of Conor making what is vulgarly known as a 'move'?"

"Precisely."

Blackie shifted reluctantly out of his chair and ambled over to a window, through whose perennially dirty panes the drunken dance of late-winter snow flurries obscured Wabash Avenue.

"Only as to the fact . . . not as to outcome. Well . . ." He paused thoughtfully and rubbed the bridge of his nose with the hand holding the depleted crystal tumbler. "I would calculate the odds against his making a move as to be of about the same order of magnitude as the odds against the sun not rising tomorrow morning."

84

"You're a nice man, Conor Clarke," Pat Slattery, her gloved hand in his, informed him, "sweet, considerate, generous, respectful, and about as much fun on a date as one of Mr. Asimov's robots."

They were walking down Michigan Avenue in the small hours of a Sunday morning. The snow flurries of the afternoon had turned into a blizzard. Spring indeed.

"Hmmn?" Conor asked absently.

"Did the Bulls win tonight?"

"I . . ." He jumped. "No, of course not."

"Orlando Wolridge made thirty-five points and they did win."

"I was joking," he said lamely.

"And I drank a lot of martinis at that bar out of which I just dragged you, right?"

"No more than usual."

"Conor, I don't drink."

"I know that," he insisted. "I was—"

"Joking?"

"As a matter of fact, yes."

"Like I say, among the males of the species currently available in this decadent city, you are in the top percentile. Infinitely better than the crop awaiting harvest at the singles' bars on Division Street. You're a wonderful kisser, you destroy my resistance—such as it is at my advanced age—instantly. I'm sure you're superb in bed. In fact, if you asked me to sleep with you—which you haven't and I don't expect you will—I might forget about my principles and say yes, out of curiosity if for no other motive. Except for one reason."

They stopped for a red light.

"And what is that, pretty Patricia?" Conor was listening to her now with an amused smile and images—vague and indistinct, to be sure—of pretty Patricia next to him in bed.

"You'd call me Diana while you were making love to me, like you have at least twenty times this evening."

"I haven't. . . ."

"Yes, you have. If I am to be loved in that ultimate and intimate sense, I want to be loved"—she laughed—"for my very own body and not someone else's. And should it go on beyond that, for my very own soul—such as it may be—and not someone else's."

"The man who finally entices you into his marriage bed with be very fortunate indeed, pretty Patricia, Young Woman Lawyer."

"Doubtless." She waved her hand, stipulating as lawyers do. "What I'm saying is that while you might just fit that job description in most respects, you have someone else on your mind. I'm not going to try to compete with her."

"I'm sorry." He held her hand more tightly. "I . . ."

"Love her very much?"

"I wasn't going to say that. I don't think I was, anyway."

"But you do. Don't try to deny it with me, Conor C. Clarke. I've been flattered once too often to see your eyes drinking me in, only to realize that it was not a redhead you were looking at at all."

"You must think I'm crazy," he said, trying to sound contrite.

"That is not the point. Maybe yes, maybe no. The point is that you have two choices."

"Which are?" They stopped because Pat had released his hand and, across the street from the snow-capped water tower, was holding his face in her hands, one on either cheek.

"Which are as follows: One. Forget about her completely and check out the available alternatives on their own merit and not as objects of comparison."

"A reasonable strategy." He kissed her lightly. Her lips were cold because of the weather and tasted of Coca-Cola and Perrier. He knew she didn't drink. Except wine at dinner. How could have I forgotten that? "And two?"

"If one doesn't work—and it sure doesn't seem to be working—then you have to decide that little things like a trumped-up indictment, libel, slander, conspiracy, et cetera, et cetera don't mean a shit and go after her like you did before."

"That would be crazy, wouldn't it?"

"Would it?" She recaptured his hand and led him further along their Michigan Avenue walk.

"Don't you think it would? I mean she's a sick, confused bitch."

"You said it was because of her father and now he's dead."

"But it's still inside of her. She might betray me again."

"That argument doesn't convince you and it doesn't convince me."

They crossed Oak Street. It was only a few minutes' walk to Pat's apartment.

"You think I'm still in love with her."

"Hopelessly," the young lawyer said flatly. "Incorrigibly."

"I'll get over it."

"I doubt it very much. She may not deserve you, Conor C. Clarke. Or maybe she does. I find myself reluctantly drawn to that possibility. But she has you. And probably always will."

He kissed her good-night at the door of her apartment building. Her invitation earlier in the walk up Michigan Avenue had been explicit. If he promised her with all his wit and charm to call her only Pat or pretty Patricia or Patty Anne, he would doubtless be admitted for what would be doubtless a rewarding day-long Saturday sexual romp.

He lacked the energy to make the promise.
And he was not sure that he could keep it.

85

Loyal and faithful Shelly took her to lunch at the Standard
Club, "where no one will recognize us except to wonder
what a nice Jewish boy like me is doing with a shiksa."

She was still not eating. But, she told Shelly, she liked
her job. "I was cut out to be a salesperson, Shel, not a
prosecuting attorney."

"You'd be good at anything you want, Diana."

Shelly took her to lunch under the pretense of keeping
her up on the office gossip, but, she was certain, really to
make sure she didn't kill herself. The temptation to end the
bitter cold inside her—much worse than the lingering
Chicago winter—was seductive. It had been especially powerful last Sunday, when, after dinner with Mama, she per-
versely borrowed Mama's Datsun and visited the halted
construction at the Cokewood Foundry. As snow flurries
stung at her face, she heard a pregnant young woman, no
more than twenty, complain, "That bitch took away our last
hope."

Somehow the life forces inside her were still stronger.
So far.

Shelly's gossip was that Donny Roscoe was returning to
private practice to earn the money needed for the college
education of his children (the oldest of whom was eight) and
that Leo Martin might join a firm specializing in criminal
practice.

"Donny's, like, forgotten about you. He can't admit that he made a mistake. It bothers Leo a lot more." Shelly passed her a plate of salad. "He always has pictured himself as the behind-the-scenes operator who kept the office functioning no matter what second-rate political hack was on top. And at the same time broke in—and broke down, if necessary—the young bloods. You deprived him of that image. So he has to leave."

"Probably did him a favor," she mused, poking at the salad.

"I see that Clarke has dropped all his complaints and charges against you."

"Damned hypocrite. Now he can pretend that he's practicing Christian forgiveness. Improve his image in the columns even more. It's all part of his game."

"You don't like him at all, do you, Diana?"

"You do?" She sunk her teeth into a tomato, as if she wished it was one of Con Clarke's vital organs.

"Well, to tell the truth, like I've been saying, I thought that he acted with a lot of class under pressure. He was innocent, you know."

"Of the charges. That doesn't mean he's not a hypocrite and a crook. Besides he made fun of your name."

"No, he made fun of Donny's inability to get any of our names right. He winked at me. Hell, I even winked back. We both came damn near breaking up."

"All a big game, damn him." She pushed the salad away, still unable to eat. "I suppose you wonder why I took such a chance with my career, with all our careers?"

"I figure"—he glanced apprehensively at the half-finished salad—"that you took a chance, based on your knowledge of him, that he'd cop a plea."

"Big chance, wasn't it?" she asked ironically.

"I suppose so. Long shot."

"The truth is, Shel"—she felt her shoulders slump—"I don't know why I did it. Yes, I thought he'd accept Donny's best and final, but that didn't matter. He'd become an obsession. I wasn't in control. Sounds weird, doesn't it?"

"You mean you were in love with him, but why then—"

"I didn't say that," she exploded. "I was obsessed. There's a difference between obsession and love. A big difference. There's nothing about him that's worth loving. He's a mean, vicious, spoiled brat."

Shelly signaled for coffee.

"You don't agree?"

"As I said, Diana, I kind of liked him and . . ."

"And what?"

"Well, you were wrong about him copping a plea. Maybe you're wrong about everything else."

"No, I'm not, Shelly," she said firmly, beginning to wonder if Sheldon Gollin had been so charmed by Con that he was keeping track of her for him.

Back at her counter in Field's basement, she glanced again at the headline on the fifth page of the *Sun-Times*: CLARKE DROPS ALL CHARGES AGAINST EX-GOVERNMENT PROSECUTOR.

The story was brief. Lee West, attorney for Conor Clarke, had confirmed that all charges had been dropped against Diana Lyons, the former government prosecutor charged with entrapment and conspiracy in the indictment of Clarke. "Mr. Clarke does not believe in holding grudges or getting even," West said. "As far as he is concerned, the whole matter is closed."

Lyons, the paper noted, had left government service and was now working as a salesperson at Marshall Field's State Street store.

Asked about bar-association citations against Lyons, West withheld comment.

"The hell he doesn't hold grudges," she muttered bitterly.

"Diana," her buyer interrupted the angry reverie. "They want to see you up in personnel."

Riding up on the escalator, Diana hoped that she might be given back her old job as assistant buyer. It would be the first step out of the cold.

Instead they told her that they had received several complaints from customers who had read the *Sun-Times* article. They were afraid that they'd have to ask her to resign for the good of the company.

Con's revenge was now practically complete. She wondered what was the easiest way to end her life.

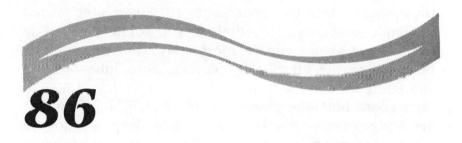

86

Blackie Ryan carried a palm in his hand as if it were a wilted swagger stick. For Palm Sunday he wore a Chicago Black Hawks jacket over his clerical shirt and trousers and a purple pompomed biretta.

"Does God find it sweet?" Con asked him.

"Revenge?" Blackie never missed an allusion to a previous conversation. "The Lady God only reserves ownership rights to revenge. It does not follow She exercises those rights. But have not you, in a notable and indeed edifying burst of Christian charity, forgiven your persecutors?"

"She was fired because the *Sun-Times* story about my dropping the charges said that she worked at Field's. She may have to move out of her little apartment on the Northwest Side across from St. Jadwiga."

"A remarkable woman. Jadwiga, that is. Or Lillian, as My Lord Cronin, who for obvious reasons these days knows the language, informs me."

"I cost her her job."

The little priest looked monumentally unimpressed. "Many ironies in the fire." He shook his head absently. "St. Jadwiga's? Well, we'll see."

"Do I look like a killer, Father Blackie?"

"As much as Sir Georg Solti looks like a quarterback."

"My own lawyers thought at first I might have put out the contract on Brod Considine."

The priest laughed so hard that his eyes watered and he had to remove his glasses and polish them, ineffectually, with a crumpled tissue. "Your Finn MacCool face during the crisis, no doubt. Ah, well, Conor Clement Clarke, we must remember that the events of Easter 1916 were precipitated by gentle poets, too. Nonetheless, you would have to be pushed a lot harder, and the most likely scenario would not be a hit by the improbably named Little Julie but you strangling the adversary at the Michigan Avenue Bridge at high noon. But"—he glanced at his watch, apparently to confirm the date—"how is it that it is late March and despite our deceptively balmy Palm Sunday you are not in, let us say, Cabo San Lucas wind surfing or engaging in some other appropriately exhausting behavior?"

"The fun has gone out of the fun times, Father Blackie."

"Still enamored of the divine Diana. Love is totally irrational, isn't it? One tells it that it has been completely killed by dastardly crime and it laughs. How odd of God to compare Herself to love. Hence, indeed—you should excuse my favorite word—divine Diana."

"Devilish Diana might be better. Anyway, you can't forgive someone who doesn't want to be forgiven, can you?"

"An absolutely convincing position. Forgive people only when they're ready and eager to be forgiven. It is not fair to be required, God-like, to authorize the rain to fall on both the just and the unjust."

"I've tried. She still hates me, still says I'm a crook, still blames me for everything."

"So." The priest shoved his small hands into the pockets of his Black Hawks jacket and pulled out a crumpled piece of paper. "Surely you have done the required seven efforts."

"Seventy times seven."

"Hmmm?" Blackie examined the paper from several

different perspectives, trying to read the note that he had made on it.

"The Scriptures say seventy times seven times."

"Really?" Blackie found a stub of a pencil and made another note on the paper and then stuffed it back into his pocket. "Surely the Jewish scriptures?"

"Jesus, as you well know."

"Indeed. A very distinguished rabbi, as our good friend Ezekiel would say. Then you have only begun the chain."

"There's no future in it, no hope, no sense, no point, no chance."

Blackie considered this litany as though he were weighing a great decision of national policy. "Even after seventy times seven, Conor Clement Clarke, the difficult and delectable Diana will still lurk in your bloodstream as possibly God's best sacrament in your life."

"How do you know that?"

"Why else would you have someone, possibly the inestimable Mr. Gollin, keeping tabs on her for you?"

"Maybe I do still want her." All purpose, all joy, all hope seemed to flow from his weary body. "What difference does that make?"

"Indeed."

"You think it's insane?"

"I don't recall saying or implying that. Perhaps it is. Perhaps not. But she's not my darkly divine Diana."

"And if she were."

The little priest made another note on his crumpled piece of paper. "Hmmm? Oh, what would I do if I were in your circumstances? Celibate advice is easy, Conor Clement Clarke, but if she were mine and I felt the way you did, I'd pursue her until hell, should there be such, freezes over."

87

That afternoon as he was jogging along the North Avenue Beach, admiring, despite himself, the scantily clad Palm Sunday beauties soaking up the first sun of spring, and noting that none of them approached the aforementioned delectable Diana for sheer delectability, Con decided that there was no hope at all in trying to fool Father Blackie.

Seventy times seven meant four hundred ninety times. But Jesus hadn't been speaking literally had he?

To the south, outlined against the bright blue heavens, the pastel Chicago skyline seemed a mystic city from another world, an illustration for a science fiction magazine.

All right, damnit, why not try again? That's what you really wanted to do all along, isn't it?

Call the wench and tell her that on the Second Saturday of Easter you intend to meet her, clad in appropriate virginal white, in front of the altar of Holy Name Cathedral and that she damn well better be there. Then, at a suitable time later that day, after large amounts of cake and lesser amounts of champagne, in the privacy of the castle you have bought for her, you propose to divest her, in more or less leisurely fashion, of the aforementioned virginal white, overcoming whatever delightful obstacles of elastic and hooks and such things that may obstruct your progress, and then to continue what you two began so well at the side of your swimming pool.

Moreover, after several days of such activity you further propose to imprison her in a suite on the QE2 and take her to Europe for a protracted honeymoon of indefinite length, with a strong concentration on warm and isolated beaches.

Let's see what the darkly divine Diana has to say about that.

His hand hesitated on the phone. Just call her up and propose after all that's happened?

I sure don't have anything to lose.

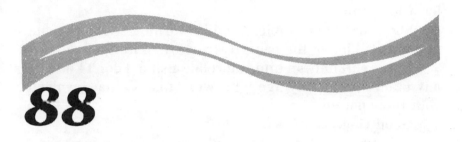

88

She watched the people streaming out of the Polish Catholic church, romanesque and cute, despite its horrid green dome, across the street from her studio apartment. Palm Sunday. She should have gone to church. But why? What reason is there for praying when God is so disgusted with you that He no longer hears your prayers?

She was still job hunting. An art-supply store on Wabash had actually offered her a job. Half the pay of Field's, barely enough to live on. She might have to find an even smaller apartment.

Mama wanted to give her more money, or even a loan if that would be easier. There was an inheritance, all in S and L accounts because Daddy didn't believe in investments. She could not accept anything from Mama. Not yet. Not ever.

She was impatient with Mama. Her grief, so hysterical during the wake and funeral, had rapidly dissolved. Mama even seemed moderately happy. Obviously she intended to remarry. Maybe she had a man on the line even now. How disgusting.

Diana wondered if she were the only one in the world who loved her father.

Poor dear man.

What did Maryjane call it? An unhealthy relationship? How idiotic.

She put her hand to her head. Another sudden throbbing headache. Was she becoming a migraine victim?

Maybe it was an unhealthy relationship.

Come on, Diana. You know it was. You've known that for a long time.

She started to tremble. A chill returning? No, a terrible thought striking at the central structure of her personality.

It was certainly an unusual relationship. I don't know of any other women my age who were that . . . that involved with their parent.

Good God.

Still quivering she grabbed for a phone book and opened to the letter *S*. So many Silvermans. "N. Silverman, M.D. 30 West Washington." Shrinkville, they used to call it at Chicago Circle.

She scribbled the number on a scrap of paper, put the book back on the stand next to her bed, looked at the number, crumpled the piece of paper, and tossed it at the waste basket.

She missed. Even her shooting eye wasn't what it used to be.

Daddy, was he the problem? Not deliberately, and with the best possible intentions, but still . . .

I couldn't bear it.

She went into the bathroom and examined carefully the bottle of Valium which her doctor in Flossmoor had given her before the indictment. She hardly needed to be tranquilized. Too much Valium and you would sleep quietly away. They might find you and pump your stomach and that was, from what the FBI had told her once, a very unpleasant experience.

Instead, she found the scrap of paper behind the cardboard waste basket and put a robe on over her bra and slip. You should be modestly dressed when you talked to a Jewish psychiatrist. Then she dialed the number she had found in the phone book. Maybe there would be an answer even on Sunday afternoon.

After three rings the phone was answered.

"Good afternoon," said the warm, reassuring voice, "this is Dr. Silverman speaking."

Diana hesitated, her whole story of misery about to rush forth.

Instead, she hung up.

89

Con showered after his run, mixed himself a margarita, though he did not believe in the solitary drinking of hard liquor, stared balefully at the phone, and determined that at most he had two attempts to check off against the four hundred and ninety that might well be charged against him.

He punched in, on his portable phone, the number Shelly had given him.

Busy signal. Well, she had someone to talk to. So, despite Shelly, her life couldn't be so bad. Another man. Probably. Why not?

He watched the Chicago Bulls in another futile TV attempt to contain Larry Bird. If the Celtics are able to draft Chris Mullen from St. John's, they'll win for the next decade.

No, I won't phone again. She has someone else to talk to.

So he punched the number again.

Answered on the first ring this time. "Diana Lyons."

Good God, why am I doing this? What was it I wanted to say?

"Con calling, Diana."

Pregnant silence. As though there were principalities and powers wrestling for her soul at the other end of the line.

"Diana?"

"Yes?"

An unreadable response. Here goes.

"It's Conor."

"I'm not deaf."

Uh-oh, sounds like the bad principalities and powers won. Now what am I supposed to say? On the second Saturday of Easter . . .

"I don't know what to say, Diana. . . ."

"Then you shouldn't have wasted your money and my time. You have a lot of money, but I don't have much time."

"I don't want it to end this way," he cried desperately.

"There never was a beginning, so how can there be an end?"

"Could we get together and talk about it? Privately I mean."

"I'm busy hunting for a job since you had me fired from my last one."

"I did not."

"Even if I wasn't job hunting, I don't want to talk to you."

"I wish you would." That's crawling pretty far out on a limb for the one who was the victim. Father Blackie will be pleased with me.

"You are an immature, spoiled brat. You were lucky this time. You'll still end up in jail where you belong."

Dead line. She sounded like she meant every word of it.

He made a mark on a sheet of paper. At the most generous estimate, three times. Four hundred and eighty-seven to go. Jesus was using Middle Eastern hyperbole, wasn't he?

90

Conor Clarke had spoken the truth about one thing: Mama was indeed a knockout. In a charcoal gray suit, with white trim, standing on the bank of the Chicago River, she managed to look like both a woman in mourning and a woman with hope in the future.

Why have I never realized how pretty she is? Was Mama a rival? Oh God, how terrible. I must make peace with her. . . . No, that's not quite it. I must permit her to make peace with me. That's why she came downtown for lunch, even though the week before Easter is the busiest time of the year for her.

And the poor thing is terrified I might reject her. Mama fragile . . . I would have never thought it possible

Diana had accepted the job at the art store at the north end of the Loop because they were nice people and because there was a lot of free time in which she could practice her own sketching, something she had neglected since high school, and because she doubted her ability to continue the job search much longer. Before she left for work the first day, she threw the Valium bottle into the trash can.

But that night she rescued it. No telling when you might need a bottle of Valium.

The conversation with Con had been disturbing and painful. He did not sound like a triumphant victor, but like a lonely little boy. What right did he have to feel lonely?

Cleansing words had hung on her lips: "I can still beat you at squash."

Such a sentence would have dissolved everything that had happened. It would have been a way to say, "I'm sorry.

Forgive me." Those terrifying words would have flowed naturally, perhaps on the squash court. They would have laughed and her obsession would begin again.

She was startled by how close she had come, nonetheless, to letting the deadly sentence slip out of her mouth.

She did not want forgiveness. She was not sorry.

Then, on the Wednesday in Holy Week, here was Mama, on her day off, come downtown to take her to lunch. Still not eating, Diana persuaded her that they should buy a hamburger at MacDonald's and enjoy the still gorgeous early-April weather with a walk along Wacker Drive on the banks of the Chicago River and across the Michigan Avenue Bridge.

"It is a beautiful, a magic city, almost like a fairy-tale city." Mama gestured with her graceful hands. "All castles and piazzas and water and handsome people, like Roma or Firenze—which I've never seen. I'm sorry I have not enjoyed it more."

Mama was no longer Mama but a beautiful and attractive woman, with interesting ideas and images and the enthusiasm of a teenager. Diana considered her as they sat in the little plaza on the river bank behind the Wrigley Building; they were watching one of the early sailboats chug along the river, eager for its summer home on the lake—like a school kid escaping for summer vacation. It was not, thank God, *Brigid*.

"Attractive" was not the right word for her mother. Mama was sexy. Funny that she had never noticed that before—not till Con had praised her figure.

"Perhaps you have forgiven me a little?" Mama said shyly.

"There's nothing to forgive, Mama. I love you."

"I was so young." Mama hardly seemed to have heard her. "He was a good man, in those days brave and happy and gentle and loving. He offered me a new life. He worked very hard and went to law school, and I had the babies, one after another. I hardly noticed the change. Even after he failed

the bar exam the first time, I did not notice. A little more bitter perhaps, but he said other men had bought passing
grades."

"That happened in those days." Diana felt her stomach
twist again. "But he did pass."

"It wasn't the same. The first time, when he opened the
envelope, he screamed that it was like being wounded at
Anzio. Soon he became different, but I didn't want to notice.

"Then he did not make money or become successful
like the other boys that went to school with him. I realized
that something had been lost at Anzio. I didn't understand
the older children. They were so different from the children
I knew in Sicily. I wanted them to respect him. The heart attacks, and the fighting . . ." She wiped her eyes with a tissue.
"I did what I could. When I insisted—like about my job, so it
would be easier for the children to go to college—he always
let me win even if it hurt him terribly. I should have fought
more. I still loved him so much. I didn't want to hurt him. If I
had defended the children, they might not have left. He
wouldn't be so disappointed and unhappy. . . ."

The heart attacks were unnecessary, Diana thought bitterly. The young resident at the St. Francis couldn't believe
that he had rejected heart surgery. Routine, he had said.

"How can I make you understand, *cara mia*? He
changed so slowly that I hardly noticed. But the man you
saw dying was not at all like the man I married or the man I
loved so much the night we conceived you."

"I know you loved him, Mama."

"As the years went on," she continued recklessly, "I
think I loved more what he used to be than what he became.
Yes, I still loved him. But can you forgive me for saying that
it is a relief to be free from what the world and life made
him?"

Talk about the candor so praised by the newspaper
marriage experts. Mama had written the book.

"It's nothing to forgive, Mama. I understand what you're
saying and why."

"Do you really?"

She was dabbing at her eyes with a tissue. Even weeping, Mama was pretty.

"Are you going to marry again, Mama?"

"You think that I betray your father, dishonor his bed?"

"I don't think that at all," she had replied hotly.

But ten minutes ago I would have thought just that.

"You Irlandesi are such romantics. I was never unfaithful, Diana, never. It would have been easy. There were opportunities. But no. I had made my promise. I would not dishonor it."

Diana extended an arm around her mother's shoulder and held her close. "Of course not."

"You are the mother and I am the child, eh? It is good to have such a sympathetic mother."

"I think you will make some man a fine wife," Diana insisted, half believing that she felt as fervently on the subject of a stepfather as her words sounded.

"We Sicilians are fatalists, not romantics. It is in our blood. We are born that way. An empty bed is a widow's death, they say. If I can find the right man, Diana *mia*, my bed will not be empty for long. Do I disgrace you?"

"You make me proud." She gulped hard. "So long as I get approval rights. I don't want you marrying the wrong man."

Was that why Conor had bought the big home with a coach house? Had he expected that Mama would be seeking and probably finding a husband? How dare he!

"I need my daughter's approval when I choose a new man for my bed?" Mama was grinning through her tears.

"Absolutely. Total veto rights."

These people, she thought, are indeed complete realists. Why didn't some of it rub off on me. If I were a realist like Mama, I'd throw myself on my knees in front of poor Conor and it would be all over.

"So it shall be. I know nothing about American men. You do."

"My record is not all that good, Mama. But I'll help as best I can."

"Such a daughter to treasure. I do not deserve to be blessed with you. I failed you."

Another deluge of tears ruined what was left of Mama's makeup. Realists? Well, sometimes.

"Don't blame yourself, Mama. You did your best."

"Not with you." Tears were streaming down her face, streaking her skillfully applied makeup. How and when did a teenage peasant bride from Agrigento learn to be chic? "I know you were being hurt more than all the others. I loved you the most, too, always sweet and thoughtful and yet becoming someone you did not want to be to keep him happy. Then, with the heart attacks, I was afraid to hurt him any more. I sacrificed you to the love I once had for him."

"I don't think—"

"That poor boy, without any real family of his own, loved you, Diana. He was so nice and so easy to hurt."

"Conor?" She was furious at him all over again for involving Mama. "When did he talk to you?"

I know, but I want to hear about it from her.

"He came to the store to buy something, back in September. He spoke in terrible Italian, but he was sweet and funny. I thought to myself, 'This one loves Diana and he wants to see what her mother is like.' So I was very friendly. I even flirted"—she smiled shyly—"only a little bit. I knew he'd make you happy. Then I saw his picture in the paper. I weep for both of you and I blame myself."

"No, Mama," she said softly, "don't blame yourself. He is a bad man. He seems charming, but he's rich and shallow and spoiled and dishonest."

"That is your father talking, Diana. He was a sweet boy and he loved you. He must still love you. . . ."

"I'm sure he doesn't."

And I'm not sure of that at all.

Mama briskly repaired the damage to her makeup. Diana offered advice at one point in the process. Mama's dark brown eyes flashed dangerously. Then she laughed.

"So I have found a mother to tell me what to do? It serves me right."

They walked down the right bank of the river and crossed in front of the *Sun-Times* Building. Mama insisted on giving her an envelope with money. Diana took it so as not to hurt her feelings and because she needed it and most of all because now she wanted Mama as a friend. "You do forgive me?" Mama pleaded.

"Forgiveness doesn't matter, Maria." She hugged the stranger who was her mother. "I want you as a friend. I forgive whatever is to be forgiven."

"You cannot mean that."

"Look, Maria, let's get this straight, so we won't let it stand in the way ever again. I do forgive you and I do love you. Maybe you did let me down sometimes, but that is over and done with, understand? I forgive it all and you must forgive yourself. Do you understand me, Maria? No more guilt?"

"You call me Maria?" The stranger-becoming-friend stared at her in astonishment.

"You're still Mama." Diana was amazed at her own skillful grace with this sad, beautiful, wonderful woman who had given her life a quarter century ago. "Now you're Maria, too, a woman like me who is becoming my friend. Maybe even"—she giggled—"Anna Maria!"

They laughed and cried together and hugged each other, and for a while the cold went away.

That afternoon in the art-supply store she forgot for a few hours about the Valium bottle in the medicine cabinet in the tiny bathroom of her apartment. Later, as she wrapped an order for a bearded, hungry-looking young man, she reflected that in some ways Mama/Maria was younger than she herself was.

I will dance at her wedding, Diana thought happily, and hummed a few bars from Wagner.

Might Maria, she stopped humming, at heart a teenage romantic really, be right about Con? If she were . . .

But no, that was impossible.

Then she also understood, in a sudden insight, the nature of the chill that was always with her. It was a chill of hatred for her own worthlessness. I should feel cold, she decided. I am worthless.

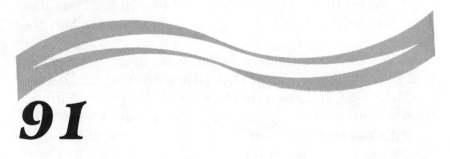

91

Was the hound of heaven chasing her? Diana wondered that afternoon after work as she wandered aimlessly through the Water Tower Mall, looking for an Easter present for Maria.

Especially because one of the pursuants even talked about hound dogs.

On the third floor, outside of Rizzoli's, Diana heard a fearsome cry from the other side of the escalators.

"Diana!"

Out of the crowd, like a racehorse breaking for the wire, emerged a young woman in jeans and a Notre Dame sweatshirt. Only when the young hoyden embraced her did she realize that it was O'Connor the Cat.

"I'm sorry, Cat." She tried to grin. "I didn't recognize you. I guess I thought you wore a swimsuit all year long."

"I wish I could," the Cat replied. "You know John, of course. And my cousin Petey. And this is his Cindasoo. That's a Coast Guard uniform she's wearing and she talks kind of funny, but we all like her."

John didn't look much like the boy they had skied with this summer. Petey could be either a Kane or a Murphy or a Ryan. And Cindasoo in her navy-blue winter uniform looked like she might be thirteen.

"C. S. McLeod, ma'am, Petty Officer, Second Class, from

Stinking Creek, West Virginia. Right proud to make your acquaintance, ma'am."

"She's Irish, but she's Protestant, but she's kinda cute anyway, isn't she, Diana? . . . WELL, when are you and Conor going to get married?"

"Never, I'm afraid." Diana fought to stop the tears that were welling up within her. "Don't you read the papers, Cat?"

"Fersure I read the papers, but what does all that gross stuff have to do with love? Don't dweeb out on us, Diana!"

Dear God, you are trying to overwhelm me with grace, carry me off in it, drown me in it. But I don't want to go.

"It's not that easy, Cat." She felt her voice choke up.

"Where Ah come from, ma'am"—Cindasoo's face was solemn—"we'uns have a saying: the first hound dog up in the morning gets the possum."

Diana had no idea how the proverb fit her situation. But nearly hysterical tears still spilled down her face as she embraced the two young women.

God would stop at nothing.

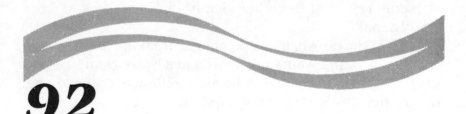

92

Conor dialed the portable phone from the comfort of the float in the basement swimming pool in his new home.

Blackie was right, as always. Why sell the house right away? It would appreciate rapidly. He could wait till the right buyer came along and make a quarter million, anyway.

What difference did that make?

Well, he was a venture capitalist, wasn't he?

In the meantime he could live in decadent splendor, floating naked in a warm pool with a large glass of Bailey's Irish Cream on ice next to him.

During Holy Week?

Well, the important thing in his life this week was arranging his own resurrection. He knew that such advice would be forthcoming if he tackled the little Monsignor again and that it would be prudent for him to report that he had begun to make progress.

"Would you ever consider coming to eleven-o'clock Mass at the Cathedral with me on Easter?" he asked the young woman who answered the phone. "The Cardinal preaches at the Easter Vigil and Father Blackie does the eleven. We could have brunch at the Ritz Carlton afterward."

She protested that it was too late to get reservations. They had been booked up for weeks.

"I am not without some influence in the Four Seasons Hotels." He raised the glass of Bailey's to his lips and considered the possibilities of the young woman, naked too, on a float next to him in the pool. During Holy Week?

Well, only after I marry her.

There was silence at the other end of the phone connection. She had not rejected him out of hand.

"I'll make a deal with you," she said finally.

You don't deal with Irish women. You simply say yes to the conditions they lay down.

"Your deal," he said, spilling the precious cream into his pool. Damn.

"You call Diana. No, that won't do. You go see her and insist that she go to Easter Sunday Mass with you. If you do your damnedest to talk her into it and she still says no, a real final and definitive no, then I'll accept your attractive offer. Otherwise, no way. I repeat, absolutely no way."

Con considered the spreading splotch of beige in the water around him. How do you wipe up spilled milk, Irish milk at that, from a swimming pool?

You don't, dummy. It filters out anyway. What would a whole pool of Bailey's be like? Decadent and messy, probably.

"I can't do that, Pat."

"I don't know what the lovely bitch will say, and note that I no longer say she's fat. Tell the truth, her boobs are really excellent. She may just be dumb enough to bury herself deeper in the grave she's already dug for herself. Regardless. Unless you're cured of her, I do not propose to waste the best years of my life, so-called, in being her surrogate."

"Pretty Patricia, I can't do that."

"My hunch"—Pat continued to ignore his protest—"is that, neurotic or not, she'll eventually say yes. In which case, I want an invitation to the wedding. Understand?"

"Listen to me, damnit. I said—"

"And I suppose that you could do a lot worse, all things considered. I hate her just at this moment, but damn her eyes, she's been classy since the shit hit the fan. So I suppose she's entitled to one more chance."

"Patricia Slattery, will you please shut up and listen."

"If she is dumb and says no—and I mean a conclusive no, do you understand?—then call me. Only, I won't wait for the call. If someone who is not in love with a dream should issue the same invitation at any point in the next day or two, I'll see you in church, Conor Clement Clarke. Have a WONDERFUL day!"

"Wait a minute. . . ."

Portable phones, even in swimming pools, were no different than any other kind. When a woman hangs up on you, she has hung up on you.

Conor groaned aloud. "I sure know how to pick them, don't I?"

93

"Large-size chartreuse envelopes, ma'am?" Diana considered the color sample sheet in front of her.

"Yeah, not letterhead size, but not legal size, either, you
know? Something in between? I like to draw wild Easter
cards for my family.... Diana ... is it you? My God!"

She looked up from her sample sheet. "It's me all
right.... Oh, Pat Slattery. I'm sorry I didn't recognize you.
You'd be surprised at the odd paper orders we get at this
time of the year."

"You look like hell.... Oh God, Di—no, you don't like
that, do you?—Diana. I'm sorry. I shouldn't have said that."

"That's all right. I do look like hell. The cold gets to me.
That's all. Would you believe lime envelopes or candy pink
or sapphire or even aquamarine?"

"It's not cold. It's like a spring day outside. I mean real
spring."

"Is it? I guess I didn't notice."

"Huh? Yeah ... I guess the sapphire will be fine. Maybe
even better. I'll take them. Do you like doing this?"

"It's not adversarial and you don't have to think and
mistakes aren't so serious, you know?"

"Right."

"You see Conor?" Dear God, why did I say something
that dumb?

"Yeah, I see him." Pat Slattery hesitated. "How much?
... No inflation here. Visa OK? ... I see him all right. And
from now on what I say is deep background, off the record,
not for attribution, and I'll deny it besides. OK?"

"OK." Her hands were trembling.

"He's a nice boy, you know. And a good date. Only one thing wrong with dating him. Know what that is?"

"No?"

"One time out of every two he calls me Patricia. And the other time he calls me Diana. Guess who he's still thinking about."

"I could easily be furious at you, Pat." With shaking hands, she carefully made out the form for her customer's credit card.

"But you're not?"

"No."

"Why not?"

"Am I on the witness stand, Counselor?"

"Yes. Why aren't you furious at me for saying some pretty dumb things in the last minute or two?"

"Because I think it's sweet of you to care about me." I will not cry. I will not.

"I don't think that I care about you. . . . No, that's not true. I guess I do. I don't know why. But I do."

"Thank you. Here's your package. Have a nice Easter."

"You too, Diana." Pat Slattery paused at the door of the shop as if she wanted to say something more. Then she thought better of it. "A wonderful Easter."

It was not, Diana decided, nearly so cold as she thought it was.

But a hint of warmth was more terrifying than the cold.

94

Conor almost lost the portable phone in the pool. Only quick wits and instant reflexes enabled him to capture it.

"Conor Clarke.... Yeah?... MJ! How did you find my new phone number?... Sure I'm going to have a monumental housewarming party in a week or two."

The problem with the phone would not have happened if he had not polished off the bottle of Bailey's as a sort of penance for having spilled some of the first glass. *I'll give up liquor for Lent next year. A bottle of Bailey's ought not to put you to sleep, not even in a heated swimming pool.*

"Yes, MJ, it's a portable phone. I'm in the pool. How about that! A house with its own pool. Come to your house for Easter dinner? Well, I don't know, I don't want to intrude...."

"With Diana? Has she agreed?... You won't invite her unless I promise to come?... Sure I appreciate it, MJ, but I don't think either of us are ready quite yet. Maybe at the lake in the summer. I certainly appreciate your concern and Gerry's too.... Yeah, well, it's still too soon."

They're all tenacious. When the women of the race make up their minds, they don't give up easily. But how come? Why don't I ask her?

All right, I will.

"I thought you hated her guts. How come you're trying to play peacemaker?... I see.... You never hated her guts ...just a little angry...All her father's fault.... And he's dead, God be good to him?... Yeah, I agree. God be good to him."

Doublethink.

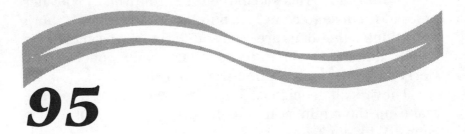

95

Diana felt Conor's fingers resting lightly on her belly, suggesting rather than teasing; protecting rather than demanding.

Protection—that's what his embrace always seemed to promise. From what? I don't know, but it doesn't matter. I need to be protected. I need him.

Dear God, she thought, how glad I am that I apologized. Without him in my bed I could not live.

Horny bitch! Sexual hunger forced you to seek forgiveness.

Well, so what?

His fingers began to explore, smoothly, delicately. She sighed. No, she would never have enough of him.

Then his demands, still tender and easy, became more demanding—breasts, belly, loins. Don't stop, darling, oh, don't stop now. Then his lips replaced his fingers, probing her most intimate secrets. Her passion rose to meet his and then raced ahead. He delayed the race, heightening her pleasure. Please stop, she wanted to shout, I cannot endure any more!

He laughed and slowed even more, driving her to the edge of madness.

Then a sound, far in the distance, stirred her from sleep.

Where is he? What happened?

Only a dream? Will I have these dreams always?

Slowly her body climbed down the mountain up which it had surged.

Will I be this easily aroused after I'm married to him?

I did apologize, did I not? We are going to be married. . . .

Yes, of course. We are lovers again. . . .

A far corner of her brain said that the reconciliation was part of the dream. But that was impossible. They had become lovers again, she was sure of that.

She struggled for more consciousness to validate her certainty. She was covered with sweat and shivering like she had a flu chill. She was exhausted as though she had made love, but frustrated as though the love had not been completed.

Then she knew it was all a dream.

She cried herself back to sleep, slipping deeper into the sinkhole of despair.

96

The next morning, her dream forgotten, Diana found the chill had returned—this time, she knew, to stay forever.

By the morning of Good Friday, it had choked out the temporary warmth Mama and daffy well-intentioned Pat Slattery had created. Now she despised Mama for her disloyalty to Daddy. How could she have said those terrible things about him?

And she bitterly resented Pat's intrusion into her private life. Let her date Conor if she wanted. Let her go to bed with him. If he ever worked up enough courage to ask her.

Oddly her art-supply store closed on Good Friday. The owners, who seemed like slightly superannuated flower children of the late sixties, turned out to be devout Catholics, deeply involved in the charismatic renewal. Both had been, they assured her, "baptized in the Holy Spirit." That made Diana feel even sadder. Her Catholic faith, which she had always prized, had somehow slipped away without her noticing it was gone. She had lost it, despite her frequent visits to the Polish church across the street, just as she had lost the rest of what she'd thought had been her character.

Wearing a tattered old terry-cloth robe, she sat in the window of her apartment on Good Friday morning, diary on her lap, staring at the baroque facade of the huge Polish church across the street.

Most women my age have kept their faith and lost their virginity, she wrote in the book, no longer using code. *I kept my virginity till I was twenty-five and then lost it and my faith—and my innocence, too. The Dirksen Federal Building was what the nuns at Mother McAuley would have called an occasion of sin.*

Maybe I should walk across the street this evening for the Good Friday service. It is stark and bleak and would fit my present mood. But would God want me in church on Good Friday—even on Good Friday? I'm not sure anymore that there is a God. Why did he permit me to become obsessed with Con Clarke? Or was it the Devil? Is there a devil? Maybe the blame is all mine, neither God nor the Devil. Maybe I'm not worth either of their attention.

She thought about the Valium bottle. There would be no one to rush her to the hospital to have her stomach pumped out.

Either the Good Friday service or the Valium bottle, she wrote in her diary. *Right now that seems like a very reasonable alternative.*

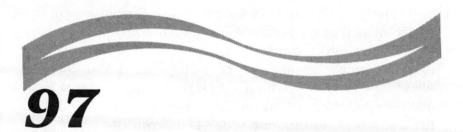

97

Monsignor John Blackwood Ryan's arrival at the Cathedral pulpit was always an event of some wonderment, to him at any rate. He seemed astonished that he had found his way to this elevated position, confused as to what he was supposed to do now that he had made it, and baffled to discover that there were people in the church waiting, actually with some eagerness, for him to begin—including, on this Good Friday evening, his superior, Chicago's handsome, haggard Cardinal Sean Cronin.

When Blackie began to preach, however, the image of a

bemused, ineffectual little man quickly disappeared. "Seldom in error," the Cardinal had said to Conor, "never in doubt."

"Consider," the Rector of Holy Name Cathedral began, "Judas.

"His worse sin was not that he betrayed the Jesus whom he loved and who loved him. We all betray those we love daily, the coward with a cruel word, the brave man with a sword."

Con wondered how many of the congregants grasped the allusion to Oscar Wilde's *Reading Gaol*. The Cardinal, assisting in plain black cassock, seemed faintly amused.

It really didn't matter. Blackie somehow had made his point. Everyone in the Cathedral, less crowded on this second evening of the Holy Week triduum than it would be at the Easter Vigil service the next night, was listening carefully.

"The worse of Judas's sins was to refuse to accept the forgiveness that was offered him twice—once at the Passover supper and again in the Garden of Olives. It was, one may reasonably assume, not easy for Jesus to offer forgiveness to the loved one who had betrayed him. We know from our own experience that the first impulse when faced with the treason of an intimate other is to even the score or to store up the memory of the other's offense in the careful account book we keep to treasure our dearly loved grievances against those whom we love.

"If it is difficult to offer forgiveness, it would seem, on the basis of the evidence, far more difficult to accept it. Thus the mystery of Judas. Poor, dumb blustery Peter, the most humble Pope in history, a man with much about which to be humble (an observation that could be made about many subsequent Popes who were and are not so willing to acknowledge their human frailties) . . ."

The Cardinal winced, but grinned, too.

". . . accepted forgiveness, if not quite with grace, at least with becoming alacrity. He lapped it up like a thirsty Snoopy. Dim, doubting Thomas would prove himself a week later to be equally avid for the restoration of love. Why not Judas?

"He certainly had his regrets. Throwing the reward for his treason on the floor of the temple treasury was a more public acknowledgment of his offense than any of the other first bishops were willing to attempt—unaccountably there were no Cardinals in those days, the Lord lacking the wisdom to establish this most crucial office.

"Having thus dramatically denounced his own guilt and responsibility for injustice, why did not Judas hasten to Calvary and accept the proffered forgiveness?

"To be offered a forgiveness we do not deserve—and if we deserve it, then it is not forgiveness but justice—is a terrifying experience as each of us can testify from our own lives. We cannot claim forgiveness, it is pure gift, pure grace, pure mercy, and—ah there's the rub—pure love. If we have betrayed the intimate other, only absurdly foolish love can possibly forgive us.

"The young persons in Erich Segal's novel *Love Story* are wrong to say that love means you don't have to say you're sorry. You do, but that merely opens the communication links, clears away the landslide rubble so that the love, which is a given, can function again. Once the plea for pardon has been made, it becomes irrelevant. The trouble with being the object of a love that is too absurdly foolish to resist is that it is terrifying to be that lovable. It is an assault on our consoling self-rejection and our soothing self-hatred. If Judas was the focus of such a love, if he were really that lovable, then he would have to live again, love again, try again, laugh again, despite his own conviction of ugliness and worthlessness. That was no mean challenge. Judas, we may have learned in school, was the victim of pride. Doubtless, but pride meant a self-rejection and a self-contempt which told him that he could never have earned again the love which he betrayed.

"Judas, you see, represents that part of our personality which wants only the love that it can earn and thus control. Peter represents that part of our personality that realizes love is unearnable and therefore surrenders helplessly to a love which is beyond merit, beyond control, beyond manipulation, beyond negotiation, beyond anything but grateful acceptance and—here's the catch: with Jesus there is always a catch—enthusiastic response. Judas thought he was not good enough to respond, so he went out and hanged himself with a rope. Peter knew that he was not good enough to respond but that it didn't matter. If you're loved with an absurdly foolish love that is irresistible, 'good enough' doesn't compute. Only acceptance and response do, an acceptance which is response and a response which is self-acceptance. We need not hang ourselves with a rope, we need not despair because love, unearnable, is nonetheless given. Love is gift, love is graceful, love is grace. And grace, needless to say, is love.

"On Good Friday the Peter in us wrestles with the Judas in us. What shall we do about the love in our lives, especially the human love that may most powerfully and passionately reflect God's love? Shall we agonize over the obligation to win it, earn it, prove ourselves worthy of it, do penance because of our failure to be worthy of it, or shall we, like Walter 'Sweetness' Payton when presented with the pigskin by one of the painfully numerous Chicago Bear quarterbacks, take our love and, in company of our beloved, run for daylight?

"In the Name of the Father and of the Son and of the Holy Spirit."

The little priest looked around, as though he were trying to figure out whether it was humanly possible to find his way back to the altar. A young acolyte bowed and led him away.

Con wished that Diana was there to hear the sermon. She was not the kind of person who would hang herself with a rope, was she?

If Jesus failed to change Judas's mind, how can I change hers?

He saw her during the veneration of the cross, after the homily and the prayers for the world and the procession down the center aisle of the Cathedral while the red-shrouded cross was unveiled with the chant "Behold the wood of the cross on which hung the Savior of the world!"

She was walking to the altar as he was returning, so she must have been in the back of the church. At first he thought it could not possibly be his *Belle* Diane—the woman was so thin, so pale, so weary and haggard. Diana was a tall woman who did not stoop to hide her height, was she not? How could this stooped woman with the sagging shoulders, in blouse and jeans, with a soiled trench coat and unruly hair, possibly be the elegant golfer who had routed him in August?

It could not be Diana. If it were, she did not recognize him when he walked past her.

He did not return to his own pew but slipped to the back of the cathedral to watch the woman return. The choir sang the "Improperia," the wondrously poetic reproaches which some genius in ages past had put on the lips of Jesus for Good Friday hymns, reproaching all his followers down through the centuries who had rejected the love he had come to offer. Translating them into English had not affected either their pathos or their beauty:

> "My people, what have I done to you?
> How have I offended you? Answer me!
> I gave you saving water from the rock,
> But you gave me gall and vinegar to drink!
> My people, what have I done to you?
> How have I offended you? Answer me!
> I gave you a royal scepter
> But you gave me a crown of thorns!
> My people, what have I done to you?
> How have I offended you? Answer me!
> I raised you to the height of majesty
> But you have raised me high on a cross!
> My people, what have I done to you?
> How have I offended you? Answer me!

The woman was indeed Diana, though a wan and suffering Diana. Con was overcome by emotion, indeed close to tears—Father Blackie's sermon, the powerful ritual of the veneration of the cross, the haunting music, and the sad Diana were too much to bear.

I want her as much as ever. Blackie and Naomi are right. I want to feed her good food and rich wine, take her to a warm and sunny place, restore her health and smile, liberate her laughter, even lose to her at golf again. And squash.

He joined the long lines for the reception of the Eucharist. Diana did not move from her pew. Is she staying away from Communion because she has sinned against me? Oh God, how ridiculous!

Father Blackie is right, as always. Forgiveness may be difficult to extend; it is certainly necessary to eliminate barriers. But once given, it is of trivial importance.

I love you, Diana. To hell with everything else.

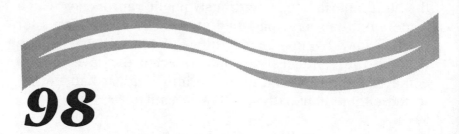

98

The Good Friday service ended with silent and deliberate anticlimax, priests and ministers scurrying out of the barren sanctuary as if they too had to pack for the journey to Emmaus.

Conor Clarke walked to the back of the Cathedral and waited for her. She remained for several minutes of private prayer to the empty altar. There was no sign on her face that the extra prayers had brought a renewal of hope. Then, shoulders bent, head down, she slipped quickly toward the door of the church.

Conor stepped behind her and took her right arm in his hand. "Can I introduce you to Monsignor Ryan, Diana?"

She glanced at him, neither surprised nor unsurprised by his presence and his words.

"All right," she said simply.

Outside, the lights in front of the Cathedral illuminated thick snowflakes, some of which were not melting when they touched the sidewalk. A snowstorm on April 5. Ah, Middle West!

The Rector had doffed his vestments, donned his Chicago Bulls jacket, and hands jammed into the jacket pockets to keep them warm, was greeting the few stragglers still leaving the Cathedral.

"It's an open question whether I ought to be here, Conor Clement Clarke," he said, shivering with the cold. "The silence of the tomb might be a more appropriate end to Good Friday than the voice of the Rector. On the other hand, as My Lord Cronin so colorfully puts it, 'If you're not back there after services, Blackwood, the lay people of God will think the world has come to an end.' "

"Monsignor Ryan, may I introduce Diana Marie Lyons."

"You certainly may." His hand emerged from the Bulls jacket and accepted Diana's tentatively extended hand. "The devastating Diana."

"Devastating?" She smiled, if only a little smile. Monsignor Blackie invariably and unfailingly charmed women. He was promptly dubbed "cute" and admired accordingly.

"Squash." He returned his hand to the jacket pocket.

"Do you play squash, Monsignor?"

"Only as a last resort."

"I bet I could beat you." A real laugh, not very vigorous but still undeniably a laugh.

"Even with hundred to one odds, I would not take the bet. Athletic women, like my three female sibs, exhaust me." He sighed his West of Ireland, asthma-attack sigh. "But then, to be honest, so do athletic men."

"May Diana and I talk with you, Monsignor, if you're not too busy."

"A pastor who is too busy has failed to give his staff the

full freedom that they will take anyway. Let's see if I can find the way back through the Cathedral to the Rectory."

Diana did not object or protest. Con's heart beat with fervent enthusiasm.

"That was a wonderful homily, Monsignor," she said respectfully.

"The Lord Cardinal is not pleased to preach on tragic days like this," he said, peering into the dim light of the empty Cathedral, as though debating whether he really could guide his guests through to the Rectory. "So he tells me at the last moment, 'See to it, Blackie!' "

"He avoids tragedy?" Diana asked, puzzled, as they walked up one of the side aisles.

"To the contrary, he has embraced more of it in his own life than most of us. Ah, I believe that if we go through the door to the Sacristy, turn right, then turn left at the staircase and then right—no, left again—we may with some luck arrive at my room. I'm afraid that, because of the day, I can promise you no refreshment save perhaps a pot of tea, McNulty's raspberry tea, however, which has always seemed to me an appropriate hint of the life of the Resurrection."

Diana giggled. Blackie's charm was working. Con's heart sang. A week or two after Easter he would join her in holy matrimony in this very Cathedral.

I've gone through that plan in my head before, haven't I? Yes, but you haven't told her about it.

Tonight I will.

They sat in the Rector's parlor while he bustled about making tea.

"You're living in Jefferson Park?" Con removed his Burberry and draped it over a chair piled high with books about William James.

Not a very poetic beginning.

She was sitting listlessly on a hassock—there weren't too many available flat spaces in Monsignor Blackie's rooms—head bowed, dirty trench coat tightly buttoned. "I borrowed my landlady's car."

"You look terribly tired"—and haggard and defeated and broken.

"I am, a little."

Blackie appeared with a Belleek teapot, cups and saucers. With considerable fumbling, he tried to rearrange them on the coffee table.

"Here, let me help," Diana offered, which was exactly what she was supposed to say. "They are very beautiful, Monsignor."

"Thank you, Diana. My sisters' ability to supply me with them exceeds my capacity to destroy them, but only just. Now then, gentlepersons"—he beamed triumphantly—"in anticipation of the Lord's Resurrection and our own, McNulty's raspberry tea!"

"Thank you, Monsignor." She smiled at him, generously enough to stir some feelings of jealousy in Con's turbulent soul. "Hmmm, *very* good."

"Indeed." He unzipped his Bulls jacket and leaned forward expectantly.

"Here goes." Con's hands were perspiring. "I may not say any of this right, but I hope you both listen to what I mean instead of what I might say."

"Indeed."

Diana stared at her tea.

"Cream or sugar, Diana." The priest reached for the Belleek vessels on the coffee table.

"What? Oh, no, thanks, Monsignor."

"Call me Blackie."

"Not Ishmael?"

"Only as a last resort."

Con understood the strategy, but he still wished that the little priest would shut up.

"You were saying, Conor?"

"I was saying"—he might as well blurt it all out—"that I love Diana, I've loved her since her first drive on the first tee at Long Beach—sheer poetry in that swing, by the way. I wrote a sonnet . . . no, that's irrelevant. I still love her. The things that have happened since then . . . they've hurt, but I love her as much as ever. I want to sweep away the past and start again. I'm not sure I know how to do that. I thought, Father Ishmael"—he was running out of breath—"you might be able to help us."

"Indeed. I don't think your position is either obscure or badly stated. Diana." He refilled her tea cup. "It is your turn at the shuttlecock."

Her head remained bowed, lips blowing on the steaming raspberry tea.

"I don't know what this conversation is all about, Father. I really should be driving back to Jefferson Park. My landlady will be worrying about her car."

"Indeed."

"Diana . . ." Con felt his Good Friday hope ebbing.

"The trouble with Conor, Monsignor Ryan, is that he is both a spoiled brat"—she finally looked up from her tea, her face contorted in disgust—"and a damned fool."

"Ah." The priest refilled his own cup and Con's, as though the most important thing in the world at that moment was to see that everyone had a plentiful supply of McNulty's raspberry tea.

"He thinks"—she put aside her cup and stood up—"that because he wants something or someone, he therefore automatically has a right to it or her. His parents indulged him. Now he expects the world to indulge him."

"He is far too fragile," Blackie said gravely, "to have been an indulged child and has been too badly hurt to think that the world owes him anything."

It's like I'm not in the room, Con thought.

"He heard your wonderful sermon, Monsignor"—she tightened the belt on her coat—"and pictures himself as Jesus and me as Judas. Well, I don't think he's Jesus and I know I'm not Judas and I don't want, pardon my language, Father, his goddamn forgiveness."

"Indeed." If the little priest was perturbed, he did not show it.

"Thanks much for the tea, Monsignor." She walked to the doorway of his suite. "It was very good. Now I must drive back to Jefferson Park before the Kennedy becomes too slippery."

"Diana . . ." Con pleaded.

"I don't want to talk about it," she said firmly.

"Diana Marie Lyons." The Rector's voice suddenly was like the blast of a trumpet or maybe the post horns in Mahler's Third.

She stopped, hand on the doorknob. "Yes?"

"Never go alone into the coldness of a snow-filled Good Friday night."

"That's how we all die, alone in the night of our own crucifixion, isn't it?"

"Only if we live that way."

"I'm too tired to rail against the failing of the light, Monsignor. Anyway, don't worry about me. I'm not Judas, I don't despise myself, and I'm not going to hang myself with a rope."

"Oh no, nothing that quick and relatively painless." The little priest was on his feet pointing his finger at her, as though he were Prince Hal on St. Crispin's Day. "That's not how Irish women destroy themselves. Don't, I repeat, don't go into the Good Friday snow alone!"

She hesitated; the transformation in the character of the little Monsignor had impressed her.

"Sorry, Monsignor, I'd rather be alone than with him. He was an obsession, nothing more."

"On the face of it, dauntless Diana, that is absurd. Conor Clarke is quite incapable of generating obsession, as should be obvious even from a cursory inspection. You fell in love with him, it is as simple, as harmless, as potentially graceful as that."

"I do not love him!" she screamed.

"Diana! I don't want an apology. I want you."

"You'll not get either." She slammed the door.

"Effective exit." Blackie shoved his glasses up on his forehead and rubbed his fingers along the bridge of his nose.

"Did I say anything wrong?" Con pleaded desperately.

"Absolutely not." Glasses still on his forehead, Blackie collapsed into his battered Victorian easy chair.

"She cut herself off."

"Certainly."

"If she acts that way, I should get rid of the ring and the Mercedes and the house I bought for her last autumn."

"Assuredly." The priest didn't seem to be giving Con his full attention.

"She has the right to resist grace."

"Undoubtedly."

"I can't force her to change."

"No way."

"She's not sorry about what happened."

"Definitely not."

"She rejects my forgiveness and my love."

"Totally."

"She is burying herself in her own icy hell."

"Unquestionably."

"Then I should forget about her?"

"Certainly not." Blackie shoved his glasses back over his eyes and bounded to the corner window that looked out over Wabash and Superior. "How did you come to that conclusion?"

Con followed him to the window. The snow was still falling, curiously golden in the street lights, precious coins cascading on Superior Street. A tall, stoop-shouldered young woman strode briskly to the corner, turned toward the parking lot, and waited for a car to pass. As she crossed Wabash, her spine seem to change to liquid and her body to shake with hysterical sobs.

"Color her despair," Blackie murmured. "I may have overestimated her capacity to survive it. You noted the curious incident, like Sherlock Holmes' dog who barked in the night, of her attending the Good Friday services at St. Jadwiga's?"

"She didn't go to the services there."

"Neither," the little priest said, drawing back the drape,

"did the dog bark in the night. That was what was curious."

"She came here because she thought I'd be here?" Con didn't want to believe it.

"Elementary, my dear Clarke."

"She's made her decision." Con was beginning to realize how deeply he had been humiliated.

"Certainly."

"She's made her bed, let her lie in it."

Diana was leaning against the wall of Randall's Restaurant, seemingly unable to rally enough strength to walk to the self-park lot a few yards away.

"A cliché unworthy of a potentially great poet, but the logic is unarguable."

"If I should put on my Burberry, which she probably hates because it's a rich man's coat, and run after her, she will reject me again."

"In all probability."

"I'd be insulted and humiliated."

"A reasonable projection."

"Then I don't have to do it."

Blackie Ryan looked at him in amazement. "That does not follow."

"I'm not going to put on my coat and run after her. She can drive back to her damn Jefferson Park landlady if she wants and freeze in her own armor of ice."

"Indeed."

"I am not going after her, Father Blackie, absolutely, certainly, and positively not." He struggled into his coat.

"Only as a last resort," the priest yelled after him as he bolted out the door and down the steps.

99

Diana had dropped the keys to the Dodge in the darkness of the parking lot and, still shaken from her fit of hysterics, was searching for them blindly on the cold and wet cement.

She had not broken down because of the loss of Con—he had been lost long ago. Rather, her pain came from the recognition that Anna Maria and the funny little priest were right: Con was a sweet and fragile young man whom she had wounded terribly, beyond any hope of undoing the pain she had caused.

She was steeped irrevocably in evil.

Then she heard the running footsteps of her own hound of heaven, pounding up the exit ramp of the parking lot. Nothing much unperturbed about his pace.

She abandoned her search for the keys and rose to face her destiny. She felt naked, defenseless, powerless, stripped of everything, completely at the mercy of the fate that was about to envelope her. She would die, cease to be, slip into nonexistence.

There was, however, no choice. She was too weary to run anymore.

The funny little priest had been right: Some passions are too absurdly foolish to resist. She would have to tell him that when she went to confession.

Daffy Diana.

She turned to face her doom. The impossible words sprung to her lips and were uttered spontaneously: "I'm sorry, forgive me."

Then the easiest and most numinous of all: "I love you."

Again Monsignor Ryan had been proven a precise

prophet: once the first two sentences had been spoken, they became irrelevant. Only the third mattered and that would matter forever.

Her doom absorbed her, overwhelmed her with a torrent of protection that was both sweet and paralyzing, possessed her so totally that she had nothing left to distinguish her self from his. He was saying something absurd about never trying to escape from him again. Didn't the poor, silly, dear man understand that escape from him was no longer an option?

Two weeks from today? That long?

Then there was a moment of the worst terror she had ever known. I cannot stand this shameful nakedness. I must hide.

She strove for hysterical tears, a last desperate covering for her disrobed self.

What emerged instead, unaccountably, was laughter.

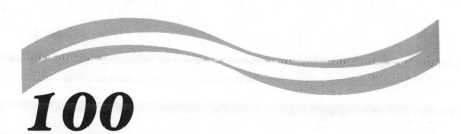

100

Monsignor John Blackwood Ryan, S.T.L., Ph.D, removed the rosary from his jacket pocket and returned it to his trousers. The young couple were holding each other, not so much clinging or even embracing any longer. If his eyes—not as nearsighted as his persona required him to pretend—were to be trusted, they were laughing together. All in all, a start of their common life with more appropriate preparatory experience than most.

He sighed and approached his liquor cabinet. He removed the Jameson's Twelve-Year Special Reserve, considered it, and then returned it. With a key he opened a secret compartment where his most treasured beverages were protected from the Cardinal and the Cathedral curates, and removed a black carton with gold trim. Inside the carton was a half-empty amber bottle with a black, red, and gold label. Black Bush single malt. Out of respect for the day, he splashed only a few drops of the precious County Antrim liquid into his County Waterford tumbler.

He turned to the saucy medieval Madonna on the wall next to John Unitas, lifted his Bushmill's to her in a respectful toast, and winked.

Sixth Song

Beloved:

Let my breasts be towers for you to scale
Above my belly's captured ivory wall.
Climb them again each day, my love, my all,
As I your victory forever hail.
Let my face be branded on your heart
That you may feel my heat in every breath,
My love, implacable as death,
My passion Yahweh's raging fire,
Impervious to the storm and flood
Of deadly friction and foolish strife
And the insidious anxieties of life,
A need burning forever in my blood.

Love Song, 8:5—8:8

epilogue

Whatever answer one may give to the problem . . . one cannot be unaware of the fact that even if it is only an anthology, in the vision of the final redactor (unless he be taken for a simpleton), Canticles does not end: true love is always a quest of one person for another; it is a constant straining toward the unity of the one who is preeminently the beloved with the companion who is the unique one.

—Daniel Lys
Le Plus Beau Chant de la Creation
(Translated by Michael V. Fox)